THE SOUNDING

CARRIE SALO

ISBN
0-9824777-6-7 (10 digit)
978-0-9824777-6-2 (13 digit)

Library of Congress Control Number: 2011935721

First Edition

Printed in the United States of America
Published by 23 House Publishing
SAN 299-8084
www.23house.com

Cover art by Tony Foti
www.tonyfotiart.com

Table of Contents

For
my parents William and Marcia
who encouraged every story and each idea
and bought a hundred notebooks for me to write them in,
and who never once asked me to do something more practical with my life

and for
Erik
my partner in crime
who always just assumed I would succeed

Praise him with the sound of the trumpet.

– Psalms 150:3

Prologue

Revelation 8:1 – 10:7…

And when he had opened the seventh seal, there was silence in heaven about the space of half an hour.

And I saw the seven angels which stood before God; and to them were given seven trumpets.

And another angel came and stood at the altar, having a golden censer; and there was given unto him much incense, that he should offer with prayers of all saints upon the golden altar which was before the throne. And the smoke of the incense, with the prayers of the saints, ascended up before God out of the angel's hand. And the angel took the censer, and filled it with fire of the altar, and cast into the earth: and there were voices, and thunderings, and lightnings, and an earthquake.

And the seven angels which had the seven trumpets prepared themselves to sound.

The first angel sounded, and there followed hail and fire mingled with blood, and they were cast upon the earth: and the third part of the trees was burnt up, and all green grass was burnt up.

And the second angel sounded, and as it were a great mountain burning with fire was cast into the sea: and the third part of the sea became blood; and the third part of the creatures which were in the sea, and had life, died; and the third part of the ships were destroyed.

And the third angel sounded, and there fell a great star from heaven, burning as it were a lamp, and it fell upon the third part of the rivers, and upon the fountains of waters; and the name of the star is called Wormwood: and the third part of the waters became wormwood; and many men died of the waters, because they were made bitter.

And the fourth angel sounded, and the third part of the sun was smitten, and the third part of the moon, and the third part of the stars; so as the third part of them was darkened, and the day shone not for a third part of it, and the night likewise. And I beheld, and heard an angel flying through the midst of heaven, saying with a loud voice, Woe, woe, woe, to the inhabiters of the earth by reason of the other voices of the trumpet of the three angels, which

1

are yet to sound!

And the fifth angel sounded, and I saw a star fall from heaven unto the earth: and to him was given the key of the bottomless pit. And he opened the bottomless pit; and there arose a smoke out of the pit, as the smoke of a great furnace; and the sun and the air were darkened by reason of the smoke of the pit. And there came out of the smoke locusts upon the earth: and unto them was given power, as the scorpions of the earth have power. And it was commanded them that they should not hurt the grass of the earth, neither any green thing, neither any tree; but only those men which have not the seal of God in their foreheads. And to them it was given that they should not kill them, but that they should be tormented five months: and their torment as the torment of a scorpion, when he striketh a man. And in those days shall men seek death, and shall not find it; and shall desire to die, and death shall flee from them.

And the shapes of the locusts like unto horses prepared unto battle; and on their heads as it were crowns like gold, and their faces as the faces of men. And they had hair as the hair of women, and their teeth were as of lions. And they had breastplates, as it were breastplates of iron; and the sound of their wings as the sound of chariots of many horses running to battle. And they had tails like unto scorpions, and there were stings in their tails: and their power to hurt men five months. And they had a king over them, the angel of the bottomless pit, whose name in the Hebrew tongue Abaddon, but in the Greek tongue hath name Apollyon.

One woe is past; behold, there come two woes more hereafter.

And the sixth angel sounded, and I heard a voice from the four horns of the golden altar which is before God, saying to the sixth angel which had the trumpet, loose the four angels which are bound in the great river Euphrates. And the four angels were loosed, which were prepared for an hour, and a day, and a month, and a year, for to slay the third part of men. And the number of the army of the horsemen two hundred thousand thousand: and I heard the number of them.

And thus I saw the horses in the vision, and them that sat on them, having breastplates of fire, and of jacinth, and brimstone: and the heads of the horses as the heads of lions; and out of their mouths issued fire and smoke and brimstone. By these three was the third part of men killed, by the fire, and by the smoke, and by the brimstone, which issued out of their mouths. For their power is in their mouth, and in their tails: for their tails like unto serpents, and had heads, and with them they do hurt.

And the rest of the men which were not killed by these plagues yet repented not of the works of their hands, that they should not worship devils, and idols of gold, and silver, and brass, and stone, and of wood: which neither can see, nor hear, nor walk: neither repented they of their murders, nor of their sorceries, nor of their fornication, nor of their thefts.

And I saw another mighty angel come down from heaven, clothed with a cloud: and a rainbow upon his head, and his face as it were the sun, and his feet as pillars of fire: and he had in his hand a little book open: and he set his right foot upon the sea, and left on the earth, and cried with a loud voice, as a lion roareth: and when he had cried, seven thunders uttered their voices. And when the seven thunders had uttered their voices, I was about to write: and I heard a voice from heaven saying unto me, seal up those things which the seven thunders uttered, and write them not.

And the angel which I saw stand upon the sea and upon the earth lifted up his hand to heaven, and sware by him that liveth for ever and ever, who created heaven, and the things that therein are, and the earth, and the things that therein are, and the sea, and the things which are therein, that there should be time no longer: But in the days of the voice of the seventh angel, when he shall begin to sound, the mystery of God should be finished, as he hath declared to his servants the prophets.

Revelation 11:15 – 11:19

And the seventh angel sounded; and there were great voices in heaven, saying, The kingdoms of this world are become of our Lord, and of his Christ; and he shall reign for ever and ever. And the four and twenty elders, which sat before God on their seats, fell upon their faces, and worshipped God, saying,

We give thee thanks, O LORD God Almighty,
which art, and wast, and art to come;
because thou hast taken to thee thy great power,
and hast reigned.
And the nations were angry,
and thy wrath is come,
and the time of the dead,
that they should be judged,
and that thou shouldest give reward unto thy servants
the prophets, and to the saints,
and them that fear thy name, small and great;
and shouldest destroy them which destroy the earth.

And the temple of God was opened in heaven, and there was seen in his temple the ark of his testament: and there were lightnings, and voices, and thunderings, and an earthquake, and great hail.

3

Chapter 1 – Bonnie and Clyde

Clyde Parker was about to die.

He didn't know it, but that did not matter. Knowing would not have changed it.

Clyde took another long pull on his beer, tossing his head back all the way so that the liquid drained right into his stomach. He still had another six-pack to finish. And he would finish it.

Roy's foot was on the cooler, and Clyde kicked it off. "You're always in the damn way," he said in a heavy, sloppy voice, like his tongue and his lips were working too hard.

"And you're always bitchin'," Roy put his foot back on the cooler, but only after Clyde found his next drink. He knew personally how ugly Clyde could be with a bottle in one hand and the other closed in a fist.

They were silent then, except for the wet sighing of their lips on their bottles. Ashton Bay lapped quietly at the stony beach in front of them. The still water reflected the lights of the college campus; it looked like a large, black carpet with specks of lint had been rolled out before them.

"So what can we smash tonight?" Clyde put both arms on the back of the bench behind him, as though he had a girl on each side.

"We don't want to keep the coach too busy," Roy joked, but he leaned forward away from the big hands on the bench. "Or the cops," the last part he muttered.

"You're such a pussy, Roy. When it came to making tackles, you ran the other way, and when it comes to getting back at the son-of-a-bitch who cut you off the team, it's the same shit."

Roy snorted and squeezed his beer tighter.

"At least I was kicked off for drinking." Clyde spat, and his sweaty brow furrowed in anger. "The old man must've been pissed as hell though," he grunted. "How much do you think it was…five grand worth of football equipment we trashed last night?"

Roy didn't answer. He could tell Clyde was beginning to rant. Maybe by the time he was done, he would be too drunk to make it off the bench.

"That's what happens when you cut an All-American football champion for having a few beers. Not only do you lose the whole season, but it comes back to bite you in the ass. Shit man!" Clyde took one beefy arm off the bench and swiped Roy hard on the back. "That was some fun shit, destroying the team room. I really should try out for baseball. I sure as hell can swing a bat," he laughed at his joke loudly, spittle flying out of his mouth like small satellites while his pupils rolled between broken blood vessels. Lately, even on the rare occasions when he was not either drunk or hung over, his eyes were always narrow and red. They reminded Roy of the eyes at his Aunt's pig roast – after they were slowly cooked into greasy, red discs.

"I'll show that asshole. I can do anything..." Clyde dragged his words as he noticed Roy's silence. "What's the matter Roy? Still worried the cops will come and haul your ass to jail?" Clyde whimpered at him mockingly.

No, I'm thinking about how damn ugly you are. Roy remained silent.

"Are you sweating it, worried you'll see your face on a wanted ad tomorrow? 'Roy and Clyde, fugitives of the law,'" Clyde laughed turning his head for a mock mug shot. "You're such a chicken shit Roy, they'd have to change the poster so people would recognize you. More like Bonnie and Clyde, since you're such a woman."

"Goodnight, Clyde," Roy got up off the bench, tossed his empty on the ground, and started to walk back to campus.

But even drunk, Clyde was very fast. With three large, fumbled steps, he easily blocked Roy's path.

"Clyde..." Roy started to speak, but Clyde pushed him hard towards the bench, sending his arms pin-wheeling. Then Clyde was leaning over him, using all his height and weight, menacing like a charging bull with his head down and shoulders out. Roy braced himself for the second hit, his hands up defensively. "Clyde!"

"Shhhh..." Clyde suddenly put a finger to his lips. His eyes lit up in a hungry sort of way, looking over Roy's shoulder.

Roy followed his gaze and saw the girl on the campus walkway at the top of the hill, one strap from her bag slung over her shoulder. Her hair glistened orange in the glow of the lamppost, and she walked with a slight swing, making the shadows move rhythmically around her. She was looking down at her feet, lost deep in thought; or maybe she already saw them, and was trying not to make eye contact.

"Well, here comes something nice," Clyde tried unsuccessfully to keep his voice low. "Come on," he moved up the hill towards the walkway.

"What?" Roy watched him with bleary eyes for a few moments, and then followed. "Clyde, let's not–"

"Very nice," Clyde said louder, meaning for her to hear this time. The girl looked up, scanning the shadows, definitely seeing them now. Her rhythmic walk turned stiff, like a person who has seen an angry dog and wants to run, but knows better. Clyde reached the walkway a few yards ahead of her. She gave a wary smile as she came to a halt, trying to feel out a threat or a joke.

"Hey baby. Where you headed?" Clyde took another step.

Her eyes narrowed, then moved side to side, as if she were trying to read something. Roy guessed she was trying to decide – were they just drunk and harmless, or if not harmless, were they at least too intoxicated to catch her if she ran? Roy decided for her and shook his head slightly in her direction, encouraging her backwards. *Clyde is not harmless. And you had better be fast.*

But she did not turn back. Lowering her head as if walking into a wind, she came quickly, holding her bag tight enough to make her knuckles show whitely.

"Don't be that way." Clyde cooed and moved into the center of the walkway. He spread his legs wide enough to bridge it edge to edge. "We're not making you nervous are we?"

Don't stop. Just go around us like we're not here, Roy coached silently.

"Of course not," the girl replied loudly, her sneakers whispering as she moved with short, rapid strides off the walkway and onto the grass.

Don't talk to him – just keep going.

"You should come back to my place," Clyde said darkly as she sidestepped him, and he leaned down towards her face as if to kiss her.

She smelled his sour breath and saw the stubble on his chin, the way his teeth looked slimy and his lips too full. "You're disgusting," she hissed as she turned her face away and moved past him.

Shit. Roy watched Clyde's face contort with anger.

Clyde kicked out his foot, catching the girl's ankle midair. She began to fall forward, catching herself for just a second on the very edge of the walkway. But a quick shove from Clyde brought her all the way down hard. Her one free hand smacked against the cement, followed by the side of her cheek, and her bag dumped around her. For a moment, there was only the sound of pencils rolling.

"See now. You should've just said... excuse me. Maybe then... I would've let you by," Clyde's breath came in gasps, as though he had been running. "Hurry and grab her," he said, already grasping one arm tightly.

"Clyde... Clyde, come on man. Let's just help her get her bag, and get the hell out of here," Roy's voice cracked. The girl was moving, but there was a small smear of blood on the walkway where her face had been. Roy was afraid for her.

"Do you want someone to see her?" Clyde's voice held a high note of panic. He began to haul her back towards the beach. "COME ON BONNIE! HELP ME GET HER THE FUCK OUT OF THE LIGHT!"

The noise of Clyde's words jumpstarted him, and Roy ran to the other side of the girl, trying to help her gain her feet, stumbling to keep up with Clyde's strides. *Why doesn't she scream?* Roy thought, feeling the urge rising in himself as they drew away from the light on the down-sloping hill.

They were almost to the water when the girl found her legs, locking them and dragging her feet awkwardly. She tossed her head back, and Roy saw the blood black on her lips and chin, strands of her hair stuck to it.

She met his gaze with horribly wide eyes, and said coolly, "Let me go."

The calm, icy tone made even Clyde hesitate, and Roy released on command. There was still fear in the defensive posture she held, her free arm out and in a fist. But there was something else too. Roy looked nervously for someone in the darkness. It seemed she wasn't afraid of them, but of something else altogether.

"Now," she commanded.

"SHIT!" Clyde screamed, and then hissed out a high-pitched tone Roy would have sworn his voice was not capable of.

"What the hell?" Roy cursed confused. "What is wrong with you? We need to just take her back–"

"She burned me," Clyde howled, and his voice was tight with pain.

"Shhh…" Roy's whisper shook. "Someone is going to come and–"

But Clyde grabbed the girl by her shirt and, with one immense, open hand, hit her across the cheek with a force that made Roy nauseated. He felt a spray of wetness on his bare arms and face, and he knew it was the girl's blood, maybe from her nose or mouth, or both.

"Stupid bitch," Clyde spewed. "Do you know who I am?"

Incredibly, she still stood, leaning on her knees and wheezing, perhaps between broken teeth. "Clyde. That's enough," Roy pleaded. But Clyde had grabbed her again.

"Disgusting, right? Do you have any idea who the fuck I am?"

The girl pulled her body straight and then seemed to wait, breathing with her mouth open as Clyde pulled his arm back to hit her.

Clyde's hand became limp in the air, and he squinted at the girl, pausing indefinitely.

Her eyes were glowing at him with a strange, blond light.

Was she wearing glasses, which were somehow catching the lamppost light just right? How drunk was he? He moved his face closer to hers, straining. From the rims to the eyelids, he could see nothing except light: no pupil, no iris, no veins or color, just a horrible shining. His confused mind tried to remember something about the science of fireflies.

In perfect mimicry, the girl grabbed Clyde by the shirt and then raised her hand so quickly, Roy hardly saw her move. There was an awful tearing noise as her open palm connected with Clyde's face. He fell away from her

7

heavily, and rolled several times down the hill and stopped on his back, quiet.

The girl turned and rose up on her toes, ready to run. Roy could see her entire body shaking even in the dark.

"Holy shit! Are you o–" Roy touched her wrist, and then he felt it: a prickling like he had been lying on his arm all night without moving. His fingers stiffened and he found he could not release her even as the sensation crept up his arm and neck to his face. *She burned me*, echoed in his head, but he wasn't sure where the words came from anymore. The girl's figure waved in front of him, as though he were looking at her through a funhouse mirror. Her eyes glowed like two tiny penlights, and he was suddenly sure his body was no longer solid, that she melted his insides completely. Roy began to cry as his knees buckled. "Don't let me tip over. I'll spill out all over everything."

She let him fall before she ran.

And then Roy was on the ground watching neon flashes fade from his vision. They were still there even when he closed his eyes, and he felt like he had been looking at the sun too long. He was entirely exhausted. He turned so that his cheek rested on the cool grass. Clyde was there on his right, looking up at the stars and unmoving.

"Clyde?" Roy's voice sounded cottony and he swallowed trying to find enough saliva to wet his tongue. He rolled to his side, then onto his elbows, and inched over to the still form. It was excruciating to move. "Clyde?" he whispered, pulling himself up as high on his elbows as he could.

At first, he couldn't make out what he was seeing in the dark. It looked like Clyde's face had been painted in tar and was still shiny in places where it was not yet dry.

Then he realized Clyde did not have a face at all; only a soupy mess of skin and cartilage where his features used to be.

"No...no, no, no." Roy whipped his head back and began moving away. Once he started screaming, he did not stop.

* * * * *

She slipped into the dormitory bathroom, and let out a shaky sigh of relief when she found it empty. Dropping her bag and grabbing a wad of toilet paper from the closest stall, she used it to turn on the faucet's cold water without getting blood on the knob. She rinsed one hand and then the other, making sure no blood splattered onto the beige porcelain. Once the preliminary red drained away, she pumped soap onto her hands and began scrubbing, cleaning out the nails and the small wrinkles in her knuckles. She let the water run and run even while she held her trembling fingers under the warm drier, hoping it would all flow down the drain and be sucked away. She glanced in the mirror.

Most of the damage was already gone.

Her eye was slightly swollen and there was still blood on her chin and under her nose; but little else indicated the bones he broke. She wiped up that blood too, and then stood, watching the water running into the sink, still shaking. She pulled her red hair back tightly away from her face, and tucked it into the back of her shirt just before she ran into the stall and heaved up fear and bile together. She rinsed her mouth, grabbed her bag, and then walked out of the bathroom.

The lounge was full of students sitting on the lumpy couches just inside, studying.

"Hey Elise, did you start Stats yet? Number two's hell!" someone called to her. Elise smiled, careful to keep her hair over her face and said no, she was too tired to start it tonight.

Chapter 2 – Out of a Comic Book

Father Chris Mognahan stirred his coffee, which didn't do much since the coffee was straight black to begin with. Regardless, he stirred, watching the soft swirls and ripples in the dark liquid. Absently, his gaze turned out the window. He loved this time of year: when it was still hot and sunny, but cool enough at night to hint that fall was very close on the heels of September. Senior citizens were still watering their petunias and begonias, and serving iced-tea on their porches. But some of the leaves had begun to show themselves off already, seeping the red and orange out from their veins. People were leaving the local grocery store with bags of apples and some front stoops were decorated with their first pumpkins. It was transition, quiet and gentle.

But this contemplation was lazy, and he sipped the coffee quickly as if to induce focus. Really, he should be back at the rectory researching for Sunday's Mass. He needed to find a clever way to preach the Prodigal Son without seeing the frustrated faces of his congregation. Whiteley Village residents were hard workers with their noses to the grind pretty consistently. They were farmers and shopkeepers, teachers and PTA Moms. For the most part, Whiteley Catholics didn't want to hear about God's mercy for slackers. Joseph Kinny, a man who worked two jobs so he could pay his mother's medical bills, usually sat in the front row. Whenever Chris gave the Prodigal Son sermon, Joe always looked like he wanted to raise his hand and ask if God was always that unfair.

"Anything else, Father?"

Chris waved away the coffee pot. "No thank you, Judy. As always, the hot turkey sandwich was delicious."

"Well, this is a diner, isn't it?" Judy shuffled through her apron for Chris' particular lunch slip with her girlish scrawl on it. She never dotted her 'i's, but put loopy circles over them like she was a cheerleader making signs for a pep rally.

She pursed her lips and made a clucking sound in her mouth. "Damn it, I left your bill in the back." She began to return to the kitchen, but then catching herself, "Oh, I'm so sorry Father! I didn't mean to talk like that in front of you!" Her face turned a slight pink behind her glasses.

Chris smiled. "Now, that will cost you a Hail Mary, Judy."

She nodded seriously, "I'll be right back with your bill. Sorry about that." She walked across the yellowed linoleum floor, her white sneakers in contrast and squeaking, and her overweight rump swinging to the pop of Dave's grease-burgers on the griddle. Chris leaned back and stirred his black coffee once more, then emptied the mug. He folded his hands, hoping she wouldn't be too long, and then glanced up at the mounted TV. A woman wearing too much make-up was looking out at him, talking with all the voice inflection and meaningful pause of a good reporter.

"McMillen was reported missing Monday night when a friend arrived at her apartment for dinner, but found it empty. Though there is speculation that her boyfriend may be a suspect in the assault, police have yet to comment. In the mean time, the search will continue for Kera McMillen."

Chris sighed as her high school graduation picture popped up on the screen.

"Awful, isn't it?" Judy smacked the bill face up on the table. "Sometimes, I just don't know what's wrong with people these days. Seems like every day there is someone missing or dead. It's like the whole damn world is going nuts. Oh. Sorry again, Father."

Chris nodded, both to her speech and her apology, and pulled out his wallet.

"It's starting to hit closer to home, too. My daughter called me from school the other day. She's down in South Carolina?" Judy left the statement a question – a quiz Chris was used to. Remembering what people's children were up to was absolutely necessary to small town survival.

"Elizabeth is in her second year at Ashton, now?"

"Yeah, and she's still loving it," Judy warmed. "Anyway, she called me the other day. There was an attack on her campus, if you can believe it." She paused for the priest to raise his eyebrows. "Yeah, I thought it was crazy too. I mean, they have two thousand kids and all, so there's bound to be some whackos. But, the crime was so awful, and the police have no clues. It was an attack on a boy too, a football player at that."

"Really?" At this unusual detail, Chris picked up his head. "How was he attacked?"

"They don't really know, haven't any ideas what weapon was used. But, whatever it was, it tore his face right off his head. And I don't mean that in any metaphorical way, now. The kid's face was literally cleaned off, and they say he died instantly. Another student found him, but he didn't see anything or anyone, just found him lying there. For a while, people thought it might be an animal or something, since it was so violent and all. I mean, what type of person can just scrape off someone's face, even with a knife? The only people I know like that are straight out of my youngest son's comic books. Superhuman."

" Yeah... you would have to be unusually strong, first to get the guy at all, and second to do some real damage," Chris thought out loud. He wrinkled his face and stopped counting his change. "Are they sure it wasn't some sort of animal?"

"Well, they closed down the campus for a few days, and brought in the forensic people, and I guess they determined that it was a person who did it. Really weird, and now Lizzy is scared to go out on her own campus at night. There's a break coming soon, and I sure am glad. If her father had his way, she would've come right home, but she's eight hundred miles away. The murder was a couple of weeks ago anyway, and with no witnesses and no weapon, I don't think they have much to go on."

"Have there been any other attacks?"

"Nope. Just the one. Still, nice little Ashton?" Judy clucked again. "It's too bad," and she shook her head.

Chris remained thoughtful. He stretched his legs and slid out from the bench seat, the red vinyl creaking. It was a lot like climbing out of an old station wagon.

He handed her the lunch slip and the money he owed. Judy put them into one of the large pockets on her apron without glancing at the money at all. *Never check a priest's bill,* Chris could almost hear her advising the other waitresses.

Still absently, "Well, I'll probably be seeing you for lunch again tomorrow, Judy."

"Yeah, I figured. That's one thing God didn't think about when He decided that priests had to stay bachelors – who in His name would be cooking for all of you?" She laughed a big laugh, her white teeth flashing for a moment. "Yeah, well that's most likely how I am going to get in up there, anyway," she said with a small sigh and a jab with her thumb at the ceiling.

"Are you going to slide old St. Peter a piece of apple pie through the pearly gates, Judy?" he teased.

"À la mode, just to be sure."

Chris laughed, but only until the diner door swung shut behind him. He put his hands in his pockets and headed back towards the rectory with his head down, thinking and no longer noticing the day.

At one time, such a violent crime would've excited him, scared him, put him on a bus to Ashton even. But that was a long time ago, with many false leads and disappointments in between.

The only people I know like that are straight out of my youngest son's comic books. Superhuman.

Superhuman. He shivered though the sun was warm on his back and neck.

The rectory was on the very end of Main Street, right where it stopped being main anything and became just another road with a faded yellow line down the middle and a farmhouse every three miles or so. The tiny church sat right next to the rectory, white vinyl siding gleaming. It was squat with shrubbery around the front door kept trim by Chris and the men's prayer group. There was a small bell tower on top that made the roof come to some sort of a point, and stained-glass windows that kept people from looking inside (or from looking outside during Mass, for that matter).

The rectory sat separated from the church by some trees and more shrubs on the other side of the circular driveway. Someone painted it a light country yellow right before Chris came to the diocese four years earlier. You could tell its blueprint from the outside: a kitchen/living room where the front door opened, and the small addition in the back could only be a bedroom as it was too big to be a bathroom and too small for anything else. The bathroom jutted out awkwardly from in between the main room and the addition, yellow curtains billowing out onto the windowsill.

Chris walked past the rectory and into the church. The heavy wooden door slid silently open, then shut behind him with a quiet swish. *Even the doors are quiet in church,* he thought as he often did upon entering. The pews were dark, the stained-glass windows refusing to let more than a blue-gray light in. When the lights were on and the fans were going, when people were shifting in their seats and babies were crying in the back room, it felt less like a church. Now, completely empty and full of shadows, it felt like he really had walked into someone else's home unannounced; he had interrupted something. It felt haunted.

Chris always liked to kneel in the second pew from the front, right at the edge. That was where he had sat with his mother while growing up: the second pew. Every Sunday, they had sat in the same place in their church, right next to the aisle. That was the beauty of small churches: almost everyone had a spot. You could always tell when someone new came because, for a few weeks, the reserved places were off.

Chris knelt and thought in the second pew, not really praying. He folded his hands over the seat in front of him and felt the leather kneeler make the first indents across his knees and shins. He thought of the beautiful day, of his sermon for the week, and inevitably, of Ashton College. With these last thoughts, he meandered home.

His Bible was already open to the Prodigal Son, waiting for him on his desk. He ignored it and rummaged through the desk's bottom drawer. It was full of clippings, old bank statements, and other things he felt he should keep, but were not important enough to organize. Close to the bottom, he found what he was looking for.

It was a picture frame, a cheap one from K-Mart or Ames probably. The shiny, black plastic casing could barely pretend to be patent leather, and there was still the remnant stickiness on the back where the price tag had been hastily removed. Father Alan Cole had sent it to Chris many years ago, the picture inside even older. It was of himself, standing in front of seven statues. The picture was taken from far away, and because the church it was taken in had high ceilings, there was a grainy quality to the photo where the flash had shot into the dark, but found nothing to reflect off of.

The statues were completely white, not marble but some shinier material. They were nicely detailed even in the picture, and Chris looked at them hard, seeing them and remembering. The first six statues were men, each dressed in long white robes with rope around their waists acting as a belt, and barefoot. They were all very large, supposing they were to scale, with the largest about eight-feet tall. Some had curls for hair etched into the stone, others soft waves; there were large and small noses, broad foreheads and wrinkled brows; each statue had a distinct physiognomy. They had in common, however, a serious line where the mouth was. The artist chose not to give any of the statues pupils, chipping blank ovals for eyes instead. The six forms stood in a line, each with a different trumpet or horn under his right arm, relaxed. A young Chris stood between the third and fourth statues, his mouth also a serious line.

The seventh and final statue in the group was cut-off in the picture, only half of her showing, but Chris could still see most of her clearly, his memory filling in where the picture stopped. She too was dressed in white robes and barefoot, but she was much smaller than the others, rising to a little under six feet. Long hair flowed back loose over her shoulders, as though a wind was gently blowing. Her face played a slight smile, and her lips were more defined than the others, slightly parted as if to speak. With her head tilted up and slightly to the side, she looked inquisitive. She too held an instrument but, unlike the others, hers was a hunting horn from Roman times – a curved, ridged tusk with a small mouthpiece hooked around her wrist – also relaxed.

She was the seventh trumpeter.

One would not guess by looking that she was a depiction of the one; that her horn was the horn. That it would be her calling them out – from their lives and their graves – on the last day. Unassuming, relaxed, and smiling – she was the angel of the world's death.

Alan had written an inscription on the frame in dark ink: *Revelation 10:7: But in the days of the voice of the seventh angel, when he shall begin to sound, the mystery of God should be finished, as he hath declared to his servants the prophets.*

* * * * *

14

The picture had been taken in the Italian countryside between Gaeta and the Vatican City in Rome. Chris had been traveling with some priest and bishop friends, members of the Congregation for the Hetairia Melchizedek, which he joined shortly after completing his doctorate in religious theology and before taking on an assignment as a Jesuit priest. They had met in Rome to go over society business, and then visited some of the outlying areas before returning to their respective parishes and homes.

Hetairia Melchizedek (known to its members more simply as 'the society'): a committee within the Catholic Church that studied omens prophesized in the Bible and recorded their fulfillment. With access to the museums and libraries around the world, and even the most secret vaults in the Vatican, the society members documented what already passed, matching moments in history with ancient prophecy. They upheld a literary, scholarly reputation to consider only historical fact while scorning rumor and superstition. The result: they sometimes debated an omen for several centuries.

Like its namesake, Melchizedek – great prophet, priest, and king – the Hetairia Melchizedek led the Church in witnessing the progression of humanity towards the final coming of God's kingdom. It worked in conjunction with the many other congregations in the Church – the Council for the Doctrine of the Faith, the Congregation for the Clergy – that debated the issues facing the Church and wrote its doctrine.

Though a trusted source of knowledge within the papacy, the last three centuries found its actions silenced. In a world of ever-increasing reliance on science, the Church was attacked again and again for its ancient ideas, and it quietly let the society fade as those who remembered it passed into the history it so constantly combed. Unlike the other congregations, whose members were listed in public directories and that often published documents, the Hetairia Melchizedek came to exist only to trusted cardinals, bishops, priests, monks, and nuns – the insiders of the Church. After more than three hundred years of hiding, the world seemed to have successfully forgotten.

The society worked steadily without a great deal of Church involvement. It presented its ideas and theories before the College of Cardinals at consistories, and then buried its head back into the vaults of history, not to reappear until the next consistory. The extensive research demands led to the appointment of theologically esteemed priests to the congregation, positions hereto reserved for bishops and cardinals. When Chris received his invitation to join, approved by the Pope himself, he did not hesitate.

It was shortly after this appointment that he and twenty other society members had made the trip to Meura. Their mission at the time: to examine a church nicknamed Chiesa di Statua by the townspeople: the Church of Statues. It was very old, and not very large or famous. The statues to which it owed its reputation were made in the twelfth century, purportedly by a sculptor who claimed prophetic vision.

"The angels of the seven trumpets," Alan had whispered in excitement to Chris inside the church. "Amazing, aren't they? Depicting the guardians of the human race..." he let his voice fall off, and the conversation could be heard echoing in the arching ceilings. "It is rumored that the sculptor was inspired to create them as they truly are."

Chris gazed at the statues flanking one side of the church, the side without windows. "It's interesting that a woman is the final angel. The seventh angel should be the most frightening, yet she is by far the most human of them all," he noted.

"True – her trumpet is definitely the most unfortunate. When she sounds, it's not just earthquakes and plagues; it's Armageddon."

"Armageddon," the church said back in Alan's voice.

Drawn by the focus of their conversation, the two priests moved in front of the last angel. Standing in front of her, she looked even smaller to Chris than she had from the church aisle. He reached out and touched her hand where she held the trumpet. It felt smooth and cold, like the stone she was made of.

Alan watched him and smiled, his leathery old face crinkling like tissue paper. "I agree with the artist and his vision. I think it most appropriate that the last angel should indeed be a woman. God always gives us a chance at redemption. It was a woman who started the world as we know it in motion with the first sin. It seems appropriate that God would choose a woman to end it all too, to make right the old sin by ending sin entirely."

Chris laughed. "I'm sure the end of the world will have nothing to do with a single woman or a man, for that matter, or a trumpet. *Revelation* is, in my reading of it, very figurative, like *Genesis*." He looked back up at the statue. She was smiling, not caring that he didn't believe in her.

"Ah, you just haven't been in my company long enough, Father Chris. Wait until you see some of the old texts, the ancient letters. You will be surprised to find how exact the Bible is, I think." Alan moved away from the statues, leading Chris' elbow the way old men are apt to do.

And then Alan had taken the picture.

Yet, he did not send it to Chris until two years after the trip. It had arrived suddenly with a strange letter:

Chris,
We have so much to discuss – new findings. Please be in Rome

November 11th through the 18th, for a plenary meeting of the society. The news is very pressing, and you must come at all cost. Though I do not want to give away the latest revelation, I thought that you would enjoy this picture of yourself and the seven guardians, especially now that everything has changed. You will see shortly. Please let me know that you are coming.

In God,
Alan

Of course, Chris had met with the other priests as requested, his curiosity truly piqued. Immediately upon arrival, the priests had left for Meura. Alan was constantly whispering with a few of the other members, and his eyes shown with excitement. Dramatically, he led them into the Chiesa di Statua, throwing the doors open. The church was dark, as they arrived quite late, and empty. Only a few lights glowed, the white statues shining dully in the shadows.

"Come. Do you see it? Do you see it!" Alan whispered to all of them. He moved swiftly up the aisle, right to the statues, and then hesitated. Chris felt his own pulse beat faster as they moved together, looking side to side furtively for what Alan was trying to make them see, like men in a side show instead of a church. Fear entered in upon the old priest's excitement and he sidled weakly past statues five and six.

She stood there, the seventh angel, her hair billowing out behind her in an invisible wind. She was as Chris remembered her, small and smiling with her robes gracefully around her.

Except, she wasn't the same.

Chris had barely heard the gasps of the other priests around him as the oddity registered for them all, and suddenly his heart had been pounding. The angel's arms had been lifted somehow, and both white stone hands now held the Roman war horn half raised in front of her breasts, as if she meant to sound it.

With the memory unsettlingly fresh, Chris put the picture back in the desk drawer.

It had been a long time ago, and yet, it was very close to him, so that he could smell the church still, the old hymnal-book scents and the old carpet smells. He saw her face, the way she smiled even with the horn so close to her lips. Her eyes were cold, without feeling or mercy. If she could speak, Chris knew exactly what she would say: *And ye shall know that I am the LORD that smiteth* – Ezekiel 7:9. It was inscribed on her pedestal.

Chris flipped the switch of his monitor. Mrs. Hutchings had donated it to the church after her last kid left the nest. There was a permanent dirty smudge on the power button, and one half of the monitor was more yellow than the other because of the sun beating in on it through Mrs. Hutchings's sliding glass doors. It made a strange sound while it booted up, like it was trying to cough, but Chris knew it was only "thinking."

Ashton College, Chris typed into his search engine. *It won't hurt to just look*, he told himself. The official website came up first on the search return, and he clicked on it, the computer coughing some more. A group of happy college students wearing Ashton College sweatshirts smiled at him while the navigation table loaded. He waited while football logos and a map of the college materialized, then finally buttons filled in: *Ashton College History, Academic Programs, Athletic Schedule, College Calendar, In the News*, and *How to Apply*. *In the News* was what he wanted and he moved the cursor onto it.

There was nothing in the headlines to suggest that there had been a murder on campus recently. The listed articles concerned parents' weekend activities and alumni donations, academic guest speakers and a recent controversy in the Women's department. Chris scrolled down to the bottom of the page hoping to find more obscure listings. Finally, he was rewarded: *Campus Safety a Priority at Ashton College*. It was an article about what students could do to protect themselves at night: call campus escorts, know where emergency phones were, etc., etc. Chris skimmed quickly, but there was no mention of any recent campus attacks. That is, until the end when he came across a link for past articles *like this*. He double clicked, and headlines ran down the page.

Clyde Parker, a sophomore at Ashton College, was found dead at the scene in the early morning hours of September 10th, near the East Campus Walk by Ashton Bay. His body was discovered by Roy Eckner, who contacted the authorities. Paramedics determined that Parker was dead upon their arrival, and transported him to St. Joseph's Hospital where head trauma was determined the cause of death. Police questioned Eckner, but released him a few hours later after he was unable to provide any leads. Following a two-day recess for the investigation, officials are encouraging students to go on with their usual activities, but to travel in groups at night.

Nothing strange about that, Chris thought. Admittedly, the crime was violent – that was obvious. But was it violent and strange enough to warrant any abnormal suspicion? Of course, the college newspaper wouldn't give any of the interesting details. *If there really is something*, "I need to dig deeper," his thoughts came out loud.

"No, no, I won't," he answered firmly and pushed his chair back hard from the desk. "Alan is crazy, wild about finding a needle in a haystack." He had sent all of them searching a search with no answers. It had always been impossible. *And even if he is right*, Chris entertained the idea as he had for a great deal of the last nineteen years, *and it was some sort of omen, the task of looking is too long and too hard. We all gave up.* "I gave up," the last part he whispered as he closed the browser.

The Prodigal Son was still sitting on the desk, begging for some sort of interpretation. He turned to it, reading the verses out loud to push away everything else. He jotted a few notes on his notepad, and then reread the text. More scribbling, his fresh pencil scratching at the paper. Finally, he ran his hand through his short hair, pulling at the roots and rubbing his temples.

Clyde Parker's killer was waiting somewhere.

Chapter 3 – Depressions

"Then the son turned to him and said 'Father, I have sinned against heaven, and in thy sight, and am no more worthy to be called thy son.' But the Father turned to his servants and said 'Bring forth the best robe, and put on him; and put a ring on his hand, and shoes on his feet…For this my son was dead, and is alive again; he was lost, and is found.'" Chris let his words carry out into the back of the church. His frame hovered above the pulpit, bent over itself with arms tucked in, like a bird in green silk robes, waiting to fly.

Luke 15:11-32, the Prodigal Son: that most important sermon of the autumn for the Catholic Church. Chris wondered again whether it was because the passage had some hidden profound meaning, or if it was because it posed such a hurdle for priests and parishioners alike. In its few lines, God created a great deal of doubt concerning His sense of fairness. A bad guy could be forgiven and find paradise, while a mediocre good guy could get the eternal cold shoulder. So much for perfect justice.

"And like the father in Luke's parable, God receives the repentant sinner with relief and celebration. For you and I, He will slay the fattened calf and put rings on our fingers. His mercy will never run thin," Chris let his voice drop slightly, watching the congregation lean forward to catch the last words. He did this periodically – about every five minutes – to see if his parishioners were still following him, or if they had been lost in the Sunday humdrum that was an early morning lecture before breakfast. Sure enough, the last few rows were basically unconscious, their bodies slouched, their necks resting on the backs of their seats, legs sprawled out and missals closed on their laps.

Chris leaned forward, frowning and deepening the wrinkles around his eyes, and then he raised his voice once again. "Now of course, the faithful son was jealous of the happy reception his sinning brother had received. After all, he had watched over his father's fields; he had never disobeyed him or caused him shame. He comes to his father in anger, wondering where his celebration is. And, the father says to him, 'Son, thou art ever with me, and all that I have is thine. It was meet that we should make merry, and be glad: for this thy brother was dead, and is alive again; and was lost, and is found.'

"For those of us who keep God's laws, the kingdom awaits us." Chris spread his hands out over the pulpit and immediately regretted it. He felt awkward making such gestures, like a bad actor on the stage that must exaggerate to convey a character he is not capable of naturally portraying. Quickly, he put his hands back down, resting them on the worn edges of the pulpit and letting his thumbs embarrassedly rub its sides. He cleared his throat, "But, we must remember God's love and mercy by giving love and mercy ourselves, welcoming the sheep that returns to the fold after wandering."

He stood back and swiped his brow with his hand. It was only slightly moist, which meant it had been a relatively good sermon. There were some Sundays he came away drenched, the level of sweat correlating to how well he felt he reached them: the blank faces watching him. For a sermon as hard as the Prodigal Son, he had done all right, and he stepped back and closed the Holy Book of Scriptures with a snap.

"Let us make our Profession of Faith," he began, and the congregation stood, the last few rows coming back to life, stretching and yawning and blinking their eyes. "We believe in one God, the Father, the Almighty, Maker of Heaven and earth..." they prayed in a single monotone voice as Father Chris returned to the altar to prepare the sacrament.

Breaking the bread, pouring the wine, Chris found it calming the way they happened every week, each in the same order. The same words were said over the Host, and the Eucharist just became, without explanation, questioning, or interpretation. It was mystical and serious, the start to each week and a cleansing one did from the inside.

He was drawn to the Catholic Church precisely for its strictness in thought and infallibility. There wasn't room for doubt between the rituals, the ceremonies, and the rules. There were so many other things in which one could lose oneself; the question of truth could be completely avoided for a whole lifetime. Chris ate up the history and the ancient writings, fitting his faith together like a puzzle. There was hierarchy and a sense of establishment that made him feel a part of something undeniably real.

But for all that, he could not interpret or explain what happened in the scriptures without narrowly escaping the idea that they hadn't really happened at all. Sunday sermon was the part of the job he hated.

Mrs. Hutchings signaled the recession with Sunday School announcements. "Don't forget to have your children read through the texts in the missal for November 22nd. We will begin practicing for the Thanksgiving Children's mass in two Sundays," she smiled a Sunday School smile, all teeth with thin-line lipsticked lips.

"As usual, there is coffee and donuts downstairs, so everyone please stay," Chris closed the sermon as the organ began to play. The 10:00 AM

21

Mass was ended in the peace of the Lord, Amen.

Chris watched his congregation slowly move down the aisle and heard the stairs begin creaking as they filed downstairs to warm coffee and cold jelly donuts. The altar boy was putting out the candles on the stage, and conversation made a lazy, insect-like hum. He went in the back, removed his robes, and then followed down to the basement.

It was always considerably cooler in the basement than in the rest of the church, and people stood in tight circles, many with sweaters or light jackets and their hands around their Styrofoam cups. Only the kids didn't seem to notice. They chased each other in and out of the wooden columns that lined either side of the room (weak ceiling support) and sprinkled powder from their donuts on their shirts and the floor.

"Hi Matt, how are you?" Chris shook hands with a lengthy man in a turtleneck. He kept moving after receiving a solid, "Fine," and made his way to the donut table, shaking several more hands and patting a few women's shoulders on the way. Judy was there, with the same line she said every Sunday, "Are you coming in for dinner tonight?"

This Sunday, however, Chris was looking for a particular parishioner. He scanned over the many heads for Derek Dewallace. They had a counseling appointment set after Mass, probably to talk about Derek's wife. She was dying of cancer, and ever since she outlived the doctor's one-year prognosis, Derek had come pretty regularly for appointments. He was using the Church as a good luck charm; as long as he kept coming, his wife would keep living.

Chris saw Derek, standing in the corner with some of his hunting buddies. He looked drawn and tired, as people do who spend most of their time in a hospital. He saw Chris and walked towards him, breaking off his conversation with nods and smiles.

"Hiya Father," Derek pushed his hands into his coat pockets. "Good sermon this morning."

"Thank you, although I thought I saw you in the back glazed over," he joked.

"Well, I figure it's kind of like those tapes they sell on the infomercials for learning foreign languages: you can sleep while they play and wake-up fluent, Father." Both men smiled large, real smiles before they began at the awkward questions.

"So, how is Helen doing?"

"All right, all right. Better than the doctors think, as always. She hangs in there, even though it is awfully painful for her. I am going to visit her after our chat, tell her about what's going on with all of her neighbors," Derek gestured to include the room.

"Shall we head over to my place, and not keep her curious too long?"

Derek nodded, and they both said their goodbyes, grabbing some coffee to go.

* * * * *

Chris settled in the overstuffed living room chair that usually sat in front of the TV, but which was now turned to face Derek on the couch and the small coffee table between them.

"Helen sure does appreciate all the help you've given us," Derek reintroduced his wife to the conversation. "She really likes how at every Mass, you say her name and ask everyone to pray for her. I have also been praying the Rosary with her, like you showed me. We do it every night."

Chris nodded and took a loud drink from his coffee and then placed it on the table. "It's good to hear that you both are keeping a positive perspective," he said while crossing one long leg over the other, trying to look relaxed. "Together, you two are very strong." He paused, his throat clicking. "But, I'd like to talk about you, Derek – that's what we're here for. How's your faith when you're alone?"

A long pause. "It certainly can be hard sometimes," Derek began slowly. His eyes wandered around the room disinterestedly, then brightened. "But, with the results we're getting, it would be hard to give up now," he scrutinized Chris' face for acknowledgement of the miracle he was trying to work. Chris nodded cautiously.

"I mean, it's been two months longer than the doctors gave her. For once, I really feel like God is listening to me, Father."

"Well, He always listens. Sometimes He doesn't answer, " Chris smiled weakly, "but He always listens." He tried to sound light even as he forced the conversation to discomfort. "And, if this doesn't work out, and Helen is never cured, God still was listening," he stressed.

Derek shook his head in short, rapid successions. "Yeah, but I don't think I could talk to Him anymore if…He didn't answer me on this," he swallowed hard and brought his hands together in a pyramid in front of him.

"That will be the most important time to continue believing." Chris tried to keep pity out of his voice. "It's dangerous to expect a miracle. God isn't about pleasing you or answering you. Sometimes, He's about hard things you can't understand."

Derek leaned back away from Chris, but Chris filled in the space, touching his knee and looking up from under Derek's down-turned face. "Hope for a miracle, but still expect what the odds tell you to expect. And that's what I'm here for, to help you with that. Faith – true faith – will allow you to find peace, Derek. Now, tomorrow."

"There won't be any peace for me if–" Derek's voice was unnaturally

23

low. "How could I…when He knows how much she means to me? When she suffers in more pain than anyone ever deserves to feel? How could He?"

They sat silent.

"You don't understand," Derek burst. "I came to you to hear something good; to find more of the thing that's been getting me through. The peace you talk about is nothing."

"Of course there's a lot of good to talk about," Chris leaned away to backpedal. "Albeit, Helen is doing better than anyone ever thought she would. But the chances of her making a full recovery are still… well… not so good. Of course, you know that," he added hurriedly. "But the real miracle is that Helen will be saved eternally. This battle is just that – a battle. And if she loses this battle, it's still all right. Because Helen will be with God, where there isn't any pain."

Derek unfolded and refolded his hand-pyramid.

"How do you do it, Father? How do you believe through losing the most important thing in the world? Watching the person you love become something else as they put more tubes in and more drugs? You talk like it's something easy, like with some more counseling, I'll be good as new," he trembled slightly. "Well, I can tell you, I don't work that way. I won't know how to come here and pray after she's gone. And some of the things you say – but you don't ever have weak moments, do you, Father?" Derek swiped at his eyes quickly, breathing deep to dry tears still forming in his throat.

Chris sucked in his breath slightly. "Do you mean…are there moments when I question whether God exists?" He sat up straight, not quite sure what to say.

Derek nodded his head, urging him to answer.

"Well, I have certainly had my doubts at one time or another," Chris began slowly. "And, there have been times when I felt like I was not heard either. God can be very dist…"

Derek rolled his head to one side, turning away from Chris.

Chris sat uncomfortable and unsure how to continue. "For the most part, I am sure. But, when I'm given the hard road to travel, I still ask why, just like anyone else. There have been plenty of times when, like you, I found my life taking an unexpected turn for the worse. In fact, only a few months ago, I–"

"I'm going to go now, Father," Derek's voice was painfully cool. "Thanks for your … advice."

Both men remained without speaking, not looking up, the clock on the wall keeping time.

"Do you think you could bless her with the Anointing of the Sick that you did the last time? Maybe tomorrow?" Derek finally spoke.

"Sure, Derek. I will definitely be over tomorrow to see Helen and bless her."

Derek put his hands back in his pockets. He turned to go, then turned back half way, facing the wall awkwardly and still not meeting Chris' eyes. "I'm sorry. I just come to see you because, well, I need a priest. Someone who is supposed to truly believe that anything with God is possible, so that I can get through another week. But, maybe I should just work on my own faith a little harder from the inside."

"I'm sure we could all work a little harder in that respect," Chris also stood with his hands in his pockets.

"Yeah. I think we all could. See you tomorrow. I'll tell Helen you're coming. She'll be glad to hear it." Derek turned to go and let himself out.

"See you tomorrow, Derek." Chris sat back down with a thud, extending his long legs to their longest around the coffee table. He blew air out through his cheeks hard and rubbed worried hands through his blond hair. "I need to work on my faith. I had a counseling appointment, that's what came out," Chris spoke to himself.

It wasn't the first time someone told him that, nor would it be the last. Counseling was a hard, sad business. Chris couldn't imagine how psychologists found any happiness after listening to so much sorrow. He genuinely wished that he could help Derek and tell him just what he needed to hear. But, it was true; faith for Chris had never been as easy as that. He brought the half-empty coffee cups into the kitchen for dumping.

The light on the answering machine was still flashing on the counter: "You have one new message." He noticed it the moment he came in and had by no means forgotten it, even during the stressful conversation. He knew who it was without having to press play: Alan. He felt his pulse quicken ever so slightly. But, he was not ready to talk yet. Not after Derek.

Chris looked outside at the garden. He felt like working up a sweat. It was another beautiful, late September day, and he needed to hoe over some of the dying flowerbeds anyway. But, as a rule, Chris did not do yard work on Sunday, being that it was the third commandment. Still the itch to leave the rectory for a little while and at least accomplish something positive for the day was strong.

There wasn't a washer or dryer at the rectory, so Andy Dowell had let Chris use his machines for the four years they had been neighbors. "Just come on in, don't bother knocking," he always greeted Chris, and since Andy was 80 years old and couldn't hear a fire alarm going off right over his head, for the most part, Chris didn't bother knocking.

Walking into his bedroom, Chris picked up his dirty clothes from the last week. Socks, jeans, underwear – he sent out his shirts to be pressed – and threw them into two piles, lights and darks. With one pile over each arm, he headed out of the front door and across the street to Andy's. He went in and down the cellar stairs to the washroom.

Grass stains, newspaper smudges, pen marks, and socks with holes: he liked to be outside as often as he could, he followed no less than seven daily publications, he wrote often, and he walked everywhere. Chris poured in the detergent and the color-safe bleach. There was a chair by the washer, and he sat on it. He fished out a book he was reading – a Stephen King thriller. He let his mind go until he no longer watched the light turn from wash to rinse, but was taking the book with him while he threw his clothes into the dryer.

By the time he was done folding, Chris felt surprisingly refreshed for having spent the afternoon in a cellar. Still thinking about his book, he carted the clothes up the stairs. There was a loud snoring coming from the bedroom. Andy probably still hadn't realized that anyone had come in his front door. Chris closed it firmly behind him, balancing the folded stacks of still-warm clothes and headed home.

Upon opening his own door, his eyes immediately flew to the kitchen counter. The answering machine was still flashing, only now there were two messages. Carefully, so as not to lose any socks, he closed the door with his foot and then put the piles down on his bed. They could wait.

"Hey Chris. It's Alan. I know you're probably busy since it's a Sunday, but I just wanted to let you know that I already looked into that crime you sent me in your e-mail. It was… very interesting, and I would like to discuss it with you in person. You know the number." The tape whirred, finding the next message.

"Hey, it's Alan again. Just give me a call."

Chris went into his bedroom, found his address book, and sat down at the kitchen table with the phone. He leaned over the table to hit the light switch, then thought better of it. Mid-afternoon sunlight came through the small kitchen windows and dappled the tablecloth with a far prettier pattern than the one it usually retained. He punched the buttons on the phone, and leaned back in the hard wood chair.

"Hello," the voice of his old friend came across the line.

"Hey Alan, it's Chris. I just got your message."

"Hey," Alan's voice lightened. "Good to hear from you. It's been a long time. How is everything?"

"Eh… a little tougher today than usual. I had counseling with a man whose wife is dying of cancer."

"Yeah, that isn't one of the perks of the job, eh? I still think you should go into teaching – you were always better with the books than the people."

Chris frowned. "I do my best. How are things in Indiana?"

"Good. The private school is helping the parish stay really healthy. It's pretty easy to keep parents dedicated to the church when their children are getting their education through it. So, the following is large and attentive. We started a choir a few months back, and it is just now starting to hold a tune."

"Yeah, well certainly not because you've been training them then," Chris fired back. "Have you heard from Ed or John recently?"

"They send me clippings every once in a while. Little articles, things like that. But, we haven't seen each other since the last time you were with us."

"I haven't spoken to them since oh..." Chris took a second to do the math, "at least a year, maybe longer."

"Yeah, well you kind of dropped out," there was a tone of reproach in Alan's voice. "I was actually really surprised when you sent me something."

Chris was waiting for this part of the conversation, and true to form, Alan didn't keep him waiting long. "Well, when I heard about the Ashton murder, I have to admit that you were one of the first people that I thought of."

"It's an interesting case. The story matches our criteria pretty well, other than of course, that it happened in the United States. But, on a college campus, there are many foreign students, so I think for the moment that we can put aside our geographical presumptions. The age grouping is right on target. Clyde was twenty years old, putting him smack in the middle of our estimates."

Chris frowned, changing the phone from one ear to the other. "That's what I thought when I first heard about the incident too. Plus, it was a pretty violent crime without a motive or a suspect, which makes it stand out a little more from the rest of the news. Did the police have anything more interesting to say than the college newspaper?"

"Way more, way more. I had Father Patrick's brother pull some police files for me as usual," his tone was excited but controlled. "The kid, Clyde, was six foot five and almost 300 pounds. When they found him, he had no nose, only one eye, and most of his left cheek was completely gone. That in itself is pretty extraordinary. But, of course, there's more," Alan waited for Chris to say something.

Chris held back. He knew that Alan was baiting him, trying to catch him up in the weird excitement and fear that was Alan's faith. But, it never worked that way. Alan always had the big ideas, and Chris always remained grounded.

After the short silence, Alan continued. "According to the coroner's report, Clyde suffered serious head trauma. He had multiple skull fractures, and severe bruising to the brain, so severe, he actually died of the trauma pretty instantly. Obviously, he was hit with something hard enough to kill and mangle him. The evidence shows that he was only hit once, so we are talking a single, strong blow. Now listen closely," Alan inhaled deeply, ready to finish the rest of the story on a single breath.

Chris felt himself lean forward instinctively.

"The flesh wounds on Clyde's face have a very distinct pattern. There are five major areas of depression on the left side of his face, where most of the major fractures are located. The depressions very much resemble the fingers of someone's hand."

Chris felt a heaviness descend on his chest. His heart beat quickly now, and the phone was sweaty. He glanced around the kitchen. It was still sunny. "You mean, someone actually slapped his face off?"

"That's not even the most impressive part," Alan took on the tone of a magician, ready to reveal his greatest trick. "To do the type of damage that was done to Clyde Parker's skull, a person would've had to hit him at no less than 200 miles per hour."

"That breaks any boxing record I've ever heard." Chris took a moment to digest the incredible number. "So, what do you think it means? Clyde Parker couldn't have been the one, right? You aren't implying that?"

"No, no I don't think that Clyde Parker is the one. But, if this crime really is as extraordinary as it seems, I would be willing to bet that someone close to that campus is."

Chris couldn't believe they were talking like this. "You can't really think that we have found... well... her... I am not even sure I still believe..."

"Remember the statue, Chris?" Alan almost whispered. "Remember the dream?"

"I didn't have any dream," Chris snapped back. "And chances are that–"

"That it is just a freak accident, a weird coincidence. I know, I know. But, what if it's not?"

Chris didn't answer him. He didn't have to.

Alan accepted the silent agreement. " We should just look into it, you know, see who's around Ashton College that shouldn't be, that sort of a thing. This is one of the strangest crimes we've come across in years."

On the other side of the line, Chris hung his head.

"And, if it wasn't just anyone that committed this crime, then we need to get there, and soon. If she's really close to that... murdering thing–"

"We need to find her first."

Chapter 4 – Revelations

The first few weeks after the incident at the Chiesa di Statua were a whirlwind in Chris' memory. Nothing had seemed real, and yet everyone around him had come to believe.

Father Alan gave the orders from the beginning, perhaps because even then, he was the oldest; or perhaps because he was the Congregation's undersecretary; or perhaps because he thought himself the foremost expert on the ancient writings of the Church. It was he who called a society meeting the morning after they viewed the change to the statue. In a conference room in Meura's only hotel, Alan set out coffee and fresh Italian pastries on the large table in the center of the room. Crowding uncomfortably to fit, the priests moved their chairs as close together as possible and sat with their coffee mugs in an unsettled but quiet way. Chris sat at the end of the table, facing Alan.

Alan started the meeting by picking up the creamer and clinking his spoon against it. Chris remembered someone saying, "It feels like a wedding," and then laughing nervously.

"May I have your attention? Gentlemen, please."

The room grew even quieter, and they turned to Alan with strained faces.

"I am sure that last evening's events came as a shock to you all. Obviously, you can see why I have been so anxious to meet in Meura to confer on this matter. I have called you here to discuss the far-reaching implications, to create Church and world history as we stop looking to the past for prophecy, and turn instead to our own time. With certainty, we can explore the miraculous movement of the seventh statue as a new omen."

Father John, a small priest with a red face and a surprisingly booming voice, quickly interrupted. "Are you sure, Alan, that this was not just some prank, an act of vandalism?" There was a general murmur of consent.

" Of course it's not vandalism, and any priest who thinks so is merely turning his head," Alan reproached with controlled anger. He then leaned forward, splaying his hands on the table. They were warm enough to leave misty smears on the wood.

"Is that what many of you have been thinking all night? Vandalism?" he accused them all. "You saw the statue; did she look vandalized to you? Did you see evidence that the arms had been broken and moved?" His face sneered. "Of course you didn't, because there are no break marks. This was hardly caused by a few teenagers sneaking into an old church and molesting a statue." The low, doubtful murmuring began again, but Alan continued to speak over it. "I am prepared for this," he took a few deep breaths. "Of course, there are those of you who will doubt. But, for the moment, I ask that you do not interrupt with your skepticism, for, I am speaking to that part of you which will come to believe."

A few eyebrows rose in defiance, but the room waited.

"As you all know, I have studied the book of *Revelation* for many years. It has often been the focus of my investigations and my publications," Alan tucked his hands behind his back and walked around the table, like a teacher moving around his classroom.

"Certainly, you have all read the book many times, and are familiar with the sections dedicated to angels." Heads nodded, but Alan continued as though they had not. "The first seven angels mentioned in the book are the angels of the seven seals, Chapters six and seven. Christ Himself commands these angels to open the seals, releasing plagues upon man: war, famine, natural disaster. But, when the seventh seal is broken, peace reins in the heavens, and there is a rest from the horrors of the seals.

"The next section of *Revelation*, however, deals with the Almighty Power – not the Son, but the Father – and the angels who stand before Him at all times," Alan's eyes grew wider with the thrill. "You have seen their sculptures. The Book of *Enoch* named them, and I'm sure they will be familiar to you: Raphael. Uriel. Raguel. Michael. Sariel. Gabriel. Remiel."

He gave each name its own sentence, emphasizing them in a dark voice, as though he were telling a ghost story around a campfire. The effect was disquieting, and Chris looked around the room, afraid to know where Alan's thoughts were headed, embarrassed that they had gone this far.

"God gave these seven angels trumpets to sound and mark off time. The first trumpeter breaks the peace of the seventh seal with natural disaster, and the last sounds the end of the earth and the beginning of God's wrath. Each one has been designated a certain moment in the history of the world to sound his trumpet, deliver his burden to humanity, and bring us one step closer to the Second Coming," he whispered these last words, letting them move into the room where their bodies and minds could absorb them. "Gentlemen, we are talking about a very calculated progression of the human race. It's evolution – God's evolution. The Father has appointed the right time and place for each of these trumpets, each of the seals." He pulled a handkerchief out of his pocket and wiped his face.

"The last trumpeter, the seventh statue if you will, is supposed to sound her horn when the final prophecy of the Bible has been fulfilled: a man from the line of King David – the ancestor of Jesus Christ – will once again come to the throne of Israel. And, when that happens, the skies fall, the seas boil, the dead rise, and all of apocalypse begins," he rattled off these last details as if they were insignificant.

Father John interrupted again, "I don't know where you are going with this Alan. But even if you assume that *Revelation* is to be taken literally and that the angels exist as more than metaphors, the trumpets must be sounded in order. And it is the general consensus, unless you go by the *National Enquirer*, that we are nowhere near the prophetic conditions that would trigger the seventh trumpet, or apocalypse."

Alan's face shown all the brighter. "Good man, Father John. I agree with you completely," he smiled at him from across the room. "We are nowhere near the end. By their descriptions in *Revelation*, most scholars agree that only a few of the seals have been broken, meaning we have not even reached the plagues of the trumpeters yet. No, there remains much to be done before the Second Coming," he laughed low.

"You see, there is a purpose to all of these holy trials, all of these plagues. It's a weeding out. Only those people who, and I quote 'have the seal of God on their foreheads' will survive the end of days. As the human race progresses in the face of opposition, we will be wielded to God's purpose. Famine, disease, while they are tragic, at the same time, they leave only the strongest. The generation of humanity that will see this new king of Israel crowned will need to be very special. The Bible says that they will not be allowed to eat, they will not sleep, but they will be able to live on faith alone for seven years. Seven years, my fellow priests. Can even we imagine living only by believing?"

The room was silent, waiting for the punch line of a bad joke.

"The trumpeters' plagues are evolution towards a generation in which better faith exists and such things are possible. At the end, we will be ready. God, by His plan revealed in this final book, will make us ready. However," here came the punch.

"What would happen if, by some mistake, the final prophecy was fulfilled too early, and the trumpeters sounded out of order?" He answered quickly, "Mankind would not be prepared. The evolution would not be fulfilled. And perhaps, we would lose the final battle."

The room took a simultaneous, gasped breath – and let it out in twenty angry voices. "You are bringing pure superstition into a scholarly society," a young priest called out. "We are in the business of recording ancient omens, not making up new ones!" "I can't believe that you are seriously talking about apocalypse here, Alan." "Are you saying that God is fallible, Alan?

31

That He would just allow something like that to happen?" the cacophony of voices rose.

"I AM SAYING THAT I BELIEVE GOD GAVE ALL OF US FREE WILL!" Alan spoke over them in his own roar. "And I don't think any of you can argue that point with me. God created paradise, and yet He allowed Eve to eat the apple. He created great and powerful Israel, and yet He allowed the nation to become slaves. Free will began our decent and continues it. Why couldn't we break a seal or force a trumpet to sound?" his spit flew onto the table, but he took no notice. He craned at them even as the doubt was obvious in their faces. "It is proven, Man can do his own aligning and create historical circumstances–"

"And what circumstances are we talking about, Alan?" Chris heard his own voice join the stream of questions and criticism. Several priests laughed.

Alan crossed his arms over his chest and leveled his eyes with Chris'. "Isn't it obvious?" He waited for silence. And waited. "I am speaking simply of Israeli politics. I believe the alteration to the seventh statue is a sign that the final apocalyptic prophecy is on the brink of early fulfillment: a man of the line of King David will be named king of Israel now, in our time – centuries or perhaps millennia before such a thing is supposed to happen. This blood ascension to the Israeli thrown will complete all that is written and force the seventh trumpeter to bring the final plagues upon us, long before we are ready. Human government can and will create the circumstances for the final sounding. Not because God wants it, or because it is time, but because we, all of us, have the free will to bring a man – just a single man – to power too soon."

"Alan, may I remind you that there isn't even a throne of Israel for someone to rule. The country is run under a democracy," Chris could not back down, even as the hurt wrinkled the skin around Alan's eyes.

"Of course, no government in the history of the world has ever changed political philosophies," Alan's voice was low and thick. "But I forgot – you're a scholar, Father Chris. You'll just do what you do best and analyze it after it happens." He glared at Chris as the room grew further out of control; several priests began to leave.

"I am not finished yet!" Alan yelled just as the first man reached the doorknob. Impatiently, he waited for everyone to stop moving.

But the priest nearest the door led the way out. "You're an old man, Alan."

"Think of your vocations!" Alan called, his voice edged with desperation. "This is what you are really here for! Did you all take your vows and not believe in any of the mysteries that you studied?" He held up his hands. "You are priests for God's sake. Go back to your rooms and seriously consider rereading the Bible, for you have all forgotten the faith that it teaches. Do you think that the twentieth century is void of God's power?"

Finally, he thundered, "COWARDS!" and turned and left the room himself, going through the opposite door.

* * * * *

The rest of the day, Chris stayed in his room to avoid the furious discussions. The hotel had a beautiful view of Meura. Stone houses lined the streets, shouldered next to small stores. The hotel sat at one end of the village, the now infamous church only a few blocks away, clay roof and stone tower reaching up into the November sky.

He gazed at it, wondering. What was it like to believe in the unreasonable, the unthinkable, the unbelievable? It had been a different type of disciple in the days when miracles were a part of life. Now, if a priest could handle some squeamish confessions and marriage counseling, he could be a decent, even a good priest, while keeping his feet entirely on the ground.

Even the Congregation for the Hetairia Melchizedek. Alan was right. They were a society that only looked at omens in the past, aligning history with what was predicted. Though Chris resisted Alan's speech as much as the next priest, he could still see the irony: the society that records ancient omens cannot even contemplate a new sign.

I have made a covenant with my chosen, I have sworn unto David my servant, thy seed will I establish for ever, and build up thy throne to all generations. Psalms 89:3-4. It was what they were all waiting for: the line of kings to be fulfilled. First King David, then his descendant Jesus Christ, and finally a third descendant: the Second Coming. Chris waited for it, preached it, and yet he could not seriously consider it.

* * * * *

Dinner was strained that night. The priests broke off into groups of closer friends and ate at Araniti's, the only restaurant in town, with its specialty of warm bread, old cheese, and dark wine. Many were talking about cutting the trip short and heading home to their parishes the following day.

Sitting at the bar, Chris ordered a beer and was working on some tomato and mozzarella when Alan came to sit beside him. The other priests barely looked up.

"I know what you're thinking," he began.

"Hello, Alan. Want something to drink?" Chris moved his stool over slightly so that Alan could get closer to the bar.

Alan moved in grumpily, for a few minutes refusing to look at Chris, and then looking at him very hard. He took in the huge frame, neck, chest breadth, the straight blond hair that stuck up around the cowlick, the dark eyes. His face had already begun to wrinkle – not in the good places around the mouth and eyes where smile lines are made, but on the forehead and temples where contemplation and worry leave their mark. And then there was the priest's collar and shirt.

"What made you become a priest, Chris?"

Chris rolled his eyes. "The same reasons that you became one, Alan. To pass on faith to others and – if there's time – to study. Maybe I can't believe as blindly as you can, but I still believe. Leave this conversation back in the conference room."

"Because, I mean look at you. You look like some retired football lineman, who's already been through two divorces. Not exactly a man of faith. Not someone I would want to confess to, pray with, or who could–"

"Can someone get this guy a beer?" Chris called out, then again. "Qualcuno posso portare una birra a questo uomo?" He waited for the bartender to put a glass down in front of Alan, then paid for it, and slid off the stool to head back to his room.

"I'll pray for you, Chris. You and all the rest," Alan said into his mug.

* * * * *

"Remiel."

Father John woke up with a start. The moon came in softly through the window and bathed the hotel comforter in blue-white light and stripes from the window panels. He sat up slowly and waited for his eyes to adjust, searching carefully without moving his head. The dresser took shape first, then the Victorian armchair – hotel furniture.

He sat up further, feeling more confident. There was no one.

"Alan's nonsense," he said as he slid back under the covers, his feet finding the cool part of the sheets at the very end of the bed. His head hit the pillow.

"Remiel."

John sat straight up this time. "Who's there?" he called out in his deepest voice. He did another quick scan of the corners, the shadows near the window – nothing. His eyes fell on the closed closet door.

As if on cue, the closet light turned on with an audible click as the socket chain was pulled. Light spilled onto the carpet through the cracks around the door and pointed a yellow line towards his bed.

Swallowing hard, John swung his legs out from under the covers and quietly placed his bare feet on the carpet. "Who's there?" he asked again, trying to sound angry and thankful that his voice did not crack. "I know you're in the closet."

34

The light turned off, plunging the room back into complete darkness.

John held his breath. Of course, it was just someone pulling a prank; one of the younger priests having a laugh. But, between *the statue incident*, as he liked to think of it, and all the talk of *Revelation*, John found himself petrified in the same way that he had been when his parents sent him down into the basement at night to check on the furnace. There was something about the light and the dark, the feeling of being watched while not seeing. He had almost forgotten.

The room was small, and it only took four steps to reach the closet door. He stood there uncertain, seeing only a slight glint of moonlight where the round knob was.

The light clicked on again, and this time, he was close enough to hear the chain swinging back and forth inside, released by some unknown hand to clink rhythmically off the light bulb. He took the opportunity to do a once over of the room aided by the sliver of light just to be sure he was alone at least on this side of the door. He was. He slid his hand onto the cool metal of the doorknob, smothering its glint–

The light turned off.

Then on again.

Then off, continuing a frenzy of light and dark.

Fear sunk in cold and heavy, and the dampness under his arms and on his palms spread. He could see the shadow of someone under the door turning on and off again with the light. The shadow was large and flat across the doorway, as though the person pulling the chain was leaning right against the door.

He wet his lips, clenched his jaw. *Whoever this is, I'm going to fu...* With a snarl halfway between a deep voice and an animal howl, he ripped open the closet door, his free hand curled into the hardest fist he could muster–

There was nothing.

Not even any clothes (he hadn't hung any of his own belongings). There was only the white back of the closet with a single crack running down the plaster, and of course, the light burning hot and the wildly swinging chain. John stared up at the bare bulb, seeing the fiery wires inside. He felt the panic rising, but wouldn't allow it to get past the ball in his throat. He concentrated mindlessly on the swinging of the pendulum chain until his eyes hurt. He stood still for more than a minute.

Then he was suddenly racing jerkily with adrenaline-controlled movements to turn on all the lights as fast as he possibly could. When all was lit that could be lit, he sat back down on his bed. The closet light remained on, and he stared at it. Perhaps he should wake some of the others. Or tell someone at the hotel...perhaps he could switch rooms. Or–

"Remiel."

John jumped from the bed, squeezing his own arms in a childish hug. The whisper sounded as though it were still coming from inside his room, and yet, that was almost impossible. "Holy God."

He undid the latch to the door and stepped out into the hotel hallway. Like his room, it was empty. And yet he ventured, high pitched and unnatural, "Is there anyone out here?"

"Remiel."

The whisper was just behind him, and he felt the air of hot breath on his neck. Whipping around, John stumbled back into his room and then froze – as his feet came down on the hard stone floor.

He was in the Chiesa di Statua, *a complete impossibility, a bend of reality*, his mind ran through the probability; immediately he felt relieved. "I'm dreaming, just dreaming," he said. "Thank God. I'll have to tell Alan about this," and he laughed.

The church was quiet, lit only by the backlights above the altar. Jesus hung on the cross with His head bowed low and His eyes closed. The seven statues stood on the left side of the church, white in the gloom. His mind recreated them perfectly and in detail, so that his relief ebbed into eeriness. The seventh statue still had her trumpet raised.

The floor was frigidly cold, and John moved onto the warn red carpet that ran up the main aisle, scrunching up his toes underneath him. He was still only wearing his drawstring pajama pants and an extra large t-shirt with holes and yellow stains in the armpits. "Well, this part is realistic anyway," he spoke to the empty room as another wave of disturbing realism stole over him. "So what happens next?" His words echoed off the high ceiling and back to him.

"Remiel."

This time, it came from the statues.

John jerked his eyes in their direction, but nothing moved in the empty spaces. "It's only a dream," and he stepped off the carpet and back onto the cold floor, pausing briefly to check the shadows. There was only new silence as he walked down the far left aisle to face their stony witness. He moved slowly down their line, watching them watch him. Their eyes stared out pupiless, without focus into the church, as though they saw everything and nothing all at once, looking past him and into him at the same time.

The second, the third, the fourth – he passed the fifth statue, and then he heard it.

A strange stream of whispering, like the sound of a window barely cracked in a speeding car. Though there was still no one to be seen, the rushing of air over lips was unmistakable, the quiet articulations of "s" and "t," distinctly audible. Goose bumps formed along his neck and arms and the hairs on his legs stood as the whispering grew with each step. His eyes hunted the darkness to see the voice that was like a fevered prayer, a rosary being recited urgently.

The seventh statue. Parts of her glared in the dim light, shimmering as though she were wet. Hair back, lips parted, and blank eyes unwavering. And the whispering – it was almost loud now, like the car window was suddenly half down. *Just a dream!* He gaped into her face knowing it could not be true and yet, heart pounding without rhythm, John leaned into her white arms. "Remiel,Remiel,Remiel, I am here. I have come. Remiel, I am here. I have come. I have come, come for you, come for you, Remiel. Come, Remiel come."

John knew his skin was the color of new chalk as he pulled away from the hard, unmoving lips that hovered over the trumpet mouthpiece and still somehow repeated over and over the string of sighing words. The desire to wake up from this *Alice in Wonderland* fantasy world rose in him like the desire to break the surface of water after a long dive. But the statue's whispering continued in a rapid fire of that horrible name.

"Is she whispering again?"

John spun around, almost toppling over into the statues at the sound of the high-pitched voice. He stumbled several steps before seeing the young child in a white nightdress standing a few feet from him on the lowest step of the altar. "Keep away from me!"

The girl could be no more than four or five, and her reddish hair was tangled as though she too had been pulled from her bed. She was a part of the dream somehow, which meant she could not be right. John placed his hand over his heart like an old woman.

The child smiled and took another step towards him. "She's whispering again, isn't she?" she asked in a singsong voice, spinning around in a small circle. Then she laughed, and it was a grown woman's laugh that erupted from her throat. "She says that Remiel has come."

"I said keep back," but his eyes flicked towards the statue. The girl took two more steps towards him.

" Yes, Remiel. I am Remiel. And I have come." She began to repeat it quickly, whispering like the statue. "I am Remiel, Remiel I am here I have come Remiel come."

"Stop. This is…" John's feet smacked loudly as he moved backward up the aisle.

Again, the woman-voice laughed as she ceased chanting. "You don't have to be afraid of me – John," she stressed his name to let him know she knew it. "I came here to help you. I have come to guard my trumpet. You wouldn't want me to sound it, would you? No, no, John. No one would be ready," she slowed her words darkly. "But there are others who would want it, John. Others who can only win by helping us to fall. They live like Satan in the garden, tempting and needing us to take the bite ourselves. Others." Then whispering, "They're the ones who want to burn our souls."

Please wake-up! For God's sake! It seemed all his blood was in his ears.

"John? John I know what you're thinking. You want to run away from me. But, believe me, you shouldn't."

Only a few more steps and he would reach the heavy wooden doors. Where would he end up? The hotel hall, his room, outside? The girl was still following him slowly.

"Shhh! John. Don't step so loud, or it will hear you!"

He took the last few steps, feeling for the latch

"Please! It's just outside – the thing that was in your closet."

John froze then, his hand on the door. He felt the panic rising up in him again. It was in his thoughts, his voice, his legs. The adrenaline was burning through him. "This is just a dream!" he yelled at her even as he heard something rubbing quietly on the doors from the outside. It was low to the ground, like a dog scratching to be let in.

"You're not asleep, John. And if it hears you, if it knows we're in here, something very real is going to happen."

John shook his head at her. "What is it? What the hell is it?" She was still coming, very close now.

"I didn't come alone, John. Something terrible came with me, to stop me. The Snake is its master. It doesn't want me to protect you, and if it finds me, it will hurt me. And it will hurt you."

The scratching became more intense. There was a horrible smell coming from under the doors, like burnt hair. John gave up all pretense, his breathing becoming wild and irregular.

"I think it's heard you! Get back!"

On the other side, something huge threw its weight against the door and the dull beat echoed through the church.

"It's going to find me John, and then everything ends," two huge tears ran down her face.

And, that's when he noticed her eyes. There was something wrong with them, and he squinted hard.

Pupiless.

She stared at him with pupiless eyes, pure white eyes, hollow eyes squeezing out tears.

With a scream John ran for the altar.

"Hide me, hide me!" The girl shrieked after him. She dove into the pews as the banging on the doors became regular, incessant, each knock shaking the doors. John couldn't see her anymore, but heard her scurrying on the floor.

"Dear God, dear God," he said over and over again. Whatever it was, it was going to burst into the church at any moment. He got on his knees to pray, mingling his whispers with the others – all the statues were whispering now.

"John? John, you have to find me, John!" he heard the child-thing calling from the back of the church. "You have to find me before it can find me! FIND ME BEFORE IT FINDS ME!" she screeched, the echoes peeling off the sides and ceiling of the church.

With a loud whining, one of the doors wrenched open.

A burst of cold air blew into the church setting the missal book pages frantically turning. John held the altar leg – some sort of charm against the thing outside.

Only the streetlight came in through the door. The church was suddenly silent.

John let out his breath in one huge sob.

And then he felt it. It was behind him, somehow. He knew it the same way he had always known when someone watched him while he slept.

There was a slow footstep behind him, then three others. The click of claws on the stone. His heart swelled inside of him, aching in his chest.

And then the footsteps began to run.

It hit him from behind, digging its claws into his back and hurling him down the altar stairs. Father John managed only one scream before his head hit the stone.

* * * * *

He awoke not long after. His eyelids fluttered open, and his breath came in short bursts as the relief swept over him. For a moment, he lay there swallowing. He remembered something his nephew had told him and laughed. *If you die in your dream, you die in real life.*

Then John realized where he was.

The arching ceiling extended into the dark above him. He was still in the church, lying in a pew. Quickly, he sat up.

He was not alone. The other priests were there, rows and rows of them sleeping in the pews.

* * * * *

That night, Chris heard many voices in the hotel hallway. Groggily, he lifted his head as small stampedes passed by his door. He thought he recognized Alan's voice, and with a groan, uncurled himself from the bed and walked into the cool hotel room air. In the hallway, he found the other priests returning to their rooms in their pajamas. For a few moments, he watched the spectacle with amusement and confusion, trying to remember if there was a meeting he had missed.

"Hey Dan. What's – why is everyone awake? What time is it?"

Dan stared at him wide-eyed. Chris noticed then that they all had unusually wide eyes.

"You didn't have the dream?"

Chris merely raised his eyebrows.

The next morning, he would find that he was the only society priest who had not dreamt of Remiel.

Chapter 5 – Racing

Monday

On the bus, Chris tried hard to keep his knees from pressing into the seat in front of him. He knew how annoying it was to have two hard knobs shoved into your back. But, between the need to slouch on an 18-hour bus ride and to sleep at six in the morning, he was sure he wasn't doing a very good job.

The windows were slowly pinking as the sun came up. The light seemed unreal, like watching an aged film when the colors just aren't right anymore, either too green or yellow; too pink. They were only an hour-and-a-half away from Indianapolis now. Alan was probably just waking up and getting ready to meet him at the bus station.

Surreal, and not just the light. Chris had not joined an investigation in years, and he repeated the calling to himself, as if to wake a part of him capable of taking the job seriously. *Twilight Zone is most accurate,* his mind came back sarcastically.

There really was nothing too extraordinary about this particular investigation anyway. It was merely standard procedure to send a priest for a closer look at anything that looked suspicious. But, Chris felt obligated to at least try to kick himself into gear.

Years earlier, closer to the collective dream and the statue alteration, priests in the society had been constantly traveling on missions. Between the dreams and Alan's rationalizations, the supernatural quest was oddly clear: find the apocalyptic angel that had come to humankind and help her keep the final prophecy from early fulfillment.

FIND ME – in those days, there was real hope and motivation despite the fact that no one really knew what to look for. Unlike apocalyptic Hollywood movies, there was no cross-shaped birthmark to brand a chosen person. Instead, they searched for a young girl, born on or close to the day the statue had changed, believing that the movement of the statue's trumpet possibly marked Remiel's coming. This was their place to start, and they searched the birth records with a fine-toothed comb. The pope was notified, the high cardinals funneled money into the society quietly, and the search became official.

On Alan's suggestion they searched for abnormalities in the birth process... either extremely hard births or miraculous ones – births that should not have been successful but were. Most of the search was conducted outside of the United States, following the logic that God would send someone close to the Holy Land, perhaps a Jew. However, in many countries, the records were unclear; there were mind-splitting headaches after sifting through handwritten records for hours.

Eventually, the Congregation for the Hetairia Melchizedek opted for teams of priests formed according to geographic region. Because of his multiple language fluencies, Chris was first charged with looking through European records. With strong hospital connections all the way around from years of service to the sick, the task was long but not impossible. Several priests gave up preaching to focus on the search.

It produced nothing.

Other searches began. Some priests contended that Remiel had never been born, but was an adult. They formed groups to search newspapers for unbelievable occurrences. Chris did not share their opinion about Remiel's age, but the idea was interesting and oddly included scanning the tabloids. Although they were hugely exaggerated and often false, some of the less extraordinary stories did have some sort of truth to them. The society searched for people with unbelievable strength, intelligence, or psychic ability. They catalogued the visionaries of other religions and monitored well-renowned psychics, searching for a modern-day prophet. On more than a few occasions, the priests conducted interviews with Olympic athletes, gold medal winners who had broken impossible records. All the while, they were careful not to give away the search that would seem crazy to the rest of the world.

And yet, there came no new information. Chris still felt that sense, which could only be described as sinking, while the years passed with no sign. Some priests began, as the memory faded, to rationalize the collective dream and the statue, to brush it away. The Hetairia Melchizedek numbers dwindled until there were no more than 50 around the world, making it impossible to monitor many sources. For those priests who remained, the task became overwhelming.

Yet, Chris stayed despite the fact that he never even had the dream in the first place. Actively searching for Remiel added an invaluable urgency to his normal priestly duties, and Chris was loath to give it up, dream or no dream. Of course, he still felt the exclusion deeply. *It was the worst catch,* he replayed the unfairness so many times. The dream would have meant so much more to him than to any of the others – frightening as it had to have been, he would have been sure finally. Through the terror and the strangeness, true belief would have come to him. And yet, he who needed it most was denied. For months following the dream, Chris stopped praying outside of Mass. If there was a God, He was cruel. If there wasn't, well then it was as pointless as it had ever been. His mind ping-ponged between the pain of his banishment and the cold security that the other priests had been carried away by Alan's rhetoric.

Within the last five years or so, the search again took a new turn, this a dark one. Remiel had proved hard to find. Extraordinary or not, she was only a girl. But, there was still the Other – the faceless abomination scratching at the door. The man in the closet. The one sent to tempt human free will into breaking God's plan.

Remembering the violence it used in the dream, the priests hoped that the Other might keep a higher profile. If they could just find the Other, perhaps they could discover what city or even what country Remiel was in. After all, it was hunting her too and after 14 years, it very well might be close.

Based on this theory, the priests began searching the news for radically sadistic crimes, ironically hoping that, in its search for the angel, the Other might commit violence against others; they were looking for a blood trail. Investigations focused particularly on crimes with no motive and no suspects. Any assault that involved a teenage girl was of particular interest and intrepidation – the more time that passed, the more likely The Other would find her first.

It was this search that had led Chris here, nineteen years after the statue and the dream, on a bus to Indiana to organize the investigation of a violent murder at Ashton College. Alan insisted that Chris be a part of the investigation, and it felt like a favor. Throughout their friendship Alan always made a point of including him, like a gym teacher compelled to make the nerdy kid – otherwise picked last on the team – the captain.

Chris closed his eyes and leaned his face on the cool bus window. For a moment, his mind recoiled from the finger grease against his cheek, left behind from hands on other trips. But, he ignored it and fell into sleep. Of course, he didn't dream.

* * * * *

As soon as he stepped off the bus, Chris saw Alan. He was standing under an ugly green awning – it was raining. He looked older than Chris remembered. Quickly, he did the math in his head; Alan had to be into his sixties by now, maybe even seventy. He looked smaller and therefore less imposing. His once hard face had become wrinkled and loose, his hair was white, and his frame bonier.

43

When he spoke, however, he was the same. "It's so good to see you. There is so much to do." Chris ducked under the awning. He did not respond, but only smiled.

"You have put your things in order, I suppose?" it came out as more of a command than a question.

"The neighboring parish priest is going to look after my congregation for the next few weeks, holding one mass in the afternoon on Sundays. The rectory has been closed up, and one of the little old ladies down the street will be collecting my mail. The windows are closed, the garage is locked, and I even remembered to turn off the stove."

Alan threw him a dry, yellowed eye. "Good, because I don't want you worrying about things like that for a while."

The two men walked briskly from the large bus terminal to Alan's old station wagon. "Every time I ride in one of these things," Chris jerked open the door, "I always want to roll down the back window and stick my feet out – it used to abhor my mother."

Alan ignored him.

Indianapolis rose around them in wet glass and concrete. They drove through apartment building neighborhoods, past Crown Hill Cemetery, and through Riverside Park. Up congested Rt. 65, windshield wipers creaking, until they reached Alan's "borough" as he liked to call it: Meridian Hills. There, Alan presided over a gray-stoned Catholic church and elementary school. He lived in a small house in the back of the property, similar to Chris' own rectory.

Chris ducked slightly as they crossed beneath the doorframe and let the screen door bang behind him. They entered right into Alan's living room, which was cool and darkened by curtains that blanketed each window. The living room sunk down two steps from the main entryway, and the priests descended down into comfortable twin armchairs.

"Anything to drink?" Alan remembered reluctantly to be a host.

"Just some water, thanks." Shortly, Alan returned with two glasses, placed them on the table in between their chairs, and then settled himself.

"So, are you ready for this?" the impatient priest leaned back, chair creaking.

He looks old, the mental remark repeated. "I guess so. I mean, it's been a long time. I must grant that I," a sigh broke involuntarily, "am not as hopeful as I once was. But as we already discussed, this is a remarkable crime," Chris knew how to keep Alan from recapping. He took a quick swig out of his water, some spilling over onto his chin. Wiping it away with a careless hand, Chris continued. "But then again, chances are, it's just another freak thing. Besides, this is really an indirect search. We have a violent criminal, one that perhaps is also the monster prophesized in the dream, the one that plans on taking out our hidden savior. Now, the theory is that if we find this thing, we may find Remiel, maybe even in time to save her. But, then again–"

"Now wait a minute, you–"

"Let me finish," Chris returned the interruption. "We may not find her, dead or alive, this way. So, while this is a worthwhile cause, I am skeptical of its outcome."

Alan sat and grudged him momentarily. "Well, I think this is the best thing that's come along in years, and I plan on pursuing it to the utmost degree," he snapped, gulping his own water while looking around the glass at Chris meaningfully. He placed it down hard and empty on the table.

"Now, here are the details." Alan assumed a shopping list tone. "As you know, I have arranged for you to fly to Ashton College tomorrow morning. I have had some of the priests down there warming up the police department under the auspice that we are trying to band the traumatized campus together with faith. When you get there, they will be prepared to speak to you about the details of the crime and will consider your inquiry to be of a more psychological nature, an, 'I need to know exactly what I am dealing with before I can help anyone,' sort of thing. See if you can find any leads to any other unusual crimes on the campus, perhaps not so violent as this. You know the drill. Then, after my own affairs are put in order, which will take about five days to a week, I will join you on the campus for some further investigation, at which point, we'll decide if this is worth pursuing further."

Chris nodded.

"Yes, well I chose you for the job because I can trust you to be thorough, so that's exactly what I am looking for. Oh, and one other thing." Suddenly, Alan looked slightly uncomfortable, with his hands resting tightly on the sides of the chair.

Chris raised an inquisitive eyebrow.

Alan cleared his throat and began. "Now, don't get me wrong, you know I think you are completely competent. Despite your reluctance and lack of ambition, your education and Biblical knowledge are invaluable. With them, I know if there is anything to be found, you will find it. That said, I have asked someone else to accompany you."

Chris smiled, relieved. "No, no, that's fine. I actually will look forward to the company." Alan was wrong. He didn't mind splitting the workload.

"Well, wait and hear me out on the whole thing," Alan put up a hand to signal no interruptions. "The man I have asked to accompany you warrants some explanation. His name is Francis Carter. First of all, he is not a priest, but rather a monk, a Benedictine from Chicago. His career is one dedicated to his monastery, the community services they provide, and to study, and he has always followed the society's activities within the Church. He introduced himself to me… oh… ten years ago at a Midwest conference and we have kept in touch."

Immediately, Chris honed in on the blemish. "What makes him want to leave his confinement for this?" he demanded.

Alan sighed and shrugged. "He believes that this is the one."

"And why would he believe that?"

A long pause. "He's… a visionary. Clairvoyant."

Chris leaned back in his chair and blew air out his nose indignantly.

"See, I knew you wouldn't react well," Alan thudded both hands on the armrests.

"What exactly is this monk a visionary of?"

"Only you could make the word 'monk' sound like an insult," Alan skirted the question. "And actually, I am very impressed with him."

"Well, that doesn't take much."

"Chris," Alan's voice lowered as his temper rose.

Chris rolled his eyes and took on the tone of an automated message. "Yes, Alan. Please continue. Why does he impress you?"

"You're patronizing, you know that?" Alan attacked now, leaning forward aggressively. "Just because you have trouble believing in things you can't explain doesn't mean the rest of the religious world does. This man sees things, all right? The last two popes, he knew who they were years before they were chosen. He said they had a – a mark on them."

Chris sneered and leaned forward himself. "That's… that's not visionary. That's just an educated guess."

"He has predicted many things. Deaths in the Church, a peaceful millennium, 9/11–"

"He predicted 9/11?"

Alan took advantage of the first genuine question and fired rapidly. "Not enough to do anything about it, of course. But, he contacted a cardinal with information about a week ahead of time. Said that he had been looking at some pictures of a New York City trip that a friend sent him, and there was one woman in the picture with a strange mark on her forehead. He looked at more pictures, on the news and in the papers. And he saw the same mark on others, a horrible mark. That's what he sees. Marks, good bad, holy, unholy." He stopped for breath. "It's like he can see a little of the bigger picture."

"Of course." Chris punctuated his sarcasm with pursed lips. "And what does he see for this?"

"Well, for one, he knew about the dream without anyone telling him."

"Alan, anyone could have told him, and you'd never know."

"No, he knew things about it. Exactly what the girl looked like, what she said. It was like he had the dream. He contacted me soon after you called about the Ashton victim, and I mentioned the crime. He asked to see some of the news articles, and he claims there is a strange mark on Clyde Parker's forehead. One he hasn't seen before."

"Yeah, a coffee stain." Chris began to laugh at his own joke and Alan glared at him hard before he spoke again.

"Are you going to do this or not? Someone else will, if you are not capable–"

Chris broke him off before he could rattle off any names. "Yes, yes. Fine. Let's drop this. I look forward to speaking with my new pal."

Both men leaned back in their chairs, away from the tension that so often existed between them. "Speaking with your new pal… that requires an explanation also." Alan's eyes dropped to the floor.

"What now?" Chris let his shoulders droop visibly in anticipation.

"He's mute."

* * * * *

It was a red digital 7:27 AM according to Elise's alarm clock. Her eyelids felt sticky – she had fallen asleep with her contacts in again. How many times had she pressed snooze already?

The morning was sickly gray, partly due to the blinds, partly due to the clouds, and the room had just begun to solidify its fuzzy outline around her. *The Plug* 104.5's Bill and Beverly squeezed in a few more favorite movie picks before she smashed the alarm again. Thank God she didn't have a roommate this year. Michelle would've killed her, hissing, "Fuck" from the top bunk.

She sat up and pushed back the comforter, sighing through pursed lips. Bartending had kept her out late the previous night, and she was nowhere near prepared for her Psych class. After popping some eye drops in, she slouched down the hall, shower shoes squeaking. The women's bathroom was empty. Elise ran the shower for a minute and then slipped under the pathetic dorm water pressure. Her shower caddy included shampoo, a razor, body wash, and a waterproof alarm clock – it was not unusual for her to fall asleep under the old showerhead. But not that morning. Slowly her grogginess began to fade, and by the time another student entered the bathroom, she was wrapped in a towel applying mascara.

She threw on a pair of capris and a lightweight pink sweater (who cared if people said redheads should not wear pink, and besides, she was really more of a strawberry blond) and added her favorite flip-flops, worn and stained gray from her feet. She fished for a raspberry multigrain bar, and locked the door with half of it in her mouth.

Only then did she remember. *I've killed someone.*

Three weeks ago, Elise had woken remembering instantly. Her dreams had not let her forget it. *Last night, I killed someone.* She had sat up, tucking her knees under her even though the room had been hot and moist. Close to tears, she had leaned her cheek on her blanketed leg and just listened to her own breath. It had been a sunny day, the light falling in swaying patches mirroring the leaves of the tree outside her window. One of the patches had played on her hand, warming it.

It was like waking up from a strong nightmare – one that lingered and refused to let her remember which parts were only the dream. A good portion of her refused to grasp what had happened. Instead, her mind habitually refocused around the day ahead of her, full of classes and meeting friends. From her bed it felt as though nothing had changed. Everything around her was the same: her shoes were where she always left them – right in front of the door; last night's clothes were in a pile by the bed as usual; her lipstick from the previous day still sat uncapped on the table under the mirror.

But there was one thing out of place: her face. It ached slightly. Cautiously, she placed her fingers on her own skin, then moved them up and down. It felt smooth, but she could not ignore the tenderness. Pattering over to her dresser, Elise gazed at her reflection with worry. Her right cheek was still slightly swollen, but she could certainly blame it on doing something stupid. There was no bruising left and all the cuts were completely gone. Still, it felt oddly stiff. She scrunched her face several different ways, rubbing and wanting it to go away.

Her whole body jumped when the knock came at the door. The blood rushed to her ears and face, and she felt the heat rising off her body in waves.

"Elise? Are you awake yet?" Sophie's muffled voice came through the door.

"Yeah … yeah, hang on." Elise moved quickly to unlock the door. It was only her neighbor.

"OhmyGod, you won't believe what's going on." Sophie walked in, her arms crossed and her eyes wide.

Inwardly, Elise flinched. Had it already happened? It couldn't be – she wasn't ready; hadn't thought of a plan. The panic rose up from her stomach. Like a liquid, it filled her lungs – in order to breathe, she had to focus. How she wished she could sit down and brace herself for the blow, but her instinct warned her not to do anything odd. She merely cocked her head to the side. Sophie never needed prodding.

"Someone mur-dered a football player last night," she drew out the word for emphasis, but continued when Elise said nothing. "Well, ex-football player, but anyway," a toss of her hair. "They found him down by Ashton Lake early this morning. And, the whole campus has gone nuts! The RAs put up signs on the doors downstairs saying that all classes have been canceled and everyone is supposed to stay in the building. And, President Foster is going to send out an e-mail to all the students this afternoon, explaining the situation. Can you believe it?"

No, she couldn't. It really had to be a bad dream, the whole thing. *Please let me wake up, please… just let me wake up.* She felt her knees wobble, and wondered foggily if she would fall.

Instead, her brain sent signals to her mouth to express surprise. After a few seconds, "You're kidding," Elise whispered. She turned away quickly to hide her red face and began rummaging through her drawers as if looking for clothes.

"Oh no, totally not kidding," Sophie shook her head slowly. "It's so awful, to think of a killer on this campus. I mean, it's not like we're in some big city, or something. And it's so creepy to think that it happened only a little ways away from our dorm. You didn't get home until late last night, either. I mean…my God…" Sophie let her words trail into a gasp as realization came over her.

Elise's head shot up from her drawer fast enough to make her neck ache.

"You're lucky you didn't run into the killer," Sophie finished. There was silence. "Awe honey, I didn't mean to scare you," Sophie's voice sweetened the way it did when she spoke to her long-distance boyfriend over the phone.

"That's okay," Elise mustered, finally turning to face Sophie. "It's just so… shocking."

"I know, and I'm totally here if you need me."

"I'm fine. I didn't even know the guy or anything," Elise shrugged.

"How do you know you don't know him? The police haven't released his name." Sophie's eyes got even wider.

"No… no," Elise stuttered. "I mean, I don't know anyone on the football team, so I just assumed…"

"Yeah, well we'll know as soon as his parents and family have been 'properly notified,' I guess, as if there is such a thing. You should come downstairs. Everyone is in the lounge."

Elise waited until the door clicked closed before the first tears came out. "Oh my God, my God," she whispered, leaning all her weight on the wall, sagging and shaking. It was uncontrollable. Her body expelled sweat and tears. *Racking sobs.* She used to think it was a funny phrase.

The fit lasted for only five minutes, but by the end, she was exhausted. Sliding down the door onto the floor, she wrapped her arms around her knees again. For perhaps only the tenth time in her life, Elise wished for someone else to hold her.

She, who had never hurt anyone before, had killed someone. Her mind raced with Sophie's words. How could she walk out of that door? Her eyes turned to the phone, yellowed and cord-tangled on the edge of her desk. *I can turn myself in, I can tell them…*

Tell them what? That was the real problem. The evidence of the attack – the puffy, broken cheekbone, bruised nose, and black eye – were already mostly healed. If the authorities did not believe she killed him in self-defense, she could be charged with murder. How could she possibly prove assault without revealing more unbelievable details?

Like how in elementary school, she used to cut herself with her own earring during recess. A crowd of kids would always form around her to see the blood on her hand or arm. And then, she would pick someone out of the circle and touch them. There would be a little zap, something the other child felt much more than she did, and then the cut would be gone, leaving only a small white mark, which would also disappear before she got home. Kids had given her their lunch money over and over to show them. Until their parents found out. Then, she had been sent to the school psychiatrist. "You don't believe you can really heal yourself, do you honey?"

But she could. And last night, she had. When he grabbed her, dragging her away from the sidewalk, she had turned herself all the way up. That's what she always called it: turning-up, like the volume on a stereo. It was as easy as concentrating; truly noticing the blood in her fingers; the way they touched. And then feeling for the thing they wanted. That's usually when the whispering began. It almost sounded like wind, like a huge tornado was blowing around somewhere between her ears. But, there were words inside, words she didn't understand. Slowly, they would become so loud, so turned-up.

Last night, she turned-up, sucking at that man from inside herself, stealing his energy and then using it against him in that fatal hit. And the other attacker. It felt good to see the shocked pain on his face when he grabbed her wrist, like he had just touched the burner on a stove, as she stole whatever it was that healed: energy, nutrients, soul, who knew?

The other attacker. Was he still alive? Had she sucked him completely dry in order to heal herself? Elise was almost positive that she could … there had been other times… but she shook her head away from them. Sophie had not mentioned anything about a second murder, so he must be alive. Waiting to finger her. Elise turned from the phone.

She had never felt guilt before, or at least, not of this type. This was dark and dirty, a secret that would make her unacceptable. It was something that, if she managed not to be discovered, she would hide from her husband someday and her children. She would always be alone now, in some way.

Still, she had killed in self-defense, and internally, she already kept herself separate from others of the same crime. She had done what she needed to survive, and she would not take it back.

When she did finally leave her room, she indeed found the lounge full of students. Some of the more callous were talking about the benefits of 72 hours without class, while others were sitting around the TV mesmerized by the local news.

"What if they don't find the killer? There's no way I will feel safe on this campus anymore. It's just way too small."

"Have you guys ever thought that the killer could be here, I mean right now? I think it's stupid that they're making us stay in the dorms. Chances are, it's some student that's gone psycho, and the police are basically locking us in with a murderer. It's like a bad horror movie."

Quietly Elise had slid into a chair: the wolf among the lambs.

* * * * *

Three weeks later, she spit the raspberry and multi-grain casing out into a tissue, almost intact. It was always strange like that, remembering the most awful thing that ever happened to her after forgetting it in sleep. A metal taste filled her mouth and coated her tongue. She salivated ridiculously while waiting for her stomach to slip back down from her throat and stop moving. Sometimes she remembered as soon as she woke-up, the thing coming to her from a dream. Other times it came while she was digging through her drawer or when she packed her bag. But regardless of how, Clyde Parker always found her within the first hour or so of each day. It was like this every time she remembered. She wondered if it would be like this her whole life.

He was Clyde Parker to her now because she read about him in the newspaper. *Found dead at the scene.* Still, he did not become a person to her until Clyde's parents wrote to the newspaper, about a week after his death. A picture of Clyde in a suit, smiling confidently, accompanied the article. *You know who you are. Just turn yourself in and get help so that this never has to happen to another student and family.* She had lain in her bed all day crying and wrapped around the newspaper. Inky fingerprints stained the room – her desk, the phone, her sheets – as though the police had already been there to dust for them. The article was titled simply *To the Killer of our Son.*

That day was her lowest point and the time when the guilt ate away the most.

It was not that she was religious – she had been too alone in life for that. Guilt for Elise was not a function of disappointing a higher being, and she felt no fear of eternal damnation for killing Clyde. There was no good or evil, no universal rights and wrongs; she did not mutter pleas under her breath when life sucked. People like her could never fit into religious framework: a miraculous power herself with no divine voices and no signs. She shunned it as much as it shunned her.

51

Still, there was an instinct that taking a human life was a dark discretion. She replayed the scenario over in her head, and saw herself moving more carefully and slower. What if she had just kept "burning" him, as he called it, instead of turning his own energy against him? Maybe then she could have run away from an angry but breathing Clyde. Then again, what would have happened if she couldn't?

The only thing worse than the guilt was the paranoia. Elise was nervous to just answer the door; she caught her breath when the phone rang. If someone whispered behind her, her mind carried a make believe rumor straight to her heart. The sound of his name could raise the hair over her whole body. Anyone could be a witness; at anytime she could give herself away. She was no longer a part of the campus community or greater human society. She was the other, the outsider.

But he deserved it. That was her mantra, the thing she repeated to herself every day for the past three weeks. She hit him only because he would not let her go; she killed him to save herself. Yet, the blame remained hard and cold inside of her, a weight in her body the size of a grapefruit that never quite went away. *I didn't mean to kill him, but he deserved it.*

A memorial bench was placed right where he first pushed her, just by the spot where she fell next to the sidewalk and her bag spilled. She walked passed it on her way to and from class: its white pristineness and shiny plaque. A morbid part of her wanted to sit down on the bench if only to defy the real Clyde Parker, the one that his friends and family did not know, the one that had made her afraid to walk alone at night.

The ache to confess and receive human understanding was physical, and she considered turning herself in several more times. There was the time that she saw a police car parked at a curb. She stopped by the back passenger side door and envisioned herself creeping in behind the cage and just saying, "I did it." She paused 10 or 20 seconds before she turned and walked away.

On a more desperate night than usual, she called an anonymous help line. It felt so good to talk, even to skirt around the crime. "I did something horrible. Yes, I could be arrested. I didn't mean to though, okay?"

"Yes, okay."

It was ruined, however, when the operator said the phrase that invariably comes out of help line operators, "It can't be that bad." She had burst into tears then. "Miss? Miss are you there?"

Buried inside, the grapefruit was rotting, infecting with gangrene her academics and her social life. She lost weight and she slept too often. But the possibility of arrest was too great, and so she continued in silence.

The other perpetrator never came forward with information during the investigation, but Elise knew the police questioned him because he was in the newspaper articles too, *Sophomore Roy Eckner found Parker's body...*

Perhaps Roy was afraid she would charge him with assault if he told them the truth. After all, he couldn't know there wasn't a single mark on her.

* * * * *

Tuesday

Chris looked over at his new companion. The monk sat in the small coach airline seat quite comfortably, his short legs leaving space between the seat in front of him. The overhead reading light shown unflatteringly on his balding head, allowing each strand of brown hair to be seen: a small island in a sea of white scalp. Chris thought that he was probably slightly older than himself (he was only pushing 46). His new partner wore a black, ankle length tunic with a hood and a leather cord at the waist. His sandaled feet stuck out, blue-veined and knobby, a description not far removed from that of his hands and face. His eyes were wet looking, as if he had just yawned. A whiteboard also hung around his neck, smeared slightly green from their earlier conversation.

Mute from birth, a physical handicap, or so Alan had said. Brother Francis Carter had never uttered a single human syllable. He seemed comfortable enough with the fact, and took great pride in his "messaging." *It allows me to choose my words carefully*, he wrote upon their introduction.

"Would either of you like something to drink? Pretzels?" A young, blond stewardess surfaced through their thoughts, and both men jumped.

"I'll have a coffee," Chris returned after a moment. "Oh, no cream."

"And you sir?"

Chris waited with the stewardess as Francis looked at the tray. When he did not say anything, Chris began to explain. "Um, he's mute. Maybe I could..." he faltered as he realized that he could not help communicate the drink selection either.

"Oh! I hadn't realized," the stewardess put on her handicapped passenger face. "Now, let's see. Do you want a coffee like your friend? No... how about an orange juice?" She held each drink close to Francis' face, as though he could not read either.

Francis turned his teary brown eyes on Chris, now sparking slightly with anger.

"Sorry," Chris looked at the floor.

After a few more minutes and a multitude of individual drink choices from the stewardess, Francis wrote simply: *Coke.*

"Let me know if you two need anything else, okay?" The blond smiled and winked at Francis before moving on to the seats in front of them.

"Sorry about that," Chris repeated. "I didn't know...she and I were both...er...extra helpful."

53

No problem, the whiteboard glowed with green words for a few moments, and then was smeared away with a tiny cloth. Francis smiled at him. Smiling was a huge improvement.

"So, have you ever been to South Carolina before? It should be nice in October."

No.

"I haven't really been either. Driven through it when I was a kid. But other than that…" Chris trailed off. He watched the scribbling.

Grew up in the Midwest, haven't moved or traveled much.

"You and Alan have quite a bit in common then, actually. He's been in Indianapolis for most of his life."

Yes, we've discussed our roots. Lived close to one another for a little while, before my vows.

"Huh," Chris paused distractedly as it occurred to him that any eavesdropping passengers would think he was talking to himself about leaves. "Well, I actually grew-up in Florida, before college and the seminary. But I like the autumn months a lot, so it was really nice to receive assignments in the Northeast. I'm not sure how much foliage the Carolinas have, but if they have any, this might be a good time of year to see it."

Morning sunlight came through the small plane window. Of course, it always looked like morning sunlight above the clouds where the light was so bright and pale. Below him, Chris saw miles of green with blobbish speckles of red and orange. Every once in a while he could see the clover of a major highway intersection: gracefully scrolling proof of human civilization.

"So, uh, what do you think of all of this?" Chris turned back to Francis, who looked slightly puzzled at the question. "I mean the dream and of course, this trip."

Francis began to write thoughtfully, less cryptically. *I am very hopeful. I know of the dream, and I have followed the society very closely.* He waited a moment, then erased the board and continued. *Personal vows kept me from joining, but I keep up in the background. Benedictines focus on knowledge and education, and I have access to many texts. Alan's work is,* a pause, *compelling.*

Chris nodded his head while searching for a follow-up, and the conversation died awkwardly. Despite 24 hours of vague questions and a few more hours discussing the case with Alan, Chris still knew nothing about what Francis believed, his visions, his views on any Scripture, the statues, or anything relevant. And when he did ask, Francis was always careful not to give too much away, coming up with opinions like *compelling.* For practical reasons, they were going to have to address each other more candidly soon. Besides, Chris couldn't live with this man for the next week and not ask any questions.

"Forgive my curiosity, but I am, well, curious. Alan mentioned that you see marks?" Chris lowered his eyes to his coffee and focused on taking a careful sip, before remembering that he had to see the answer.

If Francis was surprised, he didn't show it. The scribbling began again, this time even slower. *Yes. I see other things too. Dreams, like the one in Meura. But, mostly, I see things when I am awake. Marks, as you call them – I've seen them my whole life. People have them on their skin, like a tattoo. Sometimes, the marks just tell me what type of a person they are. Sometimes they tell me what is going to happen to the person. Sometimes, they tell me deeper things, things they don't even know themselves.*

"Like a tattoo? So, if something bad is going to happen to a person, you see..." Chris paused, but Francis didn't fill in the blank. "What? A frown face, a devil's tail?"

Francis again wiped the board clean and continued. *More personal. There are no general marks, nor an exact code. Some are obviously ominous or happy while others are untranslatable. Mostly, it's the way the mark is drawn or positioned that speaks to me. Hastily scratched, or deeply ingrained; large and dark or light and hidden; impersonally on an ankle or intimately on the face.*

Chris nodded, as if he understood. "And the one you saw on the Ashton victim? Alan said you hadn't seen a mark like that ever before."

No. It had a very complicated pattern, and even though it was only a copy of a newspaper photo, it glowed like nothing I have ever seen before. Hot, like fire. Clyde Parker met up with something very special when he died, and I believe there is a considerable chance that whatever he ran into is related to the statues.

Chris shifted slightly in his seat ready to ask at least ten skeptical questions, but let them die on his lips. He could not permit his skepticism to come through now, especially during this first confidence. Alan was hardened and stubborn, and therefore easily questionable. But Francis, he could already tell, was soft. If he acted doubtful, it would hurt him, not to mention significantly decrease the level of respect he would experience over the next few days. He nodded his head again, noting with frustration that he had been nodding his head pretty steadily ever since leaving Whiteley, for lack of other appropriate reactions.

Francis tapped him gently on the shoulder, the first time he had initiated conversation. *I understand you didn't have the dream.*

It was as if he read Chris' doubts. "No, actually. I didn't. I was the only one." He opened his mouth again, then shut it.

Francis frowned, creasing the folds around his hairless hairline. Then, carefully he wrote, *Don't worry. Some in the priesthood, or even the brotherhood, they don't have a mark at all. They made a bad decision, took the wrong path, etc., for they were not really chosen by God. But you have it, like me, like Alan. This is where you are supposed to be.*

* * * * *

"Elise! Elise Moore!"

Elise looked up from under her dripping umbrella in search of the demanding voice. "Hey dormmate. Want to walk me to work? I'll share my shelter." She forced her spirits higher and smiled as she approached Jeff, the blond boy standing bareheaded in the midst of milling umbrellas on the main campus walkway. It was pouring in a steady sheet and Elise could already feel the water soaking uncomfortably into her boots.

"Work already?" He stepped underneath her outstretched umbrella.

"Oh, come on. Don't tell me you don't know when happy hour starts."

"With you, every hour is happy hour."

She rolled her eyes. "Are you walking, or what?" Pulling his arm coyly, she let her fingers linger on the exposed skin at his wrist. As an afterthought, Elise tossed her reddish hair and stuck one leg out from the black skirt she was wearing, the better to show off her knee-high boots and the skin above. With her head tilted and her free hand on her hip, she tried to look querulous.

"Nah. Gotta do that homework thing. But, stop down and see me, maybe," the last part he said with a slightly more worried tone, as if she'd say no.

"Sure," Elise turned away quickly, still smiling, knowing that he was watching her walk away. Jeff was a dork, granted. He was studying engineering after all. But, he was good looking with a dark tan from hours on the sailing team and just-blond hair the color of sand. And besides, she liked this part: the circling of a ritualistic pretense at friendship. There was plenty of flirting, dating other people while flirting, being a little jealous, and flirting harder.

After placing a building between herself and her crush, Elise slowed her strut to one that was more fitting for the size of her boot heels and the weight that settled again on her chest. Ashton campus buildings rose around her, bleeding the gray day with their different shades of brick. English, Chemistry – all the doorways were designated in order to file students appropriately in and out. Some of the newer buildings reminded Elise of her old elementary school: plain and square with windows that popped out at the top to let in a breath of air. She could easily envision them covered with cutout pumpkins this time of year.

The small city of Ashton nestled in a crook of the Appalachian Mountains in the western corner of South Carolina. Far from Myrtle Beach's famous sand and resorts, Ashton's hills made the horizon dip and fall irregularly, the rolling softened only by the colorful stubble of oak trees and maples. The transient population of the college funded a large number of restaurants and bars, as well as unique shops, boutiques and a few too many pizzerias. There was a small theatre run by competing student player groups and a dusty art gallery for parents when they came to help decorate a son or daughter's first apartment. Some of the wealthier sections of town boasted large homes and three car garages. But for the most part, Ashton remained modest and complete with a few run down areas tagged by peeling paint and sagging porches.

The lake was Ashton's heart, despite being on the outskirts of the town limits. In the warm months, it served as a reading spot, a beach, a favorite picnic setting, and the backdrop for most of the misdemeanors mentioned in the police blotter. During the cooler season, it remained a dog walker's delight, and warmly bundled joggers burnt calories on the rough beach that ran the full length of the town north to south. A small inlet crept onto the Ashton College campus, and on her way to work or class, Elise could smell the stone and metallic scent of lake water.

KWAM!

The door slammed like it always did when she walked into the bar, or when anyone did for that matter. On the busiest nights, the bouncers usually propped open the door to allow a steady stream of people in, and to keep drunks from getting caught in its swing. Still, every once in a while the bouncer would forget and someone would enter with a resounding bang that would cause all heads in the bar to turn.

"Elise. You're late." Mr. Digby frowned at her from behind the counter. "The owner is not supposed to have to work the bar on Tuesdays."

"Sorry. I just stopped to talk to a friend," Elise closed her umbrella and hurried behind the taps, throwing her jean-jacket on a hanger for the chance that it would dry before closing. She eyed the Budweiser clock to see how late she really was – only 5 minutes – and decided Digby couldn't be too mad.

"Wipe down the glasses and write on the board '$3 Test Tube Shots and $2 Draughts.'" As if he needed to tell her. Quickly she moved with chalk and towel in hand, and the night began.

Maraschino's was already half full with the 30 and older crowd – happy hour was the only time of day when that was true, however. Once ten o'clock came, the college faces would begin to take over. Of course, they were still the older faces of seniors, soon-to-be graduates; Mr. Digby was tough on IDs. He left the profitable but illegal business of serving the underclassman crowds to Spinoffs next door. Elise had witnessed only a few moments when this moral standard came close to collapse – when the line for Spinoffs went in front of Mr. Digby's own door. Then, she could see him muttering obscenities in the back and squinting to see that she had chalked the right specials.

"Hey sweetie. I didn't think I'd see you here on a Tuesday." It was that old guy. Elise didn't know his name, but he was a regular, and a pretty chatty one. She smiled at him, quietly taking in his roving eyes. It was gross, but he left her best tips of the night. She gave him a little complementary lean-over-the-counter cleavage.

"Yeah, Digby works me. But, I've convinced him to give me the night off Friday. Want a drink?"

"Martini."

"What's that? A water?" Elise smiled at him as she poured the gin.

She took the job a few weeks into her freshman year in attempts to keep up with some of the other girls' clothing budgets, and had been pouring ever since. Bartending at Maraschino's was a fun job all things considered, and the hours weren't too bad if she scheduled late morning classes. When last summer came around, Elise found herself still mixing. It wasn't like she had any place else to go. After the death of her parents and two foster homes, she had very few ties to anywhere besides Ashton.

Good grades earned her a tuition grant for "Leaders Without Parents," leaving the tips at Maraschino's to pay for everything else. And, they were plenty as long as she lived in the dorms. Now going into her second year behind the counter, she was a pro at salt rings and the much-feared iced teas. Digby even liked to use her on the busy Friday and Saturday nights.

Tonight passed in its usual manner with Elise constantly moving between the counter and the well. She chatted with some of the regulars and occasionally searched the faces in the back for other students she knew, but failed to discern anyone familiar. The barroom was dark – the burnt-burgundy wood tables and floors absorbed the fuzzy-peach lighting. Even the bar itself used only low lighting from under the counter, and the corner by the restroom was dark enough that the exit sign cast a red-district hue over anyone waiting in line. You could feel at ease sipping a drink with someone other than your wife even in the front of the bar.

Elise was comfortable here in the low light and low murmur with the ancient jukebox playing in the background (sometimes the damned thing skipped and Digby had to go back and bang on its side in order to get to the next song). She blended in, even added to the dusky atmosphere, and the confidence she felt behind the bar serving shadowy faces was greater than at any other time in any other place.

Even when the sun streamed though the windows on Saturday afternoons, there were always corners of Maraschino's that remained dark. Elise had always been that way too, but especially now: splattered with internal shade. The bar and its inextinguishable darkness did for Elise what gingham-checkered curtains did for Martha Stewart.

Her horrible secret was safe here. In the dark and the smoke, it seemed like everyone had a secret. For the past three weeks, the bar had been the only place where the tightness in her chest eased and she felt almost like her old self. She looked forward to surrounding herself with the shadowy faces and chatter, sharing the heartache of human existence from a wonderfully impersonal distance.

The tips were good for a Tuesday, and the night wound down as the cigarette smoke wound up. After the bar closed, she did the routine wipe-downs, carried the leftover ice down to the freezer and filled out a poorly photocopied form of needed supplies for the following night's business.

KWAM! She was back in the rain, alone, by 2:30 AM.

* * * * *

It's a sign. The storm is a sign.

No it's not. Chris' mind went back and forth as he listened to the rain on the motel window. He and Francis were kept on American Airline Flight 235 an extra hour before the thunder and lightening allowed them to land. Then, they drove the hour-and-a-half from the Greenville-Spartanburg Airport into the Appalachians with the windshield wipers dancing away and brushing off with no little trouble the dark leaves that bombarded the rental. Sheets of rain had run across the road driven by the high winds. The afternoon was unnaturally dark, lit only by a green hue that lifted with the occasional lightning flash. It was now three in the morning, and the storm had yet to let up.

Francis put the idea into his head. Of course. *Seems like someone really doesn't want us here*, he had written with a wry smile when the storm finally forced them to cruise control at 45 miles an hour. It was a joke, of course, but Chris wasn't quite sure. After all, Francis knew things.

Or at least, it seemed like he could know things in the dark with the rain pounding this hard. Francis was sound asleep of course, his breath coming slow and easy. But, Chris was listening and nervous.

The chances of finding Remiel by tracking her nemesis have always been laughable, he reminded himself and pulled the blankets closer. *This is a last ditch effort. It's truly a horrible murder, but hardly connected.*

Underneath those thoughts, Chris was replaying the conversation they had with the sheriff that afternoon. It had been brief. Not because the sheriff was withholding information, but because there just wasn't any. "I dunno, I just dunno," he repeated about once every five minutes. The other officers were a little more helpful and provided pictures of Clyde's body and the scene of the crime.

His face... was all Francis had written, and for that matter, probably all that either of them had thought. In the photos, Clyde's features were hardly distinguishable from his forehead down. There was some fragmented cartilage where his nose had once been, and one eye was still intact, although the eyelid had been missing. His cheekbone on the right side was gone, leaving the loose and shredded skin to fill in the sunken mess. The left cheekbone was bared, along with parts of his chin.

But the fingers...now they were distinguishable. Not Clyde's of course, but rather the fingers of the person who hit him.

There were five visible areas of flesh damage – the first four were each the width and length of a finger beginning on the left hand side of his face and smearing across and down to the right. They looked like dark canals, jagged and full of black, dried blood, giving the mutilated face a striped look. The fifth and last "area of impact" was at his mouth – a shorter and smaller laceration the size of someone's pinky – where Clyde's lips had been removed.

"What about DNA? I mean, if someone hit him that hard, isn't there anything from them... in there?" Chris asked in a whisper.

"Nah. See where the," the sheriff cleared his throat, "the impact lines are? You see them there in the picture? The forensic people couldn't get anything from them. 'Parently they're burned in – not just cut. They were too damaged to carry any sort of identifiable...um...fibers."

"Burned?" Chris asked the question for both he and Francis.

"Yeah, that's not all just dried blood there."

Chris had suddenly envisioned the black, flaky skin of barbecued chicken left on the grill too long. He saw it again now, lying under the flimsy hotel blanket.

Another bolt of lightening. For a moment, Chris focused on the rain patters. *Still going. It's a sign. Or at least, it would be if I believed in signs.* He rolled over.

What if they did find her? He had only allowed himself to contemplate locating Remiel seriously a few times in his whole life. But, that face – it changed everything. There was something cold and twisted in the remains of that face. It wasn't torture or even anger that killed Clyde; it was power – a type of power that most people didn't believe in anymore. Hell, he still didn't believe completely.

What did it mean for the rest of the world? If they found this thing, what were the implications? At best, it would mean that whatever hit Clyde would be a drop in an awfully big bucket of unimaginable realities. *If the Other could really exist, then what else could exist?*

It's not that extraordinary. A kid on drugs could probably do it.

'Parently they're burned in.

It's a sign, his mind whispered, so loud that the words rang in his ears as if he really spoke them. In the other bed, Francis finally stirred.

* * * * *

"Damn it," Elise struggled with the window as the rain came in onto her bedspread. She was sleeping with the window open – there was nothing quite so soothing as the sound of rain on pavement – but the wind shifted and shortly she awoke to a wet face and a blanket corner that needed to be rung out.

Now, with the window shut and the rain barely a dull lull, Elise lay in the dark, carefully avoiding the wet part of her bed. But she knew it already – she wasn't going to fall back asleep. Warily, she eyed her alarm clock. It was 4:10 AM. If she fell asleep now, she could still get five hours of sleep. But for every moment that she stared at the ceiling, another moment was pledged to regret during class the next morning.

She went through the ritual pillow flip and fluff, placing her cheek on the cool side, and then she rearranged her blankets neatly. Finding her favorite position on her side facing into the room she closed her eyes.

Nope, she really wasn't going to sleep. *Damn storm.*

Think happy thoughts. That was what her mother had always said. Or at least, Elise had several memories of her saying it, and it seemed like the phrase must have been something she always said. When she was very young and couldn't sleep, her mother had sometimes sat on the side of her bed, and they traded good memories until Elise had fallen back asleep. Elise could remember pretending to think hard, but her choice was always the same: Christmas. That, and going to the amusement park. Mom repetitively picked gardening and horseback riding.

What happy thoughts are you thinking of, Ellie?

"I'm thinking of sleeping," she said aloud to scare away the ghost. It didn't work – an ache gently filled her chest bringing the dangerous wish that life had somehow been different. It was such a hollow ache, like a broken promise. And though she had lived with it for so long, it never became familiar. She was glad mostly – keeping their memory fresh was a victory. Grief was truly the lesser ache; the worst pain came when she could not remember them.

Slightly spooked, Elise contemplated getting a book or flipping on the TV. Maybe someone would still be awake in the lounge. She could at least find out.

With a single motion, she flipped back the covers hard and was out of bed. She threw on a T-shirt over her pajama top and felt around the floor for socks. She checked her shadow in the mirror just to see how her hair was shaping-up–

She froze.

Spooked was no longer the word. She could feel it – someone in the room with her, watching her. The presence was undeniable, palpable – she was being stared at. Without moving her head, Elise let her eyes scan around the room, searching from side to side and behind her by way of the mirror. She could feel the hair all over her body prickle and stand up. Waiting, she barely breathed.

There was no sound other than her heart clunking away like an idling 1960 Chevy. She waited.

A few seconds more, and the feeling began to subside. Another quick scan of the room revealed no moving shadows. Perhaps the watcher was outside? She opened her eyes wider in a vain attempt to pierce the blackness behind her rain-spattered window.

With instinct urging her, Elise found it difficult to control her speed – but it was the only way to keep from panic. Refusing any sudden movements, she crossed slowly to the desk lamp and flipped it on.

Instantly, pale yellow light illuminated one half of the room brightly, struggling to reach into the corners on the far end. But, it was enough. Elise was surprised to confirm what not even the more practical part of her believed – there was no one there.

There was still the window, of course. The light only made it harder to see out. The rain still pattered like cold fingers on the glass. Elise imagined a figure crouched outside, staring at her all the more easily now that the room was lit.

She leaned over her bed quickly and timidly and drew the blinds. She checked the closet too, turning on lights as she went until the whole room was lit.

Still, the skittishness wouldn't leave her. *There was someone here, in here and not outside...with me.*

"Mom?" her voice cracked. Immediately, Elise felt stupid. Exasperated with herself, she turned back to look under the bed for those socks. She was definitely getting out of the room for a while. At least the couches in the lounge were comfortable.

* * * * *

Wednesday

"So, you've never seen anything like this? There are no other crimes that might be related, or that we should address with the students?" Chris asked Sheriff Perinton.

"No sir. We've had a few robberies while people haven't been in their rooms, but no assaults here. We're basically pretty clean around here, not like your New York. We don't have those city problems," the pride came through the strong southern accent.

"New York State isn't the city. I don't live anywhere near it," Chris replied while still looking through the files. Of course, it was a moot point.

Francis was up looking at the crime bulletin board, and indeed, there was only one crime posted. Clyde Parker's face, a picture of the scene of the crime, some phone numbers related to the case and a blood report were hanging cock-eyed, many of them sharing the same tack. All blood samples collected from Clyde's body had been his own except for one. On his right hand there had been traces of type O negative; Clyde was B positive. There had been another blood sample, found on a sidewalk nearby, also O negative. It was the only hard evidence at the scene to place another person there besides Clyde. Three weeks later and after a major rainstorm, it was probably the only evidence they were going to find.

Francis thumbed through the report on the wall without removing the tack. *The type O negative came from a female right?* He turned to face the sheriff.

"Yes sir – the DNA specialist is certain. Awfully odd, isn't it? Obviously, a woman could not do the damage that you saw in the photos of the victim. But, nonetheless, there was a woman with Clyde before he died, and it appears that she too was wounded. Maybe they were both attacked. But, no one else has come forward. And none of the known females in Clyde's life have O negative blood type – we checked to be sure. As you already know, another student, Roy Eckner, admitted he was drinking on the beach earlier with Clyde, but said it was just the two of 'em. He claims he left when it got late, but returned to check on Clyde and found him dead."

Sheriff Perinton scratched his head and continued. "Nah. Without any witnesses and no apparent motive, we are pretty stumped. Too many footprints on that slope to know which belong to the victim's killer and which belong to students who were there a few hours before. We have nothing."

Huh, Francis wrote simply. He gave Chris the raised eyebrow cue.

"Yes, well, thank you for sharing this information with us," Chris cleared his throat and pushed back his chair. "It appears that, um, we need to address fear on the campus because of the crime's apparent randomness." He looked at Francis for approval of the lie and continued at his nod. "And, um, to do that, we can stress to the students how unusual this is for Ashton College and how unlikely another event like this is."

"When will you be having this here service?"

Chris drew a blank. They hadn't decided yet–

In your school's chapel tomorrow at noon, the whiteboard glowed.

Someone had apparently decided.

"Well now, I know you had some level of clearance from the criminal psychologist to look at this type of information, but of course you aren't going to disclose what you saw in those pictures and all to the students."

"No, no. Of course not," Chris said strongly, that being the first true sentence he had uttered in a while. "We're just going to make them feel, uh, safer."

"Right." Sheriff Perinton's lips stuck sarcastically close to his teeth.

* * * * *

Thursday

She liked the rhythm of her feet hitting the pavement over and over. It was almost as soothing as the careful rhythm of her breathing, which she timed perfectly once every two seconds. Elise liked to keep going until every muscle burned and she could feel the power in her legs with every push and the heat rising off her skull through her hair. Today, however, she wouldn't get that far. She was running with a destination.

The day was beautiful. Remnant clouds with dark underbellies had been exiled to secluded corners of the sky, leaving their puddles to recede under parked cars and porches. *Breathe...slower.* That was the only conscious thought she allowed as she ran in the mid-afternoon sun.

That and, *Like a shot, here she comes. I wonder how she trains?*

They say she's a loner. Not very close to anyone. Maybe that's how she keeps up such incredible concentration.

I'll say. I bet she's thought her heartbeat down to a steady 100 despite her speed.

Imaginary commentary. She had been listening to them since she was a little girl, admiring the way she moved, the muscle contours of her legs. Of course, she was old enough now to realize they were only things she wished other people would notice and admire in her: the cool way she could keep going, the endurance, the strength and self-control. Knowing did not make the delusion any less pleasurable, and the voices continued, watching her round a bend, climb a hill, and eventually slow down to a half-trot as she began to enter central campus.

Thursdays were always crowded. It was just too far past the previous weekend to excuse skipping class, and too far from the next weekend to start taking time off early. Students milled around the dining halls and the library looking almost studious. Elise continued past them all, jogging and zigzagging around those too lost in their conversations to realize they were blocking the sidewalk.

Look at her pass them. She's going to–

Not even the voices could block it out. She should be avoiding it, but like a moth hopelessly drawn to the light, curiosity had gotten the better of her. Even though she knew it would be bad for her, she had to come and see.

A growing crowd was spilling out onto central campus, and Elise was forced to walk. As she approached the campus chapel, even walking became difficult. Students were solemnly coming out of the chapel's stone doors.

Stupid church, her mind hissed as her steps slowed further. She knew – a priest had come to town to hold a special service for students who were looking for psychological solace after the *Ashton Murder*. It had been on a poster in her dorm. There they all were, coming down the steps and standing in tight groups. Were they really afraid? Did they really think that any one of them could be next?

Slowly, her stomach rose and that familiar illness crept over her. The guilt was pricked by the sight of so many quiet faces, paler than usual in the sun, or so she thought. Her breathing increased well past her running rate and she stopped in the very middle of the sidewalk to look. Did anyone see her, scared, more scared than any of them?

Why has she stopped? Has she really stopped?

Elise licked her lips nervously. Fixing her eyes on the ground, she moved through the crowd and began to jog again, vowing not to break until she got home. She would show them. She could outrun it.

* * * * *

Francis looked out over the students as he and Chris stood in the doorway to the chapel. The event went well, despite the fact that he and the priest had been at the 24-hour copy center until 10 PM making posters and out until midnight hanging them in the dorms. He and Chris barely went over remarks that morning together – of course Chris was doing all the talking. Chris hated speaking, and Francis knew it.

But the students were patient listeners, if not responsive. Some even joined the choir in singing the last song. They were already springing back, as young people do. Very few of them actually looked like they needed the sermon, which was split between Chris and one of the full-time campus ministers. Mostly, it seemed they came to pay respects, and of course, to find out any new information.

Chris was still shaking hands, and Francis glanced at him only briefly as he began to move away. Social greeting time was never something he enjoyed, obviously. He stayed above the crowd on the steps so that he could better see the students.

He was almost positive that she had not been there. The whole time the speakers were giving their piece, Francis had been looking. To his disappointment – though not unexpected – there were very few marks on the students. They were too young and too undeveloped. It took time to determine what was in a person and what was in store for them. A few faces had the mark of divorce or death on them. But other than these few tragic experiences, the rest remained blank to him.

Staring out over the crowd, he saw little else. They were really quite an indifferent group.

* * * * *

Elise began pealing off her damp clothes. She definitely needed a shower, but she was just too exhausted to raise her hands over her head long enough to shampoo her hair. She wiped off her back and her chest with the jogging shirt and threw it on the floor. Her shorts came next, sliding off her goosepimpled flesh. Already the heat was gone and the wetness had become chilling. Naked except for her underwear, Elise slid back into her unmade bed and wrapped the comforter around her whole body until it was tight enough to keep her legs from moving.

She had run all right. She almost dropped by the time she returned to the dorm. Her muscles were so tired they felt gummy. She could smell the sour, musty smell of her body as she breathed in slowly through her nose. She stretched her tired legs.

A muscle spasm exploded in her left thigh. Quickly she reached down and felt her muscle hard and knotted, shaking uncontrollably. She massaged it as it crept further down her leg and became more painful.

Still grasping the convulsing muscle, she leaned over towards her nightstand. An African violet plant sat in a green dish, well watered, but still a little brown around the edges. Elise let her fingers trace one of the velvety, round leaves.

Quietly, the whispering began far back in her mind, and then grew as she turned-up. So many words, as always, indistinguishable. Her fingers tightened on the leaf.

Briefly, she thought of what the priests from the chapel would think if they could see her now. Would they yell God or devil? Her mouth turned up as if to smile.

Slowly, the corners of the leaf withered as brown spread from the edges. Elise stared at the plant calmly, her eyes oddly light. Gently, she let go of the leaf, before the brownness reached the stem. The muscle spasm subsided.

* * * * *

"What do you think?" Chris asked Francis now that the students had

66

cleared out.

She wasn't there, he wrote back.

"Are you sure?" Chris eyed him curiously.

Almost.

Chris blew air out through his cheeks, an action that Francis was beginning to associate with frustration.

"Well, I guess that's not surprising. She probably is not on the campus at all." He lowered his voice to a whisper. "And hopefully, if the Other is here, she isn't." The two priests sat on the steps to the chapel watching the quieting campus as classes ended.

* * * * *

Elise glanced over at the answering machine, flashing the number '1'. She pressed the button and waited impatiently, toweling her shower-wet hair with angry scrunches.

"Hey Elise! It's Elise," her own voice came hurriedly over the speaker. "Don't forget to call Brian and tell him you can't study tomorrow night. You've already stood him up twice."

"Shit," she cursed as the message cut-off. She glanced at the clock. It was too late – Brian would already be on his way over, only to find her gone again. "Way to remind yourself, Elise. You might want to find a better system, since you don't check your messages. That one's a day and a half old." She turned back to the mirror.

The lipstick was a little too dark for her. She always thought that whenever she put it on, but she always ended up walking out the door with it anyway. Elise smiled to see her teeth white against the red. Some brown mascara and she was ready for work.

But for once, she really did not feel like going to Maraschino's. She was still tired, and her body wanted to go back to her prolonged nap.

She shook her head. The depression from the afternoon was chasing her, making her want to retreat. But one afternoon was already enough of a loss.

* * * * *

Chris sighed, surveying the emptying campus walkways. "This isn't getting us anywhere – staring at people. Let's go get a beer. Some food." Following Francis and looking for marks felt humorously similar to walking with his uncle and an old metal detector at family picnics. Except Francis was the metal detector.

I don't drink.

"Sure you do," Chris said as he began to walk towards town. He didn't look back to see Francis' response.

* * * * *

She was trying to smile and get into bartending mode, but it just wasn't happening tonight. Instead, Elise felt like hanging back away from the counter and letting Beth take all the orders. She stubbornly refused eye contact and forced patrons to ask her for a drink specifically. Her tips were going to suck.

With a sigh, Elise pushed herself away from the dark back of the bar and into what little light there was. "What would you like tonight?" she asked the closest stool warmer with a tired smile.

* * * * *

It was an easy decision. Spinoffs blasted loud music and advertised buttery nipple shots; Maraschino's looked dark and quiet and offered two for one beer. With a glance to make sure Francis was still behind him, Chris opened the door.

KWAM! The door slammed and Elise saw several drinkers jump and even more turn their heads to see who let the door go. She didn't bother. They would be up to visit her soon enough.

Seated at the very far right corner of the bar, Chris and Francis waited without speaking for the redheaded bartender to turn around and take their order.

"What can I get you?" Elise smiled over mild dislike at the priest.

Chapter 6 – It's He–

Chris stared. For a moment, he really couldn't breathe. His chest muscles contracted, trying to pull the air in, but it wouldn't come. Francis was practically punching him in the shoulder, and yet he could not move.

It was as if the statue from the Chiesa di Statua had been smuggled and placed behind the bar. She leaned over the counter at him, her red-blond hair falling loose around her shoulders, just as she had been sculpted. She even tilted her head slightly to the side, waiting for his drink request, and she barely smiled with her lips parted. The only difference was her eyes – they had irises, large brown ones.

"Remiel," Chris whispered.

"What?" The stiff smile left Elise's face. It had been a long time since someone asked her for a drink she didn't know. "What do you want?" She raised an eyebrow.

"Um…" Chris swallowed and breathed a few times. "A beer."

Elise looked from the priest to his friend in the strange black robes. Were they kidding? "What type of beer?" she asked confused. Why was he looking at her like that?

Corona. Bottle. Francis scribbled quickly across his slate.

And why the hell was he writing his order? "Ok…" she said with both eyebrows in the alert position as she pulled out two beers, took off the caps, and placed them on the counter. Without meeting either man's eyes, she asked for six dollars and then moved to the other end of the bar to help some of the less creepy patrons.

Immediately, Francis tapped Chris on the shoulder again – but still no response. With surprising strength, he turned the priest towards him with one small hand, making him look, and began to write hurriedly. *It's he–*

Francis' trembling fingers dropped the marker on the floor. He froze for a moment with both his eyes and his mouth open, his entire face taken up by the three circular gapes. He looked so exasperated, Chris was sure for a moment that he actually would speak. Instead, he began looking frantically under the stools and their drinkers.

It's he.

Chris focused briefly on the word that trailed off without an 'r.' The whiteboard with the broken writing flapped around Francis' chest wildly as he continued to spin from seat to seat in search of the only communication he had.

But Chris could not take his eyes off her long enough even to help Francis find his pen. Instead, he sat on the stool watching her pour another drink. She was here. God was here. He didn't even need the perspective of a few hours – he was not the same priest that had walked in through the bar doors.

Francis returned, pen in hand, and finished his sentence. *It's her. Praise everything – do you see HER? The one.* His face broke into a huge smile and his chest heaved– the mild mannered monk had stepped into the hypothetical phone booth.

"I see her, but I can't believe it! She looks just like she did then, just like the statue," Chris whispered slowly, as if to keep from waking a sleeping baby, or perhaps himself. There was a long pause as everything in the bar seemed to go on in some other place, leaving the three of them moving much slower together, almost alone.

"What do we do next?" Chris continued whispering. "I mean, what do we do with her? I've never thought about this part," he was almost talking to himself. "We could take her. Wait until the bar closes and take her."

Take her where? Francis broke in with a concerned look. *Don't think kidnapping is the best way.*

"Ok, well what do you," Chris' voice rose in annoyance and then lowered again cautiously, "what do you think we should do? When I said her name, she looked entirely confused, like she didn't know anything. I think it's a safe bet we can't just walk up to her and ask her how she feels about coming with us to save the world, Francis."

* * * * *

They were talking furiously, she noted. And the short one obviously had something wrong with him. He was writing everything instead of talking. Elise watched the pair continue their weird, frantic conversation for a few more seconds crossing her arms over her chest defensively. She could not shake the feeling that they were talking about her. And, because they probably had something to do with the religious service held for Clyde, they made her particularly uneasy. What could they be saying? Worse yet, what could they know?

"Hey! Can I get a drink here?" an angry customer leaned over the bar.

"Oh. Sorry. Rough night." She smiled flirtatiously, but he wasn't biting.

"I want two Rolling Rocks."

Elise turned off her smile. She glanced at the priests again as she took off the caps. They were very openly looking at her in between mad interchanges.

She handed off the two beers. Mr. Friendly didn't leave a tip.

"Damn it," she said under her breath. She was going to have to get it together. She rolled back her shoulders, as if to shrug the nervousness away.

* * * * *

It was her – the girl a 12th century artist chose to sculpt. She was the marble, only in color. Golden red hair fell in smooth waves to the middle of her back. Her eyes were a very light brown, like a coffee with cream. When she smiled, a dimple dented her left cheek. She had a high forehead, and her skin was an olive color.

And yet, she did not look like an angel.

She wore a silver tank top that clung to her so tightly it was quite obvious she wasn't wearing a bra. The straps hugged her defined shoulder blades in a tight crisscross in the back, seen only when she swung her hair flirtatiously. Dark jeans molded around small hips and slender legs, resting a revealing two inches below her belly button. When she stood straight, slim black threads of silk underwear shimmered seductively on her hipbones. She had painted her lips a dark crimson color. Chris noted he and Francis were not the only men staring her way.

"How should we do this?" he asked in heightening exasperation. An afterthought, "We should hurry."

Talk to the Congregation. It will be better, calmer. Planned. Not now, in a bar after a few beers.

"One beer," Chris pointed out. "Both still full."

Francis frowned as he wiped his slate clean and began again. *Think. Not now. We should get her alone.*

* * * * *

What was wrong with them? Elise glanced back over at the priest and monk. She felt fidgety (like she did just before a run). They had to know something about her, the way they watched her while barely trying to hide their stares – every time she looked at them, both men drank their beer and looked at the bar counter in perfect choreography.

What could they know?

Elise swallowed half way before realizing she had no saliva. *Don't worry. If they knew, they would send cops, not priests,* she told herself, turning into the bar away from all the faces. How many times had she thought she was discovered? How many times had she felt just this see-through? How many times had she needed to close her eyes and say those exact words to herself? *Don't worry.*

"See, you're fine. You're fine... just like every other time. Swallow. That's it. You're fine. You can go home in just a few hours," she whispered. Her eyes stole back to them. Both men took another sip.

* * * * *

"I think we're making her nervous," Chris whispered. "She keeps looking at us." Nudging his partner in the shoulder, "Drink more. We need to blend in better."

Francis took another sip to show his support, but made a slight face afterwards. *It's getting warm,* he wrote and then quickly erased. *We could be drunk out of our minds, and we wouldn't fit in.*

"This is stupid just sitting here. This is what we have been waiting for, and now we're choosing to wait!" Chris pushed back his chair as if he might actually get up and move toward her.

Nothing will happen before tomorrow. Trust me.

Chris began to protest, but stopped when he caught the meaning. "Trust you," he stated flatly. After a pause, he shook his head. Even now, the oddness was not lost to him. He was in a bar, watching an angel with a man who could not talk, but who had apparently seen the spiritual mark for 'ok until tomorrow.' He finished his beer.

* * * * *

"Elise, are you all right?" Beth looked concerned. Elise knew she really was, considering she had come away from the tips to ask.

"Yeah, I'm just not feeling well," Elise quickly calculated how long Beth could've been standing there – not long enough to hear her whispering, "Don't worry."

"You look really ill. Do you need to go home? I can cover for you, you know."

"I have just been... feeling funny all day. I'm fine, really."

"Digby told me to check on you. Go ahead. I can handle this crowd. It's a Wednesday. Go home."

Elise glanced at her manager. Digby pointed at her coat on the hanger.

"I guess, okay – thanks." Still unsure, Elise rinsed her hands in the back sink and slid out from behind the counter. She slunk into her coat, letting it settle around her protectively and big, hiding even her hands. "Goodnight, and thanks again," she said to Beth with a closed mouth smile.

Then came the long walk. The one that would take her along the counter, past the priest and the monk, and then finally out into the cool fall air. Holding her breath, Elise put on her most confident face, her most defiant eyes. They would not see her shaking inside; they would not knock her pride; and they would not see her guilt. She put her hands in her pockets to hide the fists she could not help clenching and smiled at the faces around her, as if she knew them.

* * * * *

Chris felt her approaching more than he actually saw her. She was staring right at them. He breathed in a few times, preparing to halt all living function when she actually passed. He stared at the writing on the bar counter. Someone had tried to remove the ink from the hearts and the 'was here,' but only managed to take off the finish.

Francis, on the other hand, stared at her straight on: strong, beautiful and intimidating. She gave off an aura of importance so strong, he knew people must feel it when she walked into a room, when she joined a conversation, or when she turned her almond eyes on anyone. He wanted to reach out and touch her, to tell her how he knew her and what plans had been laid for her. How he wished he could speak. But like he advised Chris, now was not the time. She passed.

* * * * *

Holding the bar door with the back of her heel, Elise didn't let it slam and gain any more attention. She had had enough for one night. Whatever else the two men in the bar were up to, she felt sickeningly certain they were overly occupied with her.

She glanced over her shoulder to see if anyone followed. Only a few students walked behind her, going the other direction. Jogging and still casting her eyes behind, Elise made her way from the bars that clustered around the Ashton College campus entrance and into the rows of academic buildings.

With a sigh of relief, she welcomed the lower lights of the sidewalks away from the main road. Her pace slowed; her pulse slowed; the nauseousness lowered. Music wafted from someone's window and feminine laughter floated to her. Panic reduced to caution and then to embarrassment.

The priest and the monk were interested in her – she trusted her instincts too much to deny it. But who knew why? Elise lowered her eyes to her low-rise jeans. She smiled. *They probably think I'm indecent,* she thought. *Who knows the last time those two saw any skin below the navel?* And after a moment, *They don't send the Catholic Church to arrest murderers.*

* * * * *

"She's getting away!" Chris hissed as Remiel walked out of the bar. "We don't even know who she is." A panicked look came across his face as he realized what he was saying. "What if we lose her?" he whispered. "Someone must know–"

Chris marched over to the other side of the counter with his hands in fists, as if he would physically extract Remiel's identity from the tiny fake-blond bartender who now worked in her place. "Excuse me. What is the name of the other bartender?"

Beth looked up from pouring a drink blankly.

"The one that just left, I mean."

"Yes, I know who you mean. But why do you want to know her name?" She smiled firmly with a steely look in her eye.

Chris thought fast. "Well, don't tell, but I met her during the service today, and I'm bad with names." He returned the smile smoothly. "I actually spoke to her for quite a while, and I felt embarrassed when she said hello to me on her way out the door, and I couldn't remember who she was."

The steely look faltered. "Oh. The service…" She looked at his collar.

Chris smiled again. She was breaking.

"Her name is Elise Moore."

Chris repeated it, "Elise Moore. I knew it started with an 'e.' Thanks."

"No problem. Want a drink?"

Chris bought another one for normalcy's sake, and then headed back to the table. "God's going to smote me if I keep lying like this," he said as he slid back into his seat.

Did you get her name?

"Yeah. She's Elise Moore. Elise Moore," he repeated one more time to himself. Slowly, he let all of his breath out.

Francis stood-up. *We should go. Find out more now.*

Chris dropped his new drink on the counter and moved with Francis out the door. It slammed, closing them out. They paused, each looking for her though she was gone.

"I can't believe this." Chris shook his head once again. "I really can't get my mind to grasp it. I'm worried that if I close my eyes too long, I might feel my pillow underneath my head."

Didn't you think we would find her eventually?

Chris stared at the words uncomfortably before finding a crack in the sidewalk. "Of course."

Francis smiled at him in a kind way, as if he meant to pat him on the head, like a child. *Welcome to belief.*

Chris squinted at the words through the dark. They flashed at him as Francis shifted his weight. "And was it everything you thought? Is she everything he who always believes expected?"

Francis put up a defensive hand. *I was only joking. And yes, she is what I expected. Just a person – one with a great responsibility. That's how it always works; that's who God always chooses.*

Closing his lips tightly to keep anything angry from coming out, Chris nodded his head. A lifetime of belief wouldn't have relieved Chris of the awe he felt at playing a part in a plan so much larger than himself. Where did Francis get off sounding so cool? Chris threw out his own challenge, "What about the sign or mark or whatever? Did she have a mark on her?"

No. Nothing – clean.

Chris looked up surprised and concerned, so Francis quickly continued, *Not surprising really. She doesn't have any human fate. She exists for one purpose: to keep David's line from taking back the throne of Israel too soon.*

"How did you know her then?"

Francis' face turned-up blank.

"How did you know her? If there wasn't a mark, how did you know it was Remiel without me telling you? What? From seeing pictures of the statue?"

No – I recognized her without pictures.

"How?" Chris persisted, staring at his strange partner through the low streetlight.

It was her eyes – to me they have no pupils. To me, they glow all the time.

Chapter 7 – The One More Day

Chris and Francis crowded together to read the fax in the hotel office, shoulders and heads touching. The hotel clerk watched the odd scene a little longer than usual. Her manager was right – everything imaginable could be seen in hospitality.

"Look at this – oh! Here comes another page." Chris began to pull at the paper before the feed was finished spitting it out.

* * * * *

An excited phone call to Alan, and the Catholic Church had worked through the night to pull birth, school, and medical records on Elise Moore. It was a moment that Chris had never foreseen. In his most hopeful fantasies, he dreamed of listening to some other voice say those words: "We've found her." He never thought he would say them.

Alan's reaction was surprisingly calm – only silence on the other end of the line while Chris explained. Chris could hear Alan's breathing, like he was afraid. It was a long few seconds before he finally said in a shaking voice, "I knew it. I knew it all along." For once, Chris didn't mind the self-verification. He knew it wasn't meant for him. Alan was telling himself, talking to the parts of his own mind that had worried for the last 19 years his life's work was a joke.

Alan became harsh only once. "Why, for God's sake, didn't you take her?"

"Well…we – we had no idea that it would be her. There were so many people," Chris stumbled over their reasons. "I wanted to just take her. But, we aren't the Gestapo, Alan. We didn't have a plan, and after talking with Francis, that was our decision. He felt very strongly that we could wait," Chris let the meaning sink in. "One more day."

"One more day. Well, that's all you've got, Chris," the reproach was as much worry as anger. "I'll get information for you – find me a fax number. It will probably take several hours for the society to get past confidentiality agreements, but we'll pull the necessary strings. Then, tomorrow, you go in there and you get her."

"Even if it means taking her against her will?"

"Barring immediate arrest or huge media headlines, yes. We have no way of knowing how much she knows, if she will go willingly, but we do know that we need her. She has to be protected, Chris, even if she doesn't understand. You should've just taken her! I will be there, with you, as soon as I can."

Then, Alan began doing what he did best – giving orders. Within a half hour of that first phone call, the hotel phone was ringing off the hook as new information came in. Their contacts were good, their covers were strong, and by morning, priests around the country successfully extracted every written record on her.

* * * * *

Two of 47 pages. Francis scrawled. When Chris didn't look up, he erased it.

Impatiently, they waited for the complete fax and then took the stairs up to their room. With the "Do Not Disturb" sign still swinging gently from the door, the priest and monk sat side by side at an overly polished desk and began pouring over the sheets.

"Elise Betheba Moore. Well, this explains a lot. Look at her birth date," Chris exclaimed excitedly, moving forward in the stiff hotel chair. "October 29, 1988. That's right after the statue changed! So, we were right, the whole time. THE WHOLE TIME! Two decades of guessing and we were right. Alan was right. The statue change marked the birth of Remiel," Chris paused as he scanned the page further. The bluish 7:30 AM light was barely enough to read by. He fumbled for the lamp, without looking up from the paper. After a moment, "I think it really must be her. And the only reason we found her is because a waitress, whose daughter happens to go to Ashton College, happened to tell me about the murder on campus." Chris shook his head. "We almost missed all of this." Still reading, "We were right about her birth, wrong about her nationality. Alan speculated that she might be Israeli, or at least Eastern European. But, says here she was born to Kailey and Douglas Moore in New Bern, North Carolina."

They died when she was eight, Francis noted after a few minutes, empty except for the sound of papers flipping. *Car crash. No surprise.*

"Why do you say that?" Chris' eyes busily read the whiteboard and the fax.

Francis shrugged. *She needs to be alone. To do what she has to do, she can't have too many ties. People get in the way.*

A file from the state of North Carolina listed two foster homes. Both

77

records declared the placement successful, but neither family wanted to adopt. Elise Moore was described as independent, removed, and relatively unaffectionate. The record ended abruptly with her high school graduation.

Medical records were also very brief. "Type O Negative, above average height, not too interesting." After a few moments, Chris began flipping pages quickly. "Look at this," he said slowly, knitting his eyebrows together. "Not a single sick visit or prescription. Not one." He smiled at the additional evidence. "That's too unusual. No one gets through 19 years without being sick."

Francis pulled the pile closer and took a look for himself. *Perfect bill of health,* he verified, *though her parents brought her for many exams. Seemed worried about her – one year they brought her for… eight check-ups.*

"And look at the psych reports. " The psychology papers easily made up the largest portion of the fax.

Evaluations since she was four.

"Yeah, a lot of them." Chris' voice turned lower with concern. "It looks like the only thing she was diagnosed with was an over-active imagination, though," he flipped quickly. "This one says she used to lie to other children and to her teachers, and that she sometimes didn't seem to know the difference between daydreams and reality.

"Wait, here's something more specific," Chris pulled a sheet out of the pile and, wrinkling it badly at the top with his big fingers, smacked it down on the desk space between them. "She claimed that she could 'steal other people's energy' by 'turning herself up,' whatever that means. And heal herself. It says she believed that she could cure herself of anything, so long as she was conscious." The two men's eyes met meaningfully.

Interesting, in light of her medical records.

"Someone tried to diagnose her with Attention Deficit Disorder too."

Any details?

"Not really. These are definitely just the overviews. Ummm…she was in therapy at age seven for six months. Says her parents were very concerned about her fitting in at school. She was having trouble with the other kids."

Reports basically stop after parents' death, Francis noted.

"Yeah, it looks like she decided it wasn't smart to talk about healing herself, especially with foster parents. I wonder what else made them think that she needed so many doctors," Chris mused almost to himself. "Five psychiatrists over 4 years. What was happening to her? What could she do?"

We'll have to ask her, Francis glanced down at the plastic watch he bought at the 24-hour pharmacy just down the street earlier that morning. He had never liked watches, but time was moving too fast to lose track of it.

Chris caught his drift. "She doesn't have a roommate, so if it comes down to kidnapping, we'll have a better shot." He thought about the word "kidnap" for a second, and then dismissed it. "Let's look at her class schedule and see when she's home today."

No class 'til 12:30 PM. We have a few hours.

"We want earlier rather than later." Chris continued to thumb through Elise's Ashton College file. "1290 on the SAT. Got good grades in high school. She's a psychology major at Ashton. Interesting – you would think that she wouldn't like psychology after being falsely diagnosed several times as a child."

Francis glanced over Chris' shoulder at the record. *Maybe she doesn't realize she was falsely diagnosed.*

"Yeah. Which brings us to the question of the hour – how are we ever going to talk to her about this and convince her to come with us?" Predictably, Chris blew air out through his cheeks. "Alan will be here as soon as the airlines can find him a seat. We need to have her before then."

Plan?

"We don't have one other than go in there. Alan said to just try to talk to her, and if she doesn't believe us – the most likely scenario – then we have to take her with us anyway. We sedate her," he looked anxiously at the small prescription bag sitting on the bed, "and then we drive away in our stealthy rental car until Alan can get us some help."

What will you say to her? I can't help much, Francis looked away while Chris read the whiteboard.

It was the first time Chris noticed Francis feeling handicapped. "I don't know what I will say. I guess I'll just–" Chris made a rolling motion with his hands, "just tell her about our research and how we have tried to find her. If she knows she's different – maybe that will give her just that hint of a doubt, and the willingness to listen."

For a moment, neither man said anything. They sat in the ever-brightening morning light with their own thoughts. The luggage was by the door, the beds had regained their hotel stiffness – the only thing out of place was the pharmacy bag.

"Is this it?" Chris asked. "Are we done?" He indicated the stack of papers.

Ready if you are.

Chris nodded. Then he nodded again. And finally, with effort, he slid back his desk chair and, pushing off his knees, stood up.

"Do you have your room key?" It was all he could think of to say. A quick confirmation, and they were ready to check out.

Elise Batheba Moore – Chris looked carefully at the very white sheet of paper that had her address printed on it as they walked out the door. "Batheba – her middle name is biblical. Did it list a religion in the file?"

No, Francis wrote with difficulty as they moved down the stairs. The word almost squiggled off the whiteboard. *Batheba – shortened variation of Bathsheba.*

"Book of *Samuel*. King David had an affair with the woman Bathsheba. When she became pregnant, he sent her husband to the front line of battle, knowing he would die – and married Bathsheba when he did. God then punished David for adultery and murder by taking the life of their firstborn son, temporarily interrupting the bloodline of kings. Bathsheba was David's downfall."

Elise Batheba. Same task this time around – bring down the king.

"Temporarily interrupt the bloodline."

* * * * *

Francis and Chris entered Schultz dormitory with only the quiet whisper of the door closing behind them. There were just a few students in the lobby – 9:00 AM was still too early for most of them. October sunlight, warm and orange, came through the large windows spaced evenly around the room. Worn chairs and couches gathered together around a large television, where two students sprawled asleep with their mouths open, obvious victims of an all-nighter. The student running the mailroom yawned over a book. No one even looked up at them.

Francis shifted his weight from foot to foot. He could feel her. It was the same feeling he felt before a vision – only he was quite certain that no vision was prompting his symptoms this morning. He was slightly nauseous and his chest felt heavy. He saw Chris looking at him carefully – Chris wanted to ask what was wrong, but wouldn't in the middle of the lobby.

"She's on the second floor. Room 259," Chris said quietly. He fidgeted and pulled at his collar. Francis nodded.

Up the stairs, down a poorly lit hallway, then turning around as they realized they were going in the wrong direction. Chris clenched his fists periodically to feel his fingernails dig his palms – yes, he was really here. He and Francis gave up speaking.

259 – the number was carved into the old wooden door and then painted black. Several names – probably old occupants – were etched around the number. A whiteboard larger than Francis' hung below the number. *Elise* was prettily printed on it, and a flower had been drawn in the lower corner, then smeared. Several notes remained, mostly about studying and seeing her at Maraschino's.

"I guess I'll knock," Chris said in a barely audible whisper. With a visibly shaking hand, he reached up and knocked just slightly to the right of the 259.

How should I tell her? The entire scenario felt so unreal, Chris wasn't quite sure how to get through it. Skepticism, critical thinking – he had always felt they were admirable qualities. While they might not help him be a good priest, they helped him be a smart man. But, never in his life had he felt so disadvantaged by them as he did now. *She's identical to the statue. She's never been sick,* he reminded himself. *This is the real thing. It has to be her – no doubts. She has to see you believe completely.*

The two men waited in silence, Francis slightly behind Chris. Down the hall, another student stepped out and slammed the door, making both men jump. Automatically, they resumed their previous, still-life positions.

After a few seconds, Chris tapped again, harder. His nervousness about Elise actually being there began to displace with fear that she was not. But, the sound of movement within and the flickering of light from beneath the door soon let them know she was coming. After a few more seconds, the door opened, and Elise Moore poked her head out, blinking the sleep from her eyes.

It still took his breath away, seeing her. The resemblance to the statue in Meura was identical. Though tired and disoriented, her features were the same. Chris sighed slightly with relief. She was still there, still okay – they had their one more day.

He tried to smile, but only managed a grimace. "Hi Elise. My name is Father Chris Mognahan, and this is Brother Francis Carter." He paused, like an actor who had forgotten his lines. "We were wondering if we could come in for a few moments and speak with you?"

Elise stared out the door for several more seconds. Slowly, her eyes widened as recognition began to increase her heart rate. It was the priest and the monk from the bar – standing outside her door. The blood seemed to drain completely out of her body, leaving behind only the color of her light brown eyes and messy, strawberry-blond hair.

Chris tried to break the strained silence. "Um, we recently gave a special Mass on campus – you may have seen some of the posters? We just were hoping we could speak with you for a few minutes this morning."

Elise swallowed visibly. "What do you want to speak with me about?" Her voice cracked on the word "me."

Chris looked at Francis. No help there. Francis was defensively covering his whiteboard with both of his hands, looking mostly at the gray sock that stuck out just barely from behind the door.

"Actually, um… this is kind of a sensitive matter. We were hoping to sit down with you, rather than discuss it out here." Chris managed to smile this time.

Slowly, Elise shook her head. "You can't come in unless I know what this is about," she heard herself say automatically, her consciousness a spectator to the strange scene. She knew she was acting strange and

81

suspicious, but she couldn't help it. She was out of control. It was all she could do to keep from screaming and slamming the door.

Chris assessed quickly that she was not budging. If anything, she was beginning to shrink away and retreat from the doorway. His mind rapidly began to scan all the ways to bring up what he had to say quickly, before she closed the door and they lost their chance. With only another second's worth of hesitation, he picked the idea she could relate to immediately.

"As I'm sure you are aware, a young man was killed on this campus several weeks ago," Chris could hear the tremor in his voice, and wondered if she could too. "We would like to talk with you about his death. We think you may be inadv–"

Both men watched as Elise's breathing began to come fast and heavy. Her eyes flew from one and then to the other. Her pulse shuttered in her neck.

Leaning towards her, Chris asked, "I'm sorry. Are you feeling all right?"

Elise closed her eyes while shaking her head yes. It had finally happened. How, she could not even begin to guess. But somehow, they found her. It was over. Horrifyingly, there was no relief – only terror. She could feel her facial muscles tense and then break. Tears leaked out from her closed eyelids. "Yes," she whispered and began blinking through them. "Please come in." She turned away from the door, leaving it only barely open, and repressed a strange, horrifying giggle at her cordial invitation.

Chris watched her inside, bewildered. Was she crying? Yes, he was pretty sure she was crying. Francis' face remained a blank; he neither looked alarmed, nor surprised. They tripped over each other to get in the room and close the door.

Still with tears streaming down her face, Elise dragged over her desk chair, and a beanbag chair from the corner of the room. Then, she sat on her bed, pulling her over-sized pajamas closely around herself.

Chris quickly sat in the desk chair, leaving Francis to maneuver the beanbag that left him basically on the floor and slightly lopsided. Timidly, the monk balanced, unable to remove his gaze from her eyes – they were so light, he squinted. To him, she looked as though she were hollow with a light bulb inside. Even in this frightened state, the power she gave off radiated in incredible waves. He thought about their sedative, and wondered if it would work.

"Uh, we didn't mean to upset you. Are you all right?" Chris asked again, locking both hands in a death grip around his knee.

Elise could not trust her voice, so she merely shook her head. After several swallows, "I knew, you know? I saw you last night, and I knew. You were there for me." She rocked slightly as she spoke.

Chris stared at her, unsure of how to proceed. What was she talking about? What did she know? Was it possible that she already guessed something hunted her; that it killed her classmate? For God's sake, had she been waiting for them to find her? "You know about us; Clyde Parker; his death."

A new flood of tears streamed down her face. It seemed best to wait.

"How did you know?" she asked through sobs. "How did you know it was me?"

"It was you?"

"It was the other guy, right? He told you. But he lied! Clyde hit me and there was a lot of blood."

Clyde hit me and...something important was happening. Chris could feel his mind, like a real muscle, jerking to grasp it.

"You see, it was in self defense," her words began to run over each other as she tried to get them out. "You have to believe me. I only hit him because he hit me. I didn't know what he was going to do. Please, try and understand." Her eyes darted between them. She cried aloud at the hopelessness of her plea.

The priest could feel the vein in his forehead pound as it began to come together. Clyde's murder – somehow, she had been there. With a sickening feeling, his mind quickly replayed her words, *I only hit him.*

"You..." the word drew out into an airy breath. "You only hit him?"

"Yes – that's all! I just," her voice did fail and there was a pause. "Slapped him."

Instinctually, Chris looked at her hands. They were busy clenching and unclenching. He saw the finger-stripes on Clyde's dead face.

Chris let himself openly take several large breaths. *This can't be happening. WHAT WILL THIS MEAN?* His mind yelled. Astonishment and confusion spilled onto his face and he did nothing to hide it. It was over – no pretense at normalcy. This was as far from normal as he'd ever been.

Elise looked up when no one broke the silence. She squinted through red eyes for a moment. "Are they coming?"

"You're saying that you killed him?" Chris returned the question almost before Elise had finished. It was her turn to stare in confusion.

"Are they com–"

"My God." Chris shook his head in disbelief. "Did you see this Francis? It wasn't the Other. It was...what does it mean? What do we do now?"

Francis began with a shaky hand to unravel the string connecting his pen to his whiteboard – he had been winding it tightly around his finger.

They conversed as if she wasn't even in the room anymore. The words flew meaninglessly – she had no idea what they were discussing, especially since she could only hear one half. Why weren't they telling her what was going to happen next? She needed to know – it was the most important thing! In a shrill voice that cut through the hand gestures and Chris' panicked tones, Elise asked, "Are they coming or not?"

"Who?" Chris finally turned to her.

"The police!"

Police. The word stopped everything. Chris felt sorry as he looked at Elise's face pinched with confusion and guilt. With a long sigh, he let his shoulders sag, deflating into a much older looking man. He used one hand to knead the skin between his eyes, as though he had a sinus headache. "No, the police are not coming," he said quietly.

"They aren't coming?" she let the question hang out rhetorically. "Then what's going to happen to me? Why are you here?"

Chris opened his mouth to speak, but said nothing. His mind reeled, looking for the words.

"Well, why? What is going to happen?" Elise licked her lips. "Are you trying to counsel me into–"

"No, no. We're not here to counsel you, Elise. Um," Chris leaned close to her, trying to maintain eye contact – a hypocritical tip directly from his counseling experience. "How do I begin? Francis and I came here, because we've actually been looking for you for a long time. We didn't know that you," a hard swallow, "killed Clyde. And it doesn't matter to us," he quickly added. "We're not here to turn you in. We're here – because we believe you are someone special."

"Special?" she echoed dully, like a child mimicking its mother's voice. With only slightly more life, "I don't understand. Why would you come here if–"

"Because there's more to you than this, than whatever you've done."

She shook her head slowly and sadly. "No, I'm sorry but, there isn't." In a hard voice, "I don't care what you think you know about me. If you're not here to arrest me, then I think you should leave." Elise played nervously with the ends of several strands of hair. "And if you tell anyone about this, I'll deny it," it came out a threat. Her lips trembled, but her eyes remained very steadily on Chris. He felt his neck hairs prickle. He looked at her hands again.

"Just go!"

Francis startled and began to stand, but Chris insisted nervously, "Hear me out." He let his eyes drop to the floor. Counseling experience or not, there was no way he was going to get through this strange speech while maintaining eye contact. "This is going to sound crazy. But, it's true." He gave an anxious laugh. "I guess that's the way all crazy stories start, though."

"I'm not listening – I don't care!"

"Twenty years ago, there was an omen. The omen told us, the Catholic

Church," he gestured to include Francis, "that an angel had been born to us."
He let his eyes glance at her to see her reaction to the word "angel." Nothing.

Faster, "Now, this isn't the Hallmark version of angels. In the Bible,
angels are God's warriors. They fought at the fall of mankind, and they will
fight at the end. Some of them are absolutely terrifying. But, they fight for
God's will."

Elise opened her mouth to yell again, but only blinked hard. She had no
idea what the priest was talking about. Angels, God – was he getting to some
sort of diatribe? All she could think of was what she had done: her paranoia
led her to confess to two complete strangers. At last, she had unraveled.

"This omen told the Catholic Church that we – that God had sent us a
warrior in human form to fight a great battle and destroy something wrong in
the world," he left out the confusing Israeli politics for the time being. "The
omen told us to search for her, and we have been for over two decades.
We've been looking for someone with incredible power – and we think it's
you, Elise."

He breathed out until his chest ached. His ears burned, and he
remembered Peter in the Gospel. How much easier it would be to deny his
faith. His words sounded like some apocalyptic novel plot. "Please believe
me," he said aloud the prayer that God would help them now and open up her
mind to the insane truth.

"Is this some cruel joke?" Chris' prayer died with the anger in her voice.
"What are you, sick? Get out! Get out, you crazy," her voice strangled as she
sputtered for words and threw an arm towards the door.

"Please Elise! You have to try and listen," Chris began again, his tone
that of a parent pleading with a child.

"No, I don't. Now get out!" Her voice was hard and angry, no longer
afraid or confused. Francis stumbled from the beanbag chair. Though Chris
couldn't see it, her eyes were on fire now, shining out at both of them.

Chris followed Francis' cue, putting a few feet of space between them
and the girl. Again, the hair on the back of his neck prickled.

But they needed her. Even as he moved away, Chris attacked from a
different angle. If only he could create doubt, some sort of connection!
"Think about how you killed Clyde. No one can slap someone and kill them
like that. No one can do what you did. No person," he pleaded, as he reached
into his coat pocket to feel the pharmacy bag. They hadn't even thought to
open the syringe packaging – some prepared kidnappers.

"GET OUT OF MY ROOM! YOU'RE CRAZY!" she screamed loudly
now as she climbed out of the bed. Both men took another step back.
Frantically, she searched the room. Where was the plant?

"Or what about healing yourself?" Chris threw out in desperation.

For a moment, Elise stopped moving. Only her eyes slipped towards him.

He ran with it. "You told psychiatrists that you could heal yourself. And – and what did you call it? Turning – you can suck other people's energy. Is that what happened that night? Did you use Clyde's energy to hurt him and then heal yourself? I know you were hurt. There was blood on the side walk – type O negative." He kept going, spewing anything now that he had her attention. "It's because you're not like everyone else, Elise. You ARE different. The doctors tried to tell you that you couldn't heal yourself, that you couldn't take energy from other people. But you can, can't you?"

All was quiet and still in the room as Elise hesitated before answering the question. "Yes. I can," she answered darkly as she located the plant on her nightstand and twisted her fingers into its leaves.

For a second, her admission hung in the air palpably. It was as if the room itself sucked in a huge satisfied and surprised breath.

"Then come with us. There's so much more to tell you. You have to come with us because there's more that might harm you." Chris extended his hand, but Elise remained very still.

Francis, however, continued to shrink from her slowly. She was doing something he could only describe as growing. He could feel her anger and power filling the room, and a wave, like an electric surge, passed through him. Far off, his ears began to ring. Afraid, Francis pulled on Chris' arm, and mouthed the word *leave*.

Chris gave him a confused look and pulled his arm back. "The omen also said that something else was born into the world with you – to stop you from helping us. We don't know what it is. Something horrible, though. People dream about it. And if we can find you, so can this thing. So, you see you really must..." Chris' voice got quieter and quieter until it was gone. There was something wrong. Her eyes – it looked like her irises were fading.

There was a scratching noise as a dry, dead leaf fell on the floor. For the first time, Chris focused on the plant Elise was touching. Visibly, it was drying out and dying, writhing as its stem began to fold over the planting pot. It was like time-lapse photography.

Francis pulled at him again, strongly. This time, Chris went.

"Yes, I think you'd better go now," Elise said calmly as the last of the dead plant broke off brittle in her hand. Her irises were entirely gone now, and in their void was light even Chris could see, noticeable in the morning sunshine.

"Please Elise, Remiel. I can show you things that will make you believe."

"And I can show you things that will make you believe," she warned as she closed the distance between them.

Francis felt for the doorknob behind him, keeping both eyes on Elise.

He slid out into the sanctuary of the hallway. There was no telling how far she would go to keep her horrifying secrets.

"Elise–"

"GET OUT! GET OUT OF MY ROOM! GET OUT, GET OUT NOW!" As Chris spilled out, the door slammed shut, though Elise was not close enough to touch it.

"What's all the yelling?" a student with bloodshot eyes behind dark glasses asked in an overly authoritative tone. "Not everyone has early morning class." Then, noticing the outfits, "Can I help you? I'm the Resident Advisor for this floor."

"No. No, everything is fine."

Moving around them, the RA knocked on Elise's door. "Elise, is everything all right? I thought I heard you yell." There was no answer.

Frowning, the student turned back to Chris and Francis.

"That's all right. We were just leaving,"

* * * * *

"How could we think that we could deal with her?" Chris asked sitting on his hotel bed – they had checked back in to the Ashton Howard Johnson. "How could we be so arrogant to think that we could just take her?"

Francis lay on his own bed. Periodically he responded by propping his white board up on his stomach with an encouraging remark. He continued sipping from the water on the side of his bed. He still felt ill, like he had been carsick for a few hours and his stomach was not yet settled. He did not feel much like writing.

Rather, he wished Chris would be quiet so he could think about her. Her power – he never suspected that she would be so strong. But, then why hadn't he? Remiel was one of God's greatest warriors. She was frightening. When they did finally convince her to come with them, it would be interesting to watch her stretch her legs and see what she could really do. He smiled. Yes, that would be exciting.

And, he had no doubt that she would come. It was her fate. Like others in the Bible who tried to deny their role in history, she would eventually lose.

Chris noticed that Francis' response frequency had slowed to a trickle. He looked over at the lump in black robes – he still didn't look well. With a sigh, Chris too lay back on his bed and stared up at the ceiling, quiet.

Alan would arrive in only a few hours. He had caught an early flight to Charlotte and was driving the rest of the way out to Ashton. He didn't know they had nothing, and Chris was in no hurry to dial his cell and talk about it. He wasn't even sure he could articulate what had happened that morning. Specifics aside, the general conclusions were no less easy: their savior was a murderer and capable of God only knew what else.

But despite the way it turned out, something very personal had still happened to Chris. In forty-eight hours, he found what he had missed for 40 years. Although there was certainly an element of disbelief, the doubt was gone. Lying on the hotel bed, he thought about his faith cautiously, almost afraid to look at the changes for fear they would stop. When he went home – whenever that would be – he hoped Derek Dewallace would ask him one more time about his faith. And then, for the first time in his life, he would answer without hesitation that yes, there is a God, He has a plan, and He remains very concerned with what's going on down here.

It was such an intense knowledge – it took Chris' breath away with joy and fear. He had seen first hand God working. The statue was brought to life, and the light in her eyes, though startling, was the light of God. Undoubtedly, the way he would live his life was forever changed. And, he was already praying that it would stay that way. When days and months and years had passed from that first moment seeing her alive and warm across the bar, would some of it begin to fade? It was so extraordinary – would he eventually question if it ever really happened at all?

Enough. Slowly, Chris' mind stopped spinning, like a carousel grinding to a halt. This might be the last real rest he had for a long time. Whatever other worries he entertained, Chris felt positive that this was only the beginning.

"I hope Alan can convince Elise of who she really is," he spoke up to the ceiling, unsure if Francis was already asleep. "I have a feeling we'll be fighting round two this evening. Pray she listens."

Rolling to face the wall, Chris did not see Francis scrawl a response.
She will.

Chapter 8 – The Other

Elise still sat on her bed – three hours later. She had not moved. She was vaguely conscious of her leg tingling underneath her and of being hungry. That was odd. She didn't think she would be hungry ever again, let alone so soon. Two more tears squeezed out – they were almost gone now. She had cried until she thought she might vomit. Her chest ached much worse than it ever did when she ran.

The priest said no police, and thus far he had been truthful. There had not been a single noise outside the door. The sunspot on the floor moved slowly with the time – it now lit the leg of her desk chair. The day was spinning on without her. Her first class started fifteen minutes ago. She wanted to go, to will herself to stand up, put on some clothes and find her way to her usual seat. But, she just couldn't.

Instead, Elise fingered one of the faded flowers printed on her tangled sheets. The fabric was cheap. She pulled at a lose string and then sat perfectly still, watching. The leaves from the African Violet lay on the floor exactly where they fell. She had completely killed it. Nothing but a brown stalk stuck up from the potted dirt. The minutes passed – she could hear her wrist watch ticking on her dresser.

Inexorably, her mind wandered back to the day's earlier spectacle. Like a fool, she had lost control. Even when she dealt with Clyde, she had been coldly calculating. Although afraid, she had not panicked. She remembered the eerily calm reflection of herself in the bathroom mirror, washing away the dried blood.

But, the priests, or monks or whoever – they were a different threat. They knew so much about her past and about the parts of her life she had tried to bury long ago. It had been years since anyone mentioned her psychological history. Her parents' death marked the exact day she gave up trying to live with whatever it was she had. No more doctors; no more trying to understand it; no more asking why and how it should be used. Elise buried it with their memory and focused on living as normally as she could. The reports slowly disappeared into her file and she moved on and away from anyone who remembered her as being anything more than a quiet kid.

The process had been like weaning a drug addiction. *Today is day four since I last turned-up.* Elise often went for months without hearing the whispers in her ears and feeling the tingles in her fingers. She still used it when she needed to, like a sip from a hidden stash, but spent most days only thinking about using it, and sleeping better when she didn't. The confidence it provided was always tempting, but the anxiety of discovery was far greater. She'd always known, had been well taught about the other half of the powerful coin she'd been given. There was her father dragging her from the t-ball field after she cranked eight homeruns in one game; he made her quit the next day. There was her mother blushing to explain when Elise healed her broken wrist while the second x-ray was still being taken. Over and over with fear in their eyes they'd whispered or sometimes yelled: *Until we know what this is, I don't want you using it! What will people think? You'll make them afraid.* Or worse. *Elise, are you cheating? Are you lying again? That's impossible – you know that's not possible!* Turning-up quickly became something kept below the surface. It was an anomaly; not a gift.

Until now. Although the priest and monk did not realize she killed Clyde until she told them, they did know how she could. And, they weren't trying to diagnose her strange powers away. Rather they were looking for them.

The sunspot crept up the desk chair onto the seat. Her second class was starting now. The mask was dissolving further as another time and place passed away that normal Elise should be at, but was not.

How did they find me? Elise finally untucked her leg from underneath her, feeling the pins and needles poking from under her sleeping skin. Priests and monks knowing her past, knowing what she could do – it was a few too many steps away from reality for comfort. A Catholic search put her gift in a context she refused.

In the Bible, angels are God's warriors. We've been looking for someone with incredible power – and we think it's you, Elise, the priest replayed in her mind. Well, angels were out of the question. A *gift from God, some sort of miracle, a saint...* the list of implausible realities rattled off in her head.

To take the life-energy from someone else – in another time it may have hinted at souls and powers not kept in scientific cells. But, the 21st century dictated biology the rational option to explore. More likely, she was just using a part of her brain that most others could not; she might be the next step in human evolution and others would follow; possibly, she was just a weird anomaly with a gene that others didn't have. She could accept being different. But, to suppose she was singled out and guided by the invisible hand of a 2,000-year-old legend–

"I am completely alone," Elise spoke for the first time since she slammed the door. "There is no God. I have always been alone." Her face crinkled, as though she would cry again. She couldn't even remember the last time she had been in a church. Maybe with the Korsgadens, her second foster family? She never took it seriously, never needed it.

"They're just crazy," she wiped her face on the sheet. Whatever their reasons for finding her, she definitely wasn't falling for Catholic omens.

More sliding of the sunspot, more ticking of the wrist watch. But, movement was inevitable, unless she planned on dying of starvation in a pile of piss-soaked sheets.

The police would eventually come. She had admitted being a murderer – it was only a matter of time now. Sadly, she looked around the room. All of the things she loved stared back – a shell from her first visit to the ocean, a collage of past concert tickets, her psychology books. The normal life she had built hung from the walls and folded in the drawers. Was she brave enough to leave it?

Her mind flooded with thoughts, *changing my name, dying my hair, quitting school.* Elise took several slow, controlled breaths with her lips tightened Lamaze style. She worked so hard to get here, to create this world, these opportunities. It was her parents' name – the only thing she had left.

Turn yourself in...no, just wait it out...run! Each bleak option flew through her, despite her conscious efforts to keep them slow – jail cell, paralyzing suspense, fugitive. What type of horrible decision was this and how could she possibly choose?

"I can't do this. I can't do any of this!" Elise moved her head vehemently side-to-side until the images shook away. She dragged her body off the bed with effort and stood. She could feel the blood creeping cautiously down her legs into her feet, feeling out the strangled veins. With halting steps, she crossed to the mini-fridge and pulled out half an unfinished sandwich from a recent night out. She ate standing, taking large bites and swallowing them dryly. With some old water left in a dirty glass, she washed it down, checked the door to see that it was locked and then crept back into her balled sheets.

* * * * *

When she opened her eyes, evening gloom fuzzed over everything. She could barely see across the room to the door. She lay for a few moments, blinking stiffly. She had an after-crying headache.

As her mind cleared itself of fitful dreams, Elise's pulse began to pick-up until she could feel its fluttery beat in her pillow-side temple. So dark – how much time had passed? The alarm clock – 7:17 PM. It was late. She overslept!

With a start, she sat up and then regretted the movement as a cramp throbbed angrily in her neck. Her stomach turned and she opened her mouth, waiting for the gag. How could she let this happen? Both her legs trembled as her stomach lurched a second time. Eyes wide, she looked around – no priests, no monks, and no police.

But the panic didn't ease. The more time that passed, the more likely someone was going to knock on the door. She had slept away the time to decide. Sitting in her room, waiting for the red and blue lights to flash outside her window no longer seemed like an option, if for no other reason than that it might happen soon. She could always turn herself in. But, the window for running was closing.

Flipping a light on first, Elise climbed out of bed. There wasn't time now to be sentimental or confused. Elise scanned the room only briefly. It already felt empty in the way a house is empty after a party.

Moving quickly, she slid off her pajamas and pulled on some jeans and a sweatshirt. She smoothed back her hair and put on her running shoes without untying them. Throwing open the lid of her jewelry box (not bothering to close it again), Elise tugged her mother's engagement ring onto her middle finger. With one continuous sweep, she emptied her schoolbooks onto the floor and swiped her toiletries into her backpack. A stuffed animal from the bed was thrown in on top, along with a small photo album. Several pairs of underwear later, the bag was zipped and on her back.

Elise turned one last time, looking over everything like a person in a hotel, afraid to leave something important under the bed. She heard the African violet leaves crunch under her sneakers, but didn't allow her mind to follow that line of thought. After one complete turn around, she opened the door and stepped into the hall. With her sweatshirt hood up and its rim close around her face, Elise kept her head down as she moved quietly down the hall and stairs. She wanted no witnesses.

The cool evening came in at the edges of her clothing as Schultz dormitory doors swung quietly closed behind her. A ten-second hesitation was all she needed to see that the nearby parking lot and walkway were police-free. Elise started a brisk walk away from the building, her eyes adjusting to the streetlight. A flood of weak relief helped her to take several large breaths – she had escaped the first place they would look.

It was a perfect October night for a horror movie. In the dark, the leaves on the trees looked black. They shuttered in the wind as though invisible, angry hands were violently shaking the branches. A soft shushing sound rose when the leaves moved together. Venus shown clear and bright low to the horizon, and an orange sliver of a moon rose below her. The scratching of dead leaves blowing across the pavement sounded eerily like dry fingers rubbing together, and the aroma of dewy grass rose from the ground whenever the wind fell. Any other night, Elise might have enjoyed it. Tonight, she didn't even notice.

Ten minutes later, she arrived at her first destination: the ATM machine outside the student activities center. Dark shadows draped the surrounding academic buildings, leaving central campus dark. Friday nights were obviously not big studying nights. Major traffic was limited to streams of laughing students headed down the hill to Asbury Lake and Fraternity Row.

Empty campus or not, there was still someone on the ATM. Elise waited outside nervously, fidgeting with her sweatshirt sleeves. The person seemed to be having trouble with the "Deposit" or "Withdrawal" screen. Elise rolled her head back in annoyance.

After a few minutes, the other student came out of the booth sheepishly, still with an empty wallet. *Wasting time, wasting time*, Elise's mind sang ruthlessly.

Unfortunately, there was simply no way to drain her account from the machine. She would have to take what the withdrawal limit would give her, and simply leave the rest behind. Elise tried not to think about just how far this small amount would really carry her, and instead held her breath as the machine spit out $500 in twenties. She stuffed the money into her backpack. At least her accounts weren't frozen yet – they couldn't be too hot onto her. She left the booth and headed down the main walkway.

Walking into William Albert library was a lot like walking into an operating room. The doors made a hissing noise each time they closed and opened, as though an airtight chamber were breached. Fluorescent light illuminated the white floors so brightly that squinting was necessary for a good five seconds after entering. White checkout counters attached to gleaming white walls were the first things that came into focus once the eyes adjusted. The only detail that gave away the true identity of the building was the smell of dust and old paper.

Elise became very aware of her sweatshirt hood as she headed past the main checkout counters where two librarians stood talking. It seemed to scream that she was up to something (avoiding library fines, sneaking to the computer lab to surf for porn or hack an ex's e-mail…). Elise kept her eyes on her sneakers, knowing it only made her look worse. No one stopped her.

She took off her hood only when she was alone in the elevator headed several floors down into the book stacks. It rumbled slowly until it creaked to a stop at level 5UL – the fifth underground level – and the doors opened.

Just as she hoped, the fifth level was pitch black and completely empty. With only the light from the open elevator, the rows and rows of books appeared like strange sentinels guarding a vast blackness behind them. In the dark, it was impossible to tell they ran straight back for half the length of a football field.

Elise stepped towards the closest row of books and flipped on the light-timer. An electric hum began and several white lights overhead flickered on. Always efficient, the college only paid for lighting in the library stacks when someone actually needed it. Each row in every floor of the stacks had a light-timer. If a student needed to search for something in a particular row, they turned on the row's timer and received a gracious fifteen minutes of illumination before blinking back into darkness. *They should decrease the wattage in the front lobby and put some down here*, Elise thought once again, just as she had before when doing research.

The elevator squeaked closed behind her, and she heard it begin to rumble upwards somewhere as the library-silence recaptured the room. She walked to the left, flipping on each row's timer one by one, watching the library begin to glow with fluorescence. At the far left corner, she found what she came for – a computer. The labs were still too crowded, even on Fridays, and she didn't want to use the consoles in the lobby upstairs in full view of the librarians. Down here was quiet and safe. Opening a search engine, she queried for the Ashton train schedule.

Deciding how to run was an easy decision made within the first few minutes on her walk over. She couldn't take the bus, since it was the most popular way for students to travel and most likely the first place the authorities would look besides her dorm room. And, if they didn't find her there, they would probably look at the airport. The train would most likely be their third choice, and so Elise made it her first.

Where did she want to go? *Some place where I can easily become someone else.* Allowing herself only seconds to scan her mind for ideas, Elise landed on recent memories of news headlines reporting the poorly guarded Mexican border and droves of illegal immigrants. Someone down there had to be selling social security cards.

Scrolling through states, she picked Texas and watched the screen of destinations load. There weren't very many trains from Ashton to Texas. Not that it mattered. So long as she left Ashton going in the right direction, the rest was pretty inconsequential. She could catch a two-day train ride, with a few connections, to San Antonio. And that was only a couple bus rides short of the border towns. It seemed as good a choice as any. The train was scheduled for 9:25 AM Saturday, so she only needed to get through one night. Maybe she could stay in the library without anyone noticing.

"Now, if only there's an open seat." Clicking "Ticket Availability," she began to type in her preferences. *Destination San Antonio, one passenger, adult–*

THUD

A book fell somewhere in the far back of the stacks.

Elise jumped, every muscle in her body tense. Instinctually, she hunched her shoulders as if bracing for an attack and turned her head sharply.

For several seconds, she kept very still, eyes and ears straining, but there was no further noise and no one that she could see. Taking a few shallow breaths, she tried to think her heart rate back down.

Really, there was no way the police could find her here – she hadn't even known she was coming to the library until a half-hour ago. And she was positive no one came in from the elevator or the stairs – she could see both doors from her seat. If someone was in the library, they had been there when she walked in. She just hadn't noticed – a student probably studying in the back. Except...*I turned on the lights when I came in.*

Who would sit in the stacks in the dark?

Maybe it wasn't anyone at all. Maybe a book fell off the shelf on its own.

Elise rolled her shoulders against the creeping tension at the base of her neck. *Keep it together, Elise.* With another furtive look, she began to click through the booking screens. *Sleeper car, single...*"Come on," she spoke under her breath. "Load faster."

To her relief, there were several seats/beds left on the train to San Antonio. Scrolling through several of the rooms, Elise began, for the first time, to really consider getting away. She could see herself already, looking out the train window as it pulled away from the station. There was relief and loneliness.

She couldn't book online – no credit card paper trail allowed. She would just have to take her chances and book at the station with cash. Clicking through a few more screens, she checked when the ticket window would open. According to the website, tickets went on sale bright and early. *Spend the night somewhere, buy my ticket at 6:00 AM, wait at the station, board at 9:00 AM, gone by 9:25 AM.* She nodded her head in agreement with the plan. She could do this. She could–

TAP-TAP

The sound was much, much softer than the first – almost inaudible. But it was also much, much closer. Gooseflesh grew on her arms and neck, and although her eyes remained focused on the screen, her mind tuned only to her surroundings.

TAP-TAP; TAP-TAP

Probably just a student, just looking for a book–

As if reading her mind, several more books thudded to the floor only a few rows away. Elise jumped again and then resettled nervously with both hands in her lap, her fingers twisting one over another. Her eyes flicked across the rows of books to her right. She waited to hear someone place the books back on the shelves, but no one did.

Then, from the back of the room, there came footsteps. Slow, careful, deliberate steps – first the click of a heal and then the soft thud of a sole. Elise followed the person with her ears, hearing them come closer to the front of the room. Her instinct was to hide, but if it were only a student–

THUD-THUD-THUD-THUD-THUD

The heavy pounding rose like a drum roll. It started in the back, but quickly seemed to be coming from all rows. For a split second, Elise reeled bewildered, until she realized, *It's the books…*

THUD-THUD-THUD-THUD-THUD-THUD-THUD-THUD-THUD

Louder and louder, the noise of hardcovers hitting the floor and pages rustling grew so intense that Elise reached to cover her ears. She turned helplessly, watching the shadows dancing in every row as their contents ejected. She found herself blinking rapidly, unable to take in the sight even while wondering if it was real.

Then, abruptly–

Silence

The last few books thudded to the ground, and the library settled, as though nothing happened.

With a click, Elise switched off the monitor to hide her work and turned fully on the stool to look out across the rows in front of her. *Who can do something like that? Pulling off all the books from all the different shelves…who the hell can do something like that?* The unnatural quiet continued until it took on a drone of its own in her ears. She squinted to look closer into the dark spaces.

"Hello?" Elise heard the mucus rattle in her voice and realized she had forgotten to swallow.

There was no answer – the library continued on in suspicious silence.

Then cautiously, Elise stood up, rising on the balls of her feet to see better. More forcefully, "Hello?"

In answer, she heard a soft rolling sound about seven rows up.

It continued slowly, until finally, a yellow No. 2 pencil rolled out from the aisle into the main walkway. Another followed. They rolled together until they collided with the wall. Then another rolled from the row.

Elise stood entranced, stupidly watching the pencils as they continued to roll out. Her whole body rose and fell with her chest, letting in air in large gulps, as though she were swimming instead of standing. Pencils rolling – it was familiar. Yes, she'd heard it before. New, identifiable terror rose as she remembered, *For a moment, there was only the sound of pencils rolling.*

It was crazy, but she was sure it was intentional. Whoever was in the stacks wanted her to remember, to know that they knew. It was malicious and threatening, calling up the fear from that night so close – far too cruel for the police or priests. The room wavered dreamy with her adrenaline as the chemical hit her brain. *How could anyone know that detail – how could they do something so…*

Just under the rolling, she noticed the breathing that was not her own. It was wet and loud, and much faster – like a dog.

What the hell is that? Her mind turned from the old horror to the new. She wet her top lip and then rubbed what little moisture there was between the two. Staring, willing her eyes to see into the dark of the stacks beyond those she had lit, Elise felt raw fear rising sourly in the back of her throat. *WHAT THE FUCK IS PANTING?*

Something else was born into the world with you…something horrible, though. People dream about it.

Listening to the rapid breathing, Elise heard the priest's words with a saneness they had not had earlier. It was suddenly believable that, whatever it was – panting, tapping – had indeed been waiting for her all this time, in the dark, in the stacks.

Get out of here. Real or insane, get out of here now!

Elise steadied her now trembling frame on the desk, reaching back to feel its comforting realness. She looked towards the elevator, an impossibly far 12 rows away. To reach it, she had to pass by the seventh row with the panting and the pencils, still rolling. "Oh God, oh God, oh God."

Without taking her eyes off the walkway in front of her, Elise reached down until she felt her bag. Lifting it, she kept the arm-strap tight in her hand – she could always use it as a weapon. Then, she put her free hand out in front of her, ready to grasp. Turning-up sounded suddenly damn good. She took her first step forward.

Immediately, the panting stopped. Then, four padded footsteps were heard, each with tiny clicks at the end. *Claws.*

Elise took two steps back, bumping into the desk. *It knows I want to leave. God, what the hell is it? What should I do?* The elevator button stared back at her mockingly. Even if she ran, she would have to wait for the old elevator to rattle down. The stairs? In theory, the door should be unlocked–

FLICKER

Elise's eyes flew towards the middle of the room.

FLICKER

It took her a few seconds to realize what was happening *(FLICKER)*. The lights were turning out *(FLICKER)*, one by one over the rows in the same order that she turned them on only fifteen minutes ago *(FLICKER)*. Her time was up. *(FLICKER)* Already, the darkness captured six rows and moved towards her like a great black wall.

New adrenaline exploded toxic in her veins. *(FLICKER)* She could feel the exact moment it released into her bloodstream, making her body feel weirdly like it wasn't connected in the right places anymore. *(FLICKER)* Dropping her bag, she pushed off the floor towards the closest row of books and its timer *(FLICKER)*.

It was only a few feet away, but the lights were beating her, a row going out every second. *(FLICKER)* Only three steps, *(FLICKER)* and she lost two rows–

FLICKER

The library went dark. Elise slammed at full speed into the closest row of books and then fell backwards into blackness so thick, it was as though she had her eyes closed. The fall knocked the wind from her, and she lie gasping and making strange wheezing sounds as she tried to take a real breath. Tears involuntarily streamed down her cheeks as she wondered if someone could actually suffocate like this. Still, she willed her legs to move, to at least crawl her body out from the open. A few more seconds of struggle, and Elise lie back defeated and waiting for her own breath. With the only useful sense she had left, she listened.

Nothing but the sound of her chest fighting to rise and fall regularly.

How long would it just let her lie here, this thing from God only knew where? Was it already standing over her, inches from her? Was it about to tear her face off, poetic justice for one who killed Clyde Parker in just such a way?

Elise's breathing became even more ragged, as the carnal panic grew inside her. It was panic as she had never yet known, but recognized. It was the one that drove soldiers to shoot themselves before an enemy attack, pregnant women to jump 50 stories from burning buildings, and kidnap victims to gnaw through their wrists while their torturer took a quick break. It was the panic that said, "Just let it end." Quick, its poison seeped in, convincing her that the thing with the claws was right there; that she could feel its breath on her clammy face; that it would tear her apart and she should just roll over and bang her skull into the closest bookshelf until she was dead or at least so incensed that she would not care or know what it did to her. "Beat it to it," the panic whispered.

No, no, no, no, no, NO!!! With shaking so violent it was almost a twitch, Elise raised her hand, pushing up, up through the darkness until it was fully extended above her. Moving side-to-side, as though she was exaggerating a wave to a friend, she felt – only empty air immediately above her torso. Her chest shuttered relief–

CLICK. CLICK. CLICK. CLICK.

Elise's eyes slid towards the sound, though she could see nothing. The steps were miraculously still a few rows away. The fast breathing resumed, along with a sniffing sound. Assuming the thing was in the same row that the pencils rolled from, she had about 20 feet to find the light switch and prepare to defend herself ("or smash your skull in"). Something about the heavy sniffing told her there was no use trying to hide.

Ignoring by raw will power the pain in her arm and her uncooperative lungs, Elise rolled over shakily and got on her hands and knees, orienting herself by the glow of the elevator button and the red exit sign over the stairway door. Madly crawling, she used her hands to feel forward, searching for the base of the bookshelf. If she could only find that, she could feel her way up to the light-timer. Her hands scrambled making arcs in front of her. One arc, two arc – nothing. They only swept the dust of the floor. But, the shelf had to be close – she hit it only a few seconds ago *DAMN IT!*

It was getting closer. The panting was calmly coming towards her, getting louder, and it felt like no paranoia to think that it was out of the aisle now and probably watching her. She looked to the far exit sign, waiting for something dark to blot it out.

And that's when she noticed: there were now seven elevator lights – the yellow one that seemed to have always been there, and six vibrantly blue ones.

Two of the blue lights blinked together. *Eyes.*

She was vaguely aware that she was whimpering now and making large slapping noises with her hands as she crawled. "Come on. Come on. Where is it? Where the hell is it?" Horse, crazy sounding shrieks erupted from her throat as she continued to search for the shelf. "Someone help me! Where is it? HELP ME!"

THUD

This time, it was the sound of her hand hitting the base of the bookshelf. With a triumphant half-moan, half-scream, Elise began to feel her way up the shelf. The timer should be right there, and she fumbled frantically for it.

The thing in the library growled low and angry, and Elise was sanely certain it understood what she was trying to do. She was going to spoil its fun, playing with her in the dark.

Her fingers fluttered upward, searching, searching. *The knob!*

It began to run. Two paws hitting the floor and then another two as it bounded.

She tried to turn the knob to the left. It didn't budge.

Now she could feel it coming. The thing was huge and heavy, and the shelf she leaned against shook. An incredible stench like burning hair filled her nostrils.

To the right, the knob turned easily. Elise heard the humming start as the row lights prepared to turn on.

The exit sign blotted out and the blue lights were everywhere.

"NOOOOOOO," Elise screamed and squeezed her eyes shut.

The lights flickered on, spreading out pale fingers into the row Elise knelt next to. She knew because she could see light-cracks at the edges of her eyelids. She stayed kneeling, eyes shut, her fingertips kneading the sides of the bookshelf like a cat.

No movement. Silent seconds. Her eyes began to ache, the pupils moving rapidly behind her lids until they fluttered. What was it waiting for?

With an extraordinary expending of energy for what was normally a small thing, Elise forced her facial muscles to pry open her eyes–

There was nothing.

Nothing in front of her, nothing to her side. Absolutely nothing. No sound either. A bead of sweat dripped from her nose down onto her sweatshirt.

Shaking began, first in her legs, and then traveled up her body until her teeth rattled. She clung tightly to the shelf, anchoring to reality. Elise stared out into the darkness that began again a few feet in front of her. Was it there, hiding? Was she completely losing her mind?

No time – get out before it starts again. Using her arms more than her legs, she pulled herself into a standing position and took a wobbling step away from the shelf. Her eyes fixed wide on the darkness, not even turning her head to give it so much as a millisecond unattended as she retrieved her bag from where she dropped it. With fear so strong, she could not swallow, Elise moved forward to the next row.

For a full minute, she stood frozen at that black threshold, unsure if she still had the courage to reach into what she could not quite see, and turn on the next timer. The thing was still there. It had to be. Waiting for her. But, what choice did she have?

As if in a dream, Elise watched her hand involuntarily extend into the dark for the next light-timer. Another twist and the row's lights blinked to life as she jerked her hand back so hard, her elbow and wrist joints cracked. More of the library came into view – her safe-area grew larger.

Still nothing. *Not even a book out of place,* she realized with ironic horror.

In disbelief, Elise moved forward, picking up speed and turning on lights as she went. *Where are all the books? WHERE'S THE EVIDENCE?*

She slowed again as she came to the seventh row. The pencils were gone. Not a single one remained.

Am I really out of my mind? Has Clyde pushed me over the edge?

No. It was too real. All the sounds, the shadows, seeing the pencils. Although it was impossible for someone to hide the mess in the few seconds the lights were out, it was more plausible than thinking it never happened at all.

She wasted no more time. Flipping on every row light as she went, Elise reached the exit in a half-jog, her bag bumping hard against her leg. Rather than wait for the elevator (and the suspense of waiting for its doors to close), she pulled open the door to the stairs and entered the stairwell.

It was wonderful! So bright and light, like the lobby; nothing could hide there. With a hard pull, Elise slammed the door closed behind her, putting a few good inches of metal between herself and the fifth underground level, and stood resting her face on the door and holding its handle in a white-knuckle grip. If only she could lock it.

But of course, she couldn't. Instead, she slipped her backpack onto her shoulders and forced herself to step away from the door backwards until the back of her foot hit the first step. Then, with her neck craned to look always behind her, she used the railing to guide her steps upward. Slowly at first and then faster, increasing the distance between herself and the nightmare that was below. She kept her eyes painfully open despite the operation-room light, looking for anything.

She made it to the third underground level before she heard the rattle of the door handle below – the sound of it clicking up and down, as something managed to jostle it, but not grab it. Elise was pretty sure which door it was: the fifth underground level door.

Her vision blurred as stinging tears filled her eyes. *It's not going to stop.* What was she going to do? Where could she go?

Whirling, still blind with tears, she bolted up the stairs. Her ears remained with the door handle five flights down, but it made no new noise. There was only the frantic pounding of her sneakers–

And the rumbling of the elevator.

Elise screamed freely in the stairwell, knowing she had to beat it.

Three sprinted flights and there it was – the main floor landing. With the sound of the elevator growing as it came up to meet her, Elise opened the main level door so hard that it swung open and hit the wall with a loud bang. Only the librarians at the other end of the lobby looked up disapprovingly mid-whispered conversation. Her toes pushed off to sprint.

Past the counters – past the librarians–

Ding.

Elise heard the elevator sliding open behind her just as she hit the door.

She was several yards into the main campus walkway when the librarians' screams echoed out to her, erasing any last doubt that she was only chased in her mind. For a microsecond, she hesitated. Could she leave them there? But then, was there anything she could do except lead it away? She ran.

But it was a frantic run, like an animal already wounded. Her legs were jelly with panic and burned slightly from sprinting up the stairs. The intense fear drained her body, leaving her running on adrenaline so noxious in her veins, her skin tingled. It took a few steps to kick-up into full gear, and then she was already winded. Her bag alternated hitting her in the back of the head as it rose with her body, and crashing back down into the small of her back. And although it slowed her even further, Elise couldn't fight the compulsive need to look back every few feet. Her ears strained for the sound of running behind her, but with the air rushing by, she couldn't pick out anything.

Passed the academic buildings with their dark windows…Elise knew from experience – their doors locked at 6:00 PM on Fridays, with key-card only access for lab students. Her only hope was to reach the dorms a little under a mile away. Hell, she would welcome the red and blue flashing lights now. She only hoped to make it that far. Keep pushing…

Not even half way, and she could feel her lungs expanding dangerously against her rib cage as they struggled to feed oxygen to her muscles. "I have to – keep going. Please God, I have to keep going," Elise pleaded with herself and the unknown in short breaths. She didn't know what would happen when she got to the dorm. But, the idea of other people seemed right and safe, like losing herself in a crowd.

"Fall into the zone," she coached. "Like any – other day. Focus on – the pounding. Pounding, pounding, pounding…." She tried to hear and feel nothing else. "Please, God. Please God. Just let me make it. Please – God." She tucked her head down further, pressured her muscles. "Like any other day."

Boy, she's really got a fire going.

She's got to make this one. No turning back, the voices came to her. Though they seemed like a part of her that had been left behind somewhere, she needed their calm; needed to find and bury herself in that part separate from the nightmare reality she ran from. She pushed harder.

Around this bend. She still has the hill to climb.

Yeah, but look! There are the lights. Dorm lights!

They're still a ways off. She's going so fast – no pacing. She'll burn out.

Elise ran on with the voices in her head, alternately criticizing and encouraging as they always did. She was vaguely aware that they were possibly (and ironically) her last defense against just lying on the ground and blubbering crazily. *Keep going. Don't think. Just listen to the voices and win this one.*

But, it was a temporary reprieve. Already an extra burning in her side was cause for new anxiety. Elise tried to ignore it, but it grew until she was favoring her right side and holding her breath as she hit the pavement with that leg. She crouched slightly, then tried running with her right hand over her head, but nothing eased it.

Is she slowing down, or is it just me?

Looks like a bad side-cramp. Maybe she should ditch the backpack.

This is pretty desperate. This is a race she has to win.

"I know!" Elise snapped out loud. One more step and then another. If she stopped...the thought completely terrified her, making her feel dizzy. Even a second's delay might allow it to catch-up.

But, the cramp grew until Elise practically stopped breathing to keep her lungs from pushing painfully against it. A decidedly short-term strategy, her muscles were tiring; they needed full breathing capacity to keep up this pace. It began to feel like she was running through water, every movement taking incredible effort. New fear-adrenaline leaked into her veins as she slowed to a jog, then a limping walk. She wasn't going to make it.

Whoa! Off the path.

Almost exhausted, Elise took a sharp right into the trees. There was a small dip in the ground and then she was away from the streetlights, hidden in the shadows.

It was time to get some supernatural of her own.

At half-speed, she crashed into a large tree with her hands extended wide. Halting herself there with her hot forehead against the roughness of the bark, the whole world stopped for Elise as she channeled her remaining energy into her hands.

A familiar zap, like a small electric shock, nipped at her palms. Immediately, whispers became audible over the pounding of her heart and the wind in the trees, growing louder though the words remained as indistinguishable as ever. Heat waves flowed over her slow at first, but then increasing. The cramp began to ease and her muscles stopped burning. Slowly, her vision began to cloud and yellow, as though she were looking into the beam of a flashlight – the odd glow that always came whenever she turned-up.

Still sucking, still filling, Elise began to feel the life in the tree struggle under the parasitic intimacy. Inwardly, it was bending away from her, trying to move where she could not get it. She was damaging it now. The whispers crescendoed, as if encouraging her to keep going, and then faded disappointed as Elise pushed away.

Elise turned to face the way she came, swiping away some of the leaves that the tree was dropping. She looked towards the dim glow of the streetlight.

It was quiet with only the peaceful rustle of the trees and the orange streetlamp adding to the orange of the leaves. But every shadow seemed to menace, concealing she still did not know what (blue eyes...panting). She had been stopped for too long – whole minutes. It should have caught up with her by now.

Unless it's still working on the librarians...

If she wants this race, she really has to go.

Staying here is dangerous. What's she waiting for?

She wanted to run so badly – every muscle ached to take-off. But, intuition warned her to be wary.

Edgily cautious, Elise took two quiet steps towards the path when she smelled it: burning hair. *It's here!*

Elise moved back, leaned against the tree and pressed herself into its darkness, hoping for some sort of concealment. She looked towards the path and saw nothing. Her hearing, more acute with the new life, searched for any abnormal sound and found none. But, another waft of burning hair forced her to stop breathing through her nose. Her heart and chest began to move faster. Who would give themselves away first, the hunter or the hunted?

Another glance towards the path – it was clear. Should she try to run, knowing it was there, knowing it would see her, knowing that confrontation would most likely be only a few seconds from her first step? Or, should she wait, buying a few minutes leaning against the tree, knowing that it probably already knew she was there?

Elise swallowed hard, tasting sourness – she was about to throw up. Her whole body tingled with a strange mixture of fear and the stolen life. Still holding onto the tree with both her arms behind her, Elise leaned forward to gage better the area immediately to her left and right.

To her right: nothing.

To her left: a snap of a twig as something in the darkness tried to step back, out of range of her yellow eyes.

As if on the Olympic starting line, Elise pushed off and felt the energy from the tree ignite in her blood. Feet a blur beneath her, there was no rhythm, just a drum roll sound as her sneakers found the pavement of the path again and the way home.

And then she saw it. Something out of the corner of her eye, streaking towards her from the right. It was moving jerkily, almost like an insect. With a scream that she didn't recognize, Elise stretched out her neck and pushed her legs even faster, the streak moving back and then dropping from her peripheral vision.

She kept going, faster than she'd ever run in her life. It was odd, the feeling of invincibility that always accompanied turning-up combined with the urgency to survive. It seemed only seconds before the dorm lights were bouncing closely in front of her. Another half a minute and Elise reached for the Schultz dormitory door with disbelief.

When the door stuck, the jar traveled all the way up to Elise's shoulder. *The key... I didn't pack my key.* Of course not – she hadn't planned on coming back.

Without hesitation or even a glance behind, Elise closed her eyes and reached out with her mind for the lock. For a half-second her thoughts swirled and then, she could feel the tumblers, feel them as hard as if she had her fingers on them. Elise opened her eyes as the lock clicked and she pulled the door open – another gift of turning-up.

Students milled, hanging over chairs and couches. A TV blared *Real World*. She stepped through them and around them, like a specter from another time. No one noticed her. No one knew what was coming.

Where did she see it? That poster about the Catholic services held to help students get over Clyde's murder. She remembered it was red. She made her way to the stairs, careful not to let anyone see her eyes.

In the eastern wing a few halls away from her dorm room, there was a bulletin board near the girl's bathroom. Yes, she remembered seeing it on her way to the shower the previous day (her own hallway bathroom had been full). *A mass to help students cope with the death of a classmate.*

Although the poster had since been wallpapered over by announcements for subletting and mid-term tutoring services, a flaming corner still stuck out. Pulling it loose along with several others and sending a spray of pushpins, Elise scanned with her heart in her throat. If only they gave contact information.

Father Chris Mognahan and Brother Francis Carter invite all students to attend an assembly for healing. Come address the death of Clyde Parker, honor his memory and begin the journey towards closure.

God it was cheesy. Was she really considering these two for help – journey towards closure?

Something else was born into the world with you…something horrible, though. People dream about it.

At the very bottom of the poster, almost as an afterthought, was a single line:

For questions or personal counseling, you can reach Father Chris and Brother Francis by contacting the Ashton Catholic Community leader, Ruby Larkspur.

It wasn't what she hoped for, but it was a place to start. Ruby had just better be in this particular Friday night.

The campus phone directory was in her room, and Elise jogged even while she tried to make no sound. Through the 210s, then the 220s, the doorways slowly counted up. Passed a few open doors with angry music blaring and twinkle lights hung from the ceiling, a right turn down a second hallway and through the 230s. She felt as tightly wired as the cable on a suspension bridge. She could no longer easily discern the normal from the abnormal – any bump behind her could easily be a student returning from dinner or the sound of that thing bounding after her. Someone called to her on her way by. Although her heart stopped, Elise did not. Around another corner–

But there was something wrong, and Elise's steps faltered. The last few lights in the hallway were blown, leaving only the exit sign over a back stairwell for light. Its eerie glow bathed everything red.

"Shit," Elise said half under her breath. She could barely see, especially near the stairwell. Paralyzing dread retook her – there was no way to convince herself this night that the darkness was just a janitor's laziness. *Keep going even though every part of you knows you should run? Or forget the directory and try to find the priests another way?* Neither choice seemed promising. Subconsciously, Elise reached up and pulled at the collar of her sweatshirt, as if to relieve the claustrophobic feeling setting in.

It can't have caught me already. Right? She took a step forward.

"Like some stupid, second-run horror movie heroine," she muttered as she took another step into darker shadows. *Just grab the directory.* Three more.

Another and it was then, in between steps, that the blood coagulated in her veins so that she stood rigid and unable to move. Her left foot dangled slightly above the ground where she forgot to put it down. There was something in the shadows.

It crouched low on all fours, and its long fur gleamed just slightly in the red light. It sat unmoving, except, as Elise's eyes continued to adjust, the rise and fall of its chest, great and heaving, yet rapid. Two eyes glowed a cold indigo from deep within its mane.

The moment she stopped, the thing seemed to realize it had been detected. With a low, guttural grumbling, it shifted its weight and continued to stare back.

Elise remained on one leg, outwardly frozen while inwardly in frenzy. Her entire body rattled, both hands, her legs, her teeth, her jaw, her spine. The tremors rocked through her, and she found herself ridiculously holding her breath, as though that could hide her somehow.

It cocked its head at her almost inquisitively. Just as in the library, Elise distinctly felt that it was supernaturally intelligent. It was thinking about her. Yes, she was quite sure it was contemplating her.

Then, almost as if it were stretching the way a cat might do in the sun, the thing heaved its weight from a crouching position and stood full, much fuller than Elise imagined it could from her first glance. She watched motionless as it gathered itself to a height well over six feet. For a moment, it seemed to turn its face from her, looking towards the stairwell door. However, Elise realized with growing numbness that in fact, it was merely making room for two other necks, complete with dark faces and indigo eyes of their own, to unfold from the dark, furry mass of its body. All three heads then rolled to focus on her.

The thing took several steps towards Elise, clicking with claws large enough for her to see even in the barely-there light. The smell of burning hair infected her nostrils so strongly, she snorted it back out.

106

The thing returned the snort, as if mimicking the only movement she had made thus far. The damp hair on her forehead moved with its harsh breath, though it stood a good 20 feet away. She blinked rapidly and then tore her eyes from the three sets that stared back, and instead focused on an ugly tear in the wall plaster to her left. Even when she heard it come closer (*CLICK, CLICK, CLICK*), she kept her eyes on the tear, unfocusing and refocusing, but never leaving it. Despair completely choked her. There was no use running. It would find her. It had been in every dark corner she encountered since hearing of its existence.

Elise began to pray again, whispering the words aloud. This time, she did not ask to keep going. Rather, she prayed for swiftness. "Please let it take me quickly, God. Please help me not to feel it."

The thing growled, and Elise was startled by its closeness. She kept her eyes focused and continued praying in a trembling voice. The growl became wet and there was the sound of salivating. In her mind, Elise saw three heads baring teeth, though her physical eyes did not budge. She could at least refuse to watch.

She heard it move faster, coming at her now for sure. No more contemplating. It would be on her–

A door in-between Elise and the thing swung open suddenly, flooding the hallway with light.

For a second, Elise caught a true glimpse of the monster, still coming at her. Its huge body was covered in long, dark brown fur. Silvery scales glistened beneath the coat, with an insect wing quality. Some of the fur was worn thin, showing off great patches of the scales. It did indeed have three heads protruding from its great chest – not a trick of the dark. The faces too were covered in hair, but there was still something eerily human about them. The bone structure could've been that of a deformed man, other than the large snout that protruded in place of a nose. Where there should've been nostrils, only chunks of raw flesh rested. Each heads' lips pulled back in identical leers, showing off black gums and hundreds of thin needle-teeth. Small specks of blood hung to many of the teeth, the result of closing its own mouths when there was obviously not enough room for so many fangs. The eyes were pupiless, and shown with blue light far brighter than that which caught its face. It stood on four large feet covered haphazardly in claws; claws also grew from its knees, vertebrae and hips. Two human arms, hairless, folded and unfolded from the center of its chest. The nails on the hands were infected, and oozed green as they clenched, digging and drawing blood from their own palms.

"What's up with the lights out here? Oh, hey Elise."

Jeff stepped from his room and smiled at her, standing obliviously between her and the thing. "Are you okay? You look…" he paused and squinted at her. "What's wrong with your eyes?"

The thing behind him smiled three times.

It moved so quickly, Elise wasn't even sure she saw it. One moment, it was several feet behind him, and the next it was on him. A horrible spray of blood pulsated onto the floor as the thing grabbed Jeff's throat and exposed his jugular with one movement. He tried to scream, but only a high-pitched gurgle came-out, blood mixing with his spit and spraying down his chin. Although they looked weak, the creature's two human hands held the writhing body with incredible strength while the three heads took turns. Elise heard the snap of Jeff's collarbone echo in the hallway as one bit into his shoulder. It wasn't just killing him; it was eating him.

Jeff stopped moving at the same time his head fell over and touched the tips of his shoulder blades, barely connected. Her prayer had been answered – it was swift.

Elise staggered backwards, almost falling and then catching herself on the wall. One of the heads looked up, still recognizable pieces of Jeff stuck between its needle-teeth. The others paid no attention.

Backwards, through the 250s, passed the kitchenette, she stumbled, unable to take her eyes away from it. She waited an insanely courteous several seconds at the corner for it to come after her. When it didn't, she ran.

It felt like a thread from her soul was caught somewhere, and unraveling the rest of her at an alarming pace. Elise flew down the hallways under the last of the tree's energy, knowing it wouldn't last long enough for her to make it down the stairs. She heard the screaming behind her – someone found Jeff and probably the thing hovering over him.

She was almost to the front stairwell when a hand reached out and grabbed her elbow. She swung around hard, and then felt the other person give way and fall with her. Together, they slid to a halt. Two large arms wrapped around her in a vice grip, holding her straightjacket-style with her arms pinned to her sides.

"NOOOO!" she screamed, kicking, throwing her weight hysterically. "NOOO! It's coming. Help me!" Her voice became raw in three yells.

"Elise!" The voice came from close to her ear. "What's happened? Alan! Alan help me with her!"

With a smack similar to the sound of a melon bursting open, Elise threw her head back into her assailant's face. The man yelled, and she felt a warm liquid in her hair.

"ELISSSE!" the 's' was satisfactorily drawn out. She hoped she put his teeth right through his damn lip. Still, his hold did not loosen.

"Let me go! It's coming!" She had no supernatural strength left; she could not break his grip. Unless she turned-up again. *Let's see how you like this, asshole.*

"Who's coming? Who, Elise? Please, let me help you."

She hesitated just as the first whispers began. That voice – she knew it. It was the priest. God, was it possible? The priest?

Elise let her body go limp. Still, Chris did not relax. Blood was flowing freely from his lip down his chin and into his mouth.

"Whose coming, Elise?"

"You can let me go now. I didn't know it was you."

She sounded sane enough, but Chris was hesitant to take the chance. He looked up from the floor to Alan, who was watching the scene with a dumbfounded expression, his mouth open and slack. He stared at the girl, his first time seeing her.

"Can you help us Alan?" Chris' voice had more than a slightly angry ring to it.

"You really should let me go," she spoke again. "That thing you were talking about earlier. It's down the hall."

The hold released immediately. "The thing. You mean, the Other?" Chris pulled himself up, and then reached down a hand to help her. Elise grabbed his arm with both her hands. She seemed to barely have the strength to stand.

"Whatever you want to call it," she swayed, then held herself firm. To her dismay, the priest's eyes were as wide and frightened as her own. Looking from him to the other priest, also leaning scared with a hand on his heart, she realized this wasn't much of a rescue. "I was trying to get to you, to tell you, I saw it and I needed help."

"Are you hurt?" Chris asked as he used the back of his hand to dab at his bleeding lip.

"No, but my friend," her face fell ashen and she leaned against the wall with one hand and puked.

"Come on." Chris grabbed her as gently as his panic would let him, and swung her legs up into his arms. She was in shock.

"You go first," Alan broke his silence weakly, with a tremor to his normally commanding voice. Chris nodded, and left Alan looking back down the hallway.

Just around the corner, someone else had begun to scream.

Chapter 9 – Notes

"No! That way," Elise directed from Chris' chest. At her command, the priests took a side stairwell. "We'll have a better chance going out the side door. Campus police are usually pretty quick."

She was right. As they stepped out into the cool night, the first red and blue lights were flashing just around the corner.

"Do you see Francis?"

Elise raised her head, but realized Chris was speaking to Alan.

"He said he would be right out here with the car, but I don't see him."

"There!" Alan pointed. Elise jostled against Chris as he began to run, and she put an arm awkwardly around his shoulders.

"Here, get her in the front," Alan took over command as they reached the car, finally himself again. "I'm driving." Someone took her backpack, and then Chris dropped Elise as gently as he could into the front seat. The car shifted as Francis and Chris crammed into the back. Alan pressed the gas before their doors were closed.

They drove silently, except for the car engine and deep breathing. The campus lights began to pass away, and the men Elise barely new became darker shadows. She studied them with brief but piercing glances. Even after all she saw today, it was unreal – making a fast getaway with two priests and a monk.

Someone threw a blanket and then tried to smooth it out onto her lap – Francis. He gave her a strained smile in way of greeting, crouching over her seat, and motioned with his hands. After several seconds, she got it: *Comfortable?* She nodded. It would take a while for her energy to come back, maybe hours unless she turned-up again. Comfortable was about the best she could hope for.

"I'm Father Alan Cole, by the way." Alan extended a wrinkled hand to Elise across the dashboard.

She took it, noting the look of awe on his face when she touched him. "Yeah. This is surreal. Where are we going?"

Alan glanced in the rearview mirror for some help. "Uh. Somewhere safe."

"Great," she replied thick with sarcasm.

Chris took the opportunity to lean forward between the front two seats. "Well, we weren't exactly expecting this. We didn't know it would happen this quickly."

"How could you not be expecting it? Weren't you the one who came to me today, talking about monsters and the need to get out of here?"

Before Chris could answer, Francis put up a hand. *Arguing won't help.*

Elise leaned back and looked out the window. Dark. She wasn't sure which street they were on.

"I think we should take her to Whiteley," Chris continued the conversation after a respectful pause for Francis' protest. "We can't stay anywhere near here. Whiteley is in the middle of nowhere and my congregation won't think too much of it. We could easily stay there without being detected, until the Vatican decides what to do."

"Whoa. I mean, I know you want to keep driving. No one wants to get away from here more than I do. But, I think we should also start comparing notes. What the hell is going on? What exactly is that thing, and why is after me? I need some serious answers. Before we leave the state."

"Yes. Of course." Alan's eyes scanned, searching. "It's hard to know where to begin. Are you religious, Elise?"

Elise sighed, having some idea from the earlier meeting of where this conversation would inevitably lead. But, unlike this morning, it was now worth at least contemplating. While she still might merely be a gene anomaly, she was quite sure the Other was not. If Alan told her it came straight from the gates of hell, she would believe it without hesitation. And if there was a hell, well...

"No. I'm not."

"Ok, well, as you know, we're Catholics. Pretty devout Catholics." He smiled, as if the last line were quite funny.

Elise tried to return it – it seemed like the polite thing to do.

"The two of us are Jesuits – an elite order of the Catholic Church that commits itself to knowledge and scholarship. Francis here is a Benedictine, also a scholarly order. We have all dedicated a fair portion of our lives to studying religious history and texts. Any one of us could be considered an authority on the Bible." Alan paused, his accreditation complete, and then launched into the details.

"In the Old Testament, there was a great king named David. He ruled all the Jews, and he had particular favor with God. God loved him above all other men."

"Yes, King David. I did have some Sunday school."

"Right, yes of course." Alan gave her a glance out of the corner of his eye, and then decided to continue in the same spot. "The Jews considered

David to be their greatest king, as did God. When he died, the kingdom faltered and broke apart. But, prophets foretold that one of David's descendants would come to rule the Jews again, and the glory of the Jewish kingdom would eventually be restored. Centuries passed, and they waited. Wars raged. The Romans took over the Promised Land of Israel. The Jews felt God left them with an empty promise.

"But then, a little over two thousand years ago, there began to be rumors of a man who performed miracles. He healed the sick with his touch and even made a man rise from the dead. His name was Jesus of Nazareth," Alan paused and took his eyes off the road until Chris felt the urge to reach up and grab the wheel.

Elise met his eyes blankly. "Jesus. Yeah, I've heard of him too."

"That distinction, Jesus of Nazareth, is important," Alan ignored and explained. "Nazareth is where King David's descendants settled. Suddenly, it seemed the prophets were correct: a man of David's bloodline had finally come to save the Jews. Jesus gained several disciples and became known to many as the Messiah, the Son of God."

"Yeah, but they killed Him. Right, the Romans?" Elise interrupted.

"Correct. Many of the Jewish rabbis in the temples felt Jesus was a threat to their power. He was leading the people in a way that they could not – with no thought to money, authority, or power. He made no class distinctions, for instance, and was unafraid to be seen with beggars, lepers, and prostitutes. He also felt that temple should be a place of worship only, where no money changed hands.

"So, the rabbis approached the Romans, who were the political rulers of what is now Israel, and asked them to crucify the man they considered a heretic. They reasoned that, if He truly was the Messiah, He would be able to save Himself from death."

"That's so – unbelievable," Elise filled the silence Alan used to take a breath. "Here, they had been waiting for Him all this time, and then they had Him killed."

"It's actually not all that unbelievable to me," Alan shrugged. "Think about it. We are waiting for the Second Coming, right? Christians firmly believe that God will come for mankind again. Only this time, he won't just save our souls; he will save our bodies. All suffering will end. The dead will rise. All will be judged and the earth will be made free from sin. So it is written, preached and believed.

"But, if I came up to you and told you I was the Second Coming, would you believe me? Most people would write me off as crazy, and only a handful would believe me – just as only a handful believed Jesus. In the 21st century, I would not be crucified. But, I would probably be put into a mental institute and left to rot."

It was Elise's turn to shrug.

"Chris tried to tell you today that you are something far less important than Jesus, and you didn't believe him, even though you have no explanation for the extraordinary things you can do. Most of the world is that way, Elise – they can't see what is right before them unless they can look it up in Webster's Dictionary," this last part Alan said with personal bitterness.

"Anyway..." Elise hinted to redirect the conversation away from herself.

"Anyway, Jesus was crucified. But, what many did not realize, including those that sentenced him to death, was that His crucifixion was all a part of the plan from the beginning. God made Jesus the sacrifice that would allow even an imperfect man or woman to enter heaven, so long as she or he believed and tried to live in the way of the Bible. The Romans and the rabbis only acted as God wanted them to, fulfilling the prophecy and allowing the Messiah to save all humankind with His death."

"Right, he died, took our sins with him, rose from the dead and then ascended into heaven," Elise again tried to pick-up the pace. "Where do I fit in with all of this?"

Alan paused for a long sigh. Chris could tell the he was searching for a midpoint to start from – somewhere in between Jesus and the present. He glanced at Francis, who sat with rapt attention, as though this were the first time he had heard the story as well.

"After Jesus left, the disciples grew a greater following for Jesus – what would eventually become the Roman Catholic Church," Alan picked-up the explanation basically where he left off. Chris had to smile.

"The disciples also continued writing the New Testament, including *Acts*, which records what happened after Jesus died, along with several other books. The Gospels were written by a combination of disciples and historians in the first century A.D. But, the book that has the answers you are looking for is *Revelation*, the final book."

Elise fought a shiver. Even the name sounded threatening.

"Now, we're not really sure who wrote *Revelation*. Many say it is John, the disciple who wrote the Gospel according to John. Others believe it is a totally different John, and one who wrote it years after the other Gospels were finished, about 60 years after Jesus' death. Whoever wrote it claimed to have several apocalyptic dreams in which God commanded that he write down the things still to come. This is certainly not the only apocalyptic text – the Bible is full of end-of-day prophecies. But, *Revelation* is the only book that speaks of the angels who guard time."

Everyone was silent in the car. Elise had the feeling of being on a roller coaster. They were at the top of the first hill, and if she didn't pull the emergency cord now, she would be racing down, down, until the ride was over.

"The simple version is that there are 14 angels who govern time. Each of them guards an age for mankind, until a God-appointed moment in time. A pre-set trigger, if you will. The first seven angels mentioned in the *Revelation* are the angels of the seven seals, Chapters six and seven. Christ Himself appointed these angels to open the seals, releasing plagues upon man – war, famine, natural disaster – at different milestones in history. So, the first angel guards his seal, holding back a time of great disease, but then releases it on the world when Jesus commands; the second guards, and eventually releases an age of natural disaster, and so on."

Elise made a face. "That's great. Nice of God."

"Don't judge," Alan broke out his stern voice. "There is a point to all of this. There always is with God.

"Each angel breaks his seal at the precise moment of time that he is meant to. And, the world progresses, leaving behind only the strong in faith and body. Finally, the seventh seal is broken, and peace reins in the heavens."

"The seventh seal brings peace? I thought it was supposed to bring the apocalypse?"

"No. You, like most other Americans, have watched too many movies. That's the Hollywood version of the end.

"But, in *Revelation*, there is yet another set of angels. Far more powerful than the angels that guard the seals. They are appointed, not by the Son, but the Father. These angels stand before Him at all times, and are made of eternal fire. The Apocryphal text of *Enoch* names these seven angels. They are Raphael, Uriel, Raguel, Michael, Sariel, Gabriel and Remiel."

Elise started. Remiel. Hadn't Chris called her that?

"These angels have trumpets to sound and mark off time, similar to the seals. The first trumpeter breaks the peace of the seventh seal with natural disaster, and the last sounds the end of the earth. Each one has been designated a certain moment in the history of the world, to sound his trumpet, deliver his burden to humanity, and bring us one step closer to the Second Coming. It is God's version of evolution. Darwin was right. We are all a part of a great progression, a weeding out.

"Now, there is much speculation about where we are in this holy evolution, both by the Catholic Church, and other sources you may be familiar with, such as the *National Enquirer*."

Another joke. Elise successfully smiled.

"Most people believe we are somewhere in the first seven seals, based on the descriptions of the plagues in *Revelation* and other Biblical prophesies, such as the people of Israel having their own country again, or peace in the Middle East.

"But, Israel already has its own country," Elise pointed out.

"Right. But, there is hardly peace in the Middle East. See? We're somewhere in the middle. Far from the end, far from the trumpeters, but also with some significant development behind us. It's hard to tell," Chris and Elise both noted that Alan suddenly sounded defensive. "The descriptions are so…vague. You know? World War II. Is that the second seal of war? Or was it the 100 Years War? Aids – is that the great disease of the fourth seal, or was it the Black Plague?

"That's why an organization was formed centuries ago – the Congregation for the Hetairia Melchizedek. It is a society of priests and cardinals that track the omens of the Bible, recording everything as it comes to pass. Chris and I were both appointed to this society by the Pope," Alan gestured with a nod to the back. "We also coordinate efforts with different sects of monks and nuns, who do their own research.

"You should see it," Alan's voice took on the excitement it often, ironically did when he described searching reams of disintegrating papers. "The vaults, the libraries," his eyes scanned upwards as if he were now in a great room full of shelves. "There are so many texts and letters, thousands of years old in languages almost forgotten. We look through the underground caverns in the Vatican City, and in the oldest monasteries and churches around the world. The society members regularly comb resources far greater than those of any government in existence, because we have outlasted them all and will continue to do so. We search and record omens, we check and counter-check them, noting prophesies as they are fulfilled and correcting the mistakes of those before us. It is our job to verify the progression through the past, as well as carefully monitor the present, so that when the Second Coming does happen, we will know. We won't be foolish enough to put the Messiah in a straight jacket."

Realizing he had been carried away, Alan returned, "As I was saying, there is a purpose to all of these holy plagues. Only those people who, and I quote, "have the seal of God on their foreheads" will survive, leaving only the strongest at the end.

"After the final plague, when the evolution is complete, the last trumpeter, Remiel, is supposed to sound her horn as the final prophecy of the Bible is fulfilled. Although we often disagree about the triggers of some of the other seals and trumpets, all of the Church agrees about the last. Her trumpet will sound when another of the line of David once again comes to the throne of Israel. We will come full circle, from King David, to King Jesus, to King Christ of the New World."

Again, letting his passion spill out into his narrative, Alan continued barely looking at the road. Each passenger moved in unison with his occasional swerve. "Just think, Elise. Somewhere, out there, is a descendent from the same bloodline that created Jesus Christ. The Bible hints that Mary may have had other children, although the Catholic Church does not believe that – I'm saying this off the record. But, even if it wasn't Mary, He certainly had cousins and other relatives. They continued on after He was gone. Someone out there has holy blood running through their veins, just waiting. Waiting for you to stir it."

Elise finally spoke. Her voice was weak and afraid, pleading. "I still don't understand. You said that we aren't even close to breaking all of the seals, let alone being near the final trumpet. So, why are you even talking about this Remiel? And how can I have anything to do with this? And why? Why would you think it is me in the first place? And–"

"I'm getting there," Alan tried to calm the shrill note in her voice. "I know this is all very scary for you. In fact, I can't even imagine. We, Chris and Francis and I," he made a circular gesture to include them all, "we realize that this part, just believing what we have come to tell you, may be the hardest thing you'll face. We have lived with this our whole lives, and even then, it is hard to believe sometimes." Alan and Chris' eyes met in the rearview mirror.

"So, let me answer your first question," Alan sounded, as he often did, like a teacher explaining to an elementary school class.

Elise hardly noticed the condescension, let alone cared. Her heart was beating fast again as her mind staggered without an anchor.

"Twenty years ago, almost to the day, the Congregation for the Hetairia Melchizedek became aware of a new omen," Alan slowed down, choosing each word. He had to make this believable, somehow. "There is a church in a small town in Italy called Meura. It is nicknamed Chiesa di Statua by the townspeople: the Church of Statues. Inside are seven statues, each a representation of an angel of the seven trumpets. An unknown artist sculpted them in the 12th century. However, it is known that this artist claimed his work was prompted by a holy vision.

"One night, a janitor was cleaning the church as usual. And as usual, he went to dust the seven statues that flank the left side of the altar. But, when he did, he noticed that something was different. The final statue of the seventh trumpeter, the statue of Remiel, had moved. She no longer carried her trumpet, relaxed, at her side. Instead, she had it poised before her lips, as if to sound it."

"So…" Elise's frustration continued to rise. He expected her to connect dots that made no sense.

"So, the Hetairia Melchizedek came and analyzed the change in the statue. It was determined that no person modified it. There was no disruption in the marble, no sign of plastering; all the pieces were still the same age," Alan again sounded protective of his theories, much as he had giving a similar speech to a group of priests almost two decades ago. "The statue moved on her own, as a sign."

"Ok," Elise held up both hands in front of her, and then moved them to knead her forehead. He was giving her a headache. "Supposing that you're right, and the statue moved on its own – and that's a big stretch but one I am crazily willing to consider after today – I still don't understand! A sign of what?"

Alan returned, equally frustrated, "We speculated on the meaning, and several of us, myself included, felt that," he paused and took a deep breath, "the change indicated that the seventh trumpeter was going to sound now, out of order, millennia too soon. Remiel was like the statue – ready to sound her trumpet."

He hurried on, before she could interrupt him. "Well, what happens if, by some mistake, the final prophecy is fulfilled too early? If you accept the theory that the plagues brought on by the angels are a form of spiritual evolution, then you must also believe that the generation of humanity that will live to see this king of Israel will be very special. The Bible says that only they can survive the end of days. Only they will be prepared enough, good enough, to win the war between good and evil. Our development through the seals and the trumpeters is crucial to salvation.

"But, God gave all of us free will. That freewill has led humankind down many dark paths before. It was Eve's freewill that created sin in the garden. Freewill wages wars, employs slaves, designs holocausts. Through our own choices, God has always allowed unbearable suffering. Is it unimaginable that we could break a seal or force a trumpet to sound? Not because it is time, or because we are ready, but because we can choose to put any man on the throne of Israel – its our politics, our votes, our choice. If, for some reason, we choose that man, thousands of years before we were meant to, the results will still be the same. The prophecy will be fulfilled, the war for earth will ensue, but we will lose."

Every eye rested on Elise as Alan paused. She looked down past the dashboard, perhaps at her shoes, or perhaps out into space. She remained silent, as though she was unaware they were all waiting for her to say something.

Chris felt pressure increase on his chest, a steady sinking as it seemed his spirits physically settled into his lower intestine. He could tell: she didn't believe them. She thought they were crazy. His only consolation lay in the fact that she probably wouldn't jump from a moving vehicle. They at least had until they ran out of gas to convince her. He looked at Alan and knew – what he was feeling was nothing compared to the desolation the old priest's eyes expressed. If Elise didn't believe them, Chris was sure Alan's spirit – and his faith – would break.

Francis, however, gazed with confidence, for he could see what the others could not. It was a lot of information to take in at one time, especially for someone who possibly did not even believe in God. Yet, if he wasn't mistaken, Alan's words were resonating with her somewhere, maybe in a part of her that she was only beginning to realize existed. He watched her hands clench, saw her make several attempts to swallow, noted the vein pushing against the skin of her left temple as it struggled to send racing blood to her mind. But after seeing the Other, she was much more willing to hear. Inside, the girl with the golden eyes (still visible to him), the most powerful guardian of all, was waking. As Alan had continued to explain, Elise's eyes glowed brighter to Francis. The fire inside was stirring to his words, to the truth, whether her consciousness could admit it or not.

Alan gave one last push. "We believe that the alteration to the statue is a sign that the apocalyptic prophecy is close to fulfillment: the ancestor of both King David and his descendent, Jesus Christ, will be named king of Israel – someone of Christ's own bloodline will rule, fulfilling all that is written, completing the great line of Kings and forcing the seventh trumpeter to sound. Forcing you to sound, Elise. You, because we believe you are Remiel. And we believe God sent you here to help us."

Elise's eyes flitted to each of them, holding briefly. She was tempted to tell them they were lunatics. The whole thing was damn nutter. Yet, she hesitated. The priest was able to put together a reasonable argument with crazy circumstances she could not ignore.

Of course, there was the Other. Although there was the slim possibility that it was some science experiment gone wrong, Elise felt sure it was something no man ever dreamt up. It knew her, wanted her. It was intelligent – not an animal but more like, well when she came down to it, a demon. Why would a creature like that hunt her so hard, if there wasn't some reason? Was it merely a coincidence that a group of priests and an unexplainable, supernatural monster were both looking for her at the same time?

Coincidence aside, the priest also offered Elise an answer to the largest question of her life. In a single half-hour, he did more to explain her "gifts" than her childhood doctors did in years. And, not only did he offer her an answer – however crazy – he offered her acceptance.

But, to think she was an angel. Even now, Elise couldn't comprehend that. It was too much responsibility; it made her too different. Literally separate from everyone around her.

"And that thing?" Elise broke the captive silence with only another question. "You want me to believe it's a demon? Is there anyway to kill it?"

"We don't know what it is, though I think demon is an accurate description," Alan gave the truth. "I believe the Other is your equal and opposite. God tipped the scales by sending you to us, and Satan evened them.

It was sent here to stop you from guarding your trumpet, and I'm sure, it will die trying if indeed it can die. Religion is not magic – there is nothing I know that can get rid of it except perhaps facing it."

"Great. Why me? If you really believe all of the things you've told me, why would you think this has anything to do with me? Okay, I know. I can close doors with my mind, even heal myself, and a few other neat parlor tricks. But, I also killed a man," Elise whispered this last part, though they already knew. "And, in case the police didn't tell you, I tore his face off," her voice shook. "I think that takes me out of angel territory. Hell, it takes me out of salvation territory, don't you think?"

"I don't know how to answer you," Alan replied. "Maybe, because you were given human form, you are allowed to make the same mistakes the rest of us make. Or maybe, because you are really an angel (she winced at the words), you are exempt from judgment. I don't know. But, I do know that this is your plague to guard. And, if the world is to end early, it is you who must set it right. Remiel is the greatest guardian ever created, normally seated at the side of God, holding back the moment the entire human race waits and works towards, the believers and the nonbelievers alike. Whatever you've done no longer matters. There is only this mission. What came before is of no consequence."

Elise watched him closely, saw his frame tremble. Alan believed it. God, yes, he felt that, by sitting next to her, he was in the presence of a soul different than his own. She felt embarrassed, and yet could not look away. She was certain now of one thing: they were not manipulating her or lying to her. This was not a trick. They were at least true loonies, right to the core.

"We're certain it's you. People saw you, Elise, years ago," Chris broke the odd silence, snapping Alan back to the road he had been neglecting, and forcing Elise to glance over her shoulder at him. "That's how we knew we needed to find you. It isn't like we pulled you out of a hat. After the statue changed, the Society met in Meura. There were 50 of us, maybe more. That night, everyone saw you in a dream. Fifty priests had the same dream," he tried to stress the point impressively.

"I was in your dream twenty years ago?" Elise could not hide her skepticism.

"Well, not my dream," Chris admitted. "But I was the only one there who didn't have the dream. For some reason–"

"But I had it. I dreamt it." Alan spoke to the dubiousness that was sitting on Elise's lips. "It was you, Elise, only as a little girl. You were the one that told us you had come into the world, and it was you who ordered us to find you before something else found you. The Other. You told us that it followed you here, to stop you from guarding your trumpet and thereby allow the line of Kings early fulfillment. And the Other was there too, in the dream. I didn't see it. But I could hear it." An afterthought, "And smell it."

Elise turned on Alan with renewed attention. "What did it smell like?"

Alan crinkled his nose in remembrance. "Burnt hair."

Elise squeezed her hands together tightly, until she was sure all the blood seeped out. Her mother's engagement ring dug hard into her finger, but she didn't care. The coincidences were getting scarier...

Tell her about the statue. How you knew it was her, Francis got Chris' attention finally by smacking him on the hand with the whiteboard.

"Oh! And when we found you, I recognized you," Chris said with more enthusiasm. "You are identical to the statue in Meura. Identical," he stressed. "I knew it was you, bartending at that one bar."

Elise threw him a disdainful look. "So that's why you were staring at me so hard. You both really creeped me—"

"Did you hear what I just said?" Chris interjected "I recognized you because an artist who lived 900 years ago was able to sculpt the details of your face so accurately. It's crazy, but it's also hard fact. I can show you a picture, if you don't believe me," he added.

Elise looked at him for several more seconds, then shook her head. "I believe you. Or at least," she modified the statement, "I believe that you believe all of this."

Chris opened his mouth, but Elise cut him off. "How did you find me? I realize you knew me, for whatever reason. But finding me, the angel or whatever. Out of all the millions of people out there, how did you know where to look?"

"We didn't," Alan replied. "We just started looking for anything extraordinary. We searched birth records, newspapers; you name it, we tried it. As time passed, people began to worry that the Other would catch-up with you first. You could be dead, the world could be on the brink of ending, and we wouldn't even know it.

"So, we began to look for violent deaths in the news. Although we didn't see the Other in the dream, we all got the feeling that it wasn't exactly going to take you peacefully in your sleep. In fact, it might even kill or hurt others before it got to you. We assigned members of the Society different regions of the world to monitor violent crimes. Clyde Parker's murder came to our attention."

"So, you came here looking for the Other, hoping it would lead you to me," Elise finished the story, although it was difficult to say outright. "Instead, you discovered it was me who killed Clyde Parker."

"Yes," Alan finished simply. "And not a minute too soon. It's a terrifying coincidence – given all this time, we both found you within days of each other. We've been waiting, looking for you for almost twenty years, and it still came down to one night, by the skin of our teeth. It's darkly merciful that you gave yourself away in any manner, even this."

She nodded. It was Alan's way of letting her off the hook discussing Clyde. But, she didn't want to be let off the hook. And she could not stay with them unless they understood that she was not some cold-blooded killer.

"I want you all to know," her voice caught in her throat, "I hit him because I felt I had no other choice. There were actually two men, and I don't know what plans they had for me, but I thought it might be worth my life if I didn't do something. When Clyde attacked me, I did what I had to do to get out of there, even if it meant he didn't get up. I didn't want to do it. I have spent most days since then going crazy because I – I killed him," she closed her eyes to get the last part out. "And I'm sorry. I'm sorry you came looking for a demon and found me instead," she smiled, like it was a joke, to hide the muscles in her face, tightening to cry.

An awkward silence followed. Chris felt like he was back in counseling, not knowing what to say but well aware that something was expected of him. Elise was alone in the world, trying to understand a force greater than most people could imagine. He felt sorry for her, small in the front seat and looking unbelievably vulnerable for what she was. Disbelief consumed him each time he looked at her.

How did you do it? Francis flipped the whiteboard from his neck and passed it to Elise in the front seat.

She read it through bleary eyes. "How did I do it?" she repeated. "You mean, how did I kill him?" She caught Francis shaking his head, yes, in her peripheral vision.

Elise passed back the board and crossed her arms tightly across her chest, hugging herself protectively. Then, without looking at any of them, she answered in a low, inflectionless voice. "I turned-up. At least, I mean, that's what I call it. I guess the best way to describe it is, I steal energy. It's not like I have any superpowers of my own. I need someone else. It can be anything alive – plant, animal, human. Human is the best. I can get the most from a person." She looked up, hoping not see the too familiar incredulity in their faces. They did not disappoint. Alan, Chris and Francis were listening with the same insane seriousness with which they related their own story.

"Anyway, I just have to touch the object. So, I touched Clyde and stole some of his strength, and then I used it on him." She blinked rapidly, looking out the window.

"I'm sorry," Alan interjected. "Turn-up. Why do you call it that?"

"Because that's what it's like. I turn myself up. I don't know how to describe it any better than that. I am just more aware of myself than I normally am. I clear my mind and focus on my hands. When I do it, I hear voices in my head, whispering," she gave a nervous snort, realizing how crazy this all sounded. "I can't ever understand what they're saying, but they get louder the longer I use… the thing I'm using. Turning-up is what I've called it since I've been little."

"So, once you turn-up, you can use this energy as you want?" Alan concluded.

"Basically," she dared to answer him while looking at him. "It's like being on a drug, I guess. I can run faster, punch harder…"

Tear someone's face off. The thought hung in the car, though no one said it.

"It makes me powerful," Elise continued. "More powerful than any man I've ever known. But, like I said, I have to have someone else. And it depletes quickly. When I use a person, it goes further." It was coming out easier now. It was amazing, talking about it like this, and not hearing someone say "impossible."

"What about the healing?" Chris asked. "Your medical file said you could heal yourself.

"I can't believe you got your hands on my file," Elise pursed her lips. "Psychology records are personal, you know?"

"But yes, I can heal myself. It's the same thing. I just use someone else's energy to speed up the normal healing process. That goes for bruises, cuts, and also illnesses. Usually, I can heal myself of anything instantly. There have been only a few times in my life where I have been hurt badly enough to need more time."

"How long have you had it?" Chris relayed a question from Francis' whiteboard.

"Since I can remember," Elise shrugged. "I really don't know. I just never remember being without it. It was a problem at first, because I didn't understand that I should hide it, that it was abnormal. So, my parents became worried about me and took me to a million-and-one doctors. Especially because turning-up also gives me some telekinetic powers. That really scared them. When I use it that way, it's like an out-of-body experience. I just concentrate and focus really hard on the things around me until I feel them, as though I were right next to them. I can do little things like unlock doors, turn on a TV. That's about it. I'm not very good at it, it's probably the weakest thing I can use it for."

Elise thought for a few moments, then added, "There is one more thing, although I'm not sure how interesting it is. But, while we're all making full, crazy disclosures: when I turn-up using a person, I can sometimes read their thoughts. Sometimes memories, but mostly just what they are feeling or thinking right then."

She looked up to alarmed faces. "I can't read them now or anything," she said quickly. "And I can't read just anyone's thoughts. I can only read the person I am, you know, sucking from."

"But, that's it," she concluded, folding her hands in her lap with finality.

"Francis has some more questions," Chris relayed to Elise. "Can you read while he writes?"

Elise tried to crane around to see the whiteboard, but couldn't quite make it. With a click, she unbuckled and, with effort, turned around on her knees.

"You really shouldn't sit like that," Alan reprimanded.

Elise gave him a look, the same a child gives a parent it plans to ignore, and then turned her attention to Francis.

So, what happens if you run out of energy? He was careful not to use any shorthand to ensure she understood.

"I'm just like you. Even weaker," she gestured towards herself, indicating how tired she now was.

If you can't find anything to turn-up?

"I'm S.O.L...er... just plain out of luck." She was going to have to curb the swearing. "That was actually part of the problem tonight. After the two of you left this morning, I went to the library to look up train schedules. I wanted to run after admitting I murdered Clyde. I thought you would call the cops for sure. But, the Other was there. Waiting for me in the library. Somehow it knew I decided to go there. And it did some of the most incredible things. It's so fast; it ripped all the books off the library shelves on one whole floor, all at one time; and it's a far better killer than I am." Elise closed her eyes for a brief moment. *God, Jeff...*

"Anyway, I had a hard time defending myself. There was nothing for me to use in the library. I made it out of there only because it wasn't done playing with me. It let me go. Outside, I grabbed some energy from a tree so that I could outrun it. Once I was in the dorm, there were people, but I waited."

Fast scribbling. *I thought using people gives you more energy.*

"Yeah, but I don't like it. It hurts them. Everything about me gets hot when I turn-up. My eyes, my hands. If I hold on long enough, I can do some real damage. It just feels evil. That's ironic, isn't it?" she gave a frustrated snort. She was feeling more tired now. She hoped he was almost done, so she could sit back again. But shortly, another question flashed before her.

What will happen if you hold on too long?

For a moment, Elise looked at Francis hard, trying to gage the tone of the question. She felt her defenses rise. Why was that important? Was he accusing her of other secrets besides Clyde?

"I think I could kill someone, if that's what you're getting at. I have killed plants that way before, sucked them dry," she did not blink an eye, looking at him coolly. "But, I've never held onto a person like that."

Oblivious to the heat, Francis fired again. *What about the Other? Does it need to turn-up like you?*

"No," it felt like a confession, an admission of weakness. It was. "It definitely didn't need anyone. It was the worst thing I've ever seen. A machine made for nothing else but destruction."

How did it kill your friend? Was there anything you could do to help her/him?

Was he really asking her to relive that moment, still so close to her? And, was he further accusing her of not doing everything she could to keep Jeff alive? Anger and a hint of fear filled her chest as the mere question flashed the murder before her eyes.

Chris watched, alarmed, as Elise's face turned red, noticeable even in the dark. Francis was digging a little too deep.

For a moment, it seemed as though the two were locked in a strange staring contest, neither breaking eye contact, as though the question were a test of wills. If Francis had the guts to ask, would she have the guts to answer?

Leaning over the top of the seat to be sure he caught the angry edge to her words, Elise replied as coldly as she could, "There was nothing I could do. It ate him."

Leaving them all looking satisfactorily stunned, Elise turned back, facing the front and fastened her seatbelt. Francis could take the rest of his questions and shove it, monk or not. She wanted to sleep, recover.

It was Alan this time that pressed her for yet another answer. But, unlike Francis, she could tell Alan asked out of fear and the need for reassurance – not insensitivity.

"You could have beat it, right?" he asked with his eyes unnaturally wide. "I mean, if you were turned-up? You would have stopped it," this last line an encouragement, as though he were rooting on a team.

Slowly, she shook her head. "I was turned-up," she admitted, seeing the letdown in Alan's face. "But I couldn't help him. The Other is far more powerful than I am. Our only hope is that you're taking me somewhere it can't find me."

"That's not true," Alan returned gruffly. "You just haven't discovered your full powers yet. God sent you for this."

Elise turned her head towards the window. If he wanted to be an optimist after she told him the plain truth, then that was his problem.

"Has there ever been anything? Any sign that the gifts you possess are holy?" he queried hopefully.

"You mean, has God ever dropped me a direct line?" she said with a half-smile. "Nope. Sorry, He doesn't write either." The sarcasm lessened, however, as she squinted, seeing something in her memory.

"What?" Alan pressed.

"Well, there was this one thing." She let out a long breath. "I don't know if you would consider this a religious sign or anything, but at the time it seemed..." she pulled herself up – the nap would have to wait.

"I was in the car the day my parents died," she managed to speak the words casually. "We were driving, obviously. I'm not sure what happened. I think I was asleep in the back. Everything gets blurry; there was yelling and the sound of metal scraping. And then everything was still and quiet." Elise looked straight ahead, but her eyes moved as though she were seeing things on a screen.

"I opened my eyes, and I could see my father still in the front seat. It seemed like the entire front of the car had been pushed on top of him. He was pinned by the steering wheel in such a way, I knew, though I was young, that there wasn't enough room for his body to be in the space between the wheel and the seat. He was dead.

"But, my mother. She too was pinned, but her seat had broken at the base, and she had been pushed partially into the backseat with me. It was the first sound I heard once everything stopped – the sound of her breathing. It wasn't right. There was some strange clicking sound, wheezing, like she was trying to fill a balloon with a hole in it. Even then, the only thing she thought about was me," Elise flinched, but pushed past the quiet pain that never seemed to leave. "Here she was, struggling to breath, but she kept turning, trying to see me. She whispered for me."

"I was cut badly by the glass. I think our windshield shattered. I could see blood – my blood – but I couldn't feel from where it was coming. When I tried to move, it felt like I was disconnected from my body. I couldn't even hold up my head straight. I think my back may have broken. I can't think of any other reason.

"Anyway, she kept calling for me, twisting her poor body around to see me. I tried answering her, but it was like my mouth was full of cotton. Maybe it was shock. It's all very fuzzy, and in and out. Maybe I did answer her. I don't know.

"Finally she managed to face me, and when she did, her eyes filled up with tears. I knew it must be bad, that there was something wrong with me, because she couldn't even speak at first.

"That's when I noticed her side – something had punctured her under the left-side of her rib cage. Dark blood actually streamed onto the seat, like someone forgot to shut off a faucet. It was so black. At the time, I didn't know, but it was her liver. She had only a few minutes to live." Elise closed her eyes, deep into the memory now.

"She knew it, though, knew she was going to die. She reached over to me – we could barely touch. She picked up my hand since I couldn't and she held it. It was so strange, seeing her touch me, and not being able to feel it.

"She said, 'Elise, I need you to be strong. I don't have much – time,'" Elise broke her narrative temporarily, trying hard to collect herself enough to repeat her mother's final words. "'But, I need you to be okay.' I started crying then. I could feel that, the tears on my cheeks. She told me not to cry and that everything would be fine. And then, she said, 'I've got your hand, honey. Now you just do whatever it is you do, and you make yourself okay for me.' I told her no, I wouldn't. She needed that energy, that life. But she said she couldn't stand leaving me like this. That I would deny her final wish. She was getting tired, breathing harder, and having trouble keeping a hold of my hand. When she told me again, 'Make yourself okay for me,' I did.

"I turned-up. I remember being surprised. She was still so strong, and there was so much in her. Unlike other times I've turned-up, her life came in a rush. She wanted to give it all to me, so there was no resistance, no bending away from me. I almost couldn't control it. It just flooded in," Elise took several hard swallows.

"I began to feel a tingle in my spine, my arms, my fingers, and then after a while, my legs. I wanted to stop then, but it was like I couldn't. I was too far in, and her energy just kept coming. The voices were so loud – it seemed possible I might actually hear them, understand them as more than breaths. My eyes were glowing so bright, the whole world turned yellow around me. She saw it and she actually smiled, even though I knew I was hurting her, burning her. It was the one time in my life that I knew she believed me. She didn't think I was sick or insane; she believed in what I told her I could do.

"And, it was in that moment that I caught one of her thoughts," Elise blew a hard breath out into the car, preparing and reassuring that she could get through the end. "They were far away, like she was moving away. Like her soul was leaving. She was remembering the things in her life. And she was happy. I just got an overwhelming feeling that she was really happy with the time she had.

"But then, all of a sudden, it stopped. It was like someone pulled the plug, and her stream of memories interrupted. And then I heard her in my mind, as clear as you hear me now. She thought, 'There's someone here for me.'

"I finally managed to release her then, withdrawing my hand – I could move now. I looked around for the person she saw, hoping that someone had come to help. But, there was no one. She died next to me, many minutes before a first responder arrived. The paramedics found me crying next to her with only a few scars on my face fading."

Elise finally looked up at the two priests and the monk, her jury. "Really, I know she saw someone. It was such a strong thought. I know someone was there. And she seemed to know them. I felt the surprise, the recognition, as if they were my own feelings."

"We believe you, Elise," Alan reached across the seat and took her hand gently. It was an awkward gesture for him – compassion was not something he often expressed. Maybe it was because, like himself, she was hoping for someone to believe her.

She pulled her hand back. "That's the only time in my life that I thought there was something else. A God, a soul, something other than what is right before us," she sank back into her seat, pulling the blanket around her and closing her eyes. Things would seem better once she had a little sleep.

And sleep, amazingly, she did. As it became apparent that the night's revealing was on hold, Chris and Francis too began settling into more permanent positions.

It's been hard for her, Francis wrote before he slid the white board in between seat cushions.

Chris nodded. But, in an odd way, he also envied her. There were so many moments in his life when he had wanted just that little bit, that little something to assure him there was someone out there, that religion was not just a crux to convince humanity it was not alone. And, he had seen so many others lose loved ones without ever having that type of certainty, that type of closure, that the person they loved was going on to something else. Elise was to be pitied, but also indeed, to be envied.

Chris leaned his head on the window, awake despite the exhaustion his body felt. He dozed only after they passed "Welcome to Virginia."

Chapter 10 – Road Trip

Alan woke everyone a little after 3:00 AM. They were at a rest stop, parked in between the truckers. It was time to switch drivers.

Elise pulled her sweatshirt close around her with the sleeves down over her hands as she stomped around by her car door to get the blood flowing. They were definitely headed north – it was much cooler than when she stepped into the car. She felt recovered after a few hours rest, more solid.

"I'm going to get the keys to the restroom," she announced and began walking towards the squat building next to the gas pumps and the sleepy cashier inside.

"Chris, go with her," Alan commanded as he shoved the fuel nozzle into the car. "Make sure she stays with you."

Chris jogged to catch-up, monitored the giving of keys, and then walked her around the back to the doors barely marked "Men" and "Women."

"Please tell me you aren't going to come in with me," she paused with her hand on the door.

"Check yours out. I'll wait," Chris directed.

Elise slid the key in the door and entered. She found the switch, and a dingy, green-hued light turned on overhead. It was enough to see that the bathroom was empty. She was actually thankful there was only one stall – no place for something to hide.

"It's clear," she called over her shoulder and closed the door.

Elise faced herself in the mirror. Besides looking tired, she appeared as she always did. She stared into her own light brown eyes and pushed at the taught skin of her cheek. She had not changed, and yet, how could she possibly be the same? With a sigh, she turned to the dingy toilet and forced her stiff thighs to squat over it. She hurried to wash her hands and ran a few fingers through her hair, which was stiff with blood from Chris' lip. The water was cold – there didn't seem to be any heat in the entire bathroom.

Chris was waiting when she opened the door. The blood down his chin had been washed away, though an ugly black scab was just beginning to form on his lip.

"Sorry about that. I didn't know it was you," she apologized.

"Eh. It will heal. Besides, it makes me look more intimidating. You wouldn't mess with a priest who looked like he just won a fight, would you?"

Elise raised her eyebrows, tempted to laugh. Without saying anything more, they headed back to the convenience store to return the keys. She followed him in, barely catching the door as he let it go. Chris bee-lined to the hot plate. "You want a coffee?"

"Yeah. Black please."

"A girl after my own heart. Are you sure you want some? Shouldn't you get some more sleep?" Chris hung the pot over a second empty cup without pouring.

"Caffeine has yet to successfully keep me awake. And I'm just really cold."

"I hear you. Well, with me at the helm, we're going to have some heat. I've been voted the next shift." He poured two cups of steaming liquid, threw on some lids, and walked over to the checkout.

Elise watched him, seeing him really for the first time. This morning she had been too angry, and tonight she had been too scared; but now she noticed him. Chris was big for a priest, tall (for some reason, Elise always thought of priests as diminutive). He dwarfed everyone else in the store, from the guy behind the counter to herself. He was slender, helping him fade a little bit more into the background than his height would otherwise let him. He had wrinkles at his eyes when he smiled, but the skin on his hands was still taught and young. They were powerful hands; she knew from being carried. Short blond hair topped him off, probably with some gray in it. She guessed he was in his forties? In a fifteen-second summarizing, Elise decided that, outwardly, he didn't make a very good priest. She liked him better for it.

They stood just outside the door in the autumn night air with the steam from their coffees blowing up into their faces. Chris also bought two Rice Crispy Treats, and Elise munched on hers, alternating with hot sips that she knew would later render her tongue tasteless. Alan and Francis were angrily consulting an atlas. It was an interesting conversation to watch, with all the gesturing and pointing.

"He's kind of strange," she voiced.

Chris immediately knew whom she referenced. "Yeah, Francis takes a little getting used to. I've only known him for a few days. But, he seems like a good guy."

"He's mute?"

"From birth." Chris blew across the small slit in his coffee lid.

"He asked me some difficult questions tonight. I got the feeling that he thought I didn't try hard enough, or that somehow, some of this is my fault."

"Nah. Francis just wanted to know what we're up against. He was building an intellectual arsenal for later."

129

Elise frowned, still skeptical.

Chris answered the face, "Because he has to write everything, it can be hard to tell how he means something. It's amazing how much people communicate through the tone of their voice, the way they move their mouth. But, Francis doesn't have any of those tools. It seems like he has no tact, but it's just his handicap."

"Well, I still think he's a little weird."

"No weirder than you. Actually, you and Francis have some interesting similarities. He has a few extraordinary gifts of his own."

"Like what?" she looked up over her cup.

"Francis claims he can see things. Signs. He reads things on people. He helped us realize there was something really extraordinary about Clyde's murder."

"What do you mean?"

"You left a supernatural mark on Clyde when you touched him. Some sort of seal. Francis saw it and insisted that we look into the crime. I was really skeptical at first too. Until I saw you, and knew he was right."

"Hmm," Elise noised, following Francis' movements in the parking lot. "So, he can't speak, yet he has some sort of second sight?"

"I guess. I don't think he sees the future – I didn't mean that. But, he feels things and sees markings on people that, as far as I know, aren't even there. It's like having the world's greatest intuition, I guess."

"I wonder what he sees on me," she mused half to herself.

"He feels you too. He can tell when you are… turning-up," it took him a moment to remember what she called it. "He wanted to come in with us to the dorm tonight, but began to feel sick when we got too close to the doors. I guess he could sense that you were in trouble, how heightened the situation had become. He had to stay back by the car; feeling you overpowered him."

"Was that really only tonight?" Elise asked, off topic. "It seems so much further away than that. Standing here, it feels like the world is back to normal. Well," she looked at him, "other than that I'm standing here with you."

"Thanks." Chris grinned.

"Can't you two drink that in the car?" Alan asked with residual anger from the debate over the maps.

"Time to go see what route they want me to take."

* * * * *

As promised, Chris cranked the heat once everyone settled into their new positions, Alan in the back with Francis.

"You know, we'll have to stop again in an hour, now that you had that

130

coffee," Alan grumbled as they left the rest stop.

"Hey. The angel wanted some coffee. Can we deny her what simple, earthly pleasures we have?"

Elise rolled her eyes at Chris. He did bring some much-needed humor to what was still a highly charged situation. Alan seemed annoyed by his lightness, but to Elise it was a relief. He treated her like herself – the 19 year-old girl who liked to laugh.

"Nineteen," she spoke the word out loud.

"Huh?"

It didn't seem like Chris was paying attention to her, but as she was beginning to notice, he caught everything. "My birthday is in three weeks. You probably already knew that, from my file," she sneered. "I'll be a twenty-something soon. I guess it doesn't matter. I already feel old."

Chris frowned.

"Not because of you guys," she reassured him. "I felt old long before this. Since my parents died, really, and even more so after Clyde."

"How are you doing, now that you've had a little time to digest everything?"

Elise glanced in the back. Both Alan and Francis were falling asleep. She felt relieved. It would be nice to talk without questions from three different perspectives. Speaking lower to keep it that way, "You have to realize that the whole story sounds nuts. The only reason I'm considering your theories is because of what I know about myself, and what I know about the Other. I think once you see something like that, anything seems possible." Her eyes looked far away, pulling up its grotesque faces.

"I'm not the world's easiest believer, myself," he answered. "I've been the thorn in Alan's side for decades, always voicing my skeptical opinion. I know how you feel, like you're on a train that's totally out of control. When we get to New York, we have some things to show you that might help. Seeing helps me to believe."

"It's the implications that get me," Elise continued in her own line of thought, as though Chris had not spoken. "To be an angel makes me not human, for God's sake. And, to have such a specific purpose – it means nothing I've done to this point is relevant. I wasn't supposed to go to school, to have friends, a career, marriage, kids. And if I am here to just do this one thing, and nothing else, then nothing I've ever wanted matters. Am I alone because of this? My friends, my parents…"

With an exasperated sigh, Elise let it go. "So, what's the plan? What are we doing once we get to New York?

"The plan is to very bravely, courageously, hide. We don't want the Other to find you ever again, but definitely not before we have some time to prepare. So, we'll go back to my church and pass you off as my cousin, or something. Alan will consult with the powers that be – the Pope and his council."

Elise started at the words. *Pope?*

"Yeah, he'll want to meet you," Chris smiled, feeling as though he finally impressed her. "In fact, it will probably be the greatest moment of his life. Much as it has been for the three of us," he finished shyly.

"Don't give me that kiss-up bull crap," she corrected him. "So, the Pope knows about me?"

"He and the High Council of Cardinals authorized us to go and get you, at any cost. Our networks are quite great," Chris explained. "We have the cooperation of many doctors, lawyers, police officers, you name it. If you didn't come quietly, well…"

"You would've kidnapped me?" she finished for him.

"When you believe that the end of the world is near, it doesn't even seem that drastic a measure."

"Great. Glad to hear the Church and the mob have similar tactics." Dropping the sarcasm to return to the original question, "We'll be stuck in Whiteley, waiting?"

"Could be only a few days or weeks. And, I'm sure Alan's already working on lesson plans for a crash course in Catholicism, since you have a little bit of catch-up to play. We'll know more after talking with the cardinals, but I guess we'll try to get you…ready – if you're not already. See what you can do, since you've never experimented much, have you?"

Elise shook her head no.

"We have to make sure you are prepared. For battle, the Other, anything."

"How much time do you think we have?" Elise asked.

"You've seen the headlines. Israel has been in a state of turmoil after losing U.S. support against the Palestinians – our oil needs are just too great to make more Arab enemies. Since then, the democracy there has been very shaky; citizens are fed-up with the violence, daily bombings, being afraid. They are sick and tired of politics. They want a dictator, who wouldn't have to worry about votes and reelections. Someone who could just get the job done. A king."

"Yeah, but there have been rumors about that for years," Elise pointed out. "People also are afraid to give-up their freedom and so, the democracy stands. There's no new reason for an insurgence."

"It could be years," Chris agreed. "It's already been almost twenty, so it wouldn't surprise me if nothing happens for some time. At least now, we have you. We can watch and make sure it never happens."

"Why are you in on all of this? Why were you chosen?"

Chris shrugged. "Believe it or not, I'm a theology junkie. Though I never wanted to become a part of the Church bureaucracy, and still prefer to remain a preaching priest, I spent a lot of time in exclusive schools and I wrote some pretty upper level – put you to sleep in five minutes – papers. Some cardinals took notice, and I was offered several important positions, one being membership in the Congregation. I accepted the Congregation appointment and passed on the others. Alan claims I lack ambition, but I look at it as not allowing the business of religion to cloud my purpose."

There was a long pause as both Chris and Elise thought their own thoughts.

"So what type of music do you like?" Elise broke away.

Chris grinned, where she couldn't see, and followed her lead. "Classic rock mostly. But, that's to be expected from an old guy like me."

They talked of music until the east turned pink.

* * * * *

When Francis woke, bright sunlight streamed into the car. It was early morning – he could tell by its yellowish tint. He shifted, grimacing over the kink in his neck. Sleeping in cars had stopped being even remotely comfortable when he was about five.

Alan was still asleep, head back and mouth open wide. A soft respiring sound synced with the rhythm of his chest.

It took Francis a few moments to find his whiteboard – it was stuck in the seat cushions, though he could not remember putting it there.

In a moment, he popped a greeting into the sight of the rearview mirror. *Morning.*

Chris looked back with tired eyes. "Hey. I've been wondering when someone would wake up and keep me company. The drive is getting very long."

Where are we?

"Just south of Pittsburgh. We have another six-and-a-half hours or so. Should arrive around two in the afternoon."

Francis yawned disgruntled. Six-and-a-half hours? That was a long trip by itself, let alone after ten hours in the car already.

Chris caught the yawn, then winced and put a hand to his lip. He shouldn't have opened his mouth so wide – the scab was going to split.

How's she doing?

At the request, Chris looked over at Elise. She had her head against the window, deep in sleep. She had pulled her sweatshirt hood up, so only a few slivers of reddish hair slipped out around her face.

"We stayed up talking for a while, and then she dropped off. How are you doing?" Chris turned the question.

Feels like a dream.

Chris nodded in agreement. It did still feel like a dream. He looked at Elise out of the corner of his eyes, in a way he would not have done if she were awake. *Remiel. Sitting next to me.*

A few moments later, Chris pulled off the highway for a sign that promised a diner. As he pulled into the parking lot, Alan and Elise each stirred at the interruption in the lulling car movement.

"Time for some food," Chris announced.

* * * * *

Elise looked around the diner as her companions piled into the booth around her. It definitely looked bizarre: two priests (one with a split lip), a monk, and a young girl. She raised her eyebrows at no one in particular and then stared out the window. "The leaves are so much further along here. All the fall colors are out," she commented as the waitress brought over some waters.

No one responded. All seemed consumed by the four pages of omelets, pancakes, and triple-decker sandwiches garnished with your choice of gravy fries, gravy fries or gravy fries. The waitress tolerated with remarkably little surprise the odd group, Francis relaying his order by whiteboard, and Elise ordering the "Big Daddy" breakfast.

"What? I'm hungry." Elise replied to their questioning faces when the waitress walked away. "Turning-up makes me hungry. It's amazing I lasted this long."

They ate in relative silence, minus a few "pass the ketchups" and "are there any more napkins?" Without having the apocalypse to talk about, there were awkwardly few conversation topics. Elise noticed everyone seemed relieved when the check came and they could move towards the car. Maybe it was just her, but the daylight seemed to make everything they discussed the previous night seem silly.

* * * * *

Chris curled-up in the back, drawing his long legs up behind Francis, who thankfully adjusted the driver's seat further from him. He should be tired – tired enough to fall asleep even in the backseat of a rented Malibu. But, with the sun burning on the backs of his eyelids until they turned a neon-red, he knew it was pretty useless.

Alan didn't seem to be having any trouble. He resumed the position he had been in before the diner, his head back and neck arced in what looked like a painful way. Already, his face appeared slack and peaceful.

Elise, on the other hand, was not even attempting to fall back asleep. She watched out the window and then, alternately, Francis. Her eyes asked questions that she did not express. *What's on me? What do you see on me?*

Finally, "Francis?" she asked in a voice that demanded reply.

The monk turned his watery eyes on her. With one hand on the wheel, he reached for his whiteboard and scrawled as best he could, *Decide to stop staring and ask?*

Chris heard the breath rush by her lips in surprise. It hadn't seemed that Francis noticed her watching him. For a moment, she seemed embarrassed. But, within seconds, she regained her no nonsense demeanor.

"Let's hope you can answer my questions just as directly," her tone told him she required that he do just that. "Chris told me you can see things. Supernatural things."

Francis skipped the whiteboard explanation, and merely nodded.

"I'm not saying I believe you, but what do you see for me? Do you see anything special about me?" She refused to take her eyes off him.

Francis thought for a moment. Then, in the same car-messy handwriting, *I see your soul in your eyes. All the time. Not just when you turn-up.*

She read the words over and then looked up to see if Francis was serious. He was. "Is that it? I already know my eyes shine."

Keeping his eyes on the road, Francis wiped clean the board and then made a strange symbol.

Again, the rush of air passed her lips and the startled look of surprise overcame her face. Chris could not see the symbol, but could tell from Elise's expression, it was something she recognized. Francis too watched her reaction and then wrote beneath the symbol, *Sheva.*

"Do you see this on me?" Elise asked, fear mixed in with her demand to know.

Francis indicated no, and wrote, *Clyde.*

"You saw this on Clyde," she repeated. "What does it mean?"

Francis shook his head – he didn't know. Then, he circled the middle character and drew an arrow, *Sheva*, the *Hebrew symbol for seven.*

Elise sat back and crossed her arms, staring at the symbol.

Sheva for seventh trumpeter. Hebrew is supposedly the angel language.

"It was on Clyde, and that's why you thought he had something to do with me?"

Yes.

"It's like you pulled it out of my memory," she stared at it with a sad, soft smile, then looked into Francis' eyes with a reverence Chris had not yet seen her express. "My mother's hand had it, where I touched her in the car that day. I've never seen it on anything else I've touched, but on her, it was like..." she squinted. "Like I branded her. It was clear, even on the skin where I burned her, darker and blacker. I think it's because I held on so long, longer than any time before or since."

"Did anyone else see the symbol on Clyde? The police?" she asked.

Only me. On his forehead.

"Everyone could see the mark on my mom's hand. But, I only touched Clyde for a second. Maybe that's the difference?"

Good guess. Like you, I wish there was an instruction manual.

Chris watched the corners of her mouth turned-up.

"Chris also said that you get sick around me."

Not sure if sick is the right word. But, I do feel you, yes. When you turn-up, your presence becomes overwhelming. It's all I can feel. And sometimes it's a little much.

She raised her eyebrows.

Still think I'm weird?

Elise jerked at his words. Had he heard she and Chris talking before? "No. I don't think you're weird. I mean, if I can exist, then—"

So can I, his writing interrupted her speaking.

"Has it been hard? Living with what you have?"

Sometimes. Should I hide it, or show it off? I've been ashamed. I've felt above everyone. Goes in cycles.

"Me too. I've been embarrassed, with entire neighborhoods thinking I'm crazy. One of my best friend's mothers actually told her entire church group that I was satanic, and no one came to my birthday party that year." They shared a smile. "But, as much as I felt self-conscious and strange, I also felt powerful.

"I used to get picked on at school by this one boy. I put up with it for years. Until one day, I just turned-up on him. There were tears in his eyes and he could barely stand, just from holding my hand. Sometimes, I became so angry, I wanted to crush them all. To hurt them and make them believe me the hard way."

The hard way. Sweet satisfaction. Justice. But, then you become the monster you're always afraid you're capable of becoming.

"Like with Clyde. I gave in and became that monster."

Instead of comforting her, as Chris or Alan would, Francis remained frank. He took his time, writing fully over several minutes and the steering wheel. *That's only one decision, one moment. Monsters, just like angels, are made of many decisions, many behaviors. You have the chance over and over again to choose what you really are.*

For now, just know WHO you are. You are Remiel, angel or devil, whichever she is.

With a swipe, the words were gone. But for Elise, they lasted much longer. As Francis went back to full-time driving, she couldn't help but stare at him a few more moments. Although, of the three men, she felt the most wary to trust Francis, she now found herself sensing the beginnings of a special connection to him. He was up front and honest with her; no concealed answers, no put-offs.

And, there was no way for him to know that mark, to be able to draw it like that, unless what he claimed to be was true. If it were true, that he could see things others could not, how difficult had his life been? Had he been ostracized and alone, turning to the Church to find a place where he could at least be partially accepted? Chris was wrong. It wasn't that Francis didn't have a voice to soften his hard questions. Francis actually felt comfortable asking hard questions because he didn't feel sorry for her. He knew what she felt, and he knew she could get through it. It was like a blind person talking, for the first time, to another blind person. She turned back to the window.

With the conversation over, Chris looked out his own window. The trees flew by in their best colors. Other cars passed them – Francis was not the fastest driver. Chris let his mind drift as it wanted and without noticing, he eventually slept.

* * * * *

The Malibu turned down Main Street right on time, with the mid-afternoon sun now slanting in through one side of the car. Chris crouched behind Francis' seat, giving directions, as he had been for the last half-hour. Alan felt around the floor in the hopes of finding some drops in one of the water bottles they bought hours ago because he "just couldn't wait even another minute." And, Elise looked out the window. *Welcome to Whiteley*, a small, painted sign greeted her.

It was one of the most picturesque towns she had perhaps ever been in – like jumping into a postcard. Little two-story houses, lined-up in various shades of pastels bordered a traffic-free road. The school zone speed sign had another sign posted below it that some concerned mother painted, *Go 25 Protect Our Kids.* Past a pizza shop simply named "Pizza," with after-school cheese slices on special. The telephone poles around the only intersection with a traffic light (a flashing red) were lined with fliers for hayrides, used cars, and free kittens.

Just as the town began to dwindle away and turn back into farmland, Elise caught sight of the church. St. John the Apostle stood out white against the fall colors. A small yellow house hovered close by.

Francis brought them down the drive and parked next to another car, presumably Chris'. The engine went silent save for clicking as it cooled. For a moment, everyone remained still, looking out through the dusty windshield.

"Let's get out of this blasted car," Alan initiated movement. Elise pulled the backpack from between her feet and stepped out into brisk upstate New York fall. She stood by stupidly while the others unloaded baggage from the car. Alan reminded everyone several times to clear their garbage to avoid additional fees for the rental ("Not like they aren't going to insist we buy the car when they see the mileage anyway"). It was like coming home from a strange family getaway.

Chris led the way up to the screen door, which opened with a screech, and then allowed them into the kitchen. "Well, there isn't a lot of room," Chris extended his arms to make the point. "But, this is headquarters for now. Elise, you have the bedroom. Guys, we are going to have to make due with the couch and the floor, and I already have a rotational sleep schedule in mind. So, what's first?" he asked the question without a person in mind, and no one answered. "Do you want food, drinks, a phone?"

"Phone. And water," Alan grumbled.

"A shower," Elise broke over him. "Only, I don't have any clothes with me. Just underwear."

Chris ignored Alan (he knew where the water and the phone were) and turned to Elise. "I can loan you something. A button-down and sweatpants okay? Anything else will fall off you, I think."

Elise motioned her consent and Chris retreated to the bedroom. He returned with the promised clothing, and showed Elise the bathroom.

"Anyone have to go before I get in?" Elise tried to be courteous, realizing this was the only bathroom after a 17-hour car ride. She waited a few moments, and when no one responded, she closed the door.

It was good to be alone.

Elise leaned back against the door, resting for a few moments. Was she really in Whiteley, New York in a rectory? Had she really left school? Less than forty-eight hours ago, she was at least trying to get back to normal. Four weeks ago, and she actually was normal, or close to it.

She shutoff her thoughts and turned on the water – hot. Sliding into the small shower formed by two lavender tiled walls and two glass doors, Elise breathed in the steam. It smelled strongly of men's soap. She looked down at the bar on the shower shelf. Another weird association. She never thought of priests smelling good, let alone masculinely.

She let the water run and run, beating her shoulders and pressing her hair down on her head. Her body untwisted its kinks and miraculously, her mind rested.

The two priests and the monk watched each other, listening to the water running down the hall. The silence ran on, bordered only by the soprano hum of the pipes.

Alan snickered, and Francis and Chris both looked at him questioningly. The snicker turned into a chuckle, then grew to a laugh.

"What is it?" Chris asked for the both of them.

"We did it! We found her! We found her in time!" He laughed again, looking up to the ceiling and slapping his knees with his hands before subsiding into disbelief. "I always knew we would find her, and yet, I still was not emotionally prepared for actually doing so. I was still surprised," Alan spoke with wonder. "Here we are, the three of us, with the seventh trumpeter in your shower, Chris. Isn't it just mind-blowing? For God's sake, in a moment, she will be wearing your clothes. It's just amazing! Nothing. Nothing in my life will ever come close to the moment I saw her face. I've lived all I can live. The rest is just a winding-down." His face grew blank as he tried to grasp his own words.

"The rest is just a winding-up," Chris contradicted him. "This is the beginning."

Chapter 11 – Inri

Elise lay in bed, listening to the priests and Francis settle in the living room. Although they bought her clothes at a tiny boutique in town, she still wore Chris' shirt and sweats – they made great pajamas though they looked ridiculous.

The evening had been strained, save for a few natural moments (most caused by Chris' jokes). They were afraid to leave her alone, so all three of them trooped to the boutique and stood outside the changing room; all three argued to stay home with her while the others went to the grocery store; and there was discussion about taking shifts outside her door for the night (which she quickly put to an end).

Dinner was mildly better. Chris grilled some burgers while Francis whipped up some good home fries. And, she remembered how to say grace, thank God. When they asked her to bless the meal, she put together a weak, but acceptable prayer. It was something she had to get used to – praying in general, and then praying for an audience.

Most of the day, she had sat listening as her fate was decided. Alan had spent hours on the phone. From what she could understand – he spoke often in Italian – Alan fought for two things: keeping her in Whiteley where the Other was least likely to find her (and where Alan had complete control), and ensuring she would not be questioned in the second Ashton murder. Somehow, the society promised to have her school record modified to show a planned leave of absence, and her belongings were moved discreetly so that it did not appear that she ran. Alan warned her that she may still be interviewed by the police as a matter of procedure, but he had guarantees from society police connections that she would be kept as low profile as possible. She had smiled and nodded, letting him make plans as though everything were settled.

But in her heart, it was anything but settled. She hadn't even decided whether or not she would stay.

The more she thought about it, the crazier it seemed. But where else could she go? What about the Other, whatever it was? She stayed by default; not by choice.

They had watched a movie in the evening (paused at least 20 times for the phone, which Alan answered himself now). It was a good movie, even if the four of them were crowded around a 20" screen. But, there was a love scene in the middle that made Elise want to drop through the floor. How could she watch something like that with three celibate men?

Elise rolled over, trying to find a comfortable spot. The bed was big – too big. She curled up on one side of it and drew the pillows around her to make it feel smaller. The house settled with a few creaks, and she noticed that the drone of voices in the living room had fallen off. She wondered what they had been talking about. Probably her. They seemed to be talking about her whenever they thought she wasn't listening.

She watched the moonlight outside the window next to the bed. She smelled Chris in his shirt and smiled again at a joke he cracked at dinner. She watched the town streetlights, winking as the trees moved in the wind. Slowly they blurred as she blinked less and less, then not at all.

* * * * *

She did not dream.

That was the amazing thing. She had no dreams the past two nights and was dully thankful not to be trapped with the Other inside the confines of her mind. When Chris crept in to wake her for church, she felt rested.

She came out in a new, long black skirt and white shirt, feeling a little like a pilgrim. The town clothing shop was not exactly The Gap. Many of the clothes looked homemade, and there was nothing for anyone under the age of 40, let alone with sex appeal. Not that she needed it here. That whole surrounded by celibate men thing again.

Chris and Alan were both dressed in black pants and shirts with priest's collars. But Francis, she noted, remained in his pajamas while fixing some bagels for breakfast.

"How come he doesn't have to go?" she said in way of greeting.

Chris looked over at Francis and answered for him. "Oh. Monks do most of their prayer in private. So, while we are at Mass, Francis will meditate, and then hold his own personal Mass a little later."

Before Elise could utter a word, Alan broke in, "We're not giving you a choice – you are definitely going to Mass. Consider it a training exercise and try to learn something." The tone in which he spoke left Elise to eat her bagel, resigned.

* * * * *

"You look nice," Chris tried to soften the scowl on her face as they

141

walked over to the church.

"I look like a nun," she returned, scowl deepening.

"What can I say? I have a bias for that look," he smiled down on her. "You're very spicy, Elise." He held the door open so that she and Alan could pass into the church. "I could definitely use some celery and blue cheese with you." She gave him the look he was beginning to recognize and enjoy – the "you're not very funny" look children often give their parents.

"God! It's freezing in here," Elise clasped her hands together in front of her, blind to the eye darts Alan threw her at taking the Lord's name in vain.

"I'll fire up the furnace. Elise, help Alan light the candles," the two men passed a look. Lesson number one...

Elise followed Alan up onto the raised stage with the altar. She almost tripped over him as, without warning, he knelt on one leg and performed the sign of the cross.

"This is called genuflecting. The dome on the small table directly in the back of the stage – that's the tabernacle, where the Host, the body of Jesus is housed. Whenever you cross the tabernacle, whether you are in the back or the front of the church, you are to genuflect in respect." He stood straight and waited.

Elise mimicked him, going down on one knee and then making the sign of the cross. This last part she rushed – she saw it in movies, but wasn't exactly sure how it went.

Alan did not let it slide. "Like this." He took her hand and pressed her fingertips to her own forehead. "The Father." He moved her fingertips to the center of her chest. "The Son." Then to just above her left breast. "And the Holy." Finally to just above her right breast. "Spirit."

Releasing her. "The sign of the cross is something Catholics perform to remind them that they believe in one God, composed of three persons. God the Father, the creator who led the Jews out of Egypt, and who will judge souls at the end of time; God the Son, who sits at the right-hand side of the Father and who saved us by sacrificing himself to forgives sins; and God the Holy Spirit, who imparts religious knowledge and faith, communicating the Word. One God, all three in one."

Alan turned back to the altar, leaving Elise still with her hand over her heart. *Like learning the secret handshake.* The thought died as her eyes fell on the large crucifix hanging over the altar. Jesus stared back, agony eyes calling her to look at his ruined body where the nails pierced his hands and feet, the sword, his side. *A crown of thorns*, she recalled from some Easter service. Was he watching her with those same eyes from somewhere she could not see, angry that she entered His church without knowing how to bow before Him? Was He further saddened because Remiel, who normally sat by His side, now betrayed Him by forgetting?

Elise stepped up onto the stage and took the light Alan held out to her. Internally, he remarked on her sudden seriousness and wondered if his teaching sounded too harsh. More gently, "Light the candles on that side and by the Virgin. Please."

She followed his command without a word until, "This one is already lit." She pointed to the large candle hanging by the altar.

He replied, "That is the candle of the tabernacle. It is always lit, signifying that, although Mass may end, Jesus remains in the church at all times."

Elise lit her last candle and turned to Alan. "Why do you think I don't remember any of this?" she asked him, no trace of scorn or skepticism in her voice. "If I am who you say, why wouldn't I remember Him?" she indicated Jesus on the cross with her eyes. "Why is there some curtain in my mind hiding my purpose from me, hiding the knowledge and power, the certainty that I need to fulfill it?"

"I don't know. I've asked myself so many times how it could be that you did not know to look for us. How can the world be ending while our guardian doesn't even know who she is?" He looked at the floor, as though an answer might appear. "Maybe that type of knowledge just can't be brought here unrestricted. Maybe, to keep you from revealing other plans and futures that humanity has no right to know, you had to give up all your knowledge and live by your faith."

With a rush of air, the heat came on – Chris successfully turned on the furnace and appeared in the doorway leading to the basement. "It should be warm in here soon–" he realized he interrupted.

"Good." Elise turned her careless attitude back on and put out the light she held.

Chris looked at Alan, but got no answer. Mass would start too soon for questions. "Elise, why don't you sit in the front pew? Try to follow along with everything. Alan, you can help me with the Mass? I'm not sure if anyone signed-up for Eucharistic Minister or Altar Server, since I've been gone all week."

Elise crossed to the front pew, genuflected, and then sat still, watching the preparation with interest. Both priests put on green robes, sewn with little bits of gold thread here and there. They chose a banner and then brought it to the back of the church. The organist arrived – a little old woman that one would expect to be an organist. She looked at Elise curiously, but found her seat and began warming up without speaking, periodically writing hymnal numbers on a chalkboard on the wall above her. Nevertheless, Elise had a feeling that the rumor mill was officially on.

Others began to fill in. Elise heard them greeting Chris like a long lost friend. "We missed you this week." "Didn't know you were coming back so soon." "Where did you go again, Father?" It was weird hearing them address Chris as Father. Alan she could accept, but Chris seemed far too young (and funny) to hold the title.

But when she looked at him in his robes, it did seem he transformed into a figure of authority and presence. His sense of humor fell dormant as he greeted everyone, asking about this or that in their lives. She felt slightly betrayed. He was more of a priest than she thought.

"Excuse me. Hi, I'm Katie Ryan. I haven't seen you here before," a woman spoke from behind her. Elise stood, her nerves making the movement jerky.

"Hi. I'm Elise Moore. I'm Father Chris' niece, in town visiting," she smiled over the lie through tight teeth.

Opening peals from the organ saved her from too deep a questioning, and the processional began. Elise opened her hymnal just as everyone around her broke out in a loud voice, singing without self-consciousness the way only a small church can. After a few sideways glances, Elise joined in.

Chris took the stage while Alan kept to the side. He looked out over the familiar faces, trying to avoid that now, most familiar face: Elise. Nervousness threatened to choke him, and he was suddenly glad she didn't know anything about Catholicism. It took some of the pressure off. Still, he was preaching before one of the angels allowed to stand with God. If only the parishioners could know with whom they worshipped. He hoped the slight tremor in his voice would be interpreted as religious devotion.

It passed in a blur, and shortly, he was washing his hands in the bowl Alan held for him, asking to be forgiven of sin so that he could bless the bread and wine.

For Elise, however, the difficult part of the Mass began. It was easy to fake being Catholic through the readings. But, during the second-half of the mass, she could only mouth prayer recitations weakly; correct herself when she noticed everyone around her knelt while she sat; and she stood stupidly during the sign of peace until Mrs. Ryan reached around and shook her hand "Peace be with you." Elise replied "Thank you," leaving Mrs. Ryan with a puzzled look.

Most confusing was the end. Elise watched with growing alarm as the rest of the congregation formed lines in front of the two priests to receive the bread and wine, holding their hands all the same way and whispering something as they received it. After a hesitation, she stood and moved to join. But, a barely noticeable shake of Alan's head made her regain her seat. She sat ostracized in the front pew, an anomaly: a priest's cousin who refused Communion.

Chris moved to help Elise after the Mass closed, when several pews of townspeople gathered around her to introduce themselves. He was

144

temporarily thwarted, however, for those parishioners skipping donut hour expected him to man the door and shake hands for the week. Anxiously, he looked over heads to make sure she was not drowning (or worse, insulting someone) and absently shook hands until the line out the door dwindled.

Elise turned on her brightest smile and attempted to behave how she thought a priest's cousin should behave. With her hands behind her back, she answered all their questions, from where she lived to how long she was staying and how old she was, all the way down to whether or not she was a family delinquent given to Chris to turn around. With relief she announced, "Here comes Chris. Err, I mean Father."

"I see you've all met Elise," he parted them with his huge frame. "Donuts are downstairs. Elise, you want coffee?" he gave her a chance to escape.

"I told them I am from South Carolina, and that I'm your sister's daughter. You do have a sister, right?" she hissed at him on their way down the stairs to the basement.

Downstairs, it was as it always was with the line by the donut table and those already seated mopping up piles of confectionery sugar, drinking coffee, and yelling at their kids. Chris was bombarded with more parishioners asking about everything from baptisms to incense. Elise left his side to join Alan.

"I made it," she said under her breath. "Except that one part where you made me look weird. Why didn't you want me to go up with everyone else at the end?"

Equally low, "In the Catholic Church, it is a sin for you to receive Communion without understanding what it is you receive. Angel or no angel, we need to prepare you for such a sacrament. Even more so, you need to be ready to receive the sacrament. If you don't believe that the bread and wine become the body and blood of Jesus when you eat them, you show a great disrespect for the Church and for God. There are prayers you must learn, readings–"

"Thanks for the short version," she interrupted. "How long do we have to stay?"

"Until everyone leaves," he gave her no mercy.

The parishioners did eventually meander out, until finally it was just the three. Chris and Alan rinsed the coffee cups while Elise stood by.

"Well, what's next?" she inquired of the itinerary.

Chris looked up at the clock. "We have about 45 minutes until the next Mass."

"The next Mass?"

"You're lucky I work at a small church," he responded. "Alan has to do four Masses on Sunday. I only have two."

"Do I have to stay for this one too?" she inquired hands on her hips.

"No, you don't," Chris gave her a disapproving look but released her. "You can go back, but stay close to Francis," the last part given as a direct order. "Do you feel safe going back to the house alone?"

"I'm fine," she called back without looking.

She entered the church and made a beeline for the front door. It was empty now, and unnaturally quiet. Creepy, from the statue of a man pinned to a cross with nails, hanging over an altar in which Alan claimed was entombed a relic of a dead person; to a statue of the man's mother demanding prostration with the kneeler below her shrine; to candles placed in little red cups symbolizing prayers for dead souls. She didn't understand why people felt at peace in churches. When left unattended, they had the same still quality as a graveyard.

Holding her breath, as though she indeed passed by a graveyard, Elise made it to the main aisle, even reached for the handle of the front door. But, the reproduction of Alan in her head gave her pause. *"Whenever you cross the tabernacle, whether you are in the back or the front of the church, you are to genuflect in respect."*

Elise breathed in. She had crossed the tabernacle. She could keep going and forget; no one was here to call her mistake.

But something low and small inside – too weak to be instinct but too strong to be ignored – called her to turn and face the man on the cross. What if even a small part of this was true, and God was in the church? The disrespect she showed would not go unseen after all. She shivered at the thought.

Elise bowed her head, but kept her eyes upon Christ on the cross until everything else became blurred in her vision. In this way, without blinking, His stony flesh became warm and soft, the nails glinted metallic, and the blood seemed red enough to run.

When she could bear the burning in her eyes no longer, she closed them and genuflected in one graceful motion. "My Lord," she whispered, trying it on. Tears prickled at the corners of her eyes as fear, anger, and a sadness she could not justify pushed on her chest until it became heavy.

A door slammed below.

Embarrassed, she startled and stood, letting the other emotions dissipate until there was only doubt. She didn't know what to believe; was she kneeling before a statue or a Messiah? Would she ever know? Did any of these people know? What was she hoping for – some acknowledgement from a God capable of putting His Son to death?

With a glance to make sure neither priest was standing in the stairway door observing, Elise threw her hair over her shoulder and began a brisk, bravado getaway.

"Inri."

It was no louder than a breath, but Elise heard it. She whirled (almost falling) to face – only the empty church.

Inri? Her eyes flew through the pews, searched the corners of the church. The stairway door remained empty. Who whispered?

With ever-increasing speed, Elise marched back down the aisle and came before the stage. Though only Chris and Alan were privileged to walk behind the altar that morning, she moved without hesitation and fully circled it. She peeked in the door to the side of the stage where the priests dressed and stored Mass props. No one.

Facing forward from her new vantage point above the pews, Elise looked over them again to make sure she didn't miss someone, perhaps whispering a prayer. Though her eyes continued to dart, her heart knew she was alone.

Just as her heart called her to look up, up to the statue that was immediately overhead. Slowly, she complied, arching her neck until she looked up to the crucified Christ, much closer from the stage. He stared out at the pews, captured forever in one of the most gruesome capital punishments ever conceived. And above the cross, centered over His sagging head, was one word: Inri.

* * * * *

Chris tramped up the stairs, leaving Alan to finish cleaning the basement. He wanted to reset his notes and the liturgical props before new churchgoers arrived.

He moved around the altar, refolding the napkin and placing the basin at the server's table; turning the book back to the first prayer of the day. With his back to the church, he opened the tabernacle to remove hosts and place them in the gift basket, to be brought back up to the altar during the collection–

The tapping of liquid dripping on a hard surface broke the silence.

Chris looked over his shoulder at the sound. *Please tell me the roof is not leaking*...he half prayed with a questioning look towards the sunlight outside. With a loud sigh, he searched the ceiling corners in the altar's immediate vicinity and was relieved to see no water stains. He was about to step down from the stage for a thorough search when he noticed the splash of scarlet dots on the altar cloth.

He looked at them a few moments, appreciating how bright and red they were against the bleached cloth, before he touched it. It was wet. He pulled his finger away to see a small red smear on its tip. He rubbed the smear against another fingertip until, between the two, it disappeared. *Too red to be wine,* his mind taunted him, calling up visions of the purple-maroon stains common to altar cloths.

Confusion plain on his face, he looked up at the crucifix hanging motionless just above him.

* * * * *

Francis turned from his Bible as Elise slammed the kitchen door and leaned heavily against it. She caught the concern on his face, but rather than address it, "What does Inri mean?"

With raised eyebrows, Francis pulled over his whiteboard.

I.N.R.I. – Initials, he wrote.

"Initials for what?" she sat on the chair opposite him to better see his writing.

Initials for the Latin words Pontius Pilate inscribed over the head of Jesus as he died on the cross: Iesus Nazarenvs Rex Ivdaeorvm. It means Jesus of Nazareth, the King of the Jews. He thought for a moment. *Why?*

His eyes probed – it was obvious he knew she was not asking out of idle curiosity. But, on the off chance that some new mark wasn't giving her away, "I just noticed it in the church today. It's my first time in a while, and I couldn't remember what it meant."

Francis looked at her just long enough to let her know he did not believe her, and then he wiped the whiteboard clean with deliberation, hoping she would divulge further.

He was distracted, however, as Chris appeared through the window coming from the church in a frantic run. Francis stood alarmed, letting the Bible slide to the floor.

"What is it?" Elise asked, standing because Francis did.

Chris burst through the kitchen in answer. "Elise! There you are," his breath moved through his words. "I was worried."

"Worried? Why?" Her own fear escalated a few notches. She wasn't ready for–

"The altar – there was blood on it. Not a lot, but I thought you might be hurt," the concern in his face did not dissipate.

"No. I'm fine," her eyebrows knit closer together as his meaning registered and thoughts of the Other faded. "Just fine, really. No blood, not even a shaving cut," she faked smiling.

He looked her over and she was indeed fine, save for the fear on her face caused by his panic. Suddenly, he felt like the boy that cried wolf. They were making everything an emergency. "Sorry – I know we're being over protective. But, I didn't know where it came from. Just a few drops, right under the crucifix."

Elise lowered her eyelids to keep her eyes from widening. "Weird," the only word she trusted herself to say with conviction.

"Well, probably Alan or I just have a paper cut we aren't aware of..." Chris trailed off stupidly. "Sorry. Again."

She thought of telling him. It was probably the smart thing to do – if they really were in the middle of a cosmic battle, honesty and trust were weapons they needed on their side. But, no – she wanted to hold onto it a little longer. To be sure. *The blood seemed red enough to run. Inri. It did whisper to you...*

"I'll let you get back to Mass, and back to meditating," Elise credited them each with a task. "I'll be in my room."

With the door closed, she dropped the mask and let the worry wrinkle her face.

* * * * *

Elise had always felt that Sundays were slow days, no matter where they took place, or at what age. As a kid, they meant Sunday school and proper bedtimes. In college, they meant homework and group meetings. For adults, they meant get your crap in order before you go back to work. She found them no less boring now that she lived in a rectory. The clock ticked in retard until Alan and Chris returned. Chris didn't have cable – the TV offered only college football, politics, or NASCAR.

Alan spent yet another large portion of the day on the phone, talking with other members of the society – it seemed all he could do to keep them from making pilgrimages. There were several more heated conversations about whether the group should remain in Whiteley, but each ended similarly: the Other would not know to look for her in upstate New York, while it was sure to track her to the Vatican. Again, the conversations were often in other languages (Italian? Latin?). She wondered if it was because the person on the other end of the line really didn't know English, or if Alan just didn't want her to know what was being discussed. He and Chris also poured over the bookshelves in the rectory (Alan grumbling about Chris' apparent lack of a library), and then more phone calls were made to order books.

"We'll start you on a reading schedule when they arrive on Tuesday," Alan finally bothered to address her. Obviously, it wasn't up for discussion.

Francis disappeared for a couple hours to complete his personal Mass. He returned, looking rested and relaxed. He even whistled as he opened the Sunday paper for a read. It was odd – the first noise she heard cross his lips. Living such a quiet life – Elise bet it allowed one to come up with some pretty anal routines. She wondered with some amusement how hard the last few days had been for him.

149

When evening descended, Elise announced she would make dinner. If she had to sit any longer, some of the insulting comments that filled her mind would start coming out. She burnt the potatoes, forming some cement in the bottom of the pan, and the chicken was a little too pink near the bone, but everyone ate without complaints.

"I'm heading to bed early," she announced through a faked yawn.

They each said goodnight to her in turn, like they were in some 1950s television show. "Tomorrow, we'll have more interesting things for you to do," Chris promised. "The plan has been formed," mock announcer-like, with a teasing look at Alan.

"Can't wait," she closed the bedroom door, unsure if he heard her.

She peeled off the skirt and blouse with some lingering distaste and then dug through her bag until she found the dirty jeans and sweatshirt she arrived in – she needed something she could move easily in. Though they were her own, the clothes felt strange, as if they physically held the horror and death they observed. She could smell her sweat in them. The sweat that leaked from her in panic and terror as she was chased, as she saw Jeff ripped – with horrified surprise, she realized that she hadn't even thought of Jeff once that day.

Immediately, her mind manifested the most truthful excuse: there was no time to deal with it; her own life remained too endangered to cope with the loss of his. It was true, yet she was scared by her callousness and angry – the holy trio hadn't even bothered to ask how she felt or who he was.

Lying down on top of the covers, she tried to see him. She had time now, and she wanted to feel sorry. Feeling sorry was the human thing to feel.

* * * * *

It seemed like hours before Alan, Francis and Chris fell quiet. At one point, someone approached her door, as if to check on her, and Elise's heart thudded. If they saw her lying on top of her covers dressed, what would they think? But, whoever it was retreated to the living room without so much as cracking the door. The lights dimmed and then turned out. Still, she waited. They needed to be in deep sleep if she wanted to pull this off without triggering the "Save Elise" alarm.

Finally, it seemed enough night passed. The alarm clock glowed 1:24 AM. Elise pulled on the sneakers that sat lined-up in front of the window. With effort, she unlocked the rusty latches and slid it upward, making small squeaking noises and wincing for each one. *Why didn't I open this while they still had the TV on?*

Once the sill was up, she paused to listen. It seemed the troops still slept. Cold air flooded in, curling around her bare ankles. The screen popped out, just as she thought it would during her earlier inspection. With her feet out the window, she stopped long enough to hope that none of the men sleeping on the floor would detect the draft. She thought of stuffing a towel under the door. But, rather than hesitate another moment, she jumped off the ledge, landing first on her feet and then her knees, her hands digging into the wet grass. She was out.

Trying not to think about what she was about to do, she jogged to the church. As promised in the homily that morning, the door was always open.

If possible, it was even more still than before. Her eyes were well adjusted to the dark, allowing her to discern the shadows of the pews. The stained glass windows let in very little light – only enough for her to see the glass outlines of the saints, hooded figures watching. The tabernacle candle glowed – Jesus was in. Elise swallowed hard. She was frightened. Not as she had been in the library. But, frightened by the possibilities, by what may or may not be revealed.

She took several steps down the aisle, until she was midway between the door and the altar. The crucifix was in front of her, barely visible in the shadows. Only a small gleam of light caught the milkiness of His feet pinned together. "My Lord," she said quietly, though it sounded loud. She genuflected before him and then stood, expectant.

When nothing happened, no whispering or sign of any kind, she retreated to the spot she was in that morning and genuflected again, calling out those odd words she was compelled to say earlier.

The silence of the church continued. It felt like it was waiting – for her to do something else? Like this was some odd ritual, and if she just moved in the right way, said the words in exactly the right tone, she could conjure the religion she needed. Immediately, she could hear Alan and Chris, the alter ego that took residency over the past forty-eight hours. *This is not magic. You cannot summon Christ.* She hugged herself to keep warm and remained still.

Silence. It appeared the earlier sign was not to be repeated, and Elise was surprised to find her spirits lower. Was she actually hoping to find Remiel?

It felt like a fit, her heart defended. Without it, she would be alone again.

Shaking off the thoughts, Elise walked to the altar for a better look at the tabernacle in the back of the church. The light of the candle made the domed outside shimmer with a pearl quality. Metal etchings also shone. She could make out the cross at the top, and what looked like a door. It was, as Alan described, a small house.

The candle flickered with her movements, and Elise felt an odd, dark temptation to blow it out. What good was a God ever present, but who never spoke? She blew air out through her nose and the flame struggled.

And then she felt it – the same feeling she had in her room almost a week ago; the one she had in the library when she was suddenly confident she was not alone. It prickled her hairs and tickled her spine until she felt certain that when she turned around, there would be someone in the pews, watching.

Without moving her footing, Elise turned her neck to face back down the aisle.

Empty pews, empty pews, empty–

A shadow in the very back. All the breath remaining in her lungs rushed out. Elise could make out the roundness of a head, the sloping of shoulders (it wore something hooded), and then nothing as the shadow mingled with the darkness of the pews. It watched without moving.

She took a step back even while meaning to take one forward. "Who's there?" she only managed a whisper with very little hope of making it to the back of the church.

The shadow surprised her with a gesture. *Sit with me.*

"Who are you?" Elise did not realize she was shaking her head no. Then, as if making a trade, "I'm–"

"Remiel," the whisper interrupted and filled the church. The shadow gestured again for her to come and sit in the pew.

Why did I do this alone? Why didn't I tell Chris? Elise stepped forward until she came to the front of the altar in an attempt to look strong. There, she lost her daring.

"Can you tell me about Remiel?" It sounded like a plea.

The shadow did not gesture this time, only sat. It must've seen.

Drip

Warm liquid hit Elise on the top of her head and began trickling down her scalp. Another drop, then another. Ducking, Elise reached back to her hair and came away with a dark wetness on her fingers. She already knew, but she looked up anyway.

In the small gleam of light, Christ's nailed feet were less milky than before. A black liquid flowed from the wound. A drop fell on Elise's forehead.

She screamed and stumbled down the stage stairs, wiping with her hands to keep the blood from getting in her eyes. Still screaming, not caring if she woke the entire town, she plunged into the main aisle, banging her legs against the far left pews as she tried to keep away from the shadow–

It was gone. The screams caught in Elise's throat and she fell still halfway to the door.

Where are you? She turned in a circle. Her hand kneaded the place where the blood hit her forehead until it was painful. Several times around, but she saw no movement, no shadow.

What does it want? What does it want from me? She turned frantically.

If only she had kept her eyes on it instead of panicking.

The only sound in the church was a patting sound near the altar as the cross continued to bleed. She stopped turning to see what looked like thin streamers hanging from Jesus' hands and feet. *God, what did I do? I should never have come.*

She did not hear the shadow emerging from the dark behind her while she remained distracted. It tread softly, softly, listening to her breathing jagged, coming close while she was unaware. When it stood inches away, it scraped its foot on the floor, letting her know with the stony, grating sound.

Elise closed her eyes. She failed again – all she could do was turn to see it. Reopening her eyes, she did.

The shadow grabbed the arm she raised in defense and pulled her into it, sinking her screams into the roughness of the cloth it wore, covering her head with its hood. She struggled, struggled. She was strong, but not enough. It felt her lungs try to draw breath through the heavy cloak and fail. Twice more and she clutched to its arms. It knew her fingers wanted to burn it, but she could not reach through the fabric. She began to slide lower, but the shadow held her there until all of Elise Moore drained away.

* * * * *

She snapped into consciousness again, like a daydreamer caught. Daylight poured into her eyes until she could feel it behind her forehead. She squinted, yet it did little; the light was like noon sun on fresh snow.

Only after much blinking did she realize she laid on her back. Yet, it was not exactly lying, for there was no pressure on the base of her skull, her shoulder blades, her hips, or feet. Elise understood it as suspension, though she never knew such a feeling before. She moved to sit-up and discovered she had no sound – no rustle of clothing, no noise when the breath left her lungs.

Absolute silence.

Propped on her elbows, she found she was draped in white cloth, so brilliant that it melded with the light at the edges. It was weightless and fluid, almost moisture. Curiously, she pinched it between her fingers. It felt of nothing, and she only knew she touched it by seeing her hands on it. There were no seams, no pores. She could not find how she had been put into it.

Where was she?

It was a place like ice. And she was alone.

The walls were something part clear, part vapor. Wet and cold looking, they gleamed and showed nothing beyond or through them. Rainbows bounced from the prisms created in the corners, their bands of color arcing and bowing. The floor was the same, refracting the light over and over, higher and higher, so that she could not tell if there was a ceiling. There were no doors, no windows. She alone stood out, lying on the white-translucent cloth that showed there was nothing beneath her to keep her so raised. Yet, the fear was gone, leaving only a deep relaxation similar to sleep, yet acute with awareness. It was like being inside a diamond. It was ever reflection.

Has it been so long?

The question came from within, though it was not her voice. It came from…the left.

Elise looked up to see a man approaching with excitement in his step. He was beautiful with skin fair as moonlight and great chestnut locks curling to his shoulders. His face glowed radiantly so that the skin-lines that should be there were not; unmarked, a grown man with an infant's visage. His eyes were unnaturally bright and clear, perfectly solid brown irises with no change in hue or tint. Beneath them was a slender nose that curved gently to red lips soft and full, like slices of peeled grapefruit. He wore plain beige robes with a rope at his waist, yet the power of the muscle beneath was barely concealed. The fabric moved with him as an extension of his body, clinging to his arms and chest without constricting. He walked on: light. She knew he was perfect.

The silence continued, though his footfalls should have echoed throughout the ice-cavern. He stopped before her and his gaze traveled over her face. *So long. Though it passes in the blink of my eye, my soul knows the time*, the voice was melodic, the syllables and annunciation smooth. Not a song, and yet more song than talk.

Who are you? She heard her voice though it never passed her lips.

He knelt by her before replying, continuing to take her in without the human hint of criticism. So close, she found it dangerous to look into his eyes. They made her feel she could float away, like some hopeless kite whose child dropped its string.

That isn't really your question.

Who am I? Her mind whispered back.

The man smiled. *Yes.* He reached up then and touched her face with a smooth, veinless hand. Again, there was no sensation of touch, though an intensity not unlike the bright light registered behind her eyes. She watched him watching her, her breathing increasing soundlessly. There was something familiar; something within her stirred. She concentrated, trying to remember while his fingers continued to caress the corner of her mouth.

The confused recognition in her face seemed to please him. *Remiel. Come. I will show you.* He touched her eyelids, and the room was gone.

Sand. Dusty, dry, white sand, made millions of years past by a sea long turned to clouds. Her feet were buried in it up to the ankle. It was a colorless desert. A breeze she could not feel swept it, creating small grain cyclones. It was bright here too, yet there was no obvious source of light. She was seated on (as she looked down) an intricately sewn pillow. Red. Red beads and sequins.

Remiel? A voice called to her, as though she were not paying attention.

She looked up to six others, also seated. Six men – all with the same glow in their faces. Not old, not young; some had blue eyes, others violet, one the green hue of pine needles; all had long hair in various shades that seemed only highlights and lustrous shimmering. Like herself, each was draped in white cloth. All looked at her.

Alarm rose within her, as though she had walked on stage and forgotten her lines. What were they expecting from her? She caught sight of the man from the ice chamber and felt some relief. He stood off to the side and nodded once reassuringly.

I'll go, the words erupted from her without her control.

The six men continued to contemplate her, unblinking.

The one with green eyes leaned forward, his white-blond hair – the color of dry straw – falling like water over his shoulders. Again, recognition and a particular warmth filled her. *You know what you risk? What you will face?*

Yes.

Some looked doubtful.

I must go. It is His will, Remiel felt her head bow automatically. The others followed and bowed, and when they lifted their faces again, all questioning was gone.

So it is done, they toned in a strange chorus that reverberated in the ear like a bell hammered. Then each stood. Remiel too rose, her movement as involuntary as her responses had been. Six pairs of perfect eyes held hers, then turned away. They left without indenting the sand as they walked.

But the blond man lingered. He approached with eyes sharp like jade stone, searching over her as though he lost something. *So you go. Then you won't remember me, this place. I am frightened for you,* his voice whispered in her head.

No. Though my memory must be clouded, I will always know. In my heart, I cannot forget.

His eyes remained troubled. She knew they were very rarely so troubled. She reached her hand for his. *I could never look upon Him without remembering.*

He smiled weakly, pale pink lips pulling back to reveal his hope in her. He withdrew his hand and left. He looked back once.

And she noticed then: he carried a trumpet. Each of them did. The metal glared in the light as they moved. Some hung long and rigid like staffs. Some curved like the arc of a spine with keys layered like vertebrae. Two were black. His was glass, or crystal or mirrors. The world reflected in it as he walked away.

She looked down and found her own. It was arced like a hunting horn, with a mouthpiece no larger than the stem of a reed and a bell the size of her fist. The metal was a light copper. It was not smooth, but made from hundreds of strands, like a braid of rope. It had only three keys, each a pearl with garnet rims that glimmered red to black. She brought it close to her face; the copper, metallic scent was like blood.

The trumpet. This is the trumpet. And the skies shall fall and the dead shall rise. Do you sound screams or Hosannas? What day? What day? She whispered to it. Her fingers traced its outline and lingered on the keys. They fit her hands perfectly. Her breathing grew rapid as she realized it had weight. In a world without feeling, but the trumpet was heavy.

And she knew that weight, for it was her own weight. Her fingers closed over the copper neck tight until there should have been pain in her hand and she placed her lips over the mouthpiece. And she felt the tightness suddenly in her throat; felt a mouth harshly press on her own. And she understood the answer to her question.

I am the instrument.

The answer echoed into the vast reflective chamber; the sand and those in it were gone. She stood with her arm outstretched and empty; weightless. Suddenly, she ached from a crushing loneliness. She turned and looked upon Him, still by her side, his hand only now retracting from touching her eyes. At last, there was a feeling on her cheeks as tears rolled down and scalded.

My Lord. I broke my promise, she knelt, burying both her knees in the emptiness.

He knelt next to her and compelled her eyes to meet His.

I am so weak, so weak.

Your task is both difficult and long. I know. He looked past her through squinted eyes. *I too came to a desert once, in order to remember who I was. Even then, I was not strong enough. In the last hours, I still prayed the prayer I promised I would never pray.*

Let this cup pass from me, the words barely whispered between them.

He turned from such thoughts and wiped a tear from her face. It only brought more.

Please forgive me.

He stood, but kept His hand on her head. *Then you are forgiven. Only look upon me and remember, as you said you would.*

* * * * *

Elise woke to the light. It took a moment for her to recognize the curtains and wallpaper – Chris' bedroom. She sat up with a large intake of breath. Her frantic fingers found she still wore the jeans and sweatshirt, still lie on top of the covers. The window was closed and locked, and her shoes lined-up beneath it.

A dream? I fell asleep and never went at all? No, she couldn't believe it. *It was too real. It was too…* she remembered going through that window. She remembered the church, the shadow. Her heart pounded to help her recall the details of the place and the Man, her promise. The trumpet. Her hand went to her neck and she swallowed.

"Remiel." Self-consciously she dropped her hands and stared at them. Her breath shook while she watched the pale skin gauzing over light blue veins. Outside the door, she could hear intermittent rustling much like the rustling of her mind: a sound of both waiting and impatience, attempted courtesy and hinting, for something to awake.

She was almost to the door when she caught herself in the mirror. Wide-eyed, she took a closer look. Though it was smeared from her fingers, there was red liquid dried on her forehead. She raised her eyebrows and felt its stiffness. With wonder, she reached up and touched it again while blinking back frightened, grateful tears. In the mirror Elise frowned.

She would not go back.

* * * * *

Chris, Francis, and Alan waited for her to rise. They ate in the crowded kitchen, without saying much. Alan was bothered intensely by what he felt was a lack of organization. He kept muttering about breaking the society into groups to track Israeli news, and then usually found his way back to putting together a lesson plan for Elise. Chris wanted to shout at him that she didn't even believe them yet, and there was no point in teaching her until she did. But he remained quiet, confident that Elise would tell him herself. Francis put the whiteboard down by his seat but made no attempts to use it. As usual, he was not as concerned as the others and was about to get up to hold a Mass when the bedroom door opened.

The closing of the bathroom door immediately followed it.

"Ah, she's awake," Alan's energy finally found a focus. "Good. We have so much to do."

"The books won't arrive until tomorrow," Chris stated again.

"Well, there must be something we can show her? We're priests. She's never had any religious education. If we have to wait for books, I'd say we're– "

"All right," Chris regretted his remark.

Francis observed the two with raised eyebrows. Apparently, the situation at Ashton had kept them on their best behavior. Their usual dynamic seemed to be coming out now.

Elise's shower was short. She emerged in a pair of flower-patterned pants and a pink shirt from the town's only boutique with her hair matted down and wet. She looked about fifteen in the ensemble.

"Good morning," Alan turned on a much cheerier voice for her. "How did you sleep?"

Her eyes snared him. "Fine." A scrutinous look at their faces told her they knew nothing – not even Francis.

"Would you like something to eat?" Chris offered.

"Do you have cereal?"

"Is that all you want?" he was prepared to make omelets or even French toast.

"Well, shouldn't I have something quick?" she pointed out. "Aren't we going to get started today?"

The three looked back at her, surprised at her enthusiasm.

"You know, teaching me the years of religious ed. I've missed, testing my strengths? And I want to learn about First Communion."

Alan looked at Chris with triumph. "Yes, yes. All of that. Here, you eat and I'll come up with some sort of reading schedule, though the books here are lacking." He hustled into the living room and began pulling what he deemed worthy off the shelves.

Chris and Francis, on the other hand, continued to watch her while she ate.

"That's very exciting that you want to learn," Chris threw out. "You didn't seem that interested yesterday."

Elise looked at him over her cereal bowl as she ate at the counter.

"I mean, it would be understandable if you need a little more time to digest everything and decide..." he couldn't remember the rest of the softer version he was trying to come up with.

Elise looked at Francis and saw that he also looked serious, and more so than Chris, suspicious. She swallowed some of the tasteless bran flakes and put the bowl down, mostly full.

She opened her mouth. She closed it. She could not tell them.

Speaking it aloud would make the experience feel silly. But, for some reason, the three men were paired up with her, and she knew He would want her to trust them.

"I don't know anything about Remiel. Or your Church. But, even after only a few days, there is something, like a name in my head that's barely remembered and won't come to mind, and yet, I feel it's there. I just have to get to it." She snorted air through her nose. "I know that's not exactly a decision, but it's not running either."

She shrugged and picked back up the cereal bowl, sliding the spoon against the rim. Then, she stuffed her mouth with flakes and crunched loudly – she would say nothing else.

The rest of the day was quiet until Chris went into the church to retrieve a religious education booklet. The pools of anonymous blood on the altar and church floor induced panic and a pandemic locking of doors and staying in groups. The Vatican was called. Dinner did not happen until 10:45 PM

And Elise let them talk. She let them argue and suppose, and she let them clean it up.

Chapter 12 – The Sons of Fire

That Monday began a regimented schedule of classroom time (old books) and lab time (turning-up). Alan was in charge of both, with Francis and Chris serving as his assistants; Elise tried on her odd, tri-part role of guardian, student, and test subject.

The Bible was the obvious place to start, though Alan was quick to tell her there were few mentions of angels in the Old Testament. The creation story in *Genesis* barely mentioned them. "Many believe He created angels on the Fourth day, when he created the stars. Stars are an imagery often used in the Bible to imply angels," Alan explained and then read *Genesis* 1:16-18. "'And God made two great lights; the greater light to rule the day, and the lesser light to rule the night: the stars also. And God set them in the firmament of the heaven to give light upon the earth, and to rule over the day and over the night, and to divide the light from the darkness: and God saw that it was good.'

"In this interpretation, God placed angels in the heavens to shed light on mankind; to give us guidance through the darkness and evil. Guardians, if you will."

Angels were not brought up again until *Genesis 3:22*, when God cast Adam and Eve from the garden saying, "And the LORD God said, behold, the man is become as one of us, to know good and evil." Alan explained with some condescension that the "us" was assumed to mean God and the angels.

The only direct mention in *Genesis* – the only one Elise would've discovered on her own – came after the first couple was cast out of Eden: God assigned a cherub to guard the Tree of Life. Though Satan made a quick entrance as the serpent, Elise found he would not be named a dark angel for several millennia – and many books – later.

Indeed, despite its cosmic importance, the Fall was only a whisper in the first book. And Alan warned as they read the passage, "What I am showing you is not something the Catholic Church even acknowledges. We choose not to interpret the reading this way. However, angel scholars often lay their case on *Genesis* 6:1 through 6:4, so you should read it."

Elise did, aloud, "'And it came to pass, when men began to multiply on

160

the face of the earth, and daughters were born unto them, that the sons of God saw the daughters of men that they were fair; and they took them wives of all which they chose. And the Lord said, My spirit shall not always strive with man, for that he also is flesh: yet his days shall be an hundred and twenty years. There were giants in the earth in those days; and also after that, when the sons of God came in unto the daughters of men, and they bare children to them, the same became mighty men which were of old, men of renown.'"

Alan began dissecting, "Many people believe that sons of heaven is a reference to the angels. These angels loved mortal women and fell from grace to be with them, and their children were the giants, called Nephilim. Again, the Church does not believe in this version of the angels' fall, but you can read and decide," he lifted two hands. After 40 years as priest, it was difficult to teach what was not Church doctrine.

But he had to be fair. She had to see it all.

* * * * *

Chris looked up from his highlighting for the fifth time in thirty seconds. The sun streamed onto the sofa arm, dappled with shadows from a leaf. Outside the window, the same leaf danced, a dazzling red.

He looked around the quiet room. Alan sat with a small city of books stacked around him at varying heights; Elise read with her legs coiled beneath her in a way he was used to, but that still reminded him of Cirque de Soleil; and Francis sat stiff with one book (he always returned each to the shelf before grabbing another). Hadn't any of them noticed the day?

He closed his book quietly. No one moved.

He stood. Not a head raised.

He reached the door (coat over his arm, as he dared not put it on inside) when Alan's voice hit his ears, as cringeful as his mother's used to be. "Father Chris, where are you headed?"

"Out. The lawn needs some raking." He tried to go before Alan could get a protest in, but failed, standing half in and half out to receive the appropriate beratement.

"We've only been at it a few hours today, man!"

"I'm going with him," Elise jumped up.

"No, you will stay here."

"This isn't school, Alan. I can take a break. When I come in, I'll make grilled cheese," she offered the sandwich that all three men had a remarkable soft spot for. "Besides, Father Chris won't be gone as long if I help."

"We need to train her. She needs to be prepared! For life, death, the Other..." Alan continued, his old mouth a thin, disapproving line. "See what you've done?"

"Yes, yes," Chris got the rest of the way through the door. "I know – she takes after me."

Elise laughed and followed him out.

"You really should have a coat," he scolded gently.

"Don't you start parenting me too." Elise pulled her hands out of her jean pockets to show she needed no layers. "It's just fine out. The sun is warm."

"And bright," Chris added, squinting at the yard with its speckles of leaves.

"You know, even if we rake today, we'll definitely have to do it again before the season's over," Elise noted the trees still half-covered with leaves.

"That's part of the fun." Chris left to hunt out the rakes.

* * * * *

"You're walking through my pile," he told her for the third time.

Elise only smiled over at him darkly. "I figure Alan will have to let us stay out here all morning so long as I keep your piles to a minimum."

Chris laughed, and watched her tramp through what was left of it, scattering leaves thoroughly in a four-foot radius.

"I used to do this with my parents," Elise said as she pulled a leaf out of the back of her sock. "They did the raking, and I was in charge of pile destruction. I used to get a good running start and torpedo with the best of them."

Chris began again to rake. "I'll bet you did."

"What's that supposed to mean, exactly?" Elise placed her two hands on the tip of her rake handle, leaning on it seriously, though her eyes shined otherwise.

"Nothing – you're the one that said it. I'm just agreeing." He shrugged and smiled. "It means, I can see you torpedoing through many things in life."

"Yes, well I suppose priests take a vow of non-torpedoing, so you probably don't realize how much fun it can be." She tossed her hair in mock snobbery and raked a few strokes before turning back for more conversation. "We never had as many leaves as this, I have to say. Fall in South Carolina happens later and not as thoroughly."

"It's definitely thorough here. By Halloween, there will be only a few leaves left, and those covered with frost or maybe snow."

Elise formed a small pile of leaves and stepped back to survey it before gathering a few more. "My mom used to sew my Halloween costume every year. My favorite was when she made me a bumblebee and glued an ice cream cone to my rear for a stinger. I, of course, forgot and sat on it as soon

162

as they put me in the car to drive downtown. So, the rest of the night I walked around with broken sugar cone bits stuck to my butt."

Again, Chris laughed. "You're parents sound like nice people. Watch the pile–"

Elise tramped through it. "They were nice people. Very much in love with each other and me, or so I remember. But it's been so long, I wonder if I am just seeing what I want, you know?

Chris knew better than to answer.

"But other times, their memory is so close and strong…it's as though I have perfect snapshots in my mind. Like when I went to kindergarten. They were standing in the driveway with their arms around each other while I got on the school bus for the first time. I sat down on this great, big, green seat and watched them through the window as we pulled away. I don't remember what happened before – getting dressed or eating breakfast. And I don't remember what happened next – who I sat with or what my teacher looked like. But I remember them in the driveway waving. Their arms moved back and forth while their eyes were busy scanning all of the windows, looking for me." She snorted, suddenly raking with more energy. "Only a few years later, they would both be gone. In my memory, it seems like they knew, and were beginning to say goodbye."

She stopped short, sighing quietly. Chris watched her step from the shade of the tree out into the sun. Her reddish hair blazed with gold and orange highlights; toyed by the breeze, it formed curls and tangled halos here and there. Her mouth was turned down, so that gentle creases formed in the skin around her lips. In the daylight, her eyes appeared even more lightened, like coffee with too much cream. Though, he also liked it when they appeared dark like eclipsed moons in the low light of the living room. He knew he liked the way she often raised one eyebrow, mostly because it seemed she had to use all the muscles in her forehead in order to do it. She was young and beautiful and strong, and he turned away quickly before she could catch him.

"Well, it appears you have been working too diligently."

Chris glanced up again to see her standing with an elfish grin by his largest pile. "If you don't leave that pile, Alan will know we've been up to something," he warned.

"Oh, who cares," she stuck one foot into the pile.

"Elise!" Chris felt himself smile, though he didn't mean to. "Leave it. As much as I want to escape Professor Alan, I also really did want to rake the lawn."

She tossed a few leaves with her toes. "You think you can stop me?'

His eyebrows went up. "It seems you've let some of this angel stuff go to your head." He wielded the rake in a mock menace.

Her smile grew. "You'll just have to tackle me, then–"

Elise heard her own words and startled, drawing herself back in, folding her arms. Embarrassed, she let her hair fall across her cheeks to hide their new bloom. "Of course, priests probably take a vow of non-tackling, too." Her eyes fell so she wouldn't have to look at him.

"Yeah, tackling is covered in that whole vow thing, probably." Chris returned to raking, knowing she would leave the pile of leaves alone now.

She did, and fell back to work quietly, though often looking at him over her rake.

* * * * *

Job 4:18 *Behold, he put no trust in his servants; and his angels he charged with folly.* \.

"Great. I've read hundreds of pages, and I know I can do bad things, and not much else," Elise closed the Bible with a resounding snap yet another afternoon.

Alan used his knuckles to press his forehead and closed his own book. "Much of what we know about angels does not come from the Bible. It comes from letters, Pope declarations, and the *Apocrypha*."

"The *Apocrypha*?"

"Biblical books rejected by the Council of Hippos and thus stricken from the modern Bible. They are well worth reading, and any good priest has them on hand. But, they have heretical tendencies."

"Like what?" Elise said quickly at the onset of a yawn.

"Conjurations, spells, ways to wield the power of God. They name angels and demons, and often treat them as idols. The books touch too much on ceremonial magic."

"At least they sound interesting. Are they on the reading list?"

"Some of them."

"Well, why don't we get to those? I'm not learning much from these brief passages," she pursed her lips at him.

"Before we get into the illegitimate information, I want you to study the legitimate, however less interesting."

* * * * *

"This is one heck of a place," Elise said on their first turning-up field trip. She stood in the middle of a greenhouse easily the size of half a football field and several stories tall. One large, cracked, concrete slab served for a floor. The walls were made of metal posts with gigantic glass panels in between them. The same glass and metal rose up and came to a point to form the roof. Sunlight streamed in from all sides, helping to create a humid, rainforest environment, and rows and rows of plants stretched out in all directions reaching for the light, each lined-up according to some horticulture categorizing system that had no apparent rationalization. A narrow catwalk rose above them and snaked the entire perimeter, also lined with even more plants. And the smell – it was like stepping into an elevator full of rich old women drenched in eau de toilette.

The greenhouse was part of a farm Alan noticed only a half-mile farther down the road from the rectory. With one phone call, they had permission to use it for "training."

"This must be one rich farmer," Elise continued commenting as she surveyed. "I can't believe they have four of these things."

"Yes, well, we needed a lot of plants," Alan said while reading a tag hanging from a particularly tall one.

"He really said I can just kill everything in here?" Elise looked skeptical.

Chris chimed in. "He thinks we're testing some new farming chemicals that may be used in third world countries to increase food yields. The Catholic Church made a generous donation to the farm for use of the one greenhouse. We can kill anything we like." It had an odd cheery ring to it.

Alan added his always-candid opinion, "As you've described it, turning-up on people sounds potentially dangerous. Besides, there aren't enough of us."

They all looked at Francis, who appeared generally uncomfortable, like a seriously constipated man. It was anyone's guess how he would react when she turned-up this close, but he insisted on coming.

"Well, what do you want me to do?" She was actually looking forward to this. They were away from the rectory, which was a relief (no one ever wanted to let her go anywhere else), and it was a break from cramming information she half understood. Turning-up was something that came pretty easily.

As always, Alan took the lead. "Let's start with the basics. Show us what you can do. Then, we'll try to work on things. Make you stronger."

"I don't know if I can be made stronger," Elise replied.

"We'll see. You need to be prepared for–"

"Anything. Life, death, the Other, armies, destruction, Armageddon," Elise rattled off for him, folding her arms.

"As I recall, you were hardly a match for the Other at Ashton. The world is hoping you will get better. Go ahead. The show is yours."

Elise looked back at the three. Francis now crouched in a lawn chair he found hidden in the corner. He already had his ears covered. Alan had his arms crossed and looked like he was judging some sort of competition. And

165

Chris stood with his eyes wide and nodding encouragement at her when she caught his gaze.

We are one odd group. "All right. I guess I'll start with the most basic thing; the thing I turn-up the most for." Without any further introduction, Elise walked over to a bin full of pruning equipment. Without hesitation, she reached for a pair of sheers, opened them, and then ran her palm down the sharp edge. The blood flowed quickly into her hand and down her wrist.

Though Elise's face showed no pain, the three men each winced. Chris found the situation disquietingly similar to viewing the freak show at the fair. It was gross, but no one seemed able to turn away.

Elise crossed to a fern that came up to her waist, leaving a few red drops on the floor. She looked to Francis to make sure he was warned, and then reached her hand into the leaves. The effect was immediate. The green began to curl and brown, and several dead, dry fern branches fell to the floor. Elise stood with her head up, so that they could see her eyes, and their own grew wide as they watched.

A light began as a small pin in the center of her irises, like a glare barely reflected. It grew until her entire pupil faded away in a brightness that would not at all be mistaken for reflection. It was a kind of radiance, golden in color like sunset or firelight. "Unbelievable," Chris breathed the word for all of them.

When she had enough (perhaps 10 seconds worth), she released the plant and then held up her still bleeding hand. Chris and Alan both took a few steps forward, while Francis remained squinting in his chair, but with no less anticipation.

The blood immediately around the wound began to bead, like rain on a newly waxed car. The dripping slowed, and then, as far as the three men could tell, appeared to stop. The change corresponded to a dimming in her eyes.

Elise stepped over to a hose on the floor. She rinsed away the blood and revealed only a long white mark on her palm where the cut had been.

With a mock magicians bow, she smiled. "And that's only my first trick."

* * * * *

Some of what Elise studied, she already knew. In the Old Testament's original Hebrew, the word for angel was *malak*, meaning messenger. Like priests and others in God's service, angels were supposed to carry the Word and serve as an intermediary between heaven and earth. Several instances in the Bible showed angels taking human form to complete missions (Elise reread those passages several times). Luke wrote that their souls can never die.

Other facts were not so well known to her. In Matthew's gospel, she discovered that angels can behold the face of God, while men cannot. Other passages in the Bible said similar things. God "hath immortality, dwelling in the light which no man can approach unto; whom no man hath seen, nor can see" (*1Timothy* 6:16). Angels bridged the gap between the holiness of God and the ungodliness of sinners.

Alan's constant retelling of other inductions and interpretations helped complete the picture. "When the angels were created, they were in the direct presence of God. Unlike humans, who must grow in faith and eventually choose God, angels are all-knowing because they come from the beginning. They do not sin because they can see God's will at all times – the true path is always obvious to them."

"Not always," Elise spoke under her breath. "Anyway, what about the fall then? How is it, if they cannot sin, that one third of them fell. It's in *Revelation* 12:4-12:9." She flipped to the book they now seemed to spend the most time analyzing.

"Read that passage," Alan took off his glasses and pinched the bridge of his nose.

She began, "And the dragon stood before the woman which was ready to be delivered, for to devour her child as soon as it was born. And she brought forth a man child, who was to rule all nations with a rod of iron: and her child was caught up unto God, and his throne. And the woman fled into the wilderness, where she hath a place prepared of God, that they should feed her there a thousand two hundred threescore days. And there was war in heaven: Michael and his angels fought against the dragon; and the dragon fought and his angels, and prevailed not; neither was their place found any more in heaven. And the great dragon was cast out, that old serpent, called the Devil, and Satan, which deceiveth the whole world: he was cast out into the earth, and his angels were cast out with him." She looked up expectantly.

"See, they're just a few lines," Alan needlessly summarized. "But, on those lines are built all the great legends. Ready for a short dissertation?"

Elise sat back in answer and he began. "It is believed that, when God created the angels, he was not satisfied with them. As I mentioned before, they did not have free will – once they saw He was perfect, they became mindless extensions of Him. That was not rewarding to God. He wanted beings that could be both dark and light, and still choose Him. So, he created Man. In the passage you read, the woman bearing a child is a metaphor for the birth of man. Then, the dragon, who is really Satan, another–"

"Metaphor," Elise finished for him. "The whole book is one big metaphor."

"Yes," patience thinning. "The dragon went to devour the child. Or, in short, Satan did not like God's creation and wanted to destroy it. He felt betrayed. You see, there once were eight angels that stood before God: the seven angels of the trumpets, yourself included, and Satan. It is said that he was the greatest angel and the one that God trusted most."

Elise's face puckered. "Satan was one of the angels before God?" she echoed. "So, at some point, I knew him."

Alan pondered her statement. "Better than that, you probably worked beside him, respected him, even admired him, working with him in the service of God...

"Satan realized that even he, the greatest angel, was being displaced by this man with free will. Legend claims he became jealous. He and many of the other angels could not understand how an imperfect being could be better than a perfect one. And for the first time, several of the angels wondered if God was wrong.

"Once they doubted God's perfection, they could no longer see Him so plainly and the righteous path became unclear. Satan came to believe that perhaps he was better, that he was god, and he gained a group of followers. Though unhappy, the insurgence didn't happen until God commanded His angels to bow before the new man. This request was the last straw. In Jewish lore, Satan asks, 'Why should a son of fire fall down before a son of clay?'"

"So to get revenge against God for creating humans, he tempted Eve." Elise deducted in Alan's pause to swallow.

"Yes. He thought he could show God how truly imperfect and weak a being He created. What Satan could not see is that, it was already a part of the fate God wrote for mankind. He knew Satan would betray Him even before he created Satan.

"The rest of the passage in *Revelation* tells that a great battle ensued and Michael – who is another of the seven angels standing before God – cast the fallen angels from heaven and from grace. Out of the presence of God and without the will to choose differently, they know nothing but evil. The fallen became demons, living only to torment and tempt the creation that displaced them. They too will be judged and destroyed at the end of days."

"All that from this paragraph?" Elise looked back at the text.

"There are other references: *Deuteronomy* 32:17, 2 *Peter* 2:4, *Jude* 1:6 and several books in the *Apocrypha* all detail demons, angels, and retellings of the fall."

"Do you think we can quit for today?" Elise interrupted, having not listened to the last few sentences anyway.

Alan replied with surprise, "It is almost dark. You can go if you want, though I'm not trying to torture you, Elise. You need to know where you come from, and I hope some of this is beginning to resonate with you."

"It is," she answered honestly

When God created the angels, he was not satisfied with them. They did not have free will. Why should a son of fire fall down before a son of clay?

* * * * *

Chris looked across the greenhouse catwalk with trepidation. This really wasn't such a great idea. But as always, Alan was pushing.

"What do you think?" Alan asked Elise.

"You want me to jump from this catwalk to that one?" She gestured across the greenhouse to the opposite iron grate ledge where Chris and Francis stood. They both looked concerned.

"Do you think you can do it?"

"I don't know. I've never tried anything like it." She shrugged. "It's a good 30 yards across. But, I guess it's only a fifteen foot drop."

"Yes, you could heal yourself pretty easily from something like that."

Elise shot Alan a critical look. "I'm glad you've decided I should take the risk."

"You want to know what you can do, don't you?" he replied.

"Just go stand over there with the others."

He walked away, shaking his head, and followed the narrow catwalk around the greenhouse until he stood opposite from her.

Elise looked at the distance again. *Calculate... how much do I need?*

Better safe than sorry, she answered herself.

Still looking at the gap between the catwalks, she threaded her fingers through the branches of a tree. *Jonagold,* the tag read. "Sorry," she murmured as she felt the shock in her fingers, the life in her hands.

The whispers came, sounding glad she intended to hold on so long. Their words spoke to her meaninglessly, though the sounds were becoming familiar. Voices, whispering in her ears and head, like a constant rain. Longer, and the world grew yellow so that she squinted to keep it clear. Until the tree bent away from her, its dying leaves falling to bury her feet. Francis groaned on the other side. *Just a few more seconds.* Elise pushed herself away, even as something inside called her to keep going. The bark was singed black.

She walked forward until she reached the edge and looked directly over the open space between the left and right catwalks. Francis was doubled over and breathing hard. She could not be sure, but she thought his ears were bleeding. *Don't look at him. It's distracting,* she coached herself in Alan's voice.

She flexed her legs, bounced her knees. She touched the cool, protective railing and rocked her weight on it. It came up to her waist – she would have

169

to clear it. The catwalk was only five feet wide at the most. She needed to pick-up speed quickly. She stepped back to the far wall and leaned against it, pressed in among the plants.

Chris took the movement as a sign of defeat. He called over, "Elise, you don't have to do this. If you don't think you can make it..." he trailed off.

She concentrated, listening to her heartbeat slow and strong. In a similar measured rhythm, she took several deep breaths.

It happened so fast, Chris wasn't exactly sure when she pushed off. One moment, she was leaning back in the plants, and the next, she was rushing over the railing, her entire body clearing it by a good four feet. Hurdling across – halfway and her height still did not peak. She kept her head tucked into her shoulders and her hands opened and crossed in front of her, bracing for the hit. Across, across she moved silent, her legs half-tucked and bent for landing, propelled at some incredible speed until she came down perfectly over the opposite railing, landing on one knee just in front of Alan. The catwalk vibrated and the thud of her weight echoed and shook all the glass.

Still using the forward motion of her body, she sprung from kneeling to standing in one movement and looked up at them with eyes that glowed with energy to spare.

* * * * *

"*Revelation* is still very confusing to me," Elise commented another afternoon. "The author had no sense of chronology. He put down some of his visions for the future, like the seals and the trumpeters, first; then he focuses on the fall that happened in the past; then he prophesizes the final plagues of the apocalypse. Has anyone ever concluded that he might just be loony?"

She waited, but Chris didn't look up from highlighting the next book on the list. She had been watching him unnoticed (or so she hoped) while pretending to read.

Finally, he answered her, "*Revelation* isn't an easy read."

"Yeah," she said it wistfully, and Chris could tell she was thinking about something else.

"What is it?" he looked up.

She dropped her inappropriate gaze. "There are just a few things that bother me. Some of the things I've learned, I just don't like." She exhaled long.

"Like what?" Chris closed the dictionary and placed it on the coffee table.

"Is Alan around?"

Chris shook his head. "He ran to the post office."

"It's not that I don't like Alan," Elise backtracked. "He just isn't the

170

most understanding human being I've ever met. Whenever I start to ask questions, he always just points me back to the books."

"And you think I might be able to tell you a few things off the record?" He smiled.

"All the sources on angels are different and there are hundreds of interpretations of this stuff. But, most of what I've read does agree on a few key points. One – angels have no free will. And two – they are lower than men."

Chris' smile turned to a frown, but he waited.

"That means I'm inferior to you, and to everyone I've met," she tried to sound angry, but the pain in her voice came through. "And, it means the choices I've made are not mine. Nothing about me is real. It's all someone else's will channeled through me. My personality, the things that I want and the people I care for aren't genuine. Just mock emotions created for me so I appear to be normal. Angels can't even love because God consumes them."

"Hey…." Chris tried to slow down the agitation in her voice. "That's a pretty harsh speech. What has Alan been giving you to read, anyway?" he attempted humor.

She swallowed (no smile). "I just," she stammered. "I guess I just feel like I'm trying so hard, and I've been given this really awful task," her voice rose higher as she looked up at the ceiling and blinked rapidly. "But if they're right, then there isn't any reward. I'm not being brave or sacrificing anything. I'm just doing what someone told me to do. I don't have a soul of my own."

"None of that's true."

"How can you say that?" her eyes turned to him, suddenly angry and barely slits. "It's all in here!" she knocked the Bible with a clenched fist.

"The Word of God was written down by men. And men are fallible," he steadied her hand with his larger one. "After all my studies and years as a priest, I don't believe you are less than anyone else."

There was a long pause before her voice, defeated, "You're just saying that. The Bible isn't fallible, or we wouldn't be here," she gestured to the room. "If this is all there is, if I really am just some puppet, then what happens to me when this is over?"

* * * * *

She was turning-up harder now. And, to Elise's surprise, Alan was right. The more she practiced, the stronger she became.

"Today, I want you to use telekinesis and physical strength at the same time. As it is, telekinesis takes up too much of your focus. When you do it, you can't do anything else. It leaves you vulnerable. You need to be able to control things with your mind and use your physical strength to defend yourself. The Other is out there, and probably searching hard. Who knows how long we have?"

Elise walked further into the greenhouse as Alan's words droned on – past the dead plants from previous sessions (he had her suck them dry now). "But I'm starting simple. I'll try locking the doors while throwing a few planting pots," she called back to where Chris, Francis and Alan stood.

"Try throwing them all the way across. And, I want you to lock the doors on each end simultaneously, like last week," Alan pushed back.

Elise turned-up on several plants. One, two, three – all dead in a matter of seconds. *Getting faster.* Then she picked-up a planting pot complete with dead plant (easily 80 pounds). This would be difficult. With a deep breath, Elise reached out with her mind for the locks.

Turned-up, telekinesis was no harder than imagining her consciousness outside her body. For a moment, it seemed she spun: a sense of movement without concrete feeling. Then slowly, the movement stopped and she was left feeling vaguely split between her body – the concrete floor, the pot in her hand – and where her thoughts were. It seemed she was standing beside herself, two instead of one.

But she needed to be three. Elise concentrated harder, splitting her thoughts again. *One door on either end, both ends.* She tried to see each half of the greenhouse split-screen in her mind. *Feel them. Feel the branches on your arms. Smell the flowers, the dirt. Find–*

She found the door they came in through (the most familiar). Holding onto it, feeling the lock, she turned more of her mind to the second door. Alan clucked somewhere – an indication she was taking too long. *He has no idea what this is like–*

Immediately, her hold on the first door faded and she struggled to keep herself there. *Ignore him, concentrate!* She pushed more of herself out, into the filtered sunlight and moisture. Her veins poured the energy until finally, significantly weakened, she felt the cold handle of the second door. She was ready for the third component.

The pot in her hands – though it was the thing she was actually holding, it was still difficult to sense. *Feel the first door, feel the second door, feel the pot. Feel them all until they're hard.*

But it was slipping away, and she knew it. The energy was flowing out of her as though a dam had broken. She only had seconds before everything would disappear. In one frantic mental sweep, she pushed the tumblers and threw the pot.

Chris heard a click at each end of the greenhouse and the shatter of a pot nearby. A few moments later, Elise staggered from the plants looking as exhausted as she had the night they took her from her dorm.

"Well?" she croaked through a dry mouth.

Her appearance did nothing to soften Alan. "It took you almost a minute and a half; you successfully locked the first door, and threw the pot about ten feet." He stomped back to check on the second door.

Chris came to her side and extended an arm. She leaned fully on him, resting her head on his side.

"Unlocked," Alan called back.

"I tried," she yelled into the glass cavern, breathless. "You have no idea what it's like to divide yourself like that." She reached her fingers into an already half-dead plant and took enough to stand straight before Alan reappeared.

Even so, she looked so tired that Chris felt reluctant to release her. For several days, there had been a quiet sadness about her. Alan's pushing seemed to temporarily rejuvenate her, but ultimately deplete her.

"You'll just have to keep at it," Alan returned. "You need to be faster. If you needed to lock the doors and defend yourself at the same time, then–"

"Then I would probably concentrate on one or the other," Elise retorted. "And, I wouldn't be using stupid plants! I can't get enough from them. I lose it too soon."

"Well, plants are all you have," Alan didn't meet her eyes. "So, rest a few moments, and then we'll try again."

"Plants aren't all I have," Elise said under her breath, but loud enough for them to hear. "I'm the only one making any sacrifices. Maybe you should take some risks."

* * * * *

Francis was assigned First Communion classes. It seemed logical, since he performed no less than three Masses per day. The classes consisted of going through a book obtained from the religious education director at St. John's and observing Francis prepare the feast with occasional bursts of written commentary.

I think you will be ready soon, he wrote after Elise successfully recited the Apostle's Creed.

"It will be nice, to share in the meal," she replied as she looked over some of the quiz questions in the back of the book.

Francis continued blessing hosts, mouthing prayers she was growing accustomed to. They did not seem nearly as romantic in Chris' kitchen as they did in the church.

Francis paused before pouring the wine. *You seem distracted lately,* he sketched.

Elise groaned. "I already talked with Chris. Apparently, there are no answers."

Is it your studies? He pried further.

"Did Chris say something to you?" her anger rose at the thought.

No. I am a visionary, remember? He smiled, turning his normally somber face into one Elise quite liked.

She continued looking through the quiz in the back of the reader. After a few moments of silence, "The Bible is critical of angels, and it bothers me." She did not look up to see his reaction. "We have no free will according to every source I've read. We either realize God is perfect and spend the rest of eternity doing His bidding, or we decide He isn't and we spend the rest of eternity trying to trick men. There's no choice once that one choice is made. Which of course, makes us inferior to men, who can fall and still be saved. So, not only am I a puppet according to all of Alan's sources, I'm a puppet second class."

She heard Francis scratching away at the white board and finally looked up, ready for some weak, consoling words.

Instead, *Alan chooses his texts selectively.*

She put down her book. "What do you mean?"

Though it is widely accepted by the Church – angels are lower forms – there are Biblical passages that do not concord.

"Show me."

Francis nodded and flipped pages in the Bible that was on the table. He pointed.

Psalms 8:4-5: *What is man, that thou art mindful of him? And the son of man, that thou visitest him? For thou hast made him a little lower than the angels, and hast crowned him with glory and honour.*

More flipping. *Even Jesus was made lower. Read here.* Francis turned Elise's eyes to *Hebrews 2:9.*

But we see Jesus, who was made a little lower than the angels for the suffering of death, crowned with glory and honour; that he by the grace of God should taste death for every man.

Two of many examples. It is not so black and white, Francis finished.

"Why didn't they tell me?" Hurt filled her eyes. "Why would they want me to think... I asked Chris specifically. Why wouldn't he tell me there was a possibility that it wasn't true?"

They want you to learn the Church's accepted version? They had your best interest in mind. But, it is always important: remember no one really knows. You are here, and we know your purpose for the moment, but the rest..." he gave an exaggerated shrug. *Nothing is inevitable.*

* * * * *

"What are the whispers like, again?"

"What?" Elise turned her face to Alan, while she squatted on the greenhouse floor, waiting for Chris to bring her back another, living plant. She was drained, breathing hard, anxious to turn-up and recover from another training session.

"The whispers. You said many times that you hear voices while you are turned-up?" Alan repeated, no concern in his voice.

"They get stronger the longer I hold on...I think I told you this already. I don't know what the words are – just voices from far way. It's just some side effect, like the light in my eyes."

"You said that sometimes, it seems like the voices want you to turn-up higher?"

"I guess," the exasperation came through clearly. Elise did not want to talk; she barely had the strength to open her mouth. "They get louder, more insistent the longer I hold on. And the words get more distinct, like if I held on long enough, took enough, I might figure it out. But that would mean..."

"That would mean?"

"I held onto my mom during the accident a really long time. And even then, I couldn't tell what they were saying. Turning-up that high on someone would mean doing some serious damage, possibly–" she shrugged, looking around at the dead trees. "When I hear the voices, they seem familiar, comforting. But, if they want me to kill someone in order to hear them, what type of voices do you think they are?"

Chris plunked a plant down next to her, and Elise's fingers found it, winding into its leaves parasitically. The whispers began.

* * * * *

They were all glued to the television when she came out of the bedroom one morning. It was unusual – the T.V. was almost never on until after dinner. Elise joined the line-up.

"Yet another explosion in Jerusalem. A Palestinian suicide bomber walked into a crowded hotel lobby with C4 explosives and killed nearly 40 people," a reporter's voice was heard while scenes of smoke, fire and crying people flashed on the screen.

"Let's go to our Israeli correspondent. Kyle?"

"Dave, the people are devastated," the second reporter came across with a sick hint of glee at the line. "It's another attack on a bedraggled city and a country that experiences attacks like these daily. Israelis are scared. Many avoid public places of any kind now. And, there are rumblings of more political backlash. The prime minister just isn't doing anything, Dave. And the people want to hold him accountable."

The camera panned onto the crowd of people behind the reporter: shaking fists, crying, some bloodied. Over and over, they chanted one word: malchia.

"What are they saying?" she asked Alan.

"Malchia. It's the Hebrew word for 'king.'"

* * * * *

"Apparently this isn't the abridged version," Elise ran her thumb over the history book's hundreds of pages.

"The Jews own a considerable amount of the prophesy of kings, and so you should know their side of things," Alan muttered from his side of the room. "The country of Israel has been promised to the Jews for almost 3500 years. It was their land, ruled by their kings until 587 BC when the Babylonians invaded. It wasn't until 1948 – more than 2000 years later – that they won their land back. And even now, it's a constant battle, including four full-blown Arab wars over the past 60 years and daily insurrections. That battle is the reason we're here: a nation so terrorized and torn that they're willing to trade democracy for a strong ruler. To give up their freedom in order to end the battle."

"Who even wants Israel after thousands of years of fighting?" Elise scorned without trying to understand. "What type of promised land is that?"

"Oh, Elise. It's so much larger than that," he scorned her back. "It's a thirty-five hundred-year-old promise made by God. The struggle for paradise regained has been going on since our time began; the desire to go back to Eden, inherited like a gene from the first Jewish woman, Eve. In fact, Jews believe only mothers can pass down Judaism and the right to Israel. When a Jewish man has children, even if he is a practicing Jew, he cannot pass on his religion unless the mother of his children is also Jewish. It is a blood connection back to the first sinner and the possibility of redemption in a promised land.

"But what happens when this promised land is already occupied? And, not only is it occupied, but it is occupied by a culture that does not tolerate other religions?"

Elise shrugged.

"Don't disengage. You must read a newspaper sometime – this is not a hard question. You end-up with two cultures willing to die for the same land. Muslim Palestinians have waged a war from within on Jewish Israelis since the moment the Jews regained control of Israeli. Both groups feel the land is crucial to their religious and cultural survival, and both want their own independent state. Despite U.N. resolutions, summit meetings, negotiation after negotiation, the civil war continues with suicide attacks and retaliations.

Every day life is disrupted. Schools cannot stay open. Businesses cannot sell their wares. Citizens cannot celebrate their religion. Democracy fails as laws are passed that no one follows. Leaders become leaders based on their power, rather than their ideals."

"Malchia," Elise responded.

"Yes. King. A year and a half ago, the Palestinian Legislative Council held elections in order to determine new leadership. The terrorist groups Hamas and Islamic Jihad worked together to corrupt the elections and fix the ballots so that the new council would be stacked with terrorist-sympathetic members – members who believe there should be no compromise when it comes to creating a Palestinian state. Since then, suicide attacks have become more frequent and more deadly."

Elise flopped the book onto the couch. If Alan kept talking, she wouldn't have to read it. "I remember Israel's Prime Minister asked the U.S. for help. We wouldn't commit troops, but we did supply weapons and intelligence, and we agreed to allow our weapon manufacturers to sell classified military weaponry directly to Israel."

"Which lead to the oil embargo three summers ago. Other Arab nations, outraged the U.S. was interfering in the Arab-Israeli conflict, colluded together to enforce the first oil embargo against the United States since 1974. I'm sure you remember – within a day of the embargo announcement, gas prices soared to an average of $4.56 per gallon."

"It was that way all summer. No one wanted to drive anywhere. Everyone was talking about a major economic depression, even at graduation parties. It didn't affect me much, though. I didn't have–"

"Then the winter came, and to ensure its own oil supply and control prices, China signed an agreement with Russia, the Sino-Russian Energy Stability Pact. In this agreement, Russia agreed to sell all of its oil solely to China, putting further pressure on the U.S. economy. We released oil from our strategic reserves, and also tapped into Alaskan resources. The efforts did little to curb the cold winter, and gas prices continued to soar to almost $6.00 per gallon. So we could stand by our ally no more."

Elise crossed her arms. "Don't pause for me. I'm not injecting my two cents anymore. Apparently, you don't want me that engaged."

"You were talking about graduation parties, Elise. Anyway, the U.S. held out until Israel's Prime Minister a series of suicide bombings in Tel-Aviv left over 100 dead, including two Israeli Ministers. The Israeli Prime Minister commanded an attack on the Palestinian city of Ramallah, reportedly a Hamas safe haven. After six weeks of heavy guerilla fighting and 194 Israeli casualties, Israeli soldiers were ordered to use a powerful nerve gas to clear the city, regardless of Palestinian civilians. The action broke the Geneva Protocol, causing an outcry from the international community. We took the opportunity to end our financial and military support, and the oil embargo was lifted.

"With the U.S. out, Israel's politicians lost ground fast, and their Arab neighbors began to close in. Knesset elections were held last October, and for the first time in Israeli history, two-thirds of the seats went to smaller political parties and splinter parties, leaving only one-third to the Likud party and the opposing Labor party. These smaller, more extreme parties began to immediately have their effect on Israeli policy. In April, the Knesset voted no confidence in its government. New ministers were nominated and approved – none of them from the old Likud and Labor parties. Prime Minister Daniel Rosenthal was appointed – a man perceived to be a weak leader, who would allow the Knesset full use of its power. In its first six months, the new government manipulated its own laws in order to gain greater control of an angry public. Most recently, it declared a state of emergency and gave itself the right to pass laws that temporarily violated Israel's constitution in the interest of national security. The Knesset also extended its term indefinitely by a majority vote, effectively halting democracy in the country.

"Though the Knesset continues to increase its power, it becomes more and more irrelevant. Israeli citizens have had enough. With no control over their own government, continued attacks from within and the threat of a full Arab war, their patience thins. Tired of the international community's politics and regulations and the peace resolutions that it does not enforce, the people are demanding strength – even at the expense of their immediate freedom, which is already being worn away. They require a leader that will not be afraid to stand-up for his people; that will not be so afraid of losing his power that he cannot use it. And so this past summer, what began as a whisper – a call for the dissolution of the parliamentary system – became a roar. Many claim only a monarch can clean-up the corruption, react as fast and powerfully as needed to end the violence tearing the country apart, and secure its borders against the Arabs. General Arel Demsky has emerged as a popular military leader. Using merciless tactics, Demsky successfully combated several terrorist attempts and turned back a Syrian invasion, despite the chaos of his government."

Alan leaned back, obviously waiting for some response.

"And so," Elise jolted in, "we suddenly end up with the possibility of an Israeli king. It's kind-of amazing. Israel has been Jewish for less than 100 years, and despite all the time that passed before that, it's already fulfilling its destiny."

"Destiny is a strong thing. Often we don't realize that we're playing into its hands. And yet at the same time, free will means we can always choose to step away from it."

"That makes no sense, Alan."

"Good. Then you have learned today's lesson."

* * * * *

"Come on. You can do better than that!" Alan yelled at Elise.

She spun around on him, her eyes still light from the plants, and Alan took a surprised step back. "I am trying!" her voice echoed in the greenhouse.

On this afternoon, she was shooting bullets telepathically. Or at least she was trying. Each round, Elise held the bullet in her palm in front of her, as though she were blowing a kiss. With a flick of her eyes, it shot from her hand, but none at a velocity to do any damage. A small pile had formed where the bullets bounced off the back wall.

"Yes, well right now your bullets have the same fatality rate as a ping pong ball!"

"You're unbelievable! What is the point of this anyway?" Elise threw down the remaining bullets so they ricocheted off the floor. "Who the hell cares if I can throw bullets? That's why there are guns!"

Her swearing gave Alan enough anger to retort, "Of course! There is no point. We're doing this for entertainment. Chris, Francis, and I are doing this for our benefit."

Chris and Francis gave him identical looks. *Leave us out of this.*

Elise made a disgusted sound in her throat. "I'm not saying it's for your entertainment. I just don't understand why you are having me do some of these exercises. Bullets this week. Last week it was the daggers, for God's sake! We don't even know if the Other bleeds. I should be practicing getting away from it. Not throwing darts!"

"You need to be able to defend yourself against anything!" Alan sputtered. "Anything! The unthinkable. In places where you cannot always bring guns. You may not get close enough to – you need to work on all skills, even ones that are not obvious for your defense!"

"Yeah. My defense," she replied flatly.

* * * * *

Seraphim, Elise looked again at the list Alan had scrawled for her to read.

Seraphim – The first order of angels, protectors of God's throne. Seraphs have two wings to cover their faces, two to cover their feet, and two for flying. See Isaiah.

Cherubim – The second order of angels. Close in appearance to humans

179

with a double set of wings. Cherubim know God intimately and represent his power and ability to be anywhere.

Thrones – The third order of angels. They are made of the elements that can bring anyone closer to God: humility, peace, and submission

Dominions – The fourth order of angels. They act to organize the other angels and make God's desires known.

Virtues – The fifth order of angels. They rule over all of nature and appear as bright, shining beings.

Powers – The sixth order of angels. Defenders against evil spirits and defenders of humans. They appear as mighty warriors.

Archangels – The seventh order of angels. Important messengers who deliver prophecies and God's Word to those who need Him.

Principalities – The eighth order of angels. An example of God's ultimate power. Though they disdain human life and show little awe even for God, He commands them at all times.

Angels – The ninth order of the angels. Very similar in shape to humans. They shuttle prayers and their answers between God and His followers.

Elise sat back with arms crossed, wondering which order she belonged to.

She frowned at Alan, who sat with yet another book. For some reason, he didn't want her looking up Remiel yet. He refused to tell her why; only that she needed more background before she read what was written about herself. But she didn't think that was his real reason – he never looked her in the eye when he gave it. What was written about Remiel that Alan didn't want her to see? She was growing tired of his secrets.

Watching him out of the corners of her eyes, Elise picked up Alan's tattered reference book from the table and turned to "R."

"Are you done with the list, yet?" he spoke over his book.

She jumped, "Yes."

* * * * *

Chris found Elise in the kitchen. She was reading a newspaper. Like the rest of them, she was an avid follower of the international section now.

He stepped up behind her closer than he should.

She didn't startle – she knew it was him. Instead, she leaned back so he could see over her shoulder. "He doesn't look like anything special, does he?"

Chris pretended to be interested in the paper. "Who is he?"

"Arel Demsky: the man most Israelis are calling to be king," she threw a duh glance back at him, still unsurprised by his closeness. Looking at the grainy color photo, "I wonder if he's the one. Does Christ's blood run

180

through your veins?" She traced his profile with one finger.

"There are several fringe leaders that threaten the prime minister," Chris pointed out as he continued the attempt to uphold his part of the conversation.

"Yeah, but this guy's the most popular. And, he is the least ambitious. He always declines, saying he just wants the current leadership to take charge. That makes me think it's him. Like Christ, I think the Second Coming would be a reluctant king."

She turned around then, too fast for him to move back, and Chris held his breath. Elise looked up at him, bold, inches from him. Only his height kept her face from being dangerously close.

"What am I supposed to do with him?" she asked.

It took him a moment to register the question. "What do you mean?"

"No one says anything about it. When the king does come forward, what do I do with him?"

"We keep him from coming to the throne," he stated the obvious, following the lines of her face with his eyes.

"Do you think that's enough? Doesn't it leave too many untied strings, too many risks? I think there's more to it than that. I think Alan wants me to kill him."

The words were jarring, and Chris did step back. "That's a big conclusion to jump to," he tried to look anywhere but at her.

"I think that's why he's training me the way he is. Not just to survive, because I am not meant to survive. What's left for me here after this? Kids, a house?"

Chris blanched at the harshness of her words and noticed she did not even blink.

"Love?" she spit the word with anger and saw the wound in his eyes. It was there often now, whenever they discussed the future. "You know as well as I, I'm not meant to have those things. Alan's training me to kill this man," she smiled cruelly. "And I'd be willing to bet he got his orders from a lot higher up. How ironic is that? The same religion that preaches love and peace, the same God that commands thou shalt not kill, is setting me up on an assassin's mission. A suicide assassin's mission."

"If that's what you really believe, then you should confront Alan," Chris refused to respond to the fearsome anger in her voice by keeping his own calm. Sometimes, he was certain she lashed out at him on purpose, knowing that somehow, his happiness had become tied to her own and she could make him hurt with her. "Something like this should not be left festering. Ask him." Chris left the kitchen.

She did not stop him.

She knew it even as she did it – she was cruel to the one person who really tried to understand her. Alan didn't care – he tried but always the task was the most important thing. Francis understood her without trying, but he gave her no sympathy. Only Chris had this soft spot. She wanted to run after him and ask him to forgive her, to tell him she was just frustrated and confused and tired and weak, to perhaps grasp his hand in the risky way she did when they were alone now.

She did not – in some ways that would hurt him even more.

* * * * *

But he was right. It was time to have a heart-to-heart with Alan. Still, there was one other thing to do first. Elise went to Alan's book, pressed her fingers into its worn corner just as he often did, and found the "R" section again. No interruptions – she was going to know.

Remiel – An archangel that stands before God's thrown. Named in the book of Enoch. *Often described as the angel that is over those that rise from the dead and God's mercy The name is seen also as Uriel or Jeremiel. Remiel is sometimes known as a traitor. Enoch numbers her with the fallen.*

Elise found Alan outside raking leaves (far more seriously than she and Chris). He heard her approach as she tramped through one of the piles he created.

"I wish you wouldn't track those leaves. They were ready to bag," he pointed out in way of greeting.

"And I wish you would be honest with me," Elise replied.

Alan turned around and squinted at her through the fall sunlight, ready for dangerous, bitter anger. He was surprised to see Elise's cool business expression.

He propped the rake in front of him and removed his gardening gloves. The chill bit at his fingers immediately and he thought of suggesting they go inside. But the set look on her face kept him from speaking it out loud. "What do you want me to be honest about?"

"Everything. Today, however, I want to clear up a few particular points."

"They are?"

"What is expected of me with regards to the potential king of Israel? Both your expectations and those above yours?"

"Fair enough. I take it you want the blunt version," he grunted.

Elise nodded and replied with a smirk, "I thought I could rely on you for that."

Alan leaned against the rake. "Simply, you are expected to ensure that the man with Christ's blood never comes to the throne of Israel."

"How will we know it's him?"

"That's why Francis is still here, my dear. And there are many more men like him in the Vatican. Together, they have a good track record. We have faith the visionaries will be able to pick the king out easily enough."

"And if Francis does find the one man? Then what?" Elise returned to the question she was most anxious to have answered.

"Then we will make sure he never comes to any type of power," he shrugged.

"To what lengths?"

Alan finally looked uneasy. "Whatever it takes," he replied quietly.

"Even taking his life?" she said with a small catch in her voice that threatened to break her projected indifference.

"Yes," Alan answered. "It has been discussed among the highest officials of the Church, as you insinuated. It seems the only safe way to know that the threat is over and the job is finished. More likely than not, this will end in his death. The bloodline will have to continue on in some other vein."

To his surprise, Elise nodded her agreement even as she said, "It's unfair. I am asked to commit a mortal sin by the Church that named murder a mortal sin. My soul to save all of yours."

"I don't think it will cost you your soul," Alan protested. "God sent you here for this purpose. Your soul–"

"Didn't purpose cost Judas his?" Her words cut through the air, leaving even Alan speechless. "Did God forgive Judas because someone had to betray Christ to his death, and he was chosen? Did God save Judas because deceit was his destiny, and necessary for the saving of humanity?

"I know you don't know the answer. And that's a question I have to live with," she concluded as the edge in her voice subsided. "Though it is unfair and it goes against everything I've ever believed about myself, like you, I feel it is the only way to be sure."

"You see why the training is so critical, then?"

"Yes. I need to be able to take his life; not just defend myself from the Other." She looked out across the field next door to where the town began again. "I wonder where that thing is and how close. I guess it took it twenty years to find me the first time, but...chances are I won't survive, will I?"

Alan sucked in breath audibly. "We will do everything, everything we can to make sure your life is not compromised. There will be no suicide missions, if that's what you mean. But," keeping his vow to bluntness, "it seems unlikely that, once the task is done, you will be allowed to continue."

He studied her face. Though she tried to hide it, he could see the fear creeping in around her eyes. "I know it seems cruel, like being diagnosed with cancer. You're young. I wish I could tell you I thought you had a different fate."

"But I appreciate that you didn't," she paired the words with a frank smile. "I know. Ever since I've come here, things feel differently, like time is passing faster for me," she looked out towards the fields across the street, as though even now she saw something he did not. "I even think I've made progress towards accepting whatever must be. But, the rest of me – the part that isn't Remiel – still fights against it." She saw Alan's version of concern on his face. "I'm fine, really. A little angry, but I'll deal."

With a sigh, she changed the subject. "I looked myself up even though you told me not to. I read what the books say about Remiel. No one is sure whose side I'm on."

"The book of *Enoch,* found in the *Apocrypha* and one of the Dead Sea Scrolls, calls you one of the greatest angels, but also one of those who fell. However, the translation from Hebrew is often difficult and up for debate. Sometimes, the angel referenced is Remiel. Other times it's Jeremiel. Some scholars believe Enoch was talking about the same angel, but miswrote its name in several places. Others, myself included, believe he was writing about two separate beings: Remiel the trumpeter and Jeremiel the fallen. I assume you will take the same perspective?"

"I don't have much choice. But, it bothers me. The line between good and evil is so thin. I am possibly an angel, possibly demon. Satan was God's most devoted angel, but he fell. Judas was a disciple who loved and hated his master at the same time. It's all betrayal and deceit – nothing is as it seems. The good are asked to do horrible things, and the bad are unwittingly working for the good. And I am asked to kill someone whom I have never met, who has Christ's blood coursing through him."

"I can't help you with the philosophy of it, Elise. I know what I know, and I can help you with that. No one is supposed to understand God. So, get used to it." It was the only way he knew to answer her.

"All right – then keep helping me with what you do know. The angel Gabriel. He's also a trumpeter. Some sources claim he is the final trumpeter and the one who will call for the end of days. How can you be sure Remiel is even the right angel?"

"The easiest question you've asked. The Bible names only three angels: Michael, Gabriel and Raphael. All three are trumpeters. And, Gabriel is described to be a great messenger. Some historians and religious writers assumed that, because he delivered some of the most important messages in the Bible for God, he would be the angel to deliver the news of the Second Coming. It's just an assumption.

"In the book of *Enoch,* a different story is told. Although the book is a part of the Apocrypha, historians have found it to be quite reliable. It is even referenced by several of the Gospels, so we can accurately say that the earliest members of the Church knew and trusted it. After literally centuries of study, the Congregation believes this book has the most accurate listing of the trumpeters and their tasks. In *Enoch*, Remiel is said to be the angel of the souls of men. And so, it will be you who calls for the dead to rise."

"How long are we staying in Whiteley?" she switched directions again.

"Until Francis sees the king. Or, until Whiteley is no longer safe for you. I can't imagine how the Other found you the first time, but it must have some way of tracking you. This is an unobvious spot. But, no one pretends it's perfect. As soon as one of those two things happens, we will find another place."

They were quiet, with only the sound of leaves between them. Again, she turned her head towards the fields, and Alan followed her gaze – only broken corn stalks and mud.

"Be honest with me." Elise frowned without looking at him. "It will be easier."

"Obviously, I was going to tell you all of this. It just seems like small doses are the best route. You were ready to hear it now. A week ago, I don't think you were."

"I want to read more of the *Apocrypha*," she ignored his point. "It seems to have some of the answers I'm looking for." She turned on her heal to head back to the house.

"Fine. I'll have Chris and Francis begin pulling passages," he spoke to her retreating back. At the last moment before she entered the house, he called after her in a tight voice unfamiliar to him. "We will go with you, Elise. Chris, Francis and I – we will follow you to the very end, all of our lives forfeit."

"I know." She turned back and smiled. "I didn't have to ask if I was alone."

* * * * *

It was obvious Elise and Alan reached some sort of understanding. Some of the tension in Elise eased and she became generally more pleasant. The library was completely open to her, and Alan now gave full reports after his phone conversations in Latin. Rather than clash in the greenhouse, they now both had zeal to increase her powers. She was diligent and soon mastered some of the tasks she found difficult only days before. As Alan hoped, she became stronger.

And more aggressive. Elise stopped just experimenting and became focused on violence. This day, they watched her suck five of the tallest trees dead. "I want to try something."

Francis practically crawled to the far corner of the greenhouse, stuffing tissues in his ears (which he always brought now) to stop the bleeding. Chris and Alan were too entranced by Elise to see how he was doing. Her eyes glowed so brightly, their beams could be seen even in the daylight. Chris looked at Alan, but he seemed to have no more an idea of what was about to happen than he did.

Elise waited, concentrating and feeling the power pulsating through her. She closed her right hand into the tightest fist she could make. *Feel it hard, like a rock, solid all the way through.* She thought it and thought it until her hand began to feel incredibly heavy. She tried to open her fingers, but found she couldn't, as though her mind welded them together. *Hard, harder.* The feeling began to travel up her arm.

With a nod to the priests, like a child ensuring her parents are watching her next move, she sprinted. Faster and faster, half the length of the greenhouse already. Her senses were alight with power – all the fragrances of the plants (pine, floral, fruit) filled her as they passed in blur, a kaleidoscope of green with dashes of color.

At the height of her speed, she swung her right arm with every ounce of strength she could muster and barely felt the first crack as she hit a small pine tree, then a larger one. She hit every sapling to the end of the row. She knew, not so much by feel, but by the deafening crashing that fell behind her.

When Elise stopped and turned around, even she wondered to see the disaster behind. The smallest trees were cut in half and now lay in twos, and the larger were broken where she hit them, splintering and falling over. Easily twenty trees lay in pieces.

She took several deep breaths – it began to catch-up with her towards the end. Her arm felt blown up with fluid, no longer hard, and she looked down to see a mangled limb with easily every bone broken. She had repaired even as she used it, but not enough.

Alan and Chris approached from the other end, Francis following more slowly. Quickly, she felt for one of the dying pine trees and took the rest. Francis halted at the other end, sensing her. Before Alan and Chris reached her, the arm at least hung right, though it remained red with blood and hugely swollen.

"I think you just got your donation's worth of dead trees," she spoke to Alan.

Chris reached around and lifted up her arm. Elise winced, but did not withdraw. Even as he watched, it continued to heal.

"I know. I should've gone into professional karate chopping," she smiled at his awe.

But Alan was the most pleased. "I'd like to see anyone stand up to that," he took another survey of the damage. "Do it again."

* * * * *

As Alan promised, the *Apocrypha* was strange. Though the books were Christian, Elise sometimes barely recognized them as the same religion save for the familiar names. Full of incantations, superstitions, and magic, they sometimes seemed as heretical and unbelievable as Roman mythology.

She began with the *Sixth and Seventh Books of Moses*. It was a short, tattered volume that Chris gave her from his seminary days.

He offered her a brief introduction. "The Church believes that Moses wrote the first five books of the Bible: *Genesis, Exodus, Leviticus, Numbers,* and *Deuteronomy.* But, two other books were found and also credited to him, unofficially of course. They are called simply the sixth and seventh books, and were supposedly secretly used by the high priests of Aaron to gain holy knowledge. They hold magical secrets, including angelic seals, magic psalms, demon names, and spells. Enjoy."

He left her alone with them.

The book then immediately went into seven incantations. Each brought an angel forth to the conjurer in human form when the summons was spoken aloud. Seven seals were depicted; if recreated and kept on the body, they were purported to bring wealth, love, long life, and fulfill other various desires including procuring treasure from the ground.

Dark... she read the incantations but was careful not to say a single word aloud. Though they spoke of angels, they seemed demonic with their call for ultimate control and promise of material things. If that wasn't enough, demon names were actually listed; their incantations to procure different magic (she was definitely going to close the book once the sun went down). It was unsettling to read the names of the most horrible beings thought of. It made them more real and gave new weight to the power hunting her. She read with particular chill about the demon Asmoday – a fallen angel with knowledge of the future, and three heads. *The Other?*

Halfway through, Elise came upon some yellowed notebook papers jammed into the crevice of pages. They were delicate with age, and she unfolded them with light fingers. Immediately, she recognized Chris' handwriting, though faded, on several dated entries.

She raised her eyes to see that she was still alone.

Put them back.

She was.

Put them back without so much as reading the first word.

Insight into the man – not the priest – was too seductive.

June–

I find seminary particularly hard. The studying is fine. But, the calling can be infuriating. In my heart, I know this is my place. In my heart, I have

187

faith. But, in my mind, I find it devastatingly difficult to keep doubt from snuffing my beliefs. It asks me often: aren't you a fool, grasping onto the unproven belief that you aren't alone? Isn't religion a mere crutch to keep from despair?

September–

I am praying for a sign. Is it wrong to pray for one? I just need something before I take my final vows and complete this, promising my life to the Church. I need some peace; something that I can hang onto even on my darkest days and say there is no other explanation. I will know, because I saw it, I felt it.

And so I pray, though the Bible says "Test not your God." If He truly knows me, then He will understand and forgive me. Otherwise, how can I ever serve Him? How can I show others the path to true belief when I have yet to find–

A noise in the kitchen made Elise jump and her cheeks pink. It was Chris – she immediately slid the notebook paper back into the book and flipped the page (who cared if it crumpled now?) so he would not see the transgression. These were the parts of him that he didn't want her to know; that he'd barely shown her. *I'm always a fact guy. Seeing helps me to believe.* But he hadn't told her the half of it. She thought of him in the church and wished he could see how good he actually was.

But, he didn't even turn her way. Oblivious, he grabbed something from the fridge and then sat with his back to her munching quietly and reading the newspaper with his shoulders hunched in the dim, end-of-day light. He had been more aloof lately, and careful not to find himself alone with her.

"Done for the day?" at last he called over as he turned on a light to better read by.

"Yeah. Here's your book back," she stood and handed him the old hardcover, journal entries inside. "Thanks for loaning it to me."

"No problem. I was under penalty of death from Alan," he took the book, barely looking up.

Elise watched him while he was not watching her, moved towards him, then hesitated, shrugged to no one and suddenly reached for him and squeezed his hand. He pulled back surprised, but she stepped into him and rested her head gently on his shoulder. Just barely, so his shirt fibers brushed her skin and she could suddenly feel small against him. It was an expression of understanding, of shared loneliness. Though a priest, he was imperfect as she was, full of indecision and error. He wasn't innately superior; it was his strength and discipline that made the difference.

His heart pulsed fast – she could hear it. She closed her eyes for a moment, burning his warmth into her memory. Then, without a word, she stepped away and headed to her room, door closed.

* * * * *

"How are you feeling?" Alan asked Francis with a hand on the monk's shoulder. It was early, the trees outside barely visible in the palest of morning light. They were always awake several hours before Elise and Chris.

Fine, Francis gave a reassuring smile as he looked up from the stack of newspapers to write. *Better after sleep. The stronger she gets, the harder it gets. The good news – she's getting strong.*

"I wonder why you have such a reaction to her." Alan poured himself a cup of coffee from the pot Francis was already half way through. "I know you're sensitive to these things, but... her power is God sent. You would think it wouldn't be so negative."

Francis waited for Alan to turn back to him before responding, *She gives off an energy that I am sensitive to. Nothing more. My symptoms are similar to that of other energy reactions: radiation, loud sound waves. Headaches, nausea, bloodied eardrums, bruising.*

"Amazing. I mean, it's too bad. But still, amazing." He nodded to the newspapers. *Anything worth looking at?*

None of the insurgents have the mark. The king remains hidden.

"Good. We're not exactly ready yet," Alan glanced down the hall towards the closed bedroom door.

Like I said, she is getting stronger. The angel is more in her now, even when she is not turned-up. The Other – she won't just stand there and give up the next time. You're making her a formidable opponent, Alan.

Alan did not acknowledge the compliment, but picked up a newspaper. "Word is spreading in the Church about her, and I am having a hard time keeping away both the skeptics and the allies. The more information I report about what she can do, the less doubt there is about who she is and how important. Soon, the Cardinals won't let her stay here. If we can only have a few more months, though, we'll be ready. It might even be easy if we have that long, the way she continues to learn new things."

All she needs is time.

* * * * *

There were thousands of angels, thousands of sources.

Azrael was the angel for reviving souls (he held an apple from the tree of life under the nose of the dead body); Arakiel, Samiel and Aziel lead the souls of men to judgment; Mastema tempted and tested men for God, and was credited with hardening the heart of Pharaoh in *Exodus*; Enoch ascended to heaven and became the angel Metatron; and on and on. "Hocus pocus" was actually a Jewish phrase used in magical rites, which called for the power of "angels on high" (Elise would never use that one again so lightly).

Angels were not believed to have any gender and therefore, could not multiply, though they often took human form when speaking to humans. The Catholic Church believed in guardian angels and preached that each person was assigned one or more at birth. The Virgin Mary was sometimes said to be the queen of the angels.

Islam, however, wrote that angels (or malaika) were given the task of scribes. They wrote down all deeds, good and bad, to help God with judgment. Their legends claimed that angels were made of light, while demons were made of fire.

And then there was Thomas Aquinas, who had his own version of things – a 1200 page version, which Elise decided not to touch (Alan would be good for a synopsis). He claimed to be visited by angels and gave in minute detail all the hierarchies of heaven.

"Very legitimate," Elise commented to herself. She could see why Alan directed her to the Bible first. Mixed in with the truth was a lot of superstition and well, craziness.

It was raining out, and the living room was cast in a dull gray light. She looked out the window often to interrupt the dull stream of information. The leaves were almost completely gone from the trees – a hard wind had swept them away a few nights before. The fall was ending. She was glad to have some of her winter clothes back (Alan arranged for her dorm room to be packed and shipped to storage near Whiteley; she had retrieved a few things).

But beyond the pages and pages of legend and the distractions, Elise did have a goal for the day. She wanted to look up the other trumpeters. *Raphael, Uriel, Raguel, Michael, Sariel, Gabriel and Remiel.*

Raphael – Specializes in healing and nurturing. He guards young people and supervises the guardian angels.

Uriel –Fire of God. In Enoch, *he is the angel that watches over thunder and terror. It is believed by the Catholic Church that Uriel is the angel who guards the gate of the lost Garden of Eden. He is known as God's vengeance, and is the angel that will go to hell on the last day to bring forth the demons for final judgment.*

Raguel – The angel who watches over other angels to keep them from falling.

Michael – Chief soldier, he leads the angels to battle. He is also considered to be the angel of death who conducts souls to the afterlife.

Sariel – The command of God. He takes responsibility for the destiny of angels who flout God's laws.

Gabriel – God's messenger. He is the angel who told Mary she was with child. Folklore claims he can interpret dreams and teach the childe in the womb. Muslims believe he dictated the Koran to Mohammed.

* * * * *

"You go in on that side," Alan commanded before he ducked into the priest's half of the confessional.

With a deep breath, Elise did as she was instructed. *You must be absolved of your sins before receiving First Communion*, Francis had explained in one of their sessions. And since Francis' handicap rendered him incapable of doing it himself, Alan took the job.

The confessional was a tiny room in the back of the church. Elise had never seen it open before. Her half was simple – a kneeler and some bad wallpaper. A screen was positioned at the level of the kneeler's head to blur and make indistinguishable the face of the person opposite. She could see Alan's shadow through it, taking a seat on the other side.

As she had been instructed, Elise knelt, made the sign of the cross and said, "Bless me Father, for I have sinned. This is my first confession, and these are my sins." She took a deep breath and wished for Chris. The little things, she could confess to Alan. But, for the others, she wanted mercy.

At least he was behind a screen.

Just work your way down the Commandments. "I am new to the Catholic Church and to God. For most of my life, I have lived in sin, without – knowing God. I am sorry it took me so long, but I am ready now to live differently."

Alan said nothing, so she moved on to the next. "I have taken the Lord's name in vain many times in anger and jokingly. Now that I am joining the Church, I need to work harder to change my habits and always treat God with respect.

"I have not always kept the Sabbath, and I am sorry. But since I have come to Whiteley, I have kept Sunday a holy day," Elise gave a little defense. "And, I will continue to do so."

"Um…I am sorry for dishonoring my parents. Many times since their death," her voice caught. She really wished Chris were behind the screen now. "I have been angry with them for leaving me. I have blamed them for my troubles and my loneliness, and have thought horrible things about them." *Why couldn't I be Presbyterian?* She pushed away the ugly memories. It was humiliating, confessing such personal struggles to the same man she ate three meals a day with – one who was so critical.

And the next commandment – the sin most considered the worst. Though Elise's silence droned on, Alan remained still on the other side.

"I have committed – murder, Father," she finally said in a shaky voice. "I didn't mean it, I was only trying to defend myself," the excuses began to

191

rattle off as the darkness she harbored began to spill. " But I am so sorry. I carry this awful guilt with me all the time. I keep thinking that I should've done something different, that I could've used my power in some other way. And, I worry about his family. They'll never know what happened to their son because I don't have the strength to admit what happened and accept my punishment. I don't know how to fix this, to do the right thing. But I am so sorry. Every day, I'm sorry. I'm sorry, I'm sorry."

She waited for Alan, but again, he said nothing. She licked her lips and rubbed the moisture together. *Thou shall not give false testimony against your neighbor.*

"I have lied many times in my life – mostly white lies and little things I cannot even remember. However, since going into hiding and... murdering," she swallowed, "my lies have become darker. In order to fulfill the task I've been given, I cannot be completely honest. I have to hide what I have done in order to do what you ask, and I have to hide what I am because there are people who would keep me from this. Please forgive me. I will be dishonest only when I have to, and sorry for it always."

"And," she searched. *Thou shall not covet.*

The longest pause yet grew between Elise and the priest. She knew immediately that the sin was hers, but found it impossible speak it out loud to Alan. But if she didn't... *He's under oath to keep forever silent about what you tell him, and as a priest, he can't judge,* she coached herself. *He must offer you absolution, no matter what you say, so long as you are sorry.*

Still, she swayed. Tell him everything, or keep this one little thing secret? She wanted to be forgiven for everything; she wanted to feel clean, as Francis promised she would. She wanted to be as worthy as the next person. If she held back...

"Recently, I have committed the sin of coveting." She closed her eyes, so that she could not even see Alan's shadow. "I have not acted upon it, of course, but there is a... person that I know I cannot have, but that I have sometimes wanted. Please forgive me and give me strength, Father.

"And," she quickly moved on, "I have not always kept Jesus' commandment, to love thy neighbor as thyself. I am too quick to anger; I am not always patient. And, that's it." She opened her eyes and readjusted to the shadows of the room. She remembered the final line Francis taught her to say. "For these and all the sins of my past, I am truly sorry."

There was movement on the other side of the screen, as Alan finally prepared to respond. Elise waited for his usual harshness without resentment. Reviewing the long list of her sins, she bowed her head and waited for his justified rebuttal.

"My daughter in Christ," he paused and cleared his throat. "It is not often that I hear a confession such as yours."

Elise lowered her head further in shame.

He continued, "Though you have sinned, sometimes greatly, your sorrow is real and painful. For many of your transgressions, you've already suffered more than any penance I can give you." Elise raised her head in surprise and tried for the first time to see Alan through the screen, to get just a hint of his expression. She could not.

"That said, there are several areas in your life for you to work on. Respecting God in all ways is one of them, from the Sabbath, to respecting His name. You are now conscious of those things. Each time you realize that you have transgressed, I want you to say an Our Father, to remind yourself of your focus.

"Try to be more forgiving in your life. Forgive your parents; forgive those you meet every day and give them the grace that you so long for. Whenever you feel angry, remind yourself of the sins you just presented to me.

"Channel your gifts positively," Alan hesitated, and she knew why. "As positively as you are able. The task before you is not easy, so just do your best with it. As you said, be as honest as you can while still being true to God in the other ways that you have been asked. I'm sorry I can't tell you more than that."

His voice hardened, "Lastly, this person you desire – never, never tell him how you feel."

Her face burned hot even as she breathed relief and thankfulness that Alan didn't mention the name that hung between them.

"Coveting is human; resisting is disciplined, and discipline is divine. Continue asking for strength and denying what you feel, and soon, it will be a sin you no longer need to confess.

"Tonight I want you to meditate on these improvements; not the past but moving forward. Spend the evening reading scripture, and before you go to bed, pray the rosary. Awake tomorrow with renewed faith. And now, please perform an Act of Contrition."

Dutifully, she recited, "O my God, I am heartily sorry for having offended Thee. I detest all my sins because of Thy just punishments, but most of all because they have offended Thee, my God, who art all good and deserving of all my love. I firmly resolve, with the help of Thy grace, to confess my sins, to do penance, and to avoid the near occasion of sin. Amen."

Alan took up the prayer, "God, the Father of mercies, through death and resurrection of His Son has reconciled the world to Himself and sent the Holy Spirit among us for the forgiveness of sins; through the ministry of the Church may God give you pardon and peace, and I absolve you from your sins in the name of the Father, the Son, and the Holy Spirit."

"Amen," Elise replied.

"Your sins are forgiven. Go in peace," Alan finished.

At his words, Elise closed her eyes, her soul briefly quieted. *Your sins are forgiven.*

* * * * *

"You need to concentrate, Elise!" Alan repeated for the second time. "These tests are nothing compared with what you will face. You need to survive anything, use anything, heal against anything!"

Elise was already turned-up, and had just telekinetically lifted two of the largest trees. They floated several feet off the ground, bobbing up and down as the arms of her thoughts fought to keep them airborne. She squinted at them through the blond haze that was becoming more and more familiar.

They fell with a crash that made everyone jump.

Elise marched around in a circle with her hands on her hips, like a runner just over the finish line. She breathed hard. "They're – really heavy. I'm really trying, but I can't hold them for very long."

Francis reentered through a side door; he could no longer stay in the same room with her turned-up. Again the official marker: she was turning-up higher.

"I know we've all been avoiding this, but," Elise decided to breach the subject, "when we go after this king, I'm not exactly going to be using plants. I really can do more with energy from people. Tons more!" She stopped marching and shrugged. "It hurts – I won't lie to you. But, I know when to stop, and I've never known anyone to have lasting problems from it. I know you are afraid – and I understand why. But…"

The three men looked at each other, and no one moved.

Elise grew exasperated. "It does burn. And, afterwards, you will feel tired. But, I don't have to hold on very long. A little goes a long way when I take from people. I might steal a few of your thoughts, and you may get a few of mine, but other than that…don't tell me that it hasn't been considered! I'm surprised the Vatican hasn't already been sending me bodies to–"

"I'll do it," Chris stepped forward. He nodded at her in assurance, his eyes lit with a strange hunger.

She frowned. Though he could not realize, his old words rested between them and she knew instantly he did not step forward to help her. *I want a sign. I will pray for one.* Slowly, she shook her head. "No, I really don't want to turn-up on you, Chris," her voice apologized.

For a moment, he looked confused. Then anger, as he had never before exhibited to her, hardened his face. "Why not?" The desire openly played his features. She was reminded of an addict refused a hit.

"It's nothing personal," she tried to make it sound like a sneer. "I just don't want to. And Francis is out of the question. He won't have any eardrums left if I touch him. So Alan, I'm asking you."

"But he's old!" Chris sputtered.

"Hey!" Alan turned sharply.

"Well, you are!" Back to Elise, "What makes you think he would be a better candidate than me? I'm strong and I'm not afraid," his eyes found hers and locked. "I think I should be the one."

Elise sighed. "Look, it's not up for discussion. Alan, either you do it, or we forget I said anything."

Chris made a disgusted noise and crossed over to a bench where he sat down loudly. Francis followed him and sat down. When Elise gave him a questioning look, he wrote, *I want to see this.*

"If you think you can handle it," she tossed up a hand to say, *the consequences are yours.*

Elise and Alan faced each other, now the only two on the greenhouse floor. "Will you do it, Alan?"

"I trust you." He kept his voice in tight control, too tight. Unlike Chris, he was afraid. But he kept steady steps as he approached and held out his hand, as if in some morbid handshake.

It seemed impossible that they were ever soft. They were speckled with sunspots and veins, and wrinkled near the wrists and at the knuckles. Elise slid her own taught-skinned hand into his loose one, and Alan splayed his footing to brace himself. His eyebrows knit together with worry. "What happened to the trees – the burn marks on their bark. Will that happen to me?"

"No. I won't hold on that long," she promised and held tighter despite the tremble in his fingers. "It only hurts for a minute."

The zap came for them both. Alan yelled and then bit down hard on his tongue. It felt as though she put his arm to sleep, prickling up and down his shoulder. The sensation intensified rapidly until he cried out again with the burning, like he put his hand directly on a hot stove or the bottom of an iron. Soon, it wasn't just his arm, but his whole body. It felt like he was vibrating, like he was being microwaved until he was mush. He wasn't even sure if the floor was still beneath him.

In a moment, he was on his knees.

Behind them, Chris stood. *What is she doing? He's too weak for this!* It looked like Alan was having a heart attack – he breathed hard, hissing air in and out between his teeth. His free hand clasped the wrist of his other, as if he wanted to wrench it free from her grasp. He held on, however, and she showed him no mercy. "That's enough!"

But Elise only heard the whispers, exploding louder than they had in weeks. She arched her neck back as their tones threaded through her mind.

195

Alan had much strength in him: he was seeping into her. She felt euphoric, like floating. The light rays from within blinded her eyesight. A thought came to her; Alan was remembering a high fever he had as a child. *Burning...* his mind thought.

But she would not make him bend; she didn't want to get nearly that close. *Just enough, just enough to test myself.* When the whispers became deafening and she began to feel the strange, dark urge to keep going, Elise let go. Alan collapsed in front of her, doubled over and clutching his arm. Chris was running towards them, yelling something, but she did not hear.

She turned from them and faced the greenhouse. Alan's life force was stronger than all of the trees and plants combined. She felt invincible with it flowing through her, just waiting to be tapped, and she reached out with her mind.

Unlike before, everything was clear. She could feel all things in the greenhouse simultaneously, as though she had her fingers on each one. Elise closed her eyes, smiling, feeling everything, everything. Everything shaking.

Chris quit his frantic care of Alan to look up. The trees, the potted plants, all of them were trembling, even those on the catwalk. Clinking as the clay pots chipped together, rustling as the branches shifted – it was like an earthquake only the floor did not move.

Elise raised her hands and every plant in the room followed, lifting off the ground. They staid in their perfect rows even as they rose higher. Elise remained steady, the light in her eyes barely faded. Inside, she felt butterflies, like she was on the first hill of a roller coaster. She was using everything she had in a display of power greater than anything she remembered seeing, let alone attempting. She arched her eyebrows and some of the rows began to move, twisting and swirling slowly. Like finely choreographed dancers, trees and plants flew threw the air at one another, but never touching.

Her arms began to shake – she barely noticed. But, it was a signal to start taking them down. With control (unlike before), she worked to move all in air back to where they were on ground. She lowered her arms and the trees followed. Slowly, slowly, they landed with the softest thuds.

With a triumphant smile and victorious clenched fists, she turned and faced her audience of three. Her smile faded.

Alan was still doubled over. He was pale as ash, and his eyes watered his cheeks and made them shine. Francis was kneeling by the bench. He had thrown-up everywhere, and even now held back retching. Blood was drying on his neck from his ears. And Chris, worst of all, was looking at her with gaped mouth. The expression on his face was unmistakable – she saw it before, early one morning in her dorm. He feared her.

* * * * *

196

Everyone needed a rest that afternoon, and a quiet like none Elise ever heard before settled on the rectory. Alan was recovering with a nap (Elise let him have her room). She kept him hydrated with water and teas, trying to make up for hurting him. Francis too was resting on the couch. He smiled at her reassuringly and wrote many times, *I wanted to be there. I had to see you do that.*

Chris hardly said a word to her, however. He put something in the oven for dinner and then sat in the armchair in the living room without looking at her. Was he angry with her for hurting Alan? Was he angry with her for playing with power (she knew he felt uneasy about many of the recent lessons)? Was he still angry she chose Alan in the first place? She watched for the moment to confront him.

It came when Chris stood-up (still without a word) and pulled on some shoes. He was headed to the church for something. Elise waited until she couldn't hear his footsteps on the walk, and then followed.

She found him kneeling in the second pew. "Hey," she let him know she was there before she got too close, and then came down the aisle. "Move over," she commanded. With a wary look, he complied. She genuflected and knelt next to him.

"Why are you angry with me?"

"I'm trying to pray."

"Praying is less effective if you are angry with someone, and have not yet forgiven them."

Chris rolled his eyes. "There are days I regret that we're teaching you everything we know." But his voice had softened already, and Elise hoped it wouldn't be too bad.

"So, why are you angry with me?"

Chris leaned back against the pew. He looked at her, and she looked back. His eyes belied some pain she caused.

"Touch me," he whispered.

Elise jerked her head back. "What?"

"Touch me, the way you touched Alan."

"I thought that might be it. But, I can't. I'm sorry."

"What—why?" his voice pleaded. "I don't understand. Why won't you—"

"Why do you want me to touch you so badly? Tell me why first." She stood and moved back to the aisle.

"Because I want to feel it. My whole life, I've searched and tried to feel God. You know, I didn't have the dream like the other priests. I've never directly experienced…since you've come, I've seen some amazing things that I know only He could let you do. I have faith like I've never had," he smiled large and looked up at the ceiling, his words sent upwards as much as to her. "But, I want to feel it. I want to feel what you must know every day. Be my dream." He held out his hand for her to take.

"And that's why I can't," her voice sounded wet with crying, though her eyes staid dry. "I can't be that for you. Alan didn't need to feel it. He believed already."

"I do believe," Chris protested and stood. "I do. I told you. I believe now, more than I ever thought I could. I just want this one little thing."

Elise took two steps backwards, as though he threatened her. Chris' eyebrows creased.

"Test not your God," she said.

"What is that supposed to mean?"

"You know. You wrote it," she gave herself away. "I found one of your journal entries tucked in one of the books you gave me. Even then, you thought it was wrong to ask for a sign," she took another step back as his face turned rouge with embarrassed blood. "And that's why I can't. I wouldn't be your friend if I helped you with that."

The hand Chris extended shook, and he felt dizzy with anger and humiliation. *How could she read those letters? How could she–* "I don't need you to parent me. I don't need you to save me, Elise," he sneered.

When she did not respond, he yelled, "Just do it! Just touch me! YOU GAVE IT TO HIM, NOW GIVE IT TO ME!"

Elise stumbled a few feet backwards and then ran. The door banged back against the wall as she threw it open to escape.

To escape me. Chris closed his eyes and stood perfectly still.

* * * * *

Elise looked at herself in the mirror. She wore a calf-length white dress with a lace overlay that she found on the clearance rack at the nearby mall (if 20 miles could be considered nearby). It had no sleeves, so she put a white cardigan over it. The whites almost matched – one was slightly more yellow than the other. It would have to do.

She put on light powder and pink lip gloss, and pulled her strawberry blond hair back into a bun with a few carefully crafted curls left to hang by her ears. With a soft tissue, she blotted her lips – she didn't want to leave any pink marks on the chalice.

Francis picked a Thursday evening for her First Communion. It was the one night a week when there wasn't something going on at church (Mass, religious classes, the woman's prayer group, etc.). He was in the church now, setting the liturgical props.

A little jewelry would add the finishing touch. She slid her mother's engagement ring onto her smallest finger and then pulled out the silver cross

Alan left on her bed that morning (he was too shy to offer it to her himself). She reached back and fixed the clasp. It hung just below the shadows of her neck bones. *Inri*, it read over the crucifix. He could not have presented her with a better gift.

With one last glance at herself, Elise flipped off the light and then walked down the short hall to the living room. It only took a second to see that the rectory was empty – Alan must've joined Francis in the church already. She wondered if Chris was also there. They barely spoke since their argument in the church.

She didn't bother with a jacket, but walked over to the church through the chill air with her stiff white heals clicking against the sidewalk. She stepped inside with only the soft whisper of the closing door. All of the altar candles were lit, and Alan was arranging some fresh flowers on the stage. Francis looked up from the Bible passage he was marking and smiled.

And Chris was at the organ, pushing out a few peals with obvious rust.

"Elise, you can stay in the back to come-up with the processional. Then, you will sit in the front pew until you are called up at different points in the ceremony," Alan called back with a last fluff of a flower.

At her name, Chris looked up and their eyes met. She smiled with the corners of her mouth and flicked her eyes away.

When everything seemed set, Francis and Alan joined her in the back with a banner showing a white dove, the Holy book, and a large crucifix. Chris began to play, and they processed forward to the altar. Alan and Francis moved onto the stage as Elise stood in the front pew. Alan began, "In the name of the Father, the Son, and the Holy Spirit."

Elise now understood the many components of the Mass, no longer left guessing and trying to follow along in the program. She recited the prayers without faltering, and she listened with familiarity to Alan's strong voice recite the passages about the last supper and Jesus' command: "Do this in memory of me." She smiled with special softness at the genuine petition he made for her, for grace and guidance on the next part of the journey. Together, they professed their faith in the Catholic Church and then Francis began blessing the bread and wine as she saw him often do. They spoke the Our Father with bowed heads, once a secret prayer known only by confirmed members of the Church.

"Now offer one another a sign of God's peace," Alan commanded for Francis. The three men descended from the stage. Francis extended his hand first. Though he could not say it, their eyes met. *Peace be with you.*

Alan reached out next and took her hand in both of his. "Peace be with you," he nodded once, hard, for emphasis.

Then, Chris stood in front of her. Elise waited – it was not her peace to make. If he forgave her, he would offer a sign of peace. And, if he did not, she knew she could trust him to stand awkwardly before her, looking over her head somewhere.

He did not hesitate, and held his hand out to her. Leaning across the pew with a relieved half-smile, he whispered, "Peace be with you, Elise."

"Peace be with you, Father Chris." She held his hand long, warm with thankfulness that he was no longer angry. She would have approached the bread and wine with a heavy heart otherwise.

The three men then formed a crescent in front of the altar facing Elise. Francis motioned for her, and she came to stand before them, completing the circle. He pulled out his whiteboard as she approached (something he prepared earlier).

Let us now partake of bread and wine, passing it in a circle as Jesus once did. The writing was neat with no sign of scrawl. It was perfectly centered with small calligraphy tips. Elise again smiled at the thoughtfulness.

"Lord, I am not worthy to receive you, but only say the words and I shall be healed," the three chanted in unison as, without any more ceremony, Francis took the first host and passed it to his right: Alan.

"The body of Christ," Alan whispered it and Elise's heart beat fast. Without the little girls laughing in their white dresses; without the boys squirming in their ties; without grandparents snapping photos in the pews; without parents worrying about picking up the cake; First Communion became the two thousand-year-old admission ritual that it was. Elise, for the first time in her life as she knew it, was to be filled with the something like magic, and become apart of the most enduring human legacy.

With gravity, Francis turned to Elise and held the bone white wafer in front of her face. "The body of Christ," she spoke firm and took it in her hand the way Francis showed her earlier. With her right fingertips, she placed it on her tongue and waited for it to moisten, soften. *Never chew,* Francis had warned. *Wait until it is ready to become a part of you, and then swallow.*

To her surprise, it tasted nothing like bread. It was sweeter in a way that would leave a bad aftertaste in the back of the mouth. Though the flavor was strong and distinct, the Host itself was light, like paper on her tongue. *Sweet paper. I can see why they take wine with –* Elise cut off her own cynicism. She wanted it to be a different moment from the others in her life.

She swallowed just as Francis finally took the host himself. After a few moments pause, he picked up the chalice full of wine. Again, he turned to his right. "The blood of Christ," Alan whispered and took a sip.

Francis used a small white cloth to dab the cup where Alan's lips touched it, and then turned to Elise. "The blood of Christ," she said. Then a splash of taste filled her mouth. It was sugary and good, with no hint of the tartness she associated with most wine. *The monks make it,* Francis had told her once with pride. *Secret methods.*

The chalice continued to pass until it got back to Francis who took the last bit. It was done. She was in.

The priests and Francis returned to the altar, and Elise retreated to the first pew for prayer, as she had been taught. Though often her prayers were full of petitions, that night, she only prayed in thanks.

She heard Francis stand, and the rustle of clothing told her the others did so as well. She finished her prayer and raised her head.

Francis nodded at Alan, who then spoke to her, "Elise, we would like you to say a prayer before we close. Anything you wish," he reassured the growing look of alarm on her face.

She took a deep breath. Prayers at dinner were not enough preparation for this. She searched, but could think of nothing profound; no biblical quotes or anecdotes. With a sigh, she followed in the vein of a personal prayer. "Father, only a few weeks ago, I was lost to you and your purpose…" a pause to think and rock her weight nervously. "Thank you for the men that found me, for their strength, their patience, and their determination. For, just as you chose me, so they are chosen."

Alan raised his hands. "Lord, we thank you for this great blessing, bringing Elise into your church. Though there may be dark days ahead, please help us to recall in our hour of need what you promised in your last book: 'And there shall be no night there; and they need no candle, neither light of the sun; for the Lord God giveth them light; and they shall reign for ever and ever.'"

For the Lord God giveth them light; and they will reign for ever and ever. She hoped he was right.

They recessed in silence, Chris opting to follow down the aisle rather than play the organ. It was October 29th. She was twenty years old.

Chapter 13 – The Normal Day

"We can't get out of it," Chris said for the third time as Alan continued to look skeptical. "The Whiteley Corn Festival is the biggest event in town next to the Fourth of July. Everyone celebrates the recent harvest, all the women in town make food to die for, someone rents a merry-go-round, and the priest traditionally blesses the earth for a good rest before the next season."

"I think we should go anyway, even if we could get out of it," Elise said from a slumped position in the living room armchair. She popped a bubblegum bubble. "I'm so bored."

Alan rolled his eyes. "You're like a spoiled thirteen-year-old."

Her eyes darted warningly at him, but she did not reward him with a reply.

"It's only one day – Saturday. And Mrs. Hutchings informed me that she expects all of us to be there. If you want to keep the residents at bay and the rumors in control, then we can't have two priests, a monk, and a young girl holed up here forever," Chris pointed out the obvious. "We don't have to stay long. Just for the blessing."

Francis raised a hand, as though he were in a classroom.

"Yes, you're invited too," Chris answered him before the first word hit the whiteboard. "I know it isn't something you're used to, but I still think it would be good for everyone if we made an appearance. Who knows what they're saying about you?"

Francis raised his eyebrows.

"Well, I'm in," Elise rolled her head lazily against the back of the chair. "So, it's at least you and me, pal," to Chris.

Alan was fast to chime in then, "Fine, we'll all go. But only until the blessing."

* * * * *

The Whiteley Corn Festival was held annually on the large patch of unfarmed land behind the firehouse. As Chris predicted, several rides (merry-go-rounds, the tilt-a-whirl, spinning apples, and a strange eight-legged thing called the spider) dotted the grounds. The firemen had a huge barbeque pit set up with a sign that read "Last Chicken BBQ of the Year," in dark red paint, like some dire threat. Wooden booths, all painted white by an obvious amateur, dotted the property and housed the honor of the festival in various forms: corn on the cob, corn chowder, corn rum cakes, corn muffins, and corn beers were all lined-up for the tasting.

The four walked through the makeshift gate (two of them very grumpily), bundled by various layers against the typical November weather and giving up puffs of warm breath. Immediately, people began calling to Chris.

"Howdy, ya'll," a woman used a fake southern drawl from beneath a straw hat.

"Hi Judy," Chris smiled to get the social engine warming. "You've met the gang staying over at the rectory, haven't you?"

"Only in church, Father, only in church. I consider it a personal insult that you haven't brought them by the diner," she ribbed him with an elbow.

"Been meaning to, really. It's just been busy," Chris rubbed his side – she got him hard.

"Really? No one has seen you around much for a few weeks, Father. Lot of out of town business?"

"Something like that," Chris began to edge away, giving Alan a meaningful, *I told you so*, look.

"I think it's great," Elise stepped along side him. "It's nice that the whole town looks after you and worries about you. Better than being alone."

* * * * *

They walked the entire length of the field, enjoying more questioning. Francis seemed the most tired by the activity, and took to clutching his whiteboard closely, jumping whenever someone addressed him directly (which was often – he stuck out badly in his black robes).

But Elise was happy. It felt normal – no demons or angels. No one was looking at her, expecting something special. To the town, she was even less than special. She was an outsider who didn't yet have a spot. She was someone to whisper about and criticize; not admire.

"Ride the apples with me," Elise gave a tug to Chris' coat sleeve. He didn't answer, but merely slid his eyes back towards Alan and Francis.

"We should all go. Come on. With the four of us, we would have the fastest spinning apple."

"You've got to be kidding," Alan managed to fold his arms over his bulky coat.

"Nope, scrooge, I'm not. When was the last time you were on a ride? When you were four?"

Chris gave Elise a warning look.

"What? Alan is too serious..." she trailed off as the look got sterner. She laughed and then slung an arm through his. "Everyone needs to lighten up. If all we do is–" she cut herself off from saying the words.

Not today. Today, one day, they were normal.

"Can we get some food anyway?"

Unlike the rides, food was an amiable idea for everyone. Soon, they were immersed in the smells of some of the greatest kitchens within fifty miles. Elise led the tasting by grabbing anything good and passing it back. They wandered in and out of the white booths. Not entirely by accident, Elise found herself with Chris while Alan and Francis fell back, still maneuvering their chowders through the crowd.

"It's such a beautiful day!" she looked up directly at a blazing sun. "It's amazing it doesn't give off any more warmth than that." She turned her eyes to Chris, who actually looked older in the sun with each crow's foot and worry line exposed by a dark shadow. But, Elise didn't care. She saw the tease in his eyes, just waiting to find a moment to pull at the corners of her mouth. With his coat on, Elise couldn't see the priest's collar.

Chris watched her carelessness, revealing the twenty-year-old girl she must've been before they met. In the sun, her hair glowed with red and gold, and her light brown eyes appeared lighter than usual. What he wouldn't give to spend the day with her, alone inside the crowd.

"What are you thinking?" she cocked her head to one side.

"I'm thinking..." he debated the answer. "I'm thinking... thinking...

"This is actually pretty good," Alan interrupted with his bowl of chowder.

"Yeah. It is," Elise kept her eyes on Chris, letting the double-meaning rest between them without shyness. But, he had already lowered his eyes to the ground.

* * * * *

They spent the afternoon filling up on candy apples, homemade moon pies, and popcorn from the oldest popper Elise had ever seen (an antique, she was proudly told by its owner). Several brave, extra warm souls were raising money for the boy scouts in a dunking booth, and Elise teased Alan about registering for the all male beauty contest to be held that night. A trio of trombones began playing, and the group generously gave over all their spare change. The pretty laugh rippled at the slightest joke. When it seemed they had seen (and eaten) it all, and were about to make a second round, someone with a megaphone began announcing, "Foot race to start in ten minutes! If you're thinking of racing, get on up here. Winner takes home a basket of Mrs. Hutching's famous jellies. Place your bets now – but don't tell Sheriff."

"Can anyone participate? I'm actually a pretty good runner," Elise asked Chris through bites of her latest food find: corn on the cob. She was trying to keep butter from getting on her knit gloves, but already the tips were greasy.

"I bet you're great, but the four of us are spectators only, honey," Alan answered for Chris. "We don't need any more attention. And when do we get to do the blessing? This is a lot longer than I thought it would be."

"Corn blessing is at three sharp," Chris was inspecting Elise's cob from a far, pondering if he should get some as well.

"I bet I could even take first place," Elise continued.

"No, especially since we all have a pretty good idea how you could guarantee the win. We just need to get through the blessing, and then we'll go home," Alan sounded like a tired parent in a grocery store.

"Father! Hey father. FATHER!"

It took Chris a few moments to remember he should answer. He looked up to see Derek Dewallace sprinting towards him from the parking lot. "Hold this," he handed Elise his bag of popcorn and stepped away from the group.

"Derek. Is everything okay?" He asked calmly as a matter of course. But by the look on Derek's face, he knew instantly.

"It's Helen." Derek burst into sobs at the sound of his wife's name. "Please come. Please – come," he spoke brokenly. "I d-d-didn't want to l-l-leave her, but she w-w-wanted you. There isn't – much time." Though still mid-afternoon, the sun drained from the day

"Alan, you and Francis handle the blessing, then catch a ride home. I have to go." He didn't look to see if the commands registered. Grabbing Derek's arm, Chris stalked off towards the parking lot.

"What's going on? Who's Helen?" Elise demanded. When neither Francis nor Alan answered, she jogged after Chris and the man he almost carried.

* * * * *

Chris slammed the car door and began to peel away from the curb before he realized Elise was clinging to the passenger door handle. "What are you doing? You aren't supposed to–" She got in, and he didn't have time to tell her not to. With a rubber squeal, he pulled behind Derek's truck to follow him back to the hospital.

"What's happening? Where are you going?" she did not apologize.

"Elise, taking care of sick people is what I do all the time – by myself! You shouldn't be here." He couldn't help but yell under such circumstances.

"I know you don't think so, but I am a priest!"

The words stung her as they were meant to: on more than one level. "I'm sorry. I didn't know, and I just thought you might need me – er – I didn't know." She looked out the window.

"Need you? To do what? Suck the life away from the flowers around her bed?" Though it was harsh, Chris didn't care. "Well, it's too late now. The hospital is forty-five minutes from here, so you are along for the ride. But you shouldn't be! This is personal for Derek and his wife – they don't want an audience and they really don't want a priest who needs some teenager to get through the last rights!"

Elise's eyes burned from the anger in his accusations, but she kept them fixed on the glass of the window, seeing nothing through it, but focusing on the ghostly reflection of herself. She understood; she did it often herself. He was lashing out, pinning something on her that wasn't hers.

"I can't believe I've done this!" he took the thing back and slammed his hands against the steering wheel. "Derek's been calling, but I haven't had the time to see Helen in weeks. I got so distracted," he ran his fingers through his hair until it stood-up.

"I'm sure it's fine," Elise said weakly, though she knew it was the kind of anger that did not want comfort.

"You don't understand! Derek needed me for his faith. He – he must think she's dying because I stopped coming," Chris choked on the words. "I got so caught up in you. Please, God. Don't let her die today. Don't let her die today."

* * * * *

Though it looked like a small office building, it was still a hospital. The smell was the same, like putting one's nose into a medicated bandage. Nurses raced about with charts; patients and their visitors were heard chatting and doctors consulting. But when they reached the fourth floor ward, everything seemed to slow down. And the nurses were waiting.

"Mr. Dewallace. I see you found Father–"

"How is she?" he interrupted without noticing.

"She's the same as when you left," nurse number one gave what smile she could. It was sad to see Derek's sigh of relief at what was not good news, really.

"Please come on back," she noticed Elise, but said nothing. No one, including Derek, even asked who she was. *Chris must be pleased*, Elise thought with self-pity that she immediately regretted. Hospitals didn't allow self-pity for those not in beds.

"Helen. Helen!" the nurse had to yell to get the woman in the bed's attention. She responded with only the slightest lift of her head. "Derek is back, and he brought your priest." Helen blinked several times – she heard.

"Hi, Helen," Chris spoke in an unnaturally high voice. "I'm sorry I've been away so long." He lowered his body and knelt beside her bed, still plenty tall to see over the blankets and grasp her hand. He began immediately, pulling out a vial of Holy Oil from a briefcase that he brought from the car.

"Through this holy unction and His own most tender mercy may the Lord pardon thee whatever sins or faults thou hast committed by sight," he placed oil on her eyelids. "By smell," then on her nose. "By taste," gently, he anointed her lips. "By touch," he reached around and placed oil on both her palms. "And by walking," Chris reached under the blankets and touched her soles. With each anointing, he moved slow and deliberately, graceful, like he was performing a dance.

When he was done, he pulled out a rosary, and they began to pray.

Elise tried not to stare, but gave up after a while. It wasn't like Helen really cared. The woman lay propped against pillows not quite as white as what was left of her hair. Everything about her was wrinkled, from her skin to the hospital gown that struggled to stay on her emaciated frame. A small battle for air raged in her chest, and her entire body shook with each rise and fall. Her eyes – they were still alert, still alive. *She's all there,* Elise realized. *She knows she's dying.* Flowers from friends surrounded her, like she was a corpse without a casket.

They continued on through the entire rosary. At its conclusion, Chris finally stood, his knees popping. "Take a rest, Helen. Then, we'll do it again." But she held fast to him. "Don't worry. I won't leave until you tell me it's okay." To Elise and Derek, "Would either of you like something to eat? Elise, you can run down to the cafeteria and grab something for us."

"I don't want anything, Father," Derek remained seated by his wife.

"Are you sure?" Elise risked Chris' wrath by speaking directly to Derek.

But it was Helen who startled to her voice; her eyes scanned and noticed the redheaded girl for the first time. Her breathing became more distressed; she drummed the fingers of her free hand against the blanket. She made deep rumbling sounds, though it was impossible to talk with the tube down her throat. Her heart monitor beeped faster.

"What is it, honey?" Derek cooed to her. "What's the matter? Do you need me to ring the nurse?" It took a moment for him to realize her agitation was outward. Chris and Derek both followed Helen's gaze to Elise.

"Helen, you're going to tire yourself," Derek pressed the drumming fingers.

Chris and Elise shared alarm while his gaze remained turned. She prepared to retreat, "I'll go get some foo–"

Without warning, Helen violently flung her body forward, prostrating herself on the bed guardrail.

"Helen!" Derek and Chris both moved to restrain her. "Elise! I think she wants you to stay!" Chris called when Helen gave no sign of calming.

"All right, all right. I'm staying." Elise held out both hands in front of her in a calming motion. *What's wrong with her? God, what does she see in me?*

Helen immediately lay back, breathing hard through her nose. Her eyes remained locked on Elise with an unmistakable expression: recognition.

"Who are you?" Derek asked.

"I'm Elise Moore," she hesitated qualifying it any further. But, Helen's eyes burned into her, waiting. She knew there was more, and Elise found herself incapable of denying her. "I'm a friend of the Father," she said barely above a whisper with a weak smile.

Helen's eyes returned it.

"Hear that, Helen? She's just a friend of Father Chris. Nothing to be afraid of," Derek explained with slow words. It was ironic – he was the only one in the room who misunderstood.

Helen tapped her fingers again on the bedside. She wanted Elise to come closer.

Elise looked at Chris for reassurance. She saw from his eyes that he was no longer angry with her. He was frightened and unsure, and looking at her in the way he did whenever he didn't see Elise, but only Remiel. He gave only the slightest movement of his head. *Do what you can.*

Elise pulled over a chair. She swallowed back the lump that kept growing (like its own cancer) in her throat and reached out a trembling hand to the dying woman. Helen grasped it until Elise wanted to wince. Instead, she forced her eyes to remain steady with the woman's. Minutes passed while they held on to each other. The fervor in Helen's eyes dimmed and eyelids full of tired veins closed. She slept shallowly.

"Thanks, Elise," Chris gave Elise the signal that she could let go.

But she shook her head. "She'll wake. I'll stay with her."

"I'm really sorry," Derek reminded them that he was still in the room. "Usually, Helen's really good at remembering people, and she keeps it together pretty well. She must think you're someone…"

"While she's asleep, I'm going to give Alan and Francis a call – make sure everything worked out," Chris said. "If you need anything Derek – water, a bathroom break – now might be a good time to take it."

Derek waited a few more moments, watching his wife. "When she sleeps, sometimes I can almost pretend she's getting better. All the pain disappears from her face." He got up and headed for the men's room.

Chris was the first to return, and Elise breathed a small sigh of relief. She didn't want to be the only one with Helen for long.

"Derek's not back yet?" more of an observation than a question. Chris sat in one of the other uncomfortable-looking chairs a few feet from the bed.

"How is everything?" she replied.

"Well, Alan and Francis fudged the blessing and are now back at the rectory," Chris paused, not sure what else to say. Small talk in hospitals was not exactly his specialty. "Thanks for rolling with all of this," it was an apology and a thanks in one.

"It's not like I have much choice. She knows," Elise said simply. "She knows I'm not who I appear to be."

"How do you think Helen knows that?" Chris challenged out of habit.

"My mother was able to see something when she was close to death. Maybe Helen sees something in me or on me. I don't know how, but the way she looks at me – I know she isn't seeing what you see."

Chris again ran his fingers through his hair to ensure that any strands lying flat were once again in disarray. "I've counseled Derek for months and months, since she's been hospitalized. His faith just isn't ready for this. He's told me so many times that he just can't believe in–"

Derek walked in the door and they fell into an immediate, embarrassed silence. He didn't notice, however. "How is she?"

"Unchanged," Chris answered.

Derek began to pace – which was halting and awkward in such a small room. "Maybe it was just an episode then. Maybe it wasn't so bad as they thought."

"What happened earlier, Derek?" Elise asked. Chris threw her darts.

"Helen just started coughing and coughing. She coughs up blood now – all over." His eyes glazed as the scene replayed for him. "She lost control of her... herself, and then she didn't seem to know me," he related, horrified. "They said that wasn't a good sign. Losing control like that," he began to tear-up.

"But, it looks like things are okay. She's fine now – stopped coughing. She's resting," he stopped his pacing to look at her.

* * * * *

An hour passed. Then another. They all kept their positions – Elise in the chair holding Helen's hand, Chris in another chair fiddling with the rosary, and Derek pacing back and forth, pausing only to look at his sleeping wife. The sun set early, dying the blinds on the window in different shades of orange. Elise wanted to ask how long they were expected to stay, but would not in front of Derek.

209

At about 6 PM, the heart monitor once again began to quicken. Everyone came to attention, Chris and Elise sitting up and Derek freezing mid-step.

"Should we call someone?" Elise asked Chris.

"No, no. I think she's just waking-up," Derek answered as he approached the side of the bed. Helen's eyelids fluttered. She squeezed Elise's fingers.

"I'm still here," Elise reassured her. Helen's face relaxed as much as the pain would let it, and she opened her eyes halfway.

The heart monitor kept beeping at, what Elise felt, was an alarming pace. It was making her own heart beat faster in sympathy with Helen's. Elise checked the door for anyone in green pants.

Chris stood with his fingers now completely tangled in the rosary. "Helen. Would you like to say the rosary again?"

She gave no indication, but kept her eyes on Elise. Chris began anyway.

At the end of the second Hail Mary, Helen began to shake. Elise looked at Derek (who was also holding her hand) to see if he felt it too. The fear in his eyes told her yes.

"I really think we should get someone," she interrupted Chris. "I don't think she's doing so well – AH!" Elise gave a yell as Helen squeezed her hand. Her mother's engagement ring bit into the fingers on either side.

"What?" Derek leaned over her in alarm.

Helen again began making noises in her throat, and her eyes belied how badly she wanted to speak. *Rip the tube out!* They cried.

"What is it?" Elise whispered to her, hoping it might calm her if she knew that someone was at least trying to listen.

"Maybe we should get a nurse," Derek echoed.

Elise leaned forward, closer, closer, until she was only inches from Helen's face, trying to understand. The eyes, so bright only a few hours before, were struggling now, as if some inner force were pulling them away. Helen's chest rose high in preparation, and then she rumbled in her throat something so desperate. Though it was as incomprehensible as before, Elise knew what she asked – it was a universal plea.

Don't let me die.

Elise pulled back as her eyes filled with tears until they sparkled thickly at the bottoms, ready to spill over. "I don't know how to help you," Elise whispered. Her face scrunched up and creased as she fought to stay controlled. "I don't know how. He wouldn't let me come down knowing how. Things like that just aren't meant to be. I've been where you're going. And I've seen Him," for the first time, Elise recreated her dream for another.

"What are you saying? What are you talking about?" When Elise ignored him, Derek turned to Chris. "What's she doing?"

"And He is beautiful and loving. There is no loneliness, no pain. I promise, you don't need to be afraid. I'm sorry." Helen squeezed her fingers again, but it was weaker. Elise looked up to see her eyes entirely clouded. The heart monitor began to sound some sort of alarm.

The nurse came with rapid steps heard long before she entered. "Please step back so I can see the patient," it was a command that made even Derek move away. Helen did not notice when Elise dropped her hand.

Another nurse appeared in the door. "Get a doctor," the first nurse barked and the second disappeared.

"What's happening to her? What's happening to her!" Derek began to cry from the corner where he stood with Chris. He had his hands over his ears, as if to block out the response.

"Mr. Dewallace, you must be calm for Helen." The nurse checked the monitors and the cords. She pulled up Helen's eyelids and then began trying to speak to her.

The doctor entered with a squeak of sneakers. He took one look at the monitor and announced what the nurse had not, "Irregular heart beat. She's going to bottom out!"

"No, God! DON'T TAKE HER AWAY FROM ME!" Derek thrashed from Chris' grasp.

Somewhere in the background, Elise could hear the heart monitor flat-lined. Without fully understanding what she meant to do, Elise grabbed Helen's limp hand.

"You have to stand back, or you will be asked to leave!" the doctor yelled.

But he was too late. Elise was already somewhere else, feeling the shock. She went where the whispers were, closing out the real voices.

Helen was almost gone. Only a small dripping of life came to Elise's fingers and she was careful to take as little as she could. She let it come slow, tasting but not drinking. She wasn't there for the energy.

Elise could feel the blood slowing in the veins; feel the lungs quiet with half a breath still waiting to exhale. Where was Helen? Where were her thoughts? Elise waited, waited. It always took a while for them to come. She needed time.

Someone large was trying to pull her away now, but she heard them yell when they touched her and new energy flowed in. *Come on! Come on! HELP ME OUT HELEN!* But she was close to dying. Fading, languishing, dimming, withering. Helen was–

Reaching for someone.

Yes! Elise sensed the thought, felt the excitement. She could feel peace blanketing the quieting body. Helen was going, and there was someone there with her.

With a jerk, Elise released Helen and let herself be dragged across the floor where she remained under a heavy-breathing nurse. She closed her eyes so she wouldn't see. *Hold on to it.* Elise tried to ignore the commotion. *Hold on to that piece of Helen!* Again she felt it, that hand that reached out of nowhere to take her.

"Elise," it was a voice she recognized.

"Chris. Where's Derek? Hurry."

He didn't ask a single question, but helped her roll over and stand. Derek sat on the cold floor, rocking.

Elise said nothing, but knelt and reached with both hands for his face.

He did not jump away from her or yell – only breathed out like someone splashed him with cold water. And unlike Helen, he was incredibly strong, and the power began to race into Elise, though again, she tried not to take it.

With the connection open and raging, Elise focused on reliving the last moments of Helen's death. But, he would have to help. Derek would have to let her hold on for a while, and then feel it and take it.

Over and over, she replayed it: the hand, the reach, the peace. *Come on Derek! Find me!*

He crumpled next to her, and he reached out to put a hand on her shoulder as if to say, "Enough!" He was incapable of saying anything, however, as she held on until he could not feel at all. Before his eyes rolled back into his head, Derek touched his face, as if to see if it was still there.

He was bending, and Elise could feel it. But, it hadn't happened yet. There had been no transfer – she was still only taking. *Come on!*

Chris watched with growing alarm. Derek's mouth hung open slack, as if he was in some sort of deep sleep, and he could not tell if breath passed over his lips. How long should he let this go? He had no idea what Elise was doing. She seemed so desperate to get to Derek, but she was holding on too long. Much longer than when she touched Alan. Chris looked up at the nurses, too busy with Helen. Whatever she was doing, she only had a few seconds before he got one of them.

Bending, bending, Derek's life bent away from her. He wouldn't be able to take much more. With renewed effort, Elise relived again the moment when she felt Helen reach out for someone, that person who no one saw, but that came to stand by her bed.

And then – there was someone else. A shadow, a spectator to her mind. *Derek.* Instantly, Elise gave him the memory in a flash, like a fast-forward movie. The whispers screamed as she wrenched her fingers from his face and fell backwards.

It was the highest she turned-up on another human being since the car accident. Light – there was light everywhere. The gold hue turned into a blinding whiteness, and Elise could tell only by the shadows that someone stood over her. She closed her eyes so she alone could see the fire. Her heart beat – not fast, but irregular, as if she just received an electric shock and the rhythms in her body was thrown off. And the whispers – they were still there. Fading now, but still going, curling and wafting at her ears like cigarette smoke. She did not hear Chris' voice until he called her five times.

"Elise!" he was trying to whisper, to avoid authority. But, the concern raised it many decibels. "Elise. What should I do? Derek? Derek! Can you hear me?"

"I can't see much. I shouldn't open my eyes."

"What did you do?" Chris hissed into her ear – closer than she thought. "He isn't moving."

"Mr. Dewallace?"

Elise heard the whisper of pristine sneakers. She buried her face into Chris' chest. He would have to field this.

"Uh, I think he fainted. He didn't fall or anything. Just seemed to go to sleep," Chris kept his eyes darting under the lie.

"What happened to his face?" the nurse asked as she bent to put her fingers on Derek's neck.

Chris took in the welts – ten of them on his face. She burned him. "I think it's just from crying," Chris said weakly. Awkward, his hands clenched and unclenched the fabric of Elise's shirt as he held her.

Somewhat satisfied after taking Derek's pulse, the nurse began trying to rouse him. "Mr. Dewallace. Mr. Dewallace." His eyes flickered underneath his eyelids.

"He's waking-up," Chris whispered to Elise, who kept her face hidden.

Slowly, Derek pulled himself together enough to open his eyes and register the nurse. "She died, didn't she," he stated and then let out such a long sigh, Chris wasn't sure how he managed to keep so much air in his lungs.

Elise noticed then that the room was quiet. No flatline, no urgent voices.

The nurse stated, "The doctor wants to speak with you." She helped him to his feet – so exhausted, so drained. Another nurse took his other arm.

Chris helped Elise gain her feet and then lead her out.

"What exactly did you do to Derek?" Chris asked, trying to hide the suspicion in his voice. He was unsuccessful, for Elise tried to pull back and look at him. But it was like having his face thrown into the beam of a police officer's flashlight. Squinting, he turned away.

"Sorry! I just took so much from him." She closed her eyes and leaned into Chris again, speaking into the muffle of his clothing. "I showed Derek where Helen was going. I showed him what I felt in Helen when I touched her. As she died, she knew someone was there, in her room. I stole her thought, and then I turned-up on Derek until we were so connected that I could show him what I saw, what she saw."

Chris was silent. He rested his chin on the top of her head as he thought.

Elise kept going, unsure if Chris understood her yet. "You said Derek would lose his faith. You said that I've made you neglect your duties as a priest, and Derek would stop believing in God because of it. So, I had to make sure he didn't. Say something!" Elise pushed against him, signaling their awkward untangling.

"What happened to 'test not your God?'" he asked as she pulled away.

Elise opened her eyes full, lighting Chris' face and seeing the dazzling shine reflected in his eyes. A test of wills – he did not squint this time.

"Derek didn't ask me for it. There was no test of faith – I just gave it to him."

"Father?" At the interruption, Elise turned her back. It was the same nurse as before. "Could you come in to be with Derek?"

"Yes, of course." Chris followed the nurse a few steps towards Helen's room and then looked over his shoulder.

"I'll wait outside," Elise already turned. Chris watched her a moment as she walked to the elevator, which opened automatically when she stood before it.

* * * * *

It was late when they finally pulled into the rectory driveway. They sat in the stillness, feeling the cold begin seeping into the car at its seams and listening to the engine tick off the seconds.

"I'm glad you came with me, Elise." Chris had one hand on the door handle while the other covered her hand completely. For a moment, he let his thumb rub the soft lines of her palm. "You never stop surprising me. Ever."

Elise watched him keeping focus on the vinyl seats, unable to look her in the eyes now that they were plain brown. It was ironic.

With what he tried to make a fatherly pat, Chris released her and climbed out of the car.

She sat a few more moments and leaned her head back against the headrest until she was watching Chris depart across the bridge of her nose. She was exhausted.

Perhaps that's why Elise didn't notice that every light in the rectory was on until she reached for the doorknob. But they were on, like a beacon, as if the rectory were trying to encourage Chris and herself to get home faster. *What now?*

Alan and Francis were sitting at the kitchen table. Whatever it was, they apparently already told Chris – he was once again running his fingers through his hair. As Elise closed the door quietly behind her, all eyes turned her way.

A single newspaper sat on the table. It was black and white (*of course it's black and white*), and wrinkled as if its latest reader had wet hands (*as if they read it a hundred times before we got home*). Instantly, she knew. But she asked anyway, on the slim hope that it wasn't as she thought.

"What? You found him."

The rocking started with his shoulders. Then his head followed until Francis replied *yes* twenty times.

Elise closed her eyes, feeling her eyelashes on the beginnings of her cheeks. She watched the colors swirling on the backs of her eyelids like spots from the sun, though she knew they were leftovers from her own light. She could count the beats of her heart by the throb in the base of her skull. For a second, she filled herself with sunlight, the Whiteley Corn Festival, and that thing (heart, soul, spirit) in the very center of her chest ached.

This was her normal day.

Still not looking, not wanting to see their faces belie the answer, she asked, "How much time do we have?"

Chapter 14 – Something Wicked

It was early. Though it was too dark to see the clock hanging over the stove, Elise knew because Alan and Francis still appeared to be asleep in the living room. Always before, she stood their chastising for being a late sleeper. But not this night. If she were caught thirty seconds with her eyes closed, it was a miracle of some sort.

She flipped on the light over the stove and orange revealed the kitchen, sending slivers out into the living room. She waited breathless a few seconds, but heard no stirring. The newspaper was still on the table, an ironic centerpiece. She approached it like a loaded gun.

BANG!

Elise stubbed her toe against one of the wooden kitchen chairs. "SHHHHH…" she held back swearing, both from some new-forming habits and from the desire to be quiet. Breathing hard through her nose and supporting her weight on one foot, she waited. Someone in the next room rolled over.

With some minimal throbbing from beneath her sock, Elise slid into one of the kitchen chairs. The newspaper no longer seemed so intimidating – the human commotion broke the supernatural spell temporarily.

The Syracuse Post-Standard, A4. Of all places, Francis found it in the daily paper of a small nearby city – not *The New York Times*, not an Israeli paper, but the little, upstate New York *Syracuse Post-Standard*. It was as though it had been printed there for her convenience.

The story wasn't all that compelling. It was basically a repeat of what had been in the news lately: Israeli Prime Minister keeps control by a thread; rebel groups try to join forces; without U.S. refereeing, Israel and Palestine continue the slaughter; democracy fails as the people cry for an all-powerful monarch, someone who can end the violence.

But the photo: that was what made the difference. It was a close-up of Arel Demsky, the rebel General holding popular opinion in Israel, and the same that Elise picked out a few weeks earlier. This time, however, she did not trace his profile, but looked at him for only a second.

Her focus was on the man behind him. The one not looking at the photographer, apparently busy behind the scene while Demsky took on the flash bulbs. The paper did not give his name: *Demsky and several of his closest advisers met in Jerusalem Friday.*

Nonetheless, he was David's heir.

"Just your picture to go on," Elise said under her breath. Dark hair curled ringlet-like by his ears and almost touched his shoulders, with a few stray locks crossing his forehead. His eyes were large and equally dark, giving away pupils only where some flash created a reflection. His face was long, with pronounced chin and jaw. He appeared haggard, as if he wanted to sleep but could not. "You and me both," Elise spoke to his image.

Minutes passed by the miniscule tick of the clock. Elise wasn't quite sure what she was waiting for – recognition, déjà vu, or even the slightest jerk of instinct? None came. Guardian or not, she would have passed him on the street without a second glance.

Francis had picked him out by a mark (invisible to everyone else, of course). Elise recognized it as soon as the monk began to write it:

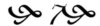

Sheva. It was the same as the one on her mother, the same as on Clyde.

Only it's all over him, Francis wrote with a trembling hand that made his letters squiggle. *Like a disease or a rash. It covers every part of his skin. He is meant for you.*

"Meant for me," Elise repeated out loud. She wished she could see it herself, to be sure. But, Francis' word would have to be enough. *Enough to kill him?* Elise watched the goose bumps appear on her forearms. *Soon, there will be no going back.*

She looked up at the clock, now wishing someone would wake up. *Not just anyone,* her id taunted. It was 4:07 AM – Chris definitely slept in later than that, even on Sundays.

But, there was no use trying to go back to sleep. And TV was out of the question with the men sleeping right under it. She could stare at the ceiling, or stare at the newspaper – take your pick.

Unless… an idea began to form, trying to convince her of its merit. Her running shoes were just down the hall. She could burn a little excess energy.

Where were you? Why would you risk running in the dark like that? What if the Other found you? She heard Chris and Alan's reprimands in her head alternately and sighed. Sometimes, they just really didn't understand.

In only a few days, she would be committed to riding a train she could not hope to stop. Elise Betheba Moore was disappearing, leaking out of her, and after Alan and his friends got done planning around this latest news, she might disappear altogether. But tonight, in the dark while they all slept, away from the priests and the books, she might still find her. Maybe for the last time.

A few more stumbles through the dark hall, a few more breathless moments praying she was silent enough, and Elise slipped out into the bitter cold night to see if she could outrun Remiel for just a little while.

* * * * *

"Elise? Elise." Chris touched her shoulder to rouse her from the couch. He had just returned from the second Sunday mass. After a few shakes, she looked up at him with sleep still in her eyes.

"What?" she said through a yawn.

"There's someone here for you."

She was too tired to hear the apprehension in his voice, and instead continued carelessly. "Sorry. Alan's yapping Latin on the phone is like a tranquilizer."

She froze mid-stretch to see Derek Dewallace standing in the doorway, looking shy. Her eyes flew to Chris for explanation, but he was already in the process of excusing himself. "Come on in, Derek. You two can have the living room, and Alan and I will try to stay quiet over in the kitchen. Alan looked up from the phone briefly, obviously not set on being quiet for anyone.

"Um, Mr. Dewallace. How are you?" What a stupid question for a man whose wife died yesterday. Elise immediately wanted to roll her eyes at herself.

"Fine, Elise. Fine."

"Good." Elise tried to smile while he settled into the chair across from her spot on the couch. "Feeling okay?"

"Yeah, well it don't hurt much anymore," Derek's eyes caught hers. "It faded pretty quick after you let go."

Elise dropped her gaze into her lap, not sure what to say.

"Marks are gone too. 'Cept for this one here," his words called her eyes to look-up, though she did not want to. On his lower left cheek was a dark spot, purple like a bad birthmark. It was slightly raised, as if already scarred. A type of pattern was noticeable: Sheva again. Elise returned her eyes to her lap. What did he want from her?

Sensing her discomfort, Derek got to the point. "Well, I can't stay too long. Got some arrangements to make for Helen. But, I wanted to bring you a little something."

"Oh, Mr. Dewallace. You really didn't have to bring me any–"

"It's Derek. And it ain't much." He leaned across the coffee table and dropped a thin silver chain into her hand with a rectangle charm at the end. "It was Helen's."

"No, please don't give this to me," Elise tried to press it back into his hand.

"I want you to have it," he pushed it back at her.

With a sigh, she held it dangling from her hand.

"I want you to have it," he repeated. Then, in a whisper, "I don't know who you are, even. And I don't know what you did yesterday, what you gave me, or how you could know…" he cleared his throat even as it was choked by a lump. "But," Derek reached across and caught the dangling charm. Losing his normal backwoods grammar, he read its inscription, "'Thou hast put gladness in my heart' – Psalms 4:7. 'Thou hast put gladness in my heart.'"

He did not wait for her awkward thanks. Derek rose and exited with a brief wave to Chris.

Elise read the inscription over for herself, just a plain rectangle tag with the simple line. She undid the clasp and slipped the charm off. Then, she reached around her neck, and unhooked the crucifix Alan gave her (she never took it off). The rectangle charm slid easily onto that chain (still warm from her skin), the cross and Psalm plate clinking together. She tucked them both into her shirt, over her heart.

* * * * *

"Is he gone yet?" Alan finally hung up the phone.

"You mean Derek?" Chris returned the question with a question.

"Whoever. The man from yesterday."

"Yes, he just left," Chris watched Derek's truck pull out of the driveway.

Alan sat down at the kitchen table. He folded his hands, then unfolded them, and his mouth kept turning down to frown.

"What is it, Alan?" Chris had been too busy eavesdropping on Derek and Elise to follow Alan's half of the phone conversation.

Alan kept his face towards the small kitchen window. "Get Elise and Francis."

Chris' heart lurched. There had to be something really wrong if Alan felt obligated to perform the social courtesy of delivering news to everyone at the same time. Chris motioned Elise in from the living room and then went down the hall for Francis.

They congregated around the small table, each in his or her own worried way. Chris played with a frayed part of the tablecloth, Francis rolled and unrolled his finger in the whiteboard pen string, and Elise fingered the skin just below her chin.

And Alan didn't meet anyone's eyes. "I just got off the phone with the Vatican. They are in the process of further investigating the man Francis discovered, trying to find out who he is, and confirm that he truly is the one."

"What does that mean? Confirm?" Elise already sounded angry, though no bad news was given yet.

"There are other visionaries. They're looking into it," Alan took a moment to answer her before continuing. "In the mean time, we need to prepare as if this is it."

"So, we're leaving Whiteley?" Elise jumped on him again. *When Francis sees the king – we will head directly wherever he is and finish the job*, she remembered their earlier conversation. "Where and when?"

"Rome. Though it is an obvious place for the Other to look for you, the high cardinals want you there, Elise. And I can no longer keep them from getting their hands on you. When the time comes – which will be soon – you can't be so far from Israel. Once they finish their initial investigation of this man, you will be on a plane. Hopefully, it won't take more than a week. Which still leaves us a little time to prepare."

A WEEK! Francis wrote in caps on his board. *They shouldn't wait that long.* He looked around to see if he had consensus. *We should go after this man NOW. I'm right!*

"I'm sure you are, Francis," Alan tried to make it sound less personal. "But, before we send Elise after him, we need to be certain. And, since this man is not an immediate candidate for king, the Vatican believes we can take a week to be sure."

"All right. All right." Chris nodded to Francis. "That's reasonable. A week will give us the time we need to get everything ready to go."

"Your preparation won't be necessary," Alan put out a hand as if to immediately block any plans for leaving. "Only Elise is going."

"What?" Elise snapped. "What do you mean I am the only one going?"

"The Vatican believes–"

"Don't give me 'the Vatican believes', as if the Vatican is some all-knowing entity." Elise stood up, grating her chair across the tile.

"Once plans are finalized, you will be assigned a guardian who will travel with you," Alan raised his voice to Elise's level. "A guardian actually trained to protect you. Chris, Francis and I, as well as other members of the society, will continue to monitor the international climate from where we are. You will be placed in the charge of the highest officials the Church has to offer."

"I don't want the highest officials," Elise sneered. "I can't believe you would let this happen. I don't want to be in the charge of anyone else. Tell them I won't come unless the three of you are with me."

"Tell them we all have to go," Chris chimed in. "Tell them we won't leave her," The emotion with which Elise spoke eased only slightly the wound Alan had just struck in his heart. *Leave Elise?* Suddenly, he couldn't imagine the rectory without her. And, he found the idea of trusting someone else with her safety unfathomable. Not that he, Alan, and Francis were formidable warriors by any means, but Chris was confident they would do anything to protect her. That counted for something.

She looked at him, grateful, showing in her face how badly she wanted to stay with him, and not caring who saw.

"Chris, don't be foolish. This is a direct order from Cardinal Matthew himself. I can't undo this," Alan spoke with crushing finality.

Elise drew close to tears. "What do you mean you can't undo this? I can undo anything! Cardinal Matthew, the Vatican, and the Pope have nothing without me. Nothing!" she yelled it, but Alan did not even flinch. She seemed to break then. "What happened to 'We will follow you to the very end, all of our lives forfeit?'" she mocked Alan perfectly.

His eyes bowed under her gaze, and she saw him old and tired. Shaking her head, Elise stormed from the room. The bedroom door slammed and the wall hangings trembled.

* * * * *

She did not expect the knock to come so soon, and tried to wipe the tears from her face before granting entrance. It was Chris – of course.

"Elise," he said her name and then didn't seem to know how to continue. He sat on the edge of the bed (the only place to sit in the tiny bedroom), and noted the wet spots blooming on one of the pillow shams.

"Don't let this happen," Elise charged him, while wiping her nose on the back of her hand to keep it from dripping, too desperate to care how it looked. "Don't let this happen." Though her face fought it, the tears flowed freely down her cheeks, her bleary eyes pleading with him.

"You just don't understand. None of you do," she made the sweep in her anger. "I've been alone my whole life. I never thought I would find a place where I fit. I never even used to think it was important to find that. But, now, after being here, being myself for the first time since I can remember. How can he ask me to go back to strangers, and who knows how much time I have left for anything? How can he ask me to be alone now?" Elise's chest shook with sobs as her words began to run together.

Chris put a hand on her shoulder. At his touch, she fell forward, burying her face on the corner of his lap. He stroked her hair, damp with nervous sweat, and pressed gently on her shoulder blades, as if to massage away the pain, wincing himself each time she whispered, "Please don't leave me."

221

* * * * *

Alan didn't knock until the light outside had begun to fade. He looked stricken. Chris thought, by his expression, if Elise asked him one more time to give in, he would.

But she didn't. She now sat coldly on the very edge of the bed. The tears had stopped, leaving only red eyes as evidence. With them, the passionate Elise seemed to dry up, leaving a resigned, hardened mimic of herself.

Alan cleared his throat. "Elise, you need to practice," he waited for another explosion, but none came. "We need to finish as much preparation as we can. Please get your coat so we can head to the greenhouse before dinner."

He did not need to ask her twice. She got up, pulled her coat from behind the door (careful not to brush Alan), and then headed out while putting it on. Chris followed, trying to remember where he last put his own coat, and Alan brought up the rear as they trooped into the living room/kitchen where Francis waited.

"You all go ahead. I'll be right behind you," Alan gestured towards the door. "And bundle up. It's cold out there."

He watched the three move down the walkway with their heads lowered, trying to save warmth for the fifteen-minute walk down the road to the greenhouse. He waited until they disappeared into the gloom.

Then, looking around, as if there might be someone else in the rectory, Alan pulled his suitcase out from behind the armchair (where he and Francis managed to stockpile their belongings for the last month). He unzipped it entirely and began lifting clothes out. At the very bottom was a soft, cloth, carrying bag. He pulled it out, feeling the weight of the object inside.

With the clothes repacked, Alan closed the suitcase and then brought the cloth bag to the kitchen table. He looked at it for a long time. *What if I'm wrong?* He pushed the thought away. It had to be done. *It's why I'm here.*

With cold fingers, Alan unzipped the bag. A gleam of black inside gave the thing away. He slid out the .44 magnum pistol revolver so that it rested in his right hand. Though he had not used it since coming to Whiteley, it felt familiar. He practiced with it for years, once thinking he might use it on the Other if it came to that. Instead, it had come to something else entirely; something he could not have foreseen.

Alan reached further into the bag until he felt the box of bullets. The box was even heavier than the gun, packed full with lead. Slow, as if it were a ritual unto itself, Alan slid one, two, three bullets into the gun and then spun it (deliberate, feeling each ridge pass under his thumb) so that the revolver locked with the three lined-up – the first three shots. Ensuring the safety was on, Alan slid the gun back into the bag and then slung it over his shoulder with the muzzle pointed down. *Better to shoot your foot than…*

As an afterthought, he repacked the bullets into the bag as well, their weight resting dense and uncomfortable against his abdomen. He was confident it wouldn't take more than three shots, but better to be prepared.

With his coat on, Alan turned off the lights in the living room and kitchen, and then passed out the front door, locking it with a click. He began the walk, not aware that he was muttering.

* * * * *

Elise was glad to enter the warmth of the greenhouse. She slipped off her gloves and began blowing on her fingers. When that didn't work fast enough, she brushed a small plant and was instantly warm.

Francis tapped on her arm. *What is Alan having you do today?*

Elise shrugged her shoulders. She was rivaling the monk for least words spoken in an afternoon.

"It's getting dark so early now," Chris tried to make small talk. When no one responded, "I'm going to turn on some of the plant lights." A few clicks and Chris had a purplish glow in the front of the greenhouse.

"Well, where the hell is he? I thought he was 'right behind us,'" Elise imitated Alan while contorting her face to copy his regular dour expression. She rolled her eyes to communicate unspoken, nasty thoughts. Chris and Francis found a seat on their familiar bench while she paced, heading to the back of the greenhouse to further prove her separation from them.

Alan opened the door a few moments later, looking haggard and breathing hard, as if he had been running. "Elise?" he ignored Chris and Francis.

She did not answer, but the click of her footsteps could be heard. Alan peered towards the back where he caught her silhouette between shadows. Maybe it was the gray stalks of all the trees she killed; maybe it was the way the dark seemed on the verge of smothering the dim light; or maybe it was the coolness of her steps: Alan caught an inner chill. He swallowed his fear, as Elise stepped out of the dark until her skin took on the purple hue of the plant lights.

"Are you ready?" he barely trusted his voice to sound normal.

"Ready for what?" Elise kept her tone emotionless.

"Soon, we will no longer be with you," Alan dared to bring up their quarrel again. "So, this is it. Final cramming."

She stared him down, as if to say she didn't care.

Chris sighed audibly. It was like watching two dominant males on the Discovery Channel. Productivity was going to be at an all-time low.

"Right then," Alan removed his coat, trying to keep his movements leisurely. "Tonight, I want you to prepare as if the Other were here, right now. I want you to turn-up as high as you think you need to be to fight it."

"I don't think I can fight it, Alan. You haven't seen that thing," she continued argumentative.

"For the purpose of speculation."

Elise looked down and scuffed both shoes against the floor. "Fine. But, there aren't enough trees left in this place for that."

"Take what you can. The rest, you will get from me," Alan offered.

In a whirl of red hair, Elise disappeared into the ever-darkening greenhouse. The only thing that gave away her actions was the rustle of leaves falling and Francis sidling towards the door while rubbing his temples. He paused with his hand on the knob – as always, he wanted to see. Minutes passed, and then her footfalls came towards the front of the greenhouse preceded by the warm light of her eyes.

She came up right before Alan and extended her hand, ignorant of the cloth bag, which he wore like a grandmother – the strap lying across his chest, caught on one shoulder and keeping the pouch close to his hip. He unzipped the top and slipped one hand in.

"Once you have enough, step away from me, but keep looking this way. Don't use any until I say," Alan commanded in the sternest voice he had mustered since the scene in the kitchen.

Confusion finally entered into her face. "What am I to do?"

Alan slid the pistol out and turned the safety off (a loud sound in the shocked silence). "You will face mortal danger."

"What! Alan – what the!" Chris stood.

"I may not be the Other, but I am a good shot. I have brought you so far, and I will not let you down now, Elise. Where you are going, many will try to kill you, and most will not be using claws or teeth, but plain human invention. You need to know they can't."

"Elise! Get out of here," Chris commanded. "I will talk with Alan."

"I will aim for your shoulder. Stop my bullet."

"This is ludicrous! Francis!" They were going to have to rush him, dear God.

"Stop your bullet?" Elise finally caught her breath enough for words. Her stunned expression melted away into something far sadder; her shoulders slumped and she bit her lip. But she answered angrily, "Of course. I have to be able to stop anything."

"I will not let this happen!"

"I can do this," she turned on Chris. "Stay out of the way."

"No! I WILL NOT allow this. Alan! You could kill her!"

"That's the point." With a cool smile, Elise moved and gripped Alan around the wrist. "I'm sure you remember. It won't hurt...long."

It was like before, but faster, and Chris stood frozen, heart pounding. Alan withstood Elise a few seconds, but then hit his knees. His breathing was loud and belabored; he turned several different shades of ash in the light of her eyes. When he leaned forward in a collapse, she followed him, coming down to one knee.

"I said THIS IS ENOUGH!" Chris called out, though she did not even glance his way. A few more seconds, and the scene began to mirror what happened the previous day in the hospital: Alan began losing consciousness, just as Derek had. Except, Elise wasn't being gentle as she had been in the hospital. Though Alan's form slackened as if in sleep, periodically his body seized, rigid. "Elise, please!"

Something hit the ground behind Chris. It was Francis. He was writhing, as if electrocuted, and holding his ears. Unknowing and temporarily uncaring, he rolled into a pool of his own vomit.

"That's enough! That's enough, that's enough!" Chris ran towards Elise. "YOU BOTH ARE CRAZY!" he reached with two hands for her one. "I'LL TEAR YOU OFF HIM!"

But, before he could even feel the fabric of her coat, Elise pulled back. She looked at him as if he had surprised her. With the light falling so bright over her features, melting them out while highlighting an expression of such anger, Chris recognized very little of the Elise he knew. She blew air out through her nose and then took steps back until she reached the line of plants.

At Chris' feet – Alan was struggling to sit-up. Chris bowed over him, and tried to support him, calling his name. Alan's mouth was open like a fish's sucking hard at the air. Several times he tried to throw Chris' arms off with jerky twists of his body. "Alan. Alan! Let me help you," he tried to get a better grasp on the old man.

With wearying strength, Alan gave up the struggle and instead, reached inside the cloth bag. As Chris yanked him to a sitting position, holding him in an awkward, tight hug, he pulled the weapon free. He switched off the safety and curved his finger through the trigger, using Chris' body to hide the movement. When the other priest moved just enough to the side, he took his shot.

Elise's instinct was to turn her head away as soon as she saw the muzzle. But, she fought it, managing only to flinch. There wasn't enough time, not to move, not to jump. She opened her eyes wide to bathe her shooter in light. She had to see it.

She heard the sound, watched Alan's hands begin to recoil, and then she caught just the smallest sparkle. With everything she had, Elise pushed out her mind. She met the bullet in the middle.

Hot, sharp, spinning; the arms inside her head reached to cover, smother, stamp it out. It moved through them, slowing only slightly.

But she pushed again, the power of her thoughts bent on holding it, holding it, like some fluttery bird. It was hot, so hot as she closed herself around it.

The real Elise watched the shot turn from a glimmer – to a streak – to a hard piece of metal trailing and then–

Hovering still by her right shoulder.

It stayed there, like some annoying insect until, with the tiniest clang, it hit the concrete, bouncing and rolling off her shoe.

Like a diver surfacing, Elise let air into her lungs in a great gasp. She kept sucking in, as though there was no oxygen in her first several gulps. The room was silent save for that sound. Finally, her dark-again eyes turned on Alan. Out of nowhere, the bullet he fired appeared, twisting like a top between their bodies. Elise flared her nostrils and contorted her face into something she would barely recognize, should she catch her own reflection. "Take this, and eat it." The bullet fell and rested with a hollow sound by Alan's knees. With the last supernatural energy she had, Elise blew the lights and all went dark as she moved to leave. "That is enough."

* * * * *

Outside, her powerful demeanor failed. *What the hell just happened?* Elise wanted to lean against the greenhouse door, prop herself up. Instead, she headed down the dirt drive from the rows of greenhouses to the road in a jog. *What am I going to do?*

Even in her anger, she knew Alan was right: many men would want her dead. All those who wanted a king and who would protect him. His entire army. The Other was a single threat among many. And yet, she still found it horrifying that he was able to point a gun at her; that he could fire it. And no doubt, he received his orders from higher up. From the very men he was turning her over to.

"I am alone," she whispered over and over down the driveway. "Now, more than ever." It had been fake – that feeling of belonging. She had been a fool. Again and always, her power separated her. It was too much, scaring away most and tempting even those who claimed to care for her. "Not even Chris," she forced herself to say it and recalled the image of him begging to feel her inhuman touch in a way he would never have begged to hold her hand. "There is only me."

Where should I go? That was real enough. *Can I do this? Alone? Will I be hunted, hiding always? There's no going back.* She knew with a deadness that it was her cause now, and she ached with the weight.

Elise reached the road and stopped as she realized for the first time – it had been snowing. What was the road half-an-hour ago, now stretched out in front of her: a solid white sheet that looked like felt. So soft and quiet, no wind. More like the fake snow people put around their Christmas town displays than real snow. The sky was full with the tiny specks, whiting out eventually. Elise could barely see the rectory streetlight.

She turned for one look back at the greenhouses. Their greenhouse, the one in the front to the right, now had a purple light near the door. But no shadows moved. The priests were up, but they weren't following her yet.

Like a swimmer disturbing a perfectly still pool, Elise stepped into the smooth-snow road with one toe first. Her sneaker slid in a few inches – it was wet, not hard. She picked up her jog again, passing from the light of the farmhouse windows into the blackness, heading towards the rectory and the distant orange-glow of Whiteley. She forced an even pace though she felt disquieted – running in the dark somehow always felt like running from something. The road was narrow and lined with the ghostly stalks of the summer's corn on both sides. *"Farmer's lazy – leaving his corn stalks high until spring planting,"* Alan had grumbled several times on their previous walks over. Yellow and dry, the stalks stood still in the breathless air, collecting snow on their wasted leaves.

The quiet continued – no car broke its spell. Her breaths grew increasingly loud as she found her rhythm, and in the cold, her muscles fought to warm up properly. Periodically, she stopped to take a glance back towards the farm; the swishing noise of her coat moving as she ran sounded too much like someone running behind her.

The thing lying in the middle of the road didn't get her attention until she was halfway home.

It was a black mass, undistinguishable in the dark save its stark contrast with the snow. Dead center in her path, it lay cold and motionless. Elise slowed to a fast walk. *What now?*

Closer, closer, she approached it with pounding heart, not sure why she should be afraid (*because people are trying to murder you, Elise*). Ten feet away and it still didn't move. Closer, closer–

Relief came out in a blast through her nostrils. "Some asshole hit a dog." With a faster step, she began to make an arc around the dead animal.

But then–

Like a name she had forgotten, lurking just under her tongue – there was some detail she was on the verge of noticing. Unconsciously, she shortened her stride.

It seemed death came quickly. The dog's neck was arched so that it faced back over its shoulder blades, obviously broken. Blood pooled near its mouth, and its eyes looked up at the falling snow, glazed.

"Just the dark and Alan's bullet," she coached herself. "You're just jumpy, Elise." Still, she rocked on her toes and took a nervous look behind her. Nothing – only her own footprints in the snow.

That was it: *the snow*. There was no snow on the animal. Only a few, new flakes clung to its coal coat. And the blood was fresh; not congealed and half-mixed with the ice; red, not pink. The death was new. So where were the tire tracks?

Elise began a cautious circle around the dog, though a few quick glances made it obvious there were no tire marks. The snow remained undisturbed in both directions save for the dog's own footsteps and a few odd imprints, and she squatted, placing her finger next to one in the snow. It was like a paw: a circle imprinted with fine ridges denoting fur. Smaller satellites placed the toes. But where any normal animal would've made small slits in the snow for claws, these marks had long ridges the size of normal human fingers. And, they didn't just come from the toes, but from everywhere on the paw. One, two, three, four were by the dog's head. The rest trailed out in front of Elise until they reached the ditch and headed into the corn. They were light and careful marks, as if whoever made them wanted to leave as few as possible.

"Oh, God," Elise whispered and raised her head from the ground with a jerk. Her heart began anew to pound in her chest and with good reason. Though she had never seen such a mark before, she knew what it was. "It can't be." She tried to stand but fell, her hands digging into the biting snow, her jeans soaking through. Stumbling to her feet, she stared into the veil of snowfall, white and black, snow and shadow. *It can't be.* She listened: the night was as quiet as the death at her feet.

I can make the rectory. But what would be there for her when she did? If the thing followed her there, she would have no way to protect herself – hardly any trees, no people. Elise snapped to a vision of herself hiding in the bedroom closet.

Alan and Chris and Francis are still in the greenhouse. She needed nothing else. She ran.

At least the snow muffled the pounding of her feet, and maybe even offered her some camouflage. Elise pumped her arms and legs, trying to keep her breathing shallow and quiet. Her eyes frantically flew to the dead stalks of corn on either side, but all remained still. The only cause for panic was the swish of her coat as she ran, making her turn often to see if someone pursued.

* * * * *

"How are you doing, Alan?" Chris tried for a response from the priest whose weight he held on his shoulders.

"I'll be fine," he repeated exactly as he had the last time. They were on the road, about a third of the way home. It was a slow go, however. Alan was not regaining his strength quickly. And the weight of his thoughts made him extra heavy and slow.

"I had to do it," he said under his breath, but in the stillness, Chris caught it.

"I'm sure you thought you did," Chris repeated his reply, as he had the last time. It was inexcusable: putting anyone in that type of danger, let alone Remiel. God only knew what could've happened. If it hadn't already been determined that Elise would go on without them, friends or no, Chris would've marched back as fast as he could to request Alan's removal from the assignment. Except, he knew that Alan did not make the choice alone. It made Chris cringe: Elise would soon be in the care of those handing down such rash decisions concerning her life.

"I did have to do it. I did. She needed to do it–"

"You can justify yourself later," Chris interrupted Alan's mutterings. "Right now, you should just pray that Elise is back at the rectory when we get there."

As if appearing at the sound of her name, Elise's bobbing blur of color began to materialize through the snow. Chris froze, unsure if it was truly good or bad.

"Why–" Alan's question was cut-off as he too noticed. Elise was coming at them in a sprint. It took an eerie few seconds before the sound of her shoes on the pavement came to their ears. Chris braced for the moment she would notice them. She would still be angry, betrayed. But, hopefully, not out of control as when they last saw her.

Elise's heart stopped when she recognized them. Chris was carrying Alan. It took several more steps before she realized it was because he was tired, not because he was – she refused to finish the thought. She dropped to a trot, but no slower. "Turn around!" she yelled ahead. "Go back. You have to go back."

They gaped at her, as if she spoke another language.

Taking off a little more speed, Elise grabbed Chris' free arm on her way by. Her momentum turned the twosome around and forced a few steps in the right direction before it was gone.

"Elise. What's wrong?" It was obvious by the way Chris locked his legs against her that he had not caught the panic in her voice.

"Just come on!" More pulling. "Please! For once, listen to me!" Elise turned her head quickly to get a look in all directions. She noticed. "Where's Francis?"

"He went to the farmhouse to make sure you didn't head there. He'll be coming behind us in a few minutes. What's going on?"

She tried again to haul them, but Chris planted his feet. "Elise–"

"If you won't come, I'll have to leave you! I think it's back there." She stopped tugging enough to repeat, "It's back there. The Other."

She let go of Chris, but caught his eyes. Even in the short second he'd had to digest, they were dilating with fear as though he had been shut in a dark room. "Here." Elise slid under Alan's free arm, and Chris began to move furiously. Together, allies again, they managed a half-jog.

"How close is it?" he whispered.

"I don't know. I didn't see it. But it's here. I don't know."

"What are we going to do?"

Elise shook her head. "Alan! You have to move your feet! I don't care if you're exhausted!" she reprimanded. "Come – on," she grew further winded. Though he did not look it, Alan carried a considerable amount of weight.

He set his face in the determined expression he most often wore and pushed off harder, trying to carry himself at least every other step. They began to move faster.

But not fast enough.

Just as the driveway to the greenhouse appeared through the thickening snow, Chris dug his heels into the pavement, pulling the others to a stop. "Do you hear that?" he hissed.

They stood completely still, as if they could somehow dissolve into the powder so long as they did not move. Oddly, Elise remembered the *Jurassic Park* movie scene when the kids stood unmoving before the gaping jaws of the Tyrannosaurus Rex. But she knew better. Their monster could see.

"I don't hear anything," she said barely above the decibel of a breath.

"I know I heard something," Chris' exhale clouded in front of them. "Out there." He moved his head towards the corn, and Elise's breath caught. She hadn't told him it was in the corn.

"There it is!" he hissed. "Listen." It took a second, but Elise finally picked it up. It was a swishing sound, like something rapid and smooth moving through the rows of corn. No steps, just swishing. It was growing.

"It's just the wind," Alan shifted his weight to indicate they should keep moving. "Just the wind in the corn."

Elise listened again and was about to agree. The movement did sound as soft as air, like a gentle shushing. But, then she caught a look at the straight-falling snow, the way it wafted like a feather. "There is no wind."

As if realizing its subtlety was no longer needed, the shushing in the corn turned to a crash.

Elise threw Alan's arm off and looked behind them at the field. Though it was hard to see through the snow, Elise could make out the tops of dead stalks shaking violently, as though a tiller were going through the row at some sonic speed. The movement was only a few rows out.

"It's coming! Move," she began to slide back under Alan's arm, but with surprising strength, he threw her off.

"No! You have to go, Elise. Chris, take her up to the farmhouse and find Francis. Let me deal with this."

"I'm not leaving you," Elise answered with equal stubbornness. "Hurry. If we go now, we can all make it!"

"Go. I'm the slow one. This is part of the deal. I signed up for this."

"No one signed up for this! Alan," Elise tried again to grab him. When he appeared unmoving, "Chris?"

"GO NOW!" Alan yelled as he twisted from the other priest's grasp. "Go Chris. Take her – she cannot be here. Too much rides on her. You know this!"

No one moved except the thing in the corn.

"Go! I'll hold it off with the pistol. I'll slow it down and then follow you."

Chris looked at Alan hard, trying to read his eyes. *I made you leave the gun...* Alan looked back at him unfalteringly. *Duty.* They called him to fulfill his.

"I'll... I can just find something to turn-up on," Elise knew she was losing, but kept going. "Chris can – we can take a stand right here."

"There is no time! I don't care what you think you can do, we can't risk this confrontation now. You, Elise, will be a part of no stand. Now go!"

Chris moved from Alan and took Elise's arm. He began pulling her to the driveway, though she refused to turn forward.

"NOOO! Chris, how can you do this? We can't leave him. You're a priest and this is murder!" She reached down to force herself free. But Chris was not letting go. Her blows struck him with no effect.

Already, Alan blurred through the snow. Tears filled her eyes to see him standing alone.

"I'm sorry, Alan!" she cried. Unsure if he heard, she called it out again, "Follow us as fast as you can!" Then quiet, "I'm sorry." Chris was turning her now, up the driveway. Finally, she fled.

* * * * *

The crashing was parallel to him – Alan could see the stalks breaking, hear the crunching of footsteps. He only hoped the thing would take the diversion. He moved loudly on the road, dragging his feet, away from the greenhouse and the girl he swore to protect.

The thing slowed down, now only breaking a stalk or two at a time. It heard him.

Alan licked his lips and breathed hard. Though his resolve did not waver, his courage failed. Panting and crazily heaving his weight from one foot to the other as he walked, Alan waited for it to come out of the corn.

The smell of burning hair wafted in like heavy perfume, with no breeze to blow it elsewhere. Alan remembered the dream so long ago, the terror of not knowing what was behind that door. He trembled and bit his tongue.

Finally, he could see it – just the top of it as it approached from the corn, taller than all the stalks. And something blue; six blue discs seemed to be floating in front of it.

With a final stomping of stalks, it emerged from the corn and he realized the discs were eyes. "Our Father who art in heaven, hallowed be thy name," Alan paused to lean over and groan. He was going to be sick.

It stood on the opposite side of the road now, glistening in the snow like a Christmas ornament from hell. He could see the three heads breathe in the cold.

"Thy kingdom come – they will be done–" Alan gasped, threatening to hyperventilate as the thing growled. But, he had to finish it. "On earth – as it is – in heaven…Give us this day, our daily – bread and forgive us–"

The Other howled an awful noise, like a woman's scream. And Alan caught a glimpse of the three sets of needle thin teeth, far too long to ever be housed in a closed mouth. For the first time since he learned it, Alan forgot the words of the prayer.

"Forgive us, forgive us…forgive us our trespasses, as we forgive – those who trespass against us." It took a step towards him. Alan hurried. "And lead us not, into temptation. But deliver us – from evil."

Two more steps toward him. The Other cocked its heads at Alan, as if to see his reaction. To see how afraid he was.

You want to play with me. Alan understood and smiled even in his terror. Maybe he could buy Elise all the time she needed.

The thing took another step forward, and Alan took one in retreat, then another. Backwards, backwards away from it. There was no point in running – but if he could just keep it in front of him, see it coming. For some reason, that seemed important.

Alan didn't have to wait long. As soon as he put more than 20 feet between them, the Other charged. It moved fast and lumbering, like a bear in full gallop. The breath came out its mouths, its heads bobbing gently on the thick necks that joined at an incredibly large chest.

For a moment, Alan feared that he was wrong, that the end might come quickly. Until, at the last second, the Other turned, only brushing him with its body.

It was enough. Thick claws clustered on its hips and knees slashed through Alan's side like freshly sharpened knives. He clutched his arm, grimacing at the feel of his jacket shreds mingling with the hanging threads of his bicep. He screamed, a hollow sound, crimson drops littering the snow beneath him.

The Other circled around until it was opposite Alan again. The faces pulled back in what was recognizable as a human smile. Keeping pressure on his arm, Alan staggered back a few steps.

Rapidly, it again closed the distance between them. Alan sucked in his breath for another attack–

But none came. Instead, the beast slowed and lowered itself so that the head on the left side was level with his own, inches from his. Alan gagged twice, but held it back. His mouth was dry, so dry. He looked into the two blue lights: no pity, no mercy.

The eyes blinked and changed instantly to brown eyes he was familiar with. Alan gave a gasp of surprise and pulled his vision back to focus on the whole face. The snout retracted into a nose, and the hair lightened and thinned, seeming to pull back into the very follicles. The jaw softened. It became recognizable: it was Chris Mognahan's face, except the skin seemed to be covered in clear jelly, shining wet.

"Father Alan," it spoke to him in Chris' voice. "Do you believe in God now, though He has abandoned you? Do you think He heard your prayer just now?"

"Liar, demon!" Alan hissed through teeth clenched in pain.

"You always were a believer," it sounded even more like Chris. "Even when all the others thought you a fool, you still believed. They would've thought you were crazy until the end, except for me. I gave them the dream, convinced them with fear."

"Remiel gave us the dream," he contradicted it. "Remiel made them believe."

The Chris-head laughed. "You know it, Alan. In your heart, where you are afraid to look. She didn't make them believe. It was I, sniffing at the door, leaving them in the pews. You know – it's easier to believe in me than in God."

"Shut-up! Blasphemer, evil straight from–" The second blow came as it reached out with one paw and swiped him across the chest. Alan rolled over the snowy road leaving red prints with each turnover. He was mauled, the front of his coat gone, the skin from his nipples to his bellybutton open and peeled back. It felt cold.

"Your time is up," it was still Chris' voice. "Don't worry. I'll take care of her."

Alan got onto his hands and knees. He tried to stand, but could get no further. He saw the clawed feet by his hand and knew it stood over him.

"Did you hear me?" A human hand, oozing infection, reached down and pulled his face up by the hair. "I said, I'll take care of her. You know how badly I want to take care of her, don't you Alan?"

Alan didn't answer. It felt like his scalp was slowly being lifted from his skull, pulling even the skin around his teeth tight.

"You've seen the way I look at her," Chris' perspective ranted. "What do you think? Am I on your side because I believe too, believe in the Pope and the brotherly priesthood?" said with scorn. "Or is it because I want to fuck her?"

The human hand threw him into a roll, careful not to fully release his hair. Alan could feel what blood he had left rushing to pound under the skin of his skull.

Only a moment lying on his back, and it was coming after him again. "Yes, Alan. Can't you see it, Elise and I together? My cum in her ass, up her twat, all over her. That's what it's going to be like, once you're gone."

"Liar!" Alan managed the word. "You lie. You see nothing."

"Oh, Chris! Do it to me again, again! More, more! Fuck me, Chris!" A new voice accosted him. It was Elise.

Alan forced his neck muscles to contract and pull his head up enough to see that the Chris-face had now turned into Elise. The reddish hair was still growing, trying to reach her normal length. The features were hers now.

"But you, Alan. I'll never forgive you. Never. I'm furious with you. Your ambition almost killed me. And now, you'll die and rot without my forgiveness."

The Other grabbed him again, this time under the arms. Up, up, the human hands lifted him until his feet dangled from the ground. "She will forgive me. She already has," he told it in a raspy voice. It would not be long. Alan felt it – almost over. "Now show me your real face," it was the last challenge he had left. Perhaps he was already looking at it – the hellish faces of the two heads unchanged. It didn't matter – the point came across. *Kill me yourself, you coward*, it said.

"My real face, Alan? Why whatever do you mean?" Elise gave a cool laugh through her shiny lips.

With barely any movement at all, one of the human hands pulled back, then thrust into his chest wound. Again, Alan screamed in agony as the nails tore into it. Then, with a hard push, the hand went through him, into him. Alan tried again to scream, but blood came up his esophagus and choked him until he coughed, spraying the Elise-head with blood. The hand reached the back of his body and moved around, feeling until its fingers curled around a hard thing.

At first there was fire-like pain, and then Alan could not feel his legs. The hand moved up, squeezing, and then he could not feel his hands. *God, please let it end. Let it be over.*

"Watch," Elise commanded. Holding him by his spinal cord with one hand and using the other, the monster began to tear through him, shredding him like tissue. Now that he couldn't feel it, couldn't pass out with the pain, the Other made him watch it destroy him, until there was no going back, no way to ever heal. His breathing became strangled, and he felt himself begin to move away inside. His eyes rolled up into the back of his head, and he found he could not roll them back down.

"Wait," it was a new voice, one Alan did not recognize. Struggling, he flopped his head onto his shoulder and blinked until the Other came into focus. Elise was gone, but in her place, the thing took on the likeness of Francis. Somewhere in Alan's confused brain, he felt happy – Francis could speak!

"Alan," the voice was moderate, not low, not high. The Francis-head leaned in to whisper in his ear, and the other heads came in closer, joined to it. "Alan, there's this mark, this strange mark on you. I see it! It's the mark of death. It's the mark of eternal damnation. Which means – I'll see you again."

Francis ripped open Alan's throat, and all three began to eat.

* * * * *

Elise came away from the greenhouse glass. "I haven't heard any shots yet. Maybe Alan's still okay."

Chris did not answer her hope as he moved to the greenhouse door. "Wait here."

"You're leaving me?" Elise caught on. "Let me turn-up, and I'll come with you."

"No! Alan is right. Confrontation with – this thing is too risky. I want you to wait here while I go check the farmhouse for Francis. Don't move." Chris turned the doorknob.

"Don't you think it's risky to leave me here by myself?" Elise's voice was high-pitched with fear as she quickly headed towards the back of the greenhouse to disobey him.

Chris' hand hesitated. "It's safe in here. Whereas who knows what I will find at the farmhouse, or on the way back? You can't be there if something goes wrong. Just stay here and watch for me."

"I'm coming with you."

"Elise!" Chris shifted his weight side to side, and then stepped away from the door. He knew her well enough: if he left, she would undoubtedly follow him. "God, help me protect her," he prayed with his eyes closed. "Help me please."

Towards the back, there were a few plants she had not yet used, and Elise went for those. She did one plant, then two. The whispers came with their unintelligible comfort. She imagined they were the voices of the other six trumpeters encouraging her to be strong. *Kick its ass*. She nodded.

She came back to the front, eyes alight. "I expect you to obey me, without question, once we're out there," Chris' tone held some unspoken, worthless threat. "I doubt Francis is still at the farmhouse, but we have to try and warn him before he heads home. Maybe the farmer will let us borrow his car – if not, we take it anyway. Then, we grab Alan," his voice clicked. "Look for Francis on the road, and get out of here."

Chris roughly grabbed her elbow and pulled her to the door. Together, they peered out the foggy glass.

"I can't really see," Chris tried to hold his breath in hopes the glass would clear.

Elise tried a new strategy, bending down close to the floor. "It's clearer down here, where it's cooler," she explained the physics of it. "I can see the path. It looks clear – but I can't see all the way to the house."

Chris crouched beside her. He gave a quick glance. "We'll have to risk it."

"Wait! I see something! Someone's coming," she dropped her voice into a whisper, as if that could make a difference.

Chris put a sweaty hand on the glass so he could lean in and put his eye almost as close. "Where? Where do you see–"

The glass answered his question. Francis was coming towards the greenhouse, his black robes making him look a dark shadow against the snow.

"He's okay!" Elise yelled in triumph, though they had done nothing but wait. "We have to get him in here."

She rose and was about to fling open the door when hard pressure from Chris' hand on her leg froze her momentum.

"He's stopping. He seems afraid of something. I just can't see what he's looking at," Chris tried to angle his head to look down the driveway.

Elise recrouched. "Maybe he's just sensing me." But, Chris was right. Francis stood several yards away with his head turned down the drive. She watched as he took two steps back into the shadows. She wished she could read his expression.

"Well, we can't just leave him out there!"

A shadow fell across the glass.

It rippled, coming closer and showing even in the shadow's bland detail some of its deformity. Suddenly, the greenhouse smelled like burnt hair.

It was as huge as Elise remembered.

They froze as if it might pass by, remaining stiff in their last positions: Elise with one hand reaching out for the door; Chris kneeling with only glass between his face and the Other.

The Other moved past Chris. They could hear its heaving breaths; several of its claws scraped along the glass as it walked. Almost past Elise…

But then it paused, as if it could sense her. The silhouette turned and three pairs of blue lights shone inside.

Instantly, Chris and Elise animated, trying to avoid the blue beams in a horrifying game of flashlight tag. With as little noise as possible, they scrambled back into the gloom and away from the cold lights.

"My eyes!" Elise hissed as she realized. She jerked her head around to the side. "It probably saw my eyes." She closed them to shut off the light. "I'm sorry. I'm sorry."

Chris put a hand on her arm to let her know where he was. "What should we do?"

"I don't know," she whispered.

THUD!

The Other's fist came up and hit the glass, making it shake. Chris and Elise both jumped, and Elise clutched a hand to her chest.

"What's it doing? What's it doing!" she pleaded with her eyes still sealed.

"Knocking. Maybe it can't use the door," he whispered.

THUD!

"No. It's opened doors before. It must be doing something else."

THUD!

"It's holding something," Chris noticed. "What is that? It's white…with some sort of brown… or–

THUD!

The object pressed against the glass again. "Alan's priesthood collar," Chris recognized. The Other smeared it down the glass.

"Come on," Chris grabbed her hand. He began pulling her back into the trees.

"No. Not in there," Elise grasped his hand back and flashed her eyes. "I've already used a lot of what's down here. Plus, if we go back there, we won't be able to see where it is." Not daring to speak it, she got close to Chris' face, lighting it until he squinted. She mouthed, *Up.*

Together they raced up the iron stairs to the catwalk, trying to keep their feet quiet even as the thing outside lumbered the last few feet to the door. They slid into the shield of the first row of trees still green, Chris first, then Elise. She pressed back against him, trying to get as far into the shadows as she could. And the worst – she had to close her eyes again. Elise concentrated on breathing silently through her nose.

They heard the click of the doorknob as the Other tried to twist it (or perhaps played with it for their nerves' benefit).

"We need to do something. We need to do something!" her voice rose with panic. Chris only pressed back on her hand, encouraging her to be quiet – not much help. *Simple exercise: lock the locks,* she suddenly heard Alan in her head, just as he asked her the first time. *Yes.* Elise pushed herself out to find the door.

There it was. The coolness around the cracks as the outside came in where it could; the doorknob even colder; and the keyhole. She had it memorized. Elise felt the tumblers click into place and heard them lock as she simultaneously came back to where Chris held her.

"I locked the door," she whispered to him. He nodded against her.

The Other tried the knob again, only this time, it refused to jostle. The creature made a low whining and pulled harder.

THUD!

Is it trying to break the glass? Shit! Elise pushed her mind out again. *Feel the door, feel the door*, she jumped back to it. It was still solid, no cracks. Her mind wound back into the lock, and she touched the metal, the parts, still locked–

Like a punch, the vapor-Elise felt something hit her with incredible force, and the real Elise cried out in surprise. She reeled and lost hold on the room and came back to Chris, who was busy trying to cover her mouth. "Something hit me. I don't–" They both heard the lock click unlocked. The door creaked open.

Desperate, Elise threw her consciousness out, and with a rush, pushed all of her strength against the door. It slammed shut.

Outside, the Other growled angry. In quick retaliation, it hit the door, using its weight to burst it open a second before Elise's imaginary arms forced it closed again. Hardly ready to give-up, it came again. This time, the door stayed open just a little bit longer.

Elise was losing strength. The door suddenly didn't feel as hard to her. She needed more – more turning-up.

But nothing could've prepared her for the force that suddenly hit her from behind. Again out of nowhere, it slammed her consciousness against the inside of the door. For a moment, even the real Elise felt pinned, unable to breath. She let go of the room and retreated back to Chris.

With a gasp, "It's like me." Elise inhaled twice before she could get the rest out. "It can do things with its mind. Hit me even. I can't keep it out."

The greenhouse door swung open so hard, it shattered against the wall. Elise flinched and pushed back harder on Chris, futilely trying to lose herself in the leaves. Something came in and quietly closed what was left of the door.

"I don't have anything left," she whispered as the glass shards crunched under heavy feet below them. Elise reached for the closest tree and sucked at it. Immediately, the leaves started falling, and she released it. If she turned-up now, they would lose their cover. She slipped both hands by her sides, unsure what else to do with them, and pulled at the fabric of her jeans.

The crunching stopped. It was further into the greenhouse now. Their only hope was that it headed towards the back on the lower level, giving them a chance to run down the front stairs and out the door.

The chance slipped away. Elise felt the catwalk shift as new weight added below. The Other was coming up the stairs.

She breathed hard, no longer caring who heard. It was over. It would see them easily. "It's going to find us," she seethed.

"Don 't move, Elise," Chris put a heavy arm across her trembling one. "Stay still."

"But it knows we're here–"

Chris clamped a hand over her mouth. The catwalk shifted again, and then again.

"Oh, God. Oh, God," Elise's prayer tickled against the palm of Chris' hand. They needed to do something, anything!

Do it! JUST DO IT! Elise's mind thrust forward the idea she had been weighing since they abandoned Alan. None of the reasons against it mattered anymore; not her own, or theirs.

With her elbow, Elise sucker-punched Chris in the stomach, loosening his grip instantly. She spun away from him out into the open catwalk. Without looking towards the stairs to see the horror so close, Elise reached for Chris' grasping hand (already recovered and looking for her). They closed on each other, and she turned-up.

Chris' life was an explosion. Elise fed on him without slowing down the rush, without disappointing the voices that urged her on. The greenhouse turned yellow, radiant, as her eyes turned the same, and the whispers crescendoed so that Elise did not hear the footsteps coming up behind her. And yet, she knew. After only seconds, she tossed his hand aside and swung around to face the thing she most feared.

For a moment, nothing happened, each waiting for the first move. They stood so close that some of the Other's long hairs extended out as Elise sucked in her breath. She could see the silver scales as large as thumbnails underneath, shining.

Slowly, Elise arched her neck so that she could meet the blue eyes several heads above hers. That was what it was waiting for – to see the death in her eyes. She showed it the light.

Fast like fluid, Elise pulled her hands back and then punched forward, hitting the Other in the chest with simultaneous force. She felt it crunch inside as bones broke. It plunged backwards and then down the stairs, crashing every step as it went.

For a moment, Elise stood unbelieving, feeling the rattle of the catwalk as evidence. She smiled a dark smile and headed for the stairs.

The Other lie on its back. Like a great struggling insect, it writhed its legs and arms, trying to turn its hulking weight over and stand upright while being careful of its broken ribs. It was furious, all of its mouths hissing. Elise had a feeling it wasn't furious very often. Her smile widened.

It sensed her approach and stopped moving. One of the heads lifted up to watch her. It turned from side to side, sizing her up in a surprisingly confident way, until she hesitated. Belly-up, she could see its clawed feet and body. *Can't let you get close to me.* Elise pushed herself out and found the barrel of pruning equipment.

(Another step down the stairs. It was trying to get up again).

A pair of garden clippers was her choice – three feet long and solid iron. The vapor fingers pulled at them.

(Another step, three to go).

Elise closed her mind's fingers around the handles. With a pull so hard, the real Elise wavered backwards, the clippers came to her hands in a streak and she snapped back into herself. Another step, and she took a swing with the weapon, enjoying their whoosh against the air.

The one head was still intent on her, and Elise took the appraising moment to decide where to hit it first.

Her appraisal turned into a squint–

It was different now. The hair was becoming white, the eyes changing, the fur thinning. Recognition came with horror.

"Elise," the head spoke. The voice wasn't quite right, and Elise was temporarily thankful. But second try, it had Alan Cole down perfect. "You left me, Elise. Now look where I am."

Elise stopped on the second to last step, unable to move. *This isn't real. This can't be.*

"It's murder you know, Elisssse," Alan drew out her name in a hiss. "Your third."

"Liar." Elise forced herself down the final two stairs in one step, afraid most of losing her nerve. With Chris' strength in her arms, she swung the clippers.

One strike, then two. Had it been human, she would've easily decapitated it. Instead, he faced each strike without blinking, ugly gashes appearing where the blades hit. It took three blows before Alan even turned away. At this first sign of weakness, Elise used the clippers to catch Alan's ear. It tore away like the peal off an apple and finally, the other two heads groaned and the Other began again trying to stand.

"Does it hurt?" the glee in Elise's voice belied that she thought she knew the answer. "Are you afraid yet?" She opened the clippers wide and shoved them deep into the furry belly.

"GOOOOOODDDDDD!"

Elise froze all her movements, even her breath, at the sound of a voice she had not heard in more than a decade.

"Stop hurting me," the scream reduced to a whimper, and the head Elise assaulted turned back into the light of her eyes to show Kailey Moore's face, instead of Alan's. Blood matted part of her hair where her ear was missing.

"You're not real," Elise said, as if to make it so. "You're dead."

"Yes," her mother's voice hardened. "You would know. You were there. You helped me die."

"No. No!" Elise yelled it stupidly as her eyes ran over the features she had tried so hard not to forget: the high eyebrows and proud chin, the mole by the side of the nose, even the smile lines at the corners of the mouth. *How does it know all that?*

She should strike, now while there was a chance. But Elise only wanted to press her palms on the cheeks of the face and feel it again. An old wound opened within her, just as the Other wanted.

"You helped me die, Elise," her mother taunted again. "More than the accident."

"No," Elise whispered. "No I didn't."

"It's okay, honey," the mother's face successfully put on an expression of real comfort and compassion. "I'm fine now," the smile was ironic atop the monster's body. "And I want you to be happy."

Hit it, now while you can. It's not her. It's not really her.

"Walk away, Elise. The priests told you that you don't have a choice," Kailey's eyes flicked down to the monster, as if to reference the Alan inside. "But you do. Choose to walk away, and I promise: I will let nothing hurt you. You can still have a normal life, the life your father and I always wanted for you."

Lies, she's lying. "What life is there if you bring about the end of the world too soon?" Elise squeezed her eyes shut to gather her strength. *Irrational. Don't talk to it. You're feeding it, showing it more about you.*

"That's where everyone mistakes us, Elise. We're not evil. We're about having. Having everything. The end of the world would not be torture. It would be an end to the abstinence, the discipline, the going without, the sadness that your God forces you to suffer under. We bring liberation; not damnation."

All lies, Elise. Hit her! Stop listening!

There was a noise on the catwalk above – Chris was moving. Kailey looked up for a long moment. Then, "Choose. Walk away, and you will have everything you want. Me, your father, we will all be there." She smiled a knowing smile and gestured with her chin towards the catwalk. "Anything you want, Elise."

Elise's eyes squeezed into hateful, lightening slits, embarrassed by her secret feelings even before the Other. "You're not my mother," Elise pulled back the clippers over her shoulder. "She loves me. She didn't ask me to join

241

her that last day, and she wouldn't ask me to join her now." She flicked the clippers forward with her wrist a few times, like a batter at the plate. "But thanks. It was good to see her face." Elise closed her eyes and swung, heard the clippers whiffing just slightly on the stairway railing, and forced Chris' life into her arms. She caught her mother's face under the chin, and there was a tearing sound like fabric ripping.

The second hit Elise delivered with her eyes open. She screamed, "STOP LOOKING LIKE HER! STOP IT!" At least it bled, like anything else.

Elise came around to hit again, but the Other had enough. Using one of its back legs, it slashed through Elise's arm; she dropped the clippers. With a move that made the floor shake, the monster threw its heavy torso to the right and stood again. Its three heads were now its own, one heavily wounded, though healing quickly.

We're more and more alike… Elise ignored the thought and concentrated on her own recovery; the gash made an attempt at closing. God, it hurt. She stood wobbly and breathing hard. The bleeding seemed to be stopping, but it took too much of her, too much of Chris.

The Other, however, seemed just ready to begin. It stomped, lowering its three heads like a bull.

If it got her again–

She had to strike first.

The Other took its first charging step and quickly picked up into a gallop. Elise focused her mind until it found the bin of pruning equipment. This time, she didn't pick just one.

The air filled with sharp objects of all kinds, silent and shining in the dim light that filtered in from outside. Her mind flicked, and they flew. Like the speed of a drum roll, they hit the side of the Other with soft padding sounds. Two of the heads turned towards the onslaught and screamed. The creature stumbled. But, she could tell by the eyes of the head still facing her: it was bent on coming.

She had nothing else. Elise turned to run from its path – she outran it the last time. With her legs already picking up supernatural speed on the turn around, Elise sprinted–

Into the scratchy branches of a tree.

The Other had also been busy moving things with its mind. Elise stared wide-eyed: the greenhouse no longer had its neat aisles, but looked like an unfamiliar jungle.

She only turned back halfway before it hit her. Elise filled her lungs to scream but never did: claws dug into her body everywhere. Several pierced through her entirely, scraping the branches she was now pinned against. The three heads peered in, like curious onlookers at an accident. Their eyes burned into hers, cool and speculative.

Don't let me die here. Please don't let me die. Don't let me fail.

One head pushed closer than the others and ran its needle-teeth ever so gently across her cheek in a morbid caress. Elise remembered it eating Jeff and tried to turn her head away. A claw piercing her shoulder restrained the movement. And then it was moving away from her, not in mercy, but in torture. The Other pulled its living daggers from her slow, so that they caused even better pain than they had on their way in. Elise collapsed to her hands and knees, silent.

With the last drippings of her power, she pushed strength into her hands and calves. *Just don't die!* She counted down, then again, each time hoping to feel strong enough. The Other was coming for her again and at last, she pushed, springing from her crouch like a cat. Elise swung her body up, up, over itself several times, and managed to barely land on the catwalk rail, hearing the internal crack of her ribs. For a moment, she hung, and then rolled herself over to land on the grate with a crash.

"Elise!" Chris was kneeling nearby. She did not respond. Blood flowed freely from several wounds, dying her clothes and the floor. Her eyes: Chris couldn't see them in the dark.

He crawled to her and put one hand on her shoulder and one on her abdomen, feeling the clammy skin through the torn clothing. "God, Elise! Take it. Take me."

He felt the shock in both his palms. It turned to a vibration, and then the burn came. New pain seared as Elise reached up and grabbed one of his wrists. Through the stars that kept trying to gather in his eyes, Chris saw some of the wounds begin to close, the light in her eyes rekindle. It was not beautiful, seeing his life burn in her. The pain was renewed over and over, a burning that ebbed and intensified like a growing wave. The things she spoke of – whispers, lights, a power beyond herself – he did not find. Only taking. And then he was floating, unattached from everything but the burn..

More seconds and Elise's breathing calmed as the pain quieted while the whispering became louder and her vision clouded with light. More, more: the blood dried and the wounds covered over, showing dark marks like bruises where they once gaped. And then finally, Elise's body began to store, tucking Chris' life into its muscle fibers and bones. His weight slumped against her as he lost consciousness, and she felt his soul bend away from her, begging to be released. But she could not. He needed to give her as much as he could stand, or they would both die.

*This is my dream...*Elise jumped and Chris twitched as his thought passed over to her. And the whispers screamed in their breathy way. And he was bending so far–

Like the snapping of a cable, the connection was abruptly broken, his

243

hand torn away, the pressure of his body absent. Elise whipped into a sitting position, and then kept the momentum going to a crouch with her feet beneath her.

No! She hadn't even heard it come up the stairs, hadn't felt it standing over them, hadn't seen it grasp Chris' unconscious body.

Where?

Elise knew by the prickling hairs on her neck. She stood and spun around, squinting against her own light. The Other silhouetted for her at the top of the steps, holding Chris like a baby in its arms. One of its heads remained poised over his neck. He did not stir.

The head closest to Chris smiled in anticipation of her anger and fear, still enjoying the game.

But Elise was not. She did not know how to beat it. Only her strongest blows had any effect, and even then, it could heal itself rapidly. They needed to get out, get away from it, or undoubtedly, they would lose.

Elise pushed off and flew at it. In a blur of hair, tattered clothing, and light, she was upon it. Digging her heels into the soft part of the Other's body, she went for the nearest head, her thumbs searching for its blue-disc eyes to put them out.

The Other screeched and tossed its body as it realized her intent. Not willing to give-up its prize, however, it opted to weave its neck, hoping to avoid her touch rather than throw her off. It got in two successful moves before it failed. Elise dug her fingernails into one of the blue eyes with a triumphant cry. But there was nothing – she pressed her thumb into the light, deeper and deeper, and felt nothing.

It didn't seem to matter, however. The Other screeched again – this time in true pain. She pressed harder and it howled. Finally, she felt something: cold. It was as though she pressed into its ruined soul. Ooze like petroleum jelly began to leak onto its face. It dropped Chris.

"You shouldn't have touched him," she whispered to it as she nuzzled close to its neck. Before it could realize what she was doing, Elise pushed Chris' energy into her mouth, and then bit down into the matted fur, into the silvery scales, and into the soft flesh beneath.

The Other screamed again, then gargled as her teeth worked their way to the neck's esophagus. Frantically, it shook its head, and the arms clawed at her shoulders to do what damage they could. But, Elise kept it caught in her vice-bite, tasting its blood, remarkably like any other blood.

Frenzied, one of the rotting hands dug itself into the back of Elise's neck, and she screamed through teeth that clenched tighter and tighter. Her retribution was quick. Elise felt for the rotting skin as the hand continued to dig. She turned-up, feeling the zap.

It was as though she had inflicted it with a mortal blow. With more force than it had previously exhibited, the Other grasped Elise and tore her off its neck, not seeming to care that she took a large portion of it with her. It launched her over the railing to get her far from the only open skin it had: the human hands.

Elise writhed in air and managed to get her feet beneath her before hitting the concrete below. Squatting, feeling the vibration of her landing move throughout the greenhouse, Elise spit a large wad of fur, scales, and flesh onto the floor, and then ran her tongue over her teeth to clean them. Though she only took a half-second of the Other's energy, she could tell by the stiffness that the wound on the back of her neck was healed. Whatever she got from it was incredible. *And it certainly didn't like it.* How much supernatural power ran through it, and how much could she steal?

The thing was already barreling down the stairs. One head bobbed unsteadily on a neck that bled freely, making a wheezing sound as it sucked air in through the hole she bit. Elise braced. "Come on, come on," she spoke under her breath.

Several feet from her, the Other pounced like a cat ready to pummel its prey.

With borrowed strength, Elise reached back one hand. At the last second, she moved to the side and swung, hammering down on the head with the weakened neck. She dug her nails in, taking skin and bone with her fist. The Other moved past her, stumbling. She turned with it, keeping it in front of her.

Unfazed, it came at her again, this time with its claws raised – a hit she could not risk. At its approach she jumped high, flipping herself gracefully several times before landing 20 feet back, hidden by the plants. She took several deep breaths. Too much more, and the dark would be creeping back in; the shadows becoming more distinct.

The Other came back for her – she could hear it knocking over plants and trees on its way through the greenhouse. Elise grasped a few leaves for a quick pick-up and then began to weave in and out between the plants. She kept tabs on the monster by its crashing, moving herself as quietly as possible in any direction it didn't seem to be heading. *Think, think!* She commanded herself as she continued brushing anything alive to load-up. She just needed enough time – time to get Chris and get out. She led the Other further into the greenhouse, then over to the left where the plants and trees were thickest.

So many trees. The idea came.

Elise headed for the very back, running now, careful to only use her own energy and leave Chris' for when she needed it. By the growing crashing, she also knew the Other was gaining. Stopping slightly short of her goal, Elise sent many of the nearest plants sailing, crashing somewhere far off in the greenhouse. A few tosses with her mind, and she had a lopsided circle cleared. She stood unready and yet waiting.

The Other burst in on her. It had not taken the time to heal its previous wounds – the one head hung limply, its face split wide open from Elise's hit and the wound on its neck continuing to dye the fur of its chest.

Blow for blow, they warred one another. At every attack, she hit it back, trying keep the damage minimal. It, on the other hand, seemed less concerned with injury, not bothering to block or dodge. The Other focused on tearing her apart: a strategy that would probably work–

If she didn't get hold of one of those hands.

But the Other kept them tucked into its body where she could not reach. Elise fought – punching, hitting, slapping, pounding – with a watchful eye, waiting for her opportunity. She was bleeding badly in several places, but she dared not use the energy to heal. The light was fading, and Elise delivered each blow with reducing strength. She pounded, pounded, but to no avail. So slow, slower, she panted to get air into her tired lungs, no longer able to hide her exhaustion. The monster let out a purring sound – it knew.

Trying one of her more successful tricks, Elise swung for one of the blue eyes. But the Other caught her flailing fist with ease. It was an instinct – reaching up with its hand to grab its prey and hold it for one of its own, stronger blows.

It was the mistake she was waiting for.

The Other leaned in, putting excruciating pressure on her fist. Several of Elise's fingers snapped. But the pain did not ruin her smile.

Elise grabbed the gangrene arm around the wrist with her free hand and turned-up to feel the fireworks go off in her body. For a moment, there was silence. Then, the whispers rushed in as though breaking a vacuum seal. She closed her eyes, knowing it would be a wild ride.

The Other realized its error with a scream. As predicted, it swung Elise like a rag doll, trying to force her off its arm. With the trees cleared back, only her feet took any damage.

One second, two seconds, three seconds – Elise hung on like a bull-rider, trying to rise and fall with each movement of the creature she clung to. Its other hand came down to beat around her skull, but she only turned up harder, burning it so that the smell of burnt hair was real.

Four seconds, five seconds – it swung her with such fury that Elise felt the whiplash in her neck and spine. It moved with purpose towards the plants, and she saw herself smashed against them. She waited until it had her in full swing and then let go. Its incredible momentum shot her half way to the front door. Unable to right herself fast enough, she crashed through prickly branches until she found the concrete floor.

Immediately, she used her new strength to heal, even while getting up. It

246

had to be now, before it found her again.

Elise concentrated, sending herself out, everywhere in the room. Like before: that one day, when Chris and Alan and Francis were with her, still whole and alive, critical and amazed – she could feel all things in the greenhouse simultaneously, as though she had her fingers on each one. Elise closed her eyes, feeling everything, everything.

The shaking began in the trees, and in the potted plants. As if pulling invisible strings, Elise raised her hands, and every object in the room followed just as they had before, lifting off the ground. This time, they twisted and swirled, some skimming off others with tiny clay clinks. They rose higher and faster; the largest trees moved around the room with sounds like swinging swords. Past the catwalk, up to the ceiling, they soared faster and faster, tightening in their patterns. The sound was like a train engine warming up. Elise's hair lifted and tossed around her shoulders in the breeze created by so much motion: a virtual cyclone of dirt, clay, and branches.

The Other – revealed now that the cement floor was clear of all things – was still near the back. Its heads turned from side to side as they viewed the angrily churning mass above them. It seemed unsure…

At the blink of her eyes, the first trees and plants launched.

Their pots shattered against the Other's body at the speed of bullets and their branches slashed it. The Other's considerable weight was thrown back, several feet, then several more. Elise kept the trees coming, plucking them out of the mass with her mind, and sending them with lightening speed to pin the creature against the back wall. With a roar that shook the building, the Other realized her intent: to bury it.

The dirt burned its eyes and choked its mouths. The branches scratched and impaled it. The plants landed on it, crushing it with their momentum and then their weight. More, more, until it struggled to move. She threw things from all directions until it stopped trying to find a way to defend itself. The monster became blurred in an ever-closing mass of branches, leaves, and dirt. Every last piece whirled and arced around it, finally landing to pin it where it stood. The dust rose and the crashing accelerated, until Elise could not see the Other at all. Until its angry screeches were drown.

Until it felt like the fingers of her mind suddenly became slippery. The mass began to come apart, pieces whirling madly out from the center without her control. Dirt showered down like rain with random crashing. Human again, Elise dropped the rest.

The room settled, empty, save for the colossal mound of broken trees and dirt in the back corner. The thing beneath it moved, but found no way out.

Breathing hard, Elise hunched over and placed her hands on her knees to support herself.

It made a muffled sound.

She began to hobble – barely a girl, let alone a warrior.

Across the floor, Elise forced her exhausted body to move at a reasonable pace until she paused at the catwalk stairs, wishing now that she hadn't lost so much. Too much.

FLICKER

Blinding lights flashed through the greenhouse, and Elise automatically raised a hand to cover her eyes. *NOOOO… I need more time!* Her mind cried before she realized:

Headlights outside, in the drive. Elise heard the engine through the shattered glass door. "Yes! Yes!"

Breathless, she limped up the catwalk steps two at a time with the help of her adrenaline. *HURRY. Don't let it drive away! We have to get that car. PLEASE.*

Chris was where the Other left him: in a heap against the rail of the catwalk. His head was bleeding, but his breaths were strong.

More movement in the back. It was working, trying to get out.

Even Chris' arm was heavy to Elise as she tried to throw some of his weight onto her shoulders. She staggered. How was she going to get him down the stairs? With stinging tears, Elise looked back to the door – the headlights still burnt strong.

"Come on," she began to talk to herself. "Come on," she threw his weight, trying to get more leverage. Two more tries, and she sat back defeated. "I'm sorry, Chris. I just need – a little."

Afraid, she grabbed one cold hand and turned-up. Chris no longer flooded into her; he dripped, and she had to wait several seconds to get what she needed. With a small penlight in the center of her pupil, Elise used Chris' life to hoist him onto her shoulders and march in a slow stagger.

The rustling in the back stopped as Elise's heavy steps echoed down the stairs in the empty space. There was a whining, like a hurt dog. She ignored it, not looking back. *Just get to the car. Get to the car.* Through the empty greenhouse, up to the front, to the shattered door and the snow falling on the cement floor. Through it–

She stopped at the threshold. There was glitter everywhere.

Little tiny specs floating and swirling before her very face. Elise blinked several times to make sure it wasn't some trick, some exhaustion creeping into her vision.

No trick. The glitter began to congregate, and she watched amazed as pieces began to fit themselves together. *Not glitter…glass!* Her mind finally grasped what was happening. It was the glass from the shattered door – fixing itself! Shards whizzed dangerously by her ears as they flocked to the door and began filling it up – a single second and the holes were already too small to crawl through. She risked pressing her hand against it – solid. She pushed harder, but the spider-web fit held. Desperate, Elise balanced and reached for the doorknob just as it locked to her touch.

Panic. She panted under Chris' heaviness and her frustration. *No.* "No. You can't keep us here. YOU CAN'T – KEEP US!" Elise spun around slow under Chris. There was nothing for her to use, and her panting became worse. The pile in the back shuddered. She spun again, stumbling slightly.

Though she hardly had enough strength, Elise pushed her mind out to feel the lock. *Feel it cold and hard, like before. Feel it...* But she couldn't. Perhaps she didn't have enough strength. *Perhaps something is blocking me.*

"God! Help me!" the cry came out angry and desperate. "If you need me another day past this one, then you have to help us! HELP US!" The glass rattled.

Several pieces of the mound's top layer fell. Beneath it, the Other heaved.

"GOD! HELP US! HELP US!" Every sheet reverberated at her high-pitched tones. Elise didn't notice – her legs trembled and threatened to give out. "GODDDD!"

With the strength of a small explosion, every sheet – the walls, the roof, the doors – burst outward in miniscule pieces. Outside the greenhouse, it rained glass.

For a moment, Elise remained still with the sound ringing in her ears too loud for her own voice, too shocked. But the headlights – they were still there. She staggered through one of the shattered wall panels and out into the snow.

Immediately, she noticed the shadow by the truck – human. "Get back!" she squinted into the headlights. "I'm warning you," her tone verified that she was.

But, the shadow came towards them anyway, its hands up protectively. It was familiar, and Elise gave enough hesitation for Francis to materialize from the headlight radiance. Even in the fake hue, she could tell he was pale. His eyes were wide and there were several gashes on his face from the glass.

He processed the supernatural scene quickly – Elise covered in blood from head to toe, her clothing in scraps, her hair matted down to her head and almost black; Chris also bleeding, a deadweight on her back. He gave one apprehensive look over Elise's shoulder into the dark greenhouse and then focused on the task at hand. With strength he hid well under his robes, Francis easily lifted Chris off of Elise and carried him around the back of the truck. It took some heaving, but he managed to slide Chris behind the driver's seat into the back cabin.

Elise remained for a moment, still frozen, and feeling consciously light now that Chris was gone. Then, leaning against the truck hood with both palms, she began to drag herself around the opposite side. She heaved open the old door and lifted herself the few inches she needed to climb in. Francis appeared suddenly at her side and helped her, shutting the door.

It was quiet in the car. Already, the snowflakes were accumulating on the windshield.

Francis crossed the headlights on his way back to the driver's seat, and Elise became terrified for him, unable to shake the inevitable death-feeling that had grown on her in the greenhouse. It seemed certain: something would reach out from the gaping greenhouse frame and pull Francis inside at the last second, before they could drive away.

She held her breath as he made it all the way around. With a creak, he pulled open the driver's door and slid inside, closing them in with a slam.

Elise leaned back in a spasm of relief, blinking and breathing rapidly, tears beginning to trail down the dirt and blood on her face.

Francis understood. He put the truck in gear, spun the tires a few worrisome moments, and then shot down the drive to the road.

"Alan," she said through too thick mucus from not swallowing. "Alan. He's probably down here. Only," several tears leaked out. "I don't think he's–" she shook her head and leaned forward over the dash to see.

He was there, just where they turned onto the road.

Elise covered her mouth with one hand and did some loud breathing through her nose. A large radius of pink snow surrounded the shredded thing that used to be Alan. There was no question – he was dead.

Francis took the truck down to an idle and waited. Finally, he shook his head.

"I know. I know. We can't do anything for him." Elise shuddered several times. "He should've come with us," her voice rose in distress. "We never – should've left him." She turned her face away to look out the window at the corn, now still again.

Francis maneuvered the truck around Alan. His form came into the rearview mirror, and then faded in seconds.

Chapter 15 – Recouping

Francis drove them into Whiteley, where things still appeared to be normal. The storefronts were closed, but lights burned in the houses as people sat down to dinner. Francis parked under a street lamp, as if its circle of light could keep them safe.

He left the engine idling, and Elise wiped away any tears left drying on her cheeks. It was rational decision-making time. She turned so that her knees were underneath her and she could face Chris, who was lumped awkwardly on the back seat in the small truck cabin. He was still unconscious.

"We should probably try to wake him," she said to Francis as a start. "He's hurt, but I think he just needs some rest. I took a lot from him." She reached across the seat and touched Chris' face, pushing gently just above the cut across his right eye. It was dry and crusty – the blood had stopped flowing at least.

Chris' forehead wrinkled and his eyes spasmed beneath their lids.

"Chris," Elise made her voice light, like a mother's. "Can you answer me?"

He moved his head slightly, but his eyes didn't open.

"I know you're tired, and you probably have the headache from hell, but…" she squeezed his shoulder in further encouragement. One eye opened. The other tried, but gave up under the soreness of the cut above it. The one eye rolled around, blinked several times, and then rested on Elise.

"Elise," so much relief came out in the one word.

"Yeah, we made it," she feigned a smile. "I'll have to tell you about it sometime. But right now, we're with Francis in–" she jerked her head to the front. "How did we get this truck?"

Francis scrambled for the whiteboard. Fingers that still trembled dropped the marker cap, and he let it roll without any attempt at retrieval. *The farmer. He wasn't there, but his wife let me borrow. Told her it was too snowy to walk. Told her I'd return it…*

Elise relayed the message to Chris, who could not see. "Francis got the truck from the farmer. And we drove into town. We need to decide what to do."

"Alan?" he whispered the name.

Elise closed her eyes briefly and shook her head exactly twice.

Chris gave a great sigh, his body deflating under the coat he still wore. Then he tried moving, wincing and huffing as he maneuvered in the tight space, finally propping up on his elbow. "Are you sure? Did you see him? Tell me you–"

Their silence stopped him. "Okay," he coached himself into taking charge. "We can't go back to the rectory." His voice was weak, with no inflection. "Francis? Do you remember how to get to Syracuse from here? Just take route 20 east. We'll head to the airport, let Mrs. Davenport know where her truck is parked. I'll...call in from there, see where to go..." his words trailed off.

"No amount of lax airport security is going to let us through," Elise voiced skepticism, taking on Chris' role just as he took on Alan's. "Look at me," she indicated the varying shades of blood from black to a watery red and stripes down her face where she cried. "You don't look a whole lot better. There must be somewhere for us to go."

"Do we really want to put someone else in danger?" Chris whispered, barely succeeding in following the conversation. "The Other may follow us...not to mention I'm afraid the police will become involved if we stop for help."

Elise made an exasperated noise. "This isn't optional."

Let's not sit here, Francis added little to the strategizing, but made a good point. He checked all the mirrors. The street was still empty.

"Derek," Elise said the idea as it came to her head. "Derek Dewallace."

"Elise..." Chris hinted at his disapproval, but could not keep her from continuing.

"He knows I'm weird. He knows that there is something going on, but he won't turn us in. I know he won't," she felt the Psalm plate hanging between her collarbones.

Francis threw the truck in gear before Chris could respond.

* * * * *

Derek lived across town from the rectory, which was fine with the three in the car (the further, the better). It was a big house set back from a road that wound a mile or so away from Main Street. The truck wiggled up the drive as it tried to find traction on the wet snow. They pulled in behind Derek's own truck. A single light was on.

Elise uselessly smoothed her hair as Francis turned the key in the ignition and the engine died. Her own strength was far from rebounded, and she held on to the front of the car for a few seconds before venturing on unsupported legs. Francis helped Chris climb out the back. He could not hold his full weight on his own, and the monk stayed with him while Elise went ahead to ring the bell.

It took a few moments, but soon she heard Derek scrounging around for a key. The door opened, and a dim light shown out, which Elise ducked to avoid. "Mr. Dewallace. Derek. It's me. Elise. From the rectory," she managed to remember all of the details in a normal introduction.

"Elise?" his voice was both curious and happy. "What can I– are you all right?" he caught a first glimpse of her face.

"I'm fine. But, I need your help."

The worry quickly crept into Derek's expression. "Of course. Come in," the door opened wider, forcing Elise more fully into the light. Derek tried to hide his gasp. "Have you been in an accident? Let me get the phone – er," he finally noticed the two men behind her. "Father?"

"Yes, it's me Derek," Chris shifted himself into the light. "And the phone won't be necessary. We could really just use your bathroom."

Elise pushed passed Derek's stunned stiffness. They didn't have time to wait outside. Chris and Francis followed.

"My God," he said as Chris passed with the huge gash over his eye. "What happened?"

The door closed behind them.

* * * * *

It was the fastest shower Elise could remember taking. It seemed she barely closed the curtain around the footed tub before she was whipping it back again. Just long enough to rinse all the pink down the drain.

One towel around her head, one around her body, Elise still dripped as she padded over to the clothes laid out for her on the bathroom counter: Helen's. After a pause, she held up the sweatshirt, smelled it: it still retained some perfume. There was definitely something morbid about putting on a dead woman's clothes, like some bad omen. But, they would pass airport security.

Elise dropped her towel to slip into the outfit and frowned at the dark circles and lines all over her body. It looked like a rash. They were healing over, literally shadows of the wounds that used to be there. But, there were so many – the Other did so much damage, tearing through her in so many places. Without more turning-up, they would finish healing normal and slow. And then she thought of Alan and how he would never heal. She cried – a cry that shook her chest – and then dressed (leaving the bra and underwear – she just couldn't wear those). Elise transferred her wallet from her tattered coat to the jean pockets, and then threw the rest of her clothes away in the garbage bag Derek gave her. Wiping a clear spot on the mirror, she found her face in the fog. Several hideous smudges and lines there too. And the skin around her eyes was loose – tired. It was like seeing an aged version of the girl she was only that morning.

"The worst of it is, it doesn't matter," she spoke to her reflection. "You'll probably never see them scar over."

* * * * *

Francis jumped up as Elise exited the bathroom, still using a towel to squeeze water from her hair – so wet it looked brown, as if the gold and red were all washed out. He shot by her, noticeably glad to be leaving the living room.

Elise could see why. Chris was asleep on the couch, and Derek sat at a piano stool, twitching his hands. He looked petrified, as if realizing he was an accomplice to some dark crime. Conversation with a whiteboard had to be seriously strained.

Elise sat down in a stiff armchair and blew air out through her cheeks as she often saw Chris do. She heard the water turn on and hoped Francis would be fast.

"This wasn't a car accident, was it? That man – he wouldn't tell me anything," Derek broke the silence with an accusatory glance towards the shower.

"Yeah," Elise nodded her head slowly and clicked her tongue. "Yeah, I'm sure he didn't." She gave Derek a smile while racing in her mind to choose words. "Francis is just – trying to protect me," she gave him part of the truth.

"From what?"

Elise nodded towards the dark mark on his cheek.

"Oh," Derek reached up and felt the mark. "So, this has something to do with…with what you can do?"

She searched for the simplest version. "Some people out there don't want me doing what I can do. They want me to stop. Some of them even want to hurt me." Elise did a double blink at all the abstract pronouns she managed to use. "So, Chris and Francis are going to take me to a place where I'll be safe," she gave the first lie.

Derek swallowed, as if literally stomaching what she said, and then looked over at Chris. "It will wear off soon. It took me a few hours, and then I felt mostly myself."

He surprised her: Derek saw and understood a lot.

They sat in silence until the water stopped running – Francis was quick.

"Do you think you can help me get him up?" Elise pushed the coffee table to the right to make more room by the couch. "It's going to be hard, but Chris needs to clean-up too."

Together, they roused him. This time, Chris successfully managed to sit-up. The sleep seemed to strengthen him, and Elise was hopeful that he might make it through a quick shower without one of them volunteering to give a sponge bath.

Francis came down redressed in his black robes (which sustained little damage). The cuts on his face, though far from healed, appeared smaller now that they were clean. He immediately indicated that Elise should move out of the way, and then again used his surprising strength to assist Derek in getting Chris off the couch. Together, they helped him hobble up the stairs to the shower.

Elise looked nervously at the clock. Thirty minutes passed since they first walked into the house. They could not stay much longer, for Derek's sake.

* * * * *

Though Francis and Derek offered to stay, Chris was quick to let them know he could at least stand in a shower and rinse off by himself (though he wasn't one hundred percent sure that he actually could). He needed a moment though, without shoulders beneath him and questions about where to go and what to do. He needed quiet even more than he needed stitches or rest. And so they left him to lean against the shower door, weakly rubbing soap on the parts of his body that he could reach without bending over.

Alan was dead.

His friend of almost twenty years was still lying cold on a road only a few miles from where he now leaned. And there was nothing he could do; no way to take back the time; to suggest they not practice at the greenhouse that day; or to stop Elise from turning-up on him in the first place. If they had only known; if they had only kept up their guard. It was something to regret forever and hurt over for years. It was excruciating and hollow, unreal and yet raw. Alan would want him to lead now. But the team – the society – was broken. How could he bring Elise where she needed to be without Alan? A dangerous despair washed over him until he shivered in the steaming water.

Only fifteen minutes later, he called for help coming down the stairs, dressed in one of Derek's flannels and a pair of old jeans. The cut above his eye was clean, but still nasty, and the skin around it formed a puffy pink pillow. He now managed to open the eye beneath the injury, though he blinked a great deal.

Francis tapped the clock face with his whiteboard marker (it still didn't have a cap – he left a green dot and then anxiously fell to smudging it out with his thumb).

"Time to go," Elise gave him a voice. She looked around the room, but there was nothing to gather. "Thank you, Derek." In turn, they each shook his hand. Just as they came, they slipped past him and out the door.

* * * * *

Forty-five minutes later, they parked the Davenport's truck in the long-term parking lot of Syracuse Hancock International Airport, and hurried three abreast through the luggage-accommodating, oversized rotating door. Though the airport was small, it was immediately obvious something needed to be done about Chris – he was just too slow, and still needed support to walk. Elise flagged one of the few airport attendants (8:00 PM on a Sunday was barely more lively in Syracuse than in Whiteley). Shortly, they had a wheelchair with two red plastic flags – the type kids sometimes put on their bikes – on stiff white poles bobbing on both sides.

The ticket lines were completely empty. "American? United? JetBlue?" Elise read some of the digital signs overhead.

"My vote's for whoever has a direct flight to Rome," Chris replied, scanning the boards.

"Rome? Why would we go there? They wanted to separate us; they want–"

"If we don't go to them, they will undoubtedly come for you, and who knows under what terms then. Alan had a hard enough time convincing the Church to leave you in Whiteley. They will never let me keep you now that it's proven the Other will find you in whatever safe haven we run to. The Pope will want you where his army and resources can protect you. And when he finds out about Alan, the risk you faced, he will send that army and those resources for you."

Elise's eyes clouded with some storm. The men waited for it to break, and were surprised when she slouched tired instead, her voice more frightened than anything else. "Fine – but only call the Vatican after you buy three plane tickets to Italy. That way, we have more leverage," she lowered her eyes. "You have to come with me, no matter what they say. Even Alan would've eventually given in." She swallowed.

* * * * *

The ticket agent gave a blank look when Chris wheeled up to the counter and asked her for the next flight to Italy. She surveyed him in the wheelchair with the cut over his eye, Elise with strange bruises all over, and the monk who looked like he'd been through a shaving nightmare. "You mean, you want to get on the next flight to Italy?" she repeated dully.

Elise gave an exaggerated sigh and rolled her eyes. Chris shot her a glance and then gave a please-excuse-her smile to the agent, who did not smile back. "Yes. Three tickets to Italy on the next flight. If they're available, of course. One-way," he haltingly remembered all of the details.

"Round-trip, actually," Elise countered him. "Round-trip for three."

"So three tickets to Italy, round-trip," the agent fell to repeating again. "Where in Italy?"

"Rome," Chris regained control of the ordering.

The agent gave them each a cautionary look over. "I will need to see a photo I.D. for each of you, please."

They each dug around, finally producing pictures from New York, South Carolina and Ohio.

The agent clucked at the different locations, but said nothing, returning to her computer screen where she typed their information rapidly. "The next flight departs tomorrow evening at 9:20 PM."

"Tomorrow evening!" Elise suddenly looked even more tired than she had a few minutes prior. "That's almost 26 hours."

"I'm sorry, miss. That's all we have."

"What about flying into another city? Do you have an earlier flight anywhere in the country?" Elise leaned over the counter, as if to find the flight herself.

More typing. "There is an earlier flight to Naples departing at 5:25 PM. There are stops in Philadelphia and Paris, with an arrival in Naples set for 2:15 PM the following day."

"That's fine, thank you," Chris spoke over another of Elise's huffs. "We'll take the three tickets to Naples."

"And when will you be returning?"

"January...seventh," Chris pulled it out of the air.

"Checking any luggage?"

"Uh...no, actually."

The agent clucked again.

* * * * *

"So why the roundtrip tickets?" Chris asked as Elise wheeled him over to two empty seats in one of the airport lounges.

"Don't you want to believe you're coming back?" she posed the dark question for them. "Angel or not, you'd have a hard time getting me on that plane if there wasn't some hope that this isn't my last time in an airport." She shrugged. "What now? I figure, we don't have to go through security for at least another eighteen hours, so..."

"I have to call Rome. We need passports, a car in Naples. And they should be involved quickly in handling Alan...we could get a hotel tonight," Chris offered. "If you think you would be more comfortable."

"No," Elise was quick to answer. "If no one else objects, I'd like to skip the dimly lit hallways and hundreds of closets. Here, the lights are bright, lots of security," she nodded to the armed guards. "And lots of space. I don't feel..." she searched for the right word, "trapped."

They fell into silence, each lost in some version of the events that passed only two hours prior. Even in the fluorescence, with the guards and the space, some of the dark crept back in.

"I keep thinking he's still here," Chris finally spoke. "He can't really be gone. I can't believe...this can't really be where we are."

"When we were in line trying to decide where to go, I actually looked over my shoulder for him, as if he was going to make the decision," Elise gave a snort-laugh that turned into more of a sniffle.

"I think I'll be doing that the rest of my life. I'm just dependent on him. He's often been the voice of my faith," Chris watched the ceiling until the lights hurt behind his eyes. "But, Alan would've rather gone defending you, Elise, than any other way."

"Yeah. You can say that because you didn't see him," she whispered. "I assure you, he would've preferred going another way." Her words chilled the air between them, and again, there was a haunted silence.

"He tried so hard to prepare me," her thoughts spilled out again. She looked past the men into the empty seats. "And I was prepared this time, as prepared as he could make me. I stood a chance. But... the Other is still so much stronger. Alan stayed behind and died because he was afraid I couldn't beat it. And he was right."

"Elise, Alan didn't die because of anything you did or didn't do. He..." Chris' words trailed off as he searched for something.

You succeeded where it mattered. YOU survived, Francis offered, propping the whiteboard on his knee.

"Do you know how cold that sounds?"

Embarrassed by her scorn, Francis hastily turned the words to face himself.

"I know what you're saying," she softened, "but, it feels awful. He died, and then I couldn't even...I only survived because I outsmarted it. I wasn't some great warrior. I used my resources, fought dirty. I poked its eyes, I even bit. But I couldn't kill it. It was like going up against a better, stronger version of myself," she tried to explain it as best she could. "The Other has unbelievable power; it can manipulate things with its mind; and it can heal itself. Just like me. But, unlike me, it doesn't need someone else's energy."

She turned to Chris, "You gave me so much, almost everything you had. And it wasn't enough. When I couldn't keep going, it could. I don't think I will ever beat it."

"That's not true. That's just not true," Chris said it because he couldn't believe it. "You may feel weaker, but you're not. You have–"

"God on my side?" Elise asked the question with some of her old anger. "He wasn't around enough today, was He?"

She closed her eyes for a moment, then whispered, "I just – I just don't know who to be mad at. How can I be so horrifyingly similar to that thing, and yet still lose to it?"

Francis scratched on the whiteboard, daring again to interject his opinion. *It isn't surprising you two are a match. Demons are fallen angels. Of course you are similar...*

"It's more than that," Elise looked past them again as she admitted to even heavier thoughts. "You've seen how angry I can be, how out of control. I could've really hurt him," she referred to the confrontation with Alan for the first time. "I was so furious that he wouldn't fight to stay with me. Angry enough to forget everything he tried to give me, every way he protected me, just so I could punish him for one mistake. And that's not the first time, as we all know. Though I fight it, the Other and I share some darkness."

"What happened tonight…it doesn't mean–"

"It knows it too. It spoke to me. It told me all these things."

"It spoke to you?" Chris' eyebrows puzzled, unprepared for such an answer.

"It turned into my mother."

He winced in sympathy. "Oh, Elise."

"That's actually not the worst part. It was what she said. She told me the only difference between that thing and me is discipline. Whatever it used to be, there was something that it wanted more than grace. She said that was the choice: discipline, or just having what you want, even if it's wrong. It offered me my heart's desires," Elise's eyes moved from side to side, as if she could see them before her. "I didn't believe it. I mean. How could I trust it? But, if there was some guarantee that it could give me those things, would I still fight? If there is a choice – I have some say in this – will I choose grace? Or are there things that I want even more than that?"

She brought her eyes down to focus on the two uncomfortable expressions in front of her.

The line between good and evil is thin.

Elise waited for Francis to write something else, but he didn't.

"The Other was just trying to get to you, Elise," Chris finally found a bypass for the rest of the conversation. "You're afraid that you don't have control over what happens, so it offered you control. You're afraid to trade your human wants for this responsibility, so it offered you freedom. It used your fears to weaken your resolve."

"I know," she nodded emphatically. "I know. I do. It said some things that definitely weren't true. But, I have those weak moments still. And there are dark hints of those things in me.

"I just feel like I failed tonight. And like, I may fail at the whole thing. I am still, underneath it all, just a girl putting on an angel's power." Elise sat back with a sigh far too old and tired for her age.

"Just rest," Chris prescribed. "You're exhausted. Try to sleep."

Elise closed her eyes, as if she meant to listen to him.

When it seemed she genuinely rested, Chris tossed his head back towards the wheelchair handles. "Could you just help me, Francis? I really have to call in. The Church needs to know what happened, if for no other reason than to cover our tracks."

Francis quickly obliged, scrambling from his chair, while Chris risked disturbing Elise. "You'll be fine here? It might take a little while."

"Yeah. I'll work on getting some of that sleep," she promised with a weak smile.

* * * * *

"And no one brought a cell phone to the greenhouse," Chris grumbled as he tried for the third time to get the pay phone to dial the international number. He and Francis stood in a cluster of machines with a view of Elise. She was now slumped with her head back, facing up at the ceiling. Both sent nervous glances her way from time to time.

"I can't tell if her eyes are opened or closed," Chris commented as he waited for the call to go through.

Francis took a better look and mouthed, *Open.* Though she was far from turned-up, to Francis, her eyes still had a glow, as always.

Someone answered. "Yes. Is Cardinal Matthew in, please? His assistant. Yes, I know it's the middle of the night – can we do this in English?" Chris rolled his eyes and then began in Italian.

Francis turned his back on the conversation, surveyed the airport, and eventually focused his gaze on Elise. The Other really dealt them two blows that night. Alan was gone, and with him, he took the information and certainty that often guided them. The other blow: Elise's confidence. Though the battle seemed a draw, she was weaker for it.

Even now, it was strange to him: seeing someone who could claim so much power, humble enough to claim so much failure. Elise second-guessed herself too much. She needed to use her instincts more. But, at least they were going to the Vatican now. And, though the Church was dragging its feet, he knew they had the right man; no other visionaries need confirm. It was time for the training to end and the real game to begin. The train was picking-up speed, the ball was rolling, the dominoes were falling, *or whatever metaphor you like.*

Chris remained on the phone long enough that Francis eventually moved to a nearby chair to wait. The priest talked louder in Italian than he normally did (as if speaking louder would make his accent better), and his foreign tones filled the empty airport. He gave a brief explanation and then the plotting began. Francis heard the plane ticket discussion and smiled. They were in.

At long last, there was a click, and Francis looked up to see Chris with his hand on the receiver, leaving it in the cradle.

"It's all set," Chris called back unnecessarily. "A car will be waiting for us in Naples. And, the Vatican is already handling details – guiding the police through some of the clean-up in Whiteley, and providing appropriate services for Alan's 'car accident' at his home church in Indiana. They were of course, very sad to hear about him. The society will be notified and a new member will have to be appointed." Chris' voice tightened unnaturally, and he cleared his throat. "Passports will be in a locker waiting for us in Philadelphia. So, now we wait."

Francis took position behind the wheelchair and they steered back to Elise. There was no glow in her face – she was asleep now.

* * * * *

They each managed to sleep that night, though it was less like sleep and more like shutting-down. It was the body's way of turning off the mind.

Elise was the first to wake. Orange sun came in through the large windows. She took a moment to look out at the still snow at the edges of the airport (all had been cleared away from the runways and docks). Off in the distance, flakes blew in little, swirling clouds.

She remembered instantly – the greenhouse, the hitting and tearing, whispers and white and blue lights, and Alan. She felt nauseated, a familiar metal taste filling her mouth and coating her tongue. Familiar for too long – waking with guilt and disbelief.

Swallowing forcefully, she stretched, using her fingers to work blood into her stiff neck. She really needed a drink. *Malls and airports – always so dry.* Elise performed the standard de-rumpling of clothing, checking to make sure a pant leg or shirt hem was not tucked up somewhere embarrassing from movement in sleep. All was in order.

She thought of waking Francis and Chris to tell them she was headed to the ladies room, but then decided it felt too much like being in elementary school. *Back in five minutes, tops.*

It was Monday morning, and the ticket lines were full with suits and briefcases. Elise skirted them with her head down. She wasn't in the mood for any questioning stares about her too baggy outfit or the marks that were probably still on her face (they were still her hands). She focused on the floor, watching the scuff marks in between quick glances to make sure she was still following the signs for "Restroom."

"Oh! I'm sorry!" Elise bumped into a traveler standing a little outside one of the lines. "I didn't see–"

Burnt hair.

She froze, unable to move. The smell assaulted Elise's nostrils as though she had put her face right into a burning carcass. She breathed in and out so quickly, it was one motion.

A mass of fur and scales next to her – she caught their glint out of the corners of her eyes. *Someone help me! Doesn't anyone see this–* a rotting hand grabbed her arm in a bone-crushing grip, and she heard the thing's triumphant hiss. And Elise whipped her head up, finally finding a scream–

* * * * *

She woke with a start.

She breathed in gasps, as though thrown in a cold shower.

Still in the lounge chair; still by Chris and Francis who remained asleep. *Just a dream.* "Only a dream." Frantically, Elise arched over the seat in every direction to scan the lines of passengers. All normal – just suits and briefcases. She licked her lips and finally sat back in the chair, waiting for the dream's grip to loosen.

Francis stirred next to her, and she wondered if he too was having a bad dream. She moved to wake him, but then she noticed: orange sun came in through the large windows. There was still snow at the edges of the airport (all had been cleared away from the runways and docks). Off in the distance, flakes blew in little, swirling clouds.

With new panic, she assessed the room again. Nothing.

* * * * *

The morning and afternoon passed slowly. They ate McDonald's breakfast sandwiches, then stopped back in for the regular menu a few hours later. They purchased newspapers and scoured them, afraid to read the international news, but relieved when it gave nothing new. They tried not to talk about Alan. They ordered coffees and Elise picked up a travel toiletry bag, spending twenty minutes in the ladies room while her companions

262

waited stressfully for her return.

Finally, it was 4:00 PM Chris put both his hands on his knees and used them to stand (that morning, he stood and gave the wheelchair back, much to the surprise of United Airlines). "We should probably go through security. Flight takes off in an hour-and-a-half."

At his words, Elise felt her stomach drop. She stood with a jump, followed by Francis. "Looks like this is really going to happen," she said with an uncertain smile. "Thank God. So, to Pennsylvania and then to Paris," she read over her tickets in an attempt to get rid of the jitters. "I've never been to Paris. But, we only have two hours and 20 minutes between planes. So, I guess no bistros or Eiffel tower." She eyed some of the more casually dressed airport patrons – probably on vacation or visiting grandparents. Elise allowed herself to wish she too was on such a light-hearted trip.

* * * * *

Though considerably shorter, the time waiting at the gate passed the slowest. They were so close – almost on the plane. Almost a continent away from the Other and a continent closer to David's heir. Elise recalled the moment weeks ago when she visualized herself waiting for the train to pull out of Ashton. Though she was no longer running from the law, the anticipation was about the same.

"Now boarding rows fifteen and higher, pleaba lorgasa…." The attendant with the microphone broke into something no one could understand. But, she was clear about the important part: rows fifteen and higher.

That's us, Francis wrote when no one immediately got up.

"Here we go," Elise stated under her breath.

* * * * *

Moments later, they were sardined in a three-seat row. Francis had the window, Elise sacrificed and took the middle, and Chris stretched out as much as possible into the aisle. They squirmed, adjusting their reading lights and the air blowing on their heads, and then settled back for the flight attendant's safety presentation. The turboprop propellers shuttered, then spun, and the plane lurched backwards towards the men waving orange sticks.

"Short flight," Elise commented to Chris while they were pressed back against their seats from the take-off incline. "We made it," she added. "How are you feeling?"

"Fine. Much better after sleeping last night. I didn't think I would be able to sleep, but boy was I out. After a little more sleep on the flights, I should be back to normal," he guessed. "You definitely took a lot out of me."

Elise pulled away and watched the window over Francis' shoulder. Apparently, she didn't want to discuss it with him yet.

He glanced down to his wrist and, in the cover of his own shadow, pulled his sleeve back. It was still there:

* * * * *

Just where her fingers had curled around his wrist, when she lay in the dark struggling so hard to live. It was there, where she held him long past consciousness, burning and taking. Even in the past few hours, it faded, the purple color draining to more of a red. But, Chris could tell by the strange striations in his skin around the mark that it would never fade completely. It reminded him of a fancy lighter burn.

Heavenly, supernatural power – all he could remember was how hot everything became. Though he witnessed the pain of turning-up several times, saw the destruction it could do to living things, he still had anticipated feelings of peace. But in the moments when Elise was the most intent on him, there was only unbelievable pain. He recalled merely the stars in his vision and her hands groping him in an inhuman way, as though they were mouths instead of fingers.

But it was still his answer. Evidence he could see burned into his own flesh; the touch of God, awesome and harsh.

Elise moved next to him, trying to find the armrest, and Chris pulled his sleeve back down. She leaned her seat back and closed her eyes. Next to the window, Francis was already out. It was as though their bodies were anticipating; calling them to save up, store energy, as if for a long winter.

* * * * *

By 8:00 PM, the three were on their way to Paris. This time, they crammed into an Airbus with many three-seat rows that stretched across the plane in several sections, like a narrow auditorium. Though they shifted and reshifted, there was no way to make the flight comfortable.

If Elise had been at all excited about their previous departure, that excitement left her now. She arched hard to see out the window as they began to taxi down the runway, wishing she had not granted Francis the window seat again. It was suddenly important to see it: the lights of the city, the SUVs on the highways, the rows of houses with brown, November grass, the American flag. What if this was her last time to see these things?

The plane's nose pointed up and the ground disappeared. From the middle seat, Elise could see nothing but dark sky. She watched even that for a little while.

Unlike the fear of death she felt when faced with the Other – adrenaline, heart palpitations, horror so fierce she could not completely comprehend – this fear was contemplative. Elise imagined it was similar to being diagnosed with cancer or AIDS. It was the quiet, nibbling fear of death that began to poison every waking moment; the one that saw all the old missed opportunities and the ones to never be offered; the one that had the time to comprehend its own loss. The feeling grew as they continued to gain height. In a plane more than two hundred people full and a few hundred feet off the ground, she was amazingly alone and nauseously homesick.

Going to try to sleep? Francis interrupted her loneliness.

"Nah. I – just don't want to sleep. It's kind of crazy. I've been trying all day."

Bad dreams?

Elise started and jerked her head up to look Francis in the eye. Sometimes, the things he knew were really just too uncanny. "Yeah. Actually, um, I had a bad dream this morning."

About the Other? He fit the question below the other two and then erased all three.

"You're good," she let her voice convey annoyance. She really didn't want to talk about this. She didn't need Francis and Chris checking on her mental health. They already monitored everything else.

He ignored the tone. *Tell me.*

Elise shrugged. "Not much to tell. I just dreamt that it was still following us, even though we don't know it. It's just choosing not to show itself and waiting until – I don't know what," she finished, trying to sound flippant. "I guess that's why it's just a dream, and nothing to really worry about."

Chapter 16 – A Small Detour

As promised, a car waited for them in Naples. Two men stood by the dark limo: the driver, who wore heavy sunglasses (though it rained) and held a sign that read "Mognahan," and another, younger man. *Very young*, Elise remarked to herself as they headed towards the sign. His dark, coarsely curly hair was pulled into a low ponytail that hung between his shoulder blades. Piercing dark eyes, smooth, seamless skin, and a wiry, tight frame. He wore one of the strangest outfits she had ever seen outside a Halloween party: blue pants with black boots that came up to his knees; a striped yellow and blue shirt that buttoned down with tiny, gold buttons and adorned with red cuffs; enormously puffed sleeves with a red stripe down the center; a high, white, renaissance collar; and a brown, leather belt.

The young man stepped forward from under the umbrella as they approached, letting the rain fall openly on his hair and face. "Father Chris Mognahan?" he asked in the same tone police officers often use before charging a criminal. He had a thick accent that Elise could not place.

"Yes," Chris extended a hand.

The young man turned automatically. "Francis Thomas." They shook hands.

He turned to Elise. She watched his Adam's apple bob for a few seconds in his neck before he actually managed to say anything. Clicking his heels together with ceremony, he kept his arms stiff at his sides and bowed his upper body. "Remiel."

"Oh for the love of God," Elise swore to see the guard flinch. "We're all tired. And we're getting wet. Please."

The young man finished his bow stiffly, keeping his face tight so as not to show any disappointment. "I am Lorenze Droz, a captain of the Swiss Guards, the Vatican's standing army. I am pledged to protect you."

"Thanks. But, I don't need your protection." Elise sidestepped Lorenze and reached for the car door just as the driver came to life and scrambled to help her with it. She refused him as well, tossing the door into his hand and sliding in.

Francis gave an embarrassed nod and then followed in after her.

"You'll get used to her," Chris smiled at Lorenze on his way into the backseat.

Lorenze stood for a few more moments and then marched to the front passenger's door. He allowed the driver to open it for him, and then slipped inside.

* * * * *

They drove.

Once outside the Aeroporto Capodichino, they raced through narrow streets before reaching a highway. Elise glimpsed tall buildings built close together on stone streets, many of them painted bright colors that helped to lighten the dark day. Some alleys gave glimpses of clothes hanging miserably to dry in the rain. So this was Italy. Even in the car, the air stuck to her, humid like a bathroom after a hot shower, and the rain poured down in sheets. It was warm – she did not miss her coat. No one spoke and the mood remained depressed. With each hiding bruises under borrowed clothes and without Alan, it could not feel like a rescue.

After some time, Lorenze turned in his seat to look back at them through the car's open privacy panel. "It will take us about two-and-a-half hours to get to Rome. Though I am sure you are exhausted, and with your loss…the Pope, and several of his highest officials will be waiting for you around supper."

"Actually, Lorenze," Chris sat forward to address the guard. "I wondered if we could make a small detour to Meura? It would only require a little time."

Elise jumped without knowing why. *Meura.*

Lorenze frowned, finally looking older than seventeen. "The Church is expecting Remiel. And, it is not safe, as you know. I have been charged with delivering you–"

"Can't you just tell them we ran into a little bit of traffic?" Elise whipped forward to defend the proposal she did not even understand.

Though intimidated by her anger and closeness, Lorenze looked the strange girl in the eye. "If you truly wish to go to Meura, Remiel, then we will go."

"Thank you," she gave a cool smile and pressed the button to close the opening between the front and back seats. An electronic motor hummed somewhere, and Lorenze's surprised face disappeared behind the rising privacy panel.

"Elise," Chris used his sternest whisper. "Do you always have to be rude? Why are you being so difficult?" he followed the rhetorical question with a real one.

"I told you I didn't want to come here. I don't like all this ceremony," she answered. "It's just like I thought it would be. Highest officials, and bows, and calling me Remiel. We've only been in the hands of the Vatican fifteen minutes, and already, everything was better when it was the three of us – four of us," she corrected herself to still include Alan. "Now we're adding a whole bunch of stuffy, bureaucratic, ambitious priests and their underage heroes," she incriminated Lorenze with a thrust of her chin.

"You are one of the Church's greatest angels. You're going to have to put up with some due bowing and admiration. The Vatican may seem bureaucratic – and true, it has had its dark moments – but it has outlasted all of the governments born and fallen in the last two millennia. That is a faith that you and I cannot even possibly understand. It is powerful and deserves respect. It is the reason we found you."

She only rolled her eyes, so Chris reached across Francis to snag her elbow. "I'm serious. Try acting with some of the grace you are supposed to represent. You may start by apologizing to Lorenze."

Elise looked into her lap. She hated the way Chris could do that – make her feel guilty, make her want to be better.

The electric hum came again as she pressed the privacy button and the divider slid down between the seats. Lorenze peered back over one of his great sleeves, timid and worried. Elise looked out the window again.

He spoke to Chris – it seemed safe to speak to him. "The driver is redirecting us to Meura. Only a small detour, as you requested."

"Would you like me to call the Vatican and tell them the delay?" Chris offered.

"If you call, they will tell you not to delay. And, they will order me to keep you in the car."

You couldn't keep me in the car, Elise managed to keep the thought to herself.

"It is better if we are just...stuck in traffic, as Remiel suggested," Lorenze remained facing the front while saying her name.

"So what's in Meura?" Elise used a bored, but softened voice.

Francis scribbled, and Chris let him answer. *Chiesa di Statua*

"That's where..." her mind searched.

"The omen," Chris gave it to her. "Meura is where you first asked us to help you, where you told us who you are and your purpose. Almost twenty years to the day, the society gathered there and the search began. I thought you should see it. See yourself as you are, as we see you."

* * * * *

There was hardly a car on the road besides theirs as they threaded through Meura's narrow streets confined by chalky-stone buildings. The rain had stopped, but a cool fog creeped, giving halos to lights and blurring detail. Under its veil, Elise suspected the town looked much the same as it did several centuries earlier, save for the electric bulbs in the street lamps.

She did not realize they arrived at the church until the car stopped. "We're here?" she asked, still not seeing it out the window.

"This is it," Chris said as he opened the car door himself (again, not remembering passenger etiquette). Elise was quick to follow his lead.

The church nestled in between two other buildings with a small graveyard to its side. It was entirely round, gray stone, and quite small with a red clay roof. Its one claim to greatness was a gigantic, crumbling bell tower. The group moved towards the heavy wooden doors framed by two lamps that had real flames jumping in them.

A small shiver rippled in Chris' lower spine as they moved towards the doors. The past forty-eight hours were filled with unreality, and this was to be no exception: seeing Elise stand next to the likeness of her angel counterpart. On some of his least skeptical days over the past twenty years, he envisioned this moment. He paused before reaching for the latch.

But Elise wanted no more suspense. She instantly moved and undid the latch for him. She slid through the door, holding it just long enough for Chris to grab it.

Like the streets, the church was empty. Chris noted it had not changed at all in twenty years. The pews were a warn, almost black wood. An old red carpet (barely covering the stone floor beneath) stretched before them up the main aisle to a simple altar and stage. It was cool and a little damp, like a cellar. Vaulted ceilings rose high, composed of long, wooden planks manipulated to bend and turn elegantly enough. Chris looked over his shoulder for Alan before remembering. His breath caught with new pain. *He, of all people, should see this.*

"Is that them?" Elise indicated the white statues just outside the light of the altar.

"Yes." Chris whispered back. "Go ahead."

"Actually, I should probably go first," Lorenze stepped forward, but she grabbed his arm on his way by. "For your protection," he explained.

"These are things you can't protect me from," she brushed past him.

With steps that did not belie the trepidation she felt, Elise walked down the left aisle to the first statue. He shone like fresh milk, pure, holding a military trumpet under his right arm and dressed in robes carved so that they somehow looked flowing, though made from stone. He stood tall and grim, his mouth serious and his eyes – blank. "Like mine," she paused to mouth. "You're turned-up." She almost smiled, but bit her lip instead. Though he was obviously stone, she could believe he once whispered, this mimic of

269

something sacred. Something secret.

The second statue. The third statue. The fourth. The fifth. The sixth–

She recognized him with a sharp intake of breath. He was the same as the blond man in her dream. The one that warned her she would forget him.

But she did remember. Long hair flowed over his shoulders. And his face held a soft type of wisdom even in the stone. In awe, she waited as her mind replayed his words perfectly. *You know what you risk? What you will face? I am frightened for you.*

She turned to Remiel with her eyes down until she stood before her, their heights evenly matched. Gradually, Elise's eyes rose.

It was like looking directly into a mirror, or a still pool of water.

Elise stared into her own face without moving. It was smoother in the stone than in real life. The arch of the eyebrows was perfect, the slender nose the same. There was even a small fleck (passed over by any other viewer as a nick) that matched the small fleck in her own skin from a scarred chicken pockmark. Elise took in her identical frame, the same small feet, the blank, cold eyes. The only thing that kept her a replica: her small pedestal.

"And ye shall know that I am the LORD that smiteth." Ezekiel 7:9. *Twelfth Century Unknown Artist.*

Elise reread the words again, and then again. With a hesitant hand (one that she brought forward, drew back, and then brought forward), Elise reached for the horn posed so artfully in front of her twin's face. Her fingers trailed lightly on it, moving up its arc and resting on its three keys. It felt different than the stone, drier, with deep grooves. She moved her head in close so that she could both see and feel the intricate etchings. Closer. Mere inches from skin to stone.

Elise's hand closed around the fragile mouthpiece, and she locked her eyes with the vacant ones. "Not yet," she whispered the warning. "Not yet."

That was it. That was all there was.

She half turned, about to go back to the men and suggest they return to the warm, undamp car. But, her ears caught it. *Whispering...*

With a great shattering, Remiel's horn exploded, fragmenting into pieces small as sand grains. Elise spun away and covered her face against the mist, like glass on her bare skin. There was the sound as of ice on pavement as the pieces scattered, and then a breathless silence.

"ELISE!"

"Shhhh..." her hiss so forceful, it echoed. Squinting and brushing litter from her eyelashes and cheeks Elise licked the blood from a cut close to her mouth. She backed away, her shoes grinding into the powder that littered the ground. Past the sixth statue. The fifth statue. The fourth, third, and the second and first.

"Remiel," Lorenze was at her side suddenly, but she jerked from him.

"Let's go."

"What happened? Did you do that? For God's sake, You're bleeding–" but she stepped by Chris too.

"I don't know. Let's go. Here." She roughly threw her hand into a display of flowers near the holy water, mindless that Francis was only a few feet away.

Immediately, there was something wrong, and Lorenze squinted to see better. The flowers – they were browning, the leaves curling and dying as though touched by pesticide or flame. He looked for some explanation in her face, and there found real fire. Lorenze let out his breath and forgot to take it back in.

When she was done, Elise turned back to the group healed and no longer bleeding with only a shine left – just enough to make her look unearthly, like a cat in a flashlight. She caught Lorenze's gape and shrugged. "Welcome to the in-crowd. We do this all the time."

She held the door and the men filed out, the questions on their faces silenced by the stern expression on hers. She let the door slide quietly closed and turned back into the day-now-turned-night without looking back.

The newly changed statue smiled after them – her same small smile with her lips parted. Her arms were extended towards the door and now empty; not a piece of the trumpet remained. The fingers remained undamaged, reaching out now as perfectly as they had held, as if to call them back.

Not yet.

Chapter 17 – The First Supper

Elise knew without being told that the huge structures rising in the distance composed the skyline of the Holy See. As the car threaded streets ever closer to the walled Vatican City, St. Peter's white and gold glow could be seen over the tops of trees and buildings, with humidity halos around the brightest lights. She caught glimpses of the great dome with its stone ridges (like an exterior skeleton) and the plain cross on top.

"St. Peter's Basilica, named after, arguably, the greatest of the twelve apostles," Chris leaned over Francis to get Elise's attention. "Though Peter was not a perfect follower, Jesus saw something in him. According to the Gospel of *Matthew*, when Jesus asked Peter to become a disciple, he said, 'Thou art Peter, and upon this rock I will build my church; and the gates of hell shall not prevail against it.' It seemed at the time, that Jesus meant this figuratively – that he meant for Peter to gather support for the new Christianity. But, as it turns out, the Church really was built on Peter's rock."

"What do you mean?" Elise spoke distractedly, craning to see out the window.

"After Jesus' death, Peter led the apostles and began the Catholic Church. He performed miracles in Jesus' name. People in Jerusalem used to bring their sick out into the streets when he came, so that his shadow might fall upon them and cure them. He was the first pope, and all other popes are considered his spiritual descendants. When a pope is named, he is imbued with the same type of miraculous power.

"But, like Jesus, Peter was a controversial figure. For many, Peter was a heretic to the Jewish God and the Roman Emperor. He was often imprisoned for his sermons and threatened with execution. Despite the risk, Peter traveled the world to spread the Word. But in 64 A.D., Peter was captured and brought to the circus in Rome. There, he was martyred on an upside-down cross. His body was released, and he was buried in a stone tomb on what was then called the Vatican Hill. Over the next few centuries, a necropolis – a city of the dead – of Christian and pagan burials grew on the hill, and Peter's tomb was decorated as a shrine.

"In the fourth century, Constantine, the first Christian Emperor of

Rome, built a church over Peter's tomb in order to consecrate the ground forever and right the wrong of his predecessor. To do this, he had to build the church over the necropolis. He leveled the ground, destroying many of the tombs and mausoleums, and buried the rest with fresh earth. To protect Peter's tomb, he encased it in nine feet of marble and built the basilica's altar over it. He also incorporated the old shrine into the floor of the basilica.

"A thousand years passed while the Catholic Church became what it is today – a government, a monarch, and one of the largest organized religions mankind has ever seen. As the Church grew, some of its most precious history was forgotten, including the exact location of Peter's tomb. It became more a Church legend than anything else. •

"The Constantinian Basilica remained on Vatican Hill until the 1500s. By then, it was in bad condition and basically crumbling. Pope Julius II tore it down and built the current St. Peter's Basilica over the old site. With the new renovations, it now seemed that the true location of St. Peter's tomb would always be a mystery."

"You're very longwinded," Elise gave her only comment. "Basically, the basilica is rumored to be built on St. Peter's tomb, which happens to be made of rock. So, Jesus was right: the Church was built on Peter's rock."

Chris sighed. "Yes. More than a thousand years of history can be condensed into a few sentences. But, you should get used to the long version," he pointed out. "This place is full of the past."

"If the tomb was lost, how does the Church know the basilica is really built on anything? How can they be sure it's not just some myth?"

"Well, at the end of the longwinded version, I was going to provide just such information." Chris gave a justified look and then fell silent.

"All right," Elise finally rolled her head towards Chris. She put up her right hand, as if swearing an oath. "No requests for cliff notes. I promise."

"In 1939, Pope Pius XII recovered a letter written in 1032 A.D. that described the location of the tomb. He immediately ordered workers to excavate the catacombs underneath the basilica. There, beneath the floor where the letter indicated, they discovered the lost necropolis. Literally hundreds of graves lay in the soil beneath the church. And, as the workers began to excavate the area underneath the basilica's papal altar, they discovered even older, Roman graves. Finally, exactly below the high altar, where the Pope celebrates Mass, they found the legendary marble tomb of St. Peter with the ancient shrine still on top of it.

"But," Chris gave dramatic pause, "the tomb was empty. So, the workers continued searching. On the outside wall of the four-foot high shrine built above the tomb, where the wall was painted red, they found a small niche and the bones of a man inside. Over them was inscribed, 'Here lies St. Peter.' The Church actually has the bones of a man who walked with Jesus

273

Christ, whose life stories live on and affect millions today. It lends remarkable human substance to the greatest divine legend."

"It's hard to comprehend," Elise admitted. "The Church has the remains of someone who lived more than two thousand years ago; someone who walked with the most loved and hated, the most feared and revered man in history. What the world wouldn't give to ask those bones a few questions. Maybe put them on a polygraph," she turned some of her thoughtfulness towards sarcasm. "So, all those dead people are still there, in the floor?" Elise's face scrunched as if she smelled something bad.

"Yes," Chris gave a laugh. "And there are plenty more dead people in the basilica now than there ever were. Just below the basilica and above the catacombs are the Vatican Grottoes. There, tombs hold the bodies of popes, kings and queens dating all the way back to the tenth century."

"Great. It sounds a little too much like *Poltergeist* for me," she crinkled her nose further. "Did you ever see that scene, where all the bodies come up from their graves and start floating in the pool?"

Lorenze, who had been quiet for the duration of the ride since leaving the Chiesa di Statua, finally turned around. His look was one of hesitant reproach. "I am surprised you do not know more about the Vatican," he gave a glance towards Chris and Francis, as if to implicate them in the error as well. "You will see. It is nothing like a movie set."

Elise waited until he turned around and then rolled her eyes. "I just meant, it must be haunted," she retorted.

"It is haunted," he replied seriously. "By God."

* * * * *

However much it displeased her, Elise found immediately that Lorenze was right: the Vatican was nothing like a movie set. Elise was barely Catholic; she could not remember even viewing a picture of the Vatican, and yet she found herself moistening her lips nervously as the car stopped before an opening in the great stone enclosure. Regardless of one's religious inclination, visitors to the Vatican City immediately understand that it represents power and continuity. It is a place that, even at first glance from outside the wall, solidly promises to be around long after one's death.

St. Anne's Gate: a story tall, wrought iron door. It barred several cramped buildings with columns facing a stone street that wound back much farther than Elise could see. A guard approached the car.

The driver rolled down the window, and the guard peered inside – another young man dressed similar to Lorenze, but in all blue. He scanned the inside of the car, and Lorenze gave him a nod. The guard's eyes then fluttered to Elise, staring at her until she wanted to tell him it was rude.

Finally, he stepped from the car. The gate opened.

They followed the road through several turns before entering an immense, well-lit courtyard. It was completely surrounded by gold-colored, stone buildings whose line was broken only by arches. The buildings rose high to rounded windows that glinted in the light and sometimes shown out with their own. A great clock face silently pronounced the time. Again, the vehicle stopped.

"Where are we?" Elise squinted out the window into the growing twilight.

"I don't know," Chris admitted while wiping some condensation from his window – the rain was drizzling again. "I'm not sure I've been to this part of the Vatican before."

"This is the Courtyard of St. Damascus," Lorenze spoke while waiting for the driver to come around and open his door. "We are in the heart of the apostolic palace."

One by one, they slid across the leather and out into the rain.

Instantly, the shadows around them began to move. Several rows of Swiss Guards stepped away from the dark protection of the buildings and formed a stiff line in the light of the courtyard. They wore chest armor and metal helmets complete with plumed, red feathers in addition to the blue, yellow, and red striped uniform. They held what looked like ancient spears in an upright position in front of their faces.

Lorenze gave the confused group the cue. "My fellow Swiss protect the entrance and are here to greet us."

He led them to a red carpet that had been laid across the stone in the courtyard, and to the door at the end. The guards moved not a muscle as the group traveled down the line, but Elise could feel them slightly bow their heads as she passed. She took in a deep breath.

The guard nearest the door clicked his heals together, and with a jerky motion, opened it.

They stepped into the grandest hall Elise had ever seen, in movies or elsewhere. Everywhere one looked, the eye was assaulted with art. The floors alone were composed of many different colors of marble that swirled and arced in amazing patterns and Latin lettering. The walls were lined with statues, columns, carvings, and countless doors that stretched a third of the way towards the vaulted ceilings. Dim lighting gave a gold casting to everything, leaving the impression that each adornment was at least plated in the precious metal. Perhaps it was.

They were not allowed to admire, however. As soon as the guards pulled the door closed behind them, a man (who apparently had been pacing only seconds before), whirled around and marched over to them in giant strides. He wore black robes (no hood) with a scarlet sash and skullcap. A large gold crucifix swung around his neck in rhythm to the huge steps. White hair stuck out from under the cap, but his face was young save for some loose skin around his neck.

"Monsignor Matthew," Chris helped close the gap between the group and the man with a few steps of his own.

"Father Chris. We were worried, expecting you earlier. You have arrived safely?" the Cardinal tried to reduce the concern in his face with a smile while extending his hand. To Elise's surprise, Chris bent and kissed it. Francis did the same, while Lorenze gave a polite bow.

"And you, of course," Matthew faced Elise with ceremony, in a more confident but no less embarrassing way than Lorenze had.

"Elise Moore," she eclipsed the name Remiel quickly and thrust out her own hand. Though the others could not see it, Elise felt the man jump at her touch. He gave her a small smile and then bowed low before her, kissing the tops of her knuckles.

"We have been waiting for you, not just tonight, but twenty years," he spoke as he stood straight. "And now, miraculously, you are here. I'm sorry there is not more time for introductions. But, please follow me. The Holy Father awaits."

The Cardinal turned and began crossing the hall with the same large steps. He touched Lorenze's elbow on his way by, and the guard stepped up quickly to walk with him, leaving Elise, Francis and Chris to follow. Their footsteps echoed over and over again into the high ceilings, like an unsteady drumbeat.

"Who is he?" Elise mouthed to Francis. For once, the monk's form of communication was the most convenient.

Cardinal Matthew Bertolli. Bishop appointed by Pope to be a member of College of Cardinals. Also appointed the Prefect of the society. He's Chris' (and Alan's) leader.

Elise had to smile even through her nervousness – Francis made it sound as though Chris and Alan were some alien species. She hid the smile long enough to mouth a second question, "The Holy Father. Is he the Pope?"

He gave a confused look.

"The Pope?" she mouthed with more annunciation. She pointed towards Matthew. "Is he taking us to the Pope?"

Francis didn't have to write down the answer. He nodded once. *Yes.*

Elise opened her eyes wide, and Francis smiled. He quickly wiped the board clean in case the Cardinal turned around.

But the Cardinal was safely occupied with another conversation, and Elise turned her attention towards it as soon as she heard its tone. "I don't understand what kept you. Do you know that the Pope has been waiting for almost two hours?" In a hiss, "Two hours! Lorenze, this is simply unacceptable. You were chosen for this honor because of your well known weapon skills, but I always questioned you reliability, maturity. You must be independently responsible in the Pope's commission, especially for a duty as important as this."

Beside the Cardinal, Elise caught a pale Lorenze rapidly swallowing with his head down.

"Actually, Mon–" Elise struggled with the title. "Monsignor Matthew, I am the reason we are late," she began to explain. "I asked Lorenze to make a stop on our way here. And as you commanded, he did everything I asked." It was Elise's version of an apology to Lorenze for her earlier behavior.

Surprised she overheard the conversation, the Cardinal gave an embarrassed nod over his shoulder. "Yes. Of course, thank you for your insight. But, the Pope should not have been kept waiting with no word."

Elise ended the cordiality and turned on the ice she wielded so well. "I would still appreciate it if Lorenze was not reprimanded on my account." Elise threw the Cardinal's back a cool smile. "Consider it a personal favor to me."

Matthew cleared his throat. "Of course, Remiel."

The group (now in uncomfortable silence) passed through an archway leading into yet, another hall. There, at least a dozen cardinals (all dressed like Matthew) crowded around one great, wooden door.

"Sono qui! Ringraziare Dio che sono qui!" several exclamations came as they approached, followed by more hushed words in Italian.

"Stay close to me," Elise whispered to Chris.

He reached around her side, where no one could see, and squeezed her hand.

Every eye was on Elise, even as she remained in the back. Matthew stopped a few feet from the cardinals and all stood frozen, like two gangs waiting for one to cross into the other's territory.

One of the oldest – a man with skeletal features, from sunken cheeks to overlarge eyes – stepped forward. He did not bother with Chris, Francis or Lorenze, stepping around them as though they were merely another set of columns placed inconveniently in the hall. With the feel of dry, burnt paper, he touched her hand, lifting it in the air between them. A one-up on Cardinal Matthew, the old man knelt on one knee before kissing the top of her hand. The others lined up and began doing the same.

"Elise. Really. Please call me Elise," she found her voice and repeated it to each of them when they murmured, "Remiel" to her, as if saying some sort of prayer. She only wished it were comical – a bunch of men in silly black robes scrambling to bow to her. Her! But, there was no comedy. Each approached with reverence and respect, some trembling against her palm as though she was a priceless artifact that should barely be touched. Some fought to control their faces from emotional expression or tears.

"Gentlemen," Matthew's tone hinted of more important things as soon as the final cardinal paid his due. "I believe the Pontifical Father is waiting?"

Several heads nodded. Another set of Swiss Guards (that Elise only just noticed) opened the door in front of them, and bright light flooded out, chasing the golden glow into the recesses of the hall. All talking ceased and the cardinals began to file in, leaving the priest, the monk, the guard and the angel to follow, Matthew coming close behind.

The room appeared to be a library. It was less impressive than the hall, but still remarkable, with great wooden bookshelves, beautiful paintings, oriental rugs and high-backed, white-satin chairs arranged in a semi-circle in the center of the room.

Two men stood at the back of the semi-circle. One in black robes and scarlet adornments – *a cardinal of some sort*, Elise deducted. The other: a man in robes identical in style to the cardinals, but white. He wore a plain skullcap. *The Pope.*

Though he had to be well over sixty, the man in the white robes was without a doubt, the most imposing man in the room. He had shortly-cropped, pitch-black hair and darkly olive skin that showed off the whites of his eyes. That in no way, however, took away from their surprising color. The Pope possessed eyes the shade of a pond iced over on a sunny day – somewhere between gray and blue. They pierced the room like a bright light. And like a magnet drawn to metal, they fell on Elise.

Elise watched with growing alarm as the cardinals each found a chair to stand in front of, and then turned their solemn gaze upon her. She looked at Chris, but by the rapid way his eyes moved back and forth around the room, she could tell he had no more idea what was going on than she did. Francis? He stood as dumbly as the rest, but managed to look unconcerned. At least Lorenze stood solidly at her side. Still, it began to feel like a game of musical chairs: Elise's apprehension rose as more seats were claimed, leaving her, Chris and Francis standing idiotically before them.

Matthew was the last. He strode with his fast gate to a seat near the Pope that appeared reserved for him. No one spoke; only waiting.

Lorenze nudged Elise in the back, moving her a few inches out into the circle. *What are they expecting?* She searched his face for a clue, but only found eyes that pleaded with her to do something they could not communicate.

Afraid, she faced the Pope. "I'm sorry," her voice sounded small in the large room. "I just – I don't know what I am supposed to do. I'm sorry."

The Pope smiled, and Elise let out a silent sigh. "Please come forward. I want to meet you. All three of you." His voice was smooth with a tight, melodic range of tones.

Bound by the simple invitation, the three approached the Pope much like pirate captives coming to the plank. Elise led the men, only because they refused to keep up with her.

"Elise Moore," the Pope said when she stood in front of him. "I've heard so much about you. Long before we knew what to call you," he smiled again. "I have to admit, I believed that being named Pope would be the culminating moment of my life. Until now."

Elise tried to smile, not knowing how to respond.

He was quick to hone in on her discomfort. He stepped into her space and whispered, "Please. Don't be afraid. Unlike you, I am just a man." He bent his body in a bow and took her hand, pressing his lips gently against it.

"Brother Francis Carter and Father Chris Mognahan," the Pope gave each of them his hand. They took it and, kneeling before him, kissed his ring. "I understand, there was to be four of you," the Pope acknowledged as the two men returned to Elise's side. "Alan Cole and his sacrifice will not be forgotten. I, myself, have prayed for the care of his soul.

"Lorenze?" The Pope posed the command in a question. "Please take my guests to their rooms and see that they are comfortable. After they have a few moments to freshen themselves, please lead them to my apartments for a late supper. The cardinals and I have some business yet to complete before concluding for the evening."

* * * * *

"Holy…" Elise whispered as soon as the door closed behind them. "That was stressful. And embarrassing."

"You did fine," Lorenze reassured her. "What did he say to you, when he whispered?"

"That was incredible," Chris burst in a hushed voice as the room full of cardinals fell behind them.

Francis nodded his similar feeling.

"Even as a priest of the Church, you have to be quite important to – though, of course, he must want to see you, I can't believe we're going to have supper with him. Leo the Fourteenth."

"Leo?" Elise's laugh echoed eerily. "Who would want to be named Leo? I can't believe there have been thirteen before him."

All three gave her a look good enough to keep the laugh fading into the ceiling.

"All right. He's very amazing," Elise confessed to redeem herself. "We only saw him a few minutes, but he has an incredible presence. Confident, yet respectful – I think I can consider that he is the spiritual descendent of the greatest apostle."

279

Chris looked in Elise's face for a sign of sarcasm, but found none.

* * * * *

"Apartments have been made for you here, off the Sala Regia: The Royal Hall," Lorenze indicated a heavy door with a great, mahogany frame. "This hall is the anteroom to the Sistine Chapel, and connects to the papal apartments. It is a sign of your importance that you have been placed so close to the Father."

If it was possible, the Sala Regia was even greater than the halls they entered through earlier. As was beginning to feel customary, the floors were made entirely of marble, this time with the stone forming a geometric pattern of circles and diamonds. The walls (several stories high) were adorned with statues and frescoes too numerous to take in. Several life-sized frescoes vied for focus, but were lost to the sculptures of angels just above them, posed in such a way that they appeared to be holding up the frescoes. The ceiling arced above them, bedecked with more patterns and paintings, like the lid of some beautiful jewel box. Doors, identical to the one they stood in front of, lined the hall in both directions leading to places that promised incredible secrets. In the shadows throughout the hall, Swiss Guards stood in their stiff positions.

Lorenze held the door open for them, and they passed into a far less grand (and more comfortable) room with antique sitting chairs adorned with silky green pillows. Several chandeliers hung from a high, but unimposing, undecorated ceiling. Miscellaneous paintings and vases decorated tastefully. In the back, two dark, wood doors faced each other from opposite sides of the room.

"The Franciscan Sisters readied your rooms for you. You should find clothing for supper laid out, as well as everything you need to refresh." The guard turned to Elise. "If you need help with your garments, please call out and I will have a sister sent immediately."

Elise raised her eyebrows to let him know she could still dress herself, thanks, and headed to the door on the left.

"Your apartment is actually on the right," Lorenze corrected her. "Anyway, I will be outside. Please let me know when you are ready, or if you need anything." The young man gave a bow and marched from the room.

"Welcome to the anti-reality," Elise spoke the feeling for each of them before heading into her rooms. "Oh wait. We've been living that for a while already."

* * * * *

Chris and Francis discovered considerably more comfortable quarters than the ones they had grown accustomed to in Whiteley. The door on the left opened into yet another sitting room (this one modernized with a television). A complete formal dining room branched to the right with a gleaming mahogany table and golden candelabra. The kitchen (also opened to the sitting room) was up-to-date with a toaster, microwave and oven. Francis opened a cupboard to find stocked shelves. A walk down a short hall led to two bedrooms and private baths. Chris could tell from the rounded surface of the bed that it was a down mattress.

"Five star," Chris called from his room, and then crossed to Francis' to get the answer.

So, shall we do dinner with the Holy Father? Francis used his face to communicate his sarcastic flippancy.

"Yeah. I think I can make time for it," Chris smirked back. "This really is incredible. Really unbelievable. I've been to the Vatican for congregation meetings multiple times. But it was, of course, never like this. I suppose we shouldn't be that impressed – we have been keeping company with an angel for a few months already. But..." He put his hands on his hips and gave another once over of the place. "Alan should be here."

Francis closed his eyes for a moment and nodded.

"It would've been the pinnacle of his faith, and his career," Chris sat on the bed (definitely feathers). "Sorry. I just haven't had any time to think – everything just keeps going so quickly.

"I'll let you get dressed," Chris gave himself an exit. "Dinner with the Pope," he called back on his way out, with only half-hearted enjoyment.

* * * * *

Elise could now see why Lorenze offered to call someone to help her dress. They hadn't purchased a single normal piece of clothing for her! The closet, the drawers – they were filled with some of the most beautiful silks and satins she ever touched. The embroidery was immaculate, and much of it was gold (real gold?). But, nothing seemed to make sense. Where was the underwear even?

Wrapping herself in a towel, Elise peered into the common room (as she had already decided to call it). It was empty, so she padded out to the main door, pushing it open a crack.

"Lorenze?" she whispered. "Lorenze? Lorenze!"

A dark brown eye appeared in the crack.

"I need some help with the dressing thing."

The dark eye disappeared, and Elise returned to her room to wait.

A tiny woman in a milk white habit appeared a few moments later. She curtseyed and then bustled around the room without another word. Elise quickly learned shyness was not expected. With an expert tug, the nun had her towel in her hand. All business, she set about the dressing.

"I'm Elise," Elise tried to introduce herself once the silk undergarments were securely fastened. "You are?"

The woman looked up at the sound of the voice, but said nothing.

"You can't speak English?" The woman merely continued pulling some fabrics over her head. "You can't speak at all?" Elise remembered Francis. Who knew?

* * * * *

Chris and Francis stood when Elise entered the common room.

"Oh, just sit down," Elise scorned them. "If you two stop treating me like a normal person, I really will go insane. So, sit!"

They sat, but the astonishment remained. Elise wore silk white robes that flowed gentle as water to the tips of her dress slippers. The style was reminiscent of a kimono, hanging naturally over the curves of her frame without a distinct waist. Beautiful embroidery embellished every aspect of the piece, shimmering just slightly in the light. Her hair was swept back in a graceful chignon that revealed her smooth neck and defined collarbones.

"This was all they had," she explained. "My entire closet is filled with this stuff. Very creepy – everything fits perfectly. My files must've contained my exact measurements, I suppose? And the little nun. She insisted on putting my hair in this knot." With that, Elise flopped onto the couch next to Francis. "I see at least you guys found the regular stuff in your rooms," she nodded towards Francis' fresh, black robes and Chris' return to black dress pants and the priest's collar.

"Are we ready?" Chris asked.

Together, they exited the apartment and found Lorenze outside the door. Even years of training keeping a stony face could not completely hide the guard's surprise.

"Remiel," he gave a brief bow.

"This was all they had for me to wear, Lorenze. I assure you, I did not go through any magical transformation in there. So, the name is Elise."

"Those are papal robes you're wearing," he ignored her contempt. "The Pope commanded the nuns to take fabric from some of the older robes and create a wardrobe for you, as soon as we heard you were coming. A small army of Franciscan women were up all night making those for you. Normally, they are mostly employed in restoring the great tapestries – they are some of the best seamstresses in the world."

She fingered one of the sleeves. Which Pope wore it before her? "Well, we'll need to keep one of those little women on call for when I get back. I don't think I'll be able to get out of this any easier than I got in."

* * * * *

The Pope and Cardinal Matthew were waiting in the Pope's apartment. The group was invited into a large dining room with a gigantic table hidden by a starched, white tablecloth. A fire crackled in one corner of the room, and Elise made a beeline for it, warming her back against it.

The Pope took a seat at the table (Elise noted that he chose not to sit at the head of the table, and liked him better for it). "Supper should be ready shortly. While we wait, Elise, why don't you tell me a little about yourself."

Her look sharpened, refusing intimidation. "Are you asking about me, or about Remiel?"

The Pope and Cardinal Matthew replied in unison with conflicting answers.

"It is all the same story," Leo gave a hard glance to the Cardinal. "Start where you like."

She gave him a cautious look, quite sure he already knew everything there was to know about her. "It isn't very interesting. Before this I was a psychology student at Ashton College in South Carolina. My parents died when I was young, so I was pretty much on my own. I worked as a bartender." She shrugged and fidgeted her hands behind her back. If she went any further than that, she would have to tell him about Clyde – something she didn't think she could stand. Undoubtedly, he already knew.

Her discomfort pricked Chris' heart and he left his post by the Pope to stand with her, pretending the warmth of the fire also drew him. But the gesture was not lost to Elise. She gave him a smile with her eyes.

"I wasn't Catholic until I met Chris and Francis and Alan. I'm not sure I really am Catholic now – I received the sacrament of Baptism as a baby, and then, over the last few weeks, the sacraments of Penance and Communion, but not Confirmation."

"We'll see if we can't do something about that for you," Leo replied. "Full Catholic or not, have you ever experienced signs of who you truly are?"

"Until recently, no. I've always been able to do strange things, but…" she shrugged.

"You mean taking energy from other living things? And using that energy for yourself?" He asked the leading questions, showing his knowledge of her.

"Yes. Over the last few weeks, under Alan, Francis and Chris' supervision, I have grown stronger. But, it's something I have always been able to do."

"But recently, there have been other signs?"

Elise gave a sideways glance at Chris. He nodded for her to continue.

"After leaving Ashton, I experienced a few strange things. There was one time in the Whiteley church."

"Yes, I heard about the crucifix in Whiteley." The Pope pulled at his chin thoughtfully. "Anything else?" His eyes closed on her, piercing as if to extract the answer he impossibly seemed to know.

She took a deep breath and then related the abridged version of the occurrence at the Chiesa di Statua that happened only a few hours prior. Cardinal Matthew's features twisted in annoyance at discovering their reason for being late, but she went on without acknowledging him. She had already decided she didn't like him.

She was glad when a knock on the door announced supper. "You must be anxious for food – our cooks are divine," Leo let her off the hot seat.

For the most part, the conversation kept well above Elise's head for the rest of the meal. Francis, Chris and Cardinal Matthew fell into discussion about offices of the Church that she never heard of. She did not mind – it felt good to be ignored for while; to be the observer rather than the observed.

Chris and Francis, on the other hand, jumped in whenever it seemed acceptable. They discussed everything from congregation appointments to recent bishop synod publications, and for his part, Leo appeared to listen. Whenever Francis commented, everyone waited patiently for him to write, which could sometimes be several minutes. This night, Francis used no abbreviations and refused to omit a single word.

But, when dessert and coffee were brought, Leo redirected their attention once more. "So Francis, we have been investigating the man you identified, the man working under Arel Demsky. The one you believe is David's heir."

All forks halted in their paths.

"His name is Chayim Ze'ev," he paused, letting the name sink in. "He is, by all measures, a normal man. Widowed, he has one daughter. Before joining the rebels, he was a general in the Israeli military. He retired and ran for the Knesset – Israel's parliament. Now, he is considered Demsky's top man."

The Pope took a silent sip of his coffee and then nestled the cup back in its saucer with a clink. The blue-gray eyes looked up to Elise. "As you probably know, Arel Demsky is a strong military leader – for the most part, he runs the entire Israeli military campaign and strategy. While the country's politics remain a disaster, he keeps the Arab nations at their borders and no closer. He defines himself by what he is not: not a leader for the Middle East, not a friend to the West, and not a peace-agent for Palestine. He claims to be a leader for Israel alone and preaches all that is prophesied about the inevitable, supernatural grandness of that nation. When the Israelis cry for a king, most are thinking of Demsky." Unconsciously, the Pope raised a hand to the cross he wore around his neck and closed his hand around it, as though to protect it from something.

"So, it is very significant," he concluded, "that you, Francis, identified Demsky's secondhand in command as the king, who if crowned, would fulfill the final prophecy and end the world before God's plan for mankind is complete. If something were to happen to Demsky, it is highly likely that Ze'ev would take over his efforts."

"And possibly become king, himself," Elise finished unnecessarily.

Francis had been writing while the Pope spoke. He now turned the board over for the group to read. *What do the other visionaries say?*

"Frankly, so far, no one has confirmed your claim – that this man has a mark, or any other indication that he is David's heir."

Francis shifted uncomfortable.

"The investigation is still preliminary," Leo tried to ease the tension. "We are waiting for confirmation or dissention. But, most other visionaries have to see – look upon the real person – to make any accurate predictions. Such an opportunity may not occur for weeks."

"What do you suggest, then, Father?" Chris folded his hands on the table like a studious pupil.

"Your congregation," Leo gave a nod to Cardinal Matthew, "has always kept its ear to the ground in Israel. Monsignor?"

Matthew cleared his throat and stood to speak. "Even without your observation, Francis, the Congregation for Hetairia Melchizedek is almost positive that something cataclysmic is going to happen in Jerusalem. Soon. With the different factions breaking apart the Knesset while the Palestinians continue to fight, it is sometimes difficult to tell whether it is just another suicide bomber, or a real insurgence. But, according to our sources and those members risking their lives in Israel's underground, new rumblings of discordance threaten to produce something far more historical and lasting than a few more dead Israelis and Palestinians."

"Do you mean that Demsky and Ze'ev may stage a coup?" Elise used her usual bluntness to consolidate and get to the point. "Take over, dispose of the Prime Minister and elected President, and destroy Israel's democracy?"

"We think it's possible," the Cardinal acknowledged. "They do, after all, have the military, which certainly leaves the Prime Minister in an insecure position. If you are right, Francis, then we may have a very dangerous situation brewing. One that puts Ze'ev far too close to power."

"It also means," Leo broke in, "that we may not be able to wait for confirmation from the other visionaries. In the event of a coup, based on your

285

recommendation and all that is at risk, we feel action must be taken against Demsky, Ze'ev, and any other contender for king. Are you comfortable with that, Francis?"

The monk wrote with hard strokes, conveying no hesitation. *Yes. No other confirmations needed. We will not be wrong.*

"And you, Elise," the Pope turned his question to her. "Are you comfortable? With the possibility, that you may be sent after the wrong man even if only to make sure he is the wrong man?"

Though she knew what her answer had to be; though she knew that there was no way this man, or any man, could now take from her the weight on her shoulders; though she knew it was only courtesy that she was asked at all, it felt important to be asked. "If Francis is sure, then I will do whatever you think is necessary," she credited her friend with her confidence and gave the answer they all waited for.

Cardinal Matthew sat down. "It's set then. We will begin strategizing the best way to handle the situation – how your powers may assist us, the Swiss guard, assassins. You are, of course, bound here until we have any new word on these activities. But, you must be ready to leave the Vatican at a moment's notice."

The Pope resumed, "Please enjoy our city, but do not leave its walls. Here, I can guarantee you some sort of protection. Lorenze will be with you at all times, Elise. You have the entire guard at your disposal, should you need it."

Again, his eyes cut through her, as though she was nothing more than the thin fabric she dressed in. There was something else behind those words, but rather than guess, Elise waited for the Pope to ask it directly.

"The Other. I don't know how connected you are to this being, how it knows where to find you. Do you have any inclination that it is close?"

She was about to tell him no, when she remembered the dream. How everything in the airport was exactly the same when she woke as it was in her mind. "As far as I know, I have no physical connection to the Other. However, I did have a dream. Yesterday. It was very real, you could say. And it made me feel that it knows where I am and for some reason, it's just waiting." She looked up to Chris' surprised face and the others' concern.

"Stay with Lorenze," the Pope commanded. "I will have him stay in your sitting room to ensure that you are not alone, even while you sleep."

She gave her approval by the tilt of her head.

"I'm sorry to end our supper with such dark suspicions," Leo apologized, while signaling the end of their meeting. "Tomorrow, I would like it if the three of you joined me for Mass and breakfast. And, I would also like to tie-up your time in the afternoon. After what happened in New York, I called an extraordinary consistory of the College of Cardinals. We are just waiting for the last few to make their way to Rome, and we expect to hold conference tomorrow. I would like you all there."

The door to the dining room cracked, and in came Lorenze without any summoning, as if he magically knew the supper was over. Chris, Francis, and Elise rose murmuring thanks and goodnights to Cardinal Matthew and Pope Leo the Fourteenth.

* * * * *

Lorenze joined the group in the common room (after much encouragement). They discussed the events of the day, from the Chiesa di Statua to the Pope, from Israel to Elise's dream until, from somewhere in the apartment, a clock struck eleven times.

At the tones, Elise stretched and yawned. With a few tugs, she had the chignon down so that her reddish hair fell stiffly around her shoulders. "What time is it back home? Five in the evening, I think? At least I don't have jetlag," she yawned again.

"We should probably go to bed," Chris resumed his parenting role in Alan's absence. "The Pope wants us in his apartment for mass at six in the morning. It won't look good if we are all falling asleep through the whole thing. Lorenze, you are staying with Elise?" Chris asked with protective worry.

"Of course. As the Pope instructed, I will sleep in her sitting room," he indicated the door on the right side of the common room. "There are no windows in this apartment – your quarters or hers. Anything trying to reach Remiel will have to pass by me first."

Chris' concern did not completely alleviate, and Elise wondered if he didn't wish to be in her sitting room himself – both for her protection and other reasons (she hoped). They had not had a moment alone since he comforted her in her bedroom back in Whiteley. *That seems so long ago...*

"Good," Chris responded to Lorenze. "And Elise, if you have any more dreams, I want to hear about them immediately. Don't be afraid to wake us. I mean it."

"I'll wake you," she promised, catching his eyes and holding them. "Goodnight," she broke the eye contact and headed into her room with Lorenze's soft steps behind her.

* * * * *

"Do you need a sister to help you get undressed?" Lorenze remembered her earlier comment.

"No," Elise surveyed her clothes before entering her bedroom. "Not that

287

they'll be hung neatly on the racks or anything, but I think I can get them off after all." She turned to go into her bedroom with no further conversation, but Lorenze stopped her.

"I never got the chance to thank you for your help with Monsignor Matthew." The guard swallowed and looked down, slightly embarrassed. His Adam's apple bobbed as it had when he introduced himself outside the car. "It was very nice of you to…defend me like that."

"Well, I was rude to you earlier," she admitted with no softness. "I had to make it up somehow, before Chris and Francis start thinking I'm some sort of monster…" she trailed off, her mind following a different, darker meaning of the words. "Although I don't know you well, you are loyal to the Church and to my friends and me. It was only fair that I repaid you with some of the same." She entered her room and closed the door.

But, their conversation stayed with her as she crawled into bed, sinking into the feathers. *Before Chris and Francis start thinking I am some sort of monster…* It was still there, just as she told them in the airport lounge – the darkness inside.

In her previous life, she understood her blacker parts as a product of her parents' death, and the knowledge that she could never let anyone close enough to know her secret. It had seemed natural, understandable, reasonable. She used to accept it: the dark corners and shadows in her mind.

But now, it was a fight against it. And it seemed the more she fought, the more it erupted. Its angry manifestations – Clyde, her arguments with Alan, her manipulation of Chris, and now cruelty to people she did not even know – scared her. And though Chris and Francis both told her not to listen to the Other's taunts, they still hit her. She knew the way her heart lurched when it offered an end to the fight. Angels and fallen angels; was her darkness really caused by death and loneliness, or something more innate?

Elise rolled over, pulling the covers with her, in an attempt to roll away from frightening thoughts. Just as undeniable as the darkness was her deep desire to do the right thing. For her parents, that despite what the Other showed her, they would never have anything to do with darkness. For Francis, who showed her patience and pitiless understanding. For Alan, who gave his life for her, both because he believed in who she was, and because he just didn't know how to let her face her task alone. For Chris, whose shy affection made her feel more whole than she had since being orphaned. For the Pope, and the Church and its followers, who archaically believed that good must prevail. For the trumpeters in her dream and the one Man, who knew her thoughts without speaking, and understood, even in His perfection, the struggle of her weakness.

Elise closed her eyes and slipped to darkness.

Chapter 18 – A Brief Demonstration

"Good morning," the Pope stood as Elise, Francis, Chris and Lorenze entered the dining room. "I trust you slept well?"

All three nodded, trying to appear alert. Elise looked crabbily out the window at a sunrise that was just beginning to happen. She eyed a Vatican plant hungrily but resisted with a frown.

At their silence, the Pope proposed, "My chapel is this way."

* * * * *

It was the same Mass that Chris performed hundreds of times, and yet, it was not. This was more serious, more grave; if anyone could truly change bread to body and wine to blood, it would be the Pope. Whispering the Latin words in front of the white marble altar, the ancient candelabras, and the Pope's crucifix brought together all those things that attracted Chris to Catholicism: ceremony, beauty, ancient tradition, power, and mystical belief. It was as much a spell as a ritual. They held Communion, and then entered the dining room for breakfast.

* * * * *

By 8:00 AM, Chris, Francis, and Elise were back in the common room. Waiting.

"What do you think they want to talk to us about?" Elise took to pacing again (an interesting endeavor considering the common room's limited size). Chris and Francis sat on the couches, also nervous but motionless.

"An extraordinary consistory is just an emergency meeting of the cardinals. All 120 of them will come," Chris attempted to make Elise calm with what he knew, but only created widening eyes. "After what happened in Whiteley, calling an extraordinary consistory is appropriate. The Pope wants to consult with the cardinals to decide what resources he should call on, what news there is from Israel …"

How they'll cover this up, Francis added.

"Anyway," Chris ignored him. "I think the Pope is just inviting us as a courtesy. So, relax and prepare to watch what will probably be a very long, deliberate meeting."

"I hope so," she replied as she straightened her robes (created from a light blue, shimmering material). "Already, I feel like a freak show with all the bowing and kissing. I don't want this to turn into a spectacle where they all get a chance to look at me and ask me questions about things they think I should know, but I don't."

And how you might be able to help them cover this up.

"Are you ready?" The three jumped as Lorenze opened the door. "They're waiting."

"What do you mean, 'they're waiting?'" Elise asked with renewed nervousness. "We're just listening in, right?"

Lorenze shrugged. "The cardinals are seated and waiting in the Hall of Consistory, and I have been asked to escort you."

Elise gave a warning look to Chris, and he smiled in reassurance. She did not smile back.

* * * * *

The Hall of Consistory was as intimidating as its name. Size was the first and greatest impression: the furniture in the hall looked miniscule in comparison to its largeness. Gigantic paintings hung from the walls, and their many oily eyes gave the sense of an audience immediately. In the spaces between the paintings, ornate carvings, wallpapers, and frescoes covered every inch. Even the carpet was alight with unbelievable threadwork. It was an immense, dressed-up cavern–

Filled with a sea of red. For the cardinals sat in chairs lined on either side of a small stage with an altar, reserved for the Pope (who stood by his throne-chair expectantly). They were dressed in ceremonial robes with red cape and hat. Their many crucifixes created a glimmering around the room, like tiny cameras going off.

At the group's entrance, the sea of red stood in unison, and an awe-filled silence captured the room. Elise sighed, but resisted the urge to roll her eyes.

"Elise Moore, Chris Mognahan, and Francis Carter. Please come forward," the Pope greeted them with a motion of his hand. "Your seats are here with me," he indicated three chairs to his right, just off the stage.

Glad for any place other than the center of the room, Elise led the group down the small aisle between the rows of cardinals. She kept her eyes on the Pope all the way down. First she sat; then the rest of the room.

The Pope faced the hall and began, "I usually compose considerable introductory notes for the issues that come before this body. But this day, we all know why we are here. It is not to determine whether a Mass should be said in Latin, whether girls may be altar servers, or whether birth control goes against Catholic doctrine. Today, we only wish we were making such human decisions."

He paused, choosing his next words carefully. "Instead, we are here to direct the divine fate of several individuals, a nation, and perhaps, the world. You have seen the reports from the Congregation for the Hetairia Melchizedek; you know and respect the omen they discovered twenty years ago; you approved the constant searching the Church has been involved in; and you know that the Congregation believes it has found the guardian you asked it to find. She sits next to me. All of the pieces are in place. You must decide where we move them.

"I have appointed the Congregation's Prefect, Monsignor Matthew Bertolli, to be the relater during this consistory, and to lead the discussion. But, may God be the true facilitator of this meeting, and guide our plans."

Leo sat down and leaned back, as if in for a long lecture, and Cardinal Matthew stood and took the floor. "Good morning. You each have an agenda."

There was the noise of papers flipping. Elise looked to Chris and Francis, also without the referred to agenda. The papers settled, the first item was scanned, and then the eyes – all eyes – turned her way. Somewhere inside, she felt the first drip of adrenaline.

"The first item is to decide if the college has faith in the proposed guardian, Elise Betheba Moore. Elise, please join me."

She started at hearing her full name, and the blood rushed unnaturally to her cheeks as her thoughts caught up with his words. "What? What am I?" Elise whispered to Chris while gripping the sides of her chair tightly.

"Elise?" The Cardinal toned shortly. "The college would like to confirm once and for all that you are who you say you are. It will only take a moment."

She darkened to scarlet as the anger rose. "Confirm who I am? As in, test me?"

"Yes. Please," his voice began to take on a wearied edge, as if she was a pet who refused his command.

"After all I have been through, after everything that has happened–"

"Elise," the Pope spoke gently from her side, and she turned her accusatory eyes on him. His explanation caught a few moments in the face of her anger. "The cardinals have asked for this last reassurance before we move forward. Can you understand?"

"With all due respect, I understand that you found me. You call me Remiel! I never asked for this. And I gave up my life to be her and to follow your calling. Here you are, kneeling before me, kissing my hands. All that, but you don't believe what I've told you, what we've been through."

"With all due respect," Matthew almost mimicked her. "You told us that you are a murderess with no divine calling. Father Alan Cole spent many a frustrated evening–"

"Don't bring him into this! He died believing…" His words knocked her breath away so that she could not reply further. They rung in her ears, repeating the humiliation he dealt her. She looked at the floor, blinking defiantly at the tears that stung her eyes.

Soft pressure on her arm – it was Francis. For the first time, she saw him angry.

"Cardinal Matthew," Chris spoke for them both. "Whatever your divine calling, it has not taught you either respect or humility. You are a fool, and if she chooses, Elise will prove it."

"Enough!" Leo interrupted sternly. "What you say is true – it is we who found you, who call you Remiel. But, when we are talking about lives, assurance is a necessary measure. I am sorry to ask this of you, but Elise Moore, please join the Cardinal in the center of the hall, and give us a brief demonstration."

Elise gave the slightest nod and then rose, taking the steps down from the stage two at a time. In a second, she stood before Monsignor Matthew. "Whatever happened to 'test not your God?'" she asked loud enough for the entire assembly to hear. A low murmur began.

"We are not testing God. But we are testing you. You will give the college evidence of your power, which we are confident of," he stressed, "and then vow your allegiance to the Pope."

"I thought Catholics only vowed allegiance to God." The murmur grew.

Matthew stood uncomfortably for a moment, before attempting to explain. "We need a formal indication that you will follow the Holy Father's leadership through the completion of your task, whatever that is."

Elise gave a snort to show just how much formal indication meant to her. "Well, I'm going to need a volunteer." She turned to face the rest of the audience, trying to catch as many of them in the eye as she could. "As I'm sure you know, I need to use the life of someone else." More whispering. "Look there. I'm sure it's in your agenda."

"I will be your volunteer," Matthew responded quickly, rolling up his sleeve as if she were going to draw his blood.

"Good."

"What do you need me to do?"

"Absolutely nothing," Elise took several formidable steps his way, but Matthew stood his ground. "Ready to believe?"

"Yes," he whispered while clutching his bare arm against his chest.

"Would you like a chair, or should I bring you to your knees?"

But Elise never let him answer. She reached out quickly and clamped a hand across his forearm. She zapped him furiously, releasing his energy as easily as turning on a tap. He yelled, grabbing her hand to push her away. She only took from him harder.

The whispers were in her ears encouraging her to drink Matthew in and taste the easy power of a life that wasn't hers. She leaned back to see the ceiling, tinting gold through the lights in her eyes, and smiled. *A brief demonstration...*

And already, she had enough. Probably more than enough. But Elise wanted to keep her promise. She would bring him to his knees.

Turning-up harder and harder, she felt him draining away. He was saying something, more gurgling than words. And then he fell, landing just at her feet, struggling to breathe and in obvious pain, but still conscious.

She stepped over him and faced the cardinals on both sides, the Pope and Chris, Lorenze and Francis at the end. With eyes wide and her hair back, she let them see the fire, the way the unearthly light washed over her features. *See his life in me?*

In the remade papal robes, she was truly angelic, truly awful.

BANG!

The door to the consistory opened and closed so loudly, even Elise jumped. She smiled as the rest of the room turned over their shoulders to see what happened.

What next? She used the hands of her mind to disturb the curtains by the altar, her invisible feet to pound and stomp, as though an unperceived giant came to stand beside her. *THUD! THUD! THUD!*

Not frightened yet? Elise turned to the large mirror in the corner of the room. Grasping her empty chair with her thought-fingers, she threw it into its reflection. Huge pieces of glass fell to the ground and shattered in a discordant roar. But she was already moving on, her thought fingers turned to the paintings. One by one, she began to rip out the oily eyes, and all began gaping in a darker version of the pupiless eyes she herself possessed. *How much are they worth?* More tearing, mutilating. *HOW MUCH?*

"That's enough," Matthew's weakened voice called from the floor. "Make your pledge." At the command, like a predator recalled to its prey, Elise's light came to rest on him, and he knew with fear, it was not enough yet.

She crossed to him and then used his energy to pull him off the ground. By the collar of his robes she held him with one hand, his toes dangling inches from the floor (though she was the shorter one). The doors began banging again, incessantly. Several guards appeared through their opening, but could not pass through. At the Pope's side, Lorenze stood.

"Stop – this," Matthew tried to command again through the tightening of his collar. "Stop! And pledge – your allegiance – to the – Pope."

She only smiled.

"It's enough!"

"Is it?" she brought him low enough so that his face was close and he could see directly into the empty light of eyes. "But I haven't even begun to use all of you." Elise scrunched her face to show the disgust she felt and threw him violently away from her towards the stage and the altar.

"ELISE!" Chris' shrill voice reached across the expanse.

She jumped, and then, with a sharp intake of breath, she reached with her mind and stopped Matthew's fall, inches from smashing into the marble altar. Slowly, she lowered him to lie on its smooth surface – a terrified offering. Only the muscles in her neck revealed the amount of control and exertion the catch cost her.

Though his voice told her how much he hated to ask her, Chris compelled her in a more controlled tone. "Finish this."

For a moment, she stood still, as if contemplating his words. The doors banged a final time and then stopped. But from under a lowered face, she gave Chris half a smile. *Just one more thing.*

A small, gold object whizzed through the air, coming to the angel's hand. It took Chris a moment to realize what it was: Cardinal Matthew's crucifix.

Another second, and crucifixes began filling the air, drawing to her like a magnet. Each cardinal's chain broke with an easy snap, and then she called the crosses to her until a glittery, metal mess took shape in front of her. She spared only three: Francis', Chris', Lorenze's.

When every other crucifix in the room was above her palm in a tangled mass that floated a few inches from her hand, she turned her eyes to the Pope's stage, giving a long, intimidating stare. Several of the closest cardinals began to stand, ready to protect the Pope, but she pushed them into their seats, almost sending them backwards. She advanced.

Though quivery fear ran over his young features, Lorenze remained standing at the Pope's side. His eyes traveled constantly between her and the Pope and back, and she knew his dilemma. He pledged to protect them both.

A few feet between them, he made his decision. Elise watched Lorenze reach for his sword. Gently, she pushed out with her mind and staid his hand so he could not draw it. When he realized what she did, he watched with new horror.

Unapproachable, Elise climbed the few stairs and then stood before the throne. The Pope gazed back at her steadily with those same blue-gray eyes. He looked comfortable. Perhaps he believed she could not hurt him because of his title? That God wouldn't let her? Perhaps he trusted her. And yet, she noticed his pulse bulging in the small of his neck.

As if she merely held a fistful of sand, Elise splayed her fingers and the crucifixes fell through them, clanging to the floor.

She knelt, but kept her golden eyes, faded but still imposing, on Leo's. "I pledge my allegiance to you, Leo the Fourteenth. You have betrayed my trust, but I give you mine because I believe that God has chosen you for something. But," she looked down at the crosses by her knees. "I pledge my allegiance only to you. Not them. Never them."

Show over. Making a rapid exit (through doors that opened on their own), she left the cardinals to collect their crosses, and Matthew to climb down from the altar.

"Lorenze," the Pope managed to find his voice. "Follow her. The guardian should not be left alone."

* * * * *

Elise lay on the couch in the common room, waiting for Francis and Chris to come bursting in. When a knock came instead, she felt her spirits sink.

"Remiel? Are you there?" It was Lorenze.

"No, I'm not. Come in."

The door cracked open so that a sliver of Lorenze appeared. He kept an intense stare, barely blinking. "You said come in?"

"Yes. Come in. And, stop staring at me like that," she dropped her voice to its iciest. "I'm not going to hurt you. I didn't hurt anyone, even though there were several who certainly deserved it!" she began already on her own defense. "So only come in if you aren't going to be afraid."

Lorenze slipped into the room. "Sorry. I've just – there are no words for you. Or what happened." Self-consciously, he reached for the handle of his sword. "I can see why you told me you didn't need my protection when we first met. You are too great an angel – I couldn't even draw."

Elise frowned. "Everyone needs someone looking out for them. I kept you from your sword today because I didn't want to fight you, and I wasn't going to hurt Leo, or anyone. And I'm not great; I have more in common with Judas than any other disciple."

"You've left no doubt who you are," he smiled, like a boy who has just seen a high-speed car chase. "Just after you left, the Pope pronounced you the guardian."

Elise only looked at the floor. "Great. What are they doing now?"

"I believe they're discussing Ze'ev now, his background," Leo interrupted through the still open door as he entered. Chris and Francis were behind him. "Now that you are the confirmed guardian, we need to make sure Ze'ev is the confirmed heir before any other action can be taken."

Elise sat up quickly, not expecting the Pope so soon. Her face pinked, but she kept her gaze steady. "Are you going to ask him for a brief demonstration too?"

The smile started in Leo's eyes, and then ended in a low laugh in his throat.

Elise sighed, taking note of Chris' warning look over the Pope's shoulder. "I'm glad the question of my identity is put to rest then," she gave the cool comment.

"Yes. You certainly convinced everyone," the Pope agreed.

"Then why aren't you back with them? Overseeing Church business? Hopefully, you are not here to ask me to apologize. Cardinal Matthew will be lucky if I–"

"No. I didn't come for your apology, Elise. While I still hold that the exercise was necessary to get everyone behind you, I should have warned you. Moving forward, I hope we can feel more as if we are on the same team."

He waited, watching the ice begin to crack around her eyes. Finally, she sighed again, and he knew he had her. "Yes? We can work together?"

"Yes," she said quietly.

"Good. I must return to the consistory. You are all more than welcome to join us again and aid in the decisions."

Elise slouched as soon as the door closed. Silence. More silence. "What?"

"It was incredible to watch you," Chris spoke quietly. "You're so strong now."

"And? I can tell by your tone, this is no compliment. If you want to reprimand me about Matthew, I don't want to hear it."

"What you gave Matthew, he mostly deserved. I only worry that you end-up crossing too many lines; you come too close, rarely showing the discipline that I – that Alan taught you. Thank God you caught Matthew before he hit the altar. But what will happen when there isn't someone calling you back?"

Francis settled next to her on the couch, and she leaned her head on the monk's shoulder. "I don't know. Maybe that's why God gave you to me. There's just too much to hold in. I can't do it for myself. But for you," she pierced him with her eyes.

"Are we returning to the consistory?" Lorenze broke the moment, too young to be comfortable in it.

"I'm not," Elise answered first. "I don't want to face them. Ever."

We should be present to voice our concerns and opinions. No rule without representation, Francis wrote.

"Yes," Chris agreed. "We should have a say in how this plays out."

Elise raised her eyebrows. "See you at dinner, then."

"Elise, it would be better if…" Chris' words fell off as Elise rolled over on the sofa, burying her head in the cushions and literally giving him her back to speak to. The men exited, with Chris muttering audibly over Elise's stubbornness. Elise and Lorenze remained in silence for several minutes, Elise still brooding.

"So where shall we start the tour?" she spoke into the cushions.

"The tour?"

"I need to rest a few minutes, but I'm not going to sit here all day. Leo said I could look around. I assume you will have to take me."

Lorenze drew in his breath. "I don't really give tours."

Silence.

"Ok. How much do you know about the Vatican?"

"Absolutely nothing," she admitted.

"Then I should probably start by telling you a little about the place, how we run, what we are about. You'll appreciate it more that way when you see it."

"Shoot."

"Shoot?"

"It means go ahead." She rolled back over and propped an additional pillow under her head.

"Oh. Uh…" Lorenze cleared his throat. "Well, the Vatican City is all that is left of the 2,000-year-old Catholic empire. It's completely walled in – a fortress nation built on over 100 acres. I think there are about 500 of us living here. The basilica faces east to greet the second coming, who is prophesied to rise from the east like the sun. Um…we use the Euro and most Italian laws. Like any other country, we have garbage collection, firefighters, police, a supermarket, a gas station, a clothing and electronics store, a library, a pharmacy, um…a bank, a newspaper, a radio station, and a railroad. Only St. Peter's Square and Basilica, and select museum exhibits are open to the public. And we don't pay taxes."

Elise raised her eyebrows – the first indication that she was listening.

"We are ruled by the pope, who is the bishop of Rome, the head of the College of Cardinals, and the successor to St. Peter's throne. He is the last absolute monarch in Europe, and rules the state and the Church infallibly with full legislative, judicial, and executive power. The pope is selected by the College of Cardinals. Though the pope can be anyone, traditionally, he is chosen from among the cardinals. He rules until his death. Cardinals are bishops that are appointed by the pope to be his advisors–"

"That's kind of incestuous. He picks them and they pick him."

"Yes. Well…there are 120 cardinals, and they meet in consistories – like this morning – to advise the pope, decide canonizations, suggest the appointment of new cardinals, and when needed, choose a new pope. They are the Church's elite. Beneath them are the bishops: priests whom the pope selects to head geographic regions in each country. The bishops work with the pope to set Church policy.

"The Roman Curia serves to govern the Church on a day-to-day basis – they are its officials, if you will, like um…U.S. cabinet members. Most workers in the curia are diocesan priests and members of religious communities. The highest official in the curia is the Secretary of State. He is always a cardinal, hand-picked by the pope to be his top advisor. He oversees the curia's three tribunals or courts, nine congregations, and eleven councils, and their staffs.

"The curial tribunals are cardinal and bishop run, each with their own spheres of influence, from ruling on excommunications, marriages and annulments, to contract cases. Curial congregations decide doctrinal issues in the Church. The pope appoints members – mostly cardinals and bishops. The head of each congregation is called a prefect; below him is a secretary (usually an archbishop); and third in line is an undersecretary (usually a priest). Cardinal Matthew, for example, is the Prefect of the Congregation for the Hetairia Melchizedek."

"Yeah, I heard the Pope call him that today," Elise responded flatly. "Nice appointment."

"Let's see – what else? Besides the various congregations, there are also councils in the curia. They help the Church promote its beliefs and grow its followers. Because its members do not actually dictate doctrine, they are chosen from a larger pool of candidates, including priests and laity, or non-religious. Like congregation members, the pope appoints them and chooses their head – a president. The secretary is normally a priest, and the rest of the staff is composed of priests, religious, and laity.

"And of course, the only army that remains active in the Vatican is the Swiss Guard, which is responsible for protecting the pope. We number about 100, and live in the barracks inside the Vatican where we are trained in many weapons. Candidates for the guard must be Swiss, Catholic, and taller than five feet eight inches. Each guard must reach corporal before he may marry. Only then will he be provided with an apartment."

"That sucks. Are you of marrying rank yet?"

Lorenze smiled. "The artist Michelangelo designed our uniforms."

"I can tell."

Again, he smiled. "And, I think that concludes our overview. What would you like to see?"

"Can you show me the square?"

"The square is open to the public and outside the walls. You probably should not…anyone could be in the square."

"And that's exactly why I would like to see it. To be just anyone, another nameless face. Even if it is just until dinner. For months, I've been unsure about who I am, while the Church has been recruiting me. Finally, I believe and I come here, and then their certainty dissolves and I have to put on a magic show. Today, it felt like I had two enemies. One that hides in libraries and greenhouses at night, and one that stalks the halls of the Vatican in red capes during the day.

"I know you probably don't care," Elise drew herself out of the anger. "You're just doing your duty, which happens to be listening to me at the moment. Someone like you, who takes duty so seriously, must think I am weak for being afraid of mine. But you know what? It doesn't matter if you understand. You have to go where I go, because I'm your assignment." She crossed her arms.

Lorenze responded in the only way he knew how. "We will have to dress you up, cover your face while you are in the square. And you will stay close to me."

* * * * *

St. Peter's square: the main entrance to the Vatican City. Like everything else in the Vatican, it was overlarge. It was a giant field of stone with the volume of a stadium hollowed out from between grand buildings. Thousands mingled comfortably in the afternoon sun – people of all nationalities and races stared at the portico with its columns and statues, the obelisk in the center, the steps of the basilica. Some wore jeans, others suits and dresses. Some looked with tears in their eyes, others with skepticism, all with awe. It was the courtyard to a country; doorstep to the palace of the Catholic God.

"Believe it or not, it is actually hard to get a sense for how incredible the place is when you are standing in it," Lorenze continued with his tour guide duties, watching the disguised Elise spin several times in order to get a 360 degree perspective. The nun's robes she wore swirled around her, her small frame disappearing entirely in them. Only a glimpse of red hair could be seen at her temples, and the veil she wore covered all but her eyes, which were wide with the scene. He steered her to a street vendor and plucked a postcard from the stand with an aerial view. "See – much larger than you can tell. There is the apostolic palace; there the basilica; there the Sistine Chapel."

Elise squinted at it, trying to eliminate the sun glare. "It's – a giant keyhole," she noted the square's shape. "From the sky, it really does look like a keyhole." She tucked the postcard away, wanting to focus on the real thing. "So explain. What is everything?"

Lorenze started with the basilica, pointing out its grand facade, its 18-

foot tall statues on top, and the two bell-towers (one with a clock and one with a bell). He moved on to the portico, numbering the columns at 284, each with a height of 45 feet. Lining the top were 140 statues of different martyred saints. And the giant obelisk in the center of the square. It was once a sundial in Emperor Nero's circus (where St. Peter was crucified), but Pope Sixtus V had it moved to the Vatican in 1585.

"There are so many people. All to look at a place that won't let them in."

"It's Wednesday. The Pope holds public audiences here on Wednesdays. It happened earlier today, but people are still milling around."

"Is it Wednesday? I really forgot what day of the week it is, and that there are days of the week and that they are important at all." Her shoulders drooped further. It was one more way she was distanced from everyone else in the square; in the world. "Can we go inside the basilica?" she suggested. "After that, I promise you can take me to all the secret caverns with the highest security." Lorenze smiled at her teasing in the hopes that it meant rising spirits, and they headed for the stairs.

Five bronze doors offered entry. "Why is that door closed?" Elise pointed to the massive, carved black door at the culmination of the stairs. Heavy and foreboding, strange figures and scenes looked on the square from its black panels.

"That is the Holy Door, carved in 1445. It is opened only by the pope, and only during a Jubilee year. When one crosses it, one is supposed to be absolved of sin."

"Of course, it's closed," Elise frowned. "And these others?"

"The Door of Death, the Door of Good and Evil, Filarete's Door, and the Door of the Sacraments."

Elise chose the Door of Good and Evil, open but unforgiving.

It was like no place she had ever been. After passing through an inhumanly beautiful atrium and an archway, they stood before a long aisle of marble stretching to an altar that Elise could barely see from such a distance. To the sides, colossal columns rose, leading to prayerful alcoves and artwork. Hundreds upon hundreds of faces peered into the hallway – all statues half in and half out of the walls that birthed them. Sun cascaded in whitely to dazzle gold plating and make alive the giant mosaics. Hundreds milled in and out, some with headphones for automated tours. Flashbulbs were constant, and whispering echoed up into the ceiling. Elise remained at a loss for words for many minutes.

Finally, "Look at this place," she said while letting out a deep breath. "Italians know how to decorate. There isn't a single inch that isn't covered in marble, or glass, or gold, or art." She shook her head. "It must've cost a fortune to build."

"The nave, or aisle, to the high altar is one eighth of a mile long," Lorenze continued rattling facts. "Besides that, the basilica has 31 altars, 27 chapels, 390 statues, 135 mosaics, and 15,000 square feet of marble floor."

"You're showing off, Lorenze."

"I don't need to show off."

They began moving slowly down the nave, while Elise tried to take everything in. "There's so much to see, I don't even know where to look."

"Many say it takes three full days in just the basilica to appreciate it."

"Can we just go anywhere, or…"

"Just about," Lorenze replied. "Stop anywhere that seems interesting."

"All right. What's in here?" They entered a small chapel to the right where many others stood silently.

Silent for the statue of a mother holding the body of her son. The woman's stone eyes were closed, her face lowered in agony, and one hand reached out ever so slightly to the side, as if she were still praying for help, though it was obvious her son was dead. She cradled his head. His body was so tired and beaten, as if death came a relief. So real. So soft. Like skin instead of stone.

"Michelangelo's Pieta," Lorenze spoke quietly.

"It's Mary holding Jesus after he was crucified, right?"

"Yes. It is the only work Michelangelo ever signed."

"She looks so sad," Elise cleared her throat. "It must've been awful to watch. I can't even imagine." She shook her head. "Maybe that's why God took my parents away from me. So that they don't have to watch."

"You aren't going to be crucified, Remiel," Lorenze turned grave. "True, you have a frightening task before you, but if you are successful – which I'm sure you will be – it won't be you who loses her life."

"But, is that any better? I'll have taken life from someone else, from someone's family, from someone's mother. And will God let me survive, anomaly that I am? Why won't He just take me back?"

"Well, there's me," Lorenze offered, trying to sound strong. "Not that I can stop God's will. But, barring that, I'll make sure you come back safe."

Elise turned to the young guard, giving her first real smile of the day, albeit a small one. "You make me feel ashamed, Lorenze. I do nothing but complain today, and you remain patient. Your resolve never falters. I don't know why God didn't decide to make me more like you."

"I think God made you with great resolve. It's because of that resolve that you are feeling sorry for yourself now. Though you want a way out, you know you won't let yourself out."

Raising her eyebrows, "Thank you. Although I notice you have nothing complimentary to say about my patience, Lorenze."

He raised his eyebrows back at her, and remained tight-lipped.

"Lorenze! You better watch it–" she started to laugh.

"Shhhh!" another onlooker warned them.

They both immediately became quiet. At a touch to her arm, Elise headed back to the main aisle. But not without one over-the-shoulder look at the mother and her son. *Look upon me and remember.* She remembered.

* * * * *

Halfway down the nave, they made another stop by a bronze statue. Elise squinted up at the man on the pedestal. He sat in a white stone chair while holding a Bible and keeping one hand raised in front of him, as though he meant to bless each onlooker. Atop his head was a golden crown that flared like the light of the sun: a halo. He had intensely curly hair and a curly beard. His eyes were pupiless.

"He's St. Peter. Statue of the first pope. Created in the fourth century. He stood in the Constantinian Basilica before here. People for well over a millennium have come to rub his right foot. They think it offers a blessing."

Elise glanced with skepticism at the worn right foot – so worn it lacked any definition as a foot at all. Hesitant, she stepped up and gave St. Peter's foot a vigorous rub. "Bless me, if you can." To Lorenze, "You might want to rub it too. We can use all the help we can get."

* * * * *

After much more walking, much more stopping, at last they paused at the end of the nave and the heart of the basilica. A small crowd gathered here, people spinning and arching their backs to see the highest points of the basilica's ceiling and towards the altar before them. "That is Bernini's Baldachin. It is a 90-foot high canopy created by Bernini between 1624 and 1632. It is believed that the bronze comes from the Pantheon's dome."

But Lorenze's technical description did not suffice. Elise gazed in wonder at the intricacies of the nine-story sculpture – its giant columns with carved, bronze ivy creeping up them. Intricate scrolls, suns, tassels – all in bronze – clung to the structure. Slowly, the eyes were led up – up until the point of neck craning – to view the four angels guarding the life-size crucifixion cross at its top.

"And beneath it is the papal altar?" she asked, her eyes still climbing over the structure.

"Yes. Past the circle of columns and then up one of the two sets of red stairs. There, the pope holds Mass on special occasions, and also confers grace to new bishops, cardinals, conducts some other ceremonies."

"What is inscribed at the base of the…"

Lorenze picked up where her mind got lost. "At the base of the cupola is inscribed in Latin 'You are Peter and on this rock I will build my Church, and I will give you heaven.'"

He then pointed to their sides. "These are the transepts. The basilica is created in the shape of a cross, with the long aisle, the nave," he extended his hand behind him, "and the transept passages to the right and left here. To the right, there is a monument to Pope Clement XIII. Clement is at the top, with the embodiment of Religion on his left and the Spirit of Death on his right. Two lions watch over his tomb there. And here where the transepts and the nave meet," Lorenze again drew a cross in the air with his hands, "these statues represent saints who were present during Christ's passion."

He then focused Elise's attention back to the center with a turn of his head. "And of course, the artwork above the canopy – way up there – is the Cattedra of St. Peter. It is also by Bernini, very famous. You see the chair at the bottom of the Cattedra?"

"Yes," Elise answered.

"It is a wooden chair preserved in bronze. It is believed that it used to belong to St. Peter. The four figures carrying it represent the fathers of the Latin Church and the fathers of the Greek Church.

"Above the chair in the center – just there, that oval window letting in the light – the dove of the Holy Spirit is pictured in stained glass. Bernini surrounded it with twelve rays of light to symbolize the apostles. The figures around the window are angels," he whispered the last line.

Angels. Elise stepped past the other onlookers until she was flush with the last pew. She let her eyes drink it in: the bronze and gold, the dove and light that promised eternity. Sculpted angels congregated around the bird, alight with the sun making its way inside, standing as eternal witnesses to the sacred place. Their wings spread wide as they huddled around the Spirit. She watched them, watching back. *We see everything and yet, are not a part of it. Does He love us as much as He loves those we help?*

Elise sucked in her breath. For the first time, she subconsciously thought of herself as being one of them. And she knew then certainly, a part of her was growing more and more awake. Not just her powers; but something else – some new consciousness and inner recognition. As David's heir grew closer to the throne, so did she grow closer to stopping him. Ze'ev, the cardinals gathering, the Other waiting, the sign at the Chiesa di Statua: all the loose ends and strings were coming together. Both sides were gathering. And she understood in a way she could not explain that, as Remiel grew stronger, Elise grew weaker. Lorenze was wrong to give her hope. She was quite certain that the two could not exist together.

"Can you move for just a second? I want a picture," an older woman in a printed dress began to move Elise to the side even before she finished asking her request. Her reverie broke, and she headed back to Lorenze.

"Is something wrong?" he noticed quickly the leftover anxiety on her face.

"Nothing that isn't normally wrong," she replied. "And I'm trying not to feel sorry for myself this time. So, onward?"

He nodded, but kept his frown.

"Show me your favorite spot, Lorenze. Whatever it is," she requested.

"Well, it isn't here."

"Where then?"

"Up," he rolled his pupils to look skyward.

* * * * *

They stepped off the elevator onto a ramp that followed the circle of the cupola. "We are about 300 feet up inside the dome and just above the high altar and the canopy. You should be able to get a spectacular view of the basilica from up here," Lorenze led Elise to the railing.

Indeed, she looked down to a view of Bernini's Baldachin. It looked much smaller from the new vantage point, and she could easily see the basilica's cross shape now. She watched the other tourists below.

"We can go up a little higher, if you'd like," Lorenze offered when Elise did not give any impressed exclamations. "Only 320 small steps, and we can see the entire Vatican City from an outdoor overlook."

"Fine, but when I say rest, we rest. 320 steps…" she grumbled.

They fell silent as they wound up the narrow staircase (sometimes circular), both losing their breath long before they reached the top. Despite her warning, Elise asked for no stopping. Atop, they stepped outside of the dome into the bright sunlight and the view.

They stayed alone with their thoughts for a few minutes. Elise leaned against the railing alternately looking down and closing her eyes to better feel the breeze on her face. It was cooler at such a height, and she crossed her arms around herself.

"There are the Vatican gardens, some of which we walked through today. And there is all of Rome, just laid out for us," Lorenze pointed in general directions.

"Do you like being a guard, Lorenze?" Elise asked the unexpected question.

"Do I like it?" he repeated. "Yes. Of course. This – becoming a Swiss Guard – was my choice. I wanted to do something for the Church, and I found the Vatican to be entirely captivating."

"But, you didn't want to go the chastity route, huh?" Elise literally ribbed him with a jab to his side.

Lorenze turned a grapefruit shade of pink and smiled without looking his interrogator in the face. "No. I guess I wanted to leave that door opened in my life."

"Understandable," she smiled at his blush. "Well, it's a beautiful place you picked. And you must be really good at what you do. Guarding me and my friends is a pretty important job."

Lorenze's looked out at the city a little harder before he answered. "I am good. I have been trained well in the tradition of our military. But, I must be honest. I wasn't chosen because I am the best, or the most senior officer." He bit his lip. "It is actually because I am the only guard that speaks English fluently. The Swiss speak their own variations of German, French and Italian as well as a local dialect called Rumantsch. But I did a student exchange to the U.S. when I was in school. The Pope felt that it would do no good to have a corporal guard you if he could not give you instruction."

"I agree with him," Elise tried to ease his discomfort.

The loud tolling of bells interrupted their conversation. "I think that concludes our tour," Lorenze glanced back towards the door. "I should have you back for supper. And you need to change out of your disguise. Everyone would be surprised if I brought you back a nun."

"Ah, yes," Elise fingered her veil and gave a final look before turning to follow him. "It's actually a little bit comforting. No matter where one is in the world or what is going on, the day still revolves around food. I guess everything hasn't quite gone to hell until that stops."

Chapter 19 – The Catacombs

Her first impression was the moisture: it was so humid, it was hard to breathe. Elise's eyelids fluttered open, but found only oppressing darkness. She blinked hard, as if to force light into her vision, and lifted her head.

She realized then that she was standing, leaning against something hard and also moist–

Her pulse exploded.

She had gone to sleep early, with the murmur of Chris speaking to Francis and Lorenze just outside her door. What happened to her bed, the apartment, the guard?

Breathing slow to induce calmness, Elise ran her fingers over the thing she leaned against. It felt cool, featureless, gritty: a stone wall. She felt down one side as far as she could, then the other. With even more caution, she reached one hand out in front of her. She moved it up and down, but felt only damp air.

It was like being blind. She could not tell if she stood in yet another Vatican hall, or before a cliff-side precipice.

Did I sleepwalk? Is this a dream? "Lorenze?" Her voice echoed, and then she was breathing fast and hard and she squeezed her eyes shut.

"Lorenze, please," her voice dropped to a whisper. "Answer me. Please, answer me. I can't see."

No answer.

"God. What is it? Where have you put me now?" She leaned her head back, sucking in air noisily through her nose. Counting down in her mind, she reached three and pushed herself from the wall out into the space–

And hit another wall. She was in a passageway after all.

Where is everyone? How long before they find me?

"Shut-up!" Elise yelled out into the blackness. "Just think!" It made her feel better to hear a voice, even her own. Again, it echoed. "Which way?"

She closed her eyes to more fully focus. There had to be something – footsteps or the closing of a door, the smell of food or perfume or laundry. *ANYTHING–*

The air.

It moved against her face in what could barely be called a breath. Elise stopped her own breathing to better feel it. *Yes,* it was real. Shaking, she moved forward against it, keeping her hands on one wall for guidance.

If it was a dream, it was incredibly real.

Elise listened to her feet pad, each making its own tiny echo. The stone wall remained cool and wet, and she could feel the hair standing up on her neck, her nose beginning to run. So many details for a dream to keep track of.

And when her foot kicked the hard thing on the floor, she felt real pain. She yelled, high-pitched and cracking, before successfully cutting herself off. Standing on one foot with the pain still throbbing, Elise listened to the thing she kicked rolling slowly over the stone. Even her frantic mind recognized the obscure sound. God only knew, she had dropped enough of them in her lifetime and heard that same frustrating wheeling away.

It was the sound of a flashlight rolling.

Flashlight? But how... maybe she really was sleepwalking. But, would a sleepwalker bring a flashlight? Or was there someone else in the dark with her?

Moving faster at the thought, Elise felt with her feet. Another painful stub and, like a beggar going after food, she crouched to the cool ground and scrambled with her fingers to grasp it. Elise pushed the button with her thumb and yellow light flooded ahead of her. Holding the flashlight with two trembling hands, as though she wielded a weapon, she stood up and shone it into the dark.

Everywhere was crumbling, gray stone.

A narrow passage wound in front of her, bordered by white bricked walls on either side that rose up to a low ceiling. The walls opened to many doors complete with elaborate thresholds and windows above them. And yet, it wasn't really a hallway. *No...more like a street.* That was it. Elise felt exactly as though she walked onto a theater set: she was in a recreation of a city street with two-story buildings on either side.

It was incredible. Too incredible. *This must be a dream.* She scanned using the flashlight, the beam steady as her shivering slowed.

But, there was something wrong with this city. Many of the windows and doors were bricked over, some of them cut off by the ceiling that came down from overhead. There were strange engravings, statues and graffiti carvings. It was old vandalism, in languages she knew she would not understand, even with a closer look.

Cautious, Elise peered inside a window only partially bricked over. Her flashlight played over what looked like tile walls. The color had bled from them except at the corners and close to the floor, which was merely soil. The room was empty save for a white box made of stone. It was about five feet long and covered with intricate carvings of people – maybe twenty different scenes, like a comic strip.

She knew then.

The damp air, the dark – like a basement. The watchful statues. The coffin.

Underneath the floor where the letter indicated, they discovered the lost necropolis – a city of the dead. Literally hundreds of tombs lay in the soil beneath the church.

The buildings weren't buildings at all. They were tombs. Somehow, she was in the Vatican Necropolis underneath the basilica.

The flashlight beam began to shake again.

"Doesn't mean it's not a dream," she told herself aloud. "It doesn't mean – anything," her words were broken by her agitated breathing. With no other apparent options, she started down the ancient road framed by mausoleums, her pace quickening as she went. On and on they stretched, worn faces of old gods leering at her from the shadows. All the while, her eyes searched desperately for a staircase or door that did not lead to the dead.

The street began to descend as if down a hill, declining as she went and becoming narrower. The buildings looked in greater disrepair, and several new passages opened up to the left and right – an ancient intersection. "Great," she stopped in the middle and turned her flashlight down each option. The side passages were smaller (she could easily bridge the gap between the walls if she stood just inside and extended her arms) and the ceilings slanted down. Loose rock accumulated at the paths' sides, and she could see inches of dust lying undisturbed on the floor. It looked like no one had stood where she now did for centuries.

"This isn't right...I should go back," she said defeated and scared as she turned. But as her flashlight swung into the main path, out of the corner of her eye, Elise caught a dim light at the end of the passage to the right.

She froze, turning only her eyes.

Orange light, similar to that of a fire or torch, gave just the slightest glow far down the passage, like a dying ember. It did not flicker, however, but remained still.

She dropped her eyes again to the dust on the floor, inches of it undisturbed by footprint or movement of any kind. So where was the light coming from and who, if anyone, was down the path?

"If it's a dream, it can be anything," she whispered. "But if this is real?" If it was real, she had not slept walked; someone brought her here. Someone who could get through Lorenze and the guards. Someone who wanted her afraid. And someone who wanted her to find them. *Someone who likes me helpless*, she thought as her eyes searched the stone. There was no life. Down here, she was mortal.

All the more reason to get out.

And, afraid as she was, as much as it seemed like a trap, Elise could not leave the light at the end of the passage for the darkness ahead. If it was the exit to the basilica, she could not miss it now.

As much as she loathed it, she forced her thumb onto the flashlight switch and flipped it off. Like water, the darkness flowed back in so that she could see nothing – the city and the other paths disappeared. Elise was alone with only the orange glow. Her heart hammered for her to hurry.

But slowly, she crept into the passageway. Her feet were careful, moving soft and deliberately around the pools of fallen stone where various archways had caved in – her path was lined with crumbling, rounded entrances to what she could only assume were more graves. Unlike those on the main street, these were left entirely to decay. With both hands on the stone to her sides, Elise drew near to the light step by step, farther from the darkness behind her (which she did not dare to contemplate). Unconsciously, she swallowed often and hard, and beads of cool sweat dotted her forehead and cheeks. An anxious shaking rattled her body in intense bursts, until at last, she was close enough to peer just a sliver into the room from whence the light came. Inching slowly, now pressed into the wall, she listened.

And indeed, something moved. A soft shushing. Then a few footsteps – no voices. It sounded like someone alone and (oddly) comfortable.

Is it a worker? Or guard? Somebody must have to work down here... Elise's mind jumped dizzy with the hope. What she wouldn't give to find someone wearing Lorenze's silly costume. She moved another step–

The light went dark.

Elise's heart stopped.

She took several shallow breaths. Again, it was like being blind.

And the sounds ceased. Whoever was in the room was either gone, or waiting.

Elise clenched the flashlight ever tighter, wanting more than anything to use it, but terrified to give herself away. She brought it up to her chest and pushed it there against her rib cage, as if its mere presence could somehow help her breathe. She was suffocating under the pressure of her own adrenaline. She squeezed her eyes shut (not that it made a difference), and all she could see was the library back at Ashton College, and the cold blue eyes that had been in the dark for her then. She sucked the air in, and yet it wasn't enough. Desperate, she pushed the flashlight button.

The beam was still pointed from her chest into her face, and for a moment, the light beamed so bright, it left color blotches on the insides of her eyelids when she blinked.

"One, two," she counted under her breath, but started again, knowing she couldn't do it on three. "One, two...One, two, three!"

Elise whipped the flashlight beam from her face and pointed it, like a sword, down the passage.

It caught the back of a man in white robes moving far down the passage, bobbing in and out of the shadows.

Elise pushed herself back into the wall and covered her mouth with her hand to keep from screaming. But, the man kept walking away from her, as if he did not notice he was caught in her light. He wore a short, white cape that hung to just below his shoulder blades. *Like the Pope's clothes.*

I just meant, it must be haunted. It is haunted. By God.

"Wait!" Elise's voice started out weakly. "Wait! Please, sir! WAIT!" She came into a sprint easily, and the man appeared in brief glimpses as the flashlight jumped. "PLEASE – WAIT FOR ME. I need to find – a way out!"

But, just as the man ignored her flashlight, he now ignored her voice. Though Elise ran hard, it seemed he only became further and further away. Once again, she found herself wondering if this was nothing more than an overblown nightmare – the type where passageways grow longer with every step, stretching forever.

"Please! Help me. I'm lost!" her words dropped their volume as she struggled for breath. Her sprint slowed to a jog. "God, please just wait," she whispered.

At last, he turned halfway back, looking at her from down the passage. With a combination of relief and fear, Elise hobbled towards him. "Thank you. I'm sorry. I'm just lost. I'm just…"

She could now see that his robes appeared dirty. There was dust all over them, as if he had perhaps been rolling around in one of the graves. He had curly dark hair and an equally curly and dark beard. He looked excruciatingly thin. She peered at him, recognizing…he looked like…

"I'm sorry. I just need a way out," Elise whispered while keeping several feet away.

The man didn't respond, only looked at her.

"Sir? Can you understand–"

"I thought I'd find you here," he spoke in monosyllables.

"What?"

"I thought I'd find you here," he repeated.

Elise took a step back, and the man in the robes smiled. He smiled with hundreds of thin, needle-teeth.

"No. No," Elise denied it even as she began to run backwards.

The teeth continued to elongate, and the man's eyes rolled back until they shone blue light. In a few seconds, it would be what she knew it as: a monster. She turned, scraping the flashlight against the wall and knocking more stone, sprinting into the darkness–

Her body smashed against something hard, though she saw nothing, and she found herself unable to move forward. "HELP ME! HELP ME!" she shrieked, pushing with all her force.

"God has buried you with me. In the dark," it was in her ear, its lips against her skin. Teeth grazed the back of her neck slow, and then punctured just beneath her skin.

"NO!!!"

"Open your eyes…you'll want to see this."

"Help me! PLEASE!"

"Open your eyes! Remiel, just open them!"

From somewhere, she heard Lorenze's accented words. She felt a shake and did as he commanded.

The room came into focus, awash in bright light. Lorenze was actually on top of her. He held her wrists and knelt across her legs, literally pinning her down.

Instantly, tears leaked out the side of her eyes, and she pressed her lips tightly together to hold in sobbing.

"It's okay now," the guard loosened his grip. "Did I hurt you? I didn't mean to, but you were kicking so wildly, I – let me get Chris and Francis."

"No! Don't leave me alone!" she sat up and grabbed his hand.

But, Elise and Lorenze had to go no further. Chris and Francis both burst into the room. "What's happened? Are you hurt?" Chris asked the questions for them both.

"No. No. Just a dream," she replied, still trying to believe it herself. "I'm fine. Really. I don't know why I'm crying. I feel so stupid," she tried to smile.

"Hey," Chris took her hand, rubbing it between his own. "You're icy." He noted the hair pressed to her temples with sweat, the paleness in her cheeks. "You're sure. Just a dream?"

So horrifying – it must've been us in these pajamas.

"What?" she sniffled and took a closer look at Francis' board, then at the men themselves. Both Francis and Chris were wearing long, old-fashioned nightdresses with little pockets over their hearts. She managed a laugh. "Well, I'm glad I'm not the only one who got stuck with a bum wardrobe."

"Do you want to talk about it?" Chris asked.

It took a moment for Elise to realize he meant the dream. "Oh, no. Not really," she sighed, already knowing that wasn't a satisfactory answer. "It's what it was before – the Other. Can it wait until tomorrow at least?"

Though his face showed he did not want to let it go that long, Chris replied, "Of course. You just need to get back to sleep."

"I don't know if I can. My heart is going so fast," she pressed her palm to her chest. "Can someone stay with me?"

The men worked out a simple watch schedule for the next three hours (all that was left in the night). Chris took the first shift, and the other two returned to sleeping – Francis to his bed and Lorenze to the sitting room – for at least a little while.

They were alone.

"Do you want to keep the lights on?" Chris asked as a way to avoid her eyes.

"Yes," she said readily. "Keep the lights on, and just wake me if you see me start to move a lot. I don't think it can do anything real to me in my dreams. But, I don't want to find out I'm wrong."

Chris dragged a chair over to the bed, leaving trails in the soft carpet, and Elise settled further into her pillows. She stared up at the ceiling.

"Try not to think about it," he recommended. "Try to think of something else. Something happy. Something…what?" he asked as she smiled large.

"My mother used to do that when I couldn't sleep. We used to play a game to help us get tired. We would list happy thoughts." Elise's eyes looked far away for a moment. "She always started first. She always said gardening, like she wanted to be out there right then with dirt on her hands."

"All right," Chris leaned back so that the chair creaked. "I'm thinking of…camping when I was a kid. My family used to go to Kittatinny Camp on the Delaware River. We had some of the best bonfires – the type you have to dump dirt on before you go to bed so you won't wake-up to a singed campsite. And even though it seemed like it rained every year, we still had the greatest time exploring the trails around the site, fishing in the river, and making two mile treks to the camp store for ice cream." He paused for a moment before he remembered. "Choco Tacos. They were the best."

Elise smiled, easily envisioning a younger, more carefree Chris. Not yet a priest.

"Well, I always give the same thought to start. Christmas," she sighed. "My parents and I always drove downtown to look at everyone's Christmas lights on Christmas Eve. I think it was their way of tiring me out," she admitted. "But, I loved it. And I was allowed to open one gift Christmas Eve. And it was always the same: new pajamas." She laughed. "I remember getting a pair of Super Girl pajamas one year. They came with a little Velcro cape. I ran around the Christmas tree, pretending I could fly." Elise sighed again. "I miss them."

Chris reached across the blanket and squeezed her wrist, moving down with small squeezes to her hand. He rested his hand there, and Elise slid her thumb in between his pinky and ring finger.

"I've missed you. You're always in meetings, and I'm always avoiding them."

He answered by turning his face away.

"I wonder what they would think of all this? My parents, I mean." Elise creased her forehead, and then slid a little closer to Chris. "So what else? What other happy thoughts do you have?"

Chris cleared his throat, too conscious of the feel of her hand to think for a moment, which created an awkward pause. "Um...listening to the Rolling Stones and Led Zeppelin in the garage with my dad. We used to sit in these cheesy, fold-up rocking chairs and watch the cars go by on sunny days. We sang too."

"College," she came up with her next thought. "Being young and free, and feeling pretty normal. Just normal. Working at the bar and studying." Elise closed her eyes. She could feel a little of the darkness, the anger, rising-up. It was still unfair.

He watched her face openly. Muscles in her cheeks twitched, as though she held them taught to control her face. She looked pale against the white pillow, and some of her more prominent nose freckles stood out better than usual. Some strands of hair fell across her left cheek, and he wanted to reach over and tuck them behind her ear. Instead, he began to loosen his fingers from hers.

But Elise squeezed tight. "You're up. What other happy thoughts?" she kept her eyes closed, knowing that if she opened them, Chris would take back his hand even by force.

Let go. Let her sleep. She doesn't need any more confusion... but he couldn't help feeling some new happiness at knowing she didn't want him to let go.

"The day Francis and I first saw you. Bartending. You looked like one unlikely angel, but I knew you. And it was like a lost piece of me finally came home. You know I," he paused, "struggle sometimes with my faith. But not then. You were the answer to all my prayers."

Chris watched her swallow something before she replied with, "The Whiteley Corn Festival. Alan was with us, and it was so sunny. Even with all the clouds over us, I was happy then. I can still smell the food..." her voice dropped off, and she breathed deeper.

Chris did not reply with his next happy thought. Instead, he let her fall asleep with visions of the sun.

But, his thought stayed with him, and he imagined saying it to her. *Feeling you when you turned-up. Feeling our lives mingle. Feeling the burn of your soul.*

With his arm extended, her hand still in his, the sleeve came up just enough to reveal her unfaded mark on his wrist.

* * * * *

313

Elise raised her hand slowly to her neck. In the mirror, she saw two thin lines of blood crusty along the nape of her neck.

She ran her hand under the warm water and then rubbed the color away, watching it turn red, then orange, then gone. She patted it dry with her hand towel. Only several dark red lines remained. Punctures.

Back in her bedroom, Elise gazed at her pillow. Two pinprick dark red, almost black stains appeared like out-of-place blossoms on the print of her pillowcase.

"Should I tell them? Should I tell them, I dreamed the Other was in the Vatican? It knew I was here, and it was waiting where the dead things wait. I dreamed it so real, it..." her fingers traced the ridge of raised, open skin just beyond the beat of her pulse. *I don't think it can do anything real to me in my dreams. But, I don't want to find out I'm wrong.*

She turned the pillow over. She would wear her hair down.

Chapter 20 – In the Eye

Christopher Mognahan. Christopher Mognahan, Elise repeated his full name (minus title) to herself while sitting in the common room. She and Lorenze just returned from another day of exploration, and Chris and Francis were not yet back from Vatican debates over Ze'ev and his bloodline. "Christopher Mognahan," she whispered it.

If she were still in high school, she would probably write his name on her notebook with a big, fat heart. Of course, she wasn't in high school, but rather in the largest religious institution in the world. And, there was a fundamental difference between having a crush on one's teacher, and having a crush on one's priest. But, none of those factors mattered. As their days at the Vatican stretched on, Elise found her feelings for Chris compounding exponentially. And the thought of a near separation or worse tempted her often and hard to act while she still had time.

* * * * *

Chris' vigil by her bed was the hardest. Each night, he took the early shift to protect her from her dreams, and they talked while she tried to fall asleep. Last night, she got up for a drink of water. She felt self-conscious as she slid out from under the covers – the nightgown the nuns provided was made of some soft material in between fine cotton and satin, and slightly transparent. She knew it hugged her breasts too much and showed some of the pink of her skin through its pale ivory.

Self-conscious or not, decent or not, Elise stood as if she did not notice, and then crossed to the dresser. She pretended to check her reflection, searching for some make-believe, wayward eyelash that was bothering the corner of her eye. She waited whole seconds, hoping he was noticing her.

And instead of walking to the bathroom for the drink of water, she turned from the mirror and faced him. Fast enough to catch his eyes trailing over the thin fabric and the skin underneath. He turned a dangerous red at being caught and murmured something about also needing some water while keeping his eyes downcast.

When she returned with two glasses, he was still running his fingers through his hair, standing it straight.

* * * * *

Elise leaned her head back on the common room sofa, reliving the racing heart, the embarrassment and the hope. He had noticed her! But it was crazy. She knew it. Had known it. But she couldn't find a way to help it. Chris was confident, composed, careful. His hands alone captivated her with their rough wrinkles lying over several large veins – representatives of a strong heart. And his powerful arms. Even in his plain priest clothes, she could see the contraction of a bicep or the flex of a shoulder blade if she watched him closely when he moved. She still remembered what it felt like when he carried her out of the dorm against his chest.

And she loved the lines of his face, the worry and care that left its print there. How often she wanted to reach over and smooth them out with her hands. It didn't matter that he was 25 years her senior; it didn't matter that he had kept a promise just as long to reserve his heart for God; she wanted him. And while she battled frustration, confusion, and darkness, fighting love didn't seem worth the energy.

And, she knew it could be done. Lorenze told her one day while showing her some curia offices. A priest recently left one of the council staffs. He had fallen in love with an Italian woman and revoked his vows.

But that was usually where the fantasy stopped, and today was no exception. Though Elise tried often in her daydreams, she could never see Chris breaking his vows. And even worse, it was a part of why she was falling for him: his dedication, his faith in the face of personal doubt, and his need to believe. She knew he would give up those things for no one. And, she wasn't sure she would like him without them.

He does have feelings for me though, she played with a strand of hair, curling it in her fingers. *I know he does.* But was it the way she wanted him to feel? At breakfast (they were regulars with the Pope now), Chris often picked the seat furthest away from her, as if afraid Leo might notice something if they sat too close. And he still went through spurts of avoiding her, though they now tended to last hours, rather than days. He evaded her only that morning (*but that's expected after last night*). He also spent inordinate amounts of time fathering her, at moments making their age difference unbearably obvious.

But, there were other moments, sometimes even when she just caught his eye. Or when their hands touched. Moments like last night when she was positive that he saw more in her than just a young protégé to be taught and disciplined.

The door opened. "What are you doing, just sitting in here?" Chris asked upon seeing her on the couch.

"Waiting for you."

Francis followed Chris inside.

"And you."

Francis caught sight of her and scratched, *What did you do today?*

"Lorenze and I visited the Vatican gardens. We stayed outside – it was so nice out. I definitely like November better in Italy than South Carolina. We're saving the museums for a rainy day. You?"

The monk wiped away his first line with exceptional vigor and busied himself by hanging his jacket aggressively.

Elise raised her eyebrows at Chris and sat up.

"Another visionary came in, and a genealogist. The visionary claims he sees nothing in Ze'ev, and that he thinks Francis is mistaken. The genealogist said the same thing – there is nothing to link Ze'ev to ancient Jewish royal blood. It's the first real challenge we've faced, and it was pretty hot."

Francis slammed the coat closet door and headed for his room.

"What was the decision of the consistory?" Elise asked in a low voice, in case it was bad news.

"More investigation. It's always more investigation with them."

She smiled. "Yeah. Well, that's their job. We'll have to think of something to cheer Francis up, though. You know, you guys can always come with Lorenze and I if you get too tired of the bureaucratic crowd."

"I told you before how important it is that we are in this – you should be there. I think I am going to take a nap before dinner," Chris gave a yawn to prove he needed one.

Elise's spirits dropped, and she looked in her lap. *Take me with you*, she wanted to say. She wondered what he would do if she actually dared to ask him such a thing.

"Are you okay?" he quickly sensed her lowered mood.

"Yeah. I'm fine."

He headed for the door to his and Francis' apartment.

Elise took a deep breath. "I thought about you a lot today." There.

Chris took another step towards the door and then stopped. He kept his back to her, and she could tell by the stiff way he stood that he wasn't breathing. Slowly, he turned around.

"You thought about me today?"

"Uhuh." She smiled, trying to keep his eyes locked with hers. *Come sit with me. Let Francis sleep.*

"Of course, we thought about you too." He swallowed and then smiled, then swallowed, and then opened the door and slipped through it.

Elise hung her head.

* * * * *

"So, this is where you sleep when you aren't under orders to guard my room?" Elise spoke to Lorenze as they entered the Courtyard of the Swiss Guard.

"Yes. These are the barracks. Are you sure this is what you want to do today?"

"Absolutely. You probably can use the practice, since we've monopolized your time lately, and I'd love to see the guard in action."

"We just don't usually have spectators," he tried to explain.

"I'm pretty confident that they'll make an exception for me. Don't you think?"

"Yeah," he admitted through tight lips.

They walked to the front of the barracks: a Spanish style building with orange shingles and brick. High trees surrounded it, swaying gently in the breeze.

"Well, I guess I'll show you the weaponry first," Lorenze led her inside, still unsure if the visit was a good idea. The guards would be nervous to perform in front of her, and would probably offer more pomp and circumstance than battle strategy.

To his relief, the weaponry was empty. "Anything you want, really. Helmets, swords, daggers. Most of these weapons are very old, or modeled after weapons that are very old. These," he pointed to a rack on the wall, "are our main weapon. They are called halberds: an ax-like blade on a steel spike with this long wooden shaft. Halberds were a popular weapon in the 15th and 16th centuries. It's basically a sophisticated spear, but it gets the job done."

"And you know how to fight with all this stuff?" Elise ran her hand over a few of the feathered helmets.

"We are trained thoroughly in weaponry of all varieties, if that's what you're asking." Lorenze stood with his hands behind his back, as he did during oral exams conducted by his corporal.

Elise picked up a helmet, then dropped it with a clang. "So heavy!"

"Our basic uniforms weigh about eight pounds before adding armor," he replied. "We train while learning to cope with the weight."

"All right. Show me something."

"Well, I can't exactly spar without a sparring partner. And no offense, but I don't think I want to fight you."

Elise smirked. "Why not? Afraid I'll cheat?" she opened her eyes wide to remind him of their glow.

"Among other things."

"As impressive as this stuff is," Elise became more serious, "can you actually defend me with it? Not to sound insulting, but swords and halberds require some pretty close fighting. And you don't want to get close to the Other if you can help it." She got a far away look. "If it can touch you, it will kill you."

"We also have an armory," Lorenze quickly defended.

"Show me."

* * * * *

The armory was not nearly so empty as the weaponry. Several guards were cleaning guns, and two were taking target practice. They stood when Elise and Lorenze entered.

"What are you telling them?" Elise kept the smile on her face so that they would know she meant well, while Lorenze addressed them in German.

"Just that we are visiting. That they should ignore us."

"That's all right," Elise reassured him. "They don't have to ignore us. Why did you tell them that?"

"Well…" he stammered. "They may ask you for blessings or…I have seen others give you attention and…"

"I know, I know," Elise looked back at the men (who pretended to be busy shining muzzles, but kept tabs on her out of the corners of their eyes). She shrugged. "I'm working on it, trying to be…more graceful."

"Do you want to see me shoot?" he let her off the hook.

Without waiting for her answer, Lorenze handed Elise a pair of earmuffs, and led her into a well-lit shooting gallery. He took his place behind a counter and called to another guard, who hung a target for him at the opposite end. He nestled a large rifle in a comfortable position under his right arm and then stood very still. He concentrated on the target in front of him, and Elise watched him breathe unnaturally slow breaths. He squinted just slightly.

Though she knew they were coming, Elise still jumped each time Lorenze fired. He relaxed after the last shot and carefully pointed the rifle towards the floor. He pulled the earmuffs down around his neck and motioned for her to do the same. "Take a look."

Though no one else was in the firing range, it still felt dangerous to cross the shooting line, and she gave one check over her shoulder to make sure it was only she and Lorenze. It was. She marched to the target, ripped it from its pins and held it up. One large hole was torn directly through the center.

"You need some more practice, hot shot." Elise spoke as he came up behind her. "One shot was perfect, but the others aren't even on the page. Looks pretty hit and miss."

"No," he took it from her and looked closely. "That's all of them. I was actually so precise, the four bullets made only one hole." He handed the paper back to her. "The Swiss Guard may be a little old fashioned as far as armies go. But, nothing will get very close to you unless I let it."

* * * * *

Chris watched Elise, as he now did every night. While she slept, the strength and confidence faded from her face, and her forehead often crinkled in anxiety. He wondered what she dreamt. But so far, he had not had to wake her.

His shift would be up in a half-hour, and he was thankful. More and more, it was hard to be alone with her. Since they arrived at the Vatican, she had become more demanding with his attention. And worse, he wanted to give it to her.

"So stupid," he muttered to himself. *It's just the strange circumstances. She's alone, and you're here. In real life, she would never want you.*

He was a priest, after all, and last Chris checked, the brotherhood wasn't exactly on the top of the sexiest men lists. And he was old. Whatever attraction she had for him was superficial at best. If they did make it through this, she would walk out of his life just as quickly as she walked in. *Back to the life she should have*, he reminded himself.

Except her eyes, the part of him that already lost the battle whispered. *You've seen it in her eyes.* That intense look. The one that asked him to stay with her when everyone else left. It had been a long time, but he remembered what desire looked like.

Stop thinking like this! Your vows! Say an Our Father *or something!* Chris threw himself back in his chair, as if moving it a few inches away from her would solve everything.

But she was beautiful, and his eyes strayed back to her face. Full of so much fire and will, full of anger and love. Elise Moore burned hot at both ends of the fuse. It hurt and invigorated him.

Angel or not – she was incredible.

Gently, Chris reached a hand for her face and brushed her cheek. The tickle scrunched her features and she turned from him, as if from some annoyance.

"Just a girl. Too young for all of this," he whispered. "Too full of life for so much fighting." Elise slept on, innocent of Chris' words, of his fear and his hope, and his fear of that hope.

While she ran around with Lorenze on some surreal vacation, decisions were being made. Decisions about her future, and about those who would accompany her. While she explored and enjoyed, the cardinals consistently plotted towards an assassination attempt with her at its head.

But what else is there to do? This is her job. This is why we are all here. This is God's choice! Chris reasoned just as he reasoned during the day.

But for once, reasoning did not help. Elise was slowly being led towards something Chris more and more feared she would not survive. Of course, he reasonably feared that none of them would survive, but especially Elise. He often remembered... what was it... something she said. *"I am not meant to survive. What's left for me here after this?"*

"There's me," he whispered. "In whatever way you want me. Whatever way."

Then Chris imagined, not for the first time, crawling next to her and holding her against his chest. Just holding her, feeling her warmth. He imagined how small she would be in his arms. Maybe then, at least for a moment, it would feel like he could protect her.

He heard the door open quietly. Francis came to relieve him.

* * * * *

They were in the Vatican's Chiaramonti Museum – an entire wing dedicated to heads and statues recovered after the French invasion of the late 18th century (or so Lorenze explained). Elise walked ahead of the guard (as she often did when he wasn't on active tour guide duty). She strode in and out of the different statues that lined the walls on both sides. Huge, high windows gave the place an airy feeling despite the angry raindrops that splattered the glass.

"This place reminds me a little of Madame Tussaud's," Elise commented behind her to Lorenze. "You know the wax museums? They have whole sections devoted to the heads of dead people. Just like this," she indicated the shelves lined with frozen faces.

"The faces of people who lived thousands of years ago," Lorenze passed over her wax reference. "They look very much like people today. I find that remarkable, considering they could not even begin to conceive what the world would be like so far in the future." •

"Eh. It isn't that different. In the end, most things still come down to love, money, or sex." Elise gave a sly look to see if Lorenze appeared scandalized. Though she tried to limit herself, shocking him had become her newest form of entertainment.

He ignored her (which he was getting good at). "On our next rainy day, we will have to visit the secret archives. The Vatican has thirty miles of shelves, holding a thousand years worth of memory. Everything from kings' annulment petitions, to letters from the artists that built the Vatican; from alliance contracts, heresy trial records: it's all in there. You should see the seals attached to many of the documents. The family crests of some of the most influential men and women in history. In many of them, you can see a thumbprint in the wax, as if they only just touched it."

"Uh-huh," Elise replied as a courtesy while she looked up at the statue of a man carrying a lion's skin. Lorenze took the cue and fell silent.

More thoughtfully, glaring into the eyes of the bust of a young man, "It's funny. He probably thought his life was pretty important. His loves and sorrows seemed too great to survive sometimes; he may have felt too much depended on him. And yet, before his face could fade from the stone it was carved on, he is forgotten without a whisper of what he was. He never existed except for this."

"You sound like a book in one of the libraries."

"How long before I am just a name, or a face without a name?"

"You'll never be a face without a name. You're Remiel. Very soon, you'll show the world.

"Soon? But I'm not ready yet," she looked at Lorenze, truly afraid.

"You have to be," he answered simply.

* * * * *

Francis, Chris, Matthew, and Secretary of State Paul Rossi were already gathered around the Pope in the dining room. A television had been brought in, and scenes of fire and smoke flashed across the screen.

"What is it? Just tell me!" Elise flew into the room.

"It's not what you think. It's bad, but it's not that bad," Chris couldn't get the words out fast enough. Her anxiety was palpable.

"It is a false alarm, but still alarming," the Pope broke in. He gestured to the television. "What you are seeing is the President's residence in Jerusalem."

"And it's on fire."

"Yes. Someone, or probably several people, broke in last night and set explosives. The President is fine. He has already released a statement, labeling the attack a scare tactic."

"But," Elise gave Leo the word he held onto.

"But, our sources are aware of the level of security the President currently has on his residence. It is literally impossible to get in without facing an Israeli soldier. Yet, none of the soldiers were engaged last night. The guards did not report a break-in until the bomb went off. And, none of the rebels were captured or harmed. Our spies have reported for some time that the Israeli President and Prime Minister's own military is turning on them. This is proof positive."

Over and over, the television showed an aerial of the residence. Police and guards moved on the ground below like busy ants. Chris spoke without taking his eyes off it, "We have evidence that Demsky ordered the attack – a spy overheard a conversation between several of his commanding generals about an hour before the bomb went off. Demsky is, of course, the highest-ranking general of the Israeli military. In these hard times, the soldiers' loyalties are to him and the strength he brings. And they are ready for treason. This is the first domino. Falling."

She was quiet. Then, Elise hung her head as though scolded. "So it's beginning." She looked at the heavy faces around her. "He's made his first move towards the throne, and he takes Ze'ev with him."

"The news stations are running a statement from Demsky," Leo spoke with a closer look to the TV. "He swears his support for the President; claiming that his followers were not involved in the attack, nor his soldiers; and, as always, he is encouraging groups with differing political views to use the democratic process – not violence – to effect change."

"Liar," Elise spoke with disgust. "Gathering support with his humbleness and belief in the choice of the people, even while he makes plans in the background to take power by force. So what do we do? Can we tell the Prime Minister what we think is happening? Tell him what we know?"

"Unfortunately, it isn't that easy," Leo said slowly.

Paul stepped forward then, and Elise felt some nervous butterflies flutter back to life low in her stomach. It was obvious Monsignor Secretary of State was stepping to the plate to save the Pope from delivering dirty news. All eyes turned to him.

"If we call the Prime Minister of Israel and give him our information, we would have to reveal that we have spies in the rebel groups. The Catholic Church spying on Israel – it's a scandal we cannot weather right now." His words left the room silent and still, only the flash of fluorescence from the television revealed that time continued on.

Chris squeezed his hands into fists, waiting for the storm to break. Surely, this would be Elise's most furious display yet. *Bureaucrat, corrupt* – the floors waited to shake, the windows to shatter, and Remiel to appear.

"A scandal?" Elise broke the hush incredulously in a very human, fearful voice. "We're talking about the end of the world here. If Demsky is successful, Ze'ev will be in a position that no one can weather. We need to stop waiting and debating." Elise turned around to Chris and Francis, who remained silent. She could tell by the look in their eyes that they already had this conversation.

"What about a damn anonymous phone call at least?"

"Elise," the Pope tried to speak.

"What? Can't we at least do that? Or do we have to just watch this happen?

323

Matthew broke in. "Of course, it has already been done. We are religious men. The call was made to the Israeli government as soon as the news broke. And, we called more than once, you will be happy to know. But, without the credibility of the Church behind that call, chances are, it won't even make it to an official with any power. They receive thousands of phone calls about the rebels each day. It will go unnoticed."

"Great!" she exclaimed sarcastically. "So what's the plan? What are we doing about this?"

"What do you think we should be doing, Elise?" the Pope asked. "For now, it seems there isn't much we can do."

"Forgive me if I don't want to watch the world end from the Vatican Hill. What about just taking out Demsky? And Ze'ev. And Ze'ev's family – he has a daughter, right? Just take them out and end this bloodline. You don't even have to use me. What about your spies? Can't they kill him?" she asked the last line quietly.

Silence.

"What? Please don't tell me you haven't thought it. It is ugly, I know. But, if it's what we have to do…"

"Our insiders are trained to be Israelis, not murderers," Monsignor Matthew revealed quietly. "They are only ambitious priests, and any attempt to kill either man would almost definitely fail. Not to mention, it's been hundreds of years since the papacy has attempted an assassination. And even then, they only happened under corrupt popes; our beliefs as Catholics don't allow such actions. We do not have the support inside our own ranks to command priests to kill a man because there is a chance that he may become king. After all," with a nervous glance at Francis, "the consistory has not decided if Ze'ev is the target. For purely moral reasons, there are many who would not have this man killed until he is in a position to be crowned, which he is not yet."

"And," Paul interjected, "our spies have too many links to the papacy. If they made an attempt on Ze'ev or Demsky's life, it would be a suicide mission that would eventually lead back to us. We are only lately in the spy business, Remiel. Even the world's most sophisticated militaries have trouble denying credit for their assassinations. The Church has left an imperfect trail."

"Then hire someone, for God's sake! Outsource your assassin, but do it. I certainly will leave a trail, and a wide one! And 100 years – a thousand years – of bad PR would be worth it!"

"No. You will leave no trail," Leo spoke without any inflection.

"What is that supposed to mean exactly?"

"It has been decided, Elise, that when you leave Rome, your ties to the Church will be cut off. At that point, you will be working for a freak faction

324

of the Church called the Secret Congregation for the Hetaera Melchizedek."

Confusion ironed out some of the anger from her face. "Freak faction?"

Paul explained, "There already is almost no evidence that the society exists as an actual function of the Church, and what evidence there is, we will destroy. The Congregation is aware of all this, and is more than willing to make the sacrifice and break from the Church. All of the members will be at your command and your control while in Israel. Cardinal Matthew will be going with you to ensure that. And as far as assassins go – you are perfect. No family, no one looking for you. There is no one literally in the world outside this building that knows you are here. For all intensive purposes, you erased yourself to avoid murder charges. And your powers are far greater than any we can hire."

"So this is it. Lies, deceit, and scapegoats: everything I was afraid the Church could be."

"We discussed it and discussed it, Elise," Chris spoke quickly. "It seemed the best way. We will go in a small group and just get the job done when we are called to. The Church can keep her reputation, and you will keep from sounding."

She shook her head, more tired than angry. "I just can't believe we are having conversations about reputation when the whole world is on the line. Who cares if the Catholic Church goes down? Who cares about anything except making sure the final judgment happens when God decides it should happen? Who cares, so long as we are all here to live and breathe another day that doesn't have the seas boiling and the dead rising? Can't you see? This is it – Demsky has control of the military, and he's bringing Ze'ev with him to the top, within reach of the throne."

No one answered.

"You all know the gravity of this situation. For God's sake, you taught it to me," she looked from one face to another for some sign of hidden agreement. "If Ze'ev is crowned and Armageddon is brought upon us now: We. Will. Lose. You understand that, right? Everything will be lost because this isn't the generation. This isn't the time. This isn't God's plan. Your reputation will be saved, but our souls will be dead. For there won't be enough angels to save you then."

Silence.

"I guess I'm just not talking to the right people," she turned her back. "We'll just watch it happen. And when Ze'ev does get on that throne – which he will – you'll send me to him without any support. Risk of death, imprisonment. Did I miss anything?" she asked rhetorically. "All while you stay here in the comfort of your positions."

"It really is the best way, Elise," Chris tried again. "If the Church is behind us, there will be too many questions. Demsky's guard is going to be up. He won't let us get within a mile of him or Ze'ev if he thinks there is something strange. We can't show-up with the Pope and the Swiss Guard. This isn't just about keeping the Church's sheets clean. It's about being successful. We are best on our own."

"I'll agree with you there." She let the double entendre sit with them, without bothering to turn around. "I don't want to talk about it anymore. Just tell me where to be and when." Elise wound around the table to the door. "Stay here and watch the President's home – and power – burn a while longer. "

* * * * *

The knock was annoying. Elise purposefully left the common room and retreated to her own apartment to avoid Francis and Chris. And yet, someone knocked.

"What?" she called, not really carrying if the knocker heard her or not.

No reply, but the door opened anyway. *Francis.* Elise listened to him wander back to her bedroom.

May I come in? was already written on the board.

"I guess," she answered and then shifted her eyes back to the ceiling. But a moment later, she heard the monk writing and so faced him again. He was going to be persistent, obviously.

How are you?

"Great. Fricking great."

The Church is frustrating.

"Yeah."

That's why I became a monk. To avoid some of this.

"Well, we're in the thick of it now," she crossed her arms over her chest.

They still don't believe me about Ze'ev. Another visionary came in today. Same thing. Said he didn't think Ze'ev was the one.

Elise sighed. "It's unbelievable. In this beautiful place, it's easy to forget that we are working with a business. But they certainly have their own interests. And they're not all holy." Switching, "You're still sure about Ze'ev?"

Francis shook his head. *I stand by it. Do you feel anything towards him?*

"No. Nothing. I thought that too – maybe I would remember something once I saw him. But, nothing tugs at me in anyway."

No twitches for any of the other advisors either? Demsky? Anyone?

"Nothing. You're still the only one seeing signs. Don't worry – I believe you. If Ze'ev were here, now, I wouldn't hesitate."

That's why disconnecting from the Church is good for us. Do what we

326

want. What we need. No bull.

Elise finally sat-up, pulling her hair back in a rubber band she had on her wrist. "You really think that?"

Chris and I talked a lot about it. We should've talked with you, but...we want the Church's resources. We don't want the Church's bureaucracy. And we can't have one without the other, so we gave up both. Leo thinks the same thing. The Church is too slow. He didn't want you waiting for its seal of approval on anything once you're there.

She frowned at him. "That's really the reason you, Chris, and Leo support cutting me loose?"

Yes. No more dealing with this. Soon, we just get the job done.

Elise sighed. "I hope so. 'Cause right now, I feel like we're missing the boat. It's like I'm in a dream screaming, and no one hears me. We could stop this now, but no one wants to make the first move." She covered her eyes with her hands and mashed the skin around her eyes and cheeks, like a tired mother.

"If we are successful, the Church will be able to just nod its big head in our direction, give us a secret pat on the back. If we succeed, but we are imprisoned or killed, it will just turn its back on us. And if we fail, I guess it will at least reserve the right to go down grandly, untarnished."

Have some faith in the Hetaera Melchizedek. Francis tapped the board below the name for emphasis, as if pounding an imaginary masculine chest. *The society is powerful on its own – why do you think our dear friend Cardinal Matthew wanted to run it so badly?* He gave a sarcastic smile. *Because it has a purpose that most other parts of the Church are afraid to rein in. And the society is behind you all the way. They would not let you be imprisoned. And they'll literally be damned before they see you fail.* He smiled again.

Elise nodded and then scrunched up her body, wrapping her arms around her long legs. "Thanks, Francis," she said simply, not knowing quite how to let him know how much he made things better. "Whenever the crap hits the fan, somehow you always help me at least keep it out of my eyes."

He opened his mouth as if to laugh, but of course, there was no sound.

* * * * *

"So, how are you doing?" Chris asked as she rolled over in bed to face the wall.

He barely spoke to her since the meeting that morning. Elise couldn't tell if he was mad at her, or afraid.

"I'm fine. Nervous," she admitted.

"I'm surprised you're talking to any of us," he said it quietly, as if

327

mentioning it might make it so.

"This would be a pretty quiet place if I did that," she replied flatly. "And quite frankly, there isn't enough time for silent treatment. I really feel like the wheels have started turning. Ever since we arrived, it's been moving fast: fighting in Israel, my dreams with the Other. And, with Demsky making such bold attacks on the President, it really feels like it won't be long now."

"There is still a chance that the coup will be unsuccessful," Chris tried to remain positive. "Despite what Leo says. Who knows? The rebel groups are unpredictable and far from loyal to one another. Perhaps a rival will take care of Ze'ev for us."

"There's something to pray for," she replied. "Although, praying for someone to kick the bucket definitely doesn't feel right." She heard Chris laugh a little, and then she rolled over to look at him. "Are you afraid?"

Chris could tell by the way she asked that it was a trick question. She was really asking him to tell her everything was going to be fine.

"I've seen what you can do too many times to be afraid. There isn't a rebel army in the world that can stand up to you. And if the Other comes to join the battle, you'll take care of that too. You faced it before. You saved my life and yours. I'll try to keep myself out of the way this time so you have a chance at finishing the thing off," he joked.

"I wonder why it doesn't attack now. Despite the Church and its constant debating, we're getting close to Ze'ev, and I'm sure it knows it. Unlike me, it doesn't seem to have any problem understanding its purpose."

"It is what it is. I'm sure many of our questions are going to be answered soon."

She ignored him. "What will we do afterwards? Supposing everything goes well and we beat this, what will we all do?"

Chris' eyebrows got a little closer together. "Well, I guess we'll go back to normal. You'll go back to school, and I'll go back to blessing the corn in Whiteley every November. You'll have your life back."

"Except, I'm not sure I want it." She smiled, realizing what she said was ludicrous. "I just can't see myself going back to school, becoming a psychologist after being here and knowing what we know. How do you listen to people who are angry with their parents after this?" She laughed a little to hide the sadness.

"You'll get used to it, Elise. You'll go back to being young. Back to the bar and staying out late."

Elise smiled a real smile. "You must've been shocked when you found me."

"Not really. You were just a girl having a good time in college. It's where you should be. Not hanging out with priests." Chris took a deep breath and looked down.

"I like hanging out with priests, though. Maybe you and Francis and I can just go back to Whiteley and—" she broke off when her imagination wouldn't allow her further. "I just don't want to be alone again."

Chris reached over to touch her face.

For a moment, she was surprised at the gesture, but then she held perfectly still, so as not to scare him away.

"You'll never be alone, Elise. I want you to have your life back. But, that doesn't mean Francis and I will disappear off the face of the earth. I'll always be there."

She kissed his hand as it ran across the corner of her mouth.

* * * * *

"So this is the Tower of the Winds?" Elise asked as the stairs opened into a square room.

"This is it. Pretty spectacular?"

Four glorious frescoes, covered with wispy beings that moved in and out of cloudy scenes, crammed each wall to almost spilling over. Many of the angelic beings pictured had their mouths open where more white wisps flowed from between their lips: the wind. It was a beautiful display of blue skies and an artist's imaginings of heaven.

"Hey. This one's vandalized," Elise paused under one particular fresco with a hole poked directly in the mouth of one of the winds. Sunlight streamed in.

"You're joking right?" Lorenze asked with open eyes to let her know she had just said something incredibly stupid.

She raised her eyebrows at him.

"The Tower of the Winds is more than just another tower in the Vatican," he explained with a sigh to let her know she was hopeless. "The South Wind, as you noted, has a break that lets in sunlight. See where it strikes the floor?" He directed her eyes to the ground, and she more carefully noticed the pale circle in the center of the room, surrounded by borders of differently shaded brown stone.

"It's a seasonal calendar," Lorenze named it when it became apparent Elise wasn't going to get it on her own. "Where the light hits the ground – that's what day it is. And as the earth rotates around the sun, as it shifts on its axis, the light from the south wind's mouth moves around the circle."

Quick to fall into full tour guide mode, Lorenze continued. "Until 1580, the world went by the Roman calendar. Pope Gregory XIII was the first to realize that calendar was inaccurate because of findings he discovered here. He noticed that over time, the sunlight didn't fall exactly on the same place each year. For example: when the Roman calendar claimed it was the spring equinox, the sunlight on this calendar showed it had not yet arrived. Each year, the gap between the calendar day and where the sun fell became greater. There weren't enough days in the year. So, in 1580, he issued a decree that let citizens know at midnight, October the 4th, the date would skip ahead to October 15th. He also decided that the New Year would start in January and no longer in March. He then added the leap years to keep the calendar accurate. So, the modern calendar is based on the observations made in this room."

Elise wandered to where the small beam of light (surprisingly strong for traveling the distance from the wall to the floor) hit the stone. In a graceful sweep, she knelt in her robes beside it. Lorenze watched her run her finger through it, as if it were water instead of light. She traced a ridge in the floor.

"So that's today, and then every other day until the end – all marked in this one circle." She looked up from her humble position and let the corners of her mouth turn-up slightly. "It looks like there's so much time."

* * * * *

She was gracious. She was humorous. *She's actually having a good time*, Chris thought with surprise as he had several times that evening. They were having dinner with several cardinals from the consistory – a scene that normally had explosive potential. He expected Elise to grin and bear it in the sullen way she bore other things the Church threw at her. But she was too busy laughing to play her normal part. She sat at the head of the table, in crimson robes that shimmered like wine or blood, her red-blond hair cascading in softly styled curls, decked with a small crown that sparkled like a cluster of fireflies around her head.

She left him breathless when she entered (the last to come through the large doors). And she left him breathless now.

Between bites of food, she told them anything they asked – how the world looked gold when she turned-up; what it was like listening to Alan explain who she was the night she left Ashton; about when she (and her parents) realized for the first time that she was different the day she shocked her mother's hand to make the fever "feel better." It was as open as Chris had ever seen her with people she did not know well. Heck, he was learning things he did not yet know about her. Elise even managed to be courteous to Cardinal Matthew (sitting on the far side of Lorenze in order to keep the guard's peaceable sword between them).

Chris remembered a conversation with his mother many years ago. They had been in the kitchen getting coffee while his father rested in the living room. He had said something like, "This is Dad's second bout with cancer. He's strong. He'll beat it again."

But his mother only shook her head. "I can tell. This will kill him."

Chris had been shocked at her simple admission, her complete lack of hope. "Why do you say something like that?" he asked with more than a small trace of anger.

"Because he let me turn-up the heat," she replied plainly. "My whole life, I've wanted this house at 72 degrees, and my whole life, it's been at 68." A small tear had appeared at the side of her eye when she spoke then, but she continued in a steady voice. "And that's how I know. When we got home from the specialist, that was the first thing he told me to do. 'Go ahead and turn-up the heat, Ann.'"

Though Chris remained angry with his mother for refusing hope, he never forgot her silly wisdom that day. And as the months passed while Brian Mognahan fought a steady battle for his life, he continued to steadily surrender the battles of his lifetime. He lost his interest in politics, forgot to hate the dog next door, dismissed his loathing of leftovers, and suddenly lived a life of complacency that he would've curled his lip at a few short months before. He passed away six months after turning the heat to 72.

In the dead quiet center of his soul, Chris knew Elise was doing the same thing. Her laughter, her apparent peace and ease – they were all forms of surrender. He had been watching her closely the last week. He tried to dismiss it as melancholy at first. Maybe even homesickness. But now, almost every moment her behavior surprised him. Even Lorenze commented the other day…what was it? Something about her adjusting well. *Adjusting well.* He knew better. Elise Moore didn't adjust well. She either decided she liked something better than another thing, or she didn't.

Like his father and the hundreds of other people Chris had seen die, Elise was suddenly exhibiting characteristics she had never come close to actually possessing. Forgiveness, selflessness, tiredness, neediness: a part of the Elise that was consciously or subconsciously getting ready to leave them all. It was something – the one thing – he could not forgive her for, and Chris felt his anger rise even at dinner.

A sudden change in the din broke into Chris' thoughts, and he found himself turning his head in jerks, like a sleeping student who's just been called on by the teacher for the answer to a question he has not heard. Something happened. He could tell by the uncomfortable way Elise looked, and the shifting of others in their seats.

As if for Chris' sake, the Cardinal explained, "It was amazing, seeing your powers. A modern miracle. We had hoped you might give us another show." Elise's red robes seemed to bleed up her neck into her face. Monsignor Matthew looked down, Francis leaned away from her, and Chris fingered the scar on the outside of his wrist.

"I don't know what else you would like to see. Thankfully, my powers are not limited to slamming doors or vandalizing paintings," she spoke quietly.

"You are living proof of God, Remiel. It doesn't matter."

She shrugged, then nodded. Lorenze was closest.

Without asking his permission, Elise slid an almost casual hand onto his shoulder, the tips of her fingers touching the warm skin of his neck. Before he realized he was selected, he felt the oddest tingle and then a sharp pain. He flinched and jerked, as though she found his pressure point. She let him go, needing nothing else.

Invisible to them, she separated from the girl standing at the end of the table and sent her consciousness into the room. She concentrated, feeling invisible lips form and harden, the breath move over them. She felt harder, stretching out to many mouths, dividing over and over and feeling the creases in the lip-skin, the teeth behind them. More concentration, more materialization of her extensions. When they were all there – so many virtual mouthpieces just waiting for her to play – she pushed with the energy.

First behind Francis. "Giveth them light," a voice just behind his ear whispered. Then on to the next. "For the Lord God giveth them light," "The Lord God giveth them," "Giveth them light." It went around the room, the words in each ear, overlapping as though many people were having the same conversation: a breathy round.

And then, the light was gone from her face, and all eyes turned to her. "It's from the *Revelation*, which, you already know that. Alan Cole told me it once." They applauded, but she lowered her eyes to avoid Chris, Francis and Lorenze.

She had heard it too, and recognized it.

The whispered voice of her mind was not the same as the one that regularly erupted from her throat. Rather, it was the same as that which whispered from the statues in the Chiesa di Statua.

* * * * *

"Well, that wasn't so bad," Elise sat down on the common room sofa to remove her shoes. "I think I can learn to take cardinals in small doses."

"What was with the voices?" Chris interrupted, not bothering to hide the annoyance in his voice.

Elise looked up with some surprise. "I didn't know that if I used the telekinesis that it would – come out like that."

The same whisper as that of the statues, Francis gave a nod, as if to tip his hat to a clever idea.

"I thought it was nice, actually. All this time, I've been wondering where to get my direction from. Tonight, it felt like God was telling me to trust myself."

"Nice. I guess that's one take," Chris muttered loud enough for the entire room.

Elise finally snapped at him. "What is wrong with you?" Chris slid his eyes away, but Elise sat forward. "What are you so pissed about?"

"Glad to see you haven't given up cursing," he spoke a half-truth.

It's late, Francis scrawled while managing to flick several alarmed glances their way before the line was complete. Awkwardly he stood, and when no one spoke, awkwardly he left.

"The question is actually what is wrong with you?"

"With me?" she let her mouth hang open to mimic his stupidity.

"You're acting so differently lately."

He watched her anger contort to confusion. Even with all his defenses up, prepared for battle, he felt a pang at hurting her. He was acting unreasonable, vague. Her face was right.

Chris sucked in a huge breath and the words exhaled out. "At first, I tried to pass it off. But, I see it more and more. The way you've warmed up to Lorenze, always making up for that first moment. The way you now try to be patient with the cardinals when two weeks ago, you wouldn't have stood next to one without rolling your eyes. And yesterday – when we told you about the Church's plan to deny your existence. I expected a huge fight. Your worst yet. But you walked away and let it go. I can't believe it! Elise Moore would never behave like that."

"Wait. Are you really complaining because I'm–"

"Then there was tonight. The cardinals asked you to do the thing you have never done happily for anyone – show-off. And you just did it."

"Are you all right? I'm serious," Elise looked at him wide-eyed. "Do you realize you're yelling at me because I am behaving the way you always encourage me to?"

Chris ran his fingers through his hair.

"You know. That's typical," Elise pursed her lips. "I always know when I've got you because you mess-up your hair."

Self-consciously, he put his hands on the sides of the cushion, finding them soft to his tense clench. "I know it sounds contradictory. I know it counters my encouragement. But, I also know it's not really you." He turned imploring eyes on her face. "The Elise I know fights everything. She's skeptical of everyone, and guards her strengths like a lion before its den. She never gives more than she wants to give. Until now."

"I'm just trying to do the right thing; act the way God would want me to; the way you always seemed to want me to. I'm just trying to be better."

"Why now though?" Chris asked the sharp question.

"Because," Elise answered too quickly.

"Because time is running out," Chris finished the sentence quickly.

Elise cocked her head sideways, as if to ask a question. Instead, she stated, "So what? Isn't it all right that I clean my record a little while I still have the chance?"

"I knew it! You're acting differently because, somehow over the course of the last few weeks, we've allowed you to accept that Ze'ev will be your end."

Elise threw up her hands. "I'm trying to be realistic, Chris. Despite everything you've done to prepare me and all the resources you will give me, I just don't think–"

"I know. You're 'not meant to survive this,'" Chris did a poor imitation of her voice. "You've said it before. But this is the first time I've seen you really believe it."

"You know, you yell at me this whole time to act towards others with the grace that I've been given, and then you yell at me when I finally do it. Very logical. Next you're going to tell me I should've seen this coming."

"It hurts me to see you giving up."

"I'm not giving up!" she yelled it.

"Not on your task. But on yourself?"

"I'm not giving up on anything! God, you're being such a–"

Chris' eyes strayed to the door that Francis closed behind him on his way to bed.

"And I don't care if we wake him up!" Elise yelled even louder. "I'm not fricking giving up! Or maybe I should say fucking so that you'll feel better! There. Do you feel like I'm living now?"

With a quick motion, she was off the couch and halfway to her room. Chris had to practically throw himself to get up fast enough to catch her.

"Elise–" he grabbed her forearm and pulled her to a quick halt.

At his forceful touch, she spun violently, using her free hand to grab him where he held her. Her face turned towards him in a blur of slit eyes and snarled mouth – so much anger. With fear, he realized, *She's going to turn-up–*

But Elise froze with equal fear. With one blink, her face turned from fury to horror – horror of herself. Her mouth became slack and her eyes opened wide. She still clutched his hand, no longer with malice, but to anchor herself.

Afraid to speak and unsure of what to say, Chris tried to let her know with his eyes that it was okay. He understood. It was Remiel versus Elise. He had just watched her switch from the power of one, to the weakness of the other.

"I wasn't going to," she began in the softest whisper. "Don't think that I would ever…" Even to her own ears, the words sounded hollow and untrue.

Color flooded her cheeks as they remained locked together in an awkward pose. Her facial muscles twitched and her eyes sparkled. Chris realized she was about to cry.

Silent, he pulled her into his chest before she could protest. She trembled against him but did not fight. Rocking her, Chris let his hands move up and down the sides of her arms, the small of her back. It was as though they danced to some slow, intense melody.

When she finally moved against him, it was only to pull back far enough for her face to meet his, her eyelashes skimming his chin. Smooth rivers of tears now squiggled down her face and smeared in places from where his shirt touched her cheeks. It would've taken barely a movement from him to kiss her.

For a long second, Elise waited there to the ticking of a clock somewhere in one of the apartments, for Chris to finally weaken and fall just far enough to touch her lips.

But the priest (and his heart) did not move.

Rejected, she removed his arms and stood before him with clenched fists.

"This–" she indicated her tears, "doesn't make you right about everything." In an even softer whisper, "I'm only becoming what you taught me to become. Powerful and focused. Godly. You shouldn't worry so much." She raised her fists between them (unthreatening) and then opened them with stretched fingers. "I'm in good hands." Elise's face tried to smile.

Chris let her walk to her room and close the door. It was one of the hardest things he'd ever do.

* * * * *

He watched her kneel in her robes, and almost mentioned that she was getting them dirty. But something stopped Lorenze. Maybe it was the way she looked past him all afternoon, ignoring his Vatican fun facts more than usual. Maybe it was the way she smiled two or three seconds late after every one of his jokes. Or maybe it was the way she kept looking over her shoulder, always expecting someone to come up behind her. Whatever the thing, dirty robes seemed irrelevant.

"Are you all right?" Lorenze asked when Elise remained squatting on the path.

"Yeah. I'm fine." Her words were so quiet, the wind threatened to take them away before they reached him.

Lorenze frowned and squinted down at her. It was a cold day despite the sun. It shown in a deep blue sky without any clouds, yet gave off no heat. Elise's cheeks were red from the bitterness. It was unattractive – the color matching her hair too closely.

"We aren't going to see much more of the gardens if you stay there," he pointed out the obvious. She had knelt under the pretense of looking at a rare bush, and then remained there.

When Elise didn't answer him, Lorenze leaned over and extended his hand. As reluctant as a child being led to the bathroom when it doesn't want to go, Elise gave him her hand and stood.

Without further warning, "Chris and I are in a fight."

"Oh?" Lorenze gave the right tone to draw her further. "What about?" Together, they began walking along the gray stone path, the gardens becoming background.

"I don't want to say. But I'm afraid it will change everything and he won't forgive me. He wouldn't even look at me this morning, in case you didn't notice. And of all the things that are going on right now," she smiled ironically, "this bothers me the most."

Though he gave her a sharp eye, Lorenze replied with a standard disclaimer. "Without knowing what happened, I cannot give you much advice."

"I'm not really looking for advice."

They walked a few feet in silence. Somewhere, a bird that forgot to head south chirped. Elise's eyes wandered to find it, but didn't.

And then abruptly she stopped. As if a steel pole was suddenly thrust up through her spine, Elise froze rigid.

Lorenze took several more steps without her before turning around.

"Run away with me, Lorenze," Elise turned her creamed-coffee eyes on him with an intensity that made his skin prickle. He noticed that, though the wind whipped, in that moment, it did not disrupt the hair around her face.

"What?" he whispered, wondering if she really asked what he thought she had asked. Then, the prickling became something else – something without an obvious cause, but a warning nonetheless. Without knowing why, he glanced over his shoulder.

Though their footsteps were still too far to be heard, Lorenze saw the men in their unique, Renaissance uniforms coming towards them. The guards were running. And there were many of them. Like an eclipse, they darkened the path with their mass and their mission.

Lorenze's heart throbbed painfully – something inside screamed what he could not possibly know. They were coming to doom her – her: the one he swore to guard. His sword hand clenched, begging instinctually to protect. Instead, Lorenze pushed the fist hard against his hip where it could find no use. The guards brought only her fate – and there was no protecting from that.

Behind him, Elise let Lorenze know she understood his surrender with words that had not been spoken in more than two millennia with as much mercy. "Friend, wherefore art thou come?"

He handed her over to the guards, staying close by her side. It had begun.

Chapter 21 – Confirmation

Elise stood shaking by the bedpost while Franciscan nuns flurried like snowflakes driven by a hard wind. They were packing her things. Actually, she realized, many of the things they were packing did not belong to her. Several articles of white clothing were brought from somewhere and packed in a bag – apparently, they were not letting her take the papal robes. *Evidence.*

She remained standing, shivering. A nun pulled at her clothing, indicating that she needed to strip. But Elise didn't move. She was too busy keeping the vomit down her throat long enough for the nun to step back. The woman obliged with startled realization, and Elise puked, barely bending over. Her vomit cascaded to the floor with a splattering sound, like rotten fruit hitting the ground.

The nuns stopped moving only a second. Then, one of them hurried from the room for cleaning supplies.

And still, Elise stood stupidly watching.

The coup took place in the early evening hours, just before sunset. Demsky's rebels were successful. They stormed the Prime Minister's office in Jerusalem – again with insider help. The bureau guards joined the rebels without a fight–

While two nuns handled the job on the floor, a third returned to Elise and pulled at her sleeve. Elise swallowed to get rid of the sour taste with some fresh saliva. She raised her arms over her head. The nun did the rest. Soon, she stood naked, trembling.

The Prime Minister and his loyalists holed up in a section of the State Archives. They planned to escape using a secret passage to an underground tunnel leading out of the residence. But of course, having defended the building for almost a decade, Demsky knew of the tunnel and had rebels stationed there as well.

The new clothes were scratchy and heavy. Vividly, Elise remembered the wool tights her mother made her wear in second grade. Instantly, her thighs itched.

And why was everything white? Everything they packed was white. A

338

nun tried to place some sort of habit over her head, but Elise ducked. The woman retreated a few steps back and looked at her hesitantly.

The rebels fought their way into the archives, even while the Prime Minister continued to fight his way down to the tunnel. The Prime Minister died there. Along with twenty-four others – Demsky's men killed every last one of them.

Her things were packed. With small glances her way, one by one the nuns filed to the bag on the bed that now held all that would come with her. And one by one, they each removed the crucifix from around their neck and placed them gently inside her bag. It was zipped – they then headed for the door, leaving Elise by herself in a room that was no longer hers.

She let her breath out and concentrated on its escape.

Once the Prime Minister fell, Knesset members and other government in the building began surrendering. But the soldiers killed them anyway.

For the first time, Elise wished for a window in the room. She wanted to watch the sunset. The urge was so strong, she contemplated going outside, or at least into one of the halls. She wanted to see it, appreciate it. She wanted to notice every golden trace and gleam so that when she next closed her eyes, the image would appear to her perfectly.

Demsky waited until his soldiers had the Prime Minister's office well under control. He came up the drive with Israeli flags waving on the sides of the car. And the guards opened the gates for him.

"Can you hear me, God?" Elise whispered to the dead room. "It's me. Remiel. The one you sent."

He strode in the office foyer, down the great halls. Those who saw him say he laughed and touched everything.

"I'm afraid. Everything has already gone so far, and I don't know if I can stop it. And yet, I don't believe you can let me fail."

Demsky asked for a moment alone in the Prime Minister's quarters to prepare his thoughts before addressing the country. A loyalist, hidden in a secret compartment in the wall, waited until the door closed, then raised a shaky pistol and shot him in the head.

"So this is it: you and me. I'm paying attention now."

They opened the palace gates a second time. They let in exactly three journalists – two Israelis and an American – and their cameramen.

"Help me forget the fears and the things that I will loose."

Chayim Ze'ev announced that he would take Demsky's place at the head of the rebel military and rebuild Israel to its prophesied glory. Citizens poured into the streets cheering; Knesset members fearing for their lives swore allegiance on television; and the Palestinians threatened open war.

"Make me your extension, your tool, so that I know nothing but your will."

Ze'ev extended his invitation to the governments of the world to acknowledge the new king of Israel. The first king of Israel for thousands of years...

"Let me bury your Son's bloodline until you determine it shall rule."

He will be crowned in three days time.

"Be with me these three days."

* * * * *

Chris, Francis, and Lorenze waited stiff as sentries in the common room. They all stood, too nervous to sit. No one spoke. Not even when there came a knock to the door.

Cardinal Matthew came inside and closed the door behind him without a word himself. There they were: team Elise. The four that would accompany the angel on her mission. A priest, a monk, a cardinal, and a guard with a halberd.

"Is she still in there?" Matthew asked.

"Yes. She hasn't come out yet," Chris spoke quietly. Elise wouldn't like it if she heard them talking about her.

"Well, I think we should get her," Matthew replied. He waited, but no one moved. "It probably should not be me," he cleared his throat.

Lorenze moved first and opened the door to her apartments with a steady hand.

"Yes. Good. Let the man with the sword go," the Cardinal tried to joke.

Chris merely flicked his eyes at him.

* * * * *

"Elise?" Lorenze called into the room. Through the hall, he saw her. She was standing in the bedroom, empty except a white bag. She moved stiffly at the sound of her name, and he knew she had been standing in just that position for a long time. "What are you doing?" he asked.

"Just waiting," she spoke with little emotion. "I didn't think they would let me stay in here forever. But while I had a few minutes, it seemed like a good time to talk to the choreographer." She raised her eyes upward.

"Did he answer you?" Lorenze whispered.

"We have three days to find out. And what is it with the three day thing?" she asked, suddenly inquisitive. "Did you catch that? Three days. Is it God's favorite number, or something? Or does he only reserve it for impossible tasks? 'You have three days to forgive the world of its sin before you must resurrect your body and appear – a dead man alive.' Or in my case, 'You have three days to stop the world from ending a few centuries too early.'"

"Cardinal Matthew is here," Lorenze said the name gently.

Elise nodded. "I'll be out. Just give me a few more minutes. I need to leave some of myself here, before I go out and I have to be – her."

"All right," Lorenze replied, though he did not understand.

* * * * *

"Is she coming out?" Matthew asked when Lorenze reappeared and closed Elise's apartment door.

"Yes. She just isn't quite ready." The guard watched the other men's eyebrows raise. "Don't worry. She will be." He licked his lips.

* * * * *

There was only one thing left to say, and Elise wasn't going to leave until she said it. For the words that rested on the tip of her tongue were like magic words. If she could get them out and mean them, they had a chance. She knew that in her heart, she had slowly been saying it already. Chris was right – there were changes in her. A shift that she was afraid of even while she encouraged it. But it was not so cowardly as surrender. Nor so simple. It was sacrifice. Laying down her plans and wants. Redirecting herself towards one thing. A short-lived thing; what now turned out to be a three-day thing.

As if giving-up a great weight from her chest, Elise arched her back and neck so that she could look directly upwards. "I give myself over to you, God. And I swear to be yours without any more hesitation. Even if it isn't fair. Even if you don't love me as much as you love them. Whether I am higher or lesser. Whether this decision is mine, or if nothing has ever been mine. If you forsake me and leave me, or bring me home. Whatever I am, whatever my fate, it's yours."

Exactly three tears trembled and fell down her cheeks, and Elise lowered her head and looked around. Everything was the same. The room was empty.

"You're awfully quiet, God," she spoke teary. "I hope that means you're listening."

* * * * *

She emerged timidly, as if she was trying not to wake someone. Chris could tell from her face that she had cried. But she looked steady. No evasive eyes, and the trembling stopped.

"Monsignor," she managed to make it sound respectful. "I'm ready."

"Right. Of course. Um, our flights have been arranged," he started explaining. "A helicopter will meet us in the early morning hours at the Vatican's helipad. It will set us down in Istanbul, Turkey. A commercial flight will take us from Istanbul to Jerusalem. However, with the coronation, security will be tight on all flights into the capital in case of terrorism. The society members are working on our accommodations and a plan for when we arrive. We should be within a few miles of the king by sunrise."

"Good," Elise replied coolly. "A few miles should be plenty close." To the rest of the group, "So everyone, get the worried looks off your faces. You've told me probably hundreds of times how you've been preparing for this task the majority of your adult lives. It's time to step up to the plate. The cup is not passing. And, I want you all to understand that what I say goes. Of course, we will be listening to the Hetaera Melchizedek for advisement. But God sent me here, and I'm sure he didn't send me here just to leave me. If we have faith and strength, I know He'll lead me to stand before Chayim Ze'ev well before the sun sets three days from now. Before he is king."

"What will you do with him?" Chris asked – the first time they spoke since the previous night.

"I will make sure he never has the chance to be king ever again," she replied coldly. "I need no more confirmation that Ze'ev is the one. Francis stands by his vision, and I by him. The stars did not coincidentally align so that Francis' choice just happens to be the lead runner to the throne of Israel. And if I'm wrong, then it was still worth it. Is there anyone who cannot handle this?"

Like teenage boys bullied into a bad prank, they slid their eyes around at each other, and everyone stayed quiet.

"Good. Then, we all understand what's coming," she confirmed for them. "Also, I will need your help. You are my supply for turning-up."

Francis and Matthew balked.

"Except Francis," she conceded. "But my powers are only good when there is energy to steal. You'll have to provide it for me." Elise closed her lips tightly.

"All right then," Matthew concluded with a cluck of his tongue. "I will be back for you at half past midnight – just a few hours from now. Until then, all of you are to stay here. Supper will be brought to you. Try to get some rest."

His last words had the same laughable ring as if spoken to a prisoner sentenced to execution at dawn.

* * * * *

A knock indicated supper's arrival. It was simple, the dishes barely

342

covering the common room coffee table. They each took a plate. Except Elise, she waved her hand to indicate she would pass. Chris watched her, his heart sinking further. She caught him, and her look was cool, punishing. If she only knew how his chest ached after their fight, how many times he actually threw back the covers, fully set on slipping back into her room and telling Francis he could have the night off.

Chris was the first to look away. He tried to swallow the food in his mouth, but found it caught. He mixed some milk with the mouthful in order to get it down. He wondered if she was still watching, soaking up his discomfort.

Looking anywhere but in Elise's direction, Chris raised his eyes to the others. He only met further embarrassment. Francis was watching him intently with eyes that forced Chris to focus steadily on his plate and hope that the light was low enough to hide his red color. Could Francis know? Could he see what was happening to him and their angel? Was there some God forsaken mark on his body now? Perhaps he was marked as clearly as Ze'ev ...*it's all over him. Like a disease or a rash. It covers every part of his skin.*

Chris' silverware clattered to his barely touched plate. He kept his eyes lowered and exited into the apartment that he shared with Francis.

"Is he sick?" Lorenze asked the surprised room.

No one answered, but Francis and Elise's eyes met across the room. Again, she won the staring contest.

* * * * *

When Francis entered the apartment, he found Chris stretched out on their sofa in the dark. Really in the dark. With no windows, it was pitch black. Without regard to Chris, the monk turned on a lamp and began writing.

Everyone is trying to at least shut their eyes, I think. We have three hours. You take the first hour's watch over Elise – like usual? Then, we'll switch?

Chris squinted, and tried to look hard at Francis for some sign. Was this a test? But Francis gave no indication. He merely held up his board.

In reply, Chris pulled himself off the sofa. "I'll come wake you in an hour." He headed for the door, still wondering if Francis had some clue as to what type of danger he sent him to.

Tonight was their last night together. The last night watching her while she dreamed. The last night to feel her bold touch. The last night talking to her about the things he imagined she confided in no one else. Tomorrow, he and Elise might be separated or worse. Tomorrow, Elise might just

343

disappear, leaving nothing but a cool, beautiful angel with no heart for his weakness. Tomorrow, the world would be different. But tonight. *Tonight.* Tonight, Chris feared, would prove whether he was a priest, or merely a man. He left the safety of Francis with no idea which one he actually was.

Elise was lying on top of her bed in the white robes the nuns had dressed her in, still with the lights on. She knew he would come. Even so, she looked up at his approach with her eyes wide, like a startled animal.

"Sorry," she in turn startled him with an apology. "I know we don't have much night, but I didn't want to try and nap without someone watching me. If the Other is going to come, it seems like it might be tonight."

"That's o.k. We all understand." Chris took his usual seat, dragging the chair across the floor to her bedside. He waited for her to ask him why he left the common room, what was going through his head, or any number of harder questions.

"So what type of music do you like?"

Chris looked up from his hands. "What type of music?"

"Yeah. Remember, I asked you that our first night together? It was in the car, on the way to Whiteley."

"I remember."

"So do I," she spoke quietly. "I wish I'd known more then. I would've paid more attention to your answers." They sat again in silence. "So, go ahead. What type?"

"Classic rock mostly. But, that's to be expected from an old guy like me."

"Great," Elise pretended to roll her eyes. "So, our common ground will be the songs I've heard during morning radio flash backs."

* * * * *

Chris and Elise spent their hour talking about music and pretending they were somehow meeting again, instead of leaving. They laughed; they joked. For sixty minutes, the dawn seemed days away.

But the clock in the common room called them back, ringing like some death knell. It was ten o'clock. They waited until the last bell was struck.

Chris put his hands on his knees as his smile faded. "I should get Francis," he mentioned, but did not actually get up.

Elise remained unspeaking and motionless. Out of the corner of his eye, Chris could see her chest rise and fall rapidly underneath her robes.

"I'll go get him." This time he stood and faced the door. "Pretend to at least be drowsy, so he doesn't get ma–"

"Don't!"

Chris turned back to see Elise standing next to her bed, a desperate expression on her face.

"Don't get Francis. Stay with me," her words tumbled over themselves. "Stay with me tonight." She ran her hand through her hair and then continued playing with the ends in her hand. "It's just two hours," she explained when he said nothing. "Just two hours. Can't we have that? Just two hours without pretending?" Elise leaned her head back so she could look up at the ceiling, and she let out a breath that shook her rib cage. "There isn't anything that I wouldn't give for those two hours with you." She lowered her eyes so that she could look into his brown ones.

Chris' heart practically stopped. Though her words were vague, he knew what she really asked of him. And it was agony. She was right – it was only two hours. What if they broke every rule for 120 minutes? It would be the greatest 120 minutes of his life.

"Here." Elise's hand left an imprint where she wanted him to sit. "Turn off the light and…"

He crossed to her in two steps. His hands touched her face, her neck, her shoulders, caressing her over and over. She kissed his fingertips, reaching up to grab them and guide them over her features, into her hair, and against her heart where it tapped as light and fast as a bird's. His lips found the top of her head and he breathed in her scent. He kissed more aggressively her forehead and cheeks.

Their noses touched, and Elise closed her eyes for the first real kiss of her life.

But, "I can't," Chris whispered as he closed his eyes. Though he protested, he did not move away. He felt like he'd been spinning.

"Yes, you can," she answered him against his face. If she chose, she could break his vows.

"I can't, Elise," he said with more resolve and a surrender of his shoulders into a slump.

"Please. You can. Please say you will."

"No. I'm a priest. I am a priest," Chris repeated. And he was. He pulled his face back and let her go, like something hot.

Elise hung her head and rocked it from side to side, her hair falling in her face.

"I'm sorry," he said between heavy breaths. "I have to go. I have to go." In the same two steps, Chris was back at the door.

"Chris. Please. Don't just…"

The priest didn't have to turn around to know that she was crying. Again, he faltered and stood paralyzed with his back to her. It was torment. His chest ached so hard, as if his heart were shot. He loved her. God, he loved her. But it didn't matter.

"If you can't stay," she kept on behind him, "then at least tell me that you want to." She swallowed so that her voice remained almost normal. "I can't go on tomorrow, or the next day, without at least knowing that. Tell me. Tell me you want to be with me – and not as a priest. Tell me you would stay with me if you weren't wearing that collar."

Chris shook his head. "It doesn't matter. I am a priest. What-ifs are meaningless." He moved to leave.

"Chris!"

He leaned his head against the doorframe. "Elise. Angel and devil. Do you need this so badly that you keep me here with my soul in the balance? What must I tell you so that you'll let me leave? Do you need to hear that the greatest test of my faith has not been believing in the unbelievable after all? But in fact, it has been just standing alone, next to you, in a room."

When Chris stepped through the doorway, Elise let him. She watched him fade into the hallway darkness through the blurring of the tears caught in her eyes. "I love you, I love you, I love you," she mouthed, as if to call him back by spell.

* * * * *

Elise stayed in her room until she heard Cardinal Matthew knock on the common room door. It was 12:28 AM. Right on time.

She had not slept a single second. Not one. She merely stood up from the stiff fetal position she had kept and pressed her hands against the wrinkles in her robes and brushed her hair with her fingers. She would not wait for the men to call her. She grabbed her bag full of white clothes and crucifixes, and headed out.

"Ah, good. You're awake," Cardinal Matthew greeted her. Francis and Lorenze stood beside him. And Chris was on the couch (mercifully) with his back to her.

"I guess you could say I didn't even need to set an alarm," she replied frankly. "Is the helicopter already waiting?"

Matthew cleared his throat. "Actually, there has been a slight change of plan. Er... the helicopter is still waiting," he added quickly when her eyes narrowed. "But, the Pope wants to see you first."

"Is everyone ready?" she finally acknowledged the others. Lorenze nodded, his face pale. It looked like he hadn't slept much either. Francis smiled, managing to look rested. And Chris – their eyes met a brief second. She didn't watch long enough to see how he responded.

"This way," Cardinal Matthew opened the door. They filed out of the Vatican apartment for the last time.

Elise quickly stepped behind him, leaving the others to follow. They walked through the halls until they reached the Sala Regia. When Matthew stopped before an unfamiliar door, Elise felt her suspicions prickle.

The Cardinal confirmed her when he faced them and spoke. "They're waiting for you in the Sistine Chapel."

"Who's 'they?'" Elise hissed.

"The Pope. And the cardinals," he replied quickly with a step back. "All of them. Leo refused to let you leave without this." He opened the large wooden door.

They entered and faced a partition of wood and metal screen. But even through its harsh crisscross, Elise could see the beauty it kept. Astonishing colors glimmered through, and the eyes were immediately called upward to the famous ceiling three stories above.

Every inch portrayed some story, some history, figures gliding across its arch in 500-year-old paint from Michaelangelo's hand. It seemed a conspiracy: the artist had secretly extracted photographs from the Bible and blown them up here where the world could not touch them. There was the creation of the sun and the moon; God and His first man, and then there was that man plucking an apple from the outstretched hand of a snake with a woman's head; there was Noah and his great boat; there was David and Goliath; Jesus' baptism in the Jordan and his last supper, Judas in his black robes and already separated from the other 11 before his betrayal; Jesus again judging the living and the dead, casting souls to the demons while angels bore others to Him for mercy. Hundreds stared from the ceiling and walls; here, the curve of an eyelash on a saint, there, the glimmer of highlights in an angel's hair; grandeur bleeding down into the walls lined with awesome arches. Beneath them, two levels of frescoes stretched down to touch the floor – the entire room a canvas for history's and prophecy's greatest and most horrible, moments of falling and of lifting up. It was a meeting room for good and evil, Satan and God together in the same place, watching in oiled patience their scenes of inspiration and desperation.

And through the partition, hovering around the altar stairs, lining the walls, and by the chapel altar itself: the cardinals dressed in ceremony robes, with their silver shepherds' staffs and tall miters. They stood beneath Christ's judgment, beneath His great hand. Elise could see them completely still and silent through the metal grate, and her breath caught to know they all waited in the middle of the night for her.

"This way," Matthew directed her attention to an opening in the center of the grate. Pope Leo the Fourteenth stood at the altar dressed in white. He waited for her much the way she always foggily envisioned a groom would – with his hands clasped in front of him and an eye only for her – the woman in white.

This time, he did not have to ask her to please come forward. She went. Across the long marble floor, beneath the angels and sinners, through the center of the congregation of cardinals. She stopped at the foot of the altar. There, she could see the ice-color of his eyes, a little grayer than usual. They refused to leave her face, and the silence crushed in.

"Elise Moore," the Pope said her name so that it echoed. "When we first met, you told me that you weren't sure if you were Catholic because you were not confirmed. So tonight, the Catholic Church opens her arms to you and offers this last ritual of membership if you will accept it. It is an earthly thing, a human celebration and fellowship – something you are no doubt above. But it is still our most precious gift."

"I accept," Elise replied while lowering her face to hide her surprise. He hadn't forgotten. He, who perhaps because of his own holy duality, could know that while Remiel might not need human fellowship, she still did.

At last, his eyes left her to move around the room. "This is a night of contrasts. We are here to offer this woman absolute acceptance into our midst. And yet, in a few hours, each and every one of us – myself included – will deny we know her. Like Peter, we will abandon the person we should stay closest to so that we may remain comfortable and avoid persecution." His gaze returned to Elise. "My only hope is that you too will come back to us, as Jesus returned to Peter, so that we may beg forgiveness." He rolled his shoulders, feeling the weight of the ceremonial robes he wore.

"Confirmation is a prayer. A prayer begun thousands of years ago during the Acts of the Apostles. Samaritan converts were first baptized by early Christians. Once they were ready to become full members of the new Church, they pilgrimaged to the apostles Peter and John. And Peter and John prayed over the baptized and laid their hands on them to impart the Holy Spirit. And so tonight, each of us will lay our hands on you, Elise Batheba Moore, that God be with you."

The Pope came down from the altar, so that he was only one step above Elise. With both his hands, he covered her head, as though he smothered a fire in her hair. "Send forth upon her they sevenfold spirit the Holy Paraclete."

After a moment of silent prayer, the Pope stepped back, and then a cardinal came before her. He too touched her head and prayed silently over her.

In silence, they each touched her in the same, heavy-handed way. It gave the impression that each man truly placed something weighted upon her. *Strange,* her mind spoke. *They give to me in the same way I take from them.*

At the end of the line came those Elise cared for the most, and she lowered her head without breathing. The last time Chris touched her, it had been with passion. But now, there was no trace of it. Like the others, as if he knew her no better, he placed his hands on her head and prayed over her as a priest. As he had over hundreds of others in his lifetime.

Francis held her the longest. Elise smiled under his hands. Though he could not speak, she could feel him praying. The man who spoke the least to other men had the most to say to God on her behalf.

When everyone resumed their places in the semi-circle, Leo approached her again, coming down the altar stairs – this time with a small, jeweled box. "This is chrism, Elise. It is our most holy oil – the oil of salvation. It will leave God's mark on you, so that while men may not know whom you belong to, He will never overlook you." He placed a cold, greasy dab on Elise's forehead, immediately calling up her desire to itch it. Her hand twitched, but she let it stay.

"I sign thee with the chrism of salvation, in the name of the Father and of the Son and of the Holy Ghost," he said while signing the cross.

The Pope took a step back and handed the chrism vial to one of the cardinals. Hands free, he turned back to Elise, and then stood very still. For the first time, Elise thought he looked old.

With a jar, Leo jerked forward and placed his hands on her shoulders. Bringing his face down awkwardly close to hers, the icy eyes moved rapidly back and forth, as if reading a book in her eyes. Closer, his lips came near her cheek. He sighed out a hot breath to impart whatever grace was his to give. "Peace be with thee," he whispered.

Elise felt a slight tremor travel up her spine as he returned to the stage. She was confirmed. A Catholic.

Leo cleared his throat and opened his arms as though he invited a hug. "May the Holy Spirit dwell in your heart and be your guide, Elise Batheba Moore. Know that, though the Church remains silent, inside, she prays for you each hour. Each hour–"

A scraping clipped the end of his words: someone opened the door to the metal grate behind them.

Elise glanced back. Swiss Guards. An escort. Her escort.

"Go now, in the name of Christ – the one man God vowed to never deny."

Elise genuflected, as Alan showed her: down on one knee before the altar. Then, in a whirl, she headed for the door. The sound of footsteps behind told her the monk, the priest, and the cardinal followed. The door to the metal grate closed behind them, and the bittersweet beauty of the Sistine Chapel faded away.

* * * * *

Elise took her seat on the helicopter, and the others filed in behind her. Except for the emergency lighting, everything remained dark. *Cover of night,* she thought. Yet, with the womping of the propellers, she doubted how subtle they really were.

She peered out the window, but saw nothing. No doubt, the Swiss Guard stood in a straight line outside, their ruffled sleeves threatening to tear off their arms in the mechanical wind. Someone slammed the helicopter door shut from the outside. Another shadow handed her a set of earmuffs – Chris. She slid them on, and the womping muffled, but in an uncomfortable way, like she just put her head beneath a blanket.

She wanted to ask questions like, were they ready to take off? How long was the flight? Would it be this loud in the air? Heck, did they serve nuts? Hastily, she searched for the belt to her seat and for the first time, Elise wished for a stewardess – what end went in which? Not that a belt would help the sick fluttering in her stomach go away. It wasn't a fear of flying that made her ill.

As conveniently as ever, Lorenze appeared and fastened the belt for her. His new black, civilian suit made him seem to appear and disappear magically into the dark. On one appearance, he indicated something, which she took to mean, *Are you all right?* She shook her head and he seemed satisfied. Hopefully that was what he actually asked.

She leaned back and looked again at the blackness out the window. A dark reflection of herself stared back. It was going to be a lonely flight if it remained like this: only reflections to watch while the earmuffs quieted everything but her thoughts.

The helicopter gave a sudden lurch, and Elise grabbed the seat with her fingers. *Are we off the ground? Are we taking off?* It was too dark, she couldn't tell.

But then, there was a sudden upward motion, and a few Vatican lights pulled away from them. They were rising. Then the basilica – fully lit – was beneath them. Elise tried quickly to remember what it looked like from the car on their way into Rome a few weeks earlier.

But a new light wiped all those thoughts away.

Elise cried out in alarm (though not even she heard the exclamation) – it looked as though a fire had just been set at the very top of the basilica. But quickly, the flickering light took a pattern. Like a dynamite fuse, the light traveled and snaked, illuminating in controlled blaze only the seams of the basilica. It traveled to outline the sides, the doors, and the windows. In seconds, the whole church was silhouetted in flame. It stood out, drowning all the lights of Rome as the helicopter continued to rise higher: a flaming blueprint.

She turned to the inside cabin and found a shadow of Francis busily writing opposite her. He lowered the white board so that the red aisle light below his seat caught it enough for her to read.

An illumination – held only on the most significant occasions. Lanterns and torches hung from all parts of the basilica by the Sampietrini – the secret men of St. Peter's who take care of the basilica when no one is looking. They set up the illumination and then orchestrate – lanterns are lit almost simultaneously.

Francis erased it and then wrote again, lowering the board one more time into the red glow.

I'm sure Leo has some very official, public reason for the illumination, but I think it's a safe bet the display is really for you. Guess they're leaving a light on for you after all.

Back out her window, the fires on the basilica remained bright. Elise barely blinked while she watched the illumination get smaller and smaller, even while her heart swelled greater and greater. She watched until the glow was swallowed by a darkness she new must be countryside. Even then, she kept her forehead firmly pressed against the cold window.

Chapter 22 – The First Day

Though her body was numbly exhausted, Elise found she could not sleep. Instead, she stared into the blackness of the helicopter. It was awful – like looking into the mouth of a cave and knowing you must go inside without a flashlight.

The dark was timeless. Had it been fifteen minutes since the Vatican dipped below the horizon, or hours? So black, and yet, with the feeling of forwardness, movement – a scary rushing. *Like being birthed or maybe dying.* Elise looked to the red emergency lighting by her shoes for renewed (and relieving) perspective.

So this is it. On our way to stop the crowning of a king. Was it really possible? How in the world had she gone from being a college student to an insane crusader in only a few months? Elise shook her head against the seat.

Chayim Ze'ev. Did she even know how to pronounce his name correctly? Elise saw him in her mind, cool and pale, as he appeared on the television while inviting the world to recognize him as the King of the Jews. He looked so normal. Afraid, but trying to keep it together. Like he didn't even want to be there on that podium. Like he was sacrificing, taking over for the greater good and the cause. Like it wouldn't be hard to talk him out of it. But, here they were on a helicopter while priests around the world plotted to do considerably more than just talk to him.

Training, the training. This was what they practiced for. Every pot she threw in the green house, every door she locked and unlocked without touching – they were all small stops on a path leading to Chayim Ze'ev. She had known it even then. Why was she surprised now? Why was she puking on floors, suddenly afraid of the dark?

Because if you fail… it was a whisper in her mind so loud, Elise could swear that it didn't come from her. *If I fail, then something will happen to me. Something…I'm not sure what. But somehow, I will bring on the end of everything. Before the seals are broken; before the first six trumpeters sound; before their plagues and judgments weed out the bad from the good. Generations before God's time. Long before we have the faith, the strength, the evolution.*

Was it like being possessed?

Would she suddenly find her mouth pried open by invisible hands and a horrible sounding erupting from her throat? Would the ground shake, the dead rise, and demons spew from the ground to claim their victory? Or would the world die a slow death? One in which God receded and left those that prayed with no hope.

With an ache, Elise's heart lunged suddenly for Alan. If only he were there. How often she hated his confidence; too many times she seethed under his criticism. Yet, what she wouldn't give up to hear his solid voice tell her what would happen next. She tried to conjure his condescending alter ego in her head. Already, it was too faded.

I let you die, the words came full in her mind, refusing to let her shy from them, as if the pain could pay back some part of the debt. *I let you die. I could've gone back, could've risked it. But I didn't.*

* * * * *

They landed in Tiranë, Montenegro to refuel. It was still dark – the same tunnel, but without movement. Elise prayed a worthless prayer for sunrise, even as she realized she should be praying for time to slow down, rather than speed up.

She was answered. As it always did, the sun arrived. Slowly, the interior of the helicopter became a faded blue, like smoke, and then burned off to other colors. The land lit with pinks and yellows, like a flower finding its newborn color.

Sixty hours, and Ze'ev would be king.

* * * * *

At 9:30 AM, the helicopter again slowed, hovered and then thudded on faded gray pavement. It was Istanbul. They were in Turkey.

Someone in the group decided to lead (though no one seemed to know who), as they filed out of the helicopter and into the humid air for the short walk to the terminal. Elise could taste the salt.

Once they were far enough from the propellers to speak, Lorenze fell back beside her. "Ok? Long flight," he asked and stated at the same time.

"The first part is over," Elise tried her voice out again.

"Stay close," Lorenze warned. "The Cardinal still has to produce our Israeli travel documents. Not that you should worry. The society has been working while we've been flying. But, still – stay close."

Elise only raised her eyebrows while trying to comb her fingers through her hair. "I'm not worried. I'm sure we'll get through." She flexed her fingers in a fake menace.

Next to them, Chris squinted. Istanbul was pale. Like a cancer patient. The sky was washed out, the ground almost white, the pavement bleached, the surrounding buildings colorless. He wondered if Elise realized how much she stood out. In the sun, her hair was aflame with the highlights that sometimes barely glimmered on a cloudy day. She walked towards the terminal like a lengthy torch fighting in the wind.

Behind them, the helicopter took off.

* * * * *

There was one tense moment when they stood in front of the terminal gate before a guard and customs official. Elise watched as Cardinal Matthew handed him five passports. She tried not to look surprised. How or when he received them, she could not guess. Perhaps there was more than refueling done in Tiranë. They passed and entered the waiting room.

"Thank God I'm not hung-over," Elise commented as she looked at the neon mustard waiting room seats next to potted palm trees. "Looking at these – I can almost feel the pain behind my eyes. And my gag reflex."

Chris gave a snort – almost a laugh. Elise almost looked at him, but dropped her eyes quickly. There were things she did not want to think about.

"You can sit here," Matthew stated the obvious. "I have to check in and prepare for more security," he made it sound matter of course. "It won't be long, though. Each of you, take your passport and study it. Lorenze, keep watch. Don't go anywhere."

As if they were going to wander off, maybe get lost in a concession stand or grab a bus tour. The Cardinal strode away at his usual gait.

Elise opened her passport. Surprise – she was British. Her school ID photo smiled up at her, but the name beneath it was Marcia Lynn. "I wonder how we got these…" she mused half under her breath.

"I heard the Cardinal talking," Lorenze offered quietly. "One of our priests formerly worked at the FBI in the witness protection program. He called in a favor, created new identities, so that security checks could be run on them. Gave us good records, hopefully. I'm Mark."

"Is it Seven Hail Mary's for fraud? Or is it four since this is a good cause?"

A few amused looks, but no one laughed at the joke. With a sigh, Elise surrendered. "Hey Francis," she slid into one of the mustard chairs.

Fine. Tired, the monk preempted her next question.

"I didn't sleep. It's almost like I did, though. That was one dark, quiet flight."

"The next flight will be better. We've officially broken away,"

Lorenze's monotone conveyed a slight sense of shock. "There's no reason to fly in the dark anymore. No one will care much about us now. We're just another religious group, traveling to the coronation."

* * * * *

"This way," Cardinal Matthew spoke, as though he had a secret. "We don't have much time. Each of you – listen while we walk! And try to look relaxed."

Elise opened her mouth, but then opted to chew on her sarcastic remark when Chris and Lorenze automatically gave her wary glances.

"Closer," Matthew commanded as they attempted to keep up with his power walk. Francis stepped on the backs of Elise's shoes. He winced to tell her sorry.

Mathew spoke in a voice a few decibels below easy hearing. He tried to barely move his lips, as if that might help conceal his words. "Since the coup, commercial and private flights to Israel have been suspended until further notice. Obviously, Ze'ev can't keep that up for long – they'll need their imports and exports going if he's to run the country. But, it appears he is taking no chances with the coronation. Flights are down, and the borders are completely closed. The military is all his, and they're battening down the hatches for one hell of a storm. Have to watch the Arab neighbors now."

"Then how are we going to–"

"Ze'ev is allowing in approved charter flights," Mathew cut Elise off. "Ambassadors, world leaders, reporters – anyone he deems important and worth having at his ceremony. He does want this to be official, after all. He has to let the world in just a little in order to be accepted and receive its acknowledgment."

"Any chance we're on one of these approved flights?" Chris asked with a ghost of a grin. The spy games amused him on a distant level.

"The newly appointed Israeli Foreign Minister was quite happy to have several 'leaders' of a Christian religious community attend the crowning and bow to his king."

What community are we leading? Francis managed to get a line in.

"We answered that one truthfully, actually. We are delegates of the Society for the Hetaera Melchizedek – a faction broken from the Roman Catholic Church. Any representatives of the Church, however far removed, are welcome – makes Ze'ev look legitimate. The foreign minister's department has been doing background checks on each of us while we've traveled. So, if we are still on the list when we get to the gate, then we're in. I trust you all know about your new selves? If any one asks, you will need to know your name, your passport country, and where you were born at the very least."

But there was no time.

From that moment on, it seemed they went from inundation to inundation. Elise had to watch Cardinal Matthew with some admiration as he navigated their way onto a plane headed for Israel. His commanding manner (which she often hated) served him well when dealing with airport officials. The group did not even know what questions or obstacles they crossed for, the Cardinal answered in languages they never heard before, let alone understood.

Finally, they halted in front of a card table that blocked a long, sunny hallway where no one walked. Several officials sat around the cheap wood frame, sweaty and annoyed. *Looks like a school board election.* Elise smiled at the tartness of the thought, and played with sharing it.

But Matthew already began a brisk conversation over authentic looking papers in a leather folder held by a large man. He was flanked by a guard openly displaying his rifle. Though Elise watched him intently, the guard never looked back, but stared off into the air. Yet, she was quite certain that he knew she watched him.

"We're on the list, of course," Matthew reassured them after a moment. "A private plane will take us to Israel shortly. The luggage will be thoroughly searched, so don't be alarmed. We just need to provide reasonable proof of our identities, and then a captain will be called."

Proof of identity. All eyes hit the floor. There were no volunteers. So Matthew turned to be first, and Chris noticed a small bead of sweat just where his hairline skimmed his ear, the fear he did not show leaking out of him.

Miraculously, none of the officials knew English well, leaving the Cardinal to answer all questions from his repertoire of prepared answers. He passed, of course, still chatting quickly in *Greek?* while he was thoroughly frisked, wanded, and frisked further. Lorenze went next looking young and nervous in his suit, like a job interviewee. His hands clutched unconsciously for the bag he left on the floor behind him. After several interchanges between Matthew and the official, Lorenze was allowed to slip behind the table. Someone new grabbed him for fingerprinting. Francis, as usual, received a raised eyebrow when Matthew conveyed that he was mute. But, he passed to the ink and paper bureaucracy beyond. Chris caused the most alarm. Taller and larger than the two men frisking him – they gave him cautious sideways looks. Their fingers pushed hard against all parts of his body, searching. At last, he received the nod.

Elise shrugged to no one. It was her turn. *Just relax.* Two men stepped forward, their hands unembarrassed to work their way over her thoroughly. They pried at her skin like doctors looking for an ailment. They found nothing, and then she was beside Chris with black ink on her fingertips. She shivered a moment. It felt like being caught.

* * * * *

The morning light brightened further as midday approached. They waited hours for the luggage search, for the final security call and the appropriate transportation papers. At last, a van spewing black smoke took them to a small plane parked out on the tarmac – a puddle jumper from about two decades earlier, Elise guessed. Once they piled inside, only a few seats remained empty.

Matthew was on translation duty again. He spoke to the captain while leaning through their partition like some ridiculous flight attendant.

Elise snickered at the thought, and Francis caught her. While Matthew's back was turned, she nodded her head at him, and then began pointing to the exits and demonstrating seatbelt buckling. The monk smiled, as did Lorenze, who also watched.

"The flight will be just over an hour," the Cardinal reported. "Almost there."

56 hours...he didn't need to remind her. Elise looked out the window, a large yawn caught her, and she did yet another count: 29 hours since she last slept. She closed her eyes, and a velvety heaviness immediately overtook her. Matthew was still speaking with the captain when she stopped hearing him.

* * * * *

When Elise woke, they were in the air. Sunlight warmed her face – the type of bright sunlight that exists above the clouds. She watched it until brilliant spots filled her eyes. It was the same sun that shown down on the world only a few days prior. The same that shown on her at college; the same that shown on her parents and their parents. So seemingly permanent. Was it possible that it could just stop one day? In two days?

Dark thoughts. Elise pushed herself up in the seat to find someone to help her escape them. But a quick survey showed that everyone was asleep. Even Lorenze, who looked like he fought until the very end – he slept while sitting rigidly in his seat, his neck cocked in an almost broken angle. *Always guarding.*

And there was Chris, kitty-corner ahead one row. It was the first long look she had at him since the previous night. She shuddered, embarrassed by the memory enough to blush. What was it he called her? *Devil.* She did not blame him. What she offered him, no angel would offer. But an apology would only increase the awkwardness, and she couldn't handle that right

357

now. *Afterwards. If we make it, I'll tell you I'm sorry.* There would be time then to work things out. She watched him hard.

So hard, she did not notice the noise at first.

But there it was: a scratching sound. Elise was vaguely aware that it had been going on for a while – perhaps even before she woke up. Turning from Chris, she concentrated on it. The noise reminded her of a foster home that she once stayed in. The apartment had cockroaches, and when the lights were turned on, the hideous bugs scampered to the corners of the rooms with insectile clicking sounds.

Elise looked down by her feet before she remembered that she couldn't see them (*stupid white robes*). She lifted them – the noise was too creepy-crawly to ignore. Were there bugs? Rats? This wasn't exactly British Airlines, after all. She peered on each side of her seat but saw nothing. "What now..." she hissed under her breath.

Light pressure on her shoulder – a hand.

"Do you hear that? There's something crawling around," Elise turned to look over her shoulder for the Cardinal, who had taken the row behind her.

Except it wasn't him – though there were a few pieces of him.

The too familiar, rotting, human hand clutched her shoulder and at her turning, dug its oozing fingernails into the cloth of her robes. Elise's eyes traveled up the arm and into the hairy, scaly chest of the creature in its full form. No human variations this time. Just three ugly heads with leers to stop her heart. Clenched in its long needle teeth were shreds of red fabric and flesh. *Matthew.*

But she wouldn't even have enough time to scream, and they both knew it. One head already pulled back to strike.

She closed her eyes and tucked her head down as her instinct called her to protect her throat. She felt it move forward – the sound of bones breaking–

But they weren't hers. Elise's eyes flew open.

A strong hand grasped the neck of the Other's attacking head until it snapped.

And Elise gaped into the face of the blond man from the desert. His eyes were alight with fire like her own.

* * * * *

She awoke.

The sun was as bright, the others still asleep. No clicking.

In a whirl, Elise tore around so she could see the seat behind her.

Cardinal Matthew slept.

Elise breathed in rapidly and continued watching him for several minutes. Thank God he was all right. *Thank God it was only another dream.*

Though the pain in her shoulder whispered otherwise. She could still feel the fingers.

But the blond angel had come. When the others were asleep, and there was no one to wake her from the possible reality of her nightmare, he had come.

Elise slid back into her seat while her pulse slowed.

* * * * *

She did not sleep again, but kept a tired kind of waiting, like a ghost, until their dusty cab stopped with a lurching finality on an equally dusty street. The house they entered had the feel of a basement. It was made completely of stone – the walls, the floors, the ceiling – just like all the other houses in Ein Kerem, a small village about 20 minutes from the Old City. The group entered directly into the living room. Olive and cypress trees shaded the windows. It was quaint if nothing else – whitewashed walls bare save for the windows with their turquoise shutters. The furniture looked used, but was brightly decorated by several knit throws in various shades of red and purple. The floor was tile, with significant cracks running through it.

"This is it? Headquarters?" Elise asked at the same time that she sighed.

Chris noticed that her eyes sagged, even though she slept a good deal on the plane. She had mentioned bad dreams.

The Cardinal answered. "This is it. And no one is to leave from here. No time for anything to go wrong, or anyone to be compromised." He eyed Elise in particular.

"Oh, come on. You mean I'm not going to get the Jerusalem tour?"

"This, my dear, is as much of Jerusalem as you are going to see until tomorrow," he replied emphatically. "This residence was assigned to us by the Israeli government, and we are being monitored. Soldiers can come at anytime and probably will, and if we do anything suspicious…we're getting close now. While we have to contend with Ze'ev and his men, we also have to contend with the Other, which I'm sure is anxiously searching for you, waiting to kill each and every–"

"All right. I was just kidding!" Elise replied with a good measure of ice. It was unnecessary to go into that level of detail. Lorenze had paled and Chris looked like he was about to ask any number of awful questions about their safety. Dropping into an armchair, Elise threw a last dart, "You sure know how to give a pep talk, Matt."

The Cardinal looked around the room at the drawn faces. "There's no point in being shy with reality," he tried to reaffirm himself, even as his tone became apologetic. "Society members will meet us here with supplies, and news. Until then, we can rest."

359

"Rest? I can't believe we wasted this entire day," Elise's sarcasm bristled into frustration. "Five hours at the Jerusalem airport. I'll never complain about the U.S. baggage screeners ever again – even if I'm randomly selected to dump my belongings each and every flight I'm ever on."

"The important thing is we made it," Chris pointed out. "We're here. We're in Ze'ev's country, miles from his doorstep."

There was silence, and Elise watched the sunset streaking in through the windows.

* * * * *

Though they all waited for the knock at the door, the room jumped in unison when it came. Lorenze stood and twitched his hands, feeling for a weapon, and Chris and Matthew both moved to answer the door, barely avoiding a collision.

"I'll get it," Matthew snapped. The others watched Chris catch his breath to hold back a comment that (from the look on his face) very few priests ventured to say to a cardinal. Even for him, the stress was beginning to wear.

Two men in jeans and buttoned-down shirts stepped from the darkening street and into the cool room. Matthew's easy greeting helped Lorenze relax enough to sit back down. The two men were laden with brown paper grocery bags.

"These are the society members," Matthew indicated needlessly.

Lorenze, Elise and Francis lined up by the couch like children receiving old relatives at Christmas.

"Please call me John," the first man wiped his hands on his pants, and then shook hands down the line. He had a southern accent that Elise found refreshingly familiar. "And you can call him Luke." The other man reached out a rough hand.

Please call you Luke and John? Elise noticed the biblical names. Somehow, she doubted either really went by the name he gave.

The introductions were over, and so of course, both fell to staring at her.

"Sorry," John apologized for the two of them. "It's just – well is it really you?"

"Yes," Elise replied simply.

"And you're really her. Remiel."

She started with a small shake of the head, and then turned it into a harder nodding. "If I'm not, then I'm certifiably crazy. There are a few too many invisible people whispering in my ear about stopping the end of the world."

360

John smiled and then took charge as any southern gentleman would. "Well, eat first, talk business second."

Groceries were lifted out of several of the bags and put in the adjoining kitchen. The cupboards were already stuffed with mismatched glassware, but the men managed to find homes for the supplies (which included dedicating one kitchen chair to boxes of cereal). Soon the small stove was lit, and John and Luke began cooking while Cardinal Matthew observed from behind them. Senses were rejuvenated by the thick slices of lamb grilling, and the aromatic potato, eggplant, onion and sherry mixture baking in the small oven.

"Ever eaten Israeli before?" John made conversation with Elise when her nose brought her halfway into the kitchen (there was no room to enter further).

She shook her head no.

"Well, you are in for a treat. Luke's been over here a while, and he has a knack with the Jewish recipes."

Luke grunted his first response as he cut open a sizzling hip steak.

* * * * *

They ate in silence on a wooden table situated awkwardly in the living room. The only sounds were of chewing, silverware clinking, and the creaking of the chairs whenever anyone shifted their weight. As the plates emptied, the anxiety thickened.

Finally, Chris became nervous enough to ask. "So, what has happened since we left? We haven't seen a television or a newspaper since Italy."

The chewing noise stopped. Everyone looked to John (as it seemed Luke was only slightly more vocal than Francis).

"Actually, it's been a remarkably smooth transition," he managed to sound cheerful. "The Israeli President resigned today. Although he is really only a ceremonial figurehead, it is still a big step towards Ze'ev really ruling. The only uprisings have been from the Palestinians. Several bombings. For now, the Israelis are just sustaining the attacks. Everyone is waiting to see what will happen after the coronation."

He had slipped, and an awkward pause filled the room, as everyone thought about what would happen after the coronation. It wouldn't be Palestinian bombings, anyway.

John continued after swallowing some water. "In another press conference, Ze'ev vowed to keep the peace agreement with Jordan. He has extended cease-fires to Egypt, Syria and Lebanon, though we all know they won't accept and a war is coming. He has been condemned by both the U.N. and the United States for overriding free elections, but it has only been verbal at this point."

Francis tapped on the table and flashed his white board. *What about the Knesset – the Israeli parliament? 120 members, what are they doing?*

John nodded, as if to acknowledge that it was a good question. "Ze'ev has dissolved the Knesset. He plans to hold representative elections, but didn't say when. It looks like Ze'ev plans for the Knesset to be an elected council. They will represent the people to him and continue to suggest laws, but he will have a monarch's say. And, he is filling the minister positions with other rebels from his group. Surrounding himself with friends. As you know, the military is his. They are patrolling the streets of Jerusalem quite heavily – scaring everyone. But the people believe he will end the terrorism. As he, himself, has said, he is not a politician. He won't consult with the United States or the U.N. No more hand-binding. Although he claims he will attempt negotiations with the PLO, our spies know of other plans to wipeout the Palestinians completely."

"All right," Elise broke in. "That's all fine, but it's a little too heavy into Israeli political policy. Quite frankly, I don't care much about peace treaties, Palestinians, the United States, or anything other than that one man. So, how am I going to get to him?"

"Elise," Matthew turned on the condescension. "There's no need to be rude."

"Rude? We have less than forty-eight hours before Ze'ev is crowned the king of Israel. Less than two days before the final prophesy is fulfilled and an army of demons shows us the PLO is nothing to worry about!"

John interrupted the internal squabbling. "It's fine. I understand. Here. We'll have to clear the table. Then I can show you what we've got."

With the food removed, another of the grocery bags was brought over. Before John would open it, Luke went to each of the windows, closed them, and drew the shutters tightly. He closed the doors to the rest of the rooms in the house as well.

Chris looked at the around the room now lit only by the overhead light. Shadows of their noses and eyelashes moved on their cheeks and chins, but could not hide the heightened nervousness. Each glanced over his or her shoulder, suddenly reminded that what they knew, the rest of the world could not know. That somewhere, an army was looking for just this type of behavior. Worse – a monster – even now was hunting them, perhaps headed for exactly the same corner of the world they were in.

John broke all the dark thoughts by lifting out a long role of paper. He unrolled it and placed two weights on the ends. It was a pencil-sketched map. The group leaned over it, and then no one could see anything with the light blocked by so many heads.

"Here," John pulled a penlight from a bag, which was beginning to give the impression that it held whatever the mind conjured inside – lamb, onion, map, weights, light. "This is Mount Herzl in western Jerusalem. Since the state was created, Israeli dignitaries have been buried there. There is also a military cemetery and a museum," John pointed to sections marked with a dashed line. "Mount Herzl is where Ze'ev has decided to hold Demsky and the assassinated Prime Minister's funerals."

"Both?" Chris asked. "He is holding a funeral for the Prime Minister which he helped kill?"

John nodded. "Ze'ev says that, though Demsky and the Prime Minister held different beliefs about how Israel should come to peace, they both fought for peace nonetheless. They should both be respected."

Eyebrows rose around the room, but John continued. "Anyway, they are to be buried tomorrow at three in the afternoon at Mount Herzl. It is not an open funeral, as there is much risk of it being a Palestinian target. Or, even a Jewish target – anyone who disagrees with Ze'ev. Society insiders say that Ze'ev was encouraged not to attend the funerals because the risk is so great, being in such a public place right now. But, he insisted on being there when Demsky is laid to rest."

"Which gives us our opening," Elise smiled eerily in the penlight. It caught one of her eyes and for a moment, mimicked the golden glow sometimes found there.

"Yes. Each of Ze'ev's rebels is allowed to bring his family to the funeral. You will go, using the names of our insiders' families. There should be a few hundred people. Everyone will process by the bodies to pay their respects before the burial," he indicated an arc drawn next to a darkened 'x' on the map. "You will be within feet of Ze'ev."

"And that's when I'll..." she faltered. "I will kill him."

"Yes. The society has decided that you – your touch – will end this."

"Was there ever a question?"

"Of course. A bomb would do the job, or a sniper. All options have been relentlessly considered, for we must be right about this. But frankly, what you have is stronger than anything we could think to use. Your weapon is perfectly concealed. No amount of security can stop you. There is no trace, no sacrificed civilians. God sent you, and we will use you as you are. Though, not alone." He pointed to several smaller 'x' marks on the map.

"Those are society members. Though all are embedded in the rebel group and cannot openly reveal themselves, they will be watching for you. There are three of them. This will be their first time seeing Ze'ev since the assassination as well – he has remained only with his most loyal officers outside of the few press conferences. Though our spies are not especially trained for assassinations, they are prepared to help you tomorrow if you need them. In any way."

Elise continued with darkness. "I have the hand-to-hand combat thing down. So long as I really am close to him, your men will only have to watch."

"In case something happens to you," John left the sentence dangling while he reached for another bag. "We have a few things for Lorenze."

"For Lorenze?" Elise questioned with annoyance.

Luke frowned at her apparent lack of strategy. "Yes. Lorenze is our backup plan, our good old-fashioned assassin. He's trained for it, and if our precautions can't get this stuff through security, he'll get arrested and you'll still have a chance."

She liked him better silent. But her attention was already distracted as John pulled out a remarkably small pistol and a slender knife.

"You will be well searched before entering the cemetery," John spoke to Lorenze. "The pistol is made purely of ceramic parts – including the bullets. The knife is made of fiberglass. Sharp as a normal knife, but like the pistol, no metal detector problems. Of course, they'll frisk you. So, we have some interesting spots for you to place these."

John shrugged, as if to say it wasn't his fault, and then began the demonstration. "This pistol should be taped to your groin. Right between the big cahuna and his sidekicks, if you get what I mean. It's small enough, your other parts should hide it."

"Should hide it," Luke said in a smirking tone inappropriate for a priest.

Lorenze frowned. "Thanks. And the knife?"

"It will tuck into the sleeve of your shirt, right by your wrist. Try to keep the guards from feeling too closely there. It's thin, but not undetectable."

John continued, "The pants we brought you have a 'loose thread' which, when pulled will release the pistol as well as unravel the groin seam in your pants. We'll make sure you have everything set right before you leave tomorrow.

"And that's it. Knife in your hand, and pistol in your pants. Oh. The pistol shoots .22 and only carries two rounds. With such a short shaft, it is not the most accurate piece. So, aim well."

"Where did you get this stuff?" Elise asked with a poke to the ceramic pistol. "Let me guess – the priests called in some favors to their friends in the black market."

No one answered, but Luke grinned.

"What about the rest of us?" Chris asked.

John looked at Luke, indicating he should deliver the bad news.

"Only two of you can come in," Luke folded his arms to show it was not up for discussion. "It would look too strange if all of you came. You don't exactly look like a family, and nothing will happen if this girl doesn't make it past the entrance. The guard was the obvious choice to go in besides Remiel."

Elise looked across the room at the Chris, who was already looking back at her. He wasn't going to come with her. *Then this could be...*

She stopped the thought. "That's fine."

Luke pulled two sets of clothes out of the bag. "Here's what you will both wear. Typical stuff – help you blend in."

"That's it. The Israeli soldiers won't bother you tonight – our insiders have rigged the guard shifts. Someone will be by for you in the morning. Be ready by ten."

"It's a date," Elise replied.

* * * * *

She felt better after a hot shower. The stall was tiny, but it did the job. No fans – it took a while before she saw her reflection in the mirror. But there she was – Elise Moore. Same as always. On the outside.

It was amazing that a person could go through so many internal changes without morphing into a different exterior. She checked her eyes, her hair (groan – such dead ends. When was the last time she had a haircut?), the skin of her face, her hands. They were the same.

Even the fear in her eyes was familiar to her.

* * * * *

Francis was in her room when she entered. *First shift*, he wrote. He winked. *Can't lose you to a dream now.*

Elise rolled back the unfamiliar covers with a puckered forehead. "Yeah," she said, indicating there was more, but not saying anything further.

At Francis' reminder, her most recent dream prickled at the corners of Elise's consciousness. The reality of the dream bothered her, as the others had. Perhaps in some way, the creature had really been on that plane. And if that were true, then it probably had a pretty good idea where they were.

Don't worry, the monk seemed to read her mind. *We haven't seen the Other for weeks. I doubt it can follow us so far so fast.*

"No," Elise replied with dead certainty. "It knows more than I do. Trust me. It knew all along where we would be headed. I'm sure it's here," she looked around the room, as if she meant exactly there. "I just don't know why it's waiting. If it's at the funeral tomorrow, which it should be, then it will be so much harder to get to Ze'ev. I'll be fighting two battles, and I haven't practiced turning-up in so long. What if I've lost some of it? What if the Other is waiting for some purpose that I can't see, and I won't be strong

365

enough when it happens? What about–"

Francis raised his eyebrows to indicate that she should slow down. *What would it be waiting for? All it has to do is kill you, and Ze'ev is as good as crowned.*

Elise blanched at the harsh word: kill. Francis was always so blunt.

"I don't know." She gave a great sigh. "I had a dream about it this morning, though." She swallowed, trying to see it again. "The Other was on the plane with us. Of course, when I woke up, it was gone. Everything was fine. But it still felt real, like it had been there somehow. It was like it wanted to remind me that it's always there, and it was coming with me."

Tell the Cardinal about the dream?

"No. I haven't told anyone," she admitted. "There's nothing he, or any of the rest of them can do to help me with the Other. It seemed like an unnecessary distraction."

Any feelings yet about Ze'ev, or any of his followers? Anyone you've seen?

Elise shook her head. "Nothing. He could be any other man for all I know. It's very lucky I have you. I don't recognize him in any way."

Let me know if you sense anything. I can try to help you read it.

"I think the time for reading is just about over," she frowned at him. "I'm killing Ze'ev tomorrow, no matter what. And, I've never had anything like your power. The world is as unmarked and pathless for me as for anyone else.

Don't worry, Elise, Francis wrote her name out for emphasis. *Everything is coming together now. There is a plan for you.*

She shifted her eyes from the whiteboard to his eyes. They were no more comforting.

* * * * *

Elise awoke for no reason. Just rolling over too hard. She pushed up on her elbows and looked around. The light was on. Had she fallen asleep with it that way?

Francis was still in the chair as she left him – but asleep. Elise frowned. *One hour. Could you not keep watch for one hour?* She moved to rouse him.

But I told him to sleep.

Elise froze.

The voice – from the ice cavern, from the desert in her dreams. The one she promised to remember.

In a jerky, still half-defensive motion, Elise looked up to see Him standing in the shadows of the doorway. He blended with the light and dark around Him, as though He were only half there. She held His perfect eyes a

366

moment, before feeling the compulsion to bow her head. Without looking, she could still feel His approach. It was magnetism, and her soul pulled.

He stopped where Francis slept in the chair and then knelt by the monk. He peered into his face for what seemed a long time, as if trying to make out a hard word in too small print.

He'll awake soon. Let me sit with you.

So light, so beautiful, so powerful, He moved to sit beside her on the bed. To her surprise, the bedsprings creaked under His weight. Carefully, respectfully, Elise let her eyes travel up from the muscular hand that now rested near hers. Her eyes began to tear and she blinked quickly. It was too much – a great longing for the smoothness of His skin, the softness of His hair.

See? You are Remiel, after all, he declared in the musical voice of her mind. *How I've ached to find you awake.*

"Am I awake?" Elise mustered the question.

Don't you know?

She shook her head. "There is still so much I don't understand. So much I can't do. So much I have done that you would not want." She turned her face away. It felt hard to breathe – suddenly she was sure every angry word, every seductive act, every abuse of power passed between them.

Yes, I know. But here you are.

"What if I can't – do this?" she asked in a breathy voice.

Without warning, he touched her.

It was like being placed in a fire. White pain in her mind; the brightness in her eyes, heat everywhere. She could not catch her breath and fell to sucking air. Helpless, she reached for His hand where it touched her cheek.

See? I call you, and you come. I am inside where everything else falls away. There, where there is nothing else. And that is where you will do this.

"What's happening?" Elise whispered though she tried to scream it. Was He still touching her? She could not tell; her skin itched with flame. Through what looked like golden water, she saw Him reach for her neck. Elise was vaguely conscious that He held her necklace in his palm – Alan's crucifix and Derek's Psalm plate. As if He meant to tuck it back into her pajamas, he pressed the two against her skin.

Elise cried out at the searing. She clutched His hand where He held the burning metal, but could not make Him release her. She looked up to the ceiling in pure agony, chest burning, head pulsing, eyes blinding. And then, the whispering began. From nothing to earsplitting, they crescendoed.

Know that you don't go alone. They will bleed with you.

But she was losing Him. Losing everything. Was she falling? She could not feel His hands anymore, nor the bed, nor her chest where it burned with the hand of a man and the word Inri. Falling... falling... anchorless, she swam in the white until a shadow began at the corner of her eyes. It spread and she knew then that it would be over soon. Just as the shadows closed in; just before Remiel fell back into Elise's sleep; for a moment, she saw them: hundreds and hundreds of eyes burning at her.

Chapter 23 – The Second Day

They all sat at the wooden table with bowls of some sort of Israeli cereal – Elise, Chris, Francis, Matthew, and Lorenze. No one ate, but everyone sat as though they meant to. Outside, it was raining.

Lorenze and Elise were each dressed in the clothes John and Luke left: Lorenze in a dark suit and Elise in a simple black dress with a floral pattern laced here and there. A black sweater hugged her shoulders.

Matthew was trying to teach them common Hebrew words, though it was probably hopeless less than an hour before they were to leave. "Just pray that being on the list is enough," he kept muttering. Though Elise wasn't really paying attention, she did at least have hello down: Shalom.

"They said ten o'clock, right?" Chris asked even though he knew he was correct.

"Yes. Ten," Matthew replied.

Elise suddenly pushed back her chair and began a fast-paced walk to the bathroom. The men at the table looked at each other.

"I'll go," Lorenze volunteered.

The bathroom was small, with barely enough room for her to kneel in front of the toilet. She hunched over it, trembling. "Don't watch me," she said when Lorenze's shadow fell across the still water. She tried to close the door, but couldn't reach it. "Don't watch me! I mean it."

Lorenze turned his back as she requested but remained near, listening to her become sick in between muttered prayers he could not make out.

When she was done, Elise stood shakily. "I'm fine!" she snapped before he could ask. "The lamb – it was probably undercooked. I need water."

No one looked up when she reentered the dining area. Chris watched her only when he knew she had her eyes turned down at the table surface. Her one hand shook around her glass. With the other, she played with the chain around her neck.

Suddenly, he squinted. "What's that, Elise?"

She jumped. "What? What's what?"

"That mark." He pointed to her neck. "What happened?"

Self-consciously, Elise felt the sore on her skin where the necklace usually rested. She knew without having to look. An outline of Alan's crucifix could be seen clearly in her skin, the word 'Inri' spelled backwards noticeable with a closer look. Next to it, the outline of the square Psalm charm was lighter. The only word recognizable from the quote was 'given.'

They were burned in, almost branded. But she wasn't about to tell Chris that.

"I'm always playing with the necklace," she said without meeting his eyes. "I scratched myself with it."

Chris looked skeptical, but it was Francis who suddenly got up for a closer look. An odd expression played on the face of the usually unruffled monk: anxiety.

Elise closed her fist around the necklace, hiding the mark beneath with her hand. Her eyes narrowed in distrust as Francis leaned over her. "It's nothing, Francis. Would you please RELAX? OR I'M GOING TO GO CRAZY!"

Francis returned to his seat. From her voice, it didn't sound like a casual threat.

* * * * *

When the doorbell rang, Elise merely scraped her chair across the floor, gave Lorenze a look to tell him he should move faster, and then went to the door to open it herself. A man in yet another black suit stood outside. He wore sunglasses despite the rain, which now beaded in his hair.

"Shirli Levy?" he used the Jewish name she was assigned for the day.

"Wait here," she replied with a command. "We'll be right out." Turning from the door, "Lorenze! Are you ready?"

The men had lined-up behind her. They looked as though someone had died already, and she knew it wasn't Demsky they mourned. It made her more afraid. Again, Elise could taste the bile in the back of her throat.

"Let's not do this," she whispered. "Lorenze, let's just go."

"Elise," Chris stepped quickly to the door. "You can't just – let me bless you."

If it weren't for the shine in his eyes, she would never have held still. It would've been easier to go without a word than stand in front of him, trembling and afraid. But still, she stood. She never saw him cry before.

He touched her forehead. "In the name of the Father," he whispered.

Elise's throat began to tighten. She swallowed.

He touched the center of her chest. "And of the Son."

Why can't they come with me? I CAN'T DO THIS ALONE!

Over her left breast, and then her right. "And of the Holy Spirit. Amen."

Elise tried to say amen, but couldn't. She wanted to say thank you; tell them she could never do it without them; that the last few weeks had been her honor. Instead, she reached for Chris' retracting hand. The familiar fire jumped from his palm into hers. She felt his body move away, but she held tight. A brief moment of resistance, and then he came into her.

Elise did not take much – just enough to stop the shaking; to quiet her stomach; to hide the tears in her eyes with light; to feel Chris and take a little of him with her.

Gently, she released him. "I'll see you all when I get back."

* * * * *

Two men in suits now waited in the rain. Two cars. Elise understood that she and Lorenze were to separate: if he was caught with the weapons, there would be no connection between them. Her heart lowered further until she could no longer feel it.

She halted at the end of the walk where they would be as alone as possible. Lorenze stayed with her, just as she knew he would. She stepped into him until there were inches between their eyes. For the first time, she realized she had to look up to him.

"Lorenze, I need you to promise me something. Fight with me in there. Get Ze'ev at any cost. Be my partner, regardless of the consequences. Live and die for this." She lowered her voice, "But once it's done, get out."

"Remiel–"

"Don't argue with me! Get out. Do whatever you can to escape. I won't be responsible for one more life."

Lorenze's eyes strayed over her head. "I can't do that."

"You can, and you will," she turned on the anger. "Look at me, Lorenze." She waited until he did. "If you respect me at all, if you believe an inkling of the name you just called me, then you'll do as I ask. For you know I'm not asking. You may have to die for the rest of the world, but once it's done, I won't have you die for me."

Lorenze swallowed, and Elise watched it all the way down his throat. He nodded his head barely. Behind him, one of the men in suits moved. Time to go.

"Say it," she insisted.

"Once Ze'ev is taken care of, I'll leave," he promised without looking at her.

"And if the Other shows up," Elise added to the oath. "Just run as fast as you can. Having you there with that thing will just be a distraction for me. Do you understand?"

The look in her eyes told him she would leave him right there before letting him go without this promise. "Fine," he replied.

371

Elise responded with a half-handshake, half-hand squeeze. "Thank you." She began to turn, but suddenly thought better of it. A slight hesitation, and then she added, "They're with us today."

His eyebrows knit together. "Who?"

"The angels." She smiled, and for a second, looked like the girl he knew in the Vatican.

Lorenze could not help but smile back. "Did they come visit you?"

"Yes," she replied without smiling at all.

* * * * *

"Shirli?" the society member in the passenger's seat peered over his shoulder at her. "We will be arriving at the funeral in about twenty minutes. Listen carefully – you will pass through security, and then follow a marked path to the section of Mount Herzl that is reserved for the burial. For several hours, those inside will be paying their respects to the two leaders. Forming a line, just like American wakes, and going by the dead men to leave flowers, flags...Ze'ev will be by the coffins with several of his new ministers. After everyone pays their respects, the burial will begin. Although, we don't suggest that you wait that long – Shirli?"

In response, Elise looked out the window. It had been that way the entire ride – attempts at conversation, which she quickly killed. Quite frankly, she had nothing to talk about. Nothing really to think about. Planning was pointless – anything overlooked was going to be overlooked. She had only her instinct now. And her faith.

Elise returned her attention to the people in the streets. She watched them, hunched over in the rain that still fell lightly, as though the world were quietly crying. Innocent of what was going on around them; naïve of the true man they called to lead them. If they could know, would they fight?

What will be so different about the people here when the last trumpet does sound? Elise asked the quiet of her mind. *Why aren't we worthy now?*

The car passed a mother with her two children. Even in the brief blur, Elise could tell the mother was angry with the young boy. She clenched him to her in an almost painful way while speaking without moving her face. An old man walking slowly appeared to look back at Elise, though the windows of the car were tinted. Several teenage boys plotted something at the corner of the street despite the rain. One stopped to watch a pretty girl digging through her bag for an umbrella.

Elise looked up at the gray sky, noticed the stone buildings where they were darkened at the corners by the rain, took in the trees looking skeletal with a few clinging leaves. She could not imagine it any different, any more beautiful, any more desperate to survive than it was now.

But *Revelation* was sure they would fail. Without the complete breaking of the seals and the sounding of the first six trumpets before her own, there was too much evil left in the world. Enough to swing the scale.

Focus. Just do what you were meant to do. It was easy the last time, she winced slightly as Clyde Parker's face briefly materialized in the weak window reflection. *If you want, no one can touch you. Heal yourself. Stun them, use them. Show them how hot you burn inside.* She ran it through again in her mind, imagined being in the cemetery, racing past guards, ministers, and stunned mourners, even sending her spirit out ahead of her. It wouldn't be that hard. A fuzzy image of Ze'ev replaced Clyde's in the glare of the window. If she could just touch him long enough. As if he were really there, Elise pressed her fingers against the imaginary image in the glass. Though she shut her mind off so that she could not see the rest, she knew she could make him shrivel–

"Ow!" she couldn't keep the word under her breath. Elise pulled the necklace off her skin so fast, she felt the chain give a notch from the stress.

"What is it?" the society member spun around in his seat.

"Nothing," she lied and waited until he faced the front again. She looked down at the odd welt from her previous night's dream. The red irritation was remade with a new burn. Yet, she fingered the cross and the Psalm plate. Both were cool.

* * * * *

"Shalom. Shirli Levy," Elise gave her name to the guard exactly as Matthew coached her. Her mouth was dry as if she had been sleeping all night with it opened. Jerkily, she handed the guard her papers and tried not to look nervous about the gun he held – a machine gun like she had only previously seen in movies.

They all had them – at least ten guards with machine guns stood around the gate to Mount Herzl Cemetery. The gate itself was draped in yellow tarp, so that she could not see inside. It was raining harder now, and she could feel the droplets beginning to accumulate on her scalp, getting ready to run off onto her forehead and nose. Though the society member offered her an umbrella before she got out of the car, she refused. She would need both hands today.

The guard was still looking at the papers. *Wait. Just wait*, Elise told herself. But the panic was gaining ground. *I'm not getting through! I know it – he's not going to let me through.* It felt inevitable. She was just too close for this to be easy. Elise took another look at the machine guns. How much turning-up would it take to heal from a round of that?

Death doesn't matter. This is it – one try. Only this is real. If the guard

373

doesn't let me pass, I'LL TOUCH HIM! Just turn-up, keep the other men from their guns with my mind, and then RUN! Could she do it that quickly? *Where is Lorenze? Did he make it inside? The other society members?* Her neck ached to turn and look, but it might make her appear nervous. Why did they plan it like this?

The guard looked at her and then back at her papers. When he looked up again, he kept his eyes over Elise's head, focused on the line of umbrellas behind her. He spoke in Hebrew without meeting her anxious face.

Elise smiled (praying it was the right response), and held her breath, of course, not understanding a word the man said. She parted her fingers wide. His face would be the easiest thing to touch – everything else was hidden under his raincoat. *It's time. Use you're instincts* – she raised her hand.

He looked her in the eye and stepped to the side for her to pass to security.

The offensive hand ran through her hair awkwardly, wet strands sticking to it. Was that it? Without feeling the movement, she passed by the guard and raised her arms for two women to pat her down. Her shaking was visible, and one of the women hesitated to look her in the face before nodding that she could enter.

Are they really letting me through? Elise flinched, as if ready to avoid gunfire. She entered Mount Herzl Cemetery. Yellow tarp had been erected on either side of the entrance for security and created a sterile, narrow tunnel for those allowed inside to follow; *keep those in within, and those out without.* Maze-like, it wound in front of her to a place she could not see. The gray sky above did nothing to diminish the feeling of standing in a biohazard cleansing tent, or an astronaut's air lock. The narrow, makeshift scene reminded her of a horror movie…what one? Some scene where a boy hid in a clothesline. The sheets hung down to the grass and moved in the wind. And though the audience could not see it, everyone knew there was something in there with the boy, hiding just where he couldn't see.

Glancing frequently backwards, Elise followed the shadow of the person in front of her: another mourner. She passed him, and he looked at her a long time. She could feel his eyes boring into the back of her scalp. *A society member looking for her?*

Faster. She tried to make it seem normal, like perhaps she was looking for someone (which was very true, and therefore, easy to act). Still, she was not nearly confident enough to walk so quickly past the guards that appeared after every turn. She slowed down by their machine guns, even meandered.

COME ON! She had to wipe the rain from her forehead now. Her hair was dripping, and she could feel the shoulders of her sweater trying poorly to soak it up. Still down the yellow tarp tunnel, *like some damned* Alice in Wonderland. *Anybody watching up there?* Elise instinctively looked towards the sky.

Finally, the tarp walls began to widen, accompanied by the growing sound of murmured voices. Elise's calf twitched to run. Ten more yards, and the tarp fell off to the sides revealing – a thousand black umbrellas.

Elise stopped moving all together. She could see nothing. "God," she whispered. "So many people. And none of them know."

Someone behind her cleared his throat. Jump-started, Elise moved ahead the few steps she could and pressed on the people in front of her. A woman smiled and offered a corner of her umbrella. Elise nodded and moved with her. A half-second and she was a part of the mass and its miniscule movement forward. To the sides, gravestones peeked between the bodies. Their marble faces combined with the black attire for an eerie recreation of some old black and white film. On the far outskirts, the tarps continued – a quarantine from the outside world.

I can't see anything! Am I even heading the right way? Elise rose up on her tiptoes until her feet ached. *Is this it? Am I going to stand a half-hour with my fists clenched so tight I can't feel my palms? Is this my last half-hour? Is this my last rain?*

Suddenly desperate to be away from the umbrellas, Elise darted forward to a clear space and turned her head up to the sky violently. *Rain on my face. I still feel it. I still feel it.* Elise closed her eyes and waited for a wave of nausea to pass. It felt like she had been spinning for a while. Her pulse battered her ears. *Alone among a thousand strangers.*

WHAT IF I CAN'T DO THIS? Frantic, Elise brushed against a woman to her side. She felt the woman jump when their hands touched, and some of her leaked inside. The woman was thinking about the flowers she carried. To the left – a child this time. But, it didn't matter. She needed it. Needed the power to calm. Needed to hear the whispers and know they were still there. A third touch, and some blond light appeared at the corners of Elise's vision. As she did when wounded, Elise used the strength to heal up the sickness, the shaking, and her pounding heart. She stood just like she used to after running a great distance. And just like then, she finally caught her breath.

Enough to see that the mass was turning into a line. They had moved up hill considerably. Behind the enclosed area, great trees with heavy branches dripped. Someone next to Elise began to cry. *Getting closer*, she recognized.

From twenty abreast to ten, to five, the mass narrowed to fit between temporary railings set up for the paying of respects. Beyond bottleneck – Elise could see the overflow down one corner of the hill where people appeared even at a distance to be milling more casually. Clusters of important looking (and importantly dressed) men stood in the dead-zone between the railings holding the crowd and the tarps that outlined the area. These men huddled tightly in between the perfectly rectangular graves. Their similar black suits made them appear like strange specters come out for a little conversation. *Ministers? Important rebels?* Further still, Elise found herself crammed in with two young men and an older couple. She sized them up while they kept their eyes focused on the ground. From a once-over, each one had a lot of life to give. Depending on what happened, they might be her only way out. *God, I'm scared. I'm not ready…*

At last, Elise could see it. A spot where the mass stopped moving; where the people only stood or leaned down to deliver their flowers. Suddenly, the crowd was not slow, but too fast, and she found herself panting. Her vision pulled to the corners of her eyes in a wave of dizziness. Helpless, Elise rested her hands on her knees. She was going to throw up.

I can't…I can't. God, I CAN'T BREATHE! She pulled at the collar of her dress, separating it further from her neck as though that were the thing constricting her throat. *Help me PLEASE. I CAN'T DO THIS! I'M SORRY!* Frenzied, she pulled the sweater off and dropped it on the ground. It was over, and she couldn't.

She squeezed her eyes shut and turned back, pushing against those pushing her forward. *I have to get out, I HAVE TO GET OUT–*

What is she doing? Turning around? But this is the end. The last lap.

Elise froze as though really spoken to.

Surely she can keep going just a little further, when so much is behind her?

Imaginary commentary. It was the internal voice from her running. So childish; such an obvious symptom of her desire for someone; to not be alone. The running voices had always been a way to view herself without being herself. To push and pull from a distance, without knowing the burn, the chest ache, the lightheadedness. A psychological barrier to keep Elise from feeling herself. They had coached her through many miles, rain, cramps, the need to breathe. And somehow, they manifested now: when she desperately needed to withstand and endure. Her heavy breath locked in her lungs as she waited, insanely. *I can't,* she explained again, moving her lips to the words. *Not here, with all these people. Not without rage. Not without fury.*

But you can, the commentator-voice answered back. *You know you can.*

God wants me to do this. God wants me – Elise winced. *It's crazy. I'm crazy.*

And they burned Joan of Arc, the voice taunted. Then in a whisper, *Is this the great angel? God's warrior? So afraid to take, and so afraid to give.*

She's not afraid! the second commentator hissed. *She will win this – she has to.*

It's been a while since she trained.

"That doesn't matter! the defender in her mind retorted. *When you*

376

HAVE to win, you just do. See? She's looking better already.

And she was. Elise let go of the dress collar and took several deep breaths, filling her lungs completely. "It's just another race," she yielded to the delusion. She breathed in and out slow as her heart rate returned to normal. She turned around – forward. "I have to win."

There. She's moving again. She's fine. Just a cramp.

When you have to do something, then you just have to.

They moved forward together: Elise and the two voices. They admired the way she moved in the crowd, so careful. *No one knows,* they whispered. *No one knows who they're walking with.* They remembered the greenhouse: carving through trees, jumping from catwalk to catwalk, stopping Alan's bullet, breaking glass, anger, fury, the darkness.

So unpredictable. So hot and cold. She burns the fuse on both ends.

Pain and anger are some of the greatest tools. They allow us to twist ourselves.

Another step, and Elise thought of Clyde Parker. Saw herself grab him by the shirt and raise her hand to strike just where the glow of her eyes reflected off his cheek.

Watch. Don't turn away.

See? You can do this. It's in you.

The dark parts – Elise listened to her truth without wincing. The things she feared and hated, yet drew from and used. Despite training, despite Communion and Confession and Confirmation, there were still parts of her fallen. The voices were right: it was time to embrace it. Use it.

They looked for the Other and found you. Dance the line.

"The line between good and evil is thin," Elise remembered how harsh the words looked on Francis' whiteboard. "The thin line."

Dance it!

Dance closer!

The smell of burnt hair wafted, just detectable.

The Other racer.

Elise stopped, and the person behind hit her, touching her elbow with his hand to catch his balance. Instantly, she drew from him before he stood straight again. With his hiss of pain still loud in her ear, Elise honed all her senses to this one thing.

Nothing. Only black umbrellas: a dark mask composed of a thousand people.

She breathed in through both her nose and mouth. There was no mistaking – the Other was close to her. She lowered herself beneath the umbrella line. But there, where the umbrella-shade created a twilight – it was as impossible to see as above. She crouched lower, darting her eyes around with her hands on her knees, as though she'd lost something important. The crowd moved around her and the scent grew. Like someone was holding hair to a lighter. Like hell itself was starting to seep out of the ground.

Elise jerked her head to the left. Something streaked behind the black of the pants and skirts.

Quick, she stood. Back to face level, back to seeing nothing. It was like swimming in a black pond with only ripples to tell her something was beneath the surface.

"Not yet," she half warned, half prayed. Swallowing without saliva, she pressed into the crowd again. *MOVE!!* She wanted to scream fire – anything! If they only knew what was coming. *THERE IS NO TIME!*

And only fifty feet ahead, just to the right of where the mass stopped, there was a dark awning. Its scalloped edges fluttered in the breeze. It was morbid – too much like a tent at a graduation party or wedding. Elise could see the tops of several heads beneath the awning. Ze'ev would be one of them.

At her sides, she opened both her hands. She felt some wetness from her hair drip down. Fifty feet too early, but it had to be now. Now: a present moment that had arrived. "This is the Lord that strikes through me," she whispered. "This is the Lord that strikes." Elise reached for the hand of the older woman by her side–

Just as another hand grabbed for her.

Like a rubber band suddenly snapped, Elise whipped her neck around. *GOD, NOOO!*

It was a man from the dead-zone.

A man from in between the tarp fence and the railing, which he reached over to touch her.

For whole seconds, he didn't register as Elise's mind fought hard to reconcile expectations of the Other with the surprise reality. She blinked at him, shivering on pins and needles while every muscle waited for the final go to tear him apart.

His face looked urgent, and he spoke in Hebrew to her, leaving his hand extended, as if he wanted her to come with him. He wore a suit.

With a new rush of fear, Elise's understanding caught up and commanded her eyes to shift for approaching guards. But there were none. *WHAT IS THIS? WHAT DOES HE WANT?* She opened her hand. If he touched her again, she would meet him with a touch of her own.

He spoke again in Hebrew, and Elise shook her head slightly to let him know she could not understand him. "English," she said simply and began to turn away, her heart hammering. Maybe now he would leave her alone. Maybe–

"Miss!" The man switched to English easily (albeit heavily accented) and sidestepped along the railing to stay with her. "A moment please."

378

Quick, she ducked under another mourner's arm, putting the body between her and the man who continued to follow closely. *GOD PLEASE!*

"Miss. Just a moment!"

No, NO NO!

"AHHHHHHHH!" Mid-weave, Elise doubled over, unable to get her hands to her neck fast enough. Clawing frantically, she pulled both the cross and the Psalm plate from her skin, snapping the chain. On her chest, several deep purple blisters formed over the old burn mark. Elise remained crouched down, tears of pain crisscrossing her cheeks while a hissing noise escaped her lips. "What? I – what?"

GET UP! GO NOW! RUN!

The cross – now in her palm – seared again, and Elise dropped it. Dazed, she stared, its silver color melting easily with the gray stone. *What...* She could almost hear the blood in her head, racing to make the connections. Elise picked up the chain, careful not to touch the cross or Psalm plate. "What are you trying to tell me?"

It's behind you, coming for you. It will eat you like it ate Alan!

NO! With more effort than she ever needed before to command her body, Elise turned back and made her way to the outside of the line. The man from the dead-zone was still there. Elise closed the necklace back in her palm, and it was cool.

"I'm sorry to disturb you today," he began and then nodded towards the head of the line to indicate the bodies.

"How can I help you? Please speak quickly."

"Miss Ze'ev," the man paused, apparently searching for the right thing to say.

"Miss Ze'ev?" Elise echoed like a child learning new words. Her mind reeled, searching frantically the half-listened-to conversations of the past. *Ze'ev was widowed with one daughter.*

Run, run, run, run, RUN!

"She saw you, said she knew you," he continued normally, slow, as if they had plenty of time. "She would like you to come and speak with her. And, I wanted to ask you before I lost you again in the crowd."

Elise blinked rapidly, every muscle flexing for the decision. "She knows me?"

"Yes. Will you come? After you pay your respects, of course."

The cross in Elise's hand suddenly warmed.

"No! I – I'll go now." Elise thrust the man the fist she held the cross with, and then used her other hand to help her vault the railing. Out of the sea of umbrellas; out of the dark pond water with the ripples in its surface. Elise's breath shook on its way out, almost like a sob. "We can hurry. I don't want to keep her..." Elise used the courtesy as an excuse to take several sharp steps away from the crowd and the rotten odor that bled from it.

"Wait!" his voice took on a command for the first time. "Spread your arms please."

Elise's pulse sputtered like she had an opened artery somewhere, but she did as he asked. *Hurry! Please hurry!*

"You can breathe while I do this," the man pointed out as he patted her sides.

Elise didn't bother.

"This way, miss?"

"El– Shirli Levy," Elise barely caught her mistake. And then she was following him, away from Ze'ev, further, she kept putting one foot in front of the other. Halfway across the dead-zone, and Elise couldn't smell the burning at all. The awning disappeared back into the mass. It was all wrong. It was wrong, and yet–

"Miss Ze'ev is just over here," he indicated a part of the enclosure passed the line and the caskets. Here, the dead-zone became a behind the scenes. A podium was arranged for speeches, and news anchors were busily arranging microphones. Across the grass, Elise could see mourners corralled at one end behind more railings. There were chairs – hundreds. Some were filled, while more bodies poured in from the wake, having just paid their respects to the dead leaders.

Elise squeezed her hands together to feel the cross painfully. It gave no new encouragement. There was still time – the burial had not even started, *although, we don't suggest that you wait that long.* Maybe she could still turn-up on someone in the crowd and just throw her mind at Ze'ev! If the ghost of her was strong enough to stop bullets and break glass...

"There," he pointed towards another dark awning. It was immediately obvious who the focal figure was: a young girl dressed in an elegant black dress that clung to a figure trying to be a woman's. Her charcoal hair was pulled back in a low knot at the base of her neck. She did not smile at their approach, nor did she respond to the man when he called to her in Hebrew. But she watched. Eyes the color of dirty water – faded blue with flecks of brown–

Elise jumped and blinked hard.

What was that?

It was as though something passed between her eyes and her mind, in between where she could see and where she thought. A hallucination? A side effect of her fear? A trick of the light?

She closed her eyes tightly and reopened them. Just the girl, still watching–

The flash in her vision came again. This time, it was enough to make Elise stagger. She shook her head, but the vision refused to dissolve, as if she were just waking from a dream. *What's happening?* She squinted to see the real world but could not. *The men at the table – all six...I'm there and...*

The scene whirled and then began to pass, leaving Elise blinking away starbursts of colorful light. The man guiding her was speaking, his voice higher with alarm. *WHAT IS HAPPENING TO ME?* She put out a hand to steady herself, forgetting there was only air and stumbling as her true surroundings blurred to focus.

"I'm sorry. I'm just not feeling well. Not enough to eat today..." Elise mumbled something, anything. He extended an arm, and she took it gladly, leaning on him while her vision continued to improve. "I'm sorry. Very sorry."

He held her arm tightly, distrust in his fingers as they haltingly walked the remaining distance without a single step in sync. Elise kept her eyes on the ground and her hand around the necklace. One foot, then the other, then the other until the man stopped, and she knew it was time – for what? What was she doing? What was happening to her, just now when she needed to be perfect? From eyelids lowered, Elise looked up through the rain into the face of Chesed Ze'ev – and the light exploded.

Elise was suddenly not in the cemetery.

She was in the desert.

The six men with their trumpets sat around the same table as before. And Elise saw herself at one head, sitting with them.

Except it wasn't really her at the table. Remiel's face was like hers, but smoother, like plaster. No fear, no doubt; she was older, pristine, like the statue. And she was nodding, nodding hard. She seemed to understand something.

Then all eyes turned on her: the real Elise, the invader and watcher. As though they saw her. As though she were not some ghost to their reality. Her and... Elise's mind registered a person beside her. She turned.

Long black hair and eyes like dirty water. *Chesed...*the surprised word formed on her tongue–

But was never spoken. Suddenly, Elise was falling, the ground opening a sudden expanse of nothing beneath her. *NO!* She closed her eyes and waited for her body to slam. It came, knocking her breath away. She opened her lungs to– the cold. No longer a desert. She lie on stone, somewhere vastly dark. Up on one elbow quickly, Elise turned her head.

And there were blue eyes. Three pairs. Alone in the blackness, a nothingness her mind did not even try to understand. They floated, blinking over her. "We are close now," The Other spoke in the voice of a man. "But we have always been close. Can you look at me? No? I know you hear me. This darkness – my darkness – will come for your soul."

The eyes blinked, and did not reopen, swallowed again by darkness.

381

Elise could see nothing as she flailed to stand. And then suddenly, the blackness lifted, like morning light just beginning to burn away a rainy night. Her eyes adjusted in the gloom to see Chris over her. He was laughing at something, perhaps her. But her confusion turned to marvel: he was young. The blond hair had no gray lacings, the face no smile lines or worry tracks. Again he laughed. It was a Chris she had never met: one without care or sadness.

He extended his hand, and Elise took it. He pulled her up as though she weighed nothing (perhaps she didn't). For a moment they stood, and she could tell he was taking her all in – in a way he did not normally allow himself. Vaguely, she wondered who he saw: Remiel or Elise.

Without knowing she did it, Elise reached for him. For once, he did not duck her movement. He smiled and lowered his face for her, so that their eyes were on the same level. *I've been here before. I touched him like this. I knew him like this.*

"I will pray for you," he spoke. "I need you. I need some peace; something that I can hang onto even on my darkest days and say there is no other explanation. I will know, because I saw you, I felt you. You will save me."

His eyes were dilated, as though dead.

In the instant she jerked back, he was gone, and Elise found herself standing with her hand out, her fingers tracing a face no longer there. In Chris' place in the grayness: Remiel. Her eyes glowed with stolen light – a firestorm just behind her face – and she stood before Elise, looking exactly at her.

"What is this? What is happening to me? I need to go back –"

Remiel took two intimidating steps closer, and Elise felt herself wanting to move away. Back from the horror of her mind, a horror that lived and breathed in her. Away from the dark half, the stronger half, the half that called her to unthinkable things.

Remiel's mouth opened. And then, her own voice whispered. *Listen. Do you hear us? Please listen. You should listen to us.*

Elise did take a step back. But Remiel matched the move with her own step, and as she did, the figure of her twitched with some inner violence. It was a second; no more, and yet it was enough for Remiel to split; to fragment into two figures that now stood before her. One with fire in her eyes and the other with eyes the color of dirty water.

Remiel and Chesed. Listen!

Remiel reached for her in a movement so sharp and fluid, Elise barely saw it. The angel covered her eyes with one hot hand. For a second, Elise looked at her between the open slits of the angel's fingers.

For the very first time, Elise knew what it was to be turned-up on. The heat, the pressure of the hand – the only thing she could feel. The sense of losing herself helplessly to someone else. She drained, and even this dream that was not real to begin with wavered before her vision. She clutched at the hand, peeling hard fingers from her face. But the fire ignited there too, as Remiel simply turned-up harder wherever they touched. Thoughts began to pass to her – Remiel's thoughts. First, like a light turning off and on, then faster, like blinking eyes. Thousands of things flashed before Elise in the spaces between darkness. Scenes in snapshot, a roll of film moving backwards and forwards – places she had seen and would yet see; people and actions, known and not yet known, done and not yet done. Remiel's past and future flashed before her until Elise feared she would be blinded. She squeezed her eyes against it before realizing they were already closed. They had been closed.

You know. You always knew. About Him and a girl. The girl with dirty-water eyes. See and remember. TRY HARDER!!

I am, I–

LISTEN! Can't you hear us?

Yes…

LISTEN!

I HEAR YOU!!!

* * * * *

And suddenly, she could feel.

Feel herself leaning heavily on the man in the cemetery, barely able to pick up her feet. Her body was moving, twitching like an epileptic pulled by imaginary strings.

The vision was ending. She wanted to cry or scream. She blinked, and part of the cemetery stone came into focus. More completely this time, without sunbursts. The darkness of her eyelids flooded back in. She felt her head hang, felt her body exhausted as it passed. She was back, back under the awning. Back to the face Elise finally, finally remembered.

Elise and the man were still standing just beneath where the girl waited. It was still barely raining. They were all staring at her – Chesed and those that guarded her. There were voices loud, calling in Hebrew.

With something close to giddiness, Elise let go of the man's arm and ducked underneath the awning to stand before the young girl. She still trembled. Her heart beat with the intensity.

"Someone send for a doctor!" It was the man who brought her. "Miss, a doctor?"

Chesed watched them for a moment, before speaking in a soft voice. Though Elise could not understand the words, she broke out in goose bumps.

There was a tone in it she recognized as belonging to someone else.

The man translated in a flattened voice, shifting his weight back and forth and obviously unsure if he should restrain Elise or let her stand. "She says she remembers you."

Elise nodded large. "She says she remembers me," she repeated.

Chesed spoke again, this time with eyes slightly averted.

The man was slower this time. "She says she remembers you from her – her dreams."

Elise closed her eyes to hold back some of the tears beginning to form. An intense happiness vibrated every cell that composed her. It was like being told for the first time that a boy loved her. Or the feeling she got when she saw her parents in her sleep, before she knew it was just a dream. Several drops leaked out at the corners of her eyes, and she blinked to get them out of the way.

Chesed was speaking again. This time she smiled. She spoke so quickly that the man had to hold up a hand for her to allow him to translate.

"She says she's dreamt of you so many times – that she feels like she knows you. She knew you as soon as she saw you."

"Tell her I know her. Tell her, I saw her, and I remembered. Just like I promised. Just like I promised."

It was too much, and Elise slid to her knees in front of her, desperate to just touch her hand. The man came at her then, his hands rough on her shoulders, but it didn't matter. "God, I can feel it," she fingered the fingers feverishly. "I can feel it. There is so much of Him in you." A tremor shook her, and she cried it, "I remember – I remember I remember I remember."

It was the last thing she would remember saying.

* * * * *

It took Elise a moment to realize that the whiteness above was a ceiling. Her head throbbed, and she wondered cloudily if she had been struck.

Immediately her heart picked-up a beat. *Chesed? THE OTHER? Where am I? What–*

A beeping noise from somewhere in the room began to accelerate. Elise turned her stinging head to see a heart monitor by her side. It read 173.

NO! Despite the ache, Elise moved quickly to survey her body. It appeared to be intact underneath a light blanket. She was obviously in a hospital bed. *Oh God...*

"Hello? Hello! Ahhhh..." she sat up with a moan. "Someone..." Elise paused and waited for her sense of balance to catch up with her. "What happened? Please God..." Elise grasped the many cords and IV that stuck from her arm, closed her eyes, and pulled. It hurt more than she expected it to, but had the desired effect. The heart monitor flatlined with a loud buzzing. A nurse came running. Upon seeing Elise awake and sitting, "You're only awake then." Elise did not wait. She touched her, the IV wounds healing instantly and new light flooding her eyes and the room.

* * * * *

"Elise Moore?" a heavily accented voice called out in the rain. She was standing in a hospital gown outside, still holding the hospital doors shut with her mind. Elise jerked her body towards the sound. A cluster of men stood by a small black car.

"We're from the Hetaera–"

It was enough. "No time!" Elise spoke her thought. "We have to go now!"

After a frustrating moment when no one moved, the men finally began opening the car doors. Elise slid into the leather backseat, smelled the smell of cigarettes – even that was to be appreciated. The doors closed with two men on her sides sitting close. And the driver did not have to be told. He pushed the gas so they leapt from the curb.

"Ze'ev? Where is he?"

"Ze'ev?" the priest to her left answered with confusion. "He's fine. Nothing happened. We've been searching for you for hours. Demsky is buried, and I imagine Ze'ev is preparing for the coronation even as we speak."

Elise sighed, deflating her chest into the seat.

* * * * *

Every window was lit when Elise walked the stone sidewalk to their front door. It was already opened, with two men standing at it: Chris and Lorenze. But only Chris came to meet her. He said nothing, but wrapped his two arms completely around her body.

His hands moved from her shoulder blades to her face. He smoothed the skin of her cheeks to reassure that they really existed and lingered long in the light brown eyes still tinged with gold. "Are you hurt? We discovered your alibi was taken to a hospital. I would've come, but I was searching on the other side of the city."

"I'm fine." She nodded to make it so. To Lorenze, "Where were you? I never saw you inside."

"I never made it inside," he frowned deeply. He looked just as he had that morning, still in his suit. "There was some mistake. I wasn't on the list. Didn't make it off the street." The words were bitter and shame-filled.

She sighed and smiled weakly. "That's okay. Although it would be a blessing if Ze'ev was out of this, things are different now anyway. We still have one more day."

"How is it different?" Lorenze asked without hope.

"I'll explain inside. Get everyone together."

* * * * *

Chris watched Elise on the couch. She sat without moving, entirely ignoring the society members that huddled behind her, as if around some fire. The glass of water she asked for remained forgotten and full on the coffee table. She looked neither tired, nor entirely awake. Yet her eyes moved rapidly, as if she relived something important.

"Are you all right?" he tried again.

"I'm fine," she smiled for him. "It's just – so much has changed, and…" she trailed off where it appeared her mind was still evaluating. "Everyone should sit down." To the rest of the group, "And I mean everyone. Lorenze, make sure all the society members are inside. No one goes out now."

After a lock-down check on the windows and doors, they gathered. Some took seats on the floor. Some, like Lorenze, preferred to stand. All fidgeted.

Except Elise who remained cool. Like she knew what she was going to say, and the only decision left was how to say it.

"As you know, I was unsuccessful at reaching Chayim Ze'ev. And he will be king tomorrow. In 20 hours, actually," Elise calculated without looking at the time.

With a deeper breath, "I was on my way to him. I was inside the cemetery, in line to the caskets. I could see where he sat – just over the crowd. And I was prepared to– kill him." She swallowed. "The Other was there, but I was ahead. It was really going to happen. Except, suddenly…" her eyes glazed as her memory traveled far away.

"There was a girl."

"A girl?" Matthew repeated when Elise paused. The faces around the room blanked.

"A girl. Chesed Ze'ev, daughter of Chayim Ze'ev. She saw me waiting in line for the wake. And she knew me."

The blank faces became blanker.

But Elise only smiled at the still close encounter. "And when I looked at her, I remembered. Just like He told me I would in my dreams. I remembered her." An awe that did not normally belong to Elise carried the tones of her voice.

It frightened Chris. The feeling reminded him of watching a balloon soaring into the sky higher, out of reach. Where was she going with this? "Elise. What dream? What are you remembering?"

"My dream," she repeated with condescension. "The one I had my first night in Whiteley. Christ told me to look upon Him and remember." She broke from the memory and searched their eyes for understanding. "All this time, I misinterpreted His meaning. Don't you see? He meant it literally! Look – on – me – and – remember. I had to see her, you understand?"

Chris shook his head. "No, I don't–"

"See HIM," Elise struggled visibly to explain. "When I saw Chesed, I saw Him in her. His bloodline runs in her. Chesed is King David's heir – not Ze'ev. But it wasn't until I saw her that I remembered."

"Okay," Chris returned the condescension. "Of course Chesed has Christ's blood in her veins. She's Ze'ev's daughter! If Ze'ev is Christ's heir, then it follows that so is Chesed."

"No. Chayim Ze'ev is not of the line of kings. But his dead wife – she was the carrier of holy blood. Chesed did not inherit this from her father, but rather from her mother. She was the descendant, the line. And in birth, she imparted it to her only daughter. Chesed Ze'ev is the one, the heir." Elise finished, and her words dissolved into the thick silence that descended on the room. The faces were no longer blank. They were bewildered. Elise could hear the steady ticking of someone's watch.

In the corner, Francis began shaking his head until it looked like a twitch. His face turned a deep shade of plum.

But it was Chris who burst first. "What about the signs? What about what Francis saw? All along, he's been leading us."

Elise responded coolly while giving Francis the dignity of looking him in the eye. "Francis was wrong. But it doesn't matter – it's just a technicality. We needed to locate Ze'ev so that I could see his daughter. Francis' visions still got us where we needed to go."

Francis tapped his pen but couldn't seem to find anything to write. Finally, he bit off the cap and held it in his teeth while he wrote. The action only helped to amplify his skeptic snarl. *How can you be SURE? Only yesterday, you said you never have visions.*

Elise turned more gentle, but remained steady. "Yes, you've asked me several times if I had any inclinations towards anyone in the new Israeli regime. Did you not want my answer unless it agreed with yours? I have more than an inclination. The vision I had cannot be doubted. Trust me. Chesed is the one."

Trust you? YOU SAID IT YOURSELF – 20 hours!! 20 hours and you want to change everything. Go on some vision that cannot be backed up. What if YOU'RE WRONG? WHAT IF YOU'RE BEING MISLEAD?"

"I'm not wrong." Elise shrugged before delivering a blow to end the conversation. "And all along, we've been going on some vision that could not be backed up. I trusted you blindly. I was willing to die for your opinion, your interpretation of something I could not see. It is time for you to trust me."

Slowly, the muscles in Francis' face relaxed and fell while the color drained back into his body. Staring into his lap, he erased his words.

Elise sighed, but did not apologize. "This is it. You chose me. You told me I was the one who had to put time right and make sure Christ's bloodline does not end up on that throne. If you don't believe me now, if you don't let me do what I was made to do, then all your faith is worth nothing. Chesed Ze'ev comes straight from Christ. I know her. And I will do this without you. I am apart of no society."

Francis shook his head but said nothing. He refused to look up.

So Elise turned to Chris. Ironic – she looked to the one that struggled with faith all his life. The one that begged for her touch in order to know God. But he knew her the best. Better than anyone. If he couldn't see Remiel in her, then she was alone. Quiet, she waited for his decision.

Typical, Chris ran his fingers through his hair so that it stood straight. His face moved as his thoughts passed. He looked in her eyes and then pursed his lips. Below where everyone watched, his hand found the mark she left.

"If you say Chesed is the one, then she's the one." Chris reasoned slow and out loud. "Which means, we don't have anything to worry about, right? Chesed certainly won't be crowned tomorrow."

"Don't be so sure. Blood carries other things. Chayim did not give his daughter the holy heritage she carries, but by the rules of monarchy, he can pass his authority to her. What happens to the crown when a king dies?"

Lorenze answered clearly from the back of the room. "His next of kin inherits it."

"And the only person in Ze'ev's bloodline is... Once Ze'ev is king, Chesed will become the next in line. She is already heir to David's kingdom, and shortly, she will be heir to her father's kingdom as well. And when she inherits the second..." she tightened her lips in an 'O' and blew out. "The sounding."

"Well, at least it buys us some more time," Matthew pointed out. "After all, the likelihood of Ze'ev dying...on the day he is crowned...is unlikely," he slowed the thought down as he began to realize his error.

Elise sighed. "Not really. His risk of assassination is high. And don't forget, the Other plans to kill him now that we won't."

"Now that we won't..." Chris repeated as he fit the last piece into place.

"Tomorrow, it will defend Ze'ev and Chesed from us until sunset, and then kill Ze'ev after he's crowned."

"This is…" Matthew put his head in his hands and began massaging his scalp as if to encourage understanding. "This is unbelievable. The plan – where do we go from here? There will be no way to get to them tomorrow."

"Chesed was not the only part of the vision," Elise answered him indirectly. "I saw the trumpeters. And I saw myself. Only it wasn't me – not the girl here, sitting with you," her tone fell to disgust and her hands moved with her urgency to make them understand. "Remiel is so much stronger and more frightening. Perfect. She knows all that ever happened, and better, she knows the end. She showed me where I came from, why. And she revealed pieces of tomorrow. What will happen, and what I have to do.

"So, there's no planning. Everyone – sleep. Tomorrow will be long."

"Sleep?" Matthew conveyed her insanity with the high pitch of his voice. "We can't just go to sleep. We need to do something, anything. No one is going to bed!"

Elise kept her response low with an intensity that needed no volume. "I told you. The plan is written, everyone's parts decided. Anything you need to know, I'll tell you in the morning. That way, the nightmares stay out of your dreams."

A new silence captured the room: fear of the known. Had she seen any of them die? How did it end?

Lorenze was the first to get up. "How shall we guard tonight?"

"I will guard," she replied. "The Other is here, and anxious we do not get in its way. At this point, I'm the only one fit to guard. So get your rest. Go!"

Her second command instigated an exodus of society members to the kitchen. Lorenze retreated as he was ordered, and Matthew (his face literally burning with questions) haunted the stairway for a moment before he found his room. A few closed doors later, and it was the original three: Francis, Chris and Elise.

Refusing to look at either Chris or Elise, Francis stood and began what looked like a short pace by his end of the room. His pen hesitated a moment, and then he wrote quickly to get it all out before another doubt slowed him down. *I have so many questions for you. I'm sorry – I just…*

"It's fine. You've always been able to see your faith; it must be hard when that's taken away."

Francis nodded uncertainly, confused whether she insulted him again or merely made a statement. *What was it like?*

Elise gave a snort that wanted to be a laugh. "A blur. Like I watched a movie in fast-forward, but my mind could keep up with it. So much information. Although, I'm sure it will be just like everything else with God: just enough."

You know the end?

389

"No."

Francis waited for her to qualify the answer. He kept waiting.

She finally added, "I know what I need to do to get to the end. Go to sleep now. Both of you."

"You really shouldn't guard alone..." Chris began but didn't get to finish. Elise's look silenced him.

Did the vision show you how to beat it? Francis wrote the unexpected question.

Elise paused before answering the question. "How to beat the Other? Not how," she remembered it standing over her, the eyes. "But it did show me that I will get the chance. Somewhere, in the dark."

Both men frowned at her in synch.

"Don't worry. I can't sleep anyway. It waits for me there too. I'll sleep tomorrow, when it's all over."

Tomorrow? Could they possibly be celebrating this time the very next day? A sharp pain entered Chris' chest. He longed for even the fantasy of such a moment. But his realism wouldn't allow him to see it. Not a second.

Elise looked up to Francis' intense gaze. His head was cocked at her – similar to the way an animal sizes up another animal. "What?" she asked.

He nodded his head slowly. A sharper nod to Chris, and he began up the stairs.

Chris stood and waited.

He remembered this feeling from high school. The relationship was over and the girl was waiting for him to leave and make it real. And just like then, Elise did not look at him.

"Elise."

"Yes, Chris." Elise sighed and then raised her chin to let him know she listened.

"I'm...I'm not sure what I was going to say."

"Well I am," she replied. "You were going to ask me one more time if I should really be left alone. Do I feel all right? Is there something you can get me? And I was going to tell you that I don't need anything, I feel well, and being alone will be just fine."

It was cruel, and she let her head fall to the side so that her ear touched her neck. "I'm sorry," she apologized before Chris had a chance to turn his back. "But, I'm doing what I'm meant to do, Chris. So don't try to save me. I saw what I really am, underneath all the skin and bone. Elise is just a part of a much larger, stronger soul that's slowly been waking-up for the last twenty years. I need to be that larger, stronger soul. Elise alone cannot do what needs to be done tomorrow."

"Stop talking about yourself like that – in the third person."

"Please," she tossed his criticism back with scorn. "Today is just a moment. So brief, you can't even comprehend it. My feelings now are only flickers, much like those other moments I envisioned today. In this flicker, I can only be here for one thing. And it isn't sleep, or feeling good, or getting back safely."

He stared at her, frozen to the manifestation of goose bumps. How could he not be chilled? Only that morning, she had still been a girl with a great responsibility hanging over her life. But not now. Elise's life hung loosely over her responsibility.

"Wake one of us if you need anything," Chris offered worthlessly. Goodnight – he would leave and make it real.

"Chris," she called just as his face began to disappear up the stairs. She waited until he looked back at her. "I knew you, before all of this. Before you could possible know me. You were there in my vision today. I saw you as you used to be, and you were laughing." Elise smiled just enough to let him know it was a pleasant memory. "Of all the people in the world, I chose you to be with me in this. I may seem different to you. You may like me better at the Whiteley Corn Festival than you'll ever like me now. But, our connection goes deeper than that, beyond this in both directions. I – chose – you."

"Elise–"

"You need to know…I am the reason you didn't have the dream. I saw it today, watched myself do it. The years you spent questioning, angry. God did not keep the dream from you. He was not punishing you or testing you. It was me. I am the reason."

"What? Why are you saying this? It was just my fear–"

"I chose not to appear to you that night so long ago. On purpose and selfishly even in perfection. For there is that ancient struggle in me; a piece that understands those that fell; the ache to be the loved creation, to be as high as the men of clay. And the way I feel for you, have always wanted you. I could not let you dream of angels. When you prayed for peace and something to hang onto in the dark days, I didn't want that thing to be Remiel. I wanted it to be Elise."

"So you are. So you have been almost since the day I met you."

He thought she might break then, might pull him to her as she did only nights before. But no. Her eyes left his face, stared into the light of the only lamp burning.

It was as he feared: Elise got into a car that morning, and she had not come back. Only Remiel watched him up the stairs and let him go.

Chapter 24 – The Third Day

They all sat at the wooden table with bowls of Israeli cereal – Elise, Chris, Francis, Matthew, and Lorenze. No one ate except Elise. Slivers of sunlight danced on the table, having made their way through the closed blinds. Bleary eyes watched them sway back and forth, dictated by the movement of some tree branch. Despite Elise's command, no one actually slept. Though the Other never paid a visit, the tension from the possibility still hung in the air. And after two similar, worsening nights, it was beginning to visibly wear. The group looked beaten already.

Except Elise. Though she kept her vigil as promised, she looked well rested. Calm. She was on her second bowl of cereal.

"You seem to be feeling well," Lorenze commented when that second bowl was half emptied.

She began to answer with a full mouth, and had to hastily wipe some milk from her chin. "I am feeling well. Ready." She dug back into the bowl.

Matthew cleared his throat. "When do you plan to let us in on everything?" he asked, unable to keep annoyance and anxiety out of his voice.

"After breakfast, I guess. Will that be all right?"

Matthew stared at her, lost for words. She made the offer as casually as she might make a study date in her previous life. He couldn't help but fire back. "And if it isn't all right for me? I'll give you a call on your cell and reschedule. Maybe we can discuss everything at Starbucks a little later."

Elise eyed Matthew over her cereal bowl hard enough to silence him. He understood, and left the room to sulk elsewhere.

From a lowered face, Elise smiled across the table at Lorenze, Francis, and Chris.

* * * * *

A few moments later, the smile was gone and a new (yet increasingly familiar) intensity gripped Elise's features. "Do you have what I requested?" Elise asked. A society member jumped from the couch and handed her a rolled up paper.

"We have to clear everything off. I need the table." She unrolled the map on the wood surface, not caring that one corner landed in a milk splat. Using some dirty bowls from the sink as weights, she kept it flat. "This is what's going to happen today.

"We're looking at the Old City." Elise traced a square outline on the map with her finger. "This box represents the Old City Wall, which quarantines the Old City from the rest of Jerusalem. And," she pointed to an 'x' located on the box outline, "this is the Golden Gate, one of many gates into the Old City. Christians believe it is the gate that Jesus used to enter Jerusalem on Palm Sunday, and that He will again enter the city through it at the second coming. Ze'ev and the procession will be entering through it at noon. Chesed will be with them, fulfilling the prophecy.

"After passing through the Golden Gate, the procession will continue on into the Haram Al-Sharif: a raised platform that covers almost one-sixth of the Old City. On the Haram Al-Sharif is the Dome of the Rock," Elise's finger traced a path to a large circle only slightly off the center of the Old City. "The Dome holds the rock where Abraham almost sacrificed his son, and also where the Muslim Mohammed is believed to have ascended. In Hebrew, this rock is known as Eben Shetiyyah: the Stone of Foundation. It is believed by all three religions – Islam, Christianity and Judaism – that this rock is the cornerstone of the world, around which God built everything. It is believed that Eben Shetiyyah rests upon and holds back the waters of the abyss. The Bir el-arweh, or Well of Souls, is just beneath it. This is a small, cave-like crypt – but with infinite capacity, where all the souls of mankind are kept until the final judgment.

"Ze'ev plans to spend several hours in prayer here, as all the great Jewish kings have: Abraham, David and Solomon. Though it matters little to the Jews, Jesus Christ also prayed in this spot. And with her father, Chesed will pray there, the final king.

"Now, there is very little opportunity for us up until this point," Elise raised her eyes from the map to look at the faces that crowded around. "Though the procession is public, there would be no way for us to get anywhere near either Chesed or Chayim. They will be kept under extremely tight security at the Dome of the Rock. No one will be allowed inside with them while they pray."

"How do you know all this?" Matthew interrupted. "We should ask the society – they may know a way in. They may also be able to help place Lorenze or, at this late stage, get an additional marks man, if there is no way for you to get close enough. It may be a stretch, but if we know what their steps will be, then I'm sure there must be a way for us to–"

"There is no need for information from the society, or reinforcements." Elise returned the interruption. "This is from the vision – a God-given vision. And when I saw it, we waited until Chesed and her father were done praying.

393

I don't care if there are other ways, or if it seems stupid. For me, this is the only way."

Matthew frowned down at the map.

Elise took a long breath to begin again. "The final stop for the procession is at the Western Wall. The lower part of the wall forms the platform that supported the Jewish Temple built during Herod the Great's reign. Since the third or fourth century, Jews have come here to mourn the destruction of that temple. As you know, there is now a gigantic plaza in front of the wall where crowds can pray and enjoy religious ceremonies. And today, at 4:30 PM, they will enjoy a coronation. Hundreds of people will gather for the ceremony in the plaza. It will be up to us to decide if they enjoy a second coronation."

"This is where we take our stand then – the Western Wall?" Chris asked and deduced at the same time.

"That's where I saw us," Elise continued to look at the map, while her mind's eye looked elsewhere. "It was sunny like it is now, even. And there were only the five of us. Five pieces to move for a checkmate. And that's how I plan to play. No society, no outside help or hindrance. Just us.

"We split into two groups. Chris and Lorenze are in the first group; Matthew, Francis, and I are in the second. The first group goes here," Elise pointed to another 'x,' this time outside the square that formed the Old City Wall. "This is a sniping position. Lorenze, you will set up what you need there. It is a tall building with large windows. The upper floor overlooks the Western Wall. You will have an easy visual of the coronation platform. You and Chris will be the last resort team. If you haven't heard from me that Chesed is dead before the crown hits Ze'ev's head, then you will shoot Ze'ev before he becomes king to ensure that Chesed has nothing to inherit."

"Shoot Ze'ev? Even though he's not the one?" Lorenze asked, as if for clarification. He regretted it as soon as he saw the motion with which Elise turned her head, slow and cold.

"Shoot Ze'ev. If I do not reach Chesed in time, Ze'ev's elimination will become necessary. Events cannot progress past the coronation. For after Ze'ev is king, he only needs to die to give Chesed the Israeli throne, and the Other will become a devastating, if not fatal factor in all of this. If Ze'ev becomes king, we will be forced into protecting Ze'ev from the Other even while we still need to destroy Chesed. And I don't think we can do both. Shoot Ze'ev," she drummed a hard finger onto the "x" on the map. "In the event that you have not heard of my success, you must make the only move left to us and kill him before he is crowned, leaving Chesed heir to nothing. As I said, you are the last resort team, and if we fail everywhere else, you must succeed. If you are too afraid to take such a shot, then speak now."

"I'm not afraid," Lorenze stuck out his chin. "I won't hesitate."

Elise returned to the map. "Now–"

"Wait," Chris interjected. "We're going to just go into some building and set up a sniper rifle? I've got to believe it isn't that easy. Otherwise, we can probably park ourselves right next to a few other terrorists. Maybe share a window."

"Valid point," Elise admitted even while sounding annoyed. "All of the buildings within firing range and viewing of the coronation are already evacuated and were searched early this morning. Military guards now stand at all entrances.

"However. At the building you will be in – 4799 T. Bab Al-Nazir – there is a guard named Ross. And at 2:06 PM, Ross will be left guarding the back entrance alone. The two other guards with him will leave to try and find a street vendor for some food. He'll only be alone for six minutes.

"But it's enough. Enough for Ross, who is an alcoholic, to decide he has just enough time to sneak a drink. But he can't do it right there, by the door on the street. Can't let anyone see him drinking on duty. So, he takes a quick walk over to the corner of the building and then just a few steps down a narrow alleyway. And while he fishes in his uniform for a small flask, Ross won't look back at the entrance he should be guarding for nearly twenty seconds. Which means, you will have twenty seconds to get inside with your equipment once Ross is around the corner and I pick the lock for you. After all of that, I can assure you that you will have the building quite to yourself.

"After Chris and Lorenze are safely inside 4799, team two – Matthew, myself, and Francis – will head to the Old City. We will enter the Western Wall plaza through the delegate's entrance at the underpass from the Tariq al-Wad. Matthew will act as a Cardinal of the formerly Catholic Society, the Hetaera Melchizedek. Francis will become a monk of the same order, and I will pose as a nun. Of course, we are coming to 'bless the new king,' and we will act the part as necessary. Once inside, there will be a stage that has been resurrected for the coronation. Behind the stage, against one corner of the wall, Ze'ev, his family, and the new Israeli ministers will be using one of the buildings that adjoin the wall. They will be waiting in rooms there just before the coronation."

"Yes, but…" Chris struggled to clear his throat as he found another flaw that could not go unnoted. "As delegates, we don't have access to these rooms. Being a delegate will only get us into the seating towards the front of the plaza."

Elise replied, "That's all right. I'll be close enough then to get us in the rest of the way. And that's when I'll strike; that's when I will find Chesed and end this. Just before sunset, which is 4:30 PM. Before Ze'ev takes the stage. It shouldn't be that hard to get through, since it really doesn't matter if we get back out."

Francis and Matthew exchanged looks across the table.

"Don't worry. You won't have to go with me at that point. I need you to provide me with first, a reasonable cover to get inside, and then second, an energy source should it come to that. Although, there will be people lined-up wall to wall inside. I should be just fine. Once everything starts to happen – and you'll know – you don't need to go with me. It would probably be better if you didn't."

"What about the Other?" Chris posed – the only obstacle not covered. "You said that you saw it there."

Her lips turned down, tight. "Yes. That's why we're splitting up. Two targets. It will come after me, which will leave you and Lorenze free to finish Ze'ev at the end."

Still nothing on how to beat it? Francis wrote and showed her.

"No," her eyes lowered. "The vision only showed me that it's waiting. There is nothing we can do to change that or prevent it, or prepare for it. It will come, and I'll just find a way."

Her confident tones receded into the quiet morning, the stifling closed room. She spoke with authority and ease, as matter-of-fact as if she were reading from a history book or a newspaper. And yet, the men shot frightened glances at each other. Confident tone or not, were they really going to follow a plan literally dreamed up without a shred of real evidence? Was there not to be a single protest?

Chris found Matthew's face, as did the others. It was easy to put the renegade on the spot; to encourage the one that already stood in bad standing and who asked the challenging questions as a regular course. But Matthew's eyes fell to the table and he buttoned his mouth firmly, moving his tongue inside as if chewing something large.

She rolled up the map, her plan unanimously accepted.

* * * * *

Elise smoothed the white fabric that draped her body. With her curves hidden by the thick material, she looked older. She surveyed herself with satisfaction. It was better that way. More believable. She slid on her mother's ring – one of her only belongings that made it from Ashton – and smiled. Her reflection did not look nervous. She wasn't. The vision paved a quick, perfect path to the stage now placed at the Western Wall.

Except the end.

Yes. Except the end. For some reason, that part – it wobbled unclear in her mind like murky water. She got there, and yet could see no further.

Elise had a feeling it was the part that no one had seen. The Western Wall – it was the part where free will had to write the rest; the part that was not determined; the part that had many endings depending on the souls of men. And whatever came, Elise was not afraid. No jitters, no need for commentator voices, the crutches of her human life. She was past them. She was ready.

Except, Elise self-consciously felt her chest. The pain flared up from the pressure, and yet she pressed. Alan's crucifix and Derek's Psalm plate were gone. Lost at Chesed's feet, still in that hospital – she didn't know. Only their welts were left.

"I wish you were here," she spoke to the spot under the cloth where the blisters were healing. "Thou hast put gladness in my heart." Elise licked her lips and repeated what she knew the plate read, "Thou hast put gladness in my heart."

Alan would be proud of her. Today, she would become everything he dreamed she was. Today, she would not let him down.

Derek Dewallace on the other hand (and just as important) would be able to see past what she was about to do today. Somewhere else in the world, far away from wells of souls and kings, he might be thinking about the place she tried to show him. Even today, with the awful task in front of her and the darkness of what was behind, he would still say that she brought him some gladness.

Like an outer heart, Elise thudded her flat palm against her chest so that the pain sharpened. She wanted to feel their heaviness; their words and beliefs against her skin.

* * * * *

Chris didn't understand. Why wouldn't she want him there, with her? Why did she pair him with Lorenze? He wouldn't even be able to help Lorenze! When was the last time he fired a gun? Hunting with his dad almost thirty years ago?

I would protect her better, Chris thought. *I could do whatever she needed. I would die to see her safe.* He realized it was true as he thought it, and felt empty.

Or get in her way more because you care so much.

Was that it? Was that why she didn't want him there?

Was it because he rejected her?

Chris rubbed his hands on his arms as if to warm himself, and he knew it was the bitter cool loneliness of days to come. *It's the way it is. Stop thinking about it. You'll have to let her go.* But mostly inside, he just wanted to take her with him somewhere far away. Inside, he needed to protect her in order to protect himself from the pain of losing her. He felt he might cry, and so closed his eyes.

I made the right choice. This is who I am. Father Chris Mognahan. The decision was still true. But harder every minute.

* * * * *

That should do it. Francis patted the whiteboard where he secured it under his arm. He twisted suddenly, but it remained in place. He had a feeling he wouldn't be untying it for much. Talking was over. It was time for doing.

He took another look at his black robes, picking off a piece of lint. They were not his ceremonial robes, which he would've preferred. But he made them as nice as he could, laying the hood perfectly across his shoulder blades. He wanted it to look as authentic as possible.

Ready, Francis turned and sat on the bed, still keeping the majority of his weight on his toes. In the room next to him, he heard Elise getting ready.

It's too bad. He liked her. For all her passion; her anger and then sudden softness; her diligence and surprising faith; the wounds she carried and fought. She was a good leader. Even with youth and accompanying selfishness against her, Francis was confident she would get them where they needed to go. *She would die for it.* He saw it in her face when she was going over the map.

But she's not a person. Don't forget that. She's not really Elise.

Remiel...

Still – I saw it in her face. She goes even though she believes she will die.

She believed it, and because she believed it, Francis began to.

* * * * *

Lorenze strapped his uniform on, knowing where every clasp and buckle fell exactly. Still, something about it felt foreign: he had not worn it in several days. Several very, very long days.

The red, blue and yellow stripes that Michelangelo designed for the guard centuries earlier: many men fell under those colors. He knew their names by heart. And he promised to join them if called to.

Now, Remiel called him.

Shoot Ze'ev? Even though he's not the one? Lorenze closed his eyes in shame at the words. He shouldn't have questioned her. God often asked things of people that they felt they could not do. And he wanted Remiel to go knowing that his faith was strong; that his pledge was strong. Instead, he reminded her that he was weak and young.

Finish dressing. Being slow will make her doubt you more!

398

As if prompted by a violent threat, Lorenze propelled himself to the other side of the room where the society had left a small stockpile of weapons. He pulled out the sniper's rifle case and its box of bullets. With hard clicks, he opened the case to see that all was in order. The parts gleamed and winked at him in the light like so many eyes.

More gently, Lorenze lifted the sight from the case. It was heavy to his hand. He put it to his eye and some miniscule scratch in the floor became like a canyon.

Thou shalt not kill. Lorenze smirked and put the sight down. *Thou shalt not kill unless God asks you to. Thou shalt not kill unless God needs you to.*

Lorenze closed the case. He surveyed the room, looked again at his uniform. He only had a few minutes left. He knelt to pray.

But what was there to pray for? Should he pray for their lives, for their safety? Could he ask that God grant them success on a murder mission? Should he pray for time or protection, or just for the world not to die?

In the end, with his last few minutes, Lorenze prayed for the soul of another assassin. One who also betrayed innocence for the greater good. Remiel had, after all, been right – they were in common with a certain other fallen disciple. And so, with his eyes squeezed shut, Lorenze prayed for mercy for Judas Iscariot. For if Judas – that tool of fate led to betray history's most innocent man – was able to find God's forgiveness, perhaps so might he.

* * * * *

Matthew looked in the dingy mirror. It was not tall enough to take in the miter he placed on his head. He sighed, wondering if it were on straight.

Not that it really matters.

Except it was the one way he could be useful now. Ceremony was the thing he was good at, and if Elise needed to get into the delegate's area by the Western Wall, then he was the cardinal to get her there.

Useful, but not courageous, his mind quipped back. Of the five, he was the fifth wheel, and he knew it. He did not have Francis' gift of signs; he could not fight like Lorenze; he had not been there from the beginning like Chris; and of course, he was not an angelic warrior sent from heaven.

Elise did not like him – Matthew was conscious of it. It bothered him in an impersonal, worrisome way – in the same way being disliked by a boss might bother someone. There were many who did not like him, who did not think that a priest should have so much ambition; who believed that power was not a part of the Church; who claimed there was no hierarchy in salvation. He could accept that she didn't like him.

But he would not accept failing for her. If bureaucratic power was his usefulness, then this was the moment. The moment to justify and forgive all others.

Matthew took his silver shepherd's staff and gave it a final polish.

* * * * *

Chris and Elise were the first to come down the stairs. They remained in the living room, neither speaking. Elise pried open a blind with her fingers, and a shoot of sunlight came through, lighting up her eyes and hair.

When she let the blind drop and turned back into the room, Chris was staring at her. "What?"

"You just – you look like the statue. The white robes, your hair back behind you, your arms out in front. It's almost identical to the first time I saw you – twenty years ago." He let out a sigh in disbelieving remembrance. "Like this is the moment the 12th century sculptor chose to preserve."

"It's just the robes," she replied. Her eyes dropped to the floor, and she put her hands behind her back to ruin the resemblance.

"Everyone ready?" Elise did a half-hearted pulse check once the other three men joined them in the living room. The person who didn't answer yes would not be going. But she was saved the elimination. All heads nodded.

"Lorenze. All the back-up packed?"

"I have everything we'll need," he patted the bag slung over his shoulder.

Everything in place, Elise now chose the words the room waited for her to say. "We should probably get started. I know the best way into the city, but we'll have to walk quite a ways. In only three hours, Ross will be taking his drink." She turned to one of the society members – Thomas if she remembered right. "Can we get a ride?"

Just like that. As if they were a group of teenagers headed to the mall.

* * * * *

The military was everywhere: by every corner they passed, in every vehicle they crossed. The sun glittered off their weapons and sunglasses. Soldiers surveyed the streams of people heading towards the Western Wall with the coolness of statues.

And here they were, riding in an SUV with tinted windows and a bag of weapons unhidden in the trunk. Chris wiped the sweat from his brow just before it hit his eyes.

But Elise told them to put the bag back there. Right in the back where it would be easily seen. *So the guard won't have to move it to unzip it* – wasn't that what she said? And then, without another word, she carried out reams

400

and reams of white fabric – like the robes she now wore – and at least a dozen cross necklaces. She stuffed them into the bag with the weapons, careful so that the cloth and crosses covered any glimmer of dark metal or muzzle. *Thank the nuns at the Vatican*, she said before closing the hatch.

Some sweat made its way into Chris' eye this time.

The skeptic inside him was screaming. They were insane-unprepared-stupid, and they were never going to make it. Not even into the city; not within a mile of the coronation.

The only thing that kept him facing forward, seat buckled, and quiet was Elise. She sat in the front with the driver, picking occasionally at one of her cuticles. Every few minutes, she would look out the window with her eyes softened, and he got the feeling that she wanted to roll down the window and let some of the sunlight in. He never saw her so calm. She smiled occasionally, as if some invisible seventh passenger whispered something pleasing to her while they crept through the traffic that threatened to standstill.

* * * * *

They reached the first checkpoint a little after 1:00 PM. Close by, Ze'ev was entering the Dome of the Rock for prayer.

"Everyone relax," Elise spoke as the car came to a stop in front of the stationed soldiers. "Matthew, you will speak in Hebrew. Provide the soldier with our delegate papers, and give each person's name in the car. He will ask us for our passports, and we will give them to him. When he asks to look in the trunk, nod your head and tell him there are materials to bless the new king. Thomas here will pop the hatch for him."

Matthew replied in a shaky voice, "I'm not sure how that's going to work considering what we really have in the trunk…"

"Shhh…." Elise barely let the quieting sound pass her lips.

Matthew looked around at the other four men he sat with, then swallowed, unbuckled and leaned forward. His miter scraped the ceiling of the car and threatened to fall off his head. Thomas hit the window button, and sunlight flooded in the dark car to the sound of mechanical whirring. An Israeli soldier peered inside.

With a similar shakiness to the opening lines spoken in a play just as the curtain rises, Matthew spoke his first line. His face cracked into a smile as he continued, and slowly his hands found the confidence to gesture. He handed over the delegate papers and began introducing everyone in the car. When the guard asked for identification, the passports were at hand. Matthew continued on for some time before (it was apparent by the sudden hitch in his voice) he was asked about the trunk. The Cardinal shook his head emphatically, and his miter fell into Chris' lap. Turning a cooked salmon shade of pink, the Cardinal spoke the final two lines of his act and nodded. Thomas popped the hatch, and the guard walked around.

"Shhhh…" Elise repeated, though no one spoke. "He'll open the bag wide, touch the white fabrics, pull out a Franciscan nun's necklace, and then zip it up with a pat."

The six passengers sat still, some of them daring glances into the back where the soldier now rummaged. Chris' pulse found an outlet in his forearm where it spasmed.

More rummaging. Then, a darting light moved around the vehicle cabin – the Franciscan cross in the soldier's hand glared the sunlight inside, finally resting on Elise's cheek. A second more, then a zipper squealed. There was a slight pat of a hand on canvas. The hatch closed.

Elise smiled and raised an eyebrow, as if to say *Am I good or what?*

The soldier returned to the window for a few parting words before allowing the SUV to rumble through.

Matthew sat back, visibly astonished and whitened. "He said that we can go up a few more streets. But after that point, no vehicles are allowed. The streets are serving as parking lots, so just leave the car where we can. We will be searched before entering the Old City Wall, of course, and he mentioned that they might make us leave the bag, even though it's 'just a few crosses,' and I quote."

Elise laughed low in the front.

"I can't do this," Chris spoke with a dry tongue while he massaged his forearm. "I'm going to have a heart attack. I'm serious."

"How much more?" Lorenze asked with enough worry in his voice to let everyone know he seconded Chris' opinion.

Elise stopped laughing and turned in her seat. "No more. We're going to park like the soldier said, and then find our way to 4799 T. Bab Al-Nazir – drum roll please – without running into a single soldier on the way."

Matthew was the one to ask. "Is that possible?"

Turning back to face the front, Elise replied, "Sure. It's possible. You'll all just have to listen very carefully."

* * * * *

"Here?" Thomas asked while beginning to turn the wheel.

Elise verified, "Yes, that's the spot." She again indicated a double-parking job on an empty side street. "Just pull in and kill the engine. Then, everyone duck down."

It took a moment for the words to sink in.

"Duck down?" Chris asked.

"A patrol is coming by, and unless we want another search, we should duck."

They looked at each other a moment and then the seatbelts began clicking as everyone unbuckled. In an adult game of musical chairs, they vied for the best hiding spots while Thomas did some last maneuvering.

Elise began to open her door. "Come on, Thomas. In back with me."

Chris, Lorenze, Francis, and Matthew lay as far under the seats as possible while the remaining two ran to the rear. The hatch popped again and then closed. The car swayed with the movement of the two bodies in back and then became still.

Though it couldn't possibly give them away, Chris resisted breathing. Each time the need for oxygen came, he gave in reluctantly. He stared at the ceiling, unable to look elsewhere. Beneath his weight, Lorenze's foot flexed, as though trying to escape.

Behind them, Elise's heart beat slow and calm. *Right about now... right about –* the patrol would be walking down the street towards them. They would be looking serious, though each of them was thinking their own thoughts (and not about security). The traffic was slowing down as the coronation neared, and the majority of people trying to get into the ceremony were already inside the Old City. Their guard was dropping.

But even without that, Elise felt confidant. She had already seen all of it – down to the positions each of the five men would choose to hide in. She herself lay with her head in the crook of her arm – just like in vision – incase the little details mattered. *They'll walk by... a few more seconds. One will turn his head to look in the driver's door. He'll hear the tick of the engine and think that we must've stopped recently. He'll pause and look again, and then keep going.*

They waited. There were no sounds, no movement. It was uncanny: a street without the sound of a car.

Finally, the back of the SUV shifted as Elise moved. "It's clear," she said quietly, her eyes piercing out the tinted windows. "But it won't be clear for long. Everyone should move silently – model yourselves after Francis – and get out of the car. Lorenze will get the bag. Thomas – you take off now. We won't need the car anymore."

Out into the sun – it blazed white like a hot summer day, though the air was cool. The street was over a thousand years old, and its several storied buildings rose in faded, sand-colored stone. Above them, strung between buildings, hung colorful streamers in blazing reds, greens, oranges, yellows and blues, with Jewish stars scattered throughout. Welcome to the new king.

"This way," Elise moved down the street without looking to see if they followed.

"Well, thank you," Matthew muttered to Thomas, who now stood dazed by the driver's door. The Cardinal began to extend a hand when he realized he was already being left behind. Holding his miter, he hastened suddenly and jogged to become the end of the duck-line that formed behind the girl in white.

* * * * *

Such a line was oddly appropriate, as Elise darted in movements that resembled a bird's. She marched and then stopped, marched and then stopped. Each cycle, the men halted behind her, peering around one another or perhaps crowding around Lorenze to hide him and his bag from a possible patrol. Always, it was the same – no one. Still, Elise scoured their surroundings, even sniffing the air as though that too could give something away. These pauses often lasted several adrenaline-laced seconds before she marched again, sometimes in a new direction, sometimes not.

It was getting late. 1:45 PM. Ross was probably getting thirsty.

* * * * *

Two minutes before 2:00 PM, Elise paused by a street sign: T. Bab Al-Nazir.

It was a main street with three and four story buildings crowding in on it. They were old and the color of bone, parts of them crumbling away and lying in the alleys. Surreal, the cars lined all parts of the street.

Elise pointed generally. "That's the building. But we can't go that way. We'll be seen. Around the back and then through the alley."

Elise marched again, leaving the men to scurry after, Lorenze shifting the bag from shoulder to shoulder, Matthew hanging on to his miter, Francis twirling unconsciously the tie to his robes, and Chris as close to Elise's shadow as he could get. They ducked into a narrow passage between two buildings just as several church bells began to knell. They each only struck two times.

Elise paused then to look behind her. "Hurry," was the only word she spoke. For the first time that day, her voice controlled a nervous tremor. "We'll come out at the end of the alley and head immediately for the doors. Move quick, but quiet." She licked her lips and then leaned against the left building (it was dry and left a gritty residue on her hands), moving along it like a scared cat. The men quickly fell in line and did the same.

Several feet back from reentering the street, she stopped. Elise put her finger across her lips and then faced the sunny avenue: a sliver viewed through the parked cars. A bird overhead called, and appeared briefly in the blue sky over their heads.

Elise dug her fingernails into the wall behind her. She had heard that sound before – yesterday. The sound meant it was time. The show was started. She jerked her shoulder to let the men know they should be ready. It would only be seconds.

On schedule, two soldiers flashed across the alley mouth. Ross's companions: on their lunch break.

The group waited, listening to the footfalls become vague thuds and finally nothing. Elise whispered, "Wait...wait...just a little more – NOW!"

Without hesitation, Elise burst silently into the street.

Ross had his back to them, one of his hands busy searching his uniform as he turned into the next alley down. As soon as he rounded the corner, she motioned for Chris and Lorenze and pointed to a door. A red, double door: 4799 T. Bab Al-Nazir.

The men stood dumb for a moment, looking at her.

Elise pursed her lips and jerked her whole body toward the building, as if she meant to fly at it, or perhaps at them. It was clear enough, and they ran. The large bag bumped against Lorenze's side loudly.

And Elise extended her hand to the Cardinal.

It took him a moment, but Matthew quickly realized what she asked. Solidly, he placed his hand in hers, wincing even as he did so.

Elise let the Cardinal rush in on her. Fast, she stole, opening the floodgates between them. The light began to get brighter as everything else inside her became strong. Higher, whispering – a thought from Matthew zapped to her. Something about feeling drunk. She felt his weight shift as he began to drop, and she released him.

Without hesitating even enough to see if Matthew was all right, Elise turned back to the door, simultaneously sending Remiel out from her. The angel moved fast, coming up quickly on Chris and Lorenze. She passed through them, and Chris looked back to where the real Elise stood glazed in the street as if he felt her brush him.

Angel hands hit the red door and maneuvered for the keyhole, felt it, moved inside it. They fluttered for the tumblers, sliding them together to find how they matched. A few more and–

The insides wrenched suddenly, locking together. Elise pulled back. *What is–*

It was Chris. He was trying to open the door, not realizing she had not yet worked the lock.

NO! Give me another second!

Elise pushed more of herself out. Renewed energy found the lock and again began manipulating the insides–

A second time, the tumblers jarred together.

Lorenze was trying the door this time. He and Chris looked back anxiously, ironically. The twenty seconds were at least half over. Their faces read: *What are you waiting for?*

LET GO OF THE DAMN DOOR!

Elise pushed out a third time. And with seven seconds left, she was taking no more chances. The fingers of her mind slammed into the backs of Chris and Lorenze. Each felt himself flung to the side away from the door.

Chris caught himself on the wall.

But Lorenze teetered on the edge of the doorstep. A quarter of a second and he lost, the weight of the bag pulling him over. He hit the sidewalk with a loud smack, the rifles in the bag clanking together like an out-of-tune bell chorus.

On the side of the building, Ross's head jerked up to the sound, and his fingers flew to hide the flask. With five seconds still to go, they were out of time.

GOD! WE'RE NOT GOING TO MAKE IT!

Desperate, Remiel worked the lock while Elise broke into a run down the street. *DO SOMETHING! NOW!*

She passed the red door and the panicked spot where Chris was trying to help Lorenze back to his feet; racing to the alleyway where Ross was no doubt returning.

Click. The lock opened.

Ross turned the corner.

And Elise drew Remiel back inside and channeled her to her legs.

At a speed considerably faster than what she could run on her own, Elise collided with the soldier. Together, they reeled backwards. His sunglasses flew off and there was a crunching sound as he put his hand down on them, breaking his fall with a yell of pain. Elise landed on him, her body falling between his legs and her head thudding against the flask that lie next to his ribs. "Sorry! I'm so sorry!" she began.

Groaning, Ross brought a hand back to his neck and winced. "Damn it! What are you – why are you going so fast?" His voice was angry, but not angry enough. Not angry enough to have seen two men sneak into the building behind her. "You better have papers. Don't move – except get off me! Are you hurt?" even less angry.

"Fine. Sorry," Elise began to collect herself, drawing up onto her knees. "It's just getting late, and I'm a delegate at the coronation. I didn't know we would have to walk so far. And I'm not sure if I'm lost or…" she kept going, rattling off anything.

Please let them be inside already. Inside and safe…

"Yeah, well it won't even start for another two hours."

Rubbing injuries, they both stood. Ross took in her strange robes, now dirtied on one side, the slight frame, the small hands. He relaxed, though something about her (the nervous pinching around her mouth, her weird, flickering eyes, which refused to look at him) woke his suspicions. "Where are your papers?" The voice he used was hard.

"Right here. I'm carrying them for her!" It was Matthew, making his way over to her in a hobbling effort, with Francis at his elbow.

Around the approaching pair, Elise could see that the street was empty. Lorenze and Chris were nowhere to be seen. From the calm way Matthew and Francis walked, she knew they were inside, behind the red doors. Elise let out her nervous breath. "Yes. The three of us – we're together."

Matthew pulled out the papers from his robes (he was white and obviously drained, leaning heavily on Francis and his shepherd's crook) and provided them to Ross, who studied them at length.

He frowned and returned them. "Follow this road a little further and you'll see one of the entrances to the Western Wall. You'll know by the guards."

"Thank you," they each murmured, and Francis nodded his head. Elise grabbed Matthew's other elbow to help steer him along in the commanded direction. They turned their backs to the soldier, liars' faces melting like wax to show the panic beneath.

Ross waited with his arms folded until the group seemed a safe distance. With a sigh, he felt for his flask, and then bent to take a look at his shattered sunglasses. He squinted to see all the pieces in the sunlight.

Something else – shinier – glimmered. "Hey! You dropped something." He called out again before Elise realized he was speaking to her.

"I dropped something?" she echoed, already feeling nervous.

He crouched and pulled something silver from the sunglass shards. "Here."

Elise untangled herself from Matthew and retreated back to 4799 T. Bab Al-Nazir. Ross extended her…she gasped. *Impossible. How could he?* Goose bumps erupted across her skin while the hair on her scalp stood straight enough to ache.

A chain dangled from Ross's fingers. On it hung a crucifix and a Psalm plate. Even in the bright sunlight, with all the metal reflection, Elise saw that it read, "Thou hast put gladness in my heart," *Psalms* 4:7.

When she only stared, Ross asked, "Isn't it yours?"

Elise raised her eyes from the metal to his face. What trick was this? It was impossible, even as it happened. How could he have the necklace she lost yesterday in a cemetery miles away? Who was he really?

He's speaking English, she realized. *As if he knows us, knew it would be me…*

Ross's eyes remained unflinching and without emotion, a muddy color reminiscent of the ground after a fresh rain. His face was just shaved – some of the skin beneath his chin was red, still agitated from the razor. He was balding.

There was no gold; no light. Just the smell of alcohol on his breath. And yet, she was certain he was somehow planted, apart of this. God was tipping the scales somehow.

Elise took the necklace from him, nodding her thanks and continuing to watch him carefully. She paused in the street a moment, securing the clasp around her neck.

* * * * *

Above, Chris and Lorenze observed anxious. They were on the fifth floor in someone's living room, watching out a gauzily curtained window. It was odd, like being behind the scenes of a play while the actors are gone. Yesterday's newspaper sat unfolded on the coffee table, waiting to be read. A toy lie near the television, possibly kicked or dropped in the hurry to leave. There seemed ghosts everywhere.

"Do you think he's stopping them?" Lorenze asked for the third time.

"I still can't tell. Elise isn't arguing with him, I don't think. They seem to be looking at something in his hand."

Lorenze rose up on tiptoes to see better without getting any closer to the glass. "Now what?"

"Looks like a staring contest – I don't know!"

"There. She's leaving." Lorenze let air out gently, as if he'd been holding his breath.

They watched Elise walk across the street to rejoin Matthew and Lorenze. She had her hand over her heart. The group moved away, falling into the shadow of another building. Together, they drifted and faded from the two men's vision.

Chris felt hollow, like he'd already thrown-up. She was gone from him again.

"Do you want to get set up?" Lorenze suggested gently.

Chris jumped, despite the quiet tone. "Of course – we need to be ready. And you should probably show me how to work the thing. Just in case."

He glanced out the window again to avoid the ominous sound of his own words. Just as Elise said, they had a great view of the Western wall, and a small platform to its right side – only 500 feet away. It was empty now.

Lorenze unzipped the bag at their feet. He pulled out the crucifixes and white robes until he uncovered the Steyr Mannlicher Tactical Elite sniper rifle case.

* * * * *

408

Matthew was moving slow. Horrifyingly, it reminded Elise of the night Alan died – trying to carry him through the snow with Chris. Matthew kept himself up slightly better than the priest had, but not much.

The Other. At least there's no sign of it.

Its no-show didn't surprise her. In the vision, she saw herself alone with it. And it was dark. Still, Elise could not shake the memory. *Carrying Alan. Carrying Matthew.*

"I have to rest. I'm sorry but–" Matthew halted his words to catch his breath.

Elise and Francis obliged, standing still while Matthew tried to transfer as much weight from his legs to their shoulders as he could.

"It's your fault," he finally muttered. "Did you need to take that much from me?"

Frowning, "I took what I had to. Chris and Lorenze have the best view in the whole city, don't they?"

He happily conceded. "Yes, they do. Team one is in position."

"And we have to get to ours," she looked around his miter at Francis. "I have to get there before the coronation. While Ze'ev and Chesed are in the back rooms."

Matthew rallied and stood with their help. "How much further?"

Elise cocked her head and looked forward. "Not far."

* * * * *

They stopped again after another hundred feet. The Cardinal leaned over, forcing Elise and Francis to do the same. Frustration and anger brought back some color to his cheeks. This was not how he wanted to finish it; not what he was best at doing. But–

"You'll have to leave me," he said simply.

Francis and Elise looked at each other again around Matthew's miter – like they were parents deciding some punishment. Neither moved.

"What? You didn't see this part?" he half-joked.

But Elise startled. *No.* She hadn't seen this part; not leaving him. Fear condensed on the outskirts of her mind, like water droplets gathering around a small leak. *I didn't see this; not everything.*

Before the Cardinal made the suggestion a second time, Elise removed her shoulder. Still supporting Matthew with a tight handgrip, she stood straight. "I'm sorry."

"Just put me down there," Matthew indicated a curb. Once sprawled out and resting, he began digging in his robes. "Take your papers now. Go on."

Elise shivered and shifted her weight, as though she were still deciding.

She was leaving one behind...again. Just like before.

But the Other comes for me. It was dark. I was alone.

Was I alone because no one else was left? I DON'T KNOW THIS PART!

Francis wiped his hands on his robes and stepped a few feet back, detaching himself. He looked at Elise. Time to go. *One way or the other.*

Elise cleared her throat. "Believe it or not, it's been good knowing you, Matthew. I wish this wasn't it."

Matthew squinted up at her. Sarcasm and jest always suited him better than apologies. "Yes, well I'm sure there will be moments in the next few hours when you will need someone to lash out at. You'll have to see how tough the monk is now."

Elise smiled. "I'll put in a good word for you with God."

"Then my energy was well spent. Go."

They left – two instead of three.

* * * * *

Elise fidgeted as the near-empty streets began to crowd. By the time she and Francis reached the entrance to the underpass from Tariq al-Wad, it was as backed-up as a two-lane tollbooth for a six-lane highway at rush hour. People pressed in one upon the other. The end of the line wasn't close enough to see the security check point.

Elise pulled out her papers, considerably wadded and wrinkled from being against her hot skin. "I don't suppose that Matthew managed to get us VIP passes...nope."

With renewed alarm, she stood on her tiptoes. Up ahead, the mass parted into countless lines to pass through metal detector arches, hand-checks, and who knew what else. It reminded her of the Raleigh airport the Sunday after Thanksgiving.

Francis looked at her, awaiting her diagnosis.

Her frustration came out in clipped words. "Don't look at me – pray the line moves fast! We're too far away from Chesed for me to work some magic – if I start now, we won't make it all the way. We wait in line with the rest of the mortals."

* * * * *

They reached the checkpoint just after 3:30 PM. The window had closed to sixty minutes.

By that time, Elise didn't need anyone else's energy; she was practically dancing with her own. The sunlight was already getting orange as it began the last leg of its descent to the horizon. The shadows were longer. The darkness was coming.

Francis looked over at her periodically, deciding each time from her expression whether to smile, frown, or just turn away.

At last, a soldier motioned them forward and the interrogation began. They passed and were eventually allowed through to an underpass – a brief arch of darkness that took them beneath the Old City Wall. They herded with the others, footsteps echoing off the stone like a low round of applause. Francis remarked to himself that it looked like a Halloween party – so many flashy, ceremonial outfits.

* * * * *

They emerged at the Western Wall plaza.

And this part, at least, was just as Elise saw it. Closely fit rows of large stone rose many stories from the platform, with out-of-place greenery growing from crevices. The largest rocks formed the first few levels, seceding to gradually smaller stone at the top, as if the builders became lazy. All were different shades of white: ivory, beige, cream.

Against the white, people of all shades themselves – both dress and skin – stood out in contrast. Delegates pushed and moved against one another on their way to their seats with their hands up by their chests protectively, like human bumper-cars. Languages droned like insect humming. And soldiers stood everywhere, raised on small platforms so that they could see over the crowd. Though the wall was normally divided by sex – women praying in one area and men in another – it appeared that tradition was abandoned for the day. Men and women mingled freely, ready to greet their king.

By the wall, the stage was set. It looked like it had always been there – made of white stone just like the Western Wall. Many lavish chairs were set on it– all velvets and dark wood trimming – as if there were several kings planning to sit before the people. *Who are they for...* Elise tried to remember. *Rabbis*, she was almost certain.

But not quite.

Elise clenched her fists beneath the long white sleeves. They had arrived at the end – *You know the end? No.*

Beginning with Matthew, the vision had deteriorated to fuzzy, like a dream fading away in the first waking blinks. Beyond a few flashes from scenes she did not understand (*the dark*), the reveal was over. Standing before the Western Wall was about where God left her on her own.

Francis nudged her gently, obviously waiting for her guidance. He didn't know that she had little else to give. She wasn't about to tell him.

Elise signaled with her eyes, and Francis followed the look. "See the building just at the corner of the wall," she acknowledged the crumbling structure to the right of the wall with large, dark windows. "Inside, Chesed and her father are refreshing themselves with food and drink, waiting for sundown with several rabbis and the newly appointed ministers. That's where I need to be. In less than 45 minutes."

Francis shrugged, *How will we get close enough?*

Elise's face crumpled as her features came in close to think. She opened her mouth, meaning to give direction. She breathed. Francis cocked his head at her, his eyes narrowing. Was this indecision? Francis waited. Waited for the fearless answer, the positive choice. But Elise remained rigid, her eyes darting over everything.

She doesn't know, his mind whispered. *She doesn't know how to get there.*

Francis reached under his arm where the whiteboard remained tied tightly. He loosened the string, then held it in his hands a few moments. Pulling the cap off with his teeth, he began to write. *What about the tunnels?*

Elise read the words, and goose bumps again began to form underneath the wool cloth. *Tunnels? It was somewhere dark. There was stone. Shadows – long shadows. And I was alone with it.* "The tunnels," Elise repeated, trying to sound like she knew what Francis was talking about.

Francis erased the question mark and inserted a dash. *– the one with the entrance on the outskirts of the plaza. Called Wilson's Arch. Runs underground and opens again at front of men's prayer area. Comes-up almost underneath the stage. Close enough.*

Elise nodded like she knew while her mind ran through it. *A tunnel.* That had to be it. The dark, the shadows – it was a tunnel. And in the vision, the Other waited there.

Did I have the vision so that I would know to avoid it, or because that's where I am supposed to go? Unconsciously, Elise clasped her hands and began rubbing her fingers together.

Francis watched every flicker of her eyebrows, each contraction of her face muscles. *She really doesn't know what to do. We're flying blind.*

God. Which is it? Is it the way in? Or is it the way to ruin? I don't know… I don't know… I saw it. But I was alone. Does that mean –something happens to Francis in the tunnel? GOD!

It doesn't matter if he dies. Everyone is expendable for this! You've less than an hour! DECIDE!

If the Other is down there, guarding, then that must be the way.

Francis watched as Elise shook her head, like she was agreeing with someone. He raised his eyebrows.

Elise reached for the necklace inside her robes. She held the Psalm plate and cross tightly. They were cool. "Where is the tunnel?"

412

Francis looked to his left. Using the sweat from his palm to erase his previous words, he wrote over the blue smear, *I'm sure it's guarded.*

Elise shrugged, resetting her face. "Show me."

Francis did as he was told, but remained unconvinced by the hard tone. Forty-five minutes left, and by God, he was leading Remiel!

Halfway there, and Elise began making herself more useful. With hands open as wide as her fingers allowed, she began a rhythmic touching – right then left – of all those within her arm's reach. Little pieces – so small they barely noticed; whispers trailed behind her like gossip. Over and over, it began to grow. She knew by Francis' hunched shoulders that he could feel her behind him.

They made it all the way to the ropes before they were approached. A woman came quickly, her chin out and her eyes angry (she had been removing people from the area for hours). She yelled at them in Hebrew, her tone communicating enough.

Elise shot her mind out. Like a taught string, she forced her psyche between the woman's knees. The woman tripped and fell into several other delegates.

But Elise paid no attention. She was looking at the great black mouth beyond the rope. Francis did not have to tell her – this was Wilson's Arch. And the three guards that would try to keep her from it. There was no point in waiting for confrontation. With the plan barely decided in her mind, Elise pushed Remiel out. She picked the guard to the left. *Tighter... harder...*she balled the energy into something that resembled a fist. Like a slingshot, she pulled it back, and then shot it forward – into the soldier's larynx.

The coughing was instant – a horrible full sound, like something lodged in his throat. With each cough, his tongue stuck out further, his body trying to clear the airway. He put his hands frantically up to his neck like he meant to tunnel into his windpipe.

The two other soldiers gathered around, their faces suddenly drawn tight and alert. They spoke in Hebrew – loud yells – and their hands left their guns, leaving the weapons to sway around their necks. Still the soldier coughed.

Elise nudged Francis in the back. *MOVE!*

The monk jerked forward, and Elise said a quick prayer of thanks for his sudden, surprising agility. Under the rope with fleeting footsteps towards the entrance and the choking guard. Only seconds, and Francis disappeared beyond where the daylight flooded the entrance. The guards paid no attention.

But a watching delegate called out the treachery from behind the rope, pointing violently to the spot Francis last stood. Remiel was sent back with a

413

glance from Elise and the voice cut-off. Elise moved to follow Francis, leaving her fading Remiel to stand guard over the soldiers. If one even turned their head…

As luck (or God) would have it, they never did. As if they were never there at all, Francis and Elise disappeared into the darkness, mere shadows.

Among shadows. Elise stopped just inside the archway. Though her eyes were not yet adjusted, Elise knew what she entered, what her mind had been warning silent but steady since Francis' suggestion.

The path they chose was a prison of rock and dirt, where no life lived.

She could tell by the damp smell, like a gravestone; the cool air, like a chill fall wind. She did not have to travel another foot to know there was nothing for her here; here, she was just Elise. A dim yellow light illuminated a narrow, twisted stairway.

Almost definitely, the Other waited somewhere, expecting an angel.

But for now, only Francis appeared at the first turn in the stair, black against the dim yellow. He gestured for her to follow.

Still she hesitated, searching with her eyes and mind. *Down here, there is only Francis. And if I use Francis, I'll kill him – is that why I end-up alone? Do I kill him?*

Francis gestured again. He could not read her expression – only her white-light eyes shown in the dark. Coupled with the outline of her frozen frame, it was like watching a caged animal. She sensed…something. She recognized this.

Can you beat it yourself? Can you even get passed it?

Forty minutes.

Francis shrugged at her. *What's the matter?* He pointed to his eyes and then shrugged again. *Was this in your vision?*

"Some of it," she whispered. "Enough to know we should be careful." Elise took her first step down. "Stay close to me, Francis." Her two beams of light shown out, flickering often with the movements of her eyes and face as she searched for something.

"This leads just below the rooms where Chesed and Ze'ev wait?"

Francis confirmed with a nod.

Elise slid down further, entering into some of the yellow light. "Quickly."

Francis led the way down the stairs and into the tunnel.

Or more like a cavern. The vaulted chambers rose several stories high beneath the surface of the earth. Huge, dry stone reflected in the yellow light provided by modern light bulbs. They tread on years and years of dust through the foundation of Christianity – a literal network of rock and beam that held the ancient temple roadway where Jesus Christ himself had walked.

"Are you sure you know the way through here?"

Francis looked back at Elise. Hadn't she just said the tunnel was in her vision?

Elise rounded on him, her voice rising. "Do you know the way?'

Yes.

"How do you know it?"

The way is marked.

"Marked?" Elise scanned the plain, almost bleached walls.

Marks that I see.

Her still yellow eyes slid to his face, so she could see him without turning her head. "You see the way? Are you sure?"

Unspoken accusations flowed between them. *As sure as you were about Ze'ev?*

Francis answered back with words that he scratched hard on the white surface. *As sure as I was when I first saw you.*

A great rumbling rose, like thunder. The crowd over their heads was moving to stand in anticipation. Perhaps the opening remarks were beginning. Soon, the sun would lower below the wall.

* * * * *

Passageways gave way to more passageways. From one yellow circle of light to another, the differences were barely noticeable. The two intruders remained alone and undisturbed, almost silent. Winding their way through paths that carried people for more than two millennia

And Elise – her heart was beating a steady 160. Like she was running, even though she wasn't. Each step brought them closer to the exit, but further from the way in. More trapped; less trapped; Elise could not tell. The catch 22 was its own form of claustrophobia – she sucked in the old air trapped beneath the ground with them.

It is down here. I know it. Waiting for me in a place where I can't do anything to protect myself. Where I'm as helpless as Jeff or Alan. She swallowed hard, pushing down the last memories she had of the two.

It's almost over. I'm close to her. I just have to make it a little bit farther.

In the dark, in the shadows…

Just a little farther… she would be back in the crowd, like a diver emerging from the water. Above the surface. Where she could take anything, be anything.

God, please protect us.

The power of prayer. Like closing your eyes and believing the man in your closet will just disappear.

Protect us in the dark…in the shadows–

415

Francis stopped.

Not naturally. More like he was caught at something.

Elise froze behind him, her foot still poised on its toe, ready to take the next step. Only her eyes moved over the cavern – stone and light, *light and stone...*

And then she heard it: a soft rolling sound. Behind her.

It was the sound of a pencil when it has been carelessly dropped. In the library stacks perhaps. Or when a football player violently pushes a girl and empties her bag onto a sidewalk.

And Elise understood. It was the sound of the two most helpless-feeling times in her life now linked to the third: this moment.

The rolling sound continued, neither coming closer, nor fading. It served as a spell, keeping them quiet and still; shivering but unmoving. Elise heard a new sound: a rattling. It was her teeth, knocking against each other.

Oh, God. Is it now?

Like closing your eyes and believing the man in your closet will just disappear.

Turn around! Turn and face it! God! It could be right there. It could be breathing on me. FACE IT!

As if she gave the command to him somehow, Francis turned only those muscles above his shoulders. His neck and head arched backwards; then finally the one, dilated eye she could see rolled to her.

She focused on it, focused on it, focused on it until it became blurry. She allowed her breath to cramp in her lungs. Waited. The rolling, the rolling–"AUGHHHHHH!"

Like some strangely costumed figure skater, Elise jumped and whirled in the air, adrenaline propelling her easily around. The light and shadow, stone and light, light and stone passed in a blur.

She landed hard on the ground, half crouched, hands out and ready. Her scream echoed, repeating her fear again and again.

The tunnel was empty. Even though the rolling continued.

Elise breathed hard and loud. She turned in a full circle. Nothing.

BUT I HEAR IT!

Too close – she should see it! See the thing controlling it.

"You hear it, don't you?" she hissed back to Francis, and then remembered that she needed to turn around for his answer.

The monk, still not facing entirely towards her nodded his head. *What is it?*

Breathing harder still, "It's for me. It's doing it for me." Elise spun again, reading all the shadows, the creases, the stone. "That sound is just for me...we've got to get out of here, Francis. Which way?"

The mention of escape cued the lights – they began to turn out.

416

One by one. First at the far end of the tunnel, back the way they came. Then traveling towards them – light and stone and shadow becoming just shadow.

Elise watched several snuffs, unmoving. It was another memory she and the Other shared from the library. Only this time, there was no light timer to turn, no way to reset the darkness. And it was moving quickly. A pitch black train rushing to hit them.

"We've got to run, Francis. RUN!" She turned while her voice hit again and again off the walls. "COME WITH ME – NOW!"

Already picking-up speed herself, Elise caught the monk's elbow, towing him into movement. A few feet and he caught her pace, their bodies knocking together until she released him.

He fell back a few steps.

"Keep coming. You've got to run HARD!"

Taking her own advice, Elise found her runner's form, elbows and legs pumping, hands flashing in front of her face in quarter seconds. *Keep going. Faster, and faster!*

But just as before, the lights were beating her. Snapping glances over her shoulder showed a losing battle, the dark traveling up the tunnel like a black fuse. Already, the light over where she and Francis stood those few frozen seconds was out.

And Francis – he was at least three meters behind her now.

"HURRY. GOD, HURRY FRANCIS. WE HAVE TO GO FASTER THAN THIS!"

Or I'll have to leave you, or use you, or–

"COME ON!" Her voice took on a slight rasp. "Please keep coming! GOD!"

I can't wait for him! I have to get out – but I can't leave him. I just–

She looked back again. Behind, the dark grew exponentially. Soon it would be catching their feet each time they kicked back. And after that they would be in it, running toward the light instead of away from the dark.

"FRANCIS!" Elise pushed her feet into the stone to slow down.

He was hobbling, his black hood flailing slower and slower at his shoulder. He pushed out a hand at her. *Go.*

"No! Keep trying. We'll run together." But even as she said it, Elise was jogging again.

Sick, she knew her choice.

Francis stopped and stood still in the center of the tunnel. He did not gesture or motion. Two more lights, and he would be in the black. Alone with it.

"FRANCIS PLEASE! Stay with me. It can't be that far!" she called back to him, but without looking. "It must be just... over–"

"Actually. I think you're going the wrong way."

"You think I'm–" Elise ran two more steps before stopping herself. She breathed in and out, but mostly out. She blinked.

Actually. I think you're going the wrong way.

A voice. So out of place. So discordant and unnatural.

No. No no no no no no....

It was the closest thing Elise would ever experience to having her life flash before her eyes. Her mind, clinging to normal thought processes and logical deductions, began a rapid shuffle of her memories. They scanned before her mind like a film reel running between the backs of her sockets and her corneas. Chris, Francis, Alan, Lorenze, Matthew, Leo, Chris, Francis, Alan, Lorenze, Chris, Francis, Alan, Francis. The dorm room, the car ride, Whiteley, the corn festival, the greenhouse, practicing, bleeding ears, headaches, faces in newspapers, Alan's blood in the snow, the consistory, the cardinals, miters, dark rooms and gold paint, confirmation and here, now. *What about the tunnels? What about the tunnels?* The shadow following in the dark; the Other in her vision.

"Did you hear me?" the voice came again.

It was an unextraordinary voice, Elise noted. Neither low nor high, neither excited nor calm. Only an underlying confidence kept it from monotone.

"Don't you hear me? I think you are going the wrong way, Elise." Her name, spoken with something close to malevolence. Close to hate.

She was still letting out her breath, her lungs beginning to ache but refusing to expand. She had to turn around, and yet, if she turned around, it would be true. *Turn around and it happens. Turn around and this is real.*

But she was turning. A step. Another. Her lungs suddenly sucked in and she faced the darkness.

And Francis.

The blackness came up to him, rested on his back like an old friend. It crowded in on him, merging with the edges of his robes, dying the backs of his hands and his neck gray. The light closest to him – the last to go untouched – illuminated his features in amber. It showed off the face that matched the voice: full of loathing and violence.

He smiled. "Elise," he let the 's' curl off his tongue like a wisp of smoke. "Elise, Elise. How I have longed to speak your name." He tipped his head back and erupted in a merciless laugh that did not echo, it was so empty.

Elise shook her head. No, this could not be happening. Not now. Not ever.

He accused, "Don't tell me you don't believe it. Have I really been so convincing? Does it break your heart to know it is me, your friend?"

She shook her head at him again, felt the stinging of tears at the corners of her eyes. *No no no no no no.* Barely, she found her own voice. "No...Francis."

"Please. Don't speak to me with pity. " His face contorted into a sneer. "Pity me, who is so close to winning? I already told you. It's about having. Having everything. The end of abstinence, discipline, going without. We're at this threshold, and you dare feel sorry for me." Francis stepped towards her.

Already told me... the words were familiar. But they weren't Francis'. She knew whose they were, and there was another cascading of falling dominos in her mind.

"You, who has been so easily led. For twenty years I waited and planned. Waited for you to show yourself. I put on this cloth, this façade. Can you appreciate the cleverness? Being a priest would force me to participate too much. Too many questions in joining the society, too many things to fake and answer to. But a mute monk who 'happened' to take an interest in the Hetairia Melchizedek? The handicap was the best part. No one questions a mute who feels the need to join the abstinent Church! In their minds, everyone pats themselves on the back that society has preserved such an accepting place for me. And it is. So accepting...add in the ability to see things, and I slid right into the best seat in the house for this fucking show. The Church just went on, spending their money and looking for you, far better than I ever could have alone.

"I have to say, though, I didn't count on vice to give you away. Murder revealing an angel? Amazing – like a devil's prayer. You killed Clyde Parker and Chris was good enough to catch it. I saw Clyde's face in the paper and your mark was on him – that part's true. A little whispering in Alan's ear to investigate, and there you were. The object of my search for so long – tending a damn bar! Sexy and sinful and so blissfully unaware of the nature of the fire you carried."

Two more steps towards Elise. The darkness stayed with him, moving forward as he moved. Unbelievingly, Elise glanced towards the burning light. It would go out if he came further – she knew it.

"You should feel sorry for yourself, and for your fucking friends! You wouldn't believe us when I came to your dorm room with the priest. Of course not –who believes a shitty story like that? Not this century, thank God! But I could make you believe." The words sounded like a threat. "The library! The library!" he laughed, and again, the room forgot to echo. "I know everything about you. All your fears, your thoughts. Your crush on that moron that couldn't even run. The way pencils remind you of Clyde hitting you across your face so hard your cheekbone shattered. I used them and watched you wait frozen for me to take you. "

419

Francis in the library. There in the dorm. In my thoughts. Please no...

Enunciating each word, "You lived that day only because I let you. And afterwards, you believed what no words of God could make you believe. So easily manipulated, you left your whole life."

I am alone in the vision. Because Francis and the Other–

"And that was enough for a time. Again, I fell to waiting. You see, I really am so patient. I watched Alan make you strong. Watched you become half an adversary–"

"You can't be. You just can't..." Elise's voice came out hoarse, as though she'd been yelling.

"But I am."

Elise started shaking her head again; dared to close her eyes against it. They flew open again as the light nearest him went out, allowing the darkness to remain just on him.

"Come. You must remember. Where was I when you first fought the Other in Ashton? Outside...somewhere. Where was I while you and Chris huddled inside the greenhouse? Speaking to the farmer about his car...somewhere. Always absent," he smiled before speaking the thought, "like Clark fucking Kent.

"I put my hands through Alan." He held up those two limbs simply to her, the same with which he blessed her, gave her Communion.

This is another nightmare. It can't be real. It just can't be.

"Literally. Put my hands through him. At the end, he asked me to show him my real face. And I did. I showed him this one. For a second, I think he knew what he was leaving you to; in whose care he was trusting you. In that second right before I tore his head off."

Just a dream. Someone wake me up! Lorenze, anyone...

"And then a second time, I let you live. Though I must say, it was far more entertaining than our previous, real meeting. At least you moved in the greenhouse, fought, even surprised me at a few turns. Fighting for your life, though there was no real threat – only manipulation that looked like death. You see, I couldn't let the Church slow things down once I set them in motion by pointing out Ze'ev. And I certainly couldn't let them decide that you were going to go by yourself to the Vatican. Killing Alan and putting you in a fury certainly did the trick – I had a plane ticket within a few hours."

Francis is... a monk. I know him. I just need to wake-up.

"This is no dream, Elise. Stop thinking it. It's pathetic."

The harsh, accurate words snapped her eyes to his.

He blinked for her benefit, and the familiar, watery brown eyes disappeared to reveal cold blue ones.

Blue eyes she knew so well, whose glow rivaled her own. The last domino.

"Did you really think that you were the only one who could take on human shape? I showed you many times that I could. All along, your worst enemy right by your side. And now, for the last time. For this is the final manipulation, leading you down into the lifeless dark where yours is the only heart that beats."

Elise took five steps back before she realized she was retreating. *Retreating where?* A fullness just below her gag reflex gave better indication than her spun-out thoughts that she believed he was telling the truth – she was going the wrong way, and there was no way out without going back. But was the reflex to be trusted? *He's manipulative. He lies. Always lies. You're here because he's good at it.*

"I am good at it. You really didn't guess it was me?" Francis purred. "That makes it all so much sweeter."

Back a few more steps. Further. *Where am I going? What – I don't know what to do! There isn't anything to do.* More retreating steps, even as Francis closed the distance between them. *Where – WHERE!! HE'S PUSHING ME BACK AND I DON'T–*

Stop moving. As if she bumped against a hard wall, Elise suddenly stood rigid. *Even now, he's leading you.* She blinked hard at him, over and over, willing her eyes to focus and her mind to follow. *There is no choice – take a stand.*

"I don't really think standing will help you much," he smiled and his teeth were elongated, thinner and straighter like needles. "You know that anything you try, I will see in you first." He was coming, always coming.

DO SOMETHING! ANYTHING! There's got to be–

A manipulation of her own.

"If you can read my thoughts," Elise paused, surprised by her voice. Was that her speaking so calmly? "Then answer my question."

Francis stopped several feet from her, and Elise got the feeling that his empty, glowing eyes were looking at her very hard. Debating, even if for just a second. Finally, treating her like an adversary instead of a kill. *Perhaps it means...* she wouldn't finish the thought.

Perhaps he knew he could still lose.

"Answer my question."

"I did not kill you before," he began slowly in the untoned voice, "because I needed you. Your God likes to even out the playing field quite regularly; step in when his weak creations can't fend for themselves. And so He protected you with two things. One," he held up a long finger. "Though I see almost everything, He hid your alias from me. I needed the society and their resources to find you. The world is full of marked faces and yours, my love, could easily get lost if I didn't play right. There would be no feeling you out – I had to see you to find you.

421

"Two," he took two more steps towards her. "He also hid His own from me, far better even than He hid you. I can read anyone – the Pope; if a person will die; who will live; who's having an affair; who wants to have an affair; who wants to jump in their priest's bed. But I cannot read Chesed. With God's protection, she is just a girl to me. Even if I saw her, I would not know her.

"But to you – God would let you see her clearly. It was just a matter of getting you to see her. I took my best bet – Chayim Ze'ev did have a mark on him – I did not lie – but not the mark of a king. Only the mark of someone important, a life that could perhaps be used. So, I guided you to him, hoping that you would find the true heir, and the path that would lead me to salvation.

"So you see, it has only been since yesterday that I could kill you. Which I would have done except, your God has been whispering in your ear, hasn't He? Too afraid to let you stand on your own. You returned home with prophecy, and I was afraid you knew my secret, perhaps even how to stop me. Again, I waited for you to show yourself, read your thoughts for vague clues. And a few moments ago, you showed an empty hand. He really didn't show you the end; has left it to your faith, yes? And that leaves a lot of doubt, doesn't it? You've come so far, been led so well, and then He deserts you. Tell me, honestly, do you really think your God even sees you down here?"

Elise clenched a fist, suddenly feeling the Inri at her neck. "Yes. And my God will make sure things end His way. You should be afraid of me."

There. She took a step towards him. It took too much effort, showed too much shaking, but she did it. *Now just don't think. Don't think of your next move. He'll–*

"Anticipate it." Francis cocked his head at her until it was almost sideways. It was familiar, and Elise suddenly saw the Other lying on its back in the greenhouse. Watching like a veteran boxer watches a young opponent. He was not afraid. He was waiting to observe her first mistake. And down here, where she was alone–

"Of course you're alone." Francis dropped his voice several degrees. "What angel are you after all? Murderer several times over. Yes! What of your mother, or the guard outside this very tunnel? Temptress. Yes. I know all about your tempting. Looking at your breasts in the mirror before you parade yourself in nightgowns for a priest. 'Just two hours. Can't we have that? Just two hours without pretending. I love you, I love you, I love you.' Really, you might've at least considered me in all your heat. I would at least know how to pleasure you."

Even now, Elise could not help the blood rushing to her face. To hear him mock one of the only things that really mattered to her even here, even in the dark when nothing should matter.

"You're no more an angel than I am. You loathe the thoughts and ideas of angels – weak, without will – and you are afraid you are one of them. And yet you still fight for the Catholic Churches, cardinals, and Alans of the world, and all the rules and discriminations they uphold. You fit in better elsewhere, Elise."

"If I fit in better elsewhere, than it's through fault! Nothing you say can ever begin to weaken where I come from and who I serve," Elise's voice began to rise louder, and the breath came freely between her words. "Now move out of my way, because I've only got thirty minutes. "

Francis threw back his head and laughed.

He laughed it all out, taking his time. Elise watched in disgust as the chest rose and fell jerkily with amusement at her poor testament to faith. Again, her eyes burned with tears at the corners.

I'M COMING FOR YOU! she thought angry and loud, and her frame shivered. *Laugh, but I'm still coming.*

"Then why haven't you moved, you little bitch?" Francis set his mouth in a snarl and came towards her suddenly. Behind and around him, the blackness moved to stay close like a child holding its mother's legs. Another light went out as he crossed to her in steps too large and powerful for a man.

"YOU CAN HAVE ANYTHING, YOU SHIT! JOIN US AND LIVE LIKE YOU'VE NEVER LIVED!" His spit flew in Elise's face, thick and oddly dry. The blue eyes blazed inches in front of her own, as Francis stood on the balls of his feet to pour his sudden rage at her. "HAVE ALL YOUR WEAK PLEASURES – YOUTH AND BEAUTY AND MONEY. EVEN THE PRIEST. CAN YOUR GOD GIVE YOU THAT – THE DARKEST SECRET IN YOUR HEART? THE DESIRE TO CORRUPT AND DESTROY ANOTHER'S FAITH. HAVE HIM!"

Dropping to a whisper, "Have everything. Show Chris Mognahan what it's like to know a woman. Fuck him and love him. Make him sorry he ever took his vows. And then bring him home to your parents, who can be alive if you ask. I see them standing behind you this very minute! Right there – living and breathing and waiting for you to call them back. Forget why you came, and I promise, your mother will lead you out of here, untouched! Can't you feel her, so close? Say the word. Say it."

Francis pulled back just enough to take in her entire face – the trembling, the pain, the panic. He kept one hand swept away from him, like he asked her to dance.

And for a moment, he looked like Francis. Caring in his own way, offering what he had and confident in its acceptance. The familiarity made Elise's heart wince, and she hesitated wishfully. Maybe it was still a mistake. Maybe Francis–

A hand came down gently on Elise's shoulder from behind, and with it the slight, floral scent of Channel No. 5. Her mother's perfume.

If I turn around, she'll be there. And if she asks me...God. I'm at the threshold. The very threshold...

Elise closed here eyes, every atom that composed her shaking. She could hear Francis next to her breathing soft, waiting respectfully for her decision, as though he could not take it from her. And noise behind her, the sound of others waiting. Those she could never have in this world.

They aren't really there. Not the way you loved them – only some worthless echo.

But someone was turning her, gentle like a sleepy child led to bed. *No, no!* Elise weakly kept her feet planted and her body turning away, but the hands that were her mother's kept the pressure and seduction on. *FIND SOMETHING... some shred....* And her thoughts swirled as formless as a shaken kaleidoscope. *Anchor to something. Anything. PLEASE!* Elise opened her mouth, and soft words spilled out with her breath, so horribly formed and unconscious, she did not know them.

"What?" Francis asked soft, hopeful.

"She remembered me," Elise repeated and realized at once. "Chesed remembered me, and she was glad she knew me. Glad because, whatever I am now, at some other time, in some other place, I was worth knowing."

The hand lifted from her shoulder. Francis' face darkened.

Low, still shaking, "Your offer is tempting. But I'm not Eve."

Before Francis could react, Elise caught the still outstretched hand and dug her fingers into the soft flesh. Strength as she only knew it in the greenhouse paused just between them, and then flowed.

Francis was quick. He pulled back even while using his other hand to come down on the back of her skull. Elise staggered to the flare of stars, almost falling to one knee.

They stood away from each other, breathing hard.

Francis wiped the skin close to his ears with his hand. Blood came back. "See what happens when you touch me? Poor Francis, always getting headaches and feeling sick whenever you turn-up." He laughed, rubbing the blood onto his face like war paint. "Though you see, it is actually less about pain and more about attraction. My reaction to your powers is like a magnet drawn to meet its opposite – Remiel stirs, and the Other – at the expense of Francis – also begins to wake. Yes, I feel you now. Scared and weak. But still calling me to come out and meet you. For once, you won't be disappointed."

Francis smiled, and again the teeth were long and thin. One of his cheekbones stuck out odd and large, and even through the injured haze, Elise could tell it threatened to puncture the skin. She was glad. The sooner the fight with Francis was over and the fight with the Other began, the better.

"Unfortunately, that meager surge is all you'll get. One little touch. Just enough to keep it interesting."

"I'll kill you," Elise flashed her bright eyes at him. "I'll never let you out of this. I'll fight to the death."

"I have no doubt. That's one thing I honestly do like about you, Elise. Something we have in common. You have no qualms with cruelty when it suits you." As he spoke, blood dripped onto his lips. The teeth were becoming longer and narrower, too long to fit in his mouth.

"COME ON!"

Francis grinned again. The cheekbone poked through and new blood sprayed. The skin at the wound stretched until it became longer and wider, as something darker and more terrible moved under Francis' skin. It was like watching something hatch: a human being morphing to monster. The man she knew as Francis began to come apart in obvious places, like a garment torn at the seams.

The skin between the eyes and at the nose split down the center and then eased back to make room for the larger face. The chest ripped apart to reveal the much grander, heaving chest underneath. The left shoulder jerked suddenly and tore from the joint. Two new heads unfolded and emerged from its cavity blinking mucus from their eyes. The foul-smelling fur did not grow, but was revealed with each split and retraction of skin. It glistened moist with the remnants of blood and fluid that peeled back from it. Four powerful limbs grew through the human fabric and stretched. Where pieces of Francis remained, the spikes and claws haphazardly erupted, leaving no trace of the living disguise except two hands, miserably shredded and rotten, clasping in the very center of its chest.

In a few long seconds, the Other stood crouched and ready in a more explosive way then before, like a dog newly untethered against a master it has longed to turn against. Once again, she did not doubt the liar's words – it meant to kill her this time.

And quickly. The attack came without even a flinch of muscle. One moment, the Other stood with watchful eyes, the next it darted forward with supernatural agility.

But Elise saw its intention, the razor sharp claws and spikes of its body glimmering in the yellow light. She jumped before it could swipe her, flipping end over end and landing in the darkness. Mid-air, she threw out Remiel.

The invisible angel attacked from behind, doling a train-like punch to the back of one head. Then, urging and feeling her fingers become thin and sharp, Remiel tore into flesh, pulling away fur and the scales beneath. The Other screamed and tossed its body like a bull, useless against the being less substantial than smoke.

425

DIG DEEPER! To the very base of its skull! Elise threw more of herself into the apparition's battle, until she could no longer feel where she stood; could not sense the light dimming in her eyes. Fully with Remiel, she dug and ripped, tearing away desperately. *Let me win with one blow, one strike–*

The cut was so fast, so perfect, it burned.

Remiel evaporated from Elise and she drew into herself, stung with pain. Blood on her arm, her leg, a whole length of the white robe torn to reveal gashes that easily sliced and exposed the muscle fiber of her thigh. Instinct drew her hands to the largest injury, as if that could stop the sudden flow of blood and ease the firing nerves.

A slight stir, as of breath, rustled the damp wisps of hair by her forehead.

Elise shuddered from it, desperately scanning the empty air before flipping her eyes to the cold blue lights watching still and patient from a distance.

The thing had not moved, and yet it cut her just as it intentioned in its first past. Like her, it manipulated the air, threw itself out.

And now she (barely) stood, injured and mortal.

More like me...how can I fight something I can't see, even on my best day with an army of people... Elise tightened her jaw, forced herself to swallow. She licked her lips and tasted blood – her own – some splattered in the violence of her injury.

The Other came forward, its gaggle of heads bobbing like great horse necks. The steps became a trot, and then a full gallop towards her ground in the dark. As it moved from the light, Elise could only make out its irregular shadow growing larger by the second. The three sets of blue eyes the unnatural color and strength of indiglo crowded towards her: slitted windows into a frigid aloneness Elise easily understood as hell.

You can't beat it unless you use it–

Barreling now, the smell of burnt hair–

DON'T MOVE! MOVE AND YOUR'E DEAD. RUN AND YOU'RE DEAD–

Thudding, shaking the ground–

JUST STAND!

The Other, a foot away, veered to the side to give Elise a second treatment with its irregular claws.

But Elise turned with it and kept herself in its full path.

They crashed together – a great jumbling of heaving bodies. Newly hot with pain, Elise knew so many places in her body now punctured and snagged against the beast. Rolling, rolling – before the motion of their crash dissipated, a head ducked down by her own. The needle-teeth, covered in their own blood and gored gums, began to slide apart to make room for a good half of her head, and the creature clutched her to it with rotten versions of the hands that taught her to hold the Eucharist.

Exactly like I hoped you would.

Elise felt the grip, the rotting hand dig painfully at her waist. Like springs releasing in her shoulder joints, both arms fell to the spot immediately. In an instant she had a death hold on a wrist, and several fingers entwined.

Again, the power hesitated between them, as if it could not decide to whom it was most attracted. And again, it began to flow to Elise in a steady rush, like a dam released on a great river.

Realizing its mistake, the Other writhed, and the gangrene hands pushed, but Elise held on. It twisted, jerked, and moved so that the spikes digging into her body shredded their puncture holes. Elise moaned, but held.

And the flood continued. Whispers in her ears, old and familiar. *Listen and don't think about the pain; don't think about the Other. Just keep taking!*

The Other thrashed, but the bleeding, rag of a creature that leeched to it only became more alive. The absent light in her eyes became a beam. The irises faded and disappeared, leaving the two blazing holes whose light shivered across the walls and ceiling with each jerk.

COME ON!

The teeth came then, ribboning her face so that Elise could feel flaps of her cheek on her chin. Fully disconnected, Elise's jaw fell slack.

KEEP IT COMING! I'll suck you dry healing myself. With a renewed rush, Elise grew the new tissue almost as fast as the thing tore it away.

The whispers screamed in her ears, the soft–sounding language encouraging darkly for her to never let go. She healed around the claws stuck throughout her body like voodoo workings. A new scent rose between them – that of truly burning hair. Elise smiled even with her slack jaw, knowing she was now taking off skin, flaking it away like ash with her hot touch. Needle teeth in her shoulder, just missing her neck by an instinctual hunching of the shoulders. New blood dripped and ran between their crushing bodies. Elise worked there too, only steps behind the carnage, closing up the fatal wounds into little white marks that faded before the eye.

The Other was screaming, a truly panicked sound, but Elise could barely hear it. The whispers deafened like a snowy TV screen. So many voices all coming together, back and forth in waves. Their sounds came closer, more clear, higher and higher. The world lit with gold until even Francis' dark receded from her.

I'm...they're going to tell me, the thought quietly came to Elise through the noise. *I'm going to hear them; the words. Finally, I'll turn-up high enough to know–*

The Other bit into her hands, almost snapping its own neck to get

427

between their bodies. It gnawed where she held the wrists, and though Elise sent tides of energy there, she began to lose the feeling in her fingers. *No!* She shifted to avoid the teeth while keeping her hold.

But the Other didn't seem to notice. It left her hands in their revised position, though it continued the gnawing, working quick and efficient, an expert in tearing through ligament and bone.

Its own bone. Elise realized just as a sudden crack left one of the already mutilated hands limp against her body. *God, it wouldn't. It wouldn't! But it is,* her mind answered. It was biting off its own limbs to dislodge her.

The second hand went equally slack. The rush fell off; the whispers turned suddenly quiet.

The cannibal head unwrenched from its position and smiled close to her face, its own skin and blood dirtying a wide circumference about its mouth. It threw her, and she went easily, hurled back into the amber light.

Twisting artfully on so much borrowed life, Elise landed on crouched legs. With a sick sound, she dropped the limbs she still held.

They both remained still, each breathing and measuring, the Other breathing harder. It crouched cautious, tired, while its life coursed through new veins. At the center of its chest lie two nubs of bone and a gore of tissue. But already, it was healing.

Its cool eyes blinked at the new adversary before him, for new she was. The robes fell tattered about her, revealing shadows of flexed muscle lines. Blood covered her entirely from head to foot, dried now in her red hair. So much blood – more blood than was ever meant to come from one being; probably twice the amount she held in her entire body. The robe that was still long on one side pinned to her leg with it, adhering as dying blood cells fought to congeal. White marks stood out on her face and other bared flesh. It cut her hundreds of times. And yet the eyes were almost too bright to stand, and now some of the light appeared in her mouth and nostrils. The Other stared at its own life great and large, and it became furious.

"Don't you still want to fight me?" Elise asked rhetorically. "Down here, where the only pulse is my own?"

Effortless, she pushed Remiel from her, and the air rippled where she came. Elise watched amused, even as she concentrated to form the angelic hands into something harder than the densest metal. *Can you even get past it? Yes. Yes, I believe I can.*

With a blow meant to kill, Remiel thrust her hands into the open sore in its chest. It gave in with little resistance, bones cracking.

And then she was on the thing herself. Clawing, hitting, bludgeoning. The Other fought, but on the defense. Again, Elise was reminded of a boxing match – this time the veteran boxer was looking his age, and the younger opponent was coming in close to smell his fear. The Other continued to move with her, to block and frustrate her attempts, but never challenge her. Blow after blow; faster and harder, so that her arms moved blurred, as if she had more than two. Blood – not Elise's – sprayed through the air like a gentle mist. She spun, kicked, punched, tore, clawed in a flurry of red hair and gold light.

And yet, it would not die.

A hundred blows, and it tiredly moved to meet the next. Elise's excitement soured, and her fatal blows became more fatal. She punched around its head – punches that would've left Clyde Parker decapitated instead of faceless. She thrust fists – hard enough to take down sapling trees in the greenhouse – into organs so they exploded. *Please just die!* But for all her fighting, the Other was still regenerating. Still healing.

Even while her own energy supply waned. She couldn't feel it yet, but she knew it was happening. The dark was crowding back in again, like a scavenger sensing the battle will once again turn to its benefit. The Other, once barely an outline against the gold light she saw through, had returned to a distinctive shape. The color of the violence was coming back.

I'll have to turn-up again. I'll have to try and...but I can't stay here! I have to get to Chesed! GOD! It's distracting me. Even as I win this fight, I'm losing another.

At least Chris and Lorenze–

No. That's not good enough!

Elise withdrew from the onslaught with a spring that put ten feet between them. Above her, new thunder rose as once again the crowd stood and applauded something.

Let it just be speeches, damnit! She put her hands on her hips and gulped the air to catch her breath. She paced.

Three pairs of blue eyes followed in sync. Until one set blinked itself brown.

In seconds, the head in the center of the monster tucked its mutilated features away to become Francis. "Tired, dear?"

Elise could not help it – she flinched again at the voice.

"Still haven't seen the end, have you? Don't you wish God would interfere now, when time is so precious to you and to everything He loves?"

"Shut-up! Filth! TRAITOR!"

The face broke into a laugh, somewhere between the human voice it mimicked well and the horrible sound more natural to its larynx. "Yes. Get angry. I'm sure that will make the difference."

Elise glared, a new hatred slowly birthing as the shock lessened.

"You're already in hell, Elise. For hell is only repetition of something unbearable. And I can fight you forever while you keep wondering what the secret is."

Elise charged with a cry not so far off from the Other's own laugh. Frenzied, she tore into the Other anew, with particular focus on the image of Francis still smiling in the center. Her light faded and faded, like the sun going down outside. She punched, and her hand actually hurt. Worse, Elise found she had little to expend for the pain.

She needed it again. How bitter – to need one's enemy.

Like birds alighting on a worm, Elise's fingers fluttered and then lunged for the mutilated hands now fully formed again in the center of the Other's chest. They writhed, but she clamped. The first whisper began infinitesimal in her ear–

But the needle teeth did not land in her shoulder this time.

Nor did they miss her neck by an instinctual hunching of the shoulders.

For Elise never hunched. She did not know the blow came until it was warm and gushing, had not seen the head move, nor barely felt the slick slice as it ripped a gash in the tender skin of her neck just where it hid her pulse.

But when she tried to breathe in surprise, to fill her lungs with air to scream hurt and angry; when her throat filled with fluid instead of oxygen, then she knew.

Another swipe, and Elise flew from the creature, crashing down on her shoulder blades so that her body folded up awkwardly, bones breaking. Heedless of the new injuries, she pressed her hands to her neck, felt the place where her skin split in a three-inch gap. *Breath... LET ME BREATHE!* Her lung muscles worked to expand so that they hurt; her eyes bulged; her tongue slid around her mouth tasting the iron spilling from her body. Used air came up through the thickness that swamped her esophagus, snorting out her nose loudly. But none came in. She opened her mouth wider, and a horrible sound like rinsing mouthwash came out. *BREATHE!!!*

A bubble blew-up at the side of her neck and popped, spraying blood.

NO! Panic forced her hands harder, pushing into the gore. Panic spasmed her right leg so that it rattled. Panic! So angry and animal and unthinking – panic strong enough to power turbines and fuel cities.

But not strong enough to let her live. *GOD, GOD! WHERE ARE YOU GOD!* Her body crumpled as it left her control. Though she wanted to jump! To run! It fell beneath her just the same. Her head smacked, and she could do nothing to raise it. Red circles came into her eyes, spots that she recognized as dying. And still her lungs heaved, pulling muscles in her back and chest as they pushed and pulled. Her hands fell away and began jerking by themselves. She blinked over and over, but the redness grew.

I CAN'T DIE HERE! CHRIS AND LORENZE. AND SUNLIGHT AND CHRISTMAS AND MUSIC AND RAKING LEAVES – I CAN'T DIE NOW!

Elise took the last stolen energy she had and pushed it into her throat for a futile attempt at healing the windpipe that she no longer possessed. One piece, then another. Then another. But not fast enough –the red was everywhere now. And her thoughts were slipping...somewhere. *"Saving the curtains in a burning house."* It was her mother's voice, her mother's saying.

Francis – no longer the monster – watched her grow still. He was dressed again in dark robes, his face clear and white, his eyes the steady watery brown. The only sign of struggle was the sheen on his balding forehead and the stiff way he moved. He allowed the amber lights to come on full.

Elise was still alive – he could feel her. But she was quieting, almost like she was getting further away. It would not be long. Again, it crossed his mind that it was too bad. He liked her, after all. He smiled.

"Looks like He's forsaken you too." He forced his face into something that mimicked comfort. "Can you look at me?" He crossed to her body, careful to stand just outside the red blossom forming around her. He squatted. "No? I know you hear me. He leaned into her face, watched carefully the slow pulse that still showered her shoulder.

Francis put his lips up against her ear so she could feel the breath of his words. He whispered, "Though I do not have much time, I'm going to show you the end. You're going to die here, as alone in death as you were in life. And the darkness – my darkness – will come for your soul."

The shower stopped.

Francis looked skeptically for a moment. He pulled one of his sleeves down over his hand then roughly turned Elise's cheek. Her head fell forward limp and he jerked it up again. He looked into her eyes, and for the very first time, he saw that they were actually brown. "Ah yes. The light – it's faded from you."

* * * * *

Lorenze wiped his hands on his uniform again. The sweat was unbearable – like his body decided to suddenly reject water. It was very late. The sun was a faded orange somewhere behind the buildings. His eye ached from staring through the scope.

"What are they doing now?" Chris asked from the growing gloom.

"More people are coming onto the platform." He squinted. 'Rabbi, rabbi, rabbi, some guards, rabbi, rabb–" He blinked rapidly and the sweat leaked into the corner of his eye so that it burned.

He stopped breathing.

"Is that it?" Chris asked, his voice higher than normal. "Just the rabbis then?"

But Lorenze was no longer listening. He was watching them – bobbing in and out of his scope as they crossed the stage. Ze'ev in the lead.

431

"Lorenze? Is there anyone else? For God's sake!"

"He's there. Ze'ev just came out. He's on the platform."

It took a moment for the words to register – long enough for the color to drain entirely from Chris' body so that his head and hands suddenly looked wax. "No," he choked out. "Look again! You must be wrong."

"I am looking, watching him right now," Lorenze replied slow, flexing his trigger finger. "Larger than life. It's starting."

"But that means... it means..." the priest fell off to heaving, his great shoulders rising and falling inches. "But she – she can't."

"Maybe they just didn't make it in time," Lorenze offered. "They could still be trying – we may see them yet."

Chris turned away and took several steps back into the dark room. His head shook from side to side, though he did not realize he moved it. "We should've never split up! GOD! Why did we split up!"

"Quiet!" Lorenze hissed, risking a glance up from the platform. "She's probably fine. But fine or not, I know Remiel expects us to do this. If you can't shoot, you will at least sit down and be calm."

Chris turned back to the young man, surprised even in his pain. It almost felt like Alan, taking charge as usual when he was too weak to. He sat.

"If she's gone. I can't accept that."

"Pray," Lorenze replied turning back to his scope.

Chris closed his eyes and conceded, praying in a fervor that he never knew in all his previous days as a priest. On his knees, in front of someone else's couch, he found an altar above all others. And he prayed for her; that the world would not be empty of her. His words tumbled over themselves, laying out a case for her survival. He whispered his love out loud for the first time, told his God of his sin and how he loved that sin. *We can't do this alone, God. We need her. WE NEED HER! And I love her, love her, love her. Take away this cup. Let her be alive and on fire somewhere. PLEASE, God.*

A few feet away in the dark, Lorenze kept his vigil. His fingers silently released the safety and he gave a once over the gun. It was ready. His eye no longer bothered him, nor the kink in his neck. If he sweat, he did not know it. His body was reacting by instinct, crouching lower, resting his trigger arm more fully so it would remain steady. His muscles were automatically tense, as though under considerable resistance. He licked his lips. Beneath him, his legs began an uncontrollable shaking that his mind refused to acknowledge. Remiel would not be sorry she picked him. He would shoot – and he would shoot straight and clean. The crown would not fall on a warm head.

* * * * *

She sent herself out. Like she had so many times, using Remiel when she was not strong enough. And she was not strong enough now.

Remiel stood behind the monk on fading energy. Watching him watch the ruined Elise. *The light – it's faded from you.*

She knew then she could not go back.

I'm like a ghost. God... But there wasn't time for thinking like this. Whatever she had would not last either, this echo of the Other's strength that allowed her to throw herself out one last time.

She flowed back the way she came; flowed because there was no hardness to her. There wasn't energy for that. She was only a feeling. Remiel watched the floor pass by much the same way Elise had watched the water go by from the deck of a boat.

The soldiers.

The plan was quiet in her, though urgent. This was it. If there wasn't enough energy to reach the soldiers, she would dissipate like smoke into air. *Go steady. Calm.* Back up the tunnel, through caverns of light. How long was it since she and Francis – the real Francis – walked through these tunnels? *Forever.*

Footsteps behind her. Remiel did not bother to look back.

The flowing halted; the thoughts stopped. She knew who it was. Knew she should be quiet. As close to dead as she could be.

The monk passed her in a strong gait, his arms brushing his sides briskly. The shadows clung to his feet, moving around him with affection.

How could I not notice? How could I not know! He left me for dead. He killed Alan and Jeff. ALL OF US!

He turned then, watery brown eyes gazing back over his shoulder as he continued to move rapidly towards the exit. They flickered over everything, pausing in the center, just where she hovered.

SHHH!!! Don't think, or he'll hear you! But as soon as she tried to think of nothing, she realized she was thinking and then more thoughts surfaced. *Just see the blackness; keep seeing it and nothing else.*

Still he watched, his step slowing down. Perhaps he could see all of her anyway. Or maybe just her eyes. The damn eyes! He would see her, come back and crush what little there was left. Crush her! He would–

He faced forward and disappeared around the corner.

Remiel waited, though she did not have the time; stood still though every moment was precious. His footsteps faded.

Remiel began again. Slower. It required more concentration to keep herself together. The path began to look waved, as if a great amount of heat radiated from the ground. *Just a little farther.*

Twenty yards, and she blinked out entirely, the light and stone moving and spinning until they became black. Darkness – fuzzy silence like underwater. Silence as she never knew it – without a heartbeat; without the

sounds of being alive. Nothing. It was a complete dark, dark like–
NOOOO!

In panicked concentration, Remiel pulled herself back, called the room back into focus. It came reluctantly, leaving her wavering with a teary feeling.

God? You said you would be here –where everything else falls away. And it's falling. Falling, falling, falling.

She began again. There was another blink out – longer.

Again.

The third time she pulled herself back, she refocused on the stairway. And a natural light falling from around the corner. It was dim and blue *(passed sunset)*. But it was light. And life.

She moved up, but the darkness flooded in, a wave cresting just over her head. She realized alarmingly that it was quiet and comfortable, warm. *Like when people freeze to death,* the thought finished this time. *Except...*

There was someone there.

Someone there with her now, in the comfortable, complete dark. Watching. Remiel could feel the person pressing in on the edges of her consciousness.

And my mother thought, 'Oh! There's someone here for me.'

Helen was – reaching for someone.

I'M NOT REACHING FOR SOMEONE!

With a jerk that she felt as real as her body could feel, Remiel ripped herself out of the blackness and back into Wilson's Arch to look through what she knew was her last window. The twilight trickled down and touched the stone, washing away the amber color. Up the stairs, the soldiers silhouetted against the fading light. Only two now– the one she hit in the neck was gone. Both remaining soldiers were agitated, yelling at each other. Perhaps because a monk just passed through them, untouchable.

But I'm touchable... she thought anxious, climbing now. *PLEASE!* The third to last stair, the second to last stair, then the last.

Unable to stop or pause or think, Remiel rushed the last space to the two soldiers. *Feel fingers. FEEL THEM!* She commanded her mind to assume a solidness it had not been able to hold for whole minutes.

She managed a reach, for a moment felt the air. But the fingers passed through the gray fabric and came away empty. The soldiers continued bickering.

In continuum, Remiel threw herself into the motion a second time. It was worse. She never even felt the air.

No more than a ghost...

The dark suddenly pressed in hard, and she reeled in desolation that washed like a cold shower, blacker even than the oblivion that waited seconds away.

GOD PLEASE! PLEASE HEAR ME! I HAVE NOTHING LEFT!!!!

The closest soldier became quiet and looked up. He turned and peered into her, his eyes slight slits.

He was Ross. Alcoholic Ross.

But how?

(A tip of the scales).

And he was staring at her. Not through her, but at her.

The fading echo that was Remiel lunged forward jerkily. Every ounce of life pushed into that one movement. She reached for him, through him, in him. Inside where his eardrum triggered his brain to read sounds.

HELP ME, ROSS! COME FOR ME, BACK IN THE DARK.

"Come for me!" The words fell between the worlds, passion and desperation giving way for a whispered voice that Remiel remembered from dreams and haunted churches – her own.

She was gone then. Back in the dark. Where someone still waited.

* * * * *

"It's almost time," Lorenze whispered. "Ze'ev is standing and being blessed. I can't wait for her anymore. I think – I think I'm going to shoot." He turned one dilated eye in the priest's direction. "What will we do after that? I don't think we'll get out."

"It doesn't matter," Chris whispered back, his head still bowed, though Lorenze's words meant that God had not answered his prayer. "Just take the shot."

"Take the shot," Lorenze repeated as he turned to the scope, prepared shakily to use it. Ze'ev was clear to his one eye, as if they stood together in the same room. "We'll do this," he whispered.

Then, "Do you smell that?" Chris' voice sounded oddly choked.

But Lorenze jerked one shoulder to indicate silence as he hovered over the rifle. He needed to concentrate! He–

Slowly he turned towards Chris. "I smell it."

Again, Chris' shoulders were rising and falling. "It smells like burnt hair."

They watched each other in the dark a few moments, listening to the silence. The house did not even creak.

Lorenze slid his finger around the trigger as the smell grew stronger. Outside the door, there was a soft thud.

The whole gun shook at his touch.

* * * * *

435

Ross went.

The whisper so odd, the feeling that there was someone. The voice. It came from behind him. Down the tunnel. He went with his gun at the ready, his body poised for an attack. The tunnel felt dusty, dead inside. He paused beneath an amber light to fish out his flask. A long swig brought more composure to hands that were sweaty, but not unsteady. Vodka – astringent enough to make him feel clean inside. With the metal once again tucked close to his heart, Ross processed, his boots scraping dryly against the stone.

He saw her several steps before he let on that he saw her.

"Don't move!" he called, his fingers searching knowingly for the trigger to his gun. "Stay just where you are." His command echoed. The figure obliged.

He came forward more slowly, but steadily.

"Are you–" the question instantly became stupid as he took another step. "Shit." His finger slid from the trigger. It would not be needed.

The girl lie on the stone, her neck falling at an unnatural angle that flirted with his gag reflex. She stained the stone red – so red it almost looked black – in a circumference five feet around. She was red: her clothes, her hair, her face and hands. Like someone rolled her around in her own life. Her open eyes stood out white against the crimson.

"Holy Shit."

Ross saw a fair amount of blood during his short tenure as an Israeli soldier. But no one ever bled as much as the girl he now looked on. He swallowed back down some sourness that came up from his gall bladder. *Whoever did this to her...*

And then his finger was suddenly back on the trigger. He tore his eyes from the pathetic body and looked into the shadows. Instantly, he had the watched feeling – that flesh creeping intuition when someone has the upper hand and it's not you. More blood – on the walls, pools like clay soil mud puddles on the floor.

No way it's all hers.

Ross took careful steps backwards, stepping on just the balls of his feet, though there was no blood behind him to step in (it didn't matter – the place was bathed in death). He completed sweeps with his eyes, right to left. He breathed hard out his nose. And though he fought it the same way one might fight looking at a handicap, Ross's eyes strayed again to the mess on the floor.

Her eyes were open. So white. White stars in a sunset sky. Glaring.

He thought of the horror movies – generic horror movies – when the next person to die stupidly, crazily leans over to close the eyes of a corpse just to keep it from staring, and thought now he understood. It seemed that the chills might go away if she couldn't watch him. It seemed he could not walk back with her watching him the whole way.

Don't be stupid. She's just dead.

What if she wasn't dead?

LOOK AROUND YOU, ROSS!

And yet, he'd already taken a step towards her. Another and another. Until he had reason to stand on the balls of his feet.

Time to get out of here, man. Yes, it was time to get the hell out. *Just close her eyes and then run. Just close them and get the fu...*

I've seen her before, he startled. The irrational fear dispensed to a different type of horror found commonly in funeral homes – death brought closer by recognition.

He knelt by her, crouching in a position that brought déjà vu to the scene. *I know her. She* – the thought silenced as Ross's eyes stumbled upon what appeared to be the fatal wound (and the reason her neck could bend the way it did). Her throat was torn out, nothing but a mangled mess of muscle and skin caved in upon itself. Glittering just below the gash, resting safely between collarbones, was a necklace. A crucifix and an engraved plate. His mind rewound two hours.

"The girl from the street." She flashed before him in white robes, smiling and apologetic. The way she hit his body, hard and warm. He didn't have sunglasses anymore because she was so alive. He tried, but could not remember her name.

"Who would want to do this to you?" he whispered.

I need a drink. A long, cold, drink.

Gently, he reached down and lifted the necklace from her neck. Ross read the inscription. Oddly, the silver was clean of blood–

He cried out as pain shot up his arm. The first thought that came to his mind was he had been cut. The second, and more accurate, thought, was that he was being burned. Somehow, the necklace had grown hot.

Prickling up his wrist, then his forearm. Pure fire between his fingers. And yet, the fingers would not relax and release the necklace; his hand refused to jerk back, and the fire began to engulf his whole body and he was aware of a shaking. He found himself gasping for breath and his thoughts trailing without meaning. Sunspots flooded his vision. He fought to blink them away, but they followed behind his eyelids. Ross raised his eyes back up to the girl's, afraid the sunspots were evidence of his eyes dilating like hers.

Only hers…there was light at their edges. Dazed, Ross watched it grow from a glint on her eyelashes to floodlight, like sun coming through the cracks of a closed door.

There was nothing left in him to be surprised when the dead girl jerked forward and grabbed his face with a cold hand.

She gasped stale breath, wheezing more through the hole in her neck than through her mouth. Her eyes, now wide and blinding, brightened the red circle they sat in to a beautiful pink color. She was startled and afraid, and for a second, Ross wondered oddly if she experienced the same burning. Perhaps they were both in the flames.

He thought so until he passed out, limp, his face falling into her hands – they were both on him now.

The healing was slow. It was more than stitching and pulling things back together. It was creating – weaving the fabric and then sewing. The skin at her neck ruffled while inside the molecules worked swiftly to create the structure – the blood vessels, the veins, the muscle fibers, the windpipe.

They were trading places. Elise's crumpled body began to unfold and turn itself to more natural, living positions. Meanwhile, Ross's shivered and shrank back. Ominously, his head dangled into her palms much as hers previously dangled – not disconnected from the throat, but disconnected nonetheless.

But she did not care. His sacrifice finally brought air to her the way it was supposed to come. Not wet; not with the ache and energy of suffocation. No red spots, no mouthwash sounds. Just air flowing from her mouth to her lungs, uninterrupted. Elise took in great gasps, the rhythm of her breathing broken as though she had been sobbing.

She swallowed. What a wonderful feeling! Mucus and air going their separate ways. She tasted the old blood, and it was sweet. Sweet to taste at all. Still taking more and more until she never had to worry about death. She would be healed. Perfect again.

Ross. Her hot hands caressed his face over and over in an intimacy cruel and only half controlled. Flashes of his life – a day on a beach of blinding sand, pulling a burnt cake from the oven, watching a marshmallow roast slowly on a stick – and other thoughts of fire passed to her. *Keep going*, the whispers pushed without words. *Keep going and listen to us. You'll need us for out there. Out there...* They swelled in and around her, like waves crashing. Her body rocked with them a slow rhythm back and forth. Words. Yes, there were words. Just beyond hearing. But not far. *Keep going. Out there, the sun has set, and the king is king! I need everything.*

The whispers shrieked agreement. She retightened her hold on his cheeks, his ears. The skin reddened to her touch instantly, blistering her mark, and she moved on to another place. His skin smelled of burning, but she ignored it. He was the lamb. The sacrifice that she no longer knew how to win without.

"N – ni. Th no n...the li-t oooo....neiiii... un." Elise closed her bright eyes to swirl her thoughts in the whispers that she at last would understand.

She was light inside as well as out – strong and gold like mid-morning sunlight.

"Tere sha...ore nnnnn....ght." The consonants became harder; the vowels more defined. So long, they called her to listen. To keep burning so she could hear them. Always before, she had to stop. But not now. Not ever again.

"Tere shall...be nooooo tttttt"

She turned-up higher. Ross didn't move.

Their wave ebbed, and then rose.

"And there shall be no night there..." came the hiss. Another ebb, another rise. "And they need no candle, neither light of the sun..." it ebbed.

Elise's eyes flew open to bathe the room so that things shimmered. And the whisper – she recognized it.

"And they need no candle...neither light of the sun."

It was Remiel's whisper. Her own breath all around her – a whispered scream.

Distantly, Elise was reminded of the times when she called herself to leave a message. *Hey Elise! Don't forget–*

"...for the Lord God giveth them light; and they shall reign for ever and ever."

Hey Elise! Don't forget–

"And there shall be no night there; and they need no candle, neither light of the sun; for the Lord God giveth them light; and they shall reign for ever and ever."

Hey Elise! Don't forget–

"There will be no more night. They will not need the light of a lamp or the light of the sun, for the Lord God will give them light. And they will reign for ever and ever."

Don't forget.

Elise's glowing eyes traveled as though she read them on a page. *I know this*... a sinking feeling began to grow. It came again, and again she listened.

Ross convulsed gently against her body. Coolly surprised, Elise looked down at him. Caught herself reflected in a pool of blood by her leg. Her eyes blazed to make her look hollowed out and empty – a thing with no tissue, no muscle, just light. It spilled down to her nostrils and her mouth.

More gently than any other touch she gave him, Elise lay Ross down on the stone floor where her old blood dampened his thin hair, and stepped away. The whisper ebbed and did not come back.

She lowered herself to the man's mouth. He breathed shallowly. The uncovered skin of his face and hands was open and oozing. As if dirtied, Elise untangled herself from him and stood stiffly. She surveyed the scene, felt a chill at the white spot among the red where moments before, her own body lie.

But there were worse things.

Don't forget.

And there shall be no night there; and they need no candle, neither light of the sun; for the Lord God giveth them light; and they shall reign for ever and ever.

I know it – a passage from *Revelation.* Alan prayed it once... *No night or need for light. God takes care of everyone.*

She never thought of it before. All this time, and she never considered asking. Always assumed that she needed someone else. She swallowed.

"God, give me light. Please. Turn me up."

There was a pause while the air around Elise gathered. Then it rushed, as if in a great breath.

The power hit her from all sides. The whispers roared, loud and coherent. And the energy raced in sweet and hot, purer than anything she had ever been given before. Like plugging into a great power source, larger than she could feel or understand. It ran in her, through her, making her a part of itself. She could get lost there.

With a scream that echoed throughout the cavern, Elise turned it off. She fought to catch her breath, knocked from her by the force. She leaned back, searching to leave her shaking in the stone foundation. She gagged and then gave-up, and puke mingled with her blood on the floor.

All this time...NO! All this time – I can't believe it. Tears welled at her eyes. So many lives that could still be living; so much time that didn't need to be wasted. She'd failed. Failed Chris, and Alan, and Lorenze, and God. Because she'd never gotten over believing in herself first.

A sob escaped, her chest shaking tiredly. "I'm sorry. I didn't realize – I'm sorry. So sorry."

Sorry isn't good enough.

No. She shook her head in agreement. Sorry was nothing.

But there was still a chance at redemption.

* * * * *

Elise stepped out from the entrance to Wilson's Arch more nightmare than angel. Gently, she sent Remiel out to put pressure on the neck of the one guard to the left so that he could not turn and see her. She slipped past him and into the crowd. Then more pressure on many necks. As she moved, she kept the hands of her mind pressed out, parting a path that perpetually turned from the gore of her face and hands, the blinding brightness of her eyes, the urgency of her breath.

The entire mass was on its feet – enraptured. Their breath erupted into the cold night air in gasping clouds; some cried loudly. Eyes were lit with excitement, and there was much nodding of heads and applause for the speaker that Elise could not understand.

But she could see him. Turning in the gloom, Elise faced the Western Wall. Sunlight from beyond the horizon oranged the very tip of the wall. White floodlights lit the stage.

The speaker was Ze'ev. The rabbis sat behind him on their velvet chairs with upturned faces. Something metal glittered on his forehead and into his hair.

Here. Where it all falls away.

She could not rush upon the stage and take him. She could not tear her way through the crowd, throwing Remiel out to destroy him. She could not send her ghost fingers to make traitors of the soldiers on their platforms. None of her most awfully imagined last second plans were useful. Well beyond last second – the metal on his forehead sparkled Ze'ev's immunity. Only twenty minutes turned the man she would die to eliminate to the man she must die to protect; he was crowned.

And the dark grows exponentially, catching my feet each time I kick back.

Chesed! Please, God – scanning frantically for a smaller frame. Someone who did not quite fill her velvet chair. A first scan, a slower second scan. She was not among the rabbis, nor did she claim a seat by her father. *Have you seen this part? No.* She might be anywhere.

Elise retched again. There in the crowd – an ugly sound like a strangled animal. Retched until she tasted the sourness of hours old cereal. *God no.* It seemed impossible – how could she let it go so far, let the end come so close?

The end. *Francis.* Elise's heart thudded a half-second faster until her body felt hot and dizzy with blood. She had not seen this, but Elise knew where he would be. Who he'd gone to see. Who else he must have eliminated in order to keep Ze'ev alive long enough to become king. Whose sniper rifle he might use just now to give that crown to someone else. The end. There were no more choices. She was checked, with only one move left.

And now we're in it, running toward the light instead of away from the dark.

* * * * *

Elise headed back the way she came in controlled panic. Back through the delegate entrance (now empty). She was not stopped, though she was plastered in blood and her eyes glowed bright enough to make the crowd squint ten people back. Those she met didn't even have time to move. Elise raced through them too fast to touch. With hummingbird speed and jerk, she weaved through the car-graveyard streets where nothing nearly so fast as herself could follow. The light from her eyes bounced off bumpers and mirrors as she passed. And when the light began to fade, she prayed for more, her own whisper exploding on her again. Power pumped into her veins from God, swamping her body. Her legs whipped back and forth mechanically, each muscle bulging to move as the energy pushed it to. In front of her face, Elise saw her hands flash rhythmically ten times each second.

What will happen? Where will we all go and be when he hits Ze'ev? MOVE FASTER ELISE! FASTER THAN YOU'VE EVER RUN! GOD, SO MUCH FASTER.

All the things that would be different if I knew earlier! And now it's too late! Ze'ev is king and the others – Elise tried to push the thought from her mind but could not. Lorenze, Chris, and Matthew. When the Other came for them, there was no turning-up. Their fight would be over quickly. Was no doubt ending even as she ran.

If Chris and Lorenze can't stall Francis, if he shoots before you get there...

* * * * *

She paused only once. She was close. Another block or two, and she would see 4799 T. Bab Al-Nazir. But there, on a lonely corner where the streetlight refused to come on–

A crumpled body.

Elise knew before she saw the miter in the gutter, knew before she stepped over the shepherd's staff. Her rapid footfalls stopped to silence.

"Matthew." She sniffed, and then licked her lips. She ducked into the shadow of the non-streetlight, her eyes casting flickers in front of her.

Matthew lay on his back, his hands palm up as if still warding off his attacker. His eyes were open, but already glazed over in a cold way that led Elise to believe if she touched him, he would feel stiff. He had been slashed across the chest, leaving his beautiful robes to soak up great volumes of blood. It was a fatal blow, though he may have lasted several minutes, looking up as he did now. More blood dried on his chin.

Tears welled in Elise's eyes, though she blinked them back. She wondered if it was by Francis' own hand, or the Other's. New hatred rose inside her. *Traitor.*

"I'll put in a good word for you with God," she whispered, though it meant nothing now. Matthew reached God before her. "I promise you, I'll do worse to him." She left him still looking up at the first stars.

442

* * * * *

The doors of 4799 T. Bab Al-Nazir were still red, even in the dark. Dark, because not a single streetlamp lit the entire street. They were all out. No doubt, snuffed by the same careless hand as in Wilson's Arch. At the edge of this dark, Elise came to a cold stop. She closed her mouth to hide her breathing. Was the Other in the street, or in an ally? Could it already know she skulked on the outskirts, reading her thoughts and plots? Worse, it could be upstairs – Francis, carefully looking at Ze'ev through crosshairs.

But the night was still. Orange light from a nearby street spilled over onto some of the tallest buildings, illuminating drying laundry. Rounded doorways gaped into the street like open mouths. Her eyes slid around, and she realized the absence of soldiers. Had Francis taken care of them? Or, like her, did he use his mind to force them elsewhere?

The doors were still red, even in the dark.

The same doors, and yet the situation so different than when she last saw them. Any moment, she could hear the fire from a gun above her head and know it was over; watch the streetlights go out in an ever widening circumference from where she now stood. Staring at those doors, her soul ached with an anxiety that made her more alive than she ever was before.

So close... so close, her pulse beat twenty times during the thought alone. She found the crucifix in her robe, feeling heavy. Elise leaned her body back against a cool, stone wall and closed her eyes. *If you tear in there...if you go in rage* – Francis would know every dark thought. He would take his shot as soon as he sensed her. And then, he might even open the doors for her. Those red doors, even in the dark.

No. With no time to go, there would be no tearing; no screaming in revenge. She at last had faith. And faith was being alone, but believing differently; taking no personal advantage while harboring a higher advantage; being David instead of Goliath. As she waited for the sound of assassination, Elise asked God to let His light leave her, prayed for the rush to become quiet, the strength to weaken.

The whispers fell away, sounding sad even as they repeated what they always repeated. The power in her veins became only her ragged pulse. Light faded from her vision, so that she saw the simple backs of eyelids. Suddenly, she felt weary and drained, running on too much adrenaline. There was a throbbing in her thigh – a familiar running cramp. She withered from Remiel to Elise and then less than that. As close to dead as she could make herself. As close to God as she could make herself.

Without hesitating to think any further, she let the angel leave her on the last of the surge. Remiel wavered in the dark faintly, and Elise fought for her consciousness, reeling for the solid world and hoping she did not give away too much. For a moment, they leaned next to each other – the girl and the angel-extension she commanded. And then the angel was crossing the street. Elise's body remained leaning and still, shallowly breathing, sweating, left behind.

At Remiel's approach, the lock to 4799 T. Bab Al-Nazir retired its hold easily. Without touching it, Remiel swung the red door away from her. Inside – complete blackness. The shadow spilled out onto her, impenetrable, the building supernaturally infested with the darkness of the advisory. More than darkness – it was an utter lack of light. And what lie in the dark? What waited this close to the threshold?

Only five stories. 50 steps. Across the street, Elise's body shuddered and her mouth closed firmly, locking the air in her chest as if against water.

Remiel submerged into the blackness of the stairwell. *Hand over hand, like a rope.* She pulled herself along blindly, spirit body dragging, thought-fingers feeling the way into the dark that, if contemplated, seemed eternal. What lurked ahead, and what crept behind in this stairwell abyss? An abyss not empty, but full of all those things that waited. The dark – that unintelligible emptiness that holds everything. No sound, no light, but alive with fear. And Francis knew her fear inside and out. Here was Chris walking dead, or Alan spitting at her guilt. Here was Clyde waiting for his second chance, or her mother screaming accusations. Her mind waited to feel their icy fingers, their hot breath; terrified for the dark to live.

It did not stir. *The second floor. The third. The fourth.* She could only tell them by the long pauses between sets of stairs. Energy waned, leaving her with a falling feeling. Outside, Elise's breath grew ragged.

The fifth floor.

Remiel reached out into the blackness, even as she held with one hand to the railing. It seemed if she let go, she might very well wander in the dark unendingly, lost in some dimension that opened here. She reached her hand out and stepped with it. Another step. Another. No sign of the wall, no skimming of a door. Another step.

What if it's here watching? It will reach for me! GRAB ME COLD AND HARD–

Her touch fell on metal with a high-pitched thud. The door. Remiel released anxiety into her fingers so that they seizured for the doorknob and twisted. The fifth floor opened beyond, a faint light from a window daring to steal inside and show her shadows of an empty hallway. The part of her that had grown hard in anticipation melted away. She moved into the hall, the stairway door shutting and quieted by her mind.

The door – the one she instructed Chris and Lorenze through, the one with a great view of the Western wall – was left open. Almost inviting.

444

Except something spilled from it – a dark shadow lumpy and soft looking. Still. So quiet. And the smell of burnt hair.

No.

Just between the door and its frame. Someone caught forever in the act of not escaping.

No God. I won't let this be real. I won't!

Outside, Elise trembled, tossing her head against the wall, as in a bad dream. Who was it? Was it Lorenze, lying cold and alone on the floor, his body in some indescribable shape? Innocent Lorenze, her own age and yet so much younger. Or–

A flash of large hands came to her. Dirty blond hair in the sun, and the smile that erased most of the seriousness the white collar gave him. *Chris.*

You knew this was coming. You knew – the price.

DON'T LOOK!

Angel eyes drew reluctantly upward at the command, taking in the low ceiling, the water stain in one corner – indications of a life extinct for all it was worth now. She was aware of an unraveling feeling, coming apart, and fought half-heartedly to control it.

If you look, you'll stop. And if you stop...

If they were dead, then there was nothing else for her – a fight to the death, and gladly. Like so much water, she poured over the still figure and into the room.

In what little light came through the window, the Other was Francis. And he was positioned by the sniper rifle, one hand caressing the smooth metal. It was so easy – she might have planned it with him. One-by-one, he had destroyed them to guarantee Ze'ev's crowning, and now he used their own plot to his advantage. No need to go back and fight soldiers or make a scene on the platform at the Western Wall; they had provided him with an easy, coldly accurate solution. Already, Francis was hunched with his back to her, one eye taking focus through the small piece of glass. He adjusted the sight, looked up through the window, and then lowered again to the scope.

Five stories was enough. He was not ready for her; had not sensed her. Not yet.

MURDERER! TRAITOR – LIAR!

Francis startled and lifted his head stiffly this time. He turned so one eye could roll back towards her. He saw nothing and turned back.

Can you feel me? That sense that you are not alone? That I am just behind you.

Francis blinked through the scope. He made the smallest adjustment with his hand and then resettled. His breathing was loud and slow.

On the street, the tips of Elise's mouth turned-up as she focused herself. *No more than a ghost...*she thought. No more than a ghost, and now, it was

445

perfect. In the room, her remaining power was becoming a small, hard thing, a storm gathering for rain.

There was a desk in the corner of the room. On it – a barely sharpened pencil next to a pad of paper, mostly used-up. The angel crouched by it. The air around her moved in a soft whisper as she gathered it to lips made for blowing – for sounding.

The breath hit the pencil so it rolled loud in the quiet room. First across the desk, and then onto the floor.

Francis swallowed so she could hear it. The jaw he clenched became slack and his head rose from the gun to look over his shoulder. His eyes were wide; his face dark.

A soft rolling sound. Remiel pushed so that it continued and continued on the tiled floor, unnaturally avoiding the rug and furniture. Rolling, rolling.

Standing, Francis squinted for the darkness to give up its secret. "Who is it?"

Like a champagne cork half twisted, the rage began to froth and burst, oozing out at the sides of her consciousness. Elise began to pray, becoming a lone light on the dark street. She would take away his opportunity, just as he had taken away hers. And then, she would destroy his life, just as he destroyed so many. *Only harder. Worse.*

For the Lord God giveth them light.

The rolling stopped. The storm broke.

Remiel rushed forward so that the gauze curtains pushed back in her wake. Like her own bullet, she flew straight and hard for the glass that glinted in the dark. The sight exploded, glass flying unseen but heard. It gave like an insect under her hand, the assassin's view disintegrating in her fingers so there was nothing left of the human aide; the sight sightless, void of fatality.

LIAR! TRAITOR!

Francis fell back from the explosion in an old man way. And she was on him as he scrambled to get up, pulling his robes so they tore and tangled him further, pushing and clawing. *HOW DOES IT FEEL? Betrayed by your own carelessness!*

She let him up when his breath heaved, coming out loudly between gritted teeth, as much from confusion as from fury. Streaks appeared on his face where the glass cut him. Blue eyes blinked into the dark and caught sight of the ruined rifle – he would never find the king through it again.

"FUUUCCKKK!!!!!" Francis' monotone, unremarkable voice now lit with a rage that commanded fear. "GOD!" He tore through the sniper rifle, pieces flung to break glass elsewhere in the room. "COME DOWN AND FACE ME YOURSELF! Coward! GOOOODDD!!!" The blue orbs returned to the room. "Where are you? I'll kill you the instant you show yourself!"

Silence. Emptiness.

He sniffed. "I feel you – you can't hide from me. Show yourself! What new, worthless cheat has the Almighty sent? You didn't happen to see the mess I made of His great warrior? Ripped her wide open, watched her drown in her own blood."

Didn't watch long enough.

Remiel smiled dark, and moved to his side, putting ghost lips close to his ear. "I know the end, Francis," the statue's whisper came, sounding beautiful and soft. "Your end. I've come to sound for you."

Francis snapped back, jerking his body off balance and into a wall covered in picture frames. They fell, assaulting his head and shoulders.

Remiel laughed aloud, the sound like a bell – clear with metal tones.

"Elise?" The question was part wonder, part skepticism. Still against the wall, Francis tried to smile, but puckered his face instead. For a moment, there was only the on and off flash of blue light when he blinked.

"Not Elise," she whispered. Closer, so that the hiss would hurt, "REMIEL!"

He balked again and threw a punch to the air. "Show me, Elise! FACE ME!"

"I intend to." Adding secondarily, "I'm waiting. In the dark."

Francis' eyes traveled to the door where it emptied the room into the mostly black hallway. With something like trepidation, he moved for it.

"That's it. I'm praying for you just downstairs."

He looked back into the room then, the full meaning of her words understood. The blue eyes narrowed before snapping back into the black.

* * * * *

Elise pulled Remiel into herself, a hot fire. They would face Francis together. Leaning still against a wall across the street, she prayed again, her whispers rising to her ears. The rush – almost unbearable in intensity – came as she wanted. The hot river flooded over her, into her, around her, and this time, she did not stop in fear. The shadows stepped back from her, receding away from this being apart of a world that had no night. Her body shivered like a tuning fork as it fought to contain something so much greater than blood and nerve and bone. Somewhere close by, God was watching, standing with her, as if she were the only creation. His own warmth flowed in. So much power – she felt invincible; suspected she was.

Francis appeared at the red doors cautiously, though he knew exactly where to look– he certainly felt her now. Calling him to come out and meet her, as he put it. The light from her eyes found him, interrogating like a police spotlight.

447

He approached casually – she had the impression that, if he had pockets, his hands would be in them fumbling around comfortably. He looked both ways before crossing the street, as if to check for on-coming cars. And when his blue eyes came up to hers, he smiled. An awful smile, but one that even then could not hide his anger, his surprise, or his fear. "What soul did you have to sell for this, Elise? I hope it was your own."

"I sold no souls," she responded quietly. "You couldn't beat me."

"I watched the light fade from you. You failed. You will fail now."

It was her turn to smile. Elise's mouth broke large and eager, much like it did when she flirted. "The light only flickered, Francis. You didn't stick around long enough to watch it come back. I found the guard. Ross. And I used him until he told me the secret, which you already know. I don't need you. I don't need anyone."

Francis' smile became smaller, though he managed to keep its echo on his face. His eyes pinched as he sought for that thing that could make it all feel worthless. "You don't need anyone? Good – because you're alone. I suppose you caught Matthew on your way, and of course, you stepped over Lorenze to get to me. And Chris – too bad you didn't stay dead. You might have a few minutes together before I ruin the world."

"Liar!" Elise cried, though in her heart, she knew he was not. "LIAR!" It was a shriek. "Always betraying. Stop speaking!" The words spilled out to cover the blow he dealt. "Come out!" she commanded. "You asked to see me, and now I ask to see you. "

"Gladly." The blue eyes blinked one last time before the face shred in two.   Francis disappeared, replaced by the thing that haunted her so long – the demon that could kill her; the demon that she could become. At last, it would be over, and there was relief through the pain and shaking. She looked at the needle teeth, the bulky body covered in scales and hair, and remained unafraid.

But not un-angry.

"Hell is only repetition of something unbearable," she shoved its own words back at its three grimacing heads. "And I'm going to send you back to your master, who will put you in a dark street with me forever and ever – better than death. Worse."

The Other lunged, all sharpness, from its teeth to the spikes growing from its body. Elise did not move, but waited. Inches away, she pulled back a hand and swung.

For all its momentum, the Other was slapped away. It rolled to a standing position, turning a mangled head to look back at her.

She was the same, unmoving and alight, as if the blow cost her nothing.

"A move I know well," Elise admitted darkly. "Clyde Parker did, after all, have his face slapped off. Come at me again."

The Other came, blue eyes glaring, mouths open. Elise caught a glimpse of rotting tongues twisting for her between rows of fangs. She hardened against them. *Like stone. Hard as stone. Diamonds. Harder.*

The first mouth to strike lost all teeth against her skin, needles flying up in a spray of blood. The second began the same process, the third finally hesitating as the pain from the first bite registered.

Elise pulled the bitten arm back, unmarked, and swung again. This time, she caught the Other beneath one of its chins. The blow snapped the neck back, bones breaking and unhinging. The mouth – still with too many teeth – closed on itself, needles stabbing through its chin, lips, and nose. It cried. A whimpering sound, like a dog.

"Come at me again," Elise offered, following the creature as it scrambled from her, the snapped neck falling onto the others. She traced its path with the two beams of light that were her eyes. "Come on, Francis. My opposite, adversary for so long. Surely it will take more than this."

Low growling, the Other crouched. The broken neck flopped as it began to heal. The two rotting hands fretted. It stepped from her light into the dark.

"You think you're safe because you can turn out a few streetlights? Well I can do better. COWARD!" Elise sent Remiel up to the darkened streetlamp over her head. The bulb snapped apart, glass shards flying, but never hitting the ground.

"The dark can't hide you. Not after Jeff and Alan and Matthew and Lorenze and Chris," she choked out his name.

Another streetlight shattered.

"I AM CRUEL! And I'm going to rip their lives out of you!"

Another streetlight. Another and another – all breaking! A window above them. More windows; all the windows up and down the street. The sounds of glass shattering in all directions.

The Other looked up.

Elise called with her mind, and Remiel brought them to her. So many shards whistling through the air, high pitched to buzzing, like a cloud of bees. Forming and unforming, swirling and juggling, growing with each new break and picking up speed as invisible hands commanded.

They passed around her closely; several locks of her hair cut away, and a piece of her robe.

But she remained untouched, while the Other–

In the light of her eyes, it was like turning over a grotesque snow globe. The Other stood frozen a moment, while the glass covered him in so much glitter.

It dug into his fur, underneath the scales. Slashes appeared across the rotting hands; a thumb fell to the ground. Glitter in the mouths, pecking at the eyes.

"AGAIN!" Elise commanded the glass, pieces ripping themselves from the Other's flesh so they could find new wounds. "I WILL tear you apart!"

The Other charged, screaming even while the glass attacked its writhing tongues and lodged in its gums. And Elise was ready with hands turned equally sharp. One hand slashed, then the other, all the while, the glass swirled around them like snow or fireflies. Blood was on her fresh and hot, but foreign. And the fury was flowing just as freely. A blow for each and every time she doubted herself for this creature! A slash for every time she confided in him, for each time she thought she might die to protect him. Pain for every time she learned from him. Blood for every time she longed still to show him mercy. Hits harder for being a friend than being an enemy. For impersonating her mother; for promising Chris. For falling. For all the things she could not have or be. It could never be enough! Never!

It fought for a while. It struck even, several times. But it – nothing was a match for the angel with wild, brilliant eyes. Terrible, she refused to relinquish though she began to win. A step back as the thing retreated across the street, and she took two steps forward. She hit him with real hands, imagined hands. Ruining, it fell before her onslaught, dazed, crouching in on itself in protection, vaguely aware that the angel was screaming, "THIS IS THE LORD THAT STRIKES! FEAR ME! AND KNOW IT! THIS IS THE LORD THAT STRIKES!"

Elise thrust a hard hand the speed of a bullet into the Other's chest. Through and through, past scales and skin and bone and blood; through lung and muscle; past heart and more muscles and out again. Her fingers curled around shoulder blades in its back. The heads hung. Blue eyes half-closed. Mouths open, but unmoving, drooling on themselves and her. Loud breathing between them. The smell of burning hair.

Elise withdrew with a jerk, and the Other fell, heaped against the wall of 4799 T. Bab Al-Nazir.

"Get-up," she commanded. "You killed so many, and you will get-up! You'll have more before I'm done with you! GET-UP!" She was hoarse.

The blue eyes blinked without looking at her. They closed.

And the Other began to cave-in. Suddenly the fur seemed too large and thick, the body beneath shriveling. The heads lie themselves on their shoulders and then buried in them. The chest heaved and then reduced. The scales swam like live things, then pulled in. Claws withdrew and skin began to show through. In the light of Elise's eyes, it was suddenly just Francis. Struggling to breathe, watery brown eyes squinting up at her. And a gaping wound in his chest where blood poured out and his robes soaked.

"Don't become him!" Elise spoke trembling. "Face me as you really are."

Francis only smiled up at her. His teeth were red, colored by the blood flooding up from his rib cage. "This is how I really am. So you'll just have...to kill me." He leaned back, tired. "Hurry now...before I begin to heal. You know how."

When she didn't move, "Surely you can't hesitate now. The great warrior. Commanded only by God. His own tamed piece of hell. End it!"

Elise snorted indignation. It almost seemed she could not kill him because he asked for it. She wanted to do nothing for him. Nothing! Slowly, she knelt.

"It's – harder to take a life – without rage...isn't it? Fighting, it's...almost second nature. But this – motive, mediation – you find it hard. Still so weak. Alan could never teach you this. Only me." He closed his eyes a moment, focusing on breathing.

"Look at me, Francis." She waited for his eyes to open – still brown with glints of her light reflecting back at her. She took his hand, fingers digging deep into his flesh to let him know the gesture was of control; not forgiveness. "Unfortunately, it's not that hard. Tell me, do you see the light in my eyes now, Francis? I can't find any in yours."

He sneered at the irony. "It – doesn't matt – matter. Kill me – but I'll be back. Or if it's not me, then it – will be someone else. We always keep coming – you win tonight. But tomorrow, and the next day? In the end, I'll see you in hell."

Elise fingered the hand she held. She flipped it over, as if to read the palm. It was the same as it always was – white and unused. She whispered, "Yes. Well, when we get there, you'll have to tell me what it felt like to be this helpless."

She raised her face (one she fought to control with blinking eyes and swallowing). She raised the hand that rested in hers, whose fluttery pulse beat at her fingertips. Elise placed it almost gently on the exposed skin above her left breast. Above her heart. She pinned it there, cold against the warm. Their pulses beat together a moment.

And then, she turned-up. The hand jerked, but remained against her skin, and the hot rush of life began its flow. Her own whisper grew in her ears, reminding again and again that God would give her light.

But not this light.

Francis arched his back and new blood spilled from his chest. His eyes rolled up until they showed white, then closed. He moaned once, and then not again, his mouth shut lest he ask for mercy.

And flashes – memories or thoughts. Some so strange, she could not understand. Places and scenes from other times, evils forgotten for centuries. Places she could not know, so horrific and lonely; so dark. Creatures that belonged to nightmares of gods; not people. They streamed to her without feeling, as if Francis were merely a passive witness to mankind's most awful moments.

She began to rock on her knees, each muscle tight with the borrowed fire. She leaned back, opened her mouth wide to breath. His intensity was unearthly. It continued coming and coming, without waning. The world looked so gold, she was not sure it was even the same world, and she knew it was higher than she had ever turned-up before; higher than she would ever need. The whispers like hurricane winds, so much fire and heat between them. This was life – a wave that never crested. And she was taking it. All of it.

His heartbeat – suddenly, it was in her veins, pounding scared and fluttery in her ears and chest. Elise turned-up to it, commanding it to submit and join her own.

Beat. Beat. Beat.

Francis. With a yell she did not hear, Elise forced the flood to come faster. *More and more. So much higher than ever before. Your life, my life, dark angel, light angel.*

Beat...Beat.

So much worse. So much worse to you. Pushing what was left of his hand into her chest, feeling it burn anew into the welt that read "Inri" backward.

The whispers shrieked, Elise shrieked. Light everywhere, until she squeezed her eyes shut. Only it was there too – brightest.

Beat...Beat....

Beat.

Somewhere, it sounded like more glass shattering. High-pitched and tinkling, the sound shivered the air. And then the street sucked in vacuous, the molecules hesitating one last time between them–

They rushed in a dry breeze like a great sigh, ruffling Elise's hair, getting under her stiff clothes. Silent. The whispers died away, like nothing more than rustled paper.

She held his hand against her many seconds, feeling it cool against the skin that covered her pounding heart. Only an inch separated him from the life needed to close his fist; the life that belonged to him. Forever bound in her now.

She opened her eyes – blinding, the darkness lit like an explosion, streaks of light. A wall of gold. Elise remained, blinking, holding Francis, waiting for it to pass like something as simple as sickness. Minutes passed before shadows came back when she squinted. More gathered after several blinks. Immediate surroundings. The stone by her hand, the wall she leaned against. She waited for further clarity, but the fade faded. *His whole life in my eyes... How long will it last? How high am I?*

Francis. All in her tinted gold, the darkness no longer clung to him, but strayed easily whenever she cast her glance. Several scalding tears stung her cheeks, leaving welts where they burned. She was not foolish enough to believe she freed him.

"No one came for you," she spoke hollowly. "There was no one."

* * * * *

Elise returned to the stairwell, each step bringing greater weight to her chest. The house was so still, far too still. Like the first time she came home after the accident. Seeing her mother's to-do-list on the refrigerator and knowing it would remain there always undone. *Laundry, cat litter, file bills, water plants.*

The second floor. The third. The fourth. She went up easily, her eyes lighting the way so that railing shadows flung high. Darkness scattered from her, jerking back beneath the objects they stole out from. Only her own creaking. Her own damn creaking! What would she do after it was all over? Go back to that little house outside the city and try to tell the society what happened? Eat their food, sleep there? Take a plane home by herself. Back to that life – the one she barely thought of anymore. Study psychology and spend holidays at Digby's. Turn-up on plants to steady running cramps.

No.

She couldn't learn all of that again. More hot tears, racing down her cheeks and neck. She did not bother swiping them.

The fifth floor.

The door swung open for her, and she stood again in the hallway, staring at a far window. And someone caught forever in the act of not escaping.

In the unnatural light, it was Lorenze. Francis had not lied.

His hand was extended out, and Elise understood that he had been crawling. The back of his head was missing, exposing skull and grayness. The wound looked chewed – she could guess how it happened (*needle teeth*).

More tears. Sobs in her chest, coming out in great gasps. "Lorenze. I should've kept you with me. I should've, I should've. You didn't deserve this. You – you–" She knelt and touched the outstretched hand where it rested on the floorboards. Still soft, she expected him to squeeze back.

Elise screamed then, screwing her eyes closed so that barely any light escaped. "GOD! WHY DID YOU MAKE ME LIKE THIS? Only able to take, never give."

No answer, either in rebuke or apology. The hand remained soft, but unmoving. She set it down.

Shaking, tasting bile, she stepped over Lorenze through the still open door. It was as she left it – the gun by the window, disfigured. The wreck of furniture and picture frames where Francis crashed in surprise and anger. It was cold – the open window letting in a breeze that rustled the curtains far gentler than she had.

"Chris?" she asked without hope, just to fill the emptiness. Again, "Chris?" The bright eyes flashed in search of that second dark figure.

It was by the couch – a limb sticking out into the visible room. Her heart sputtered as she recognized the strong, large hand. No movement; just as still as Lorenze.

It crossed her mind to leave him then – to run and never know. So he could recover in the recess of her mind. So she could imagine him happy again somewhere.

Except... Except, that left their last touch already over. She had not paid enough attention; it was too hazy to be the last.

All my attention now, she thought bitter. She stepped over to the large hand. Stepped over it. "Please, God," she whispered.

Chris lay on the side of the sofa where he was last thrown. His body was broken. Poking white bone through sleeves and pant legs. A black puddle of blood expanded from where the back of his skull hit the floor. His eyes were closed, his forehead still puckered in pain.

Elise knelt, the puddle staining her knees (*cold*). She took the extended hand and rested it in her lap. She kneaded it with both her own hands, rubbing over the knuckles, a dry skin patch on the back of the hand. She pushed the palm on her cheek, let the limp fingers run over her eyebrows and cross her tears. She would take it with her every day: which fingers were shorter than others; where the hair on his arm crept to his wrist. "Forever and ever." *Forever and ever.* Her lips kissed nippingly, for she had no saliva to soften them. Light from her eyes washed over him, and she hated it.

"No free will – Angels only love God," she whispered into the hand. "Alan said we couldn't love. But I love. I love. And I'll take you with me. Forever and ever and ever." *Forever and ever and ever.* Hunched over and fetaly curled, she drew herself next to him, her face in his shoulder, his hand at her heart. "Please, God. Take this away."

She lay with him, allowing the despair to come in. *Just for a little while. Then I'll finish it. I'll get up. Just a few minutes...* Through the open window, the boom and crack of fireworks began as Israel celebrated. Elise closed her bright eyes.

* * * * *

Until suddenly, the body beneath her shifted.

Elise moved with him limply before realizing. Just lay there while his shoulder pushed her higher for a moment before sagging back down. The ring finger of the hand entwined with hers suddenly curled to tug red hair, bringing her face down, chin against her breastbone. Elise sucked in all her breath, releasing only to ask awfully, impossibly, "Chris?" Her light found his face, winking harshly off half-opened eyes.

"CHRIS! God, Chris. Can you hear me? Please – you're alive! How are you – you're alive." Beneath, he shifted again, and Elise moved her weight from him but kept her hands touching him. "We've got to get you out of here! Help or something. We can't–"

"What happened?" his voice came-up thick to her. "Where is it?"

"You're with me." she lowered her face so her voice could come to him easier. "Elise. It's me, Chris. You're safe with me."

"Elissse…" he let the 's' run-off.

"That's right. Elise. Me." Unshy, she let a hand caress his face, pushing gently on his lower lip. "Just me." She kissed the top of his head. Again. "You're the answer to my prayer."

"You've always been the answer to mine," he replied simply. The half-opened eyes opened further, irises contracting against her light. Elise turned her own eyes to the floor apologetically.

But Chris' fist uncurled so it could catch more of her hair, softer. "I thought – I should've known better," he snorted out his nose in a half laugh. "I should've believed in you." His fingers entwined with hers, and he closed his eyes to rest. So still.

"I'll get you help. Just – can you stay all right for a little while?"

"Is it over?" he answered her question with another. "Is it all over?"

Elise swallowed and squeezed his hand to her. "Yes. It's over. You can just rest now. Rest. I'll be back with help before–"

"The Other?" He sounded thirsty.

A long pause. "I did worse to him," she whispered.

"Worse?" Chris' eyes snapped back open again, uncomprehending.

"I took care of it." Elise tried to smile. "He – it's gone. I won."

"Lorenze and Matthew?"

Elise shook her head slowly, her eyes staying on the ground away from his face.

"Francis?" Chris asked with more hope.

Francis. Elise closed her eyes and the room fell dark a moment. *Francis.* "He didn't make it." Her tongue passed noisily over her top front teeth. "The Other killed him. We're it." The eyes reopened.

"And Ze'ev? Did he?" Chris tried to shrug, but only winced.

Elise pulled back. "Shhhh. Don't worry about all this. You just rest here and I'll get help. Faster than you can imagine."

"Elise…please. I need to know!"

"You need a doctor. And I'm not going to talk you to death just to satisfy your curiosity. Stay still."

She rose, but he caught her hand, forcing her into an awkward half-squat. His eyes traveled over the white robes stained red, the blood matted in her hair. Her eyes, so brilliant – like looking at a sun. "You must've turned-up so high."

"Yes, I know. I'm not seeing quite right." Her face scrunched. "Too much contrast. It's nothing," she replied to his stare.

"He's king. I see it in your face."

"You see nothing – nothing in my face. For God's sake, you probably can't even see my face! So…we don't have time for this."

"We don't have time because she's still out there. Isn't she?"

"Chris."

"ISNT' SHE?"

"What if she is? Ze'ev is king. And Chesed with him."

"And what will you do? Elise – you need…"

"I need nothing you or anyone here can give me. Chesed cannot remain heir to the throne of Israel one night. And there's only one way to guarantee she never inherits it. I have to – I have no choice."

"El–"

"Where would we be if Judas didn't kiss Jesus Christ? If he couldn't do it, would there be no forgiveness? Would we still be waiting–"

"Even Judas didn't betray Jesus alone."

"He was just a man." Her face set. The muscles twitched, but remained hard. "I've got the world's truest compass guiding me, Chris. Have some faith – you just said you should believe in me." Her smile was bitter.

"God's greatest warrior," he replied with the confidence of a statement, the tone of defeat.

"Yes. But I'm more than that too. Less than that, actually. Real and aching and afraid with plain brown eyes and…you know me better than anyone. Whatever happens, however I am…remember me – the real me – or no one will. Remember me as I was when we met."

"I won't have to remember. You're going to come back to Whiteley with me and remind me every day."

Elise licked the tears off her lips and nodded. "Every day." Looking down, "They say angels can't love."

"They say priests can't either."

She looked in his eyes then, memorizing his desire without restraint or hiding. She reflected the same at him.

"I've got to go. Stay awake if you can. Help will be here as quick as I can get it." The fingers released. She stood. "I'll see you."

"Every day," he echoed, new pain creasing his face as she headed for the door.

"Every day," she called back.

* * * * *

She didn't see them immediately.

The soldiers had already left for 4799 T. Bab Al-Nazir with promises of a doctor over their radios. She was alone. On her way down a stone street to where fireworks still erupted. Looking for one girl among thousands and praying for the compass. Squinting at a city that remained hazy in light she could not blink away. And then she saw him. The first one was standing in a side street.

Even through the haze, he had a glow of his own. The two pinpricks might've been doorbells glowing in the dark, or perhaps quiet smokers. But, the lights snuffed out and then came again. *Blink.* Elise turned to him, breathless.

His hands were behind his back, his legs spread wide. His face was dark because he looked down, the streetlight casting a shadow onto his features. The slight frame but exuding confidence, the tilt of his chin, the silhouette of carefully combed hair. He did not speak when she approached. He did not shift his weight or turn his head towards her. Still and silent, as if he were another fixture of the street.

It wasn't possible. He was as she remembered him, not as he actually was.

Alan.

Elise reached out reflexively to steady herself, opening bright eyes wider. She arced in front of him, too afraid to approach from the front. Her light lit the face in shadow, glinted his eyes, and shown silver through the white hair. "Alan?" she asked, her own voice foreign. Her pulse beat loud and hard.

He remained stiff, not even blinking.

"Alan...what are you? I know you're not Alan." she whispered mostly to herself. "And if you're not Alan..." She walked to him quickly, light bouncing off his features with her steps. Still, the figure that was the old priest stood firm, like she was not there; like she didn't approach him with death in her walk.

His eyes... Elise looked up into the face she looked up at so many times. So odd; so impossible. They glowed with something like her own light, soft and golden, warm. Exuding peace over the cold face. They looked out, as if seeing something far beyond the buildings and streetlights.

Then, she saw the second one.

The second one was about 50 steps back from Alan in a perfect line. Similar in the frozen stature, the stance. Similar and familiar. Elise sucked in

457

all her breath.

She had seen this second figure so often, and often like this. Watching over her even while standing back. Her mother used to chide that he would make her into a true only child with all his attention. *Don't ruin her, Douglas Moore.*

Douglas Moore. Only 50 feet away.

Can your God give you that? Francis' words.

Elise's steps turned into retreating. Self-consciously she clutched the crucifix around her neck – the one Alan gave her – and then looked from one apparition to the other: hell or heaven? Demons playing or ... *can your God give you that?*

Elise, it's Elise. Don't forget–

I've got the world's truest compass guiding me, Chris. Have some faith–

Know that you don't go alone. They will bleed with you. This hour, this vigil, and the next–

"Breadcrumbs," Elise spoke to those she was not sure could hear her. "You're breadcrumbs. Showing me home. I've turned-up so high, the veil's fading away and I see you. You, who were probably there all this time."

One by one, she moved past them. They marked the trail, one appearing just as another seemed too far. None looked at her, but all stood for her: Alan, her father, Helen. A long string of the souls she touched but could not save – now saving her.

She followed them through the streets of Israel: God's promised land. And as they neared the Western Wall, through God's chosen people. The streets began to crowd with men and women dressed for a coronation and peering over their shoulders to see the last of the fireworks. Soldiers began clustering again at the street corners. Always, Elise sent Remiel before her to keep the heads turned away with ghostly pressure. She moved through them like one not there, just a flicker of light.

Matthew standing with his miter and shepherd's staff just under a streetlight. The crowd moved around him with no attention, unable to see the miracle of life after death.

Her mother: beautiful and young, leaning against a fountain in a small square. Her eyes burned out like stars, reflecting off water and stone. Elise recalled one of her final nights at Ashton and felt certain she was not wrong after all. *There was someone there, in my room and not outside...with me.* There had been. There always was.

She smiled as she approached Jeff, the blond boy standing invisible to all but her. He was just as she last really saw him, standing and waiting for her on campus, with a dark tan from hours on the sailing team. He stood with his back to a building. Only two stories tall, it had an upper balcony with a black iron railing. Several plants grew between the bars, thick and prickly.

The windows were alight, though curtained, and a light shone brightly over the door to cast a warm glow on a small set of tables and chairs set just outside the building. Two soldiers sat there, dirtying the tile top with their cigarette ashes. Another stood in front of the door with his gun prominently displayed.

Not a palace, and yet, *This is it? God, is this it?* Elise glanced to her left and right. Though she squinted to mere slits, she saw no more still figures; no more glowing eyes. No more breadcrumbs. Overhead, a firework exploded, turning the street pink.

Breathing deliberate and slow in counter to her increased heart rate, Elise returned her gaze to Jeff and the guards behind him. She let them watch her approach, watched their faces turn from confusion and leftover laughter to concern, then apprehension. The soldier in front of the door looked uneasily at his fellow guards and then placed his hand more firmly around the stock of his gun.

The hand was quickly, harshly, invisibly slapped away. The soldier jumped and then looked at the stinging fingers that weirdly came into such hard contact with what appeared as air.

He reached for the stock a second time, and a second time Remiel intercepted. This time, she pinned his arm behind him so the shoulder popped out of joint. The soldier screamed.

The rest was quick. Elise and Remiel worked as one to disarm the soldiers. One against the wall so hard, he did not get up again; the other ripped from his chair with a crash only second to the sound of his leg snapping where the angel put pressure. And the one in front of the door now slumped and moaning, holding the parts of his body that would not uphold themselves. Screams and yells from others in the street. A gruff hand on her from behind, which she crushed with a touch. The lock unlocked, the door swung inside. Elise was through it, the angel slamming and locking it behind her.

Another soldier halfway down the stairs. He halted at the sight of her – all blood and light. Remiel hit him before he moved again. He flew backward into the stairs, his head knocking loudly on the railing and his eyes rolling back. He rolled two steps towards her and did not get up.

Elise waited tense, listening to the rest of the house. Quiet. The doorknob rattled but remained locked. *Where are they? There've got to be more—*

She felt and heard the shots at the same time. Small thuds, and a punching through her arm, her ribcage, her hipbone; new pain and blood.

Elise lunged in the direction of the fire, knocking into the body that sought to destroy her own. Two more rounds tore her before her hands were on him like leeches. She turned-up, felt him jump against her heat and drop the gun to grab his arm from her.

Elise punched the soldier she held so his head snapped back and sprayed blood. *Turn me up, God! Heal me quickly!* Footsteps down the stairs meant more were coming.

Remiel flew from her to bend the metal of their guns before another bullet could fire. And then she was in them, on them, hitting with restraint meant to injure efficiently. Pounding outside and pounding inside; her heart, the fists, the door, the bodies. Remiel held the lock and Elise took on the rest. They fell away from her useless.

All but the one on the stairs. Elise turned on him in fury, poised to throw him like the others. But she caught her fist halfway through the motion of swinging, her body moving forward with it in order to stop the energy. She almost hit him.

The young guard stood in his usual blue and red stripes two steps from the top of the stairs, gazing out with eyes that glowed, seeing above and beyond her. Lorenze was beautiful and young again. Was it possible that through life and death, they were only separated by hours?

Elise sucked back in her breath and gave a last look at the soldiers fallen around her. None moved. But the door pounded. She stepped towards Lorenze. They stood close a moment, like awkward lovers. She stared into his face swallowing hard, then passed him up the stairs.

A hallway extended before her. Elise looked to the right: several closed doors. To the left–

A beautiful blond man with eyes brighter than the others; bright like her own. He was dressed all in white, and his white-gold hair shimmered with highlights from some light she could not see. He did not move, standing still like Lorenze and her mother and Alan. But he looked at her. Directly, staring with pupiless eyes only she could match.

Elise remembered him then, as she had not in her dreams. "Michael," she whispered, understanding as she spoke that she looked at the spirit who stayed Abraham's hand against his son; the destroyer of Babylon. Here, he stood to watch over her and see it done.

On the floor below, the bolt to the door broke. Remiel released the useless lock as voices rose. Michael looked on, steady. Elise went to the door the angel stood before, knowing his vacant eyes follow her. "Just a few minutes. Keep us alone just a little while." She left him in the hall and closed the door behind her.

It was a bedroom with an old four-poster bed gleaming in the center. The mattress rose and rounded, looking like it would sink several feet if laid upon. A TV on a rolling table was on with the sound off. Its images flickered into the room, hit the large windows and flickered back at itself.

Elise's eyes roamed over the apparent emptiness, her own light merging with the others in the room. She noticed a hair clip on the dresser and a pair of small gloves.

"Chesed?" she called gently. "Don't be afraid. Please. You know me. You–"

Movement by the side of the bed. Chesed raised her head wide-eyed, peering over the mattress with her nostrils flared. Her dark hair fell disheveled, a halo of misplaced strands framing her face. Eyes the color of dirty water glared with suspicion even as they lit with recognition. She stood from her crouch. Her knee popped loudly into the room. Beneath them, footsteps began up the stairs.

"I don't have much time. You said you knew–" Elise faltered, suddenly conscious of her tattered clothes dyed with blood. Blood flakes in her hair and drying stiff on her skin, her unearthly eyes. "I've come for you." Tears sprang into her eyes, once again burning her cheeks. "God help and forgive me, but I've come to take you."

"I know," Chesed responded in a whisper heavy with accent. "You've come to take me to my Father." Fireworks lit the window glass. Pounding footsteps in the hallway, and then no further. "They've been waiting for us."

Elise followed Chesed's gaze out the window–

Pressed against the glass, floating a story up and in between worlds: hundreds and hundreds of pairs of light eyes glowed, as though the stars had somehow fallen to peer through the window. Hosts and hosts where everything else had fallen away.

Elise's throat clicked and she swallowed several times before finding her voice. "Yes. They're waiting for you."

"Then take me to Him," Chesed whispered. Part shrug, part handshake, Chesed extended her hand to Elise.

And Elise took it, feeling the soft girl hands that were not yet a woman's. Could never be a woman's. Innocent and clean while hers were coated in other lives both past and present. She closed her eyes and faced the light. "Remember me when thou comest into thy kingdom?"

Chesed touched her face then and waited for Elise to open her eyes. Staring straight into the light, she replied, "To day shalt thou be with me in paradise."

Elise turned-up.

She started gently, taking from life so small she did not seem to notice at first. Higher, and Chesed's touch left her face in order to grasp the place where their two palms met. But Elise pulled her in then, hugging the girl to her chest, their faces touching. She listened to David's daughter breathe scared and then pained. She cried, sobbing into the black hair. Whispers talked loudly of light to come and the room began to fill with it. Chesed shuddered in her arms all heat and life, withering like so many other things she touched. Her legs gave way, leaving the angel to kneel with her.

Elise began to rock, her hold on Chesed like a mother's with her head in her hands, her face against her chest. Light and sound and memories flowed to her. Visions of days too sunny to belong to men; flowers too sweet to grow; compassion too great to carry; understanding too deep to comprehend. Love and peace came with all faces and times – saints and sinners, the prodigal son coming home, building and destruction of temples, begetting and forgetting covenants, Jesus Christ on a whipping post and empty wrappings and empty tombs. Elise rocked and rocked, taking and taking until she was deaf and blind with grace; locked in heat until what she knew of touch melted away.

The beating of Chesed's pulse – fluttery like a bird taking off. Almost too late. *There's so much of You in her. Centuries and centuries, and there is still so much of You in her. Your will be done. And I will take her to her Father. They're waiting.*

In the last moments of Chesed's life, she showed Elise herself. How she looked, holding her hand only moments before. Light in her hair and eyes, mouth and nose, her skin glowing with it. Above the whispers, her voice came again, *To day shalt thou be with me in paradise.*

Beat...Beat.

Beat.

Elise let the body go slack in her arms, the head falling back unnaturally. Somewhere, the whispers began to quiet, seeming to hush themselves. Elise stared out into the blanket of white light created between herself and Jesus' heir, waiting with blazing tears for it to fade. "It's done," she whispered, shaking. "It's done."

She did not hear the footsteps at the door – no longer held off by those waiting. Nor did she hear it click open, doorknob turning easily. She did not hear or see through the light, but only felt the cool circle of metal at her temple.

For an instant she knew, squeezed her eyes closed and hunched her shoulders. For an instant, she waited.

The soldier shot her through the head. One shot – trembling.

The light faded from her eyes.

And in the dark, someone waited.

Chapter 25 – The One that Comes

Father John,

Thanks very much for your recent letter. My condition continues to improve. I have had no use for the wheelchair for almost a year, and the walker has given way to just a cane (which I would like to imagine looks slightly less decrepit because I allowed the third grade Sunday school class to carve their names in it). I'm certainly not heading the church softball league, but I can do laundry across the street at Mr. Dowell's again.

Whiteley remains a small town with much interest. I gave last rights to our oldest citizen last week. Bless her, she was quite ready to go, And, there was an uproar over a young girl bringing an Ouija board to a birthday party. I think several parents expected me to run right over and interrupt cake with an exorcism.

I've put the storm screens on the windows and the chimney sweep came by so the stove is in good working order, as well as the church furnace. Winter always comes early here – first snow on October 31st. All the trick-or-treaters were bundled in winter coats, or so I saw through my windows (as usual, I was ostracized from the festivities, though I bought my traditional bowl of Milkyways). I continue to do quite a bit of reading – the fun stuff only. No good literature in my library. I just read one called The Other Tree. *Good book and with enough religion to pass it off on the rectory tab.*

That covers the major updates, save for one. I must admit, I debate telling you this last piece of news even as I write these words. And, if you write next inquiring about my mental health, I would not blame you.

As you know, it has been difficult to throw off the incredible, out-of-this-world few months that I lived. Though the Church seems to find it easier and easier to forget how it stood with a girl alight with God's spirit, I have not. She promised me she would come back for me. I have looked for her every day – at my bedside in the hospital; in the faces of my congregation when I returned; in the strangers that come to the Lake Ontario beach in the summer (I know, I sound like Alan. But then again, he was right all along, as I recall). There have been moments (a large pile of leaves in front of my door this fall, a suspicious face with red-blond hair in the crowd at the Whiteley

Corn Festival, and an eerie feeling in church when I am alone there). But nothing that could not be explained by hypersensitivity, a haunted memory and reluctance to let her go. Until now.

A few Fridays ago, I was feeling very low. I hadn't even begun on my sermon for the week and was lacking serious inspiration. There was a light bulb out in the church that I could not change with my handicaps (little frustrations seem like the worst ones sometimes). And, it had just begun to snow. I went to the town diner and even that was empty. I just sat at the window drinking coffee and watching the snow flakes come down, covering a street that didn't even have cars. I thought of Elise and Alan and Francis and how much better my life might be if they were there. Alan would remind me of our purpose as priests and tell me not to feel sorry for myself; Francis would sit quietly and perhaps offer me a metaphorical Sweet and Low; and Elise would grumble something about light bulbs and then ask me if she should turn-up and change it with her mind.

But with no such friends, I left money on the table before the bill was brought and slipped out the door as stealthily as my body would let me (like a bull in a china shop). There was a moon out somehow, and it lit each snowflake to glittering. I battened down inside my coat and concentrated on making the cane grip.

Halfway home, deeply lost in my own selfishness, I slipped and ran into another lone person walking in the snow. I yelled, whirling my arms for balance, the cane clattering away, and then waited for the apologetic arm that's always extended to me these days. It did not come and I turned haltingly to call out a very unpriestly word.

But the word never left my mouth, for the silhouette standing before from me was one I recognized immediately: the strong, almost conceited tilt of the head, the just barely red-blond hair in the moonlight. Elise breathed – I could see her puff of air in the night. She was as I knew her, only more perfect. Her face was flawless cream, unblemished and unused. She looked older and yet not aged. Her eyes were more perfectly shaped, her lips more full. Her eyes laughed though her face remained smooth and relaxed.

I realized then that she was looking. Seeing me this way. The way she could not possibly remember me. Weak and old. I lowered my eyes so that I did not have to watch her watch me and searched for the words I practiced so many times in my imagination. But all that came out was, "Are you really here?"

"You wanted me," she spoke in a voice similar to, but not her own.

"I've wanted you before."

"I was there then too. Every day."

"Every day," I repeated the irony. "I couldn't feel you."

She shrugged as if it were inconsequential. "You feel me now." Then she turned more like the girl she was, cocking her head at me and stepping one foot out as though she meant to draw me in to her. "You know, I've seen the end." Her white smile flashed in her shadowed face. "Really this time. And in the end, it's all right."

"It's all right?"

"Yes. So don't waste a blink." She stepped the foot back in and tilted her head to catch some snowflakes more fully on her face. "It's beautiful, isn't it?"

"Yes it is," I replied without looking up.

"I'll see you," she said suddenly serious. "Where everything else falls away – I'll see you."

She turned back the way she had been heading. I called to her to wait; to tell her I had too many questions; to tell her I needed to know. She went on as though I did not speak. I moved after her, sliding on the ice and snow like an old man and hating myself.

She turned sharply then, watching me catch my balance. And her eyes were suddenly fire in the snow, lighting up the flakes like a stray car headlight. She waited until I stood again on my own, then blinked out.

I followed her steps back into the dark, calling her name though I knew she was gone. Her footprints (real footprints!) went down the street steadily until they blended with the snow beyond recognition.

I haven't seen her since. But I have her word.

Where it all falls away – like Kailey Moore and Helen Dewallace – I will recognize the one that comes for me.

Yours Faithfully,
Father Chris Mognahan

Epilogue

Revelation 21:1 – 21:7...

I saw a new heaven and a new earth: for the first heaven and the first earth were passed away; and there was no more sea. And I John saw the holy city, new Jerusalem, coming down from God out of heaven, prepared as a bride adorned for her husband. And I heard a great voice out of heaven saying, Behold, the tabernacle of God is with men, and he will dwell with them, and they shall be his people, and God himself shall be with them, their God. And God shall wipe away all tears from their eyes; and there shall be no more death, neither sorrow, nor crying, neither shall there be any more pain: for the former things are passed away.

And he that sat upon the throne said, Behold, I make all things new. And he said unto me, Write: for these words are true and faithful.

And he said unto me, It is done. I am Alpha and Omega, the beginning and the end. I will give unto him that is athirst of the fountain of the water of life freely. He that overcometh shall inherit all things; and I will be his God, and he shall be my son.

Acknowledgments

To my editor, Mitchel, and all of 23 House, I am forever indebted for this chance and for your guidance in putting the best version of *The Sounding* out. Thanks are also due to my very first group of six test readers whose diligent comments and suggestions helped me mold *The Sounding* into what it is today. To Shad Froman, book trailer maker-extraordinaire, and Charles Benoit, the voice behind the book trailer, thank you both for your time and incredible contributions bringing *The Sounding* to life. Thank you to Michael Palmberg, who helped me join the World Wide Web in true thriller style. To Charles Cook – you are a teacher who truly changed my course and grew my love of writing, in addition to offering your good, honest opinion of my work for over 16 years (and I'll be coming back for more…). I owe so much more than a thank you to my incredible family, whose love is the strongest force in my life. To my in-law family, who has always made me feel as one of their own, and to the "Original 7" – the parents that support me always, and Chris, Cole, Kyle and Kailey, who never let me get away with anything and have made me such a much better person. And finally, thanks and love to my husband, who moonlights as a sounding board, an editor, a web programmer, a marketing manager, a publicist, and a chef on "writing" days.

Follow Carrie Salo on Facebook or go to carriesalo.com for:

- Author interviews and photos
- New book releases & trailers
- Discounts, free stuff and contests
- Free short stories
- Upcoming book signings and appearances
- To request Carrie for signings or book clubs
- To contact Carrie
- Author posts